KU-756-310

Our Share of Night

Also by Mariana Enriquez

The Dangers of Smoking in Bed
Things We Lost in the Fire

Our Share of Night

Mariana Enriquez

Translated from the Spanish by
Megan McDowell

GRANTA

Granta Publications, 12 Addison Avenue, London W11 4QR

First published in Great Britain by Granta Books, 2022

Originally published in Spain as *Nuestra parte de noche* by
Editorial Anagrama in Barcelona, Spain, in 2019

Copyright © Mariana Enriquez, 2019
English translation copyright © Megan McDowell, 2022
Part-title illustrations © Pablo Gerardo Camacho, 2022

Mariana Enriquez and Megan McDowell have asserted their
moral rights under the Copyright, Designs and Patents Act, 1988, to
be identified as the author and translator respectively of this work.

The text credits on page 727 constitute an extension of this copyright page.

All rights reserved. This book is copyright material and must not
be copied, reproduced, transferred, distributed, leased, licensed or publicly
performed or used in any way except as specifically permitted in writing by
the publisher, as allowed under the terms and conditions under which it was
purchased or as strictly permitted by applicable copyright law. Any unauthorized
distribution or use of this text may be a direct infringement of the author's and
publisher's rights, and those responsible may be liable in law accordingly.

Our Share of Night is a work of fiction. Names, characters, places, and incidents either
are the product of the author's imagination or are used fictitiously. Any resemblance
to actual persons, living or dead, events, or locales is entirely coincidental.

A CIP catalogue record for this book is available from the British Library.

1   3   5   7   9   10   8   6   4   2

ISBN 978 1 78378 673 2 (hardback)
ISBN 978 1 78378 935 1 (trade paperback)
ISBN 978 1 78378 674 9 (ebook)

Typeset by Patty Rennie

Printed and bound by CPI Group (UK) Ltd, Croydon, CR0 4YY

www.granta.com

MIX
Paper from
responsible sources
FSC
www.fsc.org   FSC® C171272

Who is the third who walks always beside you?

T.S. Eliot, *The Waste Land*

Contents

I

The Claws of the Living God

January 1981

I believe we lose immortality because we have not conquered our opposition to death; we keep insisting on the primary, rudimentary idea: that the whole body should be kept alive. We should seek to preserve only the part that has to do with consciousness.

Adolfo Bioy Casares, *The Invention of Morel*

I cried, 'Come out of the shadow, king of the nails of gold!'

W.B. Yeats, *The Wanderings of Oisin*

THERE WAS SO MUCH LIGHT THAT MORNING AND THE sky was so clear, its warm blue marred by a single white smirch, more like a plume of smoke than a cloud. It was already late and he needed to go and that hot day was going to be just like the next: if it rained and he was hit with the river's humidity and the stifling Buenos Aires heat, he would never be able to leave the city.

Juan swallowed a pill dry to stave off the headache he wasn't feeling yet and went into the house to wake up his son, who was sleeping under a sheet. We're leaving, he said as he shook him gently. The boy woke up right away. Do other children have such shallow, vigilant sleep? Wash your face, he said, and carefully cleared sleep from the boy's eyes. There was no time for breakfast, they could stop on the way. He loaded the already-packed bags, and debated a while among various books until he decided to add two more. He saw the airplane tickets on the table: they were still a possibility. He could lie down and wait for the date of the flight, some days later. To ward off inertia, he tore up the tickets and threw them in the trash. His long hair made his neck sweat: it was going to be unbearable under the sun. He didn't have time to cut it now, but he got the scissors from the kitchen drawer and stashed them in the same plastic box where he kept his pills, the blood-pressure monitor, the syringe, and some bandages, basic first aid for the trip. Also, his sharpest knife, and the bag full of ashes he would use later. He packed the oxygen tank: he was going to need it. The car was cool; its leather hadn't absorbed too much heat during the night. He loaded the picnic cooler, filled with ice and two bottles of cold soda, into the front seat. His son had to ride in the back; Juan would have preferred to have the boy beside him, but it was illegal, and he couldn't risk any problems with the police or the army, who kept a brutal watch over the highways. A single man alone with a child could be suspicious. The repressive forces were unpredictable, and Juan wanted to avoid any incidents.

Gaspar, he called, without raising his voice too much. When he received no answer, he went inside to look for the boy. He found Gaspar trying to tie the shoelaces of his sneakers.

'You're making a mess of it,' he said, kneeling down to help. His son was crying, but Juan couldn't console him. Gaspar missed his mother – she had done these things automatically: trimmed his nails, sewn his buttons, washed behind his ears and between his toes, asked if he'd peed before leaving, taught him how to tie his shoelaces in a perfect bow. Juan missed her too, but he didn't want to cry with his son that morning. You have everything you want? he asked. We're not going to come back for anything, I'm warning you.

He hadn't driven so far in a long time. Rosario always insisted that he drive at least once a week, just so he didn't get out of practice. The car was too small for Juan, like almost everything: pants were too short, shirts too tight, chairs uncomfortable. He checked to be sure the Auto Club's guide was in the glove box, and they set off.

'I'm hungry,' said Gaspar.

'Me too, but we're going to stop for breakfast at this great place I know. In a while, okay?'

'If I don't eat, I'll throw up.'

'And my head hurts when I don't eat. Be strong. It's just a lit-tle while. Don't look out the window or you'll get even dizzier.'

He himself felt worse than he wanted to admit. His fin-gers were tingling, and he recognized the erratic palpitations of arrhythmia in his chest. He adjusted his sunglasses and asked Gaspar to tell him the story he'd read the night before. At six years old, the boy already knew how to read quite well.

'I don't remember it.'

'Yes, you do. I'm in a bad mood, too. Let's try to change it together. Or are we going to be all pissy for the whole trip?'

Gaspar laughed at Juan's use of the word 'pissy'. Then he recounted the story of the jungle queen who sang while she walked through the trees. Everyone liked to listen to her. One day some soldiers came and she stopped singing and became a warrior. The soldiers caught her and she spent a night locked up, and then she escaped, but to escape she had to kill the guard keeping watch over her. No one could believe she was strong enough to have killed him because she was very thin, so she was accused of being a witch and they burned her at the stake – tied her to a tree and set fire to it. But in the morning, instead of a body, they found a red flower.

'A tree of red flowers.'

'Yeah, a tree.'

'Did you like the story?'

'I don't know, it scared me.'

'That tree is called a ceiba. There aren't many around here, but when I see one, I'll show you. There are a lot of them near your grandparents' house.'

In the rear-view mirror he saw Gaspar frown.

'What do you mean there are a lot?'

'That story is a legend. I've explained what a legend is.'

'So the girl isn't real?'

'Her name is Anahí. Maybe she did exist, but the story about the flowers is told to remember her, not because it really happened.'

'So did it really happen or not?'

'Both. Yes and no.'

He liked to see how Gaspar got serious and even angry, how he bit the side of his lip and opened and closed a hand.

'Do they burn witches now, too?'

'No, not any more. But there aren't very many witches now.'

It was easy to get out of the city on a Sunday morning in January. Before he knew it the tall buildings were behind them, and then so were the low houses and tin lean-tos of the shantytowns on the city's outskirts. And suddenly the trees of the countryside appeared. Gaspar was asleep by then, and Juan's arm burned in the sun just like any regular father's on a weekend of pools and picnics. But he wasn't a regular father, and people could tell just by looking into his eyes or by talking to him for a while. Somehow, they recognized the danger: he couldn't hide what he was. It wasn't possible to hide something like that, at least not for long.

He parked in front of a café advertising hot chocolate and croissants. Time for breakfast, he told Gaspar, who woke up immediately and rubbed his enormous, slightly distant blue eyes.

The woman who was cleaning the tables gave the impression she owned the place, and of being friendly and gossipy. She shot them a curious look when they sat down far from the window and near the fridge. A boy with his little toy car and his father, who was two metres tall and had long blond hair down to his shoulders. She wiped their table with a cloth and wrote their order on a notepad, as if the café were crowded with customers whose orders she had to keep straight. Gaspar wanted a hot chocolate and croissants with dulce de leche; Juan ordered a glass of water and a cheese sandwich. He took off his dark glasses and opened the newspaper that was on the table, though he knew the important news never appeared in the papers. There were no articles about clandestine detention centres or night-time clashes, no pieces on abductions or stolen children. Just stories about the 'Little World Cup' being held in Uruguay, which didn't interest him at all. Sometimes he had a hard time faking normalcy when he was distracted, when he was so hopelessly sad and worried. The night before, he'd tried to communicate, yet again, with Rosario. He couldn't. She wasn't anywhere, he couldn't sense her; she was gone in a way that he found impossible to understand or accept.

'It's hot,' said Gaspar.

The boy was sweating, his hair wet and his cheeks flushed. Juan touched his back. His shirt was soaked.

'Wait here,' he said, and went out to the car to get a dry shirt. Then he led Gaspar to the café's restroom to wet his head, dry his sweat, and change his shirt, which smelled a little like diesel.

When they got back to the table, their breakfast and the woman were waiting for them; Juan asked for another glass of water for Gaspar.

'There's a lovely campground near here, if you want to cool off in the river.'

'Thanks, but we don't have time,' said Juan, trying to sound friendly. He unbuttoned the top buttons of his shirt.

'You boys travelling alone? My goodness, the eyes on this child! What's your name, son?'

Juan wanted to say, Gaspar, don't answer, but the boy told her his name and the woman pounced, asking in an insincere, childish voice:

'And where's your mommy?'

Juan felt the boy's pain in his entire body. It was primitive and wordless, raw and vertiginous. He had to clutch on to the table and make an effort to break away from his son and that pain. Gaspar couldn't answer and looked to his father for help. He'd only eaten half a croissant. Juan thought he would need to teach the boy not to cling like that, not to him or to anyone else.

'Ma'am.' Juan tried to control himself, but it sounded threatening. 'What the hell do you care?'

'I was just making conversation, that's all,' she replied, offended.

'Oh, well, that's just great. You get mad because you won't get to have your idiotic conversation, and we have to put up with the stupid prying of a gossipy old lady. You really want to know? My wife died three months ago. She was hit by a bus that dragged her two blocks.'

'I am so sorry.'

'No. You're not sorry, you don't feel anything, because you didn't know her and you don't know us.'

The woman started to say something else, but then she walked away, sniffling loudly. Gaspar was still looking to Juan, but his eyes were dry. He was a little scared.

'It's okay. Finish eating.'

Juan himself nibbled his cheese sandwich; he wasn't hungry, but he couldn't take his medication on an empty stomach. The woman came back looking contrite, her shoulders hunched forward. She was carrying two glasses of orange juice. On the house, she said, and apologized. I certainly never imagined such a tragedy. Gaspar was playing with his red toy car, a new model with doors and a trunk that opened – a gift from his uncle Luis, sent from Brazil. Juan made Gaspar finish his hot chocolate and then got up to pay at the counter. The woman was still apologizing, and Juan felt drained. When she reached out to take the money, he held on to her wrist. He thought about marking her with a symbol that would drive her mad, that would put the idea in her head to skin her grandson's feet or cook her dog in a stew. But he held back. He didn't want to tire himself. Keeping the secret up around this trip with his son was already wearing him out, and there would be consequences. So he left the woman alone.

Gaspar was waiting for him in the doorway, wearing his father's dark glasses. When Juan tried to take them off him, the boy ran outside laughing. He caught up with him near the car and picked him up: Gaspar was light and long, though he would never be as tall as his father. Juan decided they would find a place to have lunch early, before the long stretch to Entre Ríos.

The day had been exhausting despite the utter ordinariness of the journey: light traffic, a delicious lunch at a roadside grill, and a nap in the shade of the trees, the banks cooled by a breeze from the river. The grill's owner had also been curious and tried to make small talk, but since there were no questions about his wife, Juan had decided to chat while he drank a little wine. After his nap and during the whole drive to Esquina he'd felt bad: the heat was extreme. But now, as he asked for a room and tried to make the front desk worker understand that he needed a double bed for him and another single one for his son and money was no object, he realized that it was also possible he would need assistance. He paid up front and let someone else carry the bags up the stairs. Once in the room, he turned on the TV to entertain Gaspar and lay down on the bed. He recognized his symptoms: his arrhythmia was out of control. He could hear the murmur, that sound of effort, and felt the nausea of confused valves. His chest hurt, and it was hard to breathe.

'Gaspar, hand me the bag,' he said.

He took out the monitor and checked his blood pressure; it was low, which was good. He lay diagonally, the only way his feet could fit on the mattress. Before taking his pills and trying to rest – to sleep, if possible – he pulled a sheet of paper from the hotel pad on the bedside table and, using a pen that said on the side 'Hotel Panambí – Esquina', he wrote down a number.

'Son, listen closely. If I don't wake up, I want you to call this number.'

Gaspar's eyes widened, and then his face crumpled.

'Don't cry. This is just in case I don't wake up, that's all, but I *am* going to wake up, okay?'

He felt his heart skip as if it were accelerating with a gear change. Would he be able to sleep? He brought his fingers to his neck. One-seventy, maybe more. He had never wanted to die as much as he did now, in this provincial hotel room, and he had never been more afraid of leaving his son alone.

'That's your uncle Luis's number. You have to press 9 and then you'll hear a dial tone, and only then you call your uncle's number. If I don't wake up, shake me. And if I still don't wake up when you shake me, you call him. Him first, then the man downstairs in the lobby, understand?'

Gaspar said yes, and he clutched the number in his fist as he lay down beside Juan – close, but far enough away not to disturb him.

Juan woke up sweaty from a dreamless sleep. It was night time, but the room was dimly lit: Gaspar had turned on the bedside lamp and was reading. Juan looked at him without immediately stirring: the boy had taken his book from the bag and seemed to be waiting, the paper with the phone number on the pillow beside him. Gaspar, he called, and the boy reacted with care: he put the book down, crawled over to Juan, and asked if he was okay. Just like an adult, just like he'd heard so many adults ask him when they took care of him. Juan sat up and waited a minute before answering. His heart had returned to a normal rhythm, or to what was relatively normal for him. He wasn't agitated, wasn't dizzy. I'm okay, yes, he said, and he sat Gaspar on his lap, hugged him, caressed his dark hair.

Gaspar pointed to Juan's watch.

'What time is it?'

'You know how to tell time, you tell me.'

'Twelve thirty.'

There wouldn't be anywhere to eat still open in that town. Sure, he could walk downtown, break into some closed shop or restaurant, and take whatever he wanted – opening locked doors was very simple. But if anyone witnessed him doing it, he would have to deal with them. And all those small acts built up until they became a long and exhausting chain of footprints to erase, eyes to shut, memories to make disappear. He'd been taught this years ago: it was best to try to live as normally as possible. He could do things that were impossible for most people, but every conquest, every exercise of will to achieve what he desired came with a price. In matters of little importance, it wasn't a price worth paying. Now, he just had to convince whoever was working on the night desk to fix them some food. He didn't feel hungry, and surely Gaspar didn't either. But the boy hadn't eaten, Juan had forgotten to take the sodas out of the car, and he had to behave like a father.

However, he needed to have a wash before he could leave the room – he stank. And maybe also cut his hair a little. Gaspar could use a bath too, though it wasn't as urgent. He got up from the bed with the boy in his arms and carried him to the shower, then turned on the hot water and waited a while until his suspicion was confirmed.

'No way, not with cold water!' cried Gaspar.

'Come on, it's hot out! No? Okay then, I'll clean you off with a towel after I'm done.'

Juan got into the shower and Gaspar sat on the toilet lid and told him about what he'd been reading and what he had seen from the hotel window. Juan heard his voice but didn't pay attention to what he was saying. The showerhead was too low and he had to bend over to wash his hair, but at least the hotel provided shampoo and soap. Then, with a towel around his waist, he stood in front of the mirror: his wet hair came down past his shoulders and there were dark circles under his eyes.

'Bring me the scissors, they're in the small bag.'

'Can I cut it? Just a little?'

'No.'

Juan stood looking at his reflection, his broad shoulders, the dark scar that ran down the middle of his chest, the burn on his arm. Rosario had always cut his hair, and sometimes shaved him too. He remembered her big earrings that she never took off, sometimes not even when she slept. He remembered how she'd cried once, kneeling naked on the bathroom floor, over the weight she had gained during pregnancy. How she crossed her arms when she heard something she found stupid. He remembered her shouting at him in the street, furious; how strong she was when she hit him with her fists in a fight. How many things did he not know how to do for himself? How many had he forgotten, how many had he never learned because she always did them? He combed his hair and then cut it as neatly as he could. He left one lock longer in front and used the hairdryer to see if it was a disaster. The results seemed acceptable. He had a little stubble, but it was only noticeable because he was so pale. He gathered up the cut hair, which he'd let fall on to a towel, and flushed it down the toilet.

'Let's go see if we can find something to eat.'

The hotel hallway was very dark and smelled of damp. The room they'd been given was right in the corner next to the stairs. Juan let Gaspar go out first, but instead of heading straight downstairs, the boy took off running down the hall. At first Juan thought he was making for the elevator. But then he realized Gaspar had sensed the same thing he had, though with one big difference: instead of avoiding it – Juan was so used to those presences that he ignored them – he was drawn to it and was going towards it. The thing that was hiding at the end of the hallway was very frightened and wasn't dangerous, but it was old, and like all ancient things, it was voracious and wretched and covetous.

It was the first time his son had had a perception, at least in his presence. He'd been waiting for this moment; Rosario had insisted it was going to happen soon, and she was usually right about these things. But discovering that Gaspar really had inherited his ability took his breath away, and he felt his throat closing off. He hadn't held out much hope that his son would be normal, but there in that hallway the little hope he'd clung to had vanished entirely, and Juan felt the dismay tighten like a chain around his neck. An inherited condemnation. He tried to feign calm.

'Gaspar,' he said without raising his voice, 'it's this way. Down the stairs.'

The boy turned around in the hallway and looked at him with a confused expression, as if just waking up in a strange room after sleeping for days. The look only lasted a second, but Juan recognized it. He knew he had to teach the boy how to close himself off to that floating world, to those sticky wells, how to avoid falling into them. And he had to start soon, because he remembered the terrors of his own childhood, and there was no reason Gaspar should go through the same thing.

15

My son will be born blind, the presence at the end of the hall intoned over and over; it had no hair and wore a blue dress. It didn't seem like Gaspar could hear it, though perhaps he had seen it. That's what he had been talking about in the bathroom earlier: a woman sitting in the plaza across from the hotel who stared at his window with her mouth open. Juan hadn't paid attention because the boy wasn't afraid as he told the story, and that was good. Gaspar was intuitively right: there was nothing to fear, that woman was nothing but an echo. There were a lot of echoes now. It was always like that in a massacre, the effect like screams in a cave – they remained for a while until time put an end to them. There was a long way to go until that end, and the restless dead were moving quickly, they wanted to be seen. 'The dead travel fast,' he thought.

They went down the stairs in silence to keep from waking other guests. A woman who was surely the owner of the hotel was leafing through a magazine at reception. She looked up when they came in, and then she stood; with a single quick movement she smoothed her blouse and her hair, which was dark and somewhat tousled.

'Hello there,' she said. 'Can I help you with something?'

Juan walked over to the counter and rested one hand on the phone book that was open beside the lamp.

'Good evening, ma'am. Is there by chance anything open where we could get something to eat?'

The woman cocked her head.

'You might be able to find something at the fisherman's club grill, but let me call and ask, because it's a hike to get there.'

A hike, thought Juan. Impossible – in this little town nothing could be very far. He took in the lobby walls with wood panelling halfway up, the brown laminate floor, the keys dangling from a board. Gaspar had gone over to a small tank and his finger was following a little swimming fish. No answer, said the woman, after letting it ring for a while. Okay, said Juan, guess we'll just go to bed without eating. He smiled, and noticed that the woman – who was young, not yet forty, though she looked older in the sad light of that hushed hotel – was openly staring at him. I fell asleep, he explained. It's a long drive from Buenos Aires, and I was already tired.

Outside, the silence was total. He saw the blue lights of a patrol car pass by but barely heard its engine. So, they patrolled even this tiny town?

'Excuse my indiscretion,' said the woman, coming out from behind the counter. She was fanning herself, though the ceiling fan was spinning. 'Are you in room 201? My front desk clerk told me he thought the guest in 201 wasn't feeling well. We were worried, but since we didn't hear anything and you didn't call, we didn't want to disturb you.'

'How do you know he was talking about me?'

Somewhere between shy and flirtatious, the woman replied:

'The clerk described a very tall, very blond man with a child.'

'Thanks for your concern, ma'am. I'm feeling okay now, I just needed to rest. I had surgery six months ago, and sometimes I think I'm fully recovered and I end up overexerting myself.'

And deliberately, theatrically, Juan lightly rested a hand on the dark shirt he wore unbuttoned halfway down his chest, making sure she couldn't miss his enormous scar.

'Come on,' she said. 'I'll make you some sandwiches, at least. Does the little one eat pasta? We'll just steam it with a little butter, nothing to it.'

'What's pasta?' asked Gaspar, who had left the fish tank.

'Noodles, *mitaí*,' the woman told him, kneeling down. 'You like them with butter and cheese?'

'Yeah. With sauce, too.'

'We'll see what we can do for you.'

'Can I watch you cook?'

'He likes to cook,' said Juan, shrugging his shoulders in bemusement.

An hour later Gaspar had learned to use the can opener, they'd both eaten somewhat sticky pasta with a delicious sauce and had drunk some fresh ice water, and the woman had joined them with a glass of sweet wine and a few cigarettes. When they finished, Juan offered to wash the dishes so she could return to reception, and the woman agreed; Gaspar helped dry. I hope you get well soon, she told Juan before she left. Gaspar thanked the woman with tomato sauce-stained lips, and she gave him a kiss on the forehead in return.

Gaspar didn't want to go into the room: as he stood motionless in the doorway, his eyes shone and he seemed scared.

'Daddy, there's a lady in there,' he said. Juan blinked and attuned his senses: it was the same woman from the hallway earlier.

'Come on in, don't look at her.' He took Gaspar's face in both his hands; they were so big they nearly encircled the boy's head. 'Just look at me.'

Then he sat on the floor and turned on the bedside lamp. Luckily Gaspar couldn't hear what the woman was saying. It was always better to only see. Juan listened for a moment out of curiosity. It was the same desperate and solitary repetition of death, the same echoing of death. Then he shut out her words, but didn't expel her; his son would have to learn how to do that, and fast. Juan didn't want him to be afraid a single minute longer.

'Listen to me closely now.'

'Who is it, Daddy?'

'It's not a person. It's a memory.'

He rested a hand under his son's sternum and felt his heart, fast, strong, and healthy. His mouth went dry with envy.

'Close your eyes. Feel my hand?'

'Yeah.'

'What am I touching?'

'My belly.'

'And now?'

With two fingers of his other hand, he found the vertebra behind the boy's stomach.

'My back.'

'No, not your back.'

'My spine.'

'Now you have to think about what's between my two hands, like when your head hurts and you tell me it feels like there's something in it. Okay, think about what's in here.'

Gaspar squeezed his eyes shut and bit his lower lip.

'Got it.'

'Okay, now tell the lady to go away. Don't tell her out loud. You can say it in a quiet voice if you want, but tell her as if this part of you that's between my hands could speak. Understand? It's important.'

This could take all night, Juan knew.

'I told her.'

Juan looked at the woman, who remained beside the bed, pregnant and open-mouthed, surely still talking about her first child, her eyes empty.

'Again. As if you were talking from here, as if you had a mouth inside.'

'Should I say it loud?'

Where did he get that question? The boy deserved an answer worthy of such a pertinent query.

'Yes, today you should.'

The image of the woman vanished slowly, like dissipating smoke. The air in the room seemed cleaner, as though they had opened the windows. The light from the lamp shone brighter.

'Very good, Gaspar, very good.'

Gaspar glanced around the room in search of the woman who had gone. He looked serious.

'And she won't come back?'

'If she does, you do the same thing you just did.'

Gaspar was shaking, a little from the effort, a little from fear. Juan remembered the first time he had expelled a discarnate: it had been just as easy for him, maybe even easier, given the circumstances. Hopefully this would be the only ability Gaspar had inherited. Hopefully he would never achieve the level of contact Juan was capable of. Rosario had been sure the boy would inherit all his gifts. Suddenly, the memory was so vivid that he felt it, like accidentally touching an insect in the dark: stubborn Rosario sitting on the bed in her white cotton underwear, her hair pulled back in a high ponytail. Gaspar was going to inherit everything, everything that Juan himself bore. He felt his eyes grow hot.

'Now I'm going to go back to sleep, because in a while I'll need to drive.'

'I want to sleep with you.'

'Don't be scared. Go to your bed. If you can't sleep, read your book. The light doesn't bother me.'

But Gaspar didn't want to read. He lay face up and waited for sleep to come with a discipline that was strange for his age. Juan hadn't lowered the blinds, and the few streetlights dimly lit the room, casting the shadows of tree branches on the walls. Juan waited until Gaspar's breathing indicated he was asleep, and then went over to look at him: lips parted, small baby teeth, hair plastered to his forehead with sweat.

He could do it sitting in his own bed with Gaspar beside him, but he didn't want the boy to wake up and see him. The bathroom was as good a place as any. He didn't need much: just silence, Rosario's hair, a sharp instrument, and the ashes.

Sitting on the cold tiles, he balled up the lock of Rosario's hair that he carried with him, stored in a little box. You promised me, he said in a quiet voice. And it had been a serious promise, a promise made in blood and wounds, not in sentimental words.

He took a handful of ashes from the plastic bag and scattered them on the floor in front of him so that he could draw the sign of midnight. He had done this every night since Rosario's death, always with the same result: silence. A desert of cold sand and dull stars. He had even tried more rudimentary methods, and the reply was always the same: wind blowing over the abyss.

He repeated the words, caressed the lock of hair, summoned her in the virulent language that must be used in the ritual of ashes. With his eyes closed, he saw empty rooms and corners, quenched bonfires, abandoned clothes, dry rivers, but he went on wandering until he returned to the hotel bathroom, to its silence and his son's distant breathing, and then he summoned her again. Not a touch, not a tremor, not a feint, not even a treacherous shadow. She wasn't coming and she wasn't within his reach, and, since her death, he hadn't received a single sign of her presence.

In the first days, he had made inappropriate offerings. True magic is not done by offering the blood of others, he'd been told. It is done by offering one's own, and abandoning all hope of recovering it. Juan took the razor blade he had placed beside him and cut the palm of his hand diagonally, vaguely following the line called the mind or the head. It was an unbearable wound that never healed, the worst possible kind, and for that very reason the kind that worked. When he felt the warm blood

21

in the darkness, he pressed his hand on to the sign drawn in ashes on the floor. He said the necessary words and waited. The silence was dizzying. Juan knew it was a symptom of his own loss of power. Whether it was because he was very sick or too depleted, he didn't know, but the feeling of weakness was undeniable. This kind of summons required hardly any effort: the world of the dead was very near for him, just beyond a lightweight revolving door. If it had been another ritual, almost any other, he could have questioned his ability to perform it. Not this one. This was like stretching his legs.

He washed his hand resignedly and used a towel to clean the blood from the floor. He no longer got angry when the ritual didn't work. After his first failed attempts he had cursed Rosario, he'd smashed furniture and nearly broken his fingers from punching the floor so much. Now, he just calmly cleaned up afterwards and placed the lock of hair back in its box. 'For the dead travel fast,' he thought again. It was true, in general. He, however, had so far been denied that speed.

Gaspar was still asleep, though a long time had passed: the ritual of the sign of midnight seemed short for whoever performed it, but in reality it took several unnoticed hours. Juan tended to his slashed hand. Dawn was breaking when he poured a little alcohol over the wound that never healed because he had to keep cutting and cutting in the same place, feeding blood to the ashes that brought him nothing but a stillness so suspicious that it made him imagine his wife silenced, her lips sewn shut by someone who wanted to keep them definitively apart.

The hotel breakfast was served in a dining hall with white walls and tables spread with chequered tablecloths. The décor was piscine: fish paintings, preserved fish mounted behind glass, and another fish tank, larger than the one at reception. Esquina was a sort of fishing capital. Juan had never fished a day in his life. And if the hotel's recurring theme was of aquatic fauna, he didn't understand why it was called Panambí, which means 'butterfly' in Guaraní. There were no butterflies anywhere, not even in the hotel's logo. He drank weak tea and spread dulce de leche on slices of toast for Gaspar, who was very quiet.

'What's wrong?'

'Are you mad at me?'

'No, son, I'm just in a bad mood. When you finish eating, we'll go swimming.'

Gaspar had cried all morning, until they came down to breakfast. Ever since his mother died, he had cried every day when he woke up. Sometimes he cried just because, sometimes he got angry over some silly thing, sometimes he said his head hurt or he was tired or hot. He dreamed about her, Juan knew; usually, he dreamed that her death had been a dream. Sometimes Juan let him cry alone, sometimes he sat silently beside him, sometimes he splashed cold water on his face, but he never really knew what to do. That morning, when Gaspar had calmed down after a fit of wailing and sobbing, pulling his own hair and even punching his pillow, Juan had suggested that they go to the beach. Gaspar had asked if the water was cold like at Mar del Plata. Juan explained that no, this was a river and rivers were different, more like swimming pools. It was a lie, but it worked. Juan was the one who needed to swim, and it was high time he improved on the very basic technique he'd taught his son. He himself had learned at eight years old, and then only thanks to his brother's irresponsibility; Luis hadn't known how to keep his little brother entertained when he took him on outings, and one day he'd brought him to a public pool. Juan knew swimming was forbidden – his doctor, Jorge Bradford, had told him he couldn't do any intense exercise. Bradford had never found

23

out about the afternoons at the pool, or if he had, he'd played dumb: the doctor always had contradictory attitudes, gestures of extreme generosity alternating with stinginess, and he was often unpredictable.

Bradford had taught Juan how to close himself off when he was six years old and in recovery from a cardiac crisis: many of the most important things in his life had happened in a hospital bed, amid pain, anaesthesia, and fear. Doctor Bradford used the same method Juan had taught Gaspar the night before. Doctor Bradford, who had operated on him after he'd been declared a lost cause, who had visited him every day, and who would later adopt him under the pretext of giving him the care he needed. An elegant abduction. A purchase: he had paid money for Juan. It's a miracle, Bradford had told Juan's parents, a miracle he's still alive, and he needs treatments and care that you, unfortunately, in your economic situation, cannot offer him. Juan's parents had acquiesced.

That night, lying in the hospital bed, Juan hadn't been able to turn down the volume of the voices; he felt hands touching him all over his body, inside and out, and he saw people around his bed even if he closed his eyes. And Bradford had sat him up, wet his hair with cool water, and told him more or less the same thing Juan had told Gaspar in the hotel room: use the voice between your spine and your stomach, tell them to go and they'll leave. He clearly remembered how he'd tried several times, guided by that man's dark, greedy eyes, until the silence came and the intensive therapy room was once again a place full of the wounded and dying. Bradford had stayed with him until he fell asleep. When he woke up in the morning the voices and images came back, and Bradford was still there. Again he told him what to do, and this time Juan managed it on the first try. Then Bradford wanted to know what he saw. And Juan described it all: how he would wake up and see, at breakfast, a cadaver at the table or in bed; the mouths that laughed at him, and the hand that covered his face and wouldn't let him breathe at night; the birds and insects that attacked him, flying straight at his head when he went out to the patio; the two little faces that peered at him from under the rock his mother used to prop open the door of the back shed. He'd told his parents, but they didn't seem to understand. Bradford did.

His parents were afraid of him: they tried to soothe him and then changed the subject. His brother Luis was different. He got scared, too, but he tried to help. He told Juan to think about other things. He'd taught him to swim.

Now Juan had to teach his son, too, but first he wanted to swim in the river alone for a while. He drove to the town's beachfront, which was lovely and clean and practically empty, and he sat Gaspar on the grass under a tree with the cooler beside him. He poured some soda into a plastic cup and told him, Dad's going to swim now, but if anyone comes near you I'll know, don't worry. And don't go anywhere, because I'll find you, and you know what happens then.

As he was getting into the water, a couple were making their way out. The woman, pretty in a blue one-piece suit, greeted him; the man shot him an aggressive look and took the woman by the waist. Neither of them could help but stare openly at the scar on Juan's chest. He didn't care. He swam for fifteen minutes, not enough to get agitated. He could swim for much longer, but he didn't want to be tired later when he had to drive. The river looked silvery under the sun but the water was a bit murky. He floated for a while before getting out: he sensed nothing but calm from his son. When the water came up to his knees, he waved at Gaspar and shouted, Come on, you have to learn, take off your shirt and shoes. He lay Gaspar on the water and crouched a little. I've got you, he said when he saw the boy struggling, afraid of sinking. Kick, he said, splash me, make noise.

There was something in that hot morning and the boy's slippery skin in his hands that made him feel Rosario beside him. He remembered her shivering from the cold in the English countryside, remembered her singing him a song that said *tonight will be fine*, dancing to a Bowie album and complaining that they never played good music on the radio; he remembered her neck, and her breasts, which were large but even so she never wore a bra, not even after Gaspar was born, and the mornings when he woke her up and she protested, Let me sleep, but after a while she returned his embrace, and he lifted up her legs, put them over his shoulders, and caressed her with his tongue and fingers until she was wet.

He couldn't find her. He could see that poor pregnant woman at the hotel, he could see hundreds of murder victims every day, and yet he couldn't reach her. He had said to her once when she was alive, as a joke, imitating a character in a novel, Please don't leave me alone, haunt me. He'd said it in English, 'haunt me', because there were no words in Spanish for that verb, not *embrujar*, not *aparecer*, it was haunt. She had laughed it off. He was supposed to die first – it was the most logical thing. It was ridiculous he was even still alive.

Sometimes he thought Rosario was hiding. Or that something was keeping her from reaching him. Or that she had gone too far away.

'What now?'

'Now put your head underwater. But without holding your nose.'

'I'll drown.'

'You definitely won't drown.'

They practised holding their breath above water. Gaspar filled his cheeks with air, and Juan started to feel the unmistakable pain in his temples. Too much time in the sun. But he wasn't going to leave the river until the boy learned to hold his breath.

Back under the tree, he poured cold soda into a cup and added some of the ice cubes that by now were floating in the cooler. He swallowed two pills and closed his eyes, lying back against the exposed roots until the pain retreated a little. His head was still pounding, but at least it now throbbed in a regular, slow rhythm.

'I didn't drown,' Gaspar said suddenly.

'See? Swimming is easy, you'll learn fast.'

'Are you gonna wake up?'

'I'm not sleeping, I'm resting.'

'Want a sandwich?'

'No, we'll eat later. And tonight we'll see Tali.'

'Can I make a sandwich for me?'

The best way to get one's bearings on the way to Tali's house was to keep a lookout for an old, rusty iron bridge by the highway; it had fallen out of use and had been overtaken by the unstoppable vegetation of the Argentine littoral region, with its lianas and flowers. Once you passed the bridge, you'd see the old Chapel of the Devil appear, and then you just had to go straight along a dirt road that became impassible if it was muddy. The chapel was the formal entrance to Colonia Camila. Tali loved living there, in that town of two hundred people and two corner stores.

Tali was Juan's half-sister-in-law. She was the daughter of Rosario's father, Adolfo Reyes, and his Corrientes lover, Leandra. Leandra was a middle-class woman who had gone off

27

to live in the country, had founded a temple to San La Muerte, and become famous in the region as both a healer and a great beauty. Tali's mother had died young – Juan and Rosario knew that although she'd fallen ill, her death had been far from natural – and Adolfo Reyes, who had truly loved Leandra and was also a collector of effigies of the saint (that's how they'd met, in fact), had preserved her temple. Tali saw her mother as a 'guardian' or '*promesera*', and now she continued her mother's legacy. She and Rosario had established a room dedicated to San La Muerte at the Museum of Popular Art in Asunción, part of the permanent collection; it was recognized as the best in Paraguay, in the region, and probably in the world.

For years, semi-clandestine ceremonies had been held at Tali's shrine. Colonia Camila was far away from any city, near the river but strangely isolated from any beaches or docks: it was a place where one could, with relatively little fear, follow a cult that displeased the Church and provoked alarm and distrust among laypeople. More recently, Tali had kept her sanctuary discreetly quiet. She had heard about military raids where soldiers destroyed household altars and sometimes kidnapped their owners, holding them at a station for a few nights just as a show of power. Tali was the daughter of a rich, well-connected man, and no one was going to touch her, but it didn't hurt to be careful.

Adolfo Reyes had also bought several hectares around his daughter's temple and house, because on that land stood the Chapel of the Devil, built by Don Lorenzo Simonetti. A church constructed by an Italian immigrant that, oddly, had never been consecrated. Tali cleaned it at night by the light of a kerosene lamp. Many people had seen the glare through the windows and rumours spread about what happened behind those walls, but none of them were true. Juan had confirmed as much with both Tali and her father more than once: although the church was strange, it wasn't a visited place. But Adolfo Reyes liked to have fun, and he hadn't stopped there: he had invented his own rumours, added to the stories, so many that now it was almost impossible to separate the fiction from the simple historical facts of that chapel and its forgotten town.

Lorenzo Simonetti had come to Corrientes from Italy, widowed and with eight children in tow. In 1904, a year after settling in Colonia Camila, he started to build the chapel without asking permission from the ecclesiastical authorities. It was handmade: he carved the Virgin from native urunday wood and tried to imitate the features of his wife, who had died in childbirth. He did everything else with the help of the locals – laying the bricks, building the wooden benches, installing the precarious stained-glass windows. A compatriot brought the bells over from Italy. The altar had tin flowers and plant motifs. A church of the jungle and the border, close to both Brazil and Paraguay.

Simonetti had poured all his artistic zeal into the sacristy wall. That was where he had mounted his masterpiece, which incited the locals' fear and was possibly the reason the church had not been accepted by the curia. The carvings were well preserved despite the passage of time and their somewhat faded colours. They depicted a vision of hell, a tableau of warning: children with disproportionately large heads and twisted legs performed ritual dances around bonfires, frolicking with dragons and snakes. Naked women's waists were chained by serpents. There were shocked faces, round eyes ever open, and more reptiles, especially frogs – there was a true obsession with frogs, in reference to the second plague of Egypt. This scene of the Last Judgment was finished off with the figure of a man sitting with a book, observing the horrible scenes of suffering with an impassive face.

Once he had finished, Simonetti tried to donate the church to the curia, but after two priests came to visit it, his gift was rejected. There were more negotiations, and more rejections, supposedly for bureaucratic reasons, but everyone refused to believe that explanation. It was said that the tableau represented the Salamanca, the meeting between wizards and the Devil, the criollo Witches' Sabbath, and people claimed that Simonetti had participated in those ceremonies. He died trying to convince the priests that his work was sacred. Perhaps honouring a promise, he made the sacrifice – although he wasn't old, he was ill – of walking from Colonia La Camila to Goya, where he met with a Church authority. When he returned, he lay down to rest, and by the next morning he was dead.

In the larger of Colonia Camila's grocery stores, the one that had a modest bar, it was said that people had seen Don Lorenzo's ghost dressed in black, walking towards Goya. There were also stories about a dark congregation that turned its back to the altar and knelt before the tableau of the Last Judgment.

She heard him before she saw him, at six in the evening, when the sun was lighting the sky with a yellow flame and the palm trees in the distance looked like shadows. Tali went running out in a white dress that smelled of jasmine soap brought from Paraguay, and in her hurry she forgot to put on shoes. She couldn't be sure as long as she could only hear him, but her doubts were dispelled when she looked down the small hill on which her house and temple were built, and there he was. His blond hair was tinged orange by the late-afternoon sun, and his black shirt took on a crepuscular blue shade. Even when he laughed like that, mouth open and dimples showing, even with the endearing way he bent his long legs as he slid in the mud, even when he reached out his arms to his son and said 'Come on' and the boy took little running steps beside him – even in that simple family scene, it was easy to understand why he was known as the Golden God, his arms with veins that looked like cables under the skin and his hands too large, with their slender fingers and long, wide palms.

She had never seen such a man before or after him, and now, seeing him again, he seemed so extraordinarily beautiful that her eyes went hazy. The sight of him was like a surprising sunset, when nature puts its danger and its beauty on vivid display.

'So now you like the mud, *chamigo!*' she shouted. She hoped her voice would come out firm and it did, ironic and warm at the same time. Juan recognized it immediately.

'Tali, what's with all this? We're stuck!'

Juan and his son – Gaspar, so grown up now, and so thin – were laughing like crazy. Tali couldn't believe it. She would have expected to find him just as furious and sad as when she'd seen him just a few months back. And yet here he was outside her house, bent over laughing with his feet sunk in the mud, telling his son: 'It's the famous Corrientes quicksand!'

'Just give it a try, *che*; if you fall, you can take a bath later,' she called.

She leaned against the doorway and relaxed, enjoying this unprecedented show: the Golden God having fun with his own clumsiness, pretending to sink, crying out in mock fear. Gaspar, lighter, got through the mud first, and Tali ushered him in. He looked her in the eyes, curious and alert. Hi, Tali, he said. And he turned around to cheer at a slip that almost laid his father out in the road.

'You know, Juancito, the road that comes up on the side is paved.'

'No way.'

'More or less. They put down gravel.'

31

'Why does that road have gravel? Does it lead to a big estate?'

'No, but this is Corrientes. You can't ask for logic.'

'I'll move the car later, then. I hope it isn't stuck.'

'We can push it.'

Juan leapt to reach a stretch of dry grass, and from there, two long-legged strides carried him easily to the door. Tali could finally look at him close up, and she realized the illusion of the late-afternoon light had been overly reassuring: Juan's under-eyes were dark and swollen and he had lost weight; those strange eyes of his, with their multicoloured irises – flashes of blue, green, and a little yellow – were tired and dazed. But it was Juan's extreme paleness that let her know the game in the mud was nothing but that, a game.

'If I didn't know you were alive, I'd say you were a ghost, *che*. Goddamn you're pale.'

He pretended not to hear her and hugged her tight, lifting her off the floor. He got her dress dirty, but Tali didn't care. She was feeling Juan's body again after so long, firm and fragile; it was reassuring to bury her face in that broad chest, to breathe in the smell of his shirt, heat and gasoline and insect repellent. She felt him take a deep breath of relief. Tali kept her eyes closed as she listened to his breathing and the night-time insects that were waking up and buzzing. He took her by the hand and she could sense his sadness through his fingertips, as if it emanated from him. She noticed, as well, that he had a dirty bandage over a wound on his palm. You need to change that rag, she told him, and Juan didn't answer. Gaspar was sitting on the floor, trying to clean his white sneakers.

'Don't worry, *mitaí*, I'll wash them for you,' said Tali, and then she set about resolving various issues. She took Gaspar's hand, beckoned one of the boys working in the small field behind the house over and told him to move the car on to the gravel, and then served a nice cold *tereré* on the deck table. 'I only have lemon verbena. I'll bring something for you, *mitaí*, do you like Coke?'

When she came back with the soda, Juan had stretched out as best he could in the hammock chair and had splashed a little fresh water on his face.

'You could have let me know you were coming, I would've had some food ready, gotten the house in order.'

'I didn't know if I was going to be able to make it there alone, so I hurried a little. And when I realized I was too early, I decided I'd rather visit you first than go straight to Puerto Reyes.'

'Are you okay?'

He didn't look at her. Instead, he gazed out at the red of the sunset through the trees.

'And the little one, how's he taking it?'

'Don't talk about me like I'm not here,' Gaspar protested. He set the glass of Coke on the table with a frown and crossed his arms.

'He's right there, ask him yourself.'

'Well, aren't you something, kiddo. Are you doing okay?'

'Sometimes yes, sometimes no. I miss my mom, and I get scared when he gets sick.' And with an angry, almost accusatory expression, he pointed at his father.

Tali hugged the boy and sat him on her lap, though Gaspar was already too big to be held. She didn't know how to respond, since she'd never heard a six-year-old child speak so clearly and sincerely, so she just said, Let's go change your sneakers, and asked Juan if he'd brought another pair. Sure, he replied, and I also brought him sandals, though around here he can just go barefoot. No, not barefoot, said Tali. Too many bugs.

In the bathroom she washed Gaspar's legs, changed his shoes and shirt, and listened to him talk about the animals he'd seen on the drive there, including a buck with horns. She thought it was very strange for a stag to be so far from the wetlands, but nothing could really be considered strange when Juan was around.

Tali had first met Juan in Buenos Aires. Her father had brought her there with the intention of making her study, but Tali would run away from school, throw tantrums on the floor, cry. Rosario had tried to convince her that school wasn't so bad and the two of them could have fun together. But Tali had replied it wasn't school she hated: it was the city. So, Adolfo Reyes desisted from trying to educate his younger daughter at the best school in Buenos Aires, as he was doing with Rosario, and he let her return north, to her temple and her herbs and her rural school.

She and Rosario were close friends as well as half-sisters. Tali had cried when, at eighteen years old, Rosario left for England to study, telling Tali she was going to the best university in the world and she was happy. Juan had turned fifteen by then, and he'd spent the whole summer that year in Puerto Reyes. He, too, was very sad at Rosario's departure. When she visited her father's house, Tali had been astonished to see Juan again in the cool air of the terrace overlooking the river. She had grown up seeing children of immigrants who were tall and blond like this boy: Swedes from Oberá, Germans from Eldorado, Ukrainians from Aristóbulo del Valle. On outings with her father, she sometimes lunched on sausages and admired the orchids on display in the community festivals, and she had been stupidly infatuated with many of those youths with transparent eyes and skin bronzed by the sun. But when Juan stood up from his wicker chair and kissed both her cheeks, all those men and women seemed like the practice sketches of a clumsy painter, tentative versions made by a hand that was learning, until finally it drew Juan and gave him life and said, This is it, this is what I was looking for, the perfect finish. Juan was fifteen, she was seventeen, and yet her ears burned when he sat looking at her in silence. You want to go for a walk? Tali asked him. It's not so hot out. Sure, Juan replied. They walked through the house's wild garden. She told him about the Scandinavians of Oberá and asked if his family was also from there. Juan said yes, but that they'd moved to Buenos Aires when he was born because he was very sick. Maybe you still have family around here, Tali said. Who knows, said Juan.

That night, after dining on yacare caiman with fried yuca – the speciality of Reyes' cook, Rufina – Juan tore out a page from the notebook where he'd been doodling while the others had coffee (he didn't partake) and gave it to her: it was a drawing of two dogs barking at a moon with rays that made it seem more like a sun, but it was a moon because it had a woman's face. In the distance he had drawn two low towers, one for each dog, and in front of them a lake or pond with a creature emerging from it that could be a lobster or a scorpion. Underneath the drawing he'd written the words 'La Lune', and Tali immediately recognized one of the cards from the Tarot deck Rosario read – the Moon from the Marseilles Tarot. Her sister had tried to teach her, but Tali preferred the Spanish deck.

'I can teach you, too, now that she's gone away,' Juan had told her.

'How did you know I wanted to learn?'

'Rosario told me. She said she never could explain it to you well. I'm a better teacher than she is.'

'And what does this card mean?'

'Depends on the interpretation.'

Juan slid the pencil into the pocket of his impeccable white shirt. He didn't look sick, but she knew he was gravely ill. *Why have they hidden him from me these past years?* she wondered then. She found out soon enough, and it was brutal.

She still had that drawing, that moon, those dogs.

Gaspar, clean and sleepy-looking, sat down in another of the hammock chairs. It wasn't going to rain any more, but night was falling damp and dark. Guillermito, the boy who worked in Tali's house, turned on the patio and deck lights. Juan unbuttoned his shirt and shook it to dry his sweat a little. I'll bring you the fan, offered Tali. No, don't worry, he said.

'They must be looking for you.'

'They can't find me. It's harder to keep up the secret now, but I can still do it.'

'Betty isn't coming this year, either?'

'Nothing has changed regarding her and her daughter. She can't attend the Ceremonial until they decide what to do with the girl. Things are very convenient for her, for now. We'll see what happens once they figure out what to do with her daughter, which will probably mean taking her away from Betty.'

'*Che*, you know they have new dogs there in Reyes. I'm terrified of them, they're huge, they look like horses. There's a black one that must be a metre and a half tall, named Nyx.'

'A dog can't be a metre and a half tall, don't exaggerate.'

'What's Nyx?' Gaspar asked suddenly.

'Juancito, this child is dangerous, he hears everything.'

'Nyx is the name of the Greek goddess of night. She is the night.'

'Is that in my book?'

'I don't think so, she's a forgotten god. I told you about the forgotten gods. They had very few worshippers and over time they all died out, until finally people stopped telling stories about them.'

'That's really sad.'

'It is sad, yes. But we do know some things about Nyx. She was married to Erebus, who is darkness, which is not the same thing as night. You can find darkness during the day, for example. And she had two sons, fraternal twins, Hypnos and Thanatos. Hypnos is sleep and Thanatos is death. They look alike, but obviously they're not the same.

'And do they all live together?'

'We don't know that, so imagine whatever you like.'

Juan looked at Tali and told her Gaspar was reading a book on legends. I promised I'd show him the ceiba tree, for Anahí. In a low voice, Tali said, This one's going to get pretty bored in school.

Guillermito came over to the table. I need you to go find a small mattress for Gaspar, Tali told him. Ask Karina, she's got tons. A girl hardly older than Gaspar peered around the corner of the hallway. Her knees were muddy and her hair was in two messy braids.

'Hey, Laurita, why don't you take Gaspar here to play with you a while. You want to go play with her, Gaspar? We'll call you in for dinner later.'

It took a moment for the kids to warm to each other, but then Laurita told Gaspar about her new puppy and asked if he wanted to see it, and they left. Tali noticed Juan biting his lip as he watched them go.

'It's okay, Laurita is from here, she knows the place, she'll take better care of him than you. What you're feeling is normal.'

'Nothing is normal. I can't talk to her.'

'To Rosario? Juan, you have a Ceremonial in a few days. You need to focus on that.'

Juan looked at her, his eyes mercurial in the deck's dim light. He took the bandage from his hand and showed her the wound. Tali looked at it closely: it wasn't swollen, wasn't infected.

'I can't get her to come even with the midnight sign. If I can't communicate with her using that rite, it means someone is keeping me from reaching her.'

'Can anyone do that?'

'Someone powerful could, or several people working together. I think it's multiple people.'

'Sometimes we can't reach our dead, you know that.'

'I don't think that's it this time.'

'Do you sense her anywhere?'

Juan looked at Tali and brushed a lock of hair away from his face.

'I feel nothing.'

Now that not even the kids' voices could be heard, Tali came close to Juan and reached out her hand. Come on, I'll give you a bath and clean that hand, she said. I bought a giant tub. It's like I knew I was going to need it. He got up slowly, lazily, and in the hallway that led to the bathroom Tali stood on tiptoes and kissed him and pushed him to her bedroom and closed the door with her back. It was always a little rough with Juan, even when he was trying to be gentle, and now he wasn't trying; it hurt Tali to open her legs to receive his broad body, it had hurt to fall on to the floor of her room, the wood hurt her back. There was always a moment of loving and delicate breakage, too, a push, a vertiginous slippage when she recognized the hands that grasped her hair and he was moving inside her. And there was always a dangerous moment when she had to somehow ask him to stop what began as a pleasant sensation, one of tremor and fever, and that ended up feeling like the fast advance of a tide, a wave that was warm and too deep and didn't seem at all like pleasure. He always heard her and stopped: this time he sat up, pushed her away with one hand, and made her look him in the eyes.

Afterwards, Juan lay down naked in the bed, on his side, and cried holding Tali's hand; Tali knew him well enough to listen in silence and wait. *Angá*, this must be the first time he's cried for her, she thought, but she didn't say it out loud because she knew Juan couldn't stand people feeling sorry for him. She caressed his hair, so fine and light, not darkened with age like so many blond people's. He pulled away from her carefully. Are you going to find someone, one of these days? he wanted to know. Tali lay down beside him, lit a cigarette, and offered him a drag. He smoked with eyes closed and face damp; he hadn't dried his tears. No, she said, you're my man. But I don't have Rosario's courage. There are things I wouldn't do for you.

Juan crushed the cigarette in the ashtray on the bedside table and kissed Tali; behind the nicotine and lemon verbena, she tasted the salt of his tears and the chemical aftertaste of his medication. I'm going to find Gaspar, he said, and he left, barefoot and shirtless, mud still spattered on his legs. After a while Tali heard him talking to Gaspar near the bedroom window. They were still discussing the goddess of night and her twin sons death and sleep, so similar and so different.

Tali moved over for Juan when he got into her bed that night. He'd left Gaspar asleep in the living room: the kid wanted to put the mattress there and not in a bedroom, and there was no point in arguing, he could sleep where he wanted. Juan had taken a bath, and he had that stand-offish air she knew well, so she didn't touch him. Soon he was asleep, his back to her. In the semi-darkness, she could see the scar that started at his ribs and ended on his back, the mark of one of his childhood operations. The first time she had seen him naked, she'd been so shocked by the scars that she'd almost rejected him; plus, she was older, what was she doing sleeping with a sick teenager? It had been at Puerto Reyes, in one of the mansion's many guest bedrooms. Tali remembered that first time as a careful thing; he was a virgin, and though he was as hormone-charged as any boy his age, he kept a certain distance, as if he were capable of studying the situation and avoiding adolescent nerves. And, in a way, he was. It was the illness, he'd explained to her later. Each thing he did was a negotiation, a calculation. As if he were tasked with carrying and caring for a delicate crystal treasure that he could never set aside, not even in a safe place, and that had to be moved gingerly so as not to damage or break it. He had to think out every movement in advance, always tiptoeing, always wondering if this jolt would bring the disaster, the final break.

That summer, Tali had been initiated into the Order by Adolfo Reyes, her father, and she was invited to the Ceremonial. When she saw Juan in the Place of Power, she fainted. No one noticed, they were all in some kind of trance. The fear didn't last long. Her father had talked to her about the Order for years, and he'd told her the stories of the mediums. But she never expected the medium to be Juan. They'd hidden it very well; even Rosario, who was so close, had kept the secret from her for years, and Tali understood why.

A little over a year later, Juan went to London for an operation and to see Rosario. He stayed living in England for some time, but disaster brought him back. Tali hadn't gotten angry when she found out he and Rosario were together, because she knew that's how it had to be. She merely cried, then tried to forget him; she couldn't.

Tali fell asleep at dawn, and when she woke up just a few hours later, Juan and Gaspar were in the kitchen making breakfast.

She put on a fresh dress and went over to the counter to help them. We're making something yummy, Gaspar told her. And for a moment she thought, why not? Why not take her sister's place and look after her widower and her son?

'Good morning, boys,' she said.

Gaspar was spreading butter with extreme care on to toast that was a little burnt but perfectly edible. Juan told her:

'The protection on your temple is a disaster.'

There was that contemptuous tone she hated, the superiority that always irritated her.

'I don't have your skills.'

'That's quite clear. I'll take care of it later.'

Gaspar handed her a piece of toast. It had a lot of jam, but Tali ate it anyway. Juan went on preparing the mate. Tali decided not to argue.

'Should we go to the lake today?' she suggested.

'Yeah! Let's go!' cried Gaspar. 'I know how to swim now.'

'He's learning,' said Juan.

'We could go, there are no more palometas.'

'What are palometas?'

'They're fish that are a lot like piranhas. But they only bite you, they won't eat you.'

Gaspar's eyes opened wide.

'Maybe you'll get lucky and see one,' said Juan.

'But I don't want them to bite me.'

'Don't worry about that, I'll take care of you.'

'Can I watch TV?'

Tali said sure, and brought his milk and cookies to the living room. When she came back to the kitchen, Juan was sitting at the table, smoking.

'Did you get up early?'

'I try to get up first because Gaspar wakes up crying.'

41

He looked her in the eyes, and she saw a rage so deep it frightened her. He put out the cigarette in a mug, took a notebook from his bag, and told her, We have to get that temple fixed. Then he turned to his son and said, We're going to take a walk outside, we'll be back in a bit. The kid nodded, hypnotized by the morning cartoons even though the image was filled with vertical lines and snow, thanks to the precarious aerial. Outside, Juan stood for a while in Tali's garden, which was small but had passionflowers, chrysanthemums, dahlias, forget-me-nots, wisteria that climbed up tall ferns and reached the house and ascended up the walls to the roof, purple foxgloves that looked like hoods, and some orchids hanging from the trunk of a peach tree.

Tali followed Juan to the temple, which she kept locked with a padlock. She didn't open the place much – almost all the faithful came in August, with offerings. If anyone had a special request, they came to her first, and then she would set a date for the ritual.

'Do you want to go in?'

'Not yet.'

Juan had opened his notebook and was drawing with a very small pencil, or at least one that looked very small between his large fingers. When he drew standing up he always bent his body, pushing his hips forward and curving his back. It didn't take him long, and when he was finished he lifted up his sunglasses to see if the final product was satisfactory. He wiped his damp forehead with his shirt, then approached the door of the temple and touched it, caressed it.

'Come here, Tali,' he said.

He asked her to hold the notebook so he could see the drawing, and then pulled a razor blade from his back pocket. He cut the middle finger of his right hand from the tip to the knuckle and then let his hand hang down. When the blood started to flow, he used the finger like a pen to reproduce the image in the notebook on the white-painted door. Tali looked at the seal he'd drawn. It was delicate and had Juan's characteristic geometrical correctness. Only as she was admiring the design of the protection, which looked simple but provoked an ambiguous repulsion even in her, did Tali notice the silence.

'With this you'll never need another protection again. You could leave the door unlocked if you wanted.' He fell silent and looked into Tali's eyes. 'It's a seal that was recently given to me.'

'Are you asking for protection?'

Juan looked at the bandage on his hand, soiled with blood and sweat.

'I'm seeking protection and it's offered to me, slowly, as always. As you well know, I still haven't received what I really want.'

Then he motioned with his good hand for her to give him the notebook.

'If you want to swim, I'll make you a good bandage so you can get in the water,' she said.

Later on, Tali cleaned Juan's wound in the bathroom, thinking of the dirty door and Juan's fragility; she knew an infection would be very dangerous. He let her work, and only asked her to wrap the bandage more tightly.

'You look beautiful,' he told her when she'd finished.

'Don't say that, you know I don't like it.'

'You always were beautiful. Rosario was pretty, but you're beautiful.'

'But you love her, so don't talk to me like that.'

'Oh, but falling in love has nothing to do with beauty.'

Tali put her hands on her waist and had to take a deep breath to keep from shouting.

'You know what, Juancito, you need to let me know when you're coming, because otherwise these things happen.'

'What things?' he asked, and he crossed his legs, sitting on the edge of the tub.

'The thing is that I never forget you, but I manage and I'm happy with my plants, my house, my dogs, I have my bed and some nights I imagine it's you when I hear footsteps but other nights I sleep just fine, let me tell you. And suddenly you show up here with the kid and I get all stupid, I'm such an idiot, thinking you're going to stay and we're going to be together and all that nonsense. I even get it into my head – just listen to this – that my sister would be happy if you stayed with me. My poor, dear sister. You really piss me off, asshole.'

Someone knocked gently on the bathroom door and Juan said, Come in, son. Gaspar entered shyly. Tali straightened up beside the sink and smoothed her hair, which she wore very long, almost down to her waist. Sometimes she thought she might be a little old for hair like that. Gaspar didn't even glance at her.

'What happened to your finger?'

'I cut myself outside.'

'On what?'

'On a broken bottle that was there to keep cats out of the chicken coop.'

'Does it hurt?'

'No.'

'When they cut you there it hurt a whole lot.' Gaspar pointed at Juan's chest.

'But that's totally different,' replied Juan, and Tali saw him holding back laughter. 'This is a little cut on my finger. And also, as I explained before, what hurts in the chest is the bone.'

'Right, because they sawed open the bone to operate on you.'

44

'Oh, honey, don't talk like that!' said Tali.

'They sawed it open, you didn't know?' Gaspar looked up at her, blinking as if the light bothered him. 'They cut him down the middle and then they sewed him up again. It was to cure his heart, but I don't think they cured it very good.'

Juan burst out laughing. He stood and picked his son up.

'It's just that there's no cure for your dad! You little animal, you're scaring Tali.'

'I just wanted to explain to her.'

'I already told her all about it over the phone a long time ago.'

'Then I don't need to explain.'

'No, you don't need to explain a thing.'

'Aren't we going to the water?'

'We're going right now.'

Juan kissed Gaspar's forehead and grabbed Tali's hand to lead her out of the bathroom, but she said, You all go, you two are crazy. I want to change and wash up a little before we leave. Don't make a scene, murmured Juan, and she shook her head. She needed a few minutes to herself, to look in the mirror, get the sunscreen and towels, wet her face, clean the blood from the tub, wait until her hands stopped trembling.

Let's take my car, said Tali, I'll drive. The lake was close and it was better for swimming than the river, which was treacherous along that stretch with its whirlpools and quicksand. The heat was stifling but the sky was clear, not a single rain-cloud. It still might rain later, but hopefully not, thought Tali; the January humidity could be torturous. She patted Juan's leg before starting off. He had put on a pair of khakis and seemed very uncomfortable in the Renault's seat, which was too small for him. Gaspar was silent in the back and Tali tried to draw him out by asking about the cartoons, but gave up when she received no reply. The boy was in mourning and so was she, and she well knew how sad that hot air was, the open oven of noon hitting them right in the face. His mother was dead. There was no consoling him.

She stopped the car at the roadside and got out. 'Come here, Gaspar, I want to show you something,' she told the boy through the window.

In front of a wooden sky-blue house that looked on the verge of collapse, there was a tall ceiba tree in flower. Gaspar got out grumpily, but he listened.

'This is the tree your dad was telling you about. It's Anahí's, the little native girl's.'

Gaspar walked to the trunk and stared up at the red flowers.

'There's a cat on that branch.'

'Where?'

Tali approached and looked up; a yellow cat was sleeping in the leafy shade. Gaspar still looked serious, and she knelt down to look straight into his eyes. Your mom still loves you, she told him. She can't be with you any more, but she loves you like crazy. Gaspar covered his face and started to cry and sway, and Tali let him be. She didn't look towards the car, didn't want to know if Juan was watching, if he was coming over to intervene, if he was going to be furious that she was making his son cry. She's never coming back, is she? Gaspar asked, and Tali didn't want to answer that question, but replied the way she had to: that no, his mother wasn't going to come back. Did you know she was hit by a bus? the boy asked then. Yes, don't you remember I was at the funeral? Maybe not, when you're very sad it's easy to forget things.

'There are a lot of buses here, I don't like it.'

He's scared to death, Tali realized, and she wanted to hug him, but there was nothing in the boy's attitude that authorized her to touch him. He's like his father that way, she thought; they're both like cats.

'Around here we call buses micros. They're a little different.'

She wasn't going to make him feel better with that, but at least it was true.

'Let's go to the water, okay?'

He doesn't want to be far from his dad, thought Tali. Gaspar held his hand out to her and she took it, surprised. Back in the car he was still quiet, but at least he looked out the window: before, his head had hung down. Juan said nothing, just lit a cigarette and smoked it slowly, filling his lungs with smoke as if the heat wasn't enough.

The rest of the day was calm and silent even though the beaches at the lake were full of people. Gaspar received cheers and applause when he was able to float free of the safety of his father's arms, and although he didn't eat much at lunch, he did agree to play with some boys carrying spades and buckets who invited him to dig trenches. Stay close, where we can see you, Tali told them, and the boys said, Yes ma'am, and settled in less than three metres away. Juan swam far out in the lake, and Tali, alone under the sun umbrella, finally felt calm. She was ready now to listen to what Juan had to tell her. Because, she realized, he did have something to tell her. Juan was not her occasional lover. She was no mere river witch. They were both members of the Order. They could pretend to forget that, but not for very long.

Gaspar was still digging his hole – a real crater, said the other boys' mother, who was keeping a close eye on them. A car radio was playing a melancholic *chamamé*; a fat woman was strolling along the shore with a black dog that leapt up at her and made her laugh; two young men were storing their fishing poles, bait, and catch in the back of a pick-up: they'd soon be putting the fish on a grill somewhere. Tali recognized a man who had come

47

to ask for protection two months back, and whom she had let enter the temple and pray to the saint, alone; she had blessed his skeleton figure with wine and ash. She also recognized a woman who had come to have her cards read, asking about her daughter: Tali had seen her dead, drowned, and she'd said so. One of the many girls the military had murdered and thrown into rivers, their eyes eaten by fish, their feet tangled in vegetation: dead mermaids with bellies full of lead. Tali didn't lie, she wouldn't give false hope. The fathers and mothers of young people who'd been disappeared by the dictatorship sought her out; they wanted, at least, to know how their children died, if their bodies were in a pit of bones or underwater or in a secret cemetery. The woman didn't look at her now: she was playing with a little girl. Was this the dead girl's daughter? She remembered that afternoon: it was raining, the sky was black. Unafraid of the lightning, the woman had left anyway, and Tali had watched her run down the dirt road. Then she'd gathered up the cards in the deck and sat drinking mate, looking out at the dark grey day, watching the way the wind shook the peach tree and the other trees off in the distance, by the river. *Ka'aru*, she thought, testing herself. She needed to speak more Guaraní. She was losing the language, spending too much time alone.

Juan returned, but Tali didn't see him come from the beach; he'd taken a detour to come up from behind. He dropped down beside her on the towel, and was so out of breath that after a few minutes Tali grew alarmed.

'You do realize it'll be a disaster if you have an attack here, right? Do you know what they could do to me? We'd have to go to Corrientes to find to a doctor. *Nde tavy*, you can be a real dumbass.'

Juan couldn't answer for a while, and Tali looked at him in disapproval until he got his breath back.

'Don't make a big deal of it,' said Juan, and he gulped 7up straight from the bottle.

'Gaspar is playing nicely with some boys.'

'I know. We have to talk.'

'We've needed to talk since you got here, I can tell.'

'I need your help.'

Juan sat up cross-legged, and suddenly he was no longer her friend or her lover, not even the man who made her so angry and whom she loved so much. He was the medium. Tali knew the people around them couldn't hear what he was saying, or if they did, they would hear something different, or believe they were listening to a foreign language. She knew it when the air around them seemed to tremble and the soft hairs on her arms stood up, as if instead of the sun on her skin there was ice.

Is this necessary? You're already in secret and there's no one near us.

I don't trust anyone. I don't trust myself. Gaspar is trapped. They want him to be my heir. Either he inherited my ability to summon the Darkness or I'm going to transport my consciousness into his body when the moment comes. And then, I'll still be trapped.

We already know all that. Why are you telling me again?

To collect my thoughts. And to ask you for something. I'm sure they killed Rosario. She had a fight with her mother and Florence. It was when I was in the hospital. Rosario asked them to leave us alone. She told them they couldn't keep using me, that I didn't want to summon any more and that I would never hand over Gaspar and let them use his body.

Tali felt dizzy. What she was hearing was impossible.

My sister was crazy. Angá, *how did I not stop her?*

It's inconceivable to them that I could refuse to use Gaspar's body. I told them I would, of course. Rosario told me about the fight not long before her accident. She was furious because the Ceremonial had

49

pushed me to the edge, but she put Gaspar in danger. They will test him to see if he's a medium, as always, but this time the result will be positive.

Are you sure about that? You don't think he's just sensitive?

I'm sure. If we can keep them from realizing, make the test negative as usual, then the only option is to wait for him to come of age so I can take over his body, and I know that in the intervening years I can figure out how to get him away from them. It's taking a long time and it's maddening, but I will do it.

Why didn't Rosario tell you sooner?

I spent months in and out of the hospital before they could operate on me. She didn't dare. I don't know.

Don't blame her.

I do blame her. I blame her and I also forgive her.

Can you refuse to summon?

No, they'll force me. The same way they did years ago, the time I refused because they were using prisoners as sacrifices. Sacrifices no one was asking for.

Tali looked down at her hands. She couldn't forget about that either, or about her own complicity.

They still use the hostages.

I know, but I can't confront them. They threatened to break the pact and take Gaspar, to raise Gaspar in the rites, train him, destroy him. They believe in what the Darkness tells them. They listen, and they obey. And they have no one else who can summon it. Mercedes is always looking for other mediums. She is the priestess of a god who ignores her, just as all clerics of any denomination are ignored by their gods, and always have been. But her god speaks to me. For her, it was always a kind of curse to have such an untrustworthy oracle. I believe in the Darkness. How could I not, when it's my body? When it's my body that it enters? But to believe is not always to obey. The things the Darkness tells them cannot be interpreted on this plane. The Darkness is demented, it's a savage god, a mad god.

What I want to know is if you could *refuse. If you wanted.*

Of course not, I'm a slave. I am the mouth. The Darkness can find me, it's a lost battle. Tali, I need to ask you for something. I need you to work with Stephen to block Gaspar. I'm doing what I can but it's not enough, not any more, now that I'm alone. He saw a presence yesterday, and not just any presence. I suppose it will only grow now. I need you to protect him in Puerto Reyes, I need you to hide his abilities, with Stephen's help.

They'll still want you to use his body.

We'll have years before that happens. I have time and the ability to deceive them. The hardest part will be staying alive. I need that time. Time to raise Gaspar and figure out how to get him away from the Order. I'm going to do the Ceremonial like I always have. I am the open door and it cannot close, but I have to protect Gasper. They already took Rosario, and they did it for many reasons, but above all to weaken me. 'We will take your companion so she can't help you abandon us, so she can't help you quit and betray us.' I'll never be able to stop.

And as he said that, Juan dropped the insulation that had allowed them to speak almost without moving their lips. Tali felt a kind of small whirlwind around her, and she saw sun, lake, and people all grow blurry with a golden halo around them, like mirages on the highway. Juan put a hand to her forehead and right away she could see better, and the headache, which had threatened to be intense, became a weak throb.

'Stop it!' she cried, pushing Juan's hand away from her. People turned to look and she smiled, pretending they were just playing. Juan was pale. So it was true, then. Years ago, she well remembered, it had taken him almost no effort to generate the energy to speak in secret. Now he was using his last bit of strength to make her feel better, and she could not allow it. Tali admonished herself because she had never learned to invoke secrecy too, and he'd had to exert himself alone. She put her arms around him so he wouldn't fall over. Tali didn't want Gaspar to see them touching, but now she had no choice.

'Easy now. What do you need? Tell me what to do.'

'Lay me down,' said Juan, very softly.

Tali obeyed and placed the bag under his head as a pillow. He brought two fingers to his neck and massaged it gently. He was no longer wet with lake water: he was soaked instead with sweat and panting as though he'd just run a race. Tali looked at Gaspar, who was busy building something with the dirty sand, a structure without a clear shape. The other boys were decorating it with sticks and feathers. She used a towel to wipe Juan's sweat away, at least from his face and chest.

'Open your eyes if you can,' she told him.

Juan looked at her and shifted his head on the bag. He still couldn't sit up, and his pupils were dilated.

'Call Gaspar over.'

'He'll get scared if he sees you like this.'

'Call him.'

Gaspar came running over, dirty from the water and sand: he knelt down beside his father and asked what he wanted. Nothing, said Juan, just a hug. Dummy, said Gaspar, and he wrapped his arms around Juan's neck and lay against his shoulder a while, telling him about the castle they were building near the water. Can we read stories about castles later, can we? Before bed, said Juan. I'm going back with those guys now. They're really bad at making sandcastles. I bet. I want some 7up. Take the bottle, share with them. Their names are Sebastián and Gonzalo. Okay, give them some plastic cups so you don't all drink from the bottle, that's gross.

Gaspar returned to his game with the bottle and cups and the other boys greeted him with a cheer.

They stayed until sunset. Juan didn't move from the bed Tali had improvised for him until Gaspar wanted to get in the water again for a while, before night fell, and Juan took him. He made his son swim with his head both out of the water and under. It was still a rudimentary crawl, but he did it well; he still couldn't swim on his own for long, but he did it well for as long as he could.

'He's a fast learner,' the mother of the sandcastle boys said to Juan when they came back to the beach.

Juan said yes, he was pleased. The woman, who was young, had sat with Tali drinking mate while he took Gaspar swimming; now she offered them *chipá* and croissants. You love these, said Juan as he handed a *chipá* to his son. Gaspar bit into the bread and smiled as he remembered: he had eaten this several times, years before, in Puerto Reyes. Juan ate one too, and before he put on his pants, he took his medication from the pocket. He swallowed the pills unashamedly in front of the woman; instinctively, she offered him a cup of soda to help.

'Oh, it's great how you can take them all together', she said. 'Me, when an antibiotic is really big, I can't get it down. I must have a problem with my throat.'

Juan smiled at her.

'I'm just very used to it.'

'I was just telling your wife that if you feel like it later, we all get together and play *chamamé* over there near the beach. There'll be more people coming with guitars.'

Juan shot Tali a surprised look and she explained: 'The police don't give you much grief around here when people get together.'

'The military neither,' said the woman. 'A few years back they'd

53

break everything up, but now they let it go. They're loosening up. You're invited, with the little one too, it's family-friendly.'

'Want to go?' Juan asked Gaspar. 'They're going to play music.'

'Do you want to?'

'I'm asking you.'

'Yeah.'

'You need to rest,' said Tali in a low voice, and Juan came over to her, caressed her hand and told her, Don't worry, I know what I'm doing.

'There'll be empanadas, too,' added the woman in an effort to convince Tali.

'See? That way you won't have to cook.'

'Don't be ridiculous, Juancito, please.'

They didn't stay long. Tali thought the empanadas were too greasy, but Gaspar liked them. Isn't it a little strange for a kid to eat, like, everything? she asked Juan, and he replied that honestly, he didn't know any other kids, but his son had always been like that – feeding him was the easiest thing in the world, he'd even get bored of always eating the same thing and ask for more variety. There wasn't much dancing except for a few couples who swayed lazily to 'Puente Pexoa' and 'Kilómetro 11'. The evening was heavy; across the river and beyond the trees the sky was clear, a sign that the night would be cloudy. There was a wind that provided no relief – the humid wind of a storm. The sandcastle boys' mother found them and offered them some *sopa paraguaya*, neatly cut into portions. The smoke from the grill carried the smell of meat, and Tali asked Juan for money to buy a sausage. As she was waiting in line she listened to the conversations of men who were already drunk – some of them leered at her with bloodshot eyes; in another time she would have had Juan deal with them, but now she wanted to avoid any fights. They were drinking wine that was sold by the litre in car oil cans with the edges pounded over to avoid any cuts. To distract herself from them she focused on the music, and she realized the musicians were no longer playing *chamamé*. She turned around, and through the smoke and the tenuous light given off by a few bulbs and a kerosene lantern, she saw a girl with her long hair pulled back who was singing a lovely *zamba*: *Tengo miedo que la noche me deje también sin alma, la añera es la pena buena y es mi sola compañía*. When she went back to Juan, who was sitting on a stump and smoking, he said to her, 'If she were singing that anywhere else she'd be arrested, they'd arrest us all, you're lucky here. The girl is really pretty, do you know her?' Tali hit him on the head and his blond hair fell over his face; suddenly, Juan looked like a teenager.

'No, I don't know her. And we're not sticking around here so you can get to know her.'

'You'll have to forgive me, my dear, but I much prefer *zamba* to *chamamé*,' Juan said.

The girl kept singing: *Y en cada vaso de vino tiembla el lucero del alba*. And after she greeted her listeners and introduced herself, she said she was going to sing a very sad song by a singer who was sick; she didn't name the singer, and Juan whispered to Tali that he must be banned. *No sé para qué volviste, si ya empezaba a olvidar, no sé si ya lo sabrás, lloré cuando vos te fuiste*, went the song, *y que pena me da saber que al final de este amor ya no queda nada*. Juan told her he didn't know much about music, Rosario was the one who listened to it, but he knew that song was by Daniel Toro. 'And he is indeed banned, even though they're love songs. Rosario always said it was stupid to ban him because his songs were all sappy, there was nothing political about them.'

Sappy love songs, thought Tali. And here she was brought to the verge of tears by one of those sappy songs. Rosario, you always were a mean one, *chamiga*. My sister, she thought, how I miss you.

'Still, I really don't know if things have calmed down or not,' she said. 'Every time someone comes to have their cards read, I see death, death, so much death. You know what I see? A war. Not here, but in the ocean, in the cold. I can't bring myself to tell people, because then they won't trust me any more.'

'I'm sure you're right,' said Juan.

Gaspar yawned. Time for bed, son? Did you eat enough? Yeah, the soup without water was really good. It really was delicious, Tali agreed. The girl with the guitar announced her last song, and as Tali started up the car, she heard 'Gracias a la vida'.

'That girl is brave,' said Juan. 'And come on, let's get out of here, Rosario used to spend all day listening to this with Betty and I don't want Gaspar to remember.'

Gaspar was already asleep on the back seat. The way to Tali's house was a dark dirt road, and she drove it fast: she'd gotten stuck in the mud several times. Still, the storm didn't break; it was just distant thunder, lightning, and that humid imminence. As a girl she'd been afraid of storms, but now, after so many years, she didn't mind them unless the river overflowed. The floods didn't reach her house, which was built on a hill, but almost no one else had that luxury.

'Put him in my bed,' said Tali, after turning off the light. 'I'll sleep on the mattress tonight. Your son needs you, sleep with him.'

Juan didn't argue, just undressed Gaspar and turned on the fan. The house was cool. Tali waited for Juan on the living-room sofa. Neither of them felt sleepy.

'You want to petition the saint for your health?'

'Tali, that won't do any good.'

'Such little faith, *che*, what's happened to you? Let me help you the way I know how.'

Juan sat looking at the ceiling a while. Outside, finally, it had started to rain.

'Most patients who were born with a problem like mine back then, when the surgery was experimental, have terrible lives today. The ones who don't are dead. I survived, but I'll never recover, and I have constant complications. You might say I'm lucky.'

'So, you're just going to let yourself die?'

'I tried, and I still try, many ways of curing myself, aside from medicine, and no doubt they've helped. We've already talked about this many times. I don't want to die, Tali. I'm afraid. Those like me don't pass on to death. They go to the Darkness.'

'You don't know that.'

'Yes, I do. Sometimes I choose not to believe. When I do believe it, I would do anything to avoid it.'

Juan stood up.

'Let's go see the saint. I want you to put him under my skin. Can you? Can it help me live, can it give me time?'

Tali came closer to Juan, gingerly touched the circles under his eyes, the stubble he hadn't shaved in days. Then she led him from the house by the hand.

The temple was simple. The Lord of Death was not. Tali had chosen a large skeleton effigy for the sanctuary, almost a metre tall and made of silver, wearing a black robe. She approached the figure and filled a small glass with whiskey as an offering. Then she lit three red candles. There were many more in the temple and she had to be the one to light them all, because she was its guardian.

'Don't move,' she told Juan. 'Stay there.'

Tali lit all the candles, some red, others black, and she placed before the saint some red carnations that she kept fresh in a white glass vase. She turned off the electric lights. When the small sanctuary was lit by candles it made the silver saint tremble under his black cape, his scythe just peeking out. Unlike other images that depicted him with a crown, her San La Muerte had a bare, unadorned skull. Nor did he wear a hood. The skull's eyes were lit from within by shining stones that could sometimes be seen and sometimes not, depending on how intensely the candles burned. And that night they burned like bonfires – Tali had never seen or felt them blaze like that before.

'Kneel, Juan.'

He obeyed, and Tali felt deeply grateful. Juan didn't like ceremonies. But she did, as had her sister, and she trusted in her saint. She said, in a strong and clear voice:

> Powerful San La Muerte,
> Effective advocate and protector of those
> Who invoke you,
> I pray for your intercession so that this sick man
> Will recover his health quickly.
> Powerful San La Muerte,
> Until the final moment comes,
> Allow him to live fully,
> To fulfil the mission he has been given.
> Let it be so.
> Amen.

The lights made the saint smile and Tali smiled back, showing her teeth: a mutual recognition. Then she approached the figure, touched its silver feet – warm from the heat of the day – and opened the little box made of palo santo that was on the altar beside the statue. She looked at the talismans. She had one, blessed twice, that was carved from a bullet. She had gone to get it herself from Mercedes' cemetery. Her mother had told her where to find it. She didn't want that one for Juan – it had been under the skin of a despicable man. She chose her favourite, the one she had meant to keep forever but was now going to give away. It was carved in a different style. The lord, San La Muerte, was sitting on a rock, elbows on his knees and chin in his hands. She loved that inexplicable depiction.

'I'm going to put the Lord of Patience in your body, it's what you need. It's made of Christian bone. Stand up now.'

She returned to the altar with whiskey and a razor blade that she disinfected with alcohol. The incision in his shoulder had to be less than three centimetres deep, and Tali was exact, trying not to cut too far in. Juan's skin was delicate and opened easily. She lifted the skin a little – unlike all the other devotees she had grafted the saint into, Juan didn't move or breathe sharply or make any sound at all, accustomed as he was to physical suffering – and after dunking the carving in a cup of alcohol, she carefully inserted it into the wound. She filled her mouth with whiskey, spat it over the cut, and said some words in Guaraní. She had some clean gauze, and though it was unnecessary because the cut was very small and with any luck would scar over soon, she made him a bandage.

'That's it, my love,' said Tali. 'It's the most powerful *payé* I have, and also the rune I love most. You see the light? It never burns like that, there's always at least one candle that goes out. This time not a single one did.'

'Will your lord get angry if I give you a kiss?'

'No,' Tali said, and let him kiss her. 'Do you want to leave him something? If you don't offer him anything, then he could get mad.'

Juan approached the altar, deposited a cigarette at the saint's feet, knelt down, and bowed his head. He took the bandage from his hand and let a few drops of blood fall into a dish of water that was in front of the figure. Tali realized then the enormity of what had happened. The blood of a man like Juan was an honour for her sanctuary.

Before they left, Juan took her by the waist and said into her ear:

'Can your lord watch over something? With the protection on the door, no one will be able to come in and take it. I want to leave it here.'

Juan took a small silver box from his pocket: Tali had seen it before and thought it was a pillbox for his medication. Juan opened it. Inside was a long lock of brown hair, braided and lovingly arranged in a spiral. Rosario's hair – she recognized it immediately. Tali closed the box, told Juan of course she would keep it, and placed it behind the saint, under his black tunic.

'You can come for it after the Ceremonial.'

Juan didn't answer, and Tali sensed that she was now the guardian of that relic, that she was saving it for someone or something else. Outside, it wasn't raining any more. It had been a short storm. They left. On the way back, Tali told him:

'I didn't think the saint would matter to you.'

'Why not? I've always respected him.'

'That's true, but you've never asked him for anything.'

'I need all the help I can get now.'

His breathing sounded agitated again. She entered the house first and peeked into the bedroom. Gaspar was sleeping calmly on his side. She hadn't thought about the kid at all while they were out, but as she carefully closed the door she pictured him awake and alone in the house with the storm raging outside, and she was grateful he was sleeping so soundly.

'Now I feel like a whiskey,' said Juan. Tali put ice into two glasses.

'I just brought some from Paraguay. It's pretty lousy, but if you have a craving, it'll do. Does it hurt?'

'My shoulder? No.'

'Why do you ask if I mean your shoulder? Does something else hurt?'

'My finger hurts. My hand hurts. I have some kind of bug bite on my back that hurts.'

'You should be taking antibiotics, you know.'

'I'm sure you've got some around.'

'I have, I keep them because people don't know how to take care of themselves and get infections, and I don't want anyone blaming me.'

'Well, not now, you can give them to me later.'

'Later it is,' said Tali, and she took off her damp dress and lay naked on the floor. Juan lay beside her and Tali waited with her eyes closed until he was calmer and his breathing grew less laboured.

She woke up in the morning alone on the mattress in the living room. Juan had covered her with a light sheet and brought over a fan. Tali looked at the wall clock. Six in the morning. Very early, but she couldn't sleep any more. She went to her room and looked at Juan and Gaspar as they slept. Despite the heat, they were in an embrace, Gaspar lying on his father's chest and Juan's arm around his son's waist. Tali tiptoed away to get the Polaroid camera she had bought in Asunción. The camera was loud, but she hoped the noisy fan would cover the sound. They didn't wake up when she snapped the picture, and she left the room to watch the image slowly emerge. The morning light filtering through the curtains had given it a special effect: they both looked less pale, more golden. Juan didn't like photos, and she didn't plan to show him this stolen image. When the picture dried she stashed it on top of the fridge, where he wouldn't find it.

*

Gaspar's pain was like an alarm clock for Juan, and that morning he was able to put his arms around the boy before he started crying disconsolately, caressing his hair until he grew calm. He took him to the bathroom to wash his face, then left him alone to brush his teeth. Tali had made them breakfast and left a note on the table. She'd gone into town to buy a few things she needed.

Juan wrote on the back of the note: *Thanks for everything, we're leaving, see you in Puerto Reyes.* He heated the milk for Gaspar, who hated to drink it cold. The boy had climbed up to sit on a high, backless stool. He couldn't balance and looked uncomfortable. Juan didn't say anything, didn't ask him to move to a chair. He couldn't talk that morning, his head was pounding. He had dreamed of damp hallways and handprints on walls, of the dark light that could wound and bite.

'Where're we going?'

'We're leaving.'

Gaspar pushed his milk away and spat on to the table. He hated milk skin. I don't want any more, it's gross, he said. Juan saw how his anger hardened his jaw, how he clenched his teeth. I don't want to go, said Gaspar, crossing his arms. And why not let him stay? Juan thought. Why not leave him there with Tali, let her take care of his son? He could come visit from time to time. Or not: in a few years Juan would be a distant memory and Tali would be his mother, he'd grow up amid skeletons and the mysterious church, a boy of the river who would speak Guaraní and fish for catfish. Nights of grilled pacu and sex on the sand, and fishermen would wave at him from their sailing rafts. Or he could leave Gaspar along the road, someplace near the river. Or in the doorway of a hospital or police station. There were lost kids all over the country. Abducted kids, abandoned kids. The children the military stole from their prisoners. Someone would take him. There was an epidemic of illegal adoptions. Gaspar was lucky, he'd be welcomed with open arms: he was beautiful and undamaged, or at least not damaged much. Of course, what he was imagining was impossible. They would find Gaspar in minutes once he was unprotected. Tali was Adolfo's daughter – a peripheral and rebellious Initiate, perhaps, but still part of the Order. Gaspar would never be safe with her. There was no possibility of escape. He could fantasize about running away, and often did, but in reality, not only would they both surely be caught, but he also didn't really want to renounce his power, he had to admit. Even with all the hatred, contempt, ambivalence, and repulsion he felt towards the Order, that power was still his, and he didn't possess many things. Renunciation is easy when you have a lot, he thought. He had never had anything.

'Go get dressed.'

Juan got up and said, Do as I say, go, right now, and when Gaspar refused again, sniffling with his arms crossed, Juan slapped him on the cheek with his open palm, a blow that swung Gaspar's face around, making him wobble on the stool and finally lose his balance. He fell and landed on his side with a dry thump, and the stool also toppled to the floor, barely missing him. Juan went over to him and yanked him roughly up, ignoring his cries, and saw the red mark on his cheek and his swollen lip. The pang of regret disappeared as soon as Gaspar started to cry. Stop it, he said. He grabbed his son's hair and forced him to meet his eyes, straining his neck backward. He shook the boy's head, and felt the soft, sweaty hair get tangled in his fingers. Don't be weak, nothing happened. Gaspar tried to say something: the chair, the slap; Juan raised his hand threateningly again, and the boy stopped crying. Go get changed, he repeated, and don't make me tell you again. Gaspar obeyed. He ran to the bedroom and left the door open. It was going to take him a while to get dressed – he would have to vent first, punching the pillow and shouting, I hate you, I hate you, I hate you, but Juan could put up with that.

What he couldn't put up with was that morning's sun, his exhaustion, the constant pain in his chest. He no longer knew whether it came from his most recent surgery, from anxiety, or from some mechanism in his body that was breaking down like an old, irreparable motor that struggled more and more to start up until finally it choked for good.

He went to the bedroom. In one hand he held scissors and an envelope. Gaspar had put on Bermuda shorts and a T-shirt. He was sitting on the bed trying to put on his sandals, but he still didn't know how to use Velcro.

'Let me,' said Juan, and Gaspar looked at him with dry eyes. He extended his foot so Juan could help him. His lip was swollen but not bleeding. The Franciscan sandals were new and at first Gaspar had hated them; he always wanted to wear sneakers. Maybe he had chosen them now to offer a truce. He's smart, thought Juan.

'I don't hate you,' said Gaspar. 'I'm sorry Daddy, do you forgive me?'

Juan didn't answer. He used the scissors he'd brought from the kitchen to cut a lock of Gaspar's hair, and the boy looked at him in surprise. Juan didn't explain, just cut some more and then put all the hair into the envelope. Then he drew two signs on the front: Tali would know what they meant. They were necessary to protect Gaspar. He touched his back and remembered he needed to clean the wound where Tali had inserted the skeleton saint under his skin. That region and its bones. So many bones. Like the bones in the Other Place that Juan didn't want – refused – to think about. Rosario had told him how the Guaraní had traditionally buried their dead in earthenware containers and kept them close, sometimes in their houses, because they believed they could be brought back to life. They would even keep them in those innocuous handmade baskets of braided reeds that were sold in markets and along the road-sides: the cadaver stayed there until it rotted and fell apart. Then the bones were washed and the family would store them in a wooden receptacle. Those old huts must have reeked. Rosario said that some evangelist priests had told of temples where those bones were worshipped, where the skeleton hung between two poles in a net or a hammock decorated with feathers. The place was perfumed, and the priests claimed that the skeleton was a demon and that it spoke.

'Don't forget your backpack,' he said, and got up from the bed. He went to the bathroom to put alcohol on his wound; it didn't sting. He tried not to look at himself in the mirror. Then he went to get his bag from Tali's room. Before leaving, he put the envelope with his son's hair on the table beside the note, so Tali could use it later. He waited for Gaspar in the sun of the patio.

'Is the car gonna be hot?'

Juan looked around. The green was awful, beautiful, so many shades that it was unfair to call them all by the same name. The car was parked in the shade of a willow tree.

'A little, but the sun wasn't on it, the seats won't burn.'

'If I look at the sun, my head hurts. I see those weird flowers in the sky.'

'Don't look, then.'

Juan also saw black flowers in the sky before a migraine. He and his son were oddly and exactly alike in that respect. What other things did they share? That was the question.

He started the car and struggled to manoeuvre on the gravel until they reached the highway. On the curve of the exit, he saw the checkpoint where police were stopping people and opening trunks: there was a long line of waiting cars. He glanced over as he passed, feigning curiosity, and one of the policemen waved him on: he held a gun in his hand as if he were about to use it, or needed it to defend himself. Juan sped up a little, not so much that the cop would think he was fleeing, enough to show he'd understood the order. From the back seat, Gaspar's alarmed eyes met his in the rear-view mirror.

'Come on up front,' Juan told him.

The Order had never used police or soldiers as sacrifices. Their ideological consistency was impeccable, thought Juan. They only sacrificed people their friends were after, helping them that way. He contributed, but he didn't feel complicit. He felt innocent. He was a prisoner, too.

The landscape now was dotted with pink hydrangeas, and they caught glimpses of the light reflecting off the river through the still willow branches. Beside the highway they started to see women with long hair, heavy and tangled, who sat and sold braided baskets that they wove tightly with light green and ivory reeds. The women were silent while their children ran about, dangerously close to the road. Women and baskets, willows, children, and crosses. Gaspar wanted to know about the crosses; the small, dark, malnourished children didn't interest him. They're for people who died on the road, in accidents. Are they buried here? No, the crosses are put up to remember them, they're buried in the cemetery like everyone else.

Not everyone, thought Juan, but that would have been too much information just then. Beside the sign that said BELLA VISTA 80 KM was an enormous white cross decorated with pink crepe paper, several rosaries, and ribbon for wrapping presents.

A new cross with its decoration intact, not faded yet by heat or rain. A recent death. How long until Gaspar saw one? He himself was staying closed off while they travelled: he didn't want to see an accident victim stumbling along the road, not after seeing Rosario on the metal bed in the morgue, the split femurs that had broken through the skin of her legs and peeked out pink with blood, her face smashed in where the wheel had run it over. Like a half-moon, he'd thought, because that's what it looked like from where he was, kneeling on the ground because he couldn't stand up, her features caved in, her nose destroyed, her eyes somewhere in her brain and her forehead and chin sticking out in an almost perfect half-circle. He'd covered her after a while, after caressing her unscathed arms and extended hands. Someone handed him a little plastic bag with Rosario's rings and expensive bracelets. Juan couldn't remember if that person had been a doctor or nurse, a man or woman, but he did remember asking who he needed to call. And he or she had explained patiently and clearly. Juan had taken mental notes, but before doing anything, before calling Adolfo and Mercedes, before informing the guards and the lawyers, he stopped a taxi at the hospital entrance and gave the driver the address of Gaspar's school. He couldn't do all those tasks alone. He understood that it wasn't his son who should go with him to organize the funeral. He understood that he should take care of everything and then console Gaspar, explain to him gently about his mother's death. Still, he didn't care what normal people did. None of them were normal, not Gaspar or Rosario or Juan himself.

'Mom doesn't have a cross in the street?'

'No, they don't do that in the city.'

'Why not?'

'It's only a custom along the highway.'

'Can we make one for her?'

Gaspar went quiet, his hands on the glovebox. Outside, the low trees seemed tousled, disorganized, and were definitively ugly. Juan didn't dare pass the truck that stank of fertilizer and was slowing him down. When it finally turned down a dirt road through the trees, the highway opened up on jacarandas and ceibas; suddenly everything was violet and red, and Juan breathed deeply to control the palpitations he felt in his chest and neck.

'Gaspar, hand me the water.'

The boy climbed into the back seat and passed him the glass bottle – it had originally held Orange Crush, which Gaspar loved – full of cool water. The simple Styrofoam cooler was working well.

'What's that?'

Juan looked where he was pointing.

'That's a shrine.'

He slowed down to see what saint it was: it wasn't Gauchito, it was missing the characteristic red bandanas.

It was San Güesito.

Who is it, who is it? Gaspar insisted. It's a boy your age, more or less. He was killed by some drunks. Why, was he bad? The drunks were bad, not him. He was a poor boy who lived on the street. Or not on the street, really, but around here, in the jungle, near the highway.

Gaspar sat thinking, very focused. I can't tell him the truth, thought Juan, I can't explain that they raped Güesito before killing him. How many were there? No one remembered; some said five, others ten. They'd mutilated his body and used his head for rituals. That's how he was found, bloodless and headless at the side of the road, over twenty years ago. He was buried in the Goya cemetery, and his grave was covered with all the toys he hadn't had in life.

'I don't want to get out,' said Gaspar.

Juan felt the same. He didn't like El Güesito or his effigy, a dark-skinned, half-naked figure with eyes painted on in a vaguely Egyptian style, outlined and blind. He was curious about what had been placed in the little brick house that sheltered him, but it was better to keep going.

A sign announced 78 km. He could reach Bella Vista in an hour and there was time to talk to his son on the way. It was easier in the car: the movement seemed to hypnotize the boy. They would spend the night in a good hotel in Corrientes. He needed proper sleep before attempting what he had planned. He also needed to summon a certain type of sexual energy that would be difficult to find in these small towns. He could leave that problem for later.

'Gaspar, have you seen any other women like the one at the hotel?'

'Women, no.'

Juan adjusted his sunglasses. He liked how Gaspar understood exactly what he was asking. He looked at his son, who had taken off his shirt in the heat, and saw a bruise spreading over his shoulder. From hitting the floor earlier, when he'd knocked him from the stool. Juan softly ran his finger over the dark spot.

'Well then?'

'At the river when we were eating the soup without water and there was music, a man came out of the river.'

'And how did you know he was like the woman at the hotel?'

'Because he was naked and all swollen and he couldn't be like that. Then I did what you taught me and he went away.'

'He left right away?'

'Yeah.'

Impressive, thought Juan.

'Were you scared?'

Gaspar hesitated a moment and ran a hand over his fore-head. His gesture of worry. His other one was to ball up his left hand in a fist. Many times Juan had had to make him unclench his fingers, and it was no small amount of strength that Gaspar put into that anxious tic. He's going to die young if he stays this nervous, Juan had said to Rosario once. Furious, she had yelled at him to never say such things about Gaspar. How can you be such a brute, our son is not going to die. All that seemed so distant now, the early-morning fight, Rosario taking her pillow to sleep in another room, the slam of the door and the expensive perfume on the sheets.

'I didn't like it,' replied Gaspar.

'Give me your hand and let's swear, so you'll see I'm not lying to you.'

Juan slowed the car. The highway was empty, so he could drive with one hand and look into his son's eyes.

'I swear to you they can't do anything. They're not men and women, they're echoes. You know how when you shout in the garage at home your voice comes back to you? But it's not your voice any more, the second time. This is the same. They were people once, there was a time when they were the woman from the hotel and the man from the river, but not any more. They can't do anything. They can't hurt you, because they can't even touch you. They can get near you, but they can't touch you. I swear.'

'But why do we see them?'

'There are just some people who can see them. There are people who can see many more things.'

'You see other things.'

It wasn't a question.

'Yes.'

'Me too?'

'I don't know. We can test you if you want. And, if you want, there's also a way to see those who are like the man and the woman only when you feel like it.'

'When I feel like it?'

'Sure.'

'Why would I ever feel like it?'

It was a good question. Juan laughed.

'Then I'll teach you how to never see them again.'

'Are the black flowers like the women who aren't women? Because I saw them beside the clouds and now my head hurts.'

'Where does it hurt?'

'Here, in my eye.'

Juan reached into the back seat and felt around for the bag. He had to give his son an aspirin now, before the migraine erupted. Swallow it with water, he said, and sit still with your eyes closed. Gaspar had inherited the crippling headaches from him. They were impossible to explain to the fortunate people who only suffered from regular headaches: the hammering blows beneath the skull, eyes like two stones embedded in the face, the light like a knife, every noise amplified. And the nausea.

That wasn't the worst part, for Juan. The worst was that he couldn't take away Gaspar's pain. The only suffering he could take away was the pain he himself caused.

'I need to throw up, Daddy,' Gaspar said fifteen minutes later, and Juan stopped the car at the side of the road and opened the door so he could vomit on to the asphalt. He held the boy's forehead and his hair at the nape of his neck and he felt Gaspar's body as it strained, contracting and sweating in pain. He was going to have to find someplace cool and dark so the boy could sleep; otherwise, under that noontime sun, the hours of migraine were going to be unbearable. He'd have to go back to Tali's house. He took a little ice from the cooler and ran it over Gaspar's forehead; the boy was pressing on his temples like an adult.

'Don't cry, it'll make it worse,' he told him.

Gaspar vomited again. There was nothing left in his stomach, and the effort made him tremble. Juan was so focused on holding his son's head that he didn't notice the car pulling up beside him. He heard the voice before he sensed the car's presence, and he felt annoyed with himself. Was he losing his reflexes? What was wrong with him?

'Hi there, are you okay?'

Juan turned around and saw a Peugeot beside him. The driver who had spoken was obviously from Buenos Aires, and he looked young and inoffensive. Juan was alert now as he turned his full attention to the stranger. Trustworthy, he knew it with utter certainty. Another innocent.

'My son doesn't feel well.'

'Do you need help? Here, two hundred metres on, there's a grocery. I'm staying with the family, and they have a phone.'

Two hundred metres away? In this wilderness? Juan felt a slight pang of distrust, and at the same time he perceived that the young man in the car was also making an effort. There in the north the dictatorship was less oppressive, but any thinking person at least felt alarm bells go off when faced with a strange situation. But, thought Juan, this one didn't qualify as strange: a kid getting sick on the road, in summer. That was normal. He could accept the help, and the young man acted naturally as he offered it. Nothing pointed to any danger.

'They've got the store hidden from the highway then,' said Juan. 'I don't imagine they do much business.'

'People around here know where it is. See the side road?'

His manner was casual, another reassuring sign. Juan saw

the dirt road: there was even a small wooden sign with white letters that said 'Karlen Grocery'.

'My son gets migraines. What he needs is a cool, dark place to rest, not a store with people making noise. I was going to find a hotel.'

The stranger nodded.

'The family lives there, I'm sure they'll let him borrow one of the bedrooms. It's only two hundred metres.'

Juan looked the stranger in the eyes. He had curly hair and wore glasses, though he didn't have them on now: there were marks on the bridge of his nose. His car was pretty messy: he was travelling. His beige shirt was clean. Juan would be able to use him later, if he wanted.

'I'll follow you,' he said.

Karlen Grocery appeared right away. It was a modest construction, half brick and half wood, with a large parking lot and a patio, and behind it was the white-painted family home. The store had a deck with a long table that, though it was noon, was empty. There were two men drinking something, maybe *caña*, and leaning against the railing. The stranger in the car got out first and spoke with a woman who was standing in the doorway wearing a floral housedress and apron, her grey hair pulled back. As soon as she heard what the stranger had to tell her, she came running to Juan's car. Juan had opened the driver-side door and was still moving an ice cube over Gaspar's forehead. The boy didn't turn his head: he'd already learned that would only increase the pain.

The woman introduced herself as Zulema Karlen, the owner of the grocery and the sawmill, and she told Juan that if he wanted, the boy could lie down in her son's bed, they'd be more than welcome. Could be this child is bedevilled, she said, after Juan introduced himself and Gaspar. He could very well be, replied Juan, but I don't know many people who know how to cure the evil eye. You're right about that, said Mrs Karlen. It's like they say, there's a lot of snake oil. Come on this way. My mother had headaches like that, but I've never seen them in a child. Could he have sunstroke? It's possible, said Juan. The woman's tone was vaguely critical: A man who doesn't know how to take good care of his child, she probably thought. It didn't bother Juan – she wasn't all wrong. He hadn't bought a hat for Gaspar, for example, didn't make him wear a seat belt, and if the boy annoyed him, he was capable of beating him brutally, even worse than that morning. He followed the woman, carrying Gaspar.

'My husband and son are off on the island,' said the woman, as if Juan understood what she was talking about. The house at the back had a concrete floor, and on the patio a teenage girl was sweeping with a broom made of palm leaves. The house, whose rooms were separated by curtains of plastic strips instead of doors, was surprisingly cool. Juan saw an open bottle of wine and an arrangement of plastic flowers on the table, and prayer cards to Our Lady of Itatí on the walls, delicately framed. The refrigerator hummed loudly.

'In here,' said Mrs Karlen, and she opened the plastic curtain on to a small room with a single bed and a window whose shutters were closed.

Juan had to blink to get used to the darkness, and he laid Gaspar down carefully. The woman disappeared into the kitchen and returned with a small aluminium pot with iced water and a cloth. Juan thanked her, and she asked if he wanted potatoes. Yes, said Juan, but I'll cut them myself, you have to watch the store. It'll only take a second, said the woman. I don't know how to thank you, said Juan, but Mrs Karlen ignored him.

Juan removed the pillow so it wouldn't get wet and had Gaspar lie on his side. He knew from experience that this was the best position, and it would also keep the boy from choking on vomit if his nausea returned. He soaked the washcloth in the pot of icy water and put it on Gaspar's head like a hat. Mrs Karlen brought in several thin slices of potato, and Juan placed them on Gaspar's forehead. When the boy let go of his hand, when he fell asleep with his mouth open and his eyes covered by the cold cloth, Juan thought about leaving, getting into the car and abandoning him there at that grocery store in the middle of nowhere. It would be best for you, son, he thought. He imagined Gaspar grown up, working behind the counter or maybe even sailing a *jangada*. If he abandoned his son, Gaspar would grow into a furious and silent man, but the world is full of men like that. He left the room. Outside, the girl who had been sweeping asked in a quiet voice if the boy was feeling better, and Juan told her he was sleeping and would be fine when he woke up. Good thing my brother and my dad are out, so we have room. Otherwise, I'd have given him mine, but my brother's is better. Where are they? Juan wanted to know. At the mill, on the island. You have a sawmill? It's just for making fruit boxes. For lemons and oranges. Go on, sir, if you like, and have something to eat at the store, she told him. If your son wakes up, I'll let you know. I'm going to take a nap for a couple hours, but I sleep real light.

The kindness of strangers, thought Juan. Hadn't he met too many generous and disinterested people? Was it a sign? Could he be in some kind of trap, a set-up of some kind? He closed his eyes to concentrate better while he walked towards the grocery. He couldn't sense anything lurking. The cicadas shrieked, the birds were silent, an ancient violence throbbed out in the fields, and he could also sense the more recent brutality, but nothing that was directed at him or his son. What he did feel, though, was the blast of desire from the stranger in the Peugeot, who had introduced himself as Andrés.

75

Now there were two truckers eating at the table on the grocery's deck: one was finishing a plate of pasta, while the other nibbled distractedly at a sandwich. The other two were still there, drinking and leaning against the railing, and they were talking about something called a *manguruyú*. Juan tried to remember what the word meant: it was a fish, he thought. One of the men was saying, 'I'm uglier than mackerel and cooked mate for breakfast,' and Juan smiled: the man really was ugly. His face was scarred from some childhood disease, and he was chubby and short. He reminded Juan of the typical images of *duendes de la siesta*, the evil elves used by Corrientes parents to scare their kids into being good during their midday naps.

Andrés, the stranger with the Peugeot, emerged from the grocery with Mrs Karlen, and after enquiring about Gaspar he asked what Juan wanted to drink, as if he worked there. The fact that he did not was made clear by his mannerisms, by his accent straight out of Buenos Aires' Barrio Norte, and by the quality of his clothes.

'A soda. Good and cold, if they have it.'

'They do, you can't imagine how high they crank the coolers around here.'

Juan raised an eyebrow. He could imagine.

'Do you work here?'

'I stayed with them a few days, and since they won't accept cash, I'm helping out before I take off.'

Andrés struggled to open the Crush. He was nervous. He didn't sit at the table until the two truckers left and the ones at the railing, now quite drunk, went to rest under a willow tree. Juan only then realized they were very near a lake.

'Don't you don't want to eat anything?'

'Maybe later,' said Juan, and he sat looking at the empty bottle of Crush he had downed in three gulps.

Andrés smoothed his longish curls and explained what had brought him the grocery. He was a photographer, he told Juan, on a job taking pictures of the Argentine littoral. He referred to it like that: 'a job'. He photographed people, mostly. The Karlens had let him into their private lives, and he had photographed them not only in the grocery and at home, but also at the sawmill on the Paraná island, where at night the black howler monkeys shrieked and fought. He talked about the trip on the river: by motorboat on the way there and by *jangada* back. He also talked about a dance he'd photographed just two nights before: the Karlen kids had taken him there on a tractor, because the rain had turned the dirt roads to mud. Juan listened attentively. Why Corrientes, why this area? he wanted to know.

'Because I don't know Argentina,' said Andrés. 'I lived in Italy for many years.'

'Why did you come back? Aren't you scared of the military?'

Andrés gave a start.

'Don't get paranoid,' said Juan.

'And where are you two headed?'

Juan knew he owed Andrés an explanation; plus, it was the only way to reassure him. The photographer had been friendly, though perhaps he wasn't entirely disinterested. It hadn't been easy, but eventually Juan had come to recognize the effect his appearance had on both men and women. He had learned to understand the desire of others, and to use it, even when he wasn't capable of enjoying it.

'We're going to visit my in-laws, in Posadas.'

He wasn't going to tell the truth, exactly, but he could give Andrés a believable parallel version, realistic and transparent.

'They're rich. We could have flown, but I wanted to make the trip by car. I don't know the country very well either.'

There was no point in lying anyway, because Gaspar, of

course, would talk when he woke up, and he was always oddly talkative after a migraine. So he told Andrés that he was a widower, and that it was the first time he had travelled alone with his son.

Mrs Karlen, through the grocery's door, overheard their chat and rushed to bring Juan a plate of milanesas with mashed potatoes, saying he had to eat something. Then she announced that she was also going to take a nap.

'I'll let you know if the child wakes up. And come check on him whenever you want.'

Andrés wanted to know how his in-laws got rich, and Juan told him they owned an important lumber company. Then Juan asked if he could use the hammock chair that was near the door, and Andrés said yes and brought another from inside the store. He also brought out two beers. Juan took money from his pocket and asked the photographer to add it later to the register, or wherever the Karlens kept their money. He asked for another soda. I don't want to drink alcohol before driving, he said. I thought you would stay longer. No, I have to be in Posadas tomorrow.

The photographer seemed disappointed. He went on to tell Juan how he was getting tired of photographing people, and had started to take pictures of the saints and shrines along the highway. He'd been shocked by the altar to San Güesito; much more so after learning the story behind it. That's where he'd been going when they'd met on the highway – to photograph more altars.

'I don't want to stop you,' said Juan. 'You still have good light, go on.'

'I'd rather stay here with you,' said the photographer boldly, gulping his beer. 'I'm more interested in you than anything else now.'

Juan gave a slight smile. Now he had to take the next step.

'You're brave. I don't know if I would dare try to pick some-one up here, with so many drunken bruisers around just looking to cut someone.'

'Don't you believe it. You can't imagine how much action you can get in these parts. At the dance the other night I got more tail than I did the whole time I was in Italy. They're wild.'

Juan laughed.

'Do you know the Chapel of the Devil? You should photo-graph that.'

'I did hear something. People are really afraid of it.'

'They hold masses there, even though it's not consecrated. So the story goes. Instead of wine, they use water from a tub where an unbaptized baby was bathed. You'd think it would be a cup of blood, right? But no, they'd rather drink dirty water.'

'And why do they hold masses like that?'

'Why do you think? To hurt someone. Do you take pictures at night? You could go by and see if anything's happening. If it ever is, it'll definitely be on a Friday.'

'Do you believe in that kind of thing?'

'No,' Juan lied again. 'My wife was a big believer. If you've been here a while, I don't have to tell you that everyone around here is pretty witchy. I'm going to go check on my son.'

There was total silence in the house except for the low hum of the fans. Juan went straight to the room where Gaspar was sleeping and carefully removed the thin potato slices, which were hot and dry; there was still ice in the pot, and he soaked the washcloth again. He managed to do it all without wak-ing Gaspar. He left, trying not to make any noise. When he returned to the grocery the photographer had brought out a fan from the store and was waiting for him with another soda. A Coca-Cola. He couldn't drink that either. It seemed like a joke:

Andrés wanted to pamper him, and he got it wrong every time. Plus, he had taken off his shirt. He was thin and his chest was hairless, which was surprising because his arms were dark and almost furry. The photographer was nervous. Juan did nothing to reassure him. He sat down close to him and asked to hear more about his photos. Andrés talked about the islands in the river and how afraid he'd been of the fighting monkeys. He hadn't gotten a good shot of any of them. Not that he was interested in animal photography, he said. He would only do it for the money. If *National Geographic* hired me, sure. What he liked were people and buildings. In Italy he'd grown tired of buildings, though, because everything was historic or ostentatious, but now, in the simple and seemingly uniform houses of the littoral region, he had rediscovered a taste for the places where people lived. Juan was about to tell him he should explore more, that the region had some extraordinary mansions, white stone buildings in the middle of parks full of palm trees that took up hectares of land. Instead, he asked if Andrés had been to Venice, and he listened to what the photographer had to say about the canals and the Doge's Palace. *I stood in Venice / A palace and a prison on each hand*, thought Juan, who remembered verses well. It was very hot, and he took off his shirt, slowly. He waited to see how the photographer would react – not everyone was shocked. Some people were more or less indifferent to the scars from his operations, since not everyone had enough knowledge to understand their meaning or their seriousness.

Andrés, however, understood. My God, he murmured, not out of pity, but with surprise.

'What happened to you?'

'They're scars from surgeries. I didn't get shot or anything. I'm not a wounded revolutionary.'

Andrés murmured that he hadn't thought that. And then

Juan told him everything: how he'd been born with a very serious heart defect. And that he'd been operated on several times
as a child. And again as a teenager, in Europe. And now this last
time, some six months ago.

'Six months? And you're alone out here?'

'I've recovered,' said Juan. He looked into the photographer's
eyes and leaned back into the chair.

'You don't look sick. You're really pale, sure, but you're also
really blond! And you have an incredible body. You don't look,
I don't know, weak. Really, you're sick? The recent operation
didn't do any good?'

'It did some good. But I'll never be cured. That's why I
can't drink your Coke, at least not now, because I have to drive
later.'

'The caffeine. You're brave, out on the highway with the kid
all alone. Is the scar on your ribs also from your heart?'

Juan touched it: the scar ran from his ribs round to his
back. He turned his torso a little to give a view of the whole
thing.

'Yes, this is the first one.'

'And on your arm?'

'A burn.'

'You've had all kinds of trouble.'

They looked at each other in silence.

'Thank you for showing me.'

'I wanted you to know why I might die on top of you later.'

The photographer didn't laugh.

'If you want, I can drive you to Bella Vista,' he said.

Juan stood up from the chair and approached Andrés, who
grabbed him by the hips as if to keep him from falling on top
of him.

'I don't want you to take me anywhere.'

81

Andrés ran his fingertips over Juan's flat stomach. His ears were flushed.

'I can't believe you want to be with me. You're the most beautiful guy I've seen in my life. More than beautiful.'

'Quiet,' said Juan. 'Not here, come on.'

He entered the grocery and went behind the counter, far from the deli slicer, and leaned against the fridge, which was old and noisy and painted brown to look like wood. In there, shielded by the plastic curtain, the photographer asked if his scars hurt. Sometimes, said Juan. The bone, my sternum, always hurts when it's going to rain. Promise me nothing's going to happen to you, said Andrés as he unbuckled Juan's belt. Juan let him kneel down and lower his pants. The photographer was moaning and sweating and Juan thought that if someone found them like that, they could have a bad time of it; if those drunks caught them, they weren't going to be very friendly with two fags. He grabbed Andrés hard by the hair and told him: Slower. The photographer gave a slight nod, and when he changed his rhythm Juan felt the sweat break out on his back until it almost made him slide against the door of the refrigerator that buzzed in the heat of the siesta. Then he closed his eyes and focused on the sign, focused until he was far away from heat and siesta, floating among dead stars, searching among the bones for the seal of the summons, the permission, the welcome.

Juan didn't have to tell him to swallow to the last drop; Andrés savoured it with unnerving voracity. Of all the things someone could use to hurt him, nothing was more convenient than semen, and Juan didn't want to leave a trace of it anywhere. He went over to the door to keep watch so no one would enter while the photographer masturbated in a corner. Andrés had no way of knowing what was really happening. The double current, they called it in the Order. He, like everyone, had always had companions of both sexes: the magical androgyne. The rituals, of course, were complex, and had little to do with an encounter like the one he'd just had with Andrés, but Juan, as always, walked along the edge of heresy and danger. Also, he had enjoyed it. He let the photographer kiss him on the lips, then put his shirt back on and heard Andrés go to the restroom at the back of the store to clean himself up. It was an outdoor restroom, but apparently it had a rudimentary tap, because Andrés returned with wet hands that he dried on his pants. In his own hands, Juan felt the power of the energy he had summoned. It would be enough for what lay ahead, for the invocation he wanted to perform.

'Stay tonight,' said the photographer. 'Osvaldo and his son won't be back until tomorrow.'

Juan didn't answer. He checked the time: barely two in the afternoon. Still without answering, he went to the car, where he took from his bag a few blank pages he kept for Gaspar to draw on. And his medication. His son was waking up.

When he returned to the grocery, Andrés had brought him a grapefruit Fanta. This you can drink, don't tell me you can't. Yes, this I can drink, Juan told him, and he swallowed the pills with the soda. Andrés was gazing at him with damp eyes. Juan thought he had been selfish, he should have fucked Andrés against the grocery counter until he screamed, but he was tired. He left half the soda and went to find Gaspar, who was sitting up in bed and looking around with more curiosity than fear.

'How do you feel?'

'Hungry.'

'Then you're fine.'

He picked the boy up and crossed the patio slowly. I have to buy the kid a hat, he thought. Then he asked Andrés to make a milanesa sandwich for Gaspar, and while the boy ate, Juan smoked a cigarette. He left the money for the sandwich on the counter.

'I need a portrait of you two,' said Andrés.

'No. I hate photographs.'

'I'm a good photographer, really. I'll make you famous.'

'Even worse.'

'With that body and that face, you can't hate photographs. How hard can it be? A souvenir.'

Andrés posed them against the white wall of the grocery. Gaspar left his sandwich on the table, though the photographer assured him he could hold on to it. It'll look bad, said the boy, and Andrés laughed. Juan crossed his arms; his shirt was open to the middle of his chest. Andrés went over to smooth his hair, and Gaspar put his arms around his father's leg. Before taking the shot, the photographer looked at them: the boy with round blue eyes and dark hair, a little hollow-eyed after his nap and headache, his T-shirt smooth and clean; the beautiful man who put his hands under his dark shirt and looked at the camera with a calm expression that hid his haste. His cleft chin with its deep dimple, his eyes that were mostly green but also yellow, the scar that shone a little as if smeared with a layer of wax. He took two black-and-white photos and one in colour, and when he tried to ask them to do something else, to pose differently, Juan told him absolutely not. You're gonna send us the pictures, right? Gaspar asked, as he picked at the sandwich he no longer wanted to eat.

'Have you been to Posadas?' asked Juan suddenly.

'No, but I plan to go soon.'

'We're going to be there for two weeks. My father-in-law's house is very easy to find. When you get there, look for the Hotel Savoy. It's historical, everyone knows it. It takes up half a block. The other half block is my father-in-law's house.'

Juan saw the hope in the photographer's eyes and he kept lying.

'Just ring the bell. Gaspar, finish your soda now. If you don't want to eat, leave the sandwich, or we'll put it in the cooler. Does your head hurt? No? Okay, let's go.'

The photographer walked them to the car.

'I'm going to go to Posadas and find you. You drive me crazy. I'm telling you, seriously, I'll be there.'

'Easy now,' said Juan as he got into the car. Before pulling away he told the photographer again to go to the Chapel of the Devil, don't forget, you'll like it. And please, give this to Mrs Karlen.

He handed Andrés a piece of paper. It was a short thank-you note. As he pulled away, the photographer ran after the car a little and shouted, I don't know your last name! Juan, who was driving slowly, pressed the brake. Dinesen, he said. Like the writer. What writer? asked Andrés, his hands on the window. Isak Dinesen, replied Juan. Come on now, you're a boy who was educated in Europe. The photographer remained standing there in the sunlight: Juan realized how young he was. Twenty-one, twenty-two years old. He hadn't asked his age. He didn't care. Then he pulled away again, and Gaspar put his head out the window and waved to Andrés, the grocery, and the fat dog that was barking at the car's wheels.

Gaspar talked the whole way to the city of Corrientes, and Juan tried to pay attention without getting annoyed. He remembered a cold afternoon in Buenos Aires when a chauffeur was taking him and Rosario from their house to his in-laws' apartment on Avenida Libertador – they always sent a driver even though Rosario loved to drive. He was uncomfortable in the back seat with his long legs, the closed windows stifled him, and Rosario was insisting on a monotonous guessing game with Gaspar: what has a long neck and four legs and eats leaves from the trees? A giraffe! the boy shouted, and in the closed space the noise was deafening, Gaspar's peal of laughter and his mother's infantile voice congratulating him. Juan tried to concentrate on the city outside but could not block the sensations from the street: 1978, and the slaughter was everywhere. Juan hated to leave his house. He didn't have the strength to cover the echoes and the tremor of the rampant evil: he'd never felt anything like it. It had even distanced him from his son, who was at a noisy and demanding age, very different from his adored baby from those first years. Rosario would tell him, 'Close yourself off, I'll help you,' and she didn't want to believe him when he told her the usual methods weren't enough, that the protection needed to be reinvented and he didn't have the tools to take it on. The first two years of the dictatorship had been like that: what had been unleashed felt to Juan like a direct attack. Rosario kept going: what barks and has a cold nose? What has whiskers and likes to scratch? What has eight legs and climbs the walls? And Gaspar's shouting. He remembered how the violence made him feel feverish, how he felt sure that if the boy didn't shut up he was going to snap his neck like a stem or a small animal. He had asked the driver to stop, and he got out of the car without a word to Rosario: he preferred the vibration of evil in the street, he felt like it was closer to him, and in any case it was easier to bear than the shouting in the car. Rosario followed him, and he remembered telling her, don't touch me, I'm not going back, leave me alone. Or what? she'd asked. Or I'll kill you both, he'd replied. And although he didn't think he would be capable of even hitting Rosario, at that moment he was saying what he truly felt. He walked for hours, listening and shivering, until he had to sit down on a park bench, lost and woozy, his breathing ragged and strained. The city was screaming, its air full of pleading and prayers and peals of laughter and howls and sirens and vibrating electricity and splashing, but he couldn't convince himself to go home, and there was no one to turn to besides his family.

He went home that night, when the pleas and the shrieks and the gunshots became unbearable, when he was surrounded by the echoes of murdered people with blindfolded eyes, feet bound, some with their faces or whole bodies swollen, others who dragged themselves along in burlap sacks, a legion he could not make disappear. They sought him out. They knew he could see them and recognize them. It was instinctive, they were like moths to a flame, except Juan couldn't shoo them away. Rosario was sitting in the doorway of the house, waiting for him; Gaspar was asleep inside. Don't do that to me again, she'd told him, and she dug her nails into his arm before she kissed him and started to cry. I'm going to help you improve the protection, I can't believe this affects you so much, we can move, things are calmer in Puerto Reyes. No, he'd replied, in spite of his desperation. Not Puerto Reyes. In their bedroom upstairs, she had already set out what they needed to reinforce his defences, his protection. The chalk circles on the wooden floor, the delicately drawn signs that radiated calm and power.

Now, in the car, in the unbearable heat of the Corrientes afternoon, Gaspar talked and talked and Juan tried to guide him to get more information about his abilities, but, he realized, he was failing. If he wanted to know what else Gaspar was capable of, he would have to force it. He could sound him out, certainly. But that was a tricky method, even if his son cooperated. That very night, he was going to find out for sure.

Before they entered the city of Corrientes, another group of soldiers made him slow down. Their expressions were hard as they peered into the car, and, with astonishing intuition, Gaspar smiled at them. Remarkably, one of the soldiers returned the smile; with a wave, he told Juan to keep going. Fifteen minutes later he saw the bridge, which looked delicately drawn on to a cloudless sky, and the pink boardwalk, the lapacho trees in bloom, their flowers a little wilted from the heat. Seven in the evening.

'You want to watch the sunset? We'll buy something to eat and wait for it.'

It would be an hour, at least: it was January. Juan bought two ice cream cones and took a lot of napkins from the shop: Gaspar was sloppy when he ate ice cream, and in such heat he couldn't even be blamed if it dripped over his hands and arms. They sat on a wooden bench on the paved boardwalk and looked out. The concrete pillars were a bit neglected, and the river reflected the sky, bluer than usual, with flashes of silver and brown.

Gaspar got up to collect lapacho flowers, and he made a sticky bouquet. Juan saw him stop and stare down at a cut flower – not a lapacho – that had fallen on to the sidewalk. The boy put his improvised bouquet on the ground and came over to Juan, cupping the strange flower in his hand as if it were a live creature. Juan recognized it right away. It was a passionflower, with its violet filaments, white petals, and erect pistils and stamens that looked like insects. The crown and wounds of Christ, said one of the legends that had given the flower its name. Look, Dad! cried Gaspar, who had never seen anything like it.

'It's called a *mburucuyá*. Someone must have dropped this one. Later on I'll show you a plant with more flowers.'

'There are more?'

'Sure, there are more. What, you think it's the only one in the world?'

'It's weird.'

'It has a story, you know. Like the ceiba.'

Gaspar waited for the story with the flower in his hands and his eyes very wide, made even rounder by his suspense.

'There was a Spanish girl who fell in love with a Guaraní boy. Do you know what Guaraní means?'

'Yeah, a native from around here. Like the women on the highway.'

'So, the girl's father wouldn't let her fall in love with the boy. Her father was a captain. Do you understand why he didn't want her to love him?'

'Because captains are bad.'

Juan smiled. That was true, too.

'They're bad, yes, but here the problem was that she was Spanish. You know that the Spanish didn't want to mix with the natives?'

'Mom told me they did mix together.'

'That's true, but not at first. This captain didn't want his daughter to mix. So he ordered the native boy killed.'

'The boyfriend? Really?'

'Yes. And she drove a feather arrow into her own heart and killed herself.'

Gaspar's blue eyes were full of tears. He's so different from me, thought Juan. He's got a long way to go to toughen up.

'What happened then?'

'From her wound, when she fell down dead, this flower grew.'

'Are all flowers dead girls?'

Juan looked at the sun, which was about to touch the river. He didn't see any black flowers in the sky. Were they also the memories of dead girls? The sky was orange, wrapped in flames.

'No. Do they make you sad?'

'Yeah.'

'We're both sad. Come see the sun.'

Gaspar sat down and Juan felt him put a hand under his shirt and rest it, sticky, on his chest. He's checking my heart, thought Juan. He had caught his son doing this before. When they slept together, for example: sometimes he felt the little hand on his chest, checking for heartbeats. Or else he found Gaspar's head resting on his ribs, listening. 'My little boy,' he said, caressing the anxious hand. Suddenly he felt a vivid desire to drink wine until he got drunk, until he passed out. He could even taste the bitter alcohol on his palate. 'Look at the sun, look at the colours in the sky.' Gaspar watched attentively, his eyes half-closed, and took a deep breath. The sunset over the river was brutal, almost unreal, with the purple line of the horizon and the reddened sky.

'Can I keep the flower?'

'There are tons of them around here, we'll find more. Do you like flowers? Me too.'

'Really? A kid in my class called me a fag.'

'Why did he say that?'

'Because I asked the teacher about the jasmines on the playground. They smell good.'

Next time, you bash that idiot kid's face in, thought Juan, but he said:

'There's nothing bad about being a fag.'

'Then why . . . ?'

Gaspar didn't know how to finish the question, but Juan understood.

'Because they use it to insult you, because people say "fag" the way they say "moron". Because people are stupid and mediocre,' said Juan. 'But you're different, and I'm also different.'

'What's mediocre?'

Juan didn't answer.

'Come on, we need to find a hotel. We have things to do tonight.'

Gaspar ran to the car clutching the flower, whose cross was already broken, though he hadn't noticed.

It was less than twenty blocks to the municipal cemetery, but Juan was apprehensive as they walked there. It wasn't easy to walk with Gaspar, who was in a bad mood after being woken from a deep sleep. Luckily Juan had found another door at the hotel, so they didn't have to go out the front and draw the night attendant's attention. He knew they would get there much faster if he carried Gaspar, but the boy was heavy and he couldn't afford to exert himself. He also couldn't be sure that the sex with Andrés would work as a propitiatory ritual. He was tired and confused.

You know what'll happen if you throw a tantrum in the street, Juan said, and Gaspar snivelled a little, but he walked, skipping or even running at times. It couldn't be easy for him, thought Juan, trying to keep up with a two-metre-tall man, but some things had to follow certain schedules.

The cemetery's main gates were locked, but that wasn't a problem. Just a padlock. Juan took it in his hands and traced a sign on it with his fingertips. The breach. The gates opened suddenly, as if he had pushed them, but without making a sound.

Now he had to deal with the cemetery caretaker. Gaspar, he said, I want you to wait for me here; if you move, I'll know, and it won't be fun for you. Gaspar shrugged and sat down. He was tired. Maybe he could sleep later on. They had several hours ahead of them. It was two in the morning.

Juan patted the large pockets of his pants and pricked up his senses to locate the caretaker. If anyone had been watching him in the darkness of the cemetery, tall and thin as he faced the main row of vaults, they would have seen him broaden his shoulders in concentration and sniff at the air. Something about him was different: his long fingers moved almost involuntarily, plucking secret strings, and his eyes were unfocused yet alert. He could feel the energy of the double current in his body. Andrés had been an unexpected gift. Of course, that gift wouldn't guard against intruders, nocturnal visitors, the caretaker, anyone who might catch sight of the two of them there.

He walked towards the small office. The caretaker was asleep. It was an immense stroke of luck: he had needed to catch him asleep, because he didn't think he could fight the man. Although Juan looked powerful, he had little real physical strength. The door to the office next to the chapel was unlocked, and he approached the cot where the nightwatchman lay. The man was snoring, but not just from sleep – he was also drunk. Juan smelled the potent alcohol in the air, and it grew stronger when he knelt beside the cot. *Caña* or gin. Something caustic. Was it even necessary to tie him up? Juan thought it was. He couldn't take any risks. He turned on the flashlight and placed it near the cot. He'd have to act quickly, as this was his last set of batteries. He moved the caretaker's head so he was face up: the man didn't wake, only frowned a little. Juan circled his neck with one hand and found the carotid artery, which was dilated by the alcohol and throbbing forcefully. He massaged it delicately and precisely. The caretaker stirred slightly, but under Juan's fingers the man's cardiac rhythm slowed until his heart-beats were so infrequent it seemed they weren't even there. Juan knew that now he wasn't only passed out from intoxication: he had lost consciousness. He could wake up in a while, or he could die of bradycardia brought on by the syncope. Juan didn't care either way. He stuffed the sock that he'd brought with him into the man's mouth, then tied his hands and feet with the nylon cord that had been easy to buy without raising suspicion ('It's for a package, I need a good strong one'), yet was impossible to break without great effort or use of a knife.

Before leaving the unconscious man alone, Juan searched the drawers of a small credenza and took two knives and a pair of scissors with him. They might come in handy. He left the office, and found the chapel door locked. He placed his hands on the lock and it opened for him with a creak. Altar, cross, flowers – everything was clean and in perfect order: the chapel was in use, the cemetery was holy ground. Many were not, and he'd had to learn to tell the difference. Christian demonology could work in other spaces, but never as effectively as on consecrated ground. He gathered up as many candles as he could, and also took the candelabra.

Gaspar was waiting right where he'd left him by the front gates, seated and grumpy. Juan recognized the flash of unease and curiosity in his shining eyes when he saw the candelabra. He wasn't spooked or scared. His father had left him alone at the entrance to a cemetery in the early hours of the morning, and the boy had simply sat down to wait, no matter how sulky he was. No doubt about it, he could be an exceptional Initiate – intuitive, attentive, and certainly more disciplined than Juan. And yet, he wasn't going to have that life: Juan was determined that his son would not belong to the Order, at least as long as he could avoid it. They would not have that prize.

'I've got the candelabra, you carry the candles,' he told Gaspar. The boy obeyed without question. They walked around looking for a flat patch of land, passing the mausoleums and vaults that were clustered near the entrance, as in any large municipal cemetery. Past the grave plots but still far from the wall that enclosed the cemetery, there was enough room to work. In fact, a lot of work had already been done there. Juan, trained and sensitive as he was, felt the tremor from a recent mass grave of unidentified bodies, as well as the remnants of a powerful Afro-Brazilian ritual that had been poorly executed. He chose a spot far from the place that was still littered with feathers, far from the nameless bones. As they walked, with the aid of the flashlight, he and Gaspar had gathered more candles, some almost intact, others small and mostly just drippings. They needed them all. He wasn't going to use the flashlight.

'Gaspar, I need you to stick the candles into the earth and light them.'

The boy knew how to use a lighter without burning himself. These past months, what with Juan's surgery and Rosario's death, he'd had to learn many things, including how to light a stove. Sometimes, it had simply been that no one had the time, strength, or will to heat up his milk. But also, in a fit of fury, Juan had refused to accept help, and no one had dared contradict him. Betty, Rosario's cousin who lived nearby with her daughter – another sacred child of the Order – had knocked at the door one morning, and Juan had howled at her to go away. She had not returned.

'Put them close by. Doesn't matter where.'

There were a lot of candles, and Juan was afraid Gaspar would behave like a child and start to play with them, wasting time finding some precise arrangement dictated by his game. Instead, he saw his son obey his orders with enthusiasm and a certain bureaucratic attention to detail. Juan turned around and began to draw in the earth with the knives to make the fifth seal, the one he'd seen with his eyes closed when he was with Andrés. A circle and the letters of the name of the Fifth Spirit, clockwise. Another circle around the name, and inside that, the seal: it was simple, four circles joined by lines in an

94

almost childish design, and three inverted triangles. He could draw it quickly, from memory, without making any mistakes.

The seal was soon ready; the effort it had taken, though minimal, weighed on his chest. Gaspar had lit the candles and was standing awash in their yellow light. Good, thought Juan. He only needed the triangle, the place where the Fifth would appear. He looked at the seal and knew it was going to work, even though he was not wearing white clothes or a cape, there was no incense, and the drawing was only a furrow in the earth, without the blood or golden paint that was called for – though, strictly speaking, this seal should be drawn with mercury. Where on earth was he supposed to get mercury, though? Juan had contempt for what he called the occultist cookbook. One of the candles was giving off a singular smell, it wasn't regular wax. He closed his eyes and let his body be filled by the energy summoned in the double current he'd acquired with Andrés. It was much more effective than any blade or spell.

'Gaspar,' he said in a low voice. 'Get beside me.'

Before entering into the focused state, which he was capable of attaining in seconds – 'gnosis' was the term, but he just called it concentration – he rested his hands on Gaspar's shoulders.

'I want you to hold on to me and don't let go, no matter what you hear. If you let go, I can't protect you. Understand?'

Gaspar said yes, and Juan sensed that he did understand. The portal called to him painfully, to the point that the pressure in his chest had turned into a sharp pang. He wasn't worried though – it would pass when he made the invocation.

He knelt down in the circle, and beside him, Gaspar tried to encircle his waist with his arms. The boy clutched hold of Juan's pants as if both of them were about to fall. It was, again, a correct intuition. Invocations could indeed feel like falling.

Juan called, in silence, and waited. The formula of the invocation, which he always made silently, was long, and he thought about shortening it. But Gaspar's hands on his waist told him to be careful, the whole ritual was already very messy. For the boy. Because he had to protect him.

The footsteps of the Fifth were soundless, but Juan sensed them. It was using a human form this time. Now he needed to be fast and concrete. The longer the demon was there, the harder it would be to close the door.

Gaspar raised his head and looked straight at the demon. Then he looked at Juan.

'Who's that, Dad?' he asked in a calm voice. Now it was Juan who was scared. Gaspar could see the demon, he was capable of seeing it utterly naturally, though he wasn't even remotely trained for that vision. Juan made Gaspar bury his face in his chest. Don't look any more, he said. Hold me tight.

The bare feet inside the triangle didn't touch the ground but rather floated on point, like those of a ballerina or a hanged man who'd stayed flexible. They were grey, as was the rest of the naked body, which seemed to be covered in dry mud. Juan couldn't see its face: the light from the candles didn't reach that high. He didn't need to see it to feel its displeasure: the demon was used to being summoned with all the necessary trappings, and was vaguely irritated when called by someone who omitted them.

Juan and the Fifth had met several times before. The Fifth, if it so desired, gave and cured illnesses. It had never wanted to grant health to Juan, though. It also responded truthfully about what was secret and hidden, and it was obligated to do that: it didn't know how to lie.

Without moving his lips, Juan ordered obedience. Something was falling on to the triangle. Drops of blood. The demon must be carrying something Juan couldn't see. He asked for rational replies to his questions. He heard the demon's voice resound throughout his body. In a language he couldn't translate, one he didn't know but did understand, it asked, 'Why?' Why had it been called, it wanted to know. Why was he inflicting the horror of obedience on it? Juan felt Gaspar's breathing against his chest, and also how his own body trembled, pushed to its limits: his arms shone as if they'd been submerged in water, and his forehead was dripping. He spoke to the demon in the way it was capable of understanding. He asked about Rosario. Where she was. If he could see her. If he could find her.

The demon rose a little higher. It didn't get closer: they always tried to get near and never could. It wanted the blood of whatever it was carrying to touch Juan. When it couldn't make that happen the demon grew infuriated; the grey feet stirred. The reply came quick and clear.

She belongs to those who speak to you, it said.

And then it asked to leave.

Juan lowered his head, thanked it for its answer, thanked it for coming, and placated it by reciting the formula of release aloud and in full. His voice didn't shake, though every muscle in his body was tensed to the point of pain. He heard the crackle of the candles and the slow dripping of blood on to the triangle.

The demon disappeared in silence, but as it went it unleashed a gust of wind that extinguished all the candles. Something had angered it, and it wasn't just the slipshod summons. It might have been Gaspar's presence. Juan wanted to thank it for not venting its anger on him, but it was too late. Maybe it would vent on the caretaker, if he was still alive.

She is with those who speak to you.

The shudder that ran through his body was so violent he was afraid at first that he was having a seizure, but it was only weakness. An invocation had left him this debilitated? Was he so far gone? He lay down in a foetal position without leaving the circle, holding Gaspar as tightly as he could. With the candles out he couldn't tell his son to stay inside the circle, that it was too soon to leave it – he couldn't even see the circle now, with no candlelight and a cloud blocking the moon. In any case, Gaspar didn't move from his side, didn't move from under his arm, didn't leave him alone, didn't talk to him. He waited. He cried and waited. Juan heard him whimper and couldn't console him; he could hardly breathe. As he drifted in and out of consciousness, he tried to understand the demon's words.

With those who speak to you.

Rosario was in the Darkness.

He understood. So many times she had promised that she would follow him, that she would do anything for him. Hadn't Tali said the same thing to him a few days ago? There are things I wouldn't do for you. Together forever, swore Rosario. She knew that Juan belonged to the Darkness. That he would go there after death. And she had decided to get a head start, to share that fate with him. But my love, stupid girl, we won't be you and I, there is nothing in that place but shadow and hunger and bones, that world is dead. When had she made the pact? When he was in the hospital, surely. You thought I was going to die, idiot. But she surely hadn't believed the Darkness would claim her so soon. She didn't know the Darkness's voracity even though he'd tried to explain it to her so many times, even though she herself had seen it eat. He would never find her there. There was no one there. The Darkness was a bone collector. You didn't talk to it. You didn't negotiate.

During the hours he was curled up at the back of the cemetery, on top of the seal and with Gaspar beside him, Juan dreamed. Where had Rosario seen the possibility of making a pact with the Darkness? In her chalk circles? In her cards? Her death had nothing to do with the Order, then? Rosario's death was his fault?

When the sun was just peeking out and illuminating the white crosses, Juan turned over and lay flat across the circle, his legs outside it. Gaspar was still beside him, pale and serious. He had waited, unmoving, and had never let go of his father's arm. He must be stiff. Juan wanted to say something, but the boy spoke first.

'We have to go, Dad.'

Juan sat up. Standing took an incredible effort: that hot morning, his body weighed hundreds of pounds. He looked at Gaspar. The boy seemed distant and worried, but determined. He let go of Juan's arm and took his hand.

'Let's go.' And he tugged on Juan and Juan let himself be led. He knew he could connect intimately and delicately with his son, so it felt natural to walk like that. Before leaving the cemetery, they both drank water from the tap people used to water flowers. Juan wet his hair and soaked Gaspar's head. The boy was wearing his backpack and his hands were covered in wax. He'd been so still all night long, thought Juan, that he couldn't even bring himself to scrape off the wax. Those grey-coated fingers reminded him of the demon. Surely they reminded Gaspar of it, too? He took his son's hands and started pulling off the wax. The skin wasn't burnt underneath, or even very irritated. Gaspar was going to reveal himself as a medium very soon, Juan could feel it as he was cleaning his hands. Plus, people without abilities couldn't see the Fifth. They could sense its presence, could feel unease, terror, they could even die, but seeing it was only possible by training one's gaze. If the vision came naturally, it meant the person had a true gift. Was it possible to hide something like that? If Gaspar was a medium, his life would be short and brutal. Mediums didn't last long. The contact with ancient gods destroyed them physically and mentally. Some died in the first contact, or very soon after. Most of them went irrevocably mad very quickly. There was no magic or ritual or science that could relieve them. Magic and science could help keep them alive longer than their bodies and minds could otherwise hold up, but not much longer. The mediums who survived, like him, were exceptional.

'Come on, Dad, we have to go.'

Juan ignored him and only left the cemetery gates behind – not bothering to lock them – once his son's hands were clean again. He didn't remember the guard until much later, when they were nearly at the hotel.

When Juan awoke, it was night again; he realized he had slept for over ten hours. He looked around for Gaspar in the room's semi-darkness and saw him curled up in the other bed, asleep. It was time to begin the deception.

Many hours of sleep – that always happened after contact with a demon. But his exhaustion was extreme this time. He went to the bathroom, took his medication with tap water, and washed his face. Whenever he looked in the mirror, he never saw what others saw. To him, his face was tiredness and defeat, and the scars on his chest and belly and back were a map of illness. He hated being weak, hated his body. Other people saw an exceptionally attractive man, they desired him, they were moved. Juan put the nape of his neck under the tap and wet his hair. He felt so raw and tired, despite the long hours he'd slept, that he was capable of hearing colours.

Gaspar was asleep in the foetal position with his mouth open. He hadn't gotten undressed. Juan didn't remember how they'd gotten back to the hotel, but it wasn't strange to forget.

He woke Gaspar with a hard shake of his shoulder. The boy took his time opening his eyes, but before he could focus his gaze, Juan told him:

'You were screaming! What were you dreaming about?'

Distrust, confusion. The boy knew, and it would be hard to throw him off.

'I didn't dream anything,' he murmured.

'You were dreaming something! You were shouting like crazy.'

Blinking and doubt.

'It wasn't a dream, we went to a cemetery and you made me light candles and then you told me not to look.'

'You had some awful nightmare.'

Gaspar started to cry, and Juan let him.

'It wasn't a dream!' the boy shouted, his nose running.

'But we never left this room! We took a nap, and look, we just woke up now to go eat.'

'There was a guy who was dripping blood.'

'A guy who was dripping blood. Okay, enough. You'll forget soon enough. People forget their dreams if they think about something else.'

'I promise, you fainted and I stayed there with the candles.'

'You're just scared because I'm sick. Don't worry about me so much.'

'It wasn't a dream.'

Juan felt the violence hardening in his stomach, and he thought about beating the boy until he had no choice but to believe the lies.

'Yes, it was. Tell me everything, but let's go down first, I'm dying of hunger. We're going to eat a fantastic dinner, come on.'

He picked Gaspar up to wash his face in the bathroom. The boy let him do it. He was frowning and his left hand was

101

squeezed into a fist. Juan opened it gently. If he tells me again it wasn't a dream, I'll break his finger, he thought. Gaspar took a deep breath before he started to talk: he remembered details of the long periods he'd spent awake while Juan was unconscious. Now he was afraid: Juan heard his voice shaking.

I could have killed him last night, he thought.

Gaspar went on relating his 'dream' in the elevator. And Juan, though he listened, was thinking. She is with those who speak to you. It wasn't a lie, but he could have interpreted it wrongly. There were many who spoke to him, many who had spoken to him, so why was he so convinced it meant Rosario was in the Darkness? Who else could those who spoke to him be? She belongs to those who speak to you, that was the most exact translation of what the demon had told him. It was a sphinx's riddle. And he had asked the wrong question, because he was in pain, tired, in mourning. Because he'd lost his mind. And because he'd thought, arrogantly, that Rosario would be capable of such a sacrifice for him. That she would be capable of abandoning her son.

He covered his face with his hands. Now Gaspar was talking about the demon he'd seen. A floating thing. And Juan didn't have the strength to take away the memory with a sign of forgetting, not right now.

'And did the guy talk?' Juan asked Gaspar as he felt tears dampening his hands.

'I don't remember.'

'See, we forget our dreams.'

Gaspar hadn't heard it. Maybe he was incapable of hearing it. Maybe the demon hadn't even spoken. Sometimes they stayed silent. Maybe he was the one who'd imagined hearing words.

They went into the hotel dining room and Juan dried his tears on his shirt. Some people eyed him curiously, but he couldn't care less. The waitress, who was very young, couldn't look him in the eye when he ordered: she was embarrassed to see him cry. Juan ordered *chipá* and hot chocolate for Gaspar. He didn't want anything himself. He stank, he realized now: the dried sweat had stiffened his shirt under his armpits. He hadn't even thought about showering.

'I don't want to eat,' said Gaspar when his chocolate milk and bread arrived.

Juan felt the violence ignite in his stomach. His heartbeat was too fast, and irregular: it made him dizzy, it wasn't going to let him rest. He wasn't sleepy, but he needed more hours of repose. Juan rested his hands on the tablecloth. His fingertips were blue. His lips must be blue, too. He tried to take deep breaths, but that was no solution. He needed oxygen, and soon.

'Eat fast, Gaspar. And wait for me here.'

'I don't want to be alone.'

His son's whining filled him with a rage so clear and so dark that he practically ran out of the dining room and towards the garage where the car was parked. He opened the trunk and took out the oxygen tank, which he stashed in a bag: he didn't want the other guests or hotel personnel to see it. From outside the dining room, he knocked on the window and signalled to Gaspar to finish eating immediately and come with him to the room.

Juan sat on the bed, set the tank – its white paint peeling a little – on the night table, and with a quick and practised movement opened the nozzle and brought the mask to cover his mouth and nose. He stretched the elastic behind his ears and patted the mattress beside him. Gaspar sat down and Juan leaned against the wall. The slight noise of the oxygen wasn't enough to drown out his pounding heart; the pain in his chest burned and made it even harder to breathe. So, this was all

Tali's talisman could do to help him? Would he be able to open the Darkness? Would this be the last time he did it? Gaspar watched him attentively, his round, blue eyes frightened but unsurprised, simply alert. Juan took off the mask for a second and told him:

'Bring me the hardcover book that's in the bag.'

'Are you okay, Dad?'

'I'm going to be okay. Bring it here.'

He had brought a copy of Gombrich's *The Story of Art* to look at with Gaspar. It was, as well, a safe book for the trip: any soldier who searched the car wouldn't find it suspicious. He motioned for Gaspar to open it, and, as usual, the boy flipped to the final pages: he never started at the beginning. Gaspar rested the book on the bed, on a clear space on the sheets where they could both see. And then he did something strange – at least, something he'd never done before: he peered closely at a painting – Kokoschka's *Children Playing*, Juan saw – and started to make up the story of the two children, the girl in her pink dress and the boy in a blue jacket, and blended into the story were adventures from Gaspar's school that Juan already knew and games with the girl he'd met at Tali's house. When he tired of that one, he turned some pages and went on inventing. Juan felt a shiver run through his body and he squeezed his fists to keep from losing consciousness: Gaspar was talking about a castle, and he made up a story of some princes who were locked in 'the round part' (the tower or turret, thought Juan), and he realized his son was talking now about St Paul's, Wren's cathedral in London, because the book also included architectural images. He couldn't sleep, but he could spend hours listening to Gaspar's voice: the boy understood, he did the right thing, he sustained him. He had learned this from his mother. He was imitating her. How many times had he seen her entertaining

Juan like that? She talks you back to life, Florence would say, and she was right, Rosario talked to return him to life.

Gaspar closed the book, yawned, and curled up against Juan's chest. Juan instinctively started to move him, thinking the boy's weight would hurt, but it didn't: the contact was a relief. I don't want to die in front of him, he thought.

The bathroom door was open, and in the semi-consciousness brought on by lack of oxygen Juan thought he saw his wife's legs, alive. Rosario spent a lot of time in the bathroom – she could easily spend an hour in there with the door locked. Now the room was no longer in a Corrientes hotel: Juan felt it transform into the Chelsea house where they had lived together in London. He remembered her coming out of the bathroom carrying a book and wearing her glasses, a short-sleeved shirt, and no underwear. Then the image disappeared. Gaspar suddenly got up from the bed – he wasn't asleep – and closed the bathroom door. Juan wasn't surprised by his son's intuition, but it hurt him: he didn't wish his life on Gaspar. Not even the good moments had been truly happy. He had to save him from the Order.

Gaspar put aside the art book and opened a collection of US poetry in translation. He read slowly and badly, but Juan let himself be carried along. When the oxygen was gone and he removed the mask, he looked at his fingers and saw they were no longer blue. Though the arrhythmia had taken too many hours to pass, he knew he wasn't going to die that night, and not in front of his son. He'd done it again; they had done it together.

Juan was surprised at how cheap the tickets were, though he had to admit he didn't know how to manage money, nor did he understand pricing. He travelled with a wad of bills secured with a rubber band; his whole life, he had always depended on money from Rosario's family and from the Order. How many times had they told him, 'You'll never lack for anything'? He understood his privilege and the distance that separated him from regular people. His older brother, for one: Luis had worked twelve hours a day before going into exile, and had gone to school while holding down a factory job. These past months since Rosario had died, Juan, who had never set foot in a bank, had had to make decisions: he showed Gaspar where the money was kept, explained that he could use it when he wanted and what it was for. He asked that money be brought to him once a week, by accountants or lawyers or the bodyguards themselves.

The ticket seller handed him his change through the window, and Juan felt like he was only now waking up from the months without Rosario and the slow recovery after his last surgery. It was the air, hot but strangely light – how odd, the lack of humidity here in Puerto Iguazú. It was the sense that, if he survived the Ceremonial, he and his son were going to be able to have some calm. The restorative sleep had returned some of his confidence in himself, in Stephen, in Tali. The possibility of that peace had seemed remote just a month before, when, after several sleepless nights spent trying to contact Rosario, furious with pain and worry, he had burned almost all her things in an improvised bonfire in the backyard. Gaspar had sat beside him: he had watched with dry, surprised eyes as his mother's belongings went up in flames. He hadn't tried to save anything. Later, Juan showed him the little that remained: some clothes, some photos, all the records, and the jewellery it didn't make sense to burn – valuable things that belonged to Gaspar now, like the elegant art nouveau pieces that were almost a hundred years old and that Rosario had never worn. He had also saved her deck of Tarot cards and all her relics and magical instruments, but he couldn't show those to Gaspar. Juan decided not to keep much more, not even Rosario's letters: her clothes and a lock of her hair would be enough to petition her, to ask her to visit him, as a phantom now.

If she didn't respond to his call and visit him, he thought now as he walked towards the park's train station, there were only a few possible reasons: either someone was holding her back and preventing contact, or else she had gone to a place where he couldn't reach her. That was strange: he could reach her if she was in the Darkness. He should be able to. But there were other places, many others, and so many of them were still unknown.

It had been a stupid precaution to burn everything: if someone wanted to entrap Rosario, it would still have been very easy for them to get something of hers. Many of her things, of course, were in Puerto Reyes. Her hair on the pillows, her clothes in the closets, her make-up in the drawers. But who? Why was easy: to weaken him. Who, that was more complicated. Mercedes was one candidate – she detested her daughter. Florence? Could be. But would they have dared? Rosario was the medium's wife, the mother of his heir, and she was ambitious. Wouldn't they fear reprisal?

'Is this a park?'

Gaspar pulled Juan out of his rumination. He had to stop thinking. Intuition came when he was able to divert his attention: it was a rule that always worked.

'It's a park, yes, but it has a surprise. I told you that since you were so good on this trip, I was going to give you a surprise. Now we're going to the train.'

'A train?'

'Yes, we'll take the train to the surprise. Or we can walk.'

'Only if you don't make me run.'

It was his way of saying it was hard for him to keep up: one step for Juan was a leap for his son, so he tried to slow down. It was still early. They had reached Iguazú Falls at noon, and after eating some sandwiches off the highway they had entered the waterfalls' park at one in the afternoon. It was good timing, because while the tourists were off eating lunch, they could have the Devil's Throat almost all to themselves. They started to walk along the path cut through the jungle. Juan had bought a cap with a visor for Gaspar, and sunscreen for both of them; luckily, both things were sold at roadside stands by the park entrance. They went slowly because Gaspar stopped to study every animal they saw: the coatis, a distant toucan in a tree, the motionless lizards. They reached the footbridge after walking for almost an hour. Juan was grateful for that slowness. He wasn't tired and the sun didn't affect him, but the day before had been extreme, brutal. The footbridge was a long wooden catwalk over the river, without steps. It didn't entail any significant effort, either.

Gaspar walked on tiptoe along the catwalk. Around them, everything was lush and fearsome: the trees that dipped into the water, the dark jungle in the distance, the huge, swift-flowing river. Juan thought that eventually the catwalk would have to be replaced by an iron structure: any flood would wash away that wood, no matter how well constructed it was. The water was clear in some parts, but in others the currents were dyed red, the coloured earth mixing with the river. The product, Juan thought, of incipient deforestation. In a decade or so the falls would be all red water, like cold lava or streams of watery blood. There was a lot of water now, though: just two years back, a drought had left the riverbed bare and red with just a tiny waterfall, fine like a wellspring, domestic like a shower. He had gone to see that apocalyptic scene. It was said that cadavers had been found in the riverbed then, and though Juan was sure the military was quite capable of using the falls for tossing bodies – bearing in mind, as well, that the National Park was guarded by federal forces – he didn't think any bodies had really been found. The Iguazú River was so strong along that stretch that it surely would have carried them away to wash up somewhere far from the falls.

After they'd walked two hundred metres along the catwalk, almost clear of tourists, Juan picked up Gaspar, who was trotting beside him by then. There were signs that forbade you to let children ride on your shoulders, but there was no rule against holding them in your arms. Still, Gaspar was dangerously high as Juan carried him, and he was restless. He looked down worriedly at the water flowing under the catwalk. As the noise of Devil's Throat grew louder and a flock of birds flew across the cloudless sky towards the Brazilian side of the river, he kicked a little, anxious and frightened, and said: Put me down.

'Are you scared?'

'Put me down!'

There was a tinge of hysteria in the boy's voice, and Juan complied. The catwalk was shaking a little, but it was clear Gaspar wasn't dizzy. Out of nowhere a coati ran past, and Juan had to step aside to let it pass.

'Tell me what's wrong.'

Gaspar opened his mouth and extended his hands, then brought them to his cheeks. His eyes were damp and terrified.

'Is there a monster that sucks down the water? Is there a devil? I don't want to see a devil.'

He knows how to read, thought Juan, and he'd seen the sign.

'There's no monster, it's just the name of the big waterfall.'

'I don't believe you.'

'Let's sit down.'

Along some stretches the catwalks had iron and wood benches painted a dark green, a detail added by the landscape artist Charles Blanchard, who had also designed the gardens at Puerto Reyes, Rosario's family mansion, the one Gaspar would inherit. The few other tourists around them tromped heavily over the catwalk, carrying thermoses and cameras. Juan waited: he cleaned his sunglasses on the hem of his shirt and took a long drink from the bottle of Crush he had bought at the entrance. It was warm and sickly sweet. He licked his lips.

Gaspar stood up on the bench and approached Juan in a way that could only be described as threatening. He brought his face so close that Juan saw four blue eyes filled with fear, but also determination.

'Did you bring me here to throw me to the monster?'

So that's what he thought. Of course, it could just be a fear fed by those confused days, by the unhealthy mourning he was going through – the recent months had been a nightmare for his son. But it was true: he *was* leading Gaspar straight into the arms of monsters. Juan hugged his son, not just because he was trembling, but because he had to keep him from running away, from escaping. Gaspar struggled in his arms. Juan made him sit down, and, holding his face in one hand, he forced the boy to look at him.

'Gaspar, son, it's water. It's the river, and further down it has a huge drop, and the water falls and makes a loud noise. It's beautiful. That's why I brought you here, because it's beautiful. There's a rainbow. There is no monster, and I would never throw you to a monster and let it hurt you. Never. Look at the people who are on their way there – do they seem scared? No, because there is no monster.'

The boy slightly relaxed his hands, which he had squeezed into fists, and used one to wipe his nose.

'I wanted to bring you here so you could see something beautiful,' said Juan. 'But if you want, we can leave.'

'There's a rainbow?'

'Sometimes there are two, and one time I saw three.'

He hugged Gaspar again, and this time the boy didn't resist. Juan said nothing, not wanting to confuse him. He waited until the boy's sobs and shivering had subsided. He caressed the back of his neck.

'We can come another day. If you're scared, we can go back. No problem.'

Juan watched as his son wiped his wet face on his shirt, a gesture he'd copied from his father.

'Let's go, I want to see if there's a rainbow,' said Gaspar.

Juan led him by the hand to Devil's Throat. The waterfall was visible from some two hundred metres away, before they reached the lookout, and when they caught sight of it Juan sensed Gaspar catch his breath and look at him fearfully again, but this time there was no distrust: he was frightened by the enormity and strength of the river as it plummeted, the water so powerful it was white and hung in the air, and by the noise that forced them to shout if they wanted to talk. Juan wouldn't let him lean against the railing the way other people did. 'Dad, we don't have a camera, we can't take pictures!' Gaspar yelled, his face spattered with water, and Juan resolved to buy him some postcards later on. There were two rainbows, one in the depths where the water disappeared and transformed into mist and foam, and another in the distance, a truncated rainbow that touched the highest point of the vegetation and disappeared among the branches.

On the trip back to Puerto Reyes, Gaspar babbled about the turquoise butterflies and the rainbow, and he wanted to know their legends. Juan found himself expounding on leprechauns, about Ishtar's necklace of precious stones, about the route between Asgard and Earth. Gaspar talked about the loud noise, he laughed again about how wet they'd gotten, and he wanted to know why his grandparents hadn't built their house right there. 'They couldn't,' replied Juan, 'It's a national park: it doesn't belong to anyone. It belongs to the state.'

'What's the state?'

'The land belongs to everyone, a single family can't buy it, that's what it means. But your grandparents did build a house nearby – don't you remember it?'

'Yeah,' said Gaspar, 'but only a little.' Juan thought it was remarkable how similar children and old people were: both extremes with their forgetful dementia, unable to retain people or places or situations. Gaspar had spent many months of his life in that house, ever since he was a baby. And he remembered it 'a little'. Would he forget Juan so easily too, or was it different with fathers? 'It's a very pretty house,' Juan went on. 'And it's yours. It's going to be yours when your grandparents die. Your mother didn't have any siblings.'

'Then it's yours, too. If it's Mom's, it's yours.'

'No,' said Juan. 'It's not mine. I don't have anything. Only you.'

The mansion was built in the twenties, when the Bradford family decided to expand their agricultural business – back then, mostly focused on wheat and located in the province of Buenos Aires – to include yerba mate. In that decade, the province of Misiones was in the process of being settled by colonists from Eastern Europe, Russia, Scandinavia; the Bradfords, descendants of British landowners who had possessed the most fertile lands of Argentina, distinguished themselves by knowing how to handle the local politics, and also by entering the business with significant capital of their own. It was Santiago Bradford who decided where his dream house would be built in that jungle he so loved, and into which he would disappear for days on hunting trips. It would be on the Paraná River, thirty kilometres from Iguazú Falls. Bradford bought two thousand hectares of jungle, and he hired the architect Von Plessen and the landscape artist Charles Blanchard to design the mansion, the gardens, and the walkway to the river that was to float above the trees, a kind of kilometre-long terrace with a view of the rushing water, the sun as it turned the sky into a red ember, the virgin jungle on the opposite shore.

In the north, as well, he bought three thousand hectares for yerba mate plantations. And as he was building his dream house he also founded the town, which he named Puerto Libertad, and which would grow up around the house and along the road that would later become a highway. During that time, Bradford became close friends with another owner of yerba fields, Jose Reyes, a Spanish millionaire and a widowed father of two who shared his passion for hunting. It took them months to recognize each other as members of the Order. Santiago Bradford belonged to the founding family, while Jose Reyes was merely an Initiate. The coincidence astonished them so much that they decided to become partners. In honour of his unexpected friend, Bradford decided to call his estate Puerto Reyes.

The house was ready in 1929, just before the world was plunged into an economic crisis that barely touched the millionaire class. The Bradfords had fed a planet at war, and now they were trading with the Middle East, a different world, so distant that news didn't reach it about the shocks and falls of the New York stock market.

Santiago Bradford hardly ever went back to Buenos Aires.

113

He loved the river, the sweat of the harvest, the humidity, the settlers' legends and the local ghost stories. He loved the house with its fourteen bedrooms, the Olympic pool, the mosaic tiles, the cool verandas, and the central yard, with a fountain and orchids and willows. Some of the windows had stained glass, and, surrounding the house, Charles Blanchard had planted five hundred species of plants, and had cut paths that had to be maintained or the jungle would return, ferocious, to cover everything. His sister requested a conservatory and she had it. He remembered his wife Amanda, dead so young, and how she'd laughed when those butterflies kissed her face, waving their wings of impossible colours when they alighted on her hands or shoulders.

It was hard for Santiago Bradford to believe that a person as glorious as Amanda could have given birth to Jorge and Mercedes, his first two children, dark and strange. (His third, Marta, was a normal girl, graceless, but like any other child of her class.) Mercedes, especially, was ugly and sarcastic, a girl whom no one loved or respected. Clutching at straws, he introduced her to Jose Reyes' handsome son Adolfo, a youth who was accustomed to life in the jungle and had studied in England. An impossible candidate for his surly daughter. But they understood each other. Adolfo didn't fall in love with Mercedes Bradford, but he understood that the two families wanted that engagement, and they both obliged their parents. A wife didn't have to be the woman one loved.

Adolfo used to say that Mercedes wasn't pretty and definitely was not charming, but she had a kind of madness approaching evil that attracted him: it excited him that she was capable of killing him, or at least of trying. And, most importantly, the Bradfords were high leaders of the Order, not mere members like his own family. They were of blood. The Order liked to unite its members with both blood and money, and the marriage would catapult the Reyes family upward.

By 1945, Santiago had moved almost permanently to Puerto Reyes. I'm tired of the pampa, he would say. It's all so flat, *che*. And the hunting is all the same, rodents and buzzards. He only went back to Buenos Aires because business deals were still resolved there, and because occasionally he felt stifled by the heat.

Mercedes and Adolfo were married in 1947, but never by the Church: they could put up with the gossip and didn't care about appearances. Jose Reyes died that same year, still young, drowned in the Paraná. He had taken the boat out drunk. Adolfo was left in charge of the yerba business, now the joint property of his family and his wife's. Adolfo and Mercedes lived in fear that Perón would expropriate their properties, especially Puerto Reyes, but they were lucky: the Bradfords only lost an estate out towards La Plata that they hardly used – it would be turned into a public park. The Reyes family were only forced to improve working conditions for their employees, which they did reluctantly and only for a time: they kept the overseers, the whippings, the minimal food rations, the child labour. In his dreams, Adolfo used to hear cries of '*Neike!*' It was a word that, to the workers, was far removed from what it really meant in Guaraní: strength. It was the cry used to push the *mensú* – the yerba plantation worker – to his physical limit. But Adolfo didn't like to visit the fields. He liked to drink, just as his father had: whiskey, *caña*, wine, more and more, from morning on. He liked blonde women, especially the rustic daughters of the European settlers, and he also liked the more delicate creole women. He liked to collect lamps and paintings, pipes and first editions of books – though he rarely read – and handmade Guaraní relics, amulets, talismans; he was a disciple of San La Muerte. In 1949, his sister Nora founded the first zoo in Misiones, near

Puerto Reyes. Over the years it would be transformed into an animal sanctuary, a refuge for species in danger of extinction and a mecca for the country's veterinarians. Nora moved to France, got married, and never returned to Argentina, but she left the zoo in the hands of faithful collaborators, pioneering ecologists. That same year, Adolfo and Mercedes had their only daughter, Rosario.

Adolfo focused on building a guest house at Puerto Reyes, and to gladdening Santiago's old age with another granddaughter, Catalina, whom everyone called Tali. Tali was the daughter of his Corrientes lover, the most beautiful woman he had ever seen, half indigenous and half Italian. He spent as much time with her as possible, and dreamed of her on his nights of drunkenness. They got drunk together: they'd traverse the villages looking for handicrafts, Adolfo closing business deals, and they'd try the local drinks. They brought Tali with them, first as a babe in arms and later as a toddler. Rosario went with them, too: the girls adored each other, played together, and it was very hard to separate them when the vacation ended. Mercedes, who had spent her pregnancy in bed and suffered a risky labour, couldn't have any more children, and she gave herself over to reading and travel: she tried to go to Europe once a year, where she had intense, secretive meetings in London with the Order. On some days she read about Hecate and the witches of Macbeth; on others she sewed the mouths of horned frogs shut and visited cemeteries. When she was in London she attended all the important ceremonies: her origins were peripheral geographically, but her position in the Order was anything but tangential. She was respected, important, she was of blood. And she wanted more power. Living in Argentina didn't take away from her importance: money, as the Bradfords often said, is a nation in itself.

Still, not even in her wildest dreams would Mercedes have ever thought that her brother, a gifted doctor and brilliant cardiologist, would come to tell her one night – crazed, agitated, and shouting – that he thought he'd found a medium, a very sick five-year-old boy on whom he had performed high-risk heart surgery, a true feat that would boost his reputation and be a milestone for the discipline on the continent. He was sure, he would tell her, he just *knew* the boy's power would flourish. They had to help him, take him in, raise him. They couldn't let him die. He's going to die if he stays with his family, Mercedes, they're some brutish immigrants who live in Berisso, a filthy port town. They can't even afford to live in Buenos Aires. Mercedes didn't want to believe for a long time, not even when the boy – delicate, with sinister eyes – was settled into the family building on Avenida Libertador, in Buenos Aires. She didn't want to accept it, though Santiago, her own father, did believe – he started teaching the boy magic, educating him in languages, mythology, art. She didn't want to believe, because she had dreamed of being the one to find the medium: she had worked doggedly on that project after the great disappointment of her daughter Rosario, whom the men in her family had forbidden her from training. Lazy, moralistic men, she thought. The girl didn't seem to have any ability, but abilities can also be invoked. Bah, she would say, and when the exasperation overcame her, she vented by giving Rosario beatings that left her back purple.

She didn't believe until the evidence drove them all half-mad in Puerto Reyes, and Juan elevated them – but especially her, because she was a Bradford – to unthinkable levels in the Order hierarchy. That was when the eyes of the Cult of the Shadow turned, suddenly and definitively, towards a mansion in the jungle surrounded by blood-red earth.

*

117

'So, we wasted our time and money sending you a plane ticket,' Adolfo said before even greeting Juan, who had just parked his car under the trees by the front door of Puerto Reyes. Adolfo was already drunk, but it would be a while before he turned unpleasant. The sky was threatening rain, and the house, freshly painted white, was beautiful. 'You always manage to escape when you want to, huh? Those bodyguards are useless.'

'I wanted to drive with Gaspar, I needed the time with him. Adolfo, how are you?'

'I've been better. How are you?'

Adolfo knelt down in front of Gaspar and said, Now, aren't you going to hug your grandfather? Gaspar did, unenthusiastically. His thin arms were a bit sunburnt. Mercedes emerged from the house. She walked with a limp and a cane; the femur she'd broken in a riding accident had never fully healed. She kissed Gaspar, who tried to pull away from her, and caressed his hair with both hands. My treasure, she said. Then she looked at Juan: greed twisted her smile.

His in-laws didn't know how to treat him. With the respect owed to an oracle, a medium, the one who spoke to the gods? With the nonchalance used with a family member? With the severity merited by his occasional rebelliousness? He no longer cared.

'My dear,' Mercedes greeted him. 'Your room is ready. I suppose you'll want to rest after the frightful trip you must have had. Only you would be capable of driving yourself all the way here when you can take your pick between a chauffeur and a plane.'

She'd decided not to accuse him of running away. They would change the bodyguards again, as they always did when he managed to elude them. Mercedes wore dark glasses even inside the house, but she always took them off to look at him. She seemed a bit indignant and anxious.

'You prepared a different room from the one we used to use?' he asked her.

'Of course.'

They walked along the airy main hallway of Puerto Reyes. The walls were decorated with Adolfo's hunting trophies: antlers, lynx heads with their long ears. There were also some original Rembrandt etchings, small engravings in prominent frames. Mercedes always said the collection would be ruined there in the jungle, that the artworks should be conserved in Buenos Aires. And Adolfo had complied regarding most of his pieces, except for the Rembrandts and a painting of the Battle of Curupayty by Cándido López that hung in the main hall: soldiers like black insects and, on the horizon, smoke and fire and blue sky. It was beautiful and terrible and Adolfo had roundly refused to donate it to the National Museum; nor did he want to sell it. Rosario used to shout at him, Dad, it's an outrage that this is here, all of Cándido is in the Historical or the National, it's a robbery, this is *heritage*, and he would respond, Well, let them come take it from me, then, the fuckers, I'm not going to give them shit. Rosario feigned exasperation, but Juan caught her smile: she got along with her father, despite the fights, despite the fact that he was a superficial and selfish man.

They went up to the first floor: Mercedes had ordered one of the rooms with a river view to be prepared, one that had air conditioning. Gaspar ran in, opened the backpack on the bed, and took out his toy cars.

'If you need anything, there's the bell.'

When Juan looked at the room, he recognized the effort they had made to eradicate anything that would recall Rosario. No bouquets of flowers, no incense impregnating the air with sandalwood, none of the white sheets she adored or any of the objects or ornaments from the room downstairs: Mercedes hadn't moved anything. Not the lamps or the oriental cigarette case or a single one of the photos or paintings.

'Thank you,' said Juan, and Mercedes nodded. She looked at him: her eyes were cold and distant, as if she were drugged.

'I'll be in my room.'

'I won't bother you.'

Mercedes took Juan by the arms with her bony hands, on which she wore only her wedding ring; she was austere, never dyed her hair. She could fool other people, but Juan knew she had the ability to kill. He knew she had no pity.

'Now, how could you ever bother me?'

The air conditioner was on, and the large window overlooking the garden was so clean it looked open. Other windows on the spacious first floor had a view of the golf course Adolfo had stopped maintaining, letting the jungle return it to a state of wild vegetation.

Juan took off his clothes in front of the window and lay down on top of the sheets, his arms behind his head and his eyes closed. He listened to Gaspar, who had appropriated the table and was drawing on paper he'd taken from the backpack. Juan had to get rid of him. The coming hours until the Ceremonial could not be shared with his son. He couldn't take care of the boy now, not in the way he needed, the simplest way: entertaining him, playing with him, taking him on walks. Sure, Adolfo should be capable of watching his grandson, but he was drunk. And he liked guns and boats, and, especially, he liked to talk. It was too dangerous to leave Gaspar with him.

He tried to remember what Rosario had done with Gaspar during previous Ceremonials, and he realized he didn't have the slightest idea. She hadn't told him, and he'd never thought to ask.

That had been another mistake. How many of the Ceremonial participants – how many of the cult's members – knew that Gaspar might have natural gifts? Now that the boy had manifested his ability to see, it was only a matter of time before his powers grew.

Juan took a deep breath and reached out to press the intercom to call Marcelina. She had worked in Puerto Reyes for years, and Juan trusted her. Marcelina was discreet and efficient and had an enormous capacity to pretend she didn't understand what went on in the house, to convincingly act like she turned a blind eye to her bosses' activities, and to speak only Guaraní with the other employees. She answered the intercom immediately. There was a slight tremor in her voice when she said: Yes, sir? She must feel very nervous about having to wait on him after Rosario's death, which surely had genuinely saddened her. Marcelina, he said, could you ask Señor Esteban to come up to my room? Right away, sir, said Marcelina, and Juan thought, Sir, sir, why did they make her call him that? When they were alone, she called him by his name.

Stephen insisted on being called Esteban when he was in Argentina. In Europe he used his real, English name. Juan had always called him Stephen. They'd known each other for almost twenty years, and their first, long-ago meeting had been in this very house, in Puerto Reyes. The oldest son of the Order's leader, Florence Mathers, and her husband, the recluse Pedro Margarall, Stephen had heavy eyelids and dark blue eyes, and he was tall, though he looked small beside Juan. He came in without knocking, wearing a dark brown shirt and black pants, and was very clearly angry. Juan opened his eyes, but didn't move from the bed. Gaspar looked at Stephen curiously, waved at him, and turned back to his drawings.

Stephen said loudly: 'Please, tell me I'm wrong.'

'Why can't you learn to speak like an Argentine? You spend several months a year here. And how's your little boyfriend in Misiones?'

'Splendid. What did you do in the Corrientes cemetery?'

'Were you following me?'

Stephen dropped a folded newspaper page on to Juan's bare stomach. Juan opened it. The photo was of terrible quality – a local rag printed cheaply – but he understood that Stephen's educated eye could distinguish the scratched-out symbol on the ground. The candles weren't incriminating – all the cemeteries in the region had their areas of candles and Brazilian cults; in all of them, chickens were beheaded and offered up on cardboard trays with bread and fruit.

'You didn't even cover your tracks.'

Juan started to read the article, but instead he asked:

'Are there consequences?'

'The guard is dead.'

'That wasn't my intention.'

Stephen narrowed his eyes, took the paper from Juan's hands, and started to tear it up.

'I already took care of sending something to the police and the dead man's family so they won't continue the investigation.'

Juan didn't thank him. He asked whether Mercedes, Florence, and the others knew anything. Stephen said no, they never read the local papers.

'What were you trying to find out?' Stephen asked.

Juan didn't answer. 'We're not in danger?' he asked instead.

'Not you two. The people who live around the cemetery will never have a good night's sleep again.'

'What do I care about people.'

Stephen didn't need to tell him they should start to speak in secret, and he made all the effort himself, unlike Tali.

It takes a lot of energy to invoke. One day before the Ceremonial, in your condition, it's suicide.

I needed to know if Gaspar could see it.

You're perfectly capable of finding that out without such a vulgar and unnecessary display of power.

Stephen sat at the foot of the bed. Juan could sense his anger, as well as that unconditional current that joined them together. He shook his head and pulled Stephen towards him. Stephen moved his head just enough to delicately kiss Juan's lips. Juan ran a hand through his greying hair.

It's all done. Tali started her work, too. Besides my mother, there are two other British people in the house who know what they're doing. The rest are minor Initiates. Tali will get here tomorrow. We'll meet at three in the afternoon, early, near the place of the Ceremonial.

Do I know the British people?

They're scribes, both of them. I think you've met them.

If I die after the Ceremonial, I want you to take my son to Brazil, leave him with my brother. I still haven't found the seal that will protect him.

Stephen turned his small, sharp eyes to look at Juan.

You won't die tomorrow. And I can't do that. They'll go after him. You've summoned in worse conditions.

Juan remembered the year before. Yes, it had been much worse. To keep him on his feet, Stephen had had to tie him to a kind of improvised cross. It was the second time he'd done that. His body hanging from the wood, covered by a tunic; his blond hair longer than it was now and falling over his face. Juan didn't remember what had happened after the Ceremonial. He hadn't woken up at home: they'd taken him to the hospital, first to one in Corrientes, and later, once he was stabilized, to one in Buenos Aires. He'd had to wait six more months for the surgery that had saved him, a triple bypass. He had turned twenty-eight in intensive care.

Do you think it's safe for me to leave my son with Marcelina?

Certainly. I need to tell you some things. But I want you to get him out of here first.

Juan buzzed Marcelina again and asked her to come up. So as not to embarrass her, he covered himself with the sheet and told her to pull up a chair next to the bed. Stephen stayed where he was.

'I need you to take care of Gaspar until Sunday.'

'That's a long time, sir.'

'Don't call me sir.'

'First I want to give you my condolences for Rosario. I loved her so much. We're very sad.'

'It's okay, Marcelina.'

Propped up in bed by all the pillows he'd been able to find, he told her that Gaspar already knew how to read and enjoyed it, and that he knew how to swim but she should take him only to the pool. Yes, sir, the river is treacherous and he's still very little. All his clothes are in that bag over there, on the armchair. He'll eat anything. If his head hurts, give him an aspirin and try to get him to sleep. If he asks about me, tell him I went to work. Take him to see the butterflies; he might get scared, but I don't think so. He'll love the zoo too.

Juan felt reassured by the fact that Marcelina, her husband, and their children lived in the small, very pretty house at the entrance to Puerto Reyes: they had been the estate's caretakers for years now. Gaspar would be insulated from whatever happened in the mansion, and at the same time, he would only be two hundred metres away. And well cared for.

'Tell me, Marcelina, how much is Señor Adolfo drinking? The truth.'

'Well, a lot. I'd say he goes through two bottles of whiskey a day. At night I find the bottles.'

'So, he's drunk all the time.'

'That I couldn't say.'

'Is he taking the boat out?'

'Yes, but he doesn't sail it any more, my husband does.'

'If you go out on the river, you can take Gaspar. But only with your husband. Tali tells me there are two new dogs.'

'They're huge. I won't let them get near the little one, I'm terrified of them too.'

She told him that Gaspar also liked the walkway that led to the lookout, the big one that was built above the trees. His mother and I took him out there and he asked if it could fly, said Marcelina. I'd prefer him to stay far away from the house, said Juan. Make sure nothing bites him. Don't worry. They keep the zoo up very well, and I know how to take care of children.

Juan called Gaspar over. One of his hands was balled into a fist, and Juan slowly extended each finger and massaged the palm of his hand. I'm going to work for a couple of days, he said. Gaspar peered at him uncertainly, but he nodded. And while you wait for me, Marcelina is going to take care of you. You remember her? Gaspar nodded again. Don't be scared: I'll be back in two days. That's not a long time? asked Gaspar. No, it's not long. Two nights. Count them.

'And I have my uncle's phone number.'

Juan kissed Gaspar's forehead, then indicated which bag Marcelina was to take, along with the backpack and the paper. He was surprised that Gaspar didn't ask where he was going, what kind of work he had to do, if he was going alone – all the questions that, he was sure, the boy wanted to ask and for which he had made-up answers at the ready – but he let them go without another word. Marcelina left silently. Her long hair was tied back in a ponytail that swayed, heavy and dark. She reached out her hand to Gaspar, but he didn't take it because he wanted to carry his backpack.

Stephen lay down beside Juan and imitated his posture, arms behind his head, eyes closed. They had been inseparable ever since they first met, and they had conspired and failed together. Growing up, Stephen had spent half his time with his father in Cadaqués and the other half in elite English schools. He had lived his whole life in mansions and with the utmost privilege, but he always felt a little foreign and a little orphaned.

'I'm listening,' said Juan.

They will test the child just as they did in past years, and they won't let you be there this time. It was a mistake to summon a demon in front of your son just before my mother and the inner circle test his abilities.

Gaspar thinks the vision of the demon was a dream.

And you believe that? What if he tells them about the dream? They'll know he's only confused. It was a mistake to do that, another self-destructive mistake. I'm starting to doubt the love you claim to have for your son, and I'm starting to think you're hiding something from me. If the demon had escaped your control, it could have destroyed you in front of Gaspar. Or destroyed him. It's not the whole truth that you wanted to find out if he could see it. You have other ways of testing him. Maybe you're going crazy. Why are you playing this game?

What did you find out about Rosario's death?

I haven't found anything.

I don't think you looked properly.

It's possible. I was busy with other matters. Mercedes has the underground passage full to bursting. Most of them are children. Her experiments to try to find another medium are worse than ever before, and my mother approves. They're worried because Gaspar still hasn't manifested, and they think your death is imminent. They're afraid of losing communication, since Gaspar is too young for the Rite of Transfer to be carried out on him now.

There was silence. Juan heard the hum of the air conditioner.

Listen to me. If they conclude that Gaspar isn't a medium – and they will, because we'll hide his powers – they're going to start preparations for the Rite. You know that doesn't involve any physical torture. It's very simple at this stage.

I don't want to hear any more about that. I will never hand my son over to them. The Rite cannot be done successfully. We already found that out.

What we've seen were just practice sessions. Missteps. You know that the chances of success, in your case, are very high. And you wouldn't be handing him over: you would use your son's body for yourself.

It's exactly the same thing. He would no longer exist. I'm not going to change my mind. Not even the possibility that I'll be taken to the Other Place when I die will make me change my mind. You're talking the way Rosario used to.

If he's a medium this is the only way, Juan. He's barely younger than you were when they started using you. My brother's preparation started when he was even younger than Gaspar. They'd use you both until your bodies gave out. This could have been avoided if the boy didn't exist. But he exists and he's your son. And if you don't want to use his body to carry on, I'm going to help you. Deceiving them, for now, is possible. Making the Rite fail when the time comes, also possible. We can get Gaspar away from the Order, and we can also keep them from using his body for the Rite.

My son is in danger no matter what.

He's in less danger if they don't find out he has abilities. And they won't find out, because we've worked well to hide them, and we've had help from the Other Place. Don't you trust yourself, and us? In six years, we can save him from the Rite.

127

Promise me?

Well, really you should promise yourself. The only thing that needs to happen for the Rite not to work is for you not to want to do it. To act as if it failed or to make it fail.

I can't stand being so unprotected, I can't stand this lack of power I'm feeling, I can't stand knowing that they're wrong and yet they keep on with this veneration.

How many times have we talked about this? And yet, here you are.

As if I could help it.

It was a mistake not to try to control the Order sooner. We would have done it. We didn't try seriously.

Juan looked at the ceiling. Stephen continued:

Rosario would have controlled the Order, with Gaspar and with you, and you know it.

You think they killed her because of that?

My mother is a good negotiator. And I haven't found a single reason to be suspicious. It was no secret that Rosario was rebellious.

Don't betray me, Stephen.

And don't you insult me. I'm in danger because of you.

Stephen got up from the bed. Before leaving, he placed his hands on Juan's shoulders, though he avoided looking him in the eye.

My mother once told me that your power was as great as your irresponsibility. I'll be with you forever. As long as you don't push me away, I'm with you.

Still not looking at Juan, Stephen left.

Dr Jorge Bradford asked Juan how he'd been and Juan told the truth, describing his symptoms and crises. Bradford decided to increase the dose of beta blockers and antiarrhythmics. Then Jorge examined him, using his good hand; he kept the other, mutilated one hidden in a black glove. I want you to take an anti-anxiety pill and go to sleep, Bradford said. Juan agreed: he was exhausted. But I'm going to need something stronger, he said. Bradford didn't argue and gave him a high dose of Valium. We're better prepared for your recovery than last year, he said, while Juan swallowed two pills without water. Graciela is already in the house, and another doctor is with her. We set up a very advanced intensive care room.

'All right, Jorge.'

Bradford started to add something, but stopped. For over twenty years now he'd behaved the same way towards Juan, with an indifference that disguised his devotion. Juan fell asleep naked on top of the sheets, and, possibly influenced by the air conditioner that cooled the room, he dreamed the Darkness was cold and wet, he dreamed of chattering teeth and twisted beings and fields of bodies and forests of hands and the hanged man strung up by his feet and the forest and then he couldn't walk any more, walking in the Darkness was very difficult, it was like climbing and there wasn't enough air and things took on shapes his eyes recognized but then went back to being broken and inexplicable images; the forest, however, was clear, though so far away and colourless, and in among the trees there was a clear presence, waiting, and piles of skulls, a black river that made no sound.

He woke up agitated, but not confused: Puerto Reyes was his house more than any other place was, even if he only visited once a year now. He took a quick shower and, under the water, in the steam, he thought about Gaspar. He was okay, Juan sensed. Nearby and okay. He got dressed to meet up with Stephen and Tali, and when he went out into the hallway the heat made him dizzy. It was practically solid. There was no one in the house, as far as he could hear. Somewhere, surely, Florence, Mercedes, Jorge, Anne, and the others were meeting. He couldn't hear them.

He knew every corner of the house as though he had his own private map. The same wooden stairs he was going down now had led him, when he was little, to the Place of Power. The garden where Tali had kissed him for the first time and he'd tried to contain his astonishment and joy hadn't changed much since then. He knew the number of steps on the stairs that led to the catwalk and the river.

When he left them behind, he sensed, first from the tips of his fingers and then as a sort of explosion of light in his head, something agonizing in the old tunnel that had once joined the two houses, the main mansion and the guest house. The tunnel had fallen into disuse after a flood. It was built too close to the river and it had collapsed, except for the first stretch – the part closest to Puerto Reyes – where some two hundred metres were still intact. Mercedes used that stretch to lock up children and prisoners. She had always preyed upon forsaken people, and there in the north she had an ideal hunting ground – poor, forgotten people, so abandoned they didn't even turn to the authorities if a son or a brother went missing. And for years now she'd also had the detainees her military friends handed over to her. The Darkness asked for bodies – that was the excuse she gave. But that wasn't true. The Darkness didn't ask for anything, and Juan knew it. In the Order, Mercedes was the firmest believer in the exercise of cruelty and perversion as the path to secret illumination. Juan believed, moreover, that she considered amorality to be a mark of class. The further away she got from moral convention, she thought, the more apparent her inborn superiority became. Florence no longer shared her methods, but she didn't stop Mercedes, who, as a member of one of the Order's founding families, enjoyed a certain amount of free rein to pursue her own agenda.

Tali and Stephen were waiting for him at the old gazebo surrounded by bronze statues that Adolfo Reyes had had brought over from France. Stephen was sitting on the gazebo steps and Tali, standing beside him, was smoking a cigarette. Juan kissed her on the mouth before leading her to the centre of the structure. There, near the Place of Power, he could talk to both of them out loud by creating a circle of silence. It took little effort: he was already feeding on the Darkness, could already feel how a new strength throbbed in his arteries, how his ears and skin perceived each movement with the intuition of a nocturnal animal.

'We had to do a double job,' said Tali. 'Good grief, your kid is powerful. You didn't leave me enough hair, but luckily you forgot some clothes.'

Juan smiled. He took her hand and raised her fingers to his mouth. They stank of dry, salty blood.

'How old-fashioned, Tali,' he said.

'Old-fashioned works,' Stephen said.

'Sometimes it's the only thing that works,' said Juan.

He couldn't see the Place of Power from the bedroom. Through the open window, however, wafted the smell of the candles that would mark the path in the night, though he could find it with his eyes closed. He wasn't nervous, or afraid: he barely felt anything. He was ready for the crown of shadows. Soon he would enter that dark zone where he was present yet existed no more. He was capable of re-emerging from it easily, though it hadn't always been so. Now, he was like an invited guest who is given the key so he can come and go as he pleases.

The tunic was made of black tulle; Juan let it fall over his naked body and put his hands through the armholes. His arms had to be free. Someone, possibly Florence, had ordered the two small horns of a young deer to be set into the mask. Juan looked into the mirror before going down. The attire was unnecessary, but the Order preferred such ceremonial details and Juan accepted them resignedly. He understood their effect.

He went down the stairs and saw the first candles in the yard, a path of two winding parallel lines. The silence was total except for nocturnal birds, the lapping of the river, a dog barking in the distance. As he left the perimeter of Puerto Reyes and started down the path wrested back from the jungle, he looked at his hands: they were no longer his. Now they were black, as if he had dunked them in a tar pit. Totally black up past his wrists. Their shape was also changing. Gradually and painlessly, his fingers were lengthening: at first, they seemed hit by sudden rheumatism, and in the blink of an eye the nails grew long and hard: curved golden daggers. That was his medium's mark, the physical metamorphosis that distinguished and condemned him. The god of the golden claws.

He took another step and saw the first line of Initiates. He passed among them. The Place of Power attracted him, pulled at his skin. He stepped into it and turned around, and before opening his arms he scanned the Initiates, the old ones in the first rows, the younger ones behind, some of them expectant and others filled with fear, the scribes prepared, the sacrifices waiting with their eyes blindfolded and their hands tied.

And then he saw no more.

Tali waited among the Initiates. She could see her father in the first row with Mercedes, beside the scribes, but she never would have dared to take a place there. She preferred to stay in the background.

She always attended the Ceremonial. She went for Juan's sake, but also because the thing that came with the night was divine, though she was sure it wasn't sacred. Stephen, the only one in the whole Order for whom Tali felt real affection, had listened to her attentively over the previous days as they were working together to protect Gaspar, and also to give magical strength to Juan. He wants to stop summoning, but he says he can't, Tali had said. How can he not be able to stop?

Stephen, who looked strangely aged and thin, had replied that that was a lie. He doesn't want to stop, he'd said. He could quit if he wanted to, but he's incapable of really wanting it. He has the power to hide, and he has people who would help him disappear. Or, he's not lying when he gives his excuses, but they are excuses. I don't know what it's like to be in contact with that power and I never will, but I do know it's not possible to reject it. No one could. Not even him. I don't understand, and I never will, how he's lasted so long without going crazy.

Stephen soaked Gaspar's clothing in blood and cut it into strips. He had drawn chalk symbols on the floor. His hands were filthy, as were Tali's.

I'd say he's pretty disturbed, my friend, she replied, and Stephen smiled. A little, yes. It's going to get worse as his power diminishes. Tali wanted to know if his power was waning because his health was worsening. I don't think so, said Stephen. I think there's a cycle of power, and that cycle is reaching its end. Or extinguishing. No medium has ever lasted as long as him, so really, we don't know what's happening to him, or why.

Still, Tali couldn't feel the end of that cycle now, as she stood among the candles in the unbearable jungle heat, alongside Initiates who at times collapsed to the ground, crying, shaking. She sensed him coming when they all did, but she didn't dare turn around. This was not the man she knew, the one who slept in her bed. This being who took firm steps and could sense each blade of grass as it touched his bare feet was no longer exactly a man.

Tali kept her head down until the cries, the moaning and the ecstasy of the others forced her to look.

Juan had reached the Place of Power. He was wearing a mask this time. He opened his arms and turned his head to one side: the mask had the horns of a forest animal stuck to it. He looked like an indifferent demon.

His hands: Tali saw them when he reached out. Bird claws, completely black, burnt, but sticky-looking. His golden nails shone like knives in the candlelight. How many candles? Hundreds. And then the noise of the open Darkness.

It was a panting sound, Tali thought this time, like dogs being choked by leashes, or when they are thirsty, hungry, a pack of hounds invading. The Darkness grew first around Juan as if it were steam coming off his body, and suddenly – this moment always caught Tali by surprise – it shot off in all directions and became enormous and liquid – or, rather, lustrous. It was hard to look at it: darker than the night, compact, it hid the trees, the light from the candles, and as it grew, it lifted Juan up and he floated, suspended in the blackness of wings. The scribes were writing, Tali saw them, but she didn't hear anything, nothing but panting and that flapping of wings. What did they hear, those who heard the voice of the Darkness? Juan had told her once that they didn't hear anything, it was all in their heads, that what they wrote was a kind of automatic dictation from their own minds. And if they do hear something, he'd said, it can't be anything good. Tali tried to find Stephen among the congregants, but by now it was impossible: the ranks had been broken, some people were trying to run towards the trees, but the more steadfast Initiates stopped them, and from the Darkness wafted a freezing and foul-smelling breath.

It was time for the sacrifice. Mercedes presided over it. Those who were given to the Darkness had their eyes blindfolded and their hands tied, and they stumbled. Drugged and blind, they had no idea what was before them. Maybe they expected pain. Tali saw a young, very thin man who was completely naked. He was crying, more awake than the others, and his lips trembled. Where are you taking us? he shouted, but his cries were drowned out by the panting of the Darkness and the murmuring of the Initiates.

Mercedes didn't have to do much. The Darkness was hungry, and it never refused what it was offered. Those who were given to the Darkness disappeared in one mouthful. They'd been lucky, thought Tali. She had questioned the practice, and had asked her father about it. Rosario had too. Contemptuously, he had told them the sacrifices were going to die anyway. What had gotten into them, defending those nobodies like that? Those people are marked for death, girls. We're doing them a favour.

Many members of the Order thought that, in reality, it was an honor to be sacrificed. Like the young man dressed in a black suit, despite the heat, who voluntarily approached the Darkness. He was the first. Tali saw him reach out his fingers to touch that compact black light beside Juan, at the height of his hip.

And she watched as the Darkness first sliced off his fingers, then his hand, and then, with a gluttonous and satisfied sound, took him all. The blood of the first bites spattered Juan, but he didn't move now. He wasn't going to move for a while, not until the Darkness closed.

Next came two women, hand in hand. One young, the other old. Mother and daughter? The Darkness took the old woman's head, and for a moment her decapitated body kept walking. The young woman didn't even look at her, or if she did, she wasn't shocked. She entered the Darkness resolutely and with a smile, dragging the headless body behind her, clutching its arm. They disappeared leaving only a trail of blood, the spatters that the carotid artery had sprayed over devotees in the first rows who now moved back a little, because the Darkness was coming down, down like a black sky or a bottomless throat, and it seemed to have eyes and to be able to choose.

Tali watched as it took, in one piece, a naked man who was on his knees. Then she saw how the Initiates couldn't help but raise their arms and touch the Darkness, which devoured fingers and hands. For a split second she caught sight of Stephen in the blood-spattered crowd. The candles were still lit, but they could do little to fight the black enclosure of the Darkness that descended like a mantle.

And then the withdrawal began. First, that ceiling, dark as if made of bats, started to rise, moving far away, and then it became small and surrounded Juan, who slowly lowered his arms and turned his head forward again. The Darkness didn't vanish: it receded like storm clouds, but it stayed encircling the medium and returned him gently to the ground. The Initiates – the frightened and the stunned, the calm ones and the scribes – all obeyed those with more character or experience, and they forced themselves to form back into rows. Some re-lit the candles that had been extinguished by the looming Darkness. They all pretended not to feel terror; those who trembled would claim it was from ecstasy, from emotion, from the glory of witnessing the visitation of a living god.

Juan was now kneeling on one leg and they could hear his erratic, painful breathing. He was still surrounded by a very fine black halo that, they all knew, was extremely dangerous: it cut like a scythe.

The medium rose. He walked straight, focused, his eyes very open and damp. Tali got closer. She could smell his sweat – his body was drenched under the tunic; he smelled of sea and salt and something acidic. Then she withdrew. She didn't want him to mark her. The medium raised his head and seemed to sniff the night. The fine halo around him twisted and wound and followed him vaguely, as if his body were steaming. The Initiates brought him those among them who had been wounded by the Darkness. The medium – Tali couldn't call him Juan now, she didn't recognize him – moved his black hands over the body parts and burned them. The Initiates screamed in pain as he cauterized their wounds, but only for an instant, because the loss of a member, they believed, designated them as chosen favourites. After they were healed, they cried with joy. Hands and arms lost to the Darkness were new extremities now, torn and bitten stumps. The Darkness grew smaller and smaller and more Initiates threw themselves at the medium's feet – like hungry dogs, thought Tali – offering him their naked bodies. There were many of them this time: many who were begging for a breadcrumb, jostling, some of them scratching each other. Finally, the medium acceded. In general, he marked very few people. This time he chose a thin girl with a flat chest and narrow hips who was far from the front row of howling Initiates, a girl who stood and pleaded, Please, moving her lips, a girl who was not a wolf or a submissive dog: a girl who was like a snake, with her small eyes and flat nose. The medium approached her, circled her with his slow steps, and used three of his golden nails to scratch her back with one swipe. The blood streamed down her bare legs, drew a dark belt around her: the Initiates watched open-mouthed. Later, they would say the wounds were so deep they could see her spine and ribs. The girl faltered but the medium steadied her, and with his other hand, which was gradually returning to normal – his nails were no longer yellow claws, now they were only deformed and black, rheumatic – he caressed her wounded back. And it stopped bleeding. And the wounds transformed into dark scars, as if the hand were laden

137

with time. Then he dropped the girl to the ground and walked away, slowly, towards the house. The black halo was gone. The last thing the Initiates saw was that, when he turned along the path of candles, he still had black hands. It was forbidden for them to follow him. Only Stephen and a select group were authorized to go with him. Tali was among the chosen few, because the medium had demanded it and he was granted certain whims.

The Initiates didn't know what happened afterwards, the toll the Ceremonial took on the medium's body. They had to remain beside the altar and follow Florence in the closing rites, when the mutilated ones were anointed in the circles, the blood was collected, the texts read, the dead removed. Dawn, still far away, marked the end of the Ceremonial.

Tali didn't participate in the final rituals. She ran, her dark hair loose and her white dress spattered with blood, towards the candlelit path and towards Juan. She missed Rosario more than ever at that moment, and longed for her fortitude and clear thinking.

He was taking so long to regain consciousness that Tali didn't dare get her hopes up at a tremor in his fingers or a change in his breathing. They had no choice but to wait. Bradford sounded optimistic. Dr Biedma, his disciple, seemed worried. Juan had blacked out, but his heart hadn't stopped. It had been years since that hadn't happened, thought Tali.

After ten hours, Stephen left the room. I need to sleep, he said. Tali put a hand on his back; she knew he was exhausted, and she understood why he didn't want to sleep in that sad room, with its bright light, the noisy monitor recording Juan's erratic heartbeat, his laboured breathing. Even Rosario had avoided it while Juan lay unconscious.

Tali wasn't tired. Bradford treated her with contempt, as always. To him, she was just the product of Adolfo's indiscretion with a village witch. Tali had mentally prepared a potent combination that would at least disturb Dr Bradford's sleep for a few weeks. As soon as she got home she'd do a little work on him, something brief but effective. Juan and Stephen couldn't know about it because they both always warned her about performing magic out of mere anger or annoyance. But who were they to judge her? It took some nerve, given the things they had done – and still did!

Tali looked sideways at her reflection in the windowpane. She had turned thirty years old. When people told her she was beautiful, they were referring to her heavy hair, her body that was no stranger to long walks, and the shine in her dark eyes. But she never wore make-up, didn't worry about her skin, didn't go in for rings or bracelets; when people praised her, there were always ellipses: 'But you'd be so much prettier if . . .' She felt she was getting old, that she needed to do something about the expression lines around her mouth and the stretch marks on her hips – the result of summers spent biking that had slimmed her legs. She approached the bed where Juan was still unconscious. She caressed his left hand, the wound that wouldn't scar over, but received no response. He'd been like that for a full day. Even so, this couldn't compare with the desperate hours of the year before, which she hadn't been able to stand: she'd ended up locked in a hospital bathroom, praying crazily to the saint, but above all terrified. It was Rosario who had found her and asked that she replace her beside Juan, because she needed to be with Gaspar: the boy, in a not-so-strange coincidence, was burning up with fever and they couldn't get his temperature down. She remembered her exhausted sister, her hair pulled back in a bun, her enviable determination. Looking at her, Tali had known

Rosario was destined to be the leader of the Order. What if she had been killed because of that? Juan couldn't and didn't want to understand the politics of the Order, or the extent of Rosario's ambitions. That was what he had Stephen for.

Juan pulled his hand from hers, and in a movement that seemed very fast to her, he tore the oxygen mask from his face. Before going to find Bradford, she caressed his pale lips and the skin beneath his sunken eyes, which looked as strange as they always did after the Ceremonial: more transparent, criss-crossed by burst vessels – they looked blind. Tali knew they would improve as the hours passed. She leaned over to kiss Juan's forehead, and he asked in a low voice how long he'd been out. A day, more or less, she told him. I'll be right back, she said, and opened the door. Bradford was already on the other side, as if something had alerted him. Tali left them alone. She leaned against the window in the hallway. Outside, the sky threatened another storm: purple clouds split off over the black of night, and the air seemed made of honey. Tali caressed the talisman under the thin skin of her arm, so small it looked like an insect bite or a blemish. My lord, thank you, she said, and with words no one could learn, she promised a perfect gift when she was back home, back in her temple. She had asked the saint once who the Darkness was; she'd asked at night, years ago, amid wine and candles, and the saint had replied in the cards: again and again the answer appeared in the centre of the spread. The Moon. It was the card Juan had drawn for her and the one Tali understood the least, one she always interpreted as meaning an important change, a voluntary one. But it was also about deception, confusion, reverie. Madness, even.

Bradford came out of the room and nodded to Tali to say she could go in. The doctor's hair was dirty and she felt a wave of disgust, as though she'd accidentally touched rotten meat stuck to the bottom of a dirty pot.

Juan was sitting up in bed, buttoning a clean white short-sleeved shirt. On the sheets lay a tangle of cables from the intravenous drip, the electrodes, and the other equipment he'd been hooked up to. When he looked at her, she saw his eyes were already less bloodshot; little by little they were returning to their usual yellow-flecked green. Juan beckoned her closer: his hands were shaking and he couldn't get the shirt fastened. Tali helped him. She asked if he could go out yet, and he replied that Bradford said no, but he wasn't about to stay in bed. I want you to take me for a walk, he said. Tali finished buttoning his shirt and asked if he could stand, because she couldn't hold his weight if he fell. Juan put his feet on the floor and his hands on Tali's shoulders. When he stood up, he breathed deeply to keep his knees firm. I can, he said. Where's Stephen? He's resting, but I can call him.

The room where Juan recovered from the Ceremonial was on the ground floor; otherwise Tali wouldn't have dared walk with him, since the stairs would be too much. She let him lean all the weight she could bear on her, his arm around her waist. They didn't meet anyone in the short hallway leading to the yard, or outside, when they reached the fountain and the willow. Once they were a little further from the house, Juan asked:

'Have they already tested Gaspar?'

'Earlier this afternoon,' said Tali. 'They don't tell me anything, but they do talk to Stephen. He says the kid didn't pass any of the seven tests.'

Juan looked at her with a smile that made him appear very young, like a teenager. Nowhere in his face could Tali find the being who had terrified her the night before. They sat down on a sofa, one of several Mercedes had had brought out to the garden to replace the wood and metal benches, which were so

141

uncomfortable. Tali sat at one end and Juan sat down beside her, keeping his torso upright so he could breathe better. The garden was very dark. Even with the generator running, they had to turn off as many lights as possible in order to use the air conditioner: the guest house was full and the visitors had to be kept comfortable. Still, guests were forbidden from coming to the main house where the medium stayed.

'You can't imagine how strong the kid is,' said Tali. Juan didn't reply, just let her talk. 'We had to work hard. Is it because he's little?'

Juan sat up even straighter on the sofa to answer her. The whites of his eyes were almost normal now.

'No. It should have been easy because he's little.'

'Well, it wasn't exactly Herculean, but it was tough. He kept slipping away from me!'

Juan wiped his forehead. He wasn't sweating, though the heat was damp and threatening.

'I have to ask you for a favour. I want you to keep him like that. Gaspar.'

'Of course. He'll be blocked as long as you're here.'

'That's not what I mean.'

'Juan, shouldn't we be using silence to talk?'

He shook his head. He was agitated.

'Today I can feel the plants growing, I can hear every whisper in the house, the footsteps of the guests, even the wailing of the ones Mercedes hides in the tunnel. No one is listening to us. Except Stephen, who's on his way. We're alone.'

And then he made his request: I want you to keep my son blocked forever. I need to know if you can do it. Tali told him she could try, but she also explained how painful it was to annul someone so young. When she was performing the work to block him, she had felt that she was physically hurting the boy. It was like he was shrieking, said Tali, and she remembered the shiver, the feeling she was slicing through muscle when she manipulated the doll made of blood, hair, rope, and bone. Like she was drowning a strong newborn kitten that was desperate to live. Stephen had had to draw the symbols many times because they'd faded, as if they lacked strength, as if a hand were erasing them. Maintaining that state for a long time was possible, but it would be laborious, and, Tali believed, it would be damaging to Gaspar. Not to mention lethal for her and Stephen if they were ever found out.

Juan's eyes were cold.

'They won't find out if you work in the temple. The protection sign I left there hides anything that happens inside.'

'You asshole, you didn't tell me that's why you did it.'

'Can you keep my son blocked?'

'I don't know what might happen when he grows up.'

'When he grows up, we'll see. No one is going to teach him anything. I need them to go on thinking he's no good to them. If they even suspect he is, they'll start using him.'

Stephen came into the garden along the path that led to the guest house. He knelt down in front of Juan and looked at him closely. He had slept, and he seemed relieved.

'My mother thought it was a magnificent Ceremonial, and she wants to see you as soon as you feel well. Your son is with Marcelina.'

'Tali told me Gaspar didn't pass any of the tests.'

Juan remembered the seven tests clearly. They were simple and effective. He had passed them without much effort long before he'd manifested. Gaspar would have done too, if it hadn't been for Stephen and Tali's intervention.

'The kid could be astonishing if you trained him. If you'd let me train him. Rosario wanted that, and you know it.'

'And she did train him, a lot. Gaspar reads Tarot and he's only six years old. I don't want to go back over these discussions. You and I are not going to argue about this. It's my decision. They're not going to give up, are they?'

'Of course not. They'll test the kid once a year, or whenever they consider it necessary. They haven't told me how they'll do it, but come on, you can't refuse them that.'

'I've just asked Tali to keep Gaspar blocked, and you have to help her.'

Stephen sighed.

'Look, I know that right now caution could not matter less to you, but having this conversation here is crazy.'

'Will you help her?'

'Of course I will. And now that's enough.'

Stephen took Juan's hands. Like Tali had done, he caressed the wound in one of the palms. 'I'll go get Gaspar for you,' he said.

When Gaspar came into the garden with Stephen, sleep still in his eyes, he was very serious until he saw his father, and then he ran over and climbed up on the sofa, and hugged him so hard that Tali had to look away, towards the night and its storm, the lights from the guest house, the white orchids that hung over the moss on the trees.

Juan and Gaspar slept together and spent the morning together: they had dinner and breakfast in bed, and watched TV. Juan felt the peculiar disconnection that always followed a Ceremonial: an excessive sensitivity mixed with tiredness and a certain bewilderment.

Gaspar didn't mention the tests that his grandmother, Florence, and Anne had subjected him to. Juan didn't want to ask anything. Could he have thought they were a game? He would talk eventually. In the exhaustion of the hours after regaining consciousness, Juan preferred this interlude of silence. But he knew his son well enough to know that if he wasn't talking about what had happened, it was because he was still mulling it over. And when Gaspar kept quiet in order to think, it was because something had bothered him, and he still hadn't found the words to talk about it. He needed time, and Juan was willing to give it to him. But his son did talk about other things. About the zoo he'd gone to with Marcelina. It's to take care of the animals, he said, because people hunt out of cruelty. Out of cruelty. Juan smiled: he had copied that expression from someone. He could clearly sense the work Tali and Stephen had done on his son. Juan, though, could still tell what the boy was feeling, and could still talk to him without uttering words. What he no longer perceived was the vibration that had been intensifying since the night the two of them had seen the ghost of the pregnant woman at the hotel. A tense and throbbing vibration, like a headache. Gaspar was better off without that burden.

Bradford had come in several times during the night to be sure Juan was all right. So had Dr Biedma. Gaspar had slept so peacefully beside him that he didn't even wake up any of the times Bradford had checked Juan's blood pressure. It was such a relief to pull up the sheet, to sit in bed and look out the window at the night, to leave behind the spattered blood, the hands aching from their transformation, the image of the sacrifices, their blindfolded eyes and gaping mouths.

And above all, it was a relief to take in a new certainty. He had not opened the Darkness for Rosario. No one else could open it, and he hadn't done it for her. Thus, she could not be there. The demon had confused him. He wasn't immune to its suggestions, much as he'd like to believe otherwise. What arrogance. It was a relief to know, in any case, that Rosario wasn't in the forests of hands, the fields of torsos, the bone-filled desert that she had considered a temple. Or in the valley of the hanged, where men and women were strung up by their feet, and where Eddie was spending his eternity – Eddie, Stephen's younger brother, the boy who had been trained as a medium and who had failed. There were never living beings in those wastelands, though. Only human remains. Or could there actually be someone else in the Order who was capable of opening the Darkness? Had Mercedes found a medium among the abducted people she held prisoner? Wouldn't he sense it if she had?

No, he said aloud. He couldn't keep ruminating, he'd drive himself mad. The hours after the Ceremonial were the hardest when it came to maintaining his sanity.

After breakfast, Juan took Gaspar to the wooden walkway that hung over the treetops and descended in a steep staircase to an empty beach, from where they could see the main dock of Puerto Reyes. Juan sat on the thick, dark sand and watched as Gaspar entertained himself with branches, fish bones, and his toy cars, or splashed about in the water. He had asked that no one go with him except the bodyguards, who were different from the ones in Buenos Aires, and who kept their distance. The river was nervous, swollen by the rains, brown and opaque. Marcelina had given Gaspar a plastic bucket the day before, and the boy filled it with jacaranda flowers that fell to the ground, red ceiba flowers, and all kinds of green leaves. Juan wanted to swim, but he didn't feel physically strong enough. When he extended his arms, his hands still trembled.

He might improve as the days passed, or he might not. Bradford had explained it to him: from a medical perspective, there was nothing more to be done. His heart was enlarged and failing, and it was irreversible. There was medication, and there were therapeutic advances and other palliatives. What was most likely, however, was that he would decline irrevocably until his death, in months, in a few years, in a second.

The sun made his head hurt.

'I'm gonna climb the tree!' shouted Gaspar.

Juan regretted not having brought something to drink: he was thirsty. He didn't want to ask anything of the bodyguards. He watched how nimbly his son climbed the twisted trunk of a tree, negotiating the branches until he sat mounted on a low-hanging one like a horse. He must have learned that on outings with his mother, when the two of them went hiking and left him alone and prostrate. Juan had never climbed a tree as a child. A grasping envy filled his mouth with a metal taste and he recognized the danger of the feeling, what it meant for Gaspar, for him, for what remained of his sanity.

He sensed Stephen's footsteps about a hundred metres away, on the catwalk. There was a clinking sound: he was bringing a drink, with ice. He watched Stephen gingerly balance the glasses as he descended the steep steps, and he accepted the glass with a smile. It was iced tea: Stephen detested tereré and yerba mate in general, but he greatly enjoyed the Misiones tea, much more than its hard-working cultivators ever did.

'Good morning,' said Stephen as he sat on the sand. Juan downed the tea in two gulps, and the cold drove a sharp pain into his left eye. 'They want to talk to you today. Of course, they'll respect your decision if you'd rather put off the meeting.'

'No,' said Juan. 'The sooner the better.'

Stephen complained about the heat and took off his dark shirt. He hadn't seen the sun in a while, and the thick, freckle-dotted skin on his shoulders was pale, though his forearms were tanned, like a truck driver's. On his back, twin scars began below his shoulder blades and extended to his waist, dense

147

and protruding. Juan caressed them with his fingertips: he had opened and closed those wounds himself.

Stephen had first travelled to Misiones with his mother. He was fifteen, and Florence had judged him old enough to attend. Juan was twelve at the time, tall and thin, and in those first Ceremonials he still hadn't understood that feeling in his hands, that desire to mark. Stephen showed him the way when he knelt down before him, turned around, and offered his back. Later he'd told Juan that the cut had been fast and painful: Juan remembered how his golden nails had collided with Stephen's ribs. Stephen hadn't screamed or trembled, just clutched at the grass with his hands. He had also later described the relief he'd felt when Juan's hands closed the wound, the nails like a caress. Juan remembered how Florence had cried with joy. She considered it a blessing. She felt a little envious, she'd admitted. Oh, she would have worn scars from the golden claws with pride. Florence knew the mark was a commitment between Stephen and Juan, a scar of fidelity. The idea that her oldest son's allegiance was divided between the medium and the Order wasn't entirely gratifying, but Florence respected the decisions of the Darkness and didn't question them. It was an honour that the Darkness had touched her older son, and a misfortune that it had spurned Eddie, her younger son, the greatest failure of her life. And it was a shame it hadn't chosen her.

The marked had a different status in the Order: greater access to knowledge, rituals, decisions of the inner circle. They had been touched by the gods. The young woman who had been marked the night before would now be invited to more important rituals, her whims would be granted, and, if Juan wanted, she could have a personal relationship with him. Stephen had so much freedom and access to Juan not only because he was Florence's son, but also because he was one of the marked. Over the years their bond had become intimate, both fraternal and sexual. If that bothered Florence, she had never said so out loud. Everyone knew that she would have preferred the privilege for her other son, but no one talked about Eddie any more, not since he had disappeared almost ten years ago.

Gaspar shook the branch so hard that some leaves drifted down to Juan and Stephen.

'Get down right now! I'm not going to climb up there and get you.'

There was silence, then a slow and doubtful sliding of hands and legs. The tree wasn't tall, and Juan knew his son could manage on his own. In under five minutes he was back on the beach and running towards Juan.

'It's harder to get down than climb up.'

'And that's strange?'

'Yeah, cos it's the opposite on stairs.'

One of his hands was full of leaves, and he added them to the collection in the bucket. Hi, he said to Stephen, and sat down beside him. When Gaspar started to organize and classify his flowers and weeds and leaves on the dark sand of the beach, Juan asked:

'How did it go with your grandmother yesterday? You told me a lot about the zoo but nothing about what you did with her.'

'It was boring. She said we were gonna play, but we played weird games that weren't fun. I don't like being with Grandma. I like Grandpa okay.'

'What were the games?'

Gaspar described the tests in his own way, confused and chaotic, but to Juan and Stephen, who knew them, it was easy to understand. They had covered his eyes and asked him who was in the room. Gaspar had named the people present. He didn't sense anyone else. Still with the blindfold on, they'd asked him to imagine symbols. Like what? Gaspar had asked. Like numbers. Or other things. He had talked to them about the flowers he saw before a headache.

'That doesn't count for anything?' Juan asked Stephen.

'Doesn't seem to have caught their attention. It's an aura from a migraine. They're not idiots.'

Gaspar talked as though in a dream while he piled up purple flowers, red flowers, light green leaves, dark green leaves, and bark, as though they were ingredients for the cauldron.

'Then they made me walk around a weird part of the zoo and they ran around me, I think. I don't know what game that was. Like hide and seek, but I got scared by the noises and plus some of them weren't wearing clothes and I didn't like that. Grandpa came to get me, but after a really long time. Like night time.'

'Okay. What else?'

'Then that boring part, when they made me sit on some circles in the grass. Are they chalk, Dad?'

'Yes, they're made of chalk.'

Juan thought: They used to be made of blood, son, but your mother forbade it as you got older. I'm surprised they're respecting that wish.

'And another boring thing – they wanted me to lie in a bed with my legs all twisted up, and think about things they told me, like imagining things, but I didn't really understand them. Plus, they have a hand like the one Mom had in her purse, maybe it's the same one.'

Juan frowned. He didn't like to mention that hand in front of Stephen, but he also knew the hand was hidden. If they had found it, that was a serious problem. Stephen reassured him:

'It's not the same one. Rosario's is still safe. Argentina has more than enough anonymous dead, and this house has been a clandestine prison for years.'

Juan rubbed his eyes. His neck felt stiff from his headache, and from his frustration.

'Grandma got mad because when they gave it to me, I almost dropped it, it's really heavy. Mom never let me touch it and I don't know how to hold it.'

'What do you mean she got mad?'

'She took it away from me and hit me and told me I was stupid, something like that. I don't know if she said stupid. Something mean. Anyway, I almost dropped it. It's heavy.'

'She hit you.'

Gaspar made a gesture like a slap, hitting the back of his hand on his cheek.

'It didn't hurt, though. It didn't *really* hurt.'

Juan looked at Stephen.

'One of these days I'm going to kill her,' he said. And he added: 'Gaspar, do me a favour. Make a racetrack for your cars, in a figure of eight.'

Gaspar obeyed, as if he were grateful the interrogation was finally ending. He started to work in the sand, smoothing and packing it with his shoes.

The meeting took place in the main hall of Puerto Reyes. What had been a hint of a migraine at the Paraná beach was now hammering in Juan's head, and his nausea grew with each violent, uneven pound of his heart. He sat down in the leather armchair – completely unsuitable for the heat and humidity of that room, which was too large for air conditioning and had only a ceiling fan; the chair was immediately damp with sweat. He had left Gaspar asleep in Marcelina's arms. The pain forced his eyes closed. It was too late to take a pill, and in any case, he knew he would need something very strong, but a powerful painkiller would lower his blood pressure too much, even more than the medicines Bradford had already injected him with, the tracks running up the inside of his elbow in tiny puncture wounds. From his chair he could see the painting by Cándido López. *Assault of the 3rd Argentine Column at Curupayti.* A rectangle a metre and a half long, with its little men carrying ladders, the wounded soldier on a stretcher, the man riding a white horse with his sword raised, seemingly removed from it all, the ground a swamp, the explosions in the background like low clouds, the darkened sky of war. It was beautiful. It was death at a distance, observed, childish.

Stephen was preparing cold drinks as if the conversation to follow would be a friendly and extortion-free chat, a kind of social tea. He himself, however, was drinking whiskey from Adolfo's bottomless cellar. He offered some to Juan with a lot of ice, but Juan refused it: alcohol made the pain worse. Stephen came over and ran an ice cube over the back of his neck.

'Does this help?'

Juan didn't answer. It didn't help, but he needed Stephen nearby. He had proved his loyalty a long time ago, and proved it so definitively that it was impossible to doubt.

Only Mercedes, Florence, and Anne Clarke were in the hall. The women, the leaders. Florence was wearing a floral silk dress that seemed to float around her. She was tall, and that day she was wearing almost no make-up or jewellery: her *au naturel* skin was overly white and had a greyish tinge, and her teeth, somewhat yellowed, appeared only when she smiled. She had pulled her long and indomitable red hair back into a bun. She was talking about how this time the Darkness's projection had been extraordinary. Twelve people it had touched, more than ever before. Juan wanted to know how many people had been consumed, and with unchecked pride she told him there'd been eight, and then she repeated it, *eight*, in English. She often did that, mixed English and Spanish, when she talked to Juan, who understood both languages.

'That's why we want to thank you, before anything else,' said Florence. *So grateful*, she said in English. 'Because the gods spoke, and the record of their words was extensive. We know the toll it takes on your body to do this, and we know you are full of doubt. It's normal for a medium to doubt. But we must protect the Order from the madness of the mediums. We know how they deteriorate. We know the price they pay for being the door.'

'The medium is right here,' said Juan. 'Don't speak as if you were talking about someone else. Before you tell me what you have to tell me, I need to know something, and you will answer me. I'm sick of the silence.'

The women looked up expectantly, and Juan raised his voice. Outside, the dogs were barking.

'On my trip here, I summoned an entity. My reason for doing so is not something I have to explain to you. It replied to one of my questions with words that I interpreted in a certain way. The wrong way. And I persisted in the error. The way I persisted and the difficulty I had convincing myself that I was thinking something foolish gave me a clue: my confusion was magical work. Very good magical work, because I didn't feel it. I needed to be in this house in order to realize my mistake. To understand who "those who speak to me" are. And it's you three.'

He looked closely at the women. They were calm. Anne, with her perfectly coiffed white hair, was the only one who seemed a little uneasy. She was the oldest of them, and the most scrupulous.

'You underestimate me,' he went on. 'You know it's possible that I'm reaching the end of my cycle. But, as you saw last night, the cycle still holds a great deal of power.'

Florence started to speak, but Juan raised a hand.

'Not now. I want you to tell me why you were manipulating me.'

Florence's reply was direct:

'We have Rosario,' she said. 'We have her trapped in a place where you can't contact her. *Out of reach.*'

Juan closed his eyes. His teeth were clenched tight and his jaw hurt now, too.

'Where is she?'

'We don't know that. You'll have to figure it out.'

'You performed a spell without knowing how to undo it. That's what you're telling me.'

'Yes, that's correct.' Florence crossed her arms.

'Why did you kill Rosario? To take away my power? Because you thought she wanted to take control of the Order?'

Mercedes stood up.

'We did not kill my daughter. We respect the blood. She had an accident.'

'And then you saw your chance.'

Mercedes gazed at him steadily through her dark glasses, but said nothing.

'I don't believe you,' he told her. 'Doesn't matter. Where did you send my wife?'

'We don't know and we're not lying,' Florence said. 'In the last Ceremonial, the gods spoke of different places of death. We sent her spirit to one of them. But they have not taught us yet how to find her, nor can we contact her. *We just can't. Like you.* Every year when you do the Ceremonial for us, you'll be able to ask the Darkness where that place is and how you can get her out. Sooner or later, it will give you the answer.'

'Is it a place of suffering?'

'Yes,' said Florence, coldly. 'We have to ensure our protection and your commitment. You can't leave her there, right?

You have to look for her, and you have to come here to do it, in the Ceremonial. Perhaps you can look for her on your own, too, but that's no business of ours. You only need to know that the answer you seek is here.'

Juan closed his eyes in a pretence of pain, but really he was studying the energy in the room to see if he could hurt them. When he approached Mercedes and Florence, he felt it. Something was protecting them, and it was powerful. He withdrew. When had they become so strong? The three of them had always been unremarkable as practical witches. Then he understood: it was his own power shrinking, so that what had seemed minimal before was now significant and potent. The conditions were evening out. As though in a dream, he heard Stephen's voice:

If you eliminate them, they'll never be able to tell you what they did with Rosario. Don't hurt them.

It's in the texts, they say. I can read the texts.

They'll have that particular text well hidden. We can find it, but only if you stay calm. You have other ways of looking for her that they don't know about. Don't forget that. We'll find her.

Juan had nothing to say. So, Rosario *was* in the Darkness. In a way. The demon hadn't lied, of course, and neither had he interpreted its answer entirely incorrectly. He had only lacked information.

'It's our way of ensuring that you will return and that you will continue summoning, because if you don't, you'll be abandoning her there,' Florence continued. 'And it also ensures that you will agree to attempt the Rite with your son when it becomes necessary.'

'And that you will give us the steps, so we can all perform it successfully ourselves,' added Mercedes. 'Thus far, only the medium can perform the Rite. We cannot let anything interrupt the process.'

'Rosario could have interrupted it,' said Juan. 'You thought she would have that power over me, that she would want to protect her son.'

There was no reply. Juan went on: 'Mercedes, you have no children left to move your consciousness into.'

Mercedes smiled. 'Juan, that headache has left you stupid. I don't have my daughter, but I do have my grandson.'

'Gaspar's body is mine.'

'Not if you fail. If you decide to fail – as I fear you want to – I will take him. It's the blood that matters.'

She smiled again and looked to Florence, who said:

'Juan, we've never had another medium even close to your calibre. We need to protect ourselves from what's happening to you. Mediums lose their sanity. *They lose their minds! It's happened too many times.* They become unmanageable, they rebel. We understand. But what the Darkness, our ancient god, is giving us must not be interrupted by a whim or fleeting mania. Not even by your illness. We have to protect ourselves from your power. The messages cannot stop just because you decide to turn against us. The Darkness is teaching us how to conquer death. It is teaching us how to contact other ancient gods. *Just imagine.* You must continue summoning for us. Your wife told us that you wanted to stop, and we cannot allow that. And you know perfectly well that when something must be done for the Order, I don't back down. *I'm so terribly sorry.* I'm more grateful to you than to anyone in this world. But I cannot allow you to leave us, or to exercise your power over us.'

'Do you really think I can stop summoning? That the Darkness will allow it?'

Florence cocked her head to one side and her bun almost came undone. A lock of red hair fell over her forehead.

'You could manage to stop for a time, if you wished. What

we fear is that you'll decide to end your life. *You can kill yourself*, and that would be your way to stop summoning. It wouldn't be the first time a medium committed suicide.'

'I could also die in any Ceremonial.'

'I doubt it. At least I know we can revive you, and it's a risk we must take. But if you decide to kill yourself, we'll have nothing left. Now that your wife is trapped, I don't think you'll do it, I think you will go on so that you can free her. The Darkness will reveal where she is.'

'Plus,' added Mercedes, 'don't think we will ever give up and stop testing my grandson's abilities. Maybe Rosario lied to us and maybe she didn't, it doesn't matter. She was ambitious and wanted to inherit the Order, and I can't blame her for that, but I never trusted her. Gaspar could reveal himself later.'

'Gaspar is not my heir. He's not a medium.'

'Not yet,' said Florence. 'If he is, he will be marked as you were. The left hand finds its way, its fingers have their reach. It cannot be hidden. *It radiates*. I know what you feel for the boy. I've seen you together. You are full of love for each other. We thought that the boy was talented. We still believe it, though he hasn't manifested just yet. If he is, he will be your heir. If he's not, I know it will be difficult for you to perform the Rite when the moment comes. But you will use his body, and you will want to. Who wouldn't? It's an act of love. We have children so that we can continue on, they are our immortality. I'm sorry the Rite is impossible now, with the boy still so young. I know the rules. It's better if you are the one who takes his body, right? If you decide to kill yourself, someone else can take it. You don't want that, *of course you don't.*'

Juan took a deep breath before speaking.

'These next few years, until Gaspar is of age for the Rite, I want you to leave him alone. I don't want him to hear anything from you. Nothing. I want him to be a normal child for what remains of his life.'

'Of course, my dear,' Florence said, and she shot Mercedes a warning look. Don't anger him, her eyes said. 'We won't break the agreement we've had with you and Rosario up till now: life will be normal. A medium, as you well know, is revealed on his own terms. *And it's a powerful revelation.* We will know. There are always members of the Order near you: they are already watching over your son, and they will continue to do so. If Gaspar reveals himself, they will inform us. A medium cannot be hidden indefinitely. Plus, he will be close to the girl, the black miracle. She will strengthen him, she has been touched. You don't want to bring him with you every summer for the Ceremonial? Then don't. *I agree with you.* It could be dangerous. What if the Darkness wants him, and we lose his body? It's your decision, and I won't oppose it.'

'None of you will come near him. He won't have a relation-ship with Mercedes or Adolfo either.'

Mercedes rose from her chair. Juan saw the fury in her eyes.

'He will be watched over,' Florence went on, 'and we will receive reports. It's impossible for him to escape. He'll have nowhere else to go. His body is precious and necessary. We will find ways to keep you alive until he is older and can receive you.'

'You never kept me alive. I owe this vile life to Bradford alone.'

'We will never agree about that. He has been fundamental. *But we helped too.*'

Florence kept talking, but Juan was no longer listening. He was too angry and exhausted to argue. His need for Rosario pierced him with brutal precision. They had won, and all he could do was submit. This time, he had lost. He felt the pain behind his eyes. They had Rosario, and he would have to find her. He had to, because she would have done the same for him. He stood up and walked towards the door.

'Don't follow me,' he said. 'I could kill you all. Mediums are suicidal, right? They go crazy, don't they?'

He smiled at them. He summoned the last of his strength from beneath his pain and left the room. Outside, the sunlight was white like a desert.

Juan asked Stephen to leave him alone so he could rest in his room; the pain in his head wouldn't let him think or even walk. He found Gaspar sleeping face down. He smelled of pool chlorine and his hair was wet. Juan didn't want to wake the boy. He always found it strange that the Initiates came to the Ceremonial alone. How many had come this time? Fifty, sixty? Where were their children? Because they all had children. Well, they were rich. They could pay for nannies until the kids were old enough to attend with them. And that time came soon enough, even leaving aside the case of Adela, which had been an accident. On one occasion, the Darkness, channelled through him, had torn a ten-year-old boy's arm off at the shoulder. His mother, instead of reacting with the usual ecstasy of the Initiates, had gone into hysterics, threatening to expose everything, to denounce them. Florence didn't tolerate that kind of rebellion. She had rocks tied to the woman's feet, and she was thrown into the Paraná River. Let her join the many dead hidden along Argentine river bottoms. The dictatorship's crimes were very useful to the Order, providing it with bodies, alibis, and currents of pain and fear – emotions that were easily manipulated.

Juan turned up the air conditioner a little and covered his son with a blanket. He got the syringe and the injectable painkiller from his bag: it was too late to fight the migraine with pills. He tightened his belt around his forearm to find a usable vein. He could hardly see what he was doing, his vision was so clouded by the pain. Still, he managed to inject the drug, whose effects he no longer feared: he felt fully prepared to throw himself into the river, and the idea pursued him with a buzzing sound. But if he did decide to kill himself, he would have to take Gaspar with him. Or ask Stephen to find his brother in Rio de Janeiro and leave the boy with him. But the Order would surely take Gaspar from Luis sooner or later. So that he could be a recipient for Mercedes. So that he could be the medium, once they discovered and destroyed the work Stephen and Tali had done and killed them both. They were in danger. He had designed the protection for his son with elements brought back from the Other Place, a zone of the Darkness that the Order didn't know about. But he still needed the final and definitive protection, which was slow in coming. The Lord of Patience, he thought, touching his back. He waited with his eyes closed for the painkiller to kick in. It took a long time. It wasn't going to take away all the pain, but it would allay the intensity of the pounding, the pressure in his temples, the heartbeats that seemed to pump hot iron instead of blood.

Once the pain had finally subsided a little, Juan slid a small flashlight into the back pocket of his jeans, closed the door softly behind him, and walked, trying not to make any noise, towards the entrance to the tunnel between the houses. Years ago, it had been put to all kinds of use: the servants used it when it rained, so that they wouldn't track red mud into the guest house or the main one; furniture was stored there; clandestine encounters took place there; and at some point a kind of underground washing station for dishes and clothes had been installed. But after the flood there was hardly any tunnel left: the mud had carried the bricks away and caused an avalanche.

All that remained was the first stretch, which still had the old iron gate with its padlock.

Juan opened it without a thought: there wasn't a door in existence that could withstand him. When he entered, he smelled the stench and sensed the suffering of the children who lived there. He switched on the flashlight and practically crawled along on his knees: the tunnel was low, and for a man of his height it was very cramped. Then he came upon the first child.

The boy was in an animal cage, surely brought there from the neighbouring zoo. ('They have toucans, Dad, the toucans are incredible!' Gaspar had shouted with glee.) Juan remembered when Rosario had been forced to care for a different crop of kidnapped children Mercedes had kept at one of her estates in Buenos Aires province, and he had decided to help her. They'd been held in cages then, too. Now, this first child was in a rusty, dirty pen that had possibly once held animals. His left leg was tied to his back in a position that would have required his hip to have been broken. Since he was very young (one year old? Hard to know under all the grime), the bone had surely broken easily. His neck was twisted as well because of the position of his foot. When Juan brought the flashlight closer to see him better, he reacted like an animal, his mouth open and growling; his tongue had been sliced in two, and was now forked. Around him in the cage were the remains of his food: cat skeletons and some small human bones.

Juan kept walking. There were more cages. The other boys and girls were older. Many of them stared at him with black eyes: some of them were Guaraní children who probably didn't speak Spanish. Others might be the children of men and women who were sacrificed to the Darkness. Some of them reacted to his presence by skittering to the back of their cages, while others barely opened their eyes. There were children whose teeth had been filed into sharp rows, like saws; there were children with the obvious marks of torture on their legs, their backs, their genitals; he smelled the rot of children who must already be dead. Did they leave the cadavers there so the others would get used to the smell? Rosario had been forced to bury the caged ones who had died. She'd seen festering wounds, infections, eyes where the bugs of dampness and the river crawled. He stopped after some hundred metres of cages of destroyed children, living and dead; he could tell they continued for the remaining hundred metres of tunnel. He turned back, ready to confront Mercedes, who was waiting for him at the door beside her imbunche child. Juan turned off the flashlight when Mercedes lit a weak lamp, the tunnel's only illumination.

'So, this is your new collection, Mercedes.'

'It will bring results. Our god says so, his instruction is to do it this way.'

'The god is crazy, like you.'

'I follow the orders of the Darkness.'

Juan laughed, and his laughter bounced back off the tunnel walls in obscene echoes. Some of the moribund and wounded children whimpered. From the depths of the tunnel came a dying moan.

'This is not a search for a medium, Mercedes. This was always just for your own pleasure.'

Mercedes uncrossed her arms and let them fall to her sides.

'It may not be beautiful now, but it will be! When they work together! There are many gods! Ours says so and orders the search for another medium. It's in the book!'

Juan approached Mercedes until he could see the glint of her eyes behind the dark glasses she always used, even in the semi-darkness of the tunnel.

'Where do you get them, Mercedes? Indigenous children?

The children of prisoners? Why don't you ask for a sacrifice, an offering, from the rich Initiates of the Order? Do you steal them in the night, or do their mothers sell them because they're dying of hunger? Do their fathers know where their children are before they're thrown to the Darkness? You've learned a few things from your friends' torture chambers.'

'Such compassion. Why don't you save them, then? You have the power to do it.'

Juan turned his flashlight back on and shone it directly into Mercedes' dark glasses. He wanted to look her in the eye. He wanted to blind her.

'That would only be more cruelty. They're far beyond any help.'

Juan directed the flashlight on to one of his own hands, and Mercedes started to babble and beg for mercy. She tried to run out the door, but Juan willed it sealed hermetically. She was alone in the tunnel with the golden god, the lord of the gate.

'You know where this tunnel went?' he asked her. 'It didn't go from one house to the other in a straight line. The builders had to skirt round some underground lakes, because it's very close to the river. And in one stretch, several metres past the beginning of the collapse, it reaches the Place of Power. See?'

His illuminated hand was now surrounded by black light.

'Female mediums are much more powerful,' he went on. 'They have the power to summon anywhere, they just have to figure out the particular conditions needed for concentration, or else the ritual can be performed on them. Men depend on Places of Power. There are many. Some mediums simply stumble upon them, others learn to find them. I know how to find them. I also know the radius of the power they emanate. Far from those places, we are almost normal. Although I have natural talent, it takes a lot of energy to use it. Far from the Place

163

of Power, Mercedes, you and I aren't so different. Close to it, however ...'

His hand radiated that dark, sharp light, a blade of shadow. He brought it close to her face.

'Luckily for you, this god is bored and only wants to know if you killed Rosario. If you killed your daughter. I want you to admit it, Mercedes, because this hand won't leave any skin over your bones. I don't respect the blood. I don't know what that means.'

Mercedes was trembling. Juan put his fingers between the bars of the cage next to her and with a slight movement beheaded the imbunche child, who barely moved. His hot blood soaked Mercedes' shoes.

The other children, crazed by the salty smell, bellowed.

'What else, let's see ... Who carried it out? I went to see the bus driver who hit her. He doesn't even remember the accident. He was sent. You're capable of doing that, with help, of course. Why? What did she say to you?'

Mercedes' sobbing surprised Juan. It was convulsive and sad, somewhat desperate.

'She was planning to kill me. Did you know? Didn't she tell you? I had to defend myself.'

Juan pictured Rosario and her silver bracelets, the white band in her hair, speaking Guaraní with a fluency that astonished everyone. Rosario with her expensive perfumes and her pen between her teeth when she read, the fan behind her so it would blow on her back instead of her face. Rosario with her lists and her fingers covered in ink, or in chalk.

Delicately, he drew a circle around Mercedes' mouth, and in his open palm he caught his mother-in-law's lips and teeth. Then he cauterized the wound. Mercedes' screams and those of the caged children were deafening, but he went on with his work. He licked each tooth clean and chewed the lips before Mercedes' bulging eyes. She was no longer suffering, because when the wound was closed the pain disappeared. The scars of the wounds Juan made never had the tenderness of a recent injury; they were hard and old. Then he brought Mercedes' face to his and used his tongue to clean away all the blood on her chin and neck. When he finished, he threw her to the floor.

'I should cut off the hand you hit my son with. It's nothing to you, is it? But with this' – and he opened his hand to show her the shining teeth, somewhat spoiled by tobacco stains and lead fillings – 'I have enough material to keep you from ever touching him again, or even trying to. I can also use these to control you and hurt you in other ways.'

Mercedes grunted. With her bare gums and dark glasses, she looked ridiculous, grotesque. Juan had nothing else to say to her. He left and closed the door behind him: he locked it using another sign that some members of the Order, certainly Florence, would be able to recognize and reverse. But not immediately. Mercedes would be locked in for a long time, listening to her pets die as she wandered that ghoulish tunnel, fed through the iron bars like one more zoo animal, choking on the stench of shit and decomposing children. It didn't matter. They had won and he didn't have much time, but now he knew what he wanted to know. They couldn't deceive him any more.

Juan packed his bag calmly and told Stephen he was ready to go to the airport. He couldn't drive on his own this time: the bodyguards were already on top of him and he couldn't escape them. He was having trouble breathing, and a constant, annoying cough was growing worse as the hours passed.

Mercedes still hadn't asked to be rescued from the tunnel. She was proud. Juan wanted to go before Florence found out about his little meeting with his mother-in-law. Gaspar was awake and dressed and sitting on the bed, waiting. Since he'd found out they were flying back he'd been excited but quiet, nervous. You're scared, ha ha, Gaspar is afraid the plane will crash, Juan had teased him, and his son had hit him with his fists, pretending to be mad.

Juan crossed the inner yard and the veranda to Marcelina's house. He thanked her for taking care of Gaspar and rummaged in his leather bag to find a necklace that he'd bought on a whim for Tali in the ostentatious hotel casino in Corrientes, but that he'd ultimately decided she wouldn't like much. They were hard stones from the Wanda mines, near Iguazú. The gems – blue, white, pink, green, purple – were strung together, and the necklace could be worn by looping it several times or simply letting it hang long. Marcelina was moved and tried half-heartedly to refuse the gift, but Juan put the necklace carefully around her neck, trying not to tangle the stones in her hair. It looks lovely on you, he told her. I hope you enjoy it. Marcclina fingered the stones, then reached into her front apron pocket and pulled out a caburé feather.

'For the little one,' she said.

Juan accepted the talisman on behalf of Gaspar. Then he asked Marcelina for her permission to take the things Rosario had left in her care. Marcelina ushered him into the room where she stored old junk. Juan searched until he found the box with the symbol discreetly drawn on one end. He opened it and found a plastic bag inside, an innocent grocery bag. He smiled when he saw what it contained. How smart to leave the relic with Marcelina. It was safer, even, than hiding it in Tali's temple. The Order would never have searched the belongings of a servant, not even one in Rosario's confidence.

Tali was waiting for him outside Puerto Reyes, leaning

against his car. He kissed her, taking her face in his hands. On tiptoe, she sank her fingers into his hair.

'Damn, you're kissing me like it was the last time. You still have to come by the house to pick up the relic of Rosario's you left with me.'

Juan shook his head.

'It's yours. Use it. She could give you a sign.'

Tali's dark eyes studied him.

'I don't want you to come back to this house again, not even for the Ceremonial,' said Juan.

'You don't get to give me orders, okay?'

'It's a request, not an order. A favour. Every year, when I see that you and Stephen haven't gone into the Darkness, I can breathe again. I can't ask Stephen to stop coming because this is his family and his world. I can ask you though.'

Juan hugged her again, felt her body; he let her put a hand into his pants to caress him.

'It's okay,' he said. 'I don't feel like it now.'

They looked at each other in the heat, under the sun, both of them excited and a little crazed and sad. They could hear the swollen river, a nervous bird. The house, distant and silent, seemed dead. When would the guests leave? The parking area was still full. Juan considered telling Tali about Mercedes, but it wasn't the right time. He hadn't told Stephen yet either. He would do it on the plane.

'Where's your car? I have things to give you, but I don't want them to see us.'

Tali led him by the hand to her Renault 6, which was completely coated in a layer of red dust. She unlocked the door and Juan settled into the back seat. He took from his bag the Hand of Glory that had been stored among Marcelina's clutter. It was perfectly preserved. Tali admired it, took it carefully.

'Why are you giving me this?'

'Your sister wanted it to be yours. They don't know we have a Hand of Glory, they don't even know it exists. Rosario always kept it well hidden. We both hid it.'

'You're crazy! My sister would never have given that to me.'

'Well, I'm giving it to you. You know how to use it? It will help you keep Gaspar blocked. The hand isn't enough on its own, but it will help a lot.'

'I know how to use it. Rosario didn't lend it out, but she was always good at explaining. She was generous that way, wasn't she?'

Juan smiled. She was halfway generous, yes. He motioned for Tali to put the hand away, and she stowed it in her wicker bag. A car horn interrupted them. Stephen already had Gaspar and the bags in the car. 'We have tickets!' he shouted. 'We need to be at the airport in an hour.'

'So why don't you use it yourself?' she asked him.

'I can't, it reminds me of what I did, I can't stand it. Don't fail my son, Tali,' said Juan. 'They're never going to stop watching him.'

'Don't you worry. We're going to find the way, between the three of us. And you're going to get the final sign. Be patient. The saint is going to help you with patience.'

'Gaspar will grow and change. You'll have to keep covering him to keep them from getting close.'

Tali kissed his forehead to silence him, to instil trust. Juan thought about telling her that in another life she would have been his, but he kept his mouth shut. There was no other life. He didn't want to lie.

II

The Left Hand
Dr Bradford Enters the Darkness

Misiones, Argentina, January 1983

I want to drain your entrails with kisses
Exist inside you with all my senses
For I am a pitch-black toad with two wings.

Baldomero Fernández Moreno,
'Sonnet of Your Entrails'

WHILE HE WAITS ON HIS KNEES BECAUSE HE KNOWS IT
will happen tonight, Bradford thinks how it's like all those
stupid stories about the minutes before death that his patients,
the more and the less ignorant ones – for they all become
brutish faced with death – had told him: my life is passing
before my eyes, I see my whole life before me. Though it's not
exactly my life, thinks Bradford, it's my life with *him*, because
everything that happened before him, though not without
meaning, no longer matters. He knows it will be tonight, he
feels it in the place where his missing fingers once were. The
absent fingers that the Darkness consumed long ago, they're
calling to the present fingers, and tonight the Darkness shines
– how to explain it to someone who never saw this shining
darkness emanating from that boy who is now a man and who
is spreading out his arms, pale and enormous, his head bowed?
– if only he'll raise his head before the final moment, Bradford
wants to see his yellow eyes before entering the Darkness, and
now the scars on his belly are burning, the scars the boy gave
him, a believer, when he'd touched him with those claws, nails,
talons, it's never easy to remember afterwards, sharp, black
fingers, there is nothing like them in the world, human or
animal – maybe some mechanical instrument, a prosthesis, a
disguise – the hands, in sum, had ripped at his belly and he
expected to see grey entrails scattered over the grass in the hot

night, but no, the wounds throbbed but didn't burst and didn't open and they never opened and when the boy who was a man cauterized them he did it with pure cold, and now even though he's naked Bradford can't see his scars but he feels them, cold and burning, ice that burns, everything is calling him towards the Darkness, it will be tonight, please show me your eyes, Juan, one last time.

The first time, there were dark circles under the boy's eyes, as now, as always. Bradford had just finished his specialization in cardiovascular surgery and had joined the most prestigious team in the country at the Italian Hospital. It was 1957 when they brought the boy to him, a patient at the hospital whose parents couldn't afford to continue his medical treatment. He was five years old and Bradford decided not to wait to operate. It would be his first surgery on a congenital heart disease, Tetralogy of Fallot. The child had been unforgettable from the first: he was dying, and yet he stared at Bradford defiantly, sitting up despite the urging from his parents, who, if they hadn't been so hunched over and servile, would have looked like reincarnations of Thor and Freya, but as they were, snivelling and whining about their poor little boy, how they just didn't have the money, how he's going to die, Doctor, my sister had heart problems, too – Bradford hated that vulgarity, he saw them as a couple of peasants who deserved every bit of their humiliation. Not the boy, though. His skin was blue, his lips violet, he could no longer walk. He didn't even notice his parents' degradation, he seemed focused on breathing, on living, with a will that Bradford found monstrous and that gave him the courage to operate using methods that were the most complex of the time, for both the patient and the surgeons. He relives those methods in his head now, kneeling while the Darkness extends over his head – this happened the last time too, Darkness invading the sky – and they say his power is lessening? It doesn't feel like it on this night of unbearable heat. Bradford remembers as he waits: horizontal incision from the sternum under the armpit to the third intercostal space, division of second and third cartilage, entrance into the pleural cavity, left lung apparently normal . . . and then he interrupts his own reminiscences, far removed from what is happening around him, the moans and the scribes' frenetic scribbling – Bradford has never heard the voice of the Darkness – and he tells himself that was a lie, the boy had never seemed normal inside, it was beautiful in there, beautiful to touch his cold body – the theatre was kept so cool back then that an operation was like an autopsy or an anatomy lesson, except that the organs moved, breathed, bled, throbbed – the boy was abnormal not only because of the heart defect that, once he was opened, proved to be even more intricate than his cardiologists had thought, with several other defects in addition to the Tetralogy – an interatrial communication of some ten millimetres and a quite significant anomaly in the right acute marginal branch of the coronary artery that was going to make surgical correction of the pulmonary stenosis very difficult – how had he even made it to the operating table alive? No, he wasn't normal, he was beautiful inside, and the experience of touching his labouring, hypertrophic heart had been for Bradford like discovering a nymph in a sacred forest, seeing a golden sunrise or being surprised by a flower blooming at night. The colours of the boy's insides were more intense, his blood smelled of an unknown, salty metal, his arteries were shaded with greys and blues and reds. Right pulmonary artery identified and cut. Superior vena cava, too small, left subclavian artery identified and cut, transposition of vertebral artery to thyrocervical trunk. Clip on subclavian artery at the distal point to its origin at the aorta. Two clips on left pulmonary artery, the first at the origin, the second at the entrance to the lung. Transverse incision in the wall of the pulmonary artery. Anastomosis performed with silk thread between the end of the left subclavian artery and the side of the left pulmonary artery. Almost no bleeding when the clips are removed.

That body has silk inside, thought Bradford, and he remembered how quickly the boy had recovered, pink and sitting up in bed less than a day later, but strangely, the nurses, who would have been moved in any other case, didn't really grow fond of their sick little patient – that's what they called him, *el enfermito*, how maddening, patients should be called by their names – they pretended to care about him, but it took some doing and no wonder, he was a little beast, furious at his body and at those who wanted to help him and at his parents, and he was only relieved, physically at ease, when he was with his brother, another one of those proud children for whom, Bradford thought, one had to thank Perón, a man he should hate but who inspired only indifference in him, even a little admiration – he didn't feel class conflict or any economic impact because the members of the cults of the shadow are always close to power, and as such are almost always untouched by social fluctuations. So Bradford didn't worry about Perón or his wife – that fascinating, moribund woman – and was secretly grateful for these children so full of hubris who never bowed their heads, children like Juan and his brother Luis, then almost a teenager with aquamarine eyes, who spent more time with Juan than his own parents did – they were always in a hurry, always giving the excuse that they had to work, the buses, the streetcars, putting food on the table, Bradford hated them, they stank of close quarters and smoke, and partly because of that, because he knew they were crammed into a shack on the outskirts of town, he asked for a meeting with his team leader, the hospital director, and the head of cardiology to request that they allow him to keep Juan on permanently in the hospital. He talked about unsanitary conditions in the boy's home, but also about pioneering procedures that would put the hospital at the vanguard of surgery, not just regionally but worldwide, and he wasn't exaggerating the child's good prospects: unlike most congenital heart patients, he wasn't malnourished, he was a normal size for his age – it was remarkable, he'd always been like that, even if he did lose weight at times – and he had come through the first palliative surgery with flying colours. Bradford wanted to carry out the second, more extensive corrective surgery in a few months. They agreed. The hospital's vice-director was an intimate friend of Bradford's family, and also a member of the Order, though peripheral. Gonzalo Biedma. His brilliant daughter would, in the future, be Bradford's right hand, the hand he now lacked.

That's how influence worked: he had only to ask for what he wanted, and he got it. For a long time, Bradford had thought that was all it was, influence, alliance, friendly meetings, Freemasonry by another name, with people who drank and sometimes sang around the piano, gatherings where women flaunted their heavy jewels and men shared hunting secrets and a taste for old books, meetings where at some point the conversation turned to the differences between the followers of Vishnu and those of Shiva, and the hundreds of tantric cults were discussed. For a long time, the fact that his family belonged to a Cult of the Shadow, to the Order, meant only that they moved in an international circle of money, privilege, and relationships.

He understood that the Order was different when he was eighteen years old and about to enter college, and his father had taken him to a ritual in the countryside, not at his family's estate but at Florence Mathers'. *La inglesa*, as his family called her – strange, as if they weren't English themselves, but Bradford supposed they weren't any more, not really: he'd been born in Buenos Aires and so had his father. They spoke the language, they'd gone to British schools, but they were English no longer. His father was proud: Me, I'm a good ol' mongrel, he used to say. Bradford didn't care either way. He was a surgeon and a cardiologist: sick bodies were his nation.

After the ritual, his father had told him about mediums. About the lack of mediums. About the existence of many cults of the shadow with different interpretations and practices, some of them hostile to each other, others allied. That day in the country, while some men and women were still wandering like sleepwalkers around the estate and its fields, clutching at the air and crying, startling dogs and horses, Jorge Bradford understood that this was no club. That Florence was a priestess. Jorge Bradford had seen things he couldn't explain. Things that kept him awake many nights and made him return to his father's books, which he had never scorned, but had studied with a certain disinterest. Now they were as important to him as his seminars, his medical books, his exhausting residency. He decided to spend a few months in London to hone his abilities as a surgeon and to visit the Order's large library there. Florence, the Englishwoman, who was spending time in Britain between trips, let him read the Book, with its annotations and interpretations contributed by experts. Bradford believed. He had his doubts, but they would soon be dispelled.

Now, with Bradford on his knees, a cry rings out and the Darkness takes a high Initiate. Still far away, some thirty metres away. It would come for him tonight, but he still had time. He remembered his first encounter with the Darkness, unexpected and unpleasant, like accidentally stepping into sewer water.

The second operation on the child Juan Peterson was performed five months after the palliative shunt. Hypothermia,

Bradford remembered: the blue boy again packed in ice, as beautiful as the dead. He remembered the pleasure of saw against sternum, and the stupidly woeful expression on the face of the technician wielding it – he'd had to tell her, We're saving his life, quit the theatrics, and she'd murmured something about compassion that had almost made his hands start to shake, the worst possible thing for a surgeon. That surgery had never before been performed in the country – actually three procedures: close the intraventricular communication with a patch, open the pulmonary valve to pull back the thickened muscle, and place a patch on the right ventricle and the pulmonary artery to improve circulation in the lungs. And, if he had time, he would also close the interatrial communication. He did have time: Bradford managed to finish everything in six hours, with only a few minutes of rest; he hadn't wanted to let anyone else make even the simplest sutures.

He remembered the moments before the revelation with unbearable clarity. Just when he was about to announce he had finished and they would proceed to close up, the boy's heart, which had held up for so long, barely speeding up in certain stretches, began to beat uncontrollably, arrhythmically, and Bradford recognized the ventricular fibrillation, the muscle's frantic shaking, that harbinger of death. He carefully started manual reanimation; decisiveness and delicacy would be key, and he gave the order to prepare the external defibrillator, a novel apparatus that the cardiovascular surgical team had employed with discretion and success.

But before they could use it, the electricity cut out. It was a wet blackout – that's how Bradford remembered it, as a cold wetness. The boy had undergone several minutes of manual reanimation, but he was going to need a shock. 'Lantern flashlights candles generator anything!' he yelled, and then he felt,

179

with horrible certainty, that another hand was pulling him out of the boy's body. Bradford cried out, shouting accusations at the surgical team, what were they doing, and in the dark, no less! – it was early morning – and he heard, Nothing, Doctor, we aren't doing anything, the rest of the hospital has electricity, the outage is only here in the operating room, and when someone brought a lantern to the table they all clearly saw that over the boy's open chest, above the metal keeping his sternum separated, above his stilled heart, there floated what could only be described as a piece of night, but transparent, like soot, perhaps, or thick smoke, and when the assistant surgeon tried to touch it, put his hand through it, murmuring, What the holy hell is happening here, no sooner did his fingers brush the black dust than he screamed and pulled back his hand and it was no longer his hand, now he was missing half of three fingers, the middle, ring, and index, and he was screaming and screaming, and the electricity didn't come back and Bradford wasn't about to take the same risk as his assistant, because although he didn't understand what was happening and he couldn't believe it, he knew that this slowly receding darkness was dangerous. More than dangerous. It was the Darkness his father had told him about, the one the Order's mediums summoned, the one the Englishwoman desperately sought. The boy had been in cardiac arrest for fifteen minutes and the nurses were blathering nonsense, tending to the assistant, someone was saying it had been an accident, he must have inadvertently bumped into a scalpel, which was impossible, but people would rather justify, invent, refute, and not believe what's right in front of them. Bradford held out through the stampede of people – nurses, the anaesthesiologist, scrubs – who said they'd seen the boy wrapped in darkness like a cocoon, he stayed until the darkness withdrew, and then he touched the boy's motionless heart again and whispered, Come on, you're here for a reason, if you are the voice of the gods then beat, and the heart started beating between his fingers as though it had never stopped. Bradford closed up the boy's chest on his own and in silence, not listening to the explanations, the complaints and grievances from the others – he didn't even know who they were, whether they were other doctors or directors or what. When he had finished suturing, he accidentally moved the green sheet covering the boy's arms, and then he saw the proof. The mark. A hand on the boy's arm, the mark of a hand, like a burn scar. It wasn't strange, he told himself at first: sometimes the cold of the ice used to bring on hypothermia in surgeries left burns; it was even less strange after the disaster that had occurred in the operating room. A nurse could have rested her hand there and left a mark in the cold. He studied it. It was deep and looked old. It was a scar. A left hand on the left arm, the Left Hand of Darkness. He had read about that sign. He knew what it meant.

He waited for the boy to wake up in intensive care. Ten hours. He was sure there would be cerebral lesions – he'd explained to the parents, who didn't seem to understand, just as they didn't understand anything else; oh, but the older brother did understand, where did these little immigrants get that intelligence? – he expected a coma, he expected another arrhythmia that would kill the boy once and for all. But Juan woke up around noon, and the encephalogram was normal and Bradford ordered that he not be allowed to suffer for a second, and then, since he couldn't sleep and he had to talk to someone, he almost crashed his car driving home, and in that spirit he knocked on the door of his sister's apartment, his sombre sister who occupied two floors of the same building where he lived, one of the family's Buenos Aires buildings – the most spacious, the most beautiful. Mercedes ruled over that apartment where her husband almost always left her alone – she'd married a man who was rich, fun, and unfaithful. And her daughter, Rosario, spent almost all her time at school and then in her room or with friends. Bradford liked his niece: she had the irrepressible joy of intellect. Bradford talked and Mercedes listened in a silence interrupted only by a spoon in a teacup and the enormous clock that presided over the room. Don't rush it, she said. And that was why he'd turned to Mercedes: she had sangfroid. He must be yours, if what you say happened is true. He must be ours. But there can't be any suspicious behaviour. I can't leave him with those brutes, Mercedes, those peasants. Of course not, but we need to be careful.

Oh, the plan, thinks Bradford, on his knees as he listens to more muffled moans and feels his belly burn, senses that he's out of time. I let your parents take you home. I hired people to report to me and tell me all about your sobbing mother, your drunk father, your always decent brother, the only decent one in that pathetic tin shack. About that sad school they sent you to when what you deserved was a private institute. The cardiologists told me you were improving, but they couldn't control the arrhythmia and I guessed, oh, I guessed, even before the night that joined us forever, that it was fear, that it was a panic you couldn't endure. That was the name of the nymphs' collective terror when the great god Pan appeared: panic, and that's what you felt, that horror. They brought you back to the hospital, thin but still strong, your father spouting nonsense about how he couldn't take care of you, my joy at his alcoholism and misery and at your mother's surrender, and then that first night everything was confirmed, because all those things you saw, they were worse in a hospital, of course, and I let you suffer, I needed to be sure, it was a test you had to pass, I let you reach the edge and I brought you back once – how many times, Juan, when you were older, did you joke that I was your own personal resurrector – and that night, when I knew and everyone knew that you weren't going to survive if the ventricular arrhythmia continued, we talked. What's wrong, I asked you, and you told me about men and women no one else saw and who talked to you, but also about a forest through a window and about feet that floated and about someone eating a woman's neck, and you said you didn't know who they were but they wouldn't leave. There are more of them here, you told me; here, they scream. Your eyes had lost their shine. And I taught you the simplest method of blocking what was happening to you, the one I'd never needed but that the Englishwoman taught all the Order's members. I put a hand on your stomach in just the way I'd heard her explain, and you recoiled a little, your body sick of being handled and hurt. Still, you endured it, and you learned the technique in seconds. There'd been no trick or illusion, you were the one we were waiting for, you were the medium, and when you stopped seeing what you'd been seeing you fell back on to the pillow, and gradually your breathing and your heart calmed down and you asked me, what do I do if they come back? and I said, for now, you repeat that same exercise. Oh, Juan, the trust of that first time. If only I could see your eyes one last time, before I enter the Darkness.

I brought you home with me when you recovered. We were never apart. When the Darkness you opened took my fingers, I could never again be inside you. I could only watch. Two more times. And that was all. And now the Darkness takes me: it eats my entrails first and there is no pain and I have time to think and try to see your eyes, but now they're too far away, you're far away now, and I ask the Darkness for compassion because now I hear it for the first time ever.

Compassion. And when the Darkness takes another bite and I smell its glee mixed with the scent of my blood, while I watch as it eats my hands, my shoulders, attacks my side, I remember how you told me once that the Darkness doesn't understand, that it has no language, that it's a savage or too-distant god. Will I be remembered as the man who found the medium and saved him more than once? Will they write about me, will my name be uttered in admiration? I must not think of my glory. Let it be secret if it must. I will stop pleading for compassion. There are no words from this world for the entrance into the Darkness, no words for the last bite.

III

The Bad Thing about Empty Houses

Buenos Aires, 1985–1986

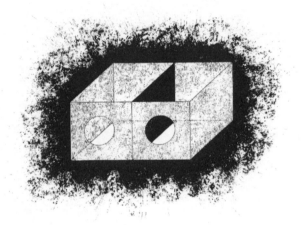

just a few years old and already i was
entirely old

Elena Anníbali, *The House of Fog*

GASPAR OPENED THE WINDOW AND FELT THE COLD, wet drizzle on his skin. It was Saturday afternoon: the neighbourhood bike shop would be open by now. He needed to bring his bike in to be fixed: he'd broken the chain and some spokes in a dumb accident that morning, when he'd clipped the kerb on the corner by his house. He liked to ride very fast, especially on Saturdays, early, when the streets were empty. He had barely hurt himself, just a few scrapes on his elbows and knees, a scratched cheek.

He tried to leave the house quietly so he wouldn't wake his father, but was surprised to see him already awake, serious but serene, coming from the kitchen with a cup of tea. As always, there were no electric lights on in the house, only the TV in the living room, which was unfurnished but for the yellow corduroy sofa that was so big it was practically a bed. When Juan saw Gaspar, he went over to him and switched on a small lamp on the floor. His other hand held a cigarette.

'You shouldn't smoke,' said Gaspar.

'Don't bust my balls.' Juan took hold of Gaspar's chin to get a look at the fresh scrape. Then he knelt down to inspect his pants, stained with grease from the bike chain.

'I fell.'

'Don't lie to me. That's your first warning.'

'I was riding fast and I hit a kerb.'

Gaspar felt how his father came closer and sniffed at him in a way that struck him as . . . possessive? Something like that. As if he could eat him, but for real. Though it was also affectionate.

'How many times have I told you why you need to be careful? We're alone. I'm sick. If they think I don't take good care of you, they'll come for you. They'll separate us. I can't be keeping tabs on you all the time.'

'I know. It was nothing.'

'Okay. Wash it well with soap.'

'I already used hydrogen peroxide and washed. You think the stain will come out of my jeans?'

'I have no idea,' Juan said, and took a long drag on the cigarette. He picked up the mug of tea he'd left on the floor and turned off the lamp. 'If it doesn't, you can buy another pair.'

'Are you okay, Dad?'

'Better. You?'

'Yeah. I'm going to the park to see if they can fix my bike. I'll probably go around to Pablo's, too.'

'Whatever you want. I'll be in my room.'

'Upstairs or down?'

Juan hesitated a moment. Finally, he said: 'Down.'

'I'll be home later to sleep. Do you have food?'

Juan didn't answer, but came over to Gaspar and slowly opened the hand he had squeezed into a fist, rubbing his palm as if to warm it.

Pablo heard and then saw Gaspar and his bike rounding the corner. As always, the sight of his friend brought an automatic smile to his face, then he forced himself to be serious: he was ashamed to show how happy he was to see Gaspar. He wasn't the only one who reacted like that. Everyone loved Gaspar, from the kiosk attendant to the corner grocer to the mechanic, not to mention almost all the parents and the girls who laughed when they saw him go by. Gaspar lived in a mansion and went to the most expensive school in the neighbourhood, which was bilingual and had its own pool, but he didn't act arrogant or make you feel like he had money, he was normal and generous and he'd lend you anything, clothes, a VCR, his video rental card, books. Gaspar's life was very different from the others': his father, who was sick and almost never left the house, didn't work. A woman came to clean and cook for them: she left their food ready while Gaspar was at school, and he almost never saw her. Other visitors – lawyers and accountants, according to Gaspar – brought money and took care of the school tuition fees and the bills. No one lived like that, with everything just taken care of, at least no one Pablo knew. Even though the Petersons were rich, they didn't live like rich people: they hardly had any things. But they never lacked for money, and if they ever needed something, those strange employees would appear right away, as if they were standing guard.

Plus, Gaspar is really cute, thought Pablo, but then he bit his lower lip because he knew he wasn't supposed to think about that. Just last week his father had grabbed him by the hair, all because Pablo had taken a long time choosing what he was going to wear to his uncle's birthday party. His dad had never done such a thing before: his mouth reeked of mate when he said: 'You wouldn't be a little bit faggy now, would you?' Pablo liked to dress well. He'd said as much to his father, who had nearly hit him for it. When they got home from the birthday party he'd come up with a plan: he listed all his clothes on the last page of a school notebook, in three columns, and then he linked everything with arrows, a kind of summary chart using different coloured pens, the way he'd learned to link sentences in class. He had to memorize the combinations or check them quickly before going out, and that way he wouldn't waste any more time trying to see if the brown corduroy pants went with the green shirt or not.

Gaspar never had those problems. Right now, Pablo was watching him walk his bike up the driveway wearing a thin, mustard-coloured sweatshirt that was a little too big for him, with blue jeans and Topper sneakers, and there was nothing so great about those clothes, but they sure looked great on Gaspar. Even if he wore something weird it came off cool: for example, he'd wear really long leather belts that hung off him. They were his father's, and sometimes he had to wrap them twice around his waist. Still, the men's buckle and the worn leather didn't look like a costume, they provided just the right touches to make him stand out from the rest. Of course, it wasn't just his clothes: it was his way of brushing his hair from his face, it was his long legs and dark blue eyes, round and seemingly innocent – at least until he smiled or got mad. Then something really weird happened, because the expression in his eyes would shift just slightly; Pablo didn't know how to describe it, but it was something he both liked and distrusted – it reminded him of his cat, the way he'd purr as you petted him and then suddenly strike for no reason, with no real intention to wound, just to make it clear that he'd gotten what he needed.

When he reached Pablo, Gaspar pulled a piece of gum from his back pocket and offered it to him, a little squashed. They started to blow bubbles on the sidewalk, under the protection of a balcony that acted as a roof, because it had started to rain.

'Will you come with me to the park?' Gaspar pointed to the bike. 'I went flying, you should have seen it, but I didn't get hurt.'

He said this calmly, and Pablo knew he probably hadn't even felt scared when he fell. There was something tough about Gaspar: they were the same age, but Pablo felt like his friend was much older. Maybe it was because he didn't have a mom, because his father was sick, because he didn't have family nearby, because he was so alone. He didn't laugh much, and he listened attentively. Pablo's mom said he was a traumatized child; Vicky's mom said he was a sad child. Then there was Adela, who rounded out their group of inseparable friends, and Adela's mom, who said: Juan is a widower and he's sick, it's not easy to raise a child alone, Gaspar is just fine.

When the downpour lessened to a drizzle, Pablo zipped up his jacket and said: 'Let's go.' The park was very close, just two hundred metres away. Thanks to the bad weather that afternoon it would be empty; when it was sunny, there was almost no room to play soccer or to sit down to drink a soda, because the whole neighbourhood spent the afternoon on the neglected grass, under the centenary trees lining the pathways of red earth. They were about to cross the street when they saw Vicky and Adela running towards them. Vicky, her dark hair loose and shining, had tears streaming down her face. Adela, who was holding Vicky's hand, was wearing a giant yellow raincoat that looked like a tent and completely covered the stump of her left arm.

'Hey, what's wrong?' asked Gaspar, and he hurried over to Vicky. She flung her arms around his neck and cried that Diana was lost; they hadn't seen her since the morning. Diana was one of Vicky's two dogs, the one she loved the most, an eight-year-old German shepherd who'd been with her for practically her entire life.

'My jerk dad let her get away,' said Vicky. And amid her tears and complaints she told them how her father had left the back door open with Diana off her leash, and how the dog had run out to the sidewalk. He'd yelled at her, but she hadn't obeyed.

193

They'd expected her to come back, but there'd been no sign of her since nine that morning.

'So now we're looking for her ourselves. Now that there aren't so many cars, maybe she's calmed down,' said Adela, brushing a lock of damp hair from her face with her only hand.

'She could be in the park,' said Gaspar.

'That's where we're going now.'

'Us too. I'll drop my bike off at the shop and go with you.'

The four of them walked down the street lined with English-style houses towards the park. Adela, as always, walked beside Gaspar. She started talking to him about dogs that came back, the dogs that waited in hospital doorways for their sick owners to be discharged, the ones that lived in cemeteries because they had stayed with their humans until the end. Adela was imaginative and theatrical and she'd been lying more and more, but her friends put up with it, and not just out of pity. She was fun. Adela lived with her mother in an apartment at the end of a passageway, a somewhat dark apartment because it was in the middle of the block and the light was obstructed by the buildings around it, and even by the trees in the neighbours' large yards. Still, it was quite a pretty house; Betty, her mother, had a good eye for choosing fabrics and art reproductions, and the furniture was simple but comfortable and colourful, sometimes covered by blankets with Andean designs. The house was kind of hippie, thought Pablo, and very different from his own, with his grandmother's old glass ornaments, orange birds and white swans, black toucans with yellow beaks and pink flamingos, all of which he was forbidden to touch. Adela didn't have a father and no one really knew why, whether he had died or left. No one dared say out loud that he could be disappeared, though some ventured to insinuate that it was the opposite, that he was a cop who had died in a confrontation.

It was also a mystery why she was missing an arm. The stump was small and proportionate, as if she had suffered a clean cut above the elbow. Adela's mother said she'd been born that way, that it was a congenital defect. A lot of kids were afraid of her, or disgusted by her. They laughed at her, called her little monster, butt-ugly, half-baked; they said she should get a job at the circus, that her photo probably appeared in medical books. It all hurt her and sometimes she cried, but she had decided to always meet the mockery with more jokes or insults. She didn't want to use a prosthetic arm. Generally, she didn't hide the stump. If she saw repulsion in another kid's eyes, or even an adult's, she was capable of touching it to their faces, or of sitting very close and brushing the other person's arm with her useless appendage until they were on the verge of tears.

Adela's version of the story of her absent arm was dramatic, typical of her. She claimed that a dog had attacked her, a black Dobermann. The dog had gone crazy – it happened with Dobermanns a lot, Adela said, the breed had a skull too small for the size of its brain, so their heads hurt all the time and it drove them mad. She said the dog had attacked her when she was two years old. She also claimed to remember it: the pain, the growling, the sound of chewing jaws, the blood spraying over the grass. She had been at her grandparents' summer house, and it was her grandfather who had murdered the dog: his aim had been excellent, because when the bullet hit the animal, it was still gripping little Adela in its teeth.

Oddly, because of the four of them he was the one who listened best and argued least, Gaspar always refused to believe this version. 'No way you remember that,' he'd tell her. 'You were two years old. I can barely remember my mom, and she died when I was six.'

'Well, this was very traumatic,' said Adela, emphasizing the word 'traumatic', which she had learned recently.

'Are you dumb or something? My mom's death was traumatic, too.'

'You must remember something.'

And Gaspar would repeat that sure, he remembered something, but very little, he wanted to remember so much more; his memories were like photos, short movie scenes with no connection. And nothing at all from when he was two. No one remembers being two, it was impossible, he insisted.

'Anyway, I don't care if you lie,' he'd say, making Adela furious. 'But with some things you have to lie better.'

Adela always came out of these arguments with her face and ears very red; she was freckled and exaggeratedly blonde, so light that her pale skin made her teeth look yellow. She had small brown eyes under nearly white eyelashes.

'You guys wait here,' said Gaspar when they reached Castelli Park.

They complied: Adela used her raincoat to dry off a wooden bench, and the three of them sat in silence. The park took up twelve blocks and had a school and two swimming pools – one outdoor and one indoor; Gaspar swam there on weekends, when the one at school was closed – as well as a rose garden and a huge fountain that sprayed streams at different heights, synchronized to give the impression the water was dancing. There was also a carousel in the playground area, but they were too big for that stuff, except maybe the swings. The girls, especially, loved the swings, and also the rose garden, with its nineteenth-century gazebo, dark green vines and red pebble pathways that stained your sneakers.

Gaspar returned quickly from the bike shop and organized

the search: Pablo would take the part of the park that went from the school to the avenue with the church; he would take the fountain and the pools; and the girls would split the rose garden and the area around the subway entrance. Really look, he told them. She could be scared. Look behind all the trees and under all the benches. The school is closed, but I'm sure there's a caretaker. Pablo, ring the bell and check with him. I'll do the same at the pool. In one hour, we meet back here. The others nodded, and before they started the search, Gaspar bent over to drink from a fountain shaped like a lion's head, made of old blue ceramic tiles. The water spilled over and left a small, bloody river over the red earthen path.

Gaspar circled the club building, its dining room open but empty of customers – surely because of the rain and the hour: people would start to arrive closer to dinner time – and went in. The owner and the only waiter both knew him: sometimes he stopped in for a snack on Saturday and Sunday afternoons after swimming, or he'd do his homework at one of the tables that had a view of the most wooded part of the park. He did that when his father was in a very bad mood, which in the past year had been more and more frequent, to the point that Gaspar had started to miss him, as if that man who lived in his house were someone else, someone who was ever more silent, violent and distant.

He asked both of them if they had seen the dog, but neither the waiter nor the owner remembered seeing a German shepherd; there were a lot of dogs that ran around the park and they knew most of them, even gave them food, but they hadn't noticed a new one. Gaspar accepted the glass of Fanta the owner offered him, then went on scouring the steps on either side of the fountain. The park was built on a small hill that rose up in the middle and ended at the outdoor pool, which was already closed until the following summer. He circled around the pool and stood looking at the diving board. He squeezed between the narrow bars – it was a little tight: even though he was very thin, he would soon be too big to fit through them – and called Diana with a whistle that he knew the dog would recognize. Nothing. He went around the pool and called again: strange, the caretaker wasn't there. Maybe he'd taken the afternoon off, since it was drizzling and no one was likely to sneak into the water. Gaspar did, sometimes: he liked to swim when it was cold outside, to emerge shivering from the water, with the pool for him alone and no one watching. His father didn't know about those escapades, of course.

He closed his eyes. His cheek hurt, and so did his knees a little; they were still bleeding a bit, he'd noticed in the bathroom, and he could already feel the skin tightening around the incipient scabs.

The dog wasn't by the fountain or the pool, so he started checking for her around the trees. There were a lot of them in the park, and Gaspar would have liked to be able to identify them, to know which was a poplar, which a loquat; he only recognized the pines. He wished they taught that kind of thing at school, instead of fractions or single-celled organisms. He did well in school because it was easy, but he got bored, he always had. He read on his own: his father could be erratic and he could be scary, but he let Gaspar read whatever he wanted. Now, he was reading *Dracula*: he had already seen about ten movie versions, and the book was totally different from them all. One phrase had stuck with him, and now the shiver he felt near the fountain wasn't just because his jacket was lightweight: that phrase seemed terrible to him. 'For the dead travel fast.' One character, a travel companion, says that to Jonathan Harker as he's on his way to the count's castle. He had looked for the book in English in his father's library while his father was distractedly drawing in one of his notebooks. He'd found it immediately and compared it with the Spanish translation, *Los muertos viajan deprisa*. The English book also said that the phrase was translated from the German, and that it came from a poem called 'Lenore'. He asked his father if he had it – he had a lot of poetry books – and his father, without pausing in his writing or drawing, without looking at him, said no. 'Is it true?' Gaspar had asked. 'Is it true that the dead travel fast?'

Juan had finally looked up and said, simply: 'Some do.'

Gaspar went running down the steps to the open area with the sculpture of the sabre-toothed tiger, then circled the park on the path parallel to Calle Mitre. Vicky and Adela were already waiting at the gazebo, near the rose garden. Their faces made it clear that they hadn't found the dog, either.

'She'll come back, Vicky,' said Gaspar. 'If you want, we can go make copies of a photo of her, and we'll put them up in stores and on lamp posts. We'll find her.'

Vicky was crying.

'She's old, she's going to get lost.'

Pablo came running up and looked at Gaspar before shaking his head.

'Are you going to offer a reward?' asked Adela. 'If you offer a reward, it's way better.'

'And what money am I going to use for that? My dad won't pay it.'

'I'll lend you money, no problem,' said Gaspar, and he asked Adela to go with him to the copy shop later.

They spent the rest of the afternoon putting together, on legal-sized paper, a 'lost dog' poster for Diana. Vicky chose a photo with a light background so the image would stand out more. Hugo, Vicky's father, joked to Gaspar that with inflation it didn't make sense to offer a reward, and Vicky got so mad she locked herself in her room, crying. Adela and Gaspar finished the poster while Pablo listened to Hugo explain how the dog had escaped. He had left the door open, it was true. Just for a minute, because he'd forgotten his umbrella and he needed it – it had been raining that morning when he went to work at the pharmacy. And something had scared the dog, something fell inside the house. Maybe Virginia, Vicky's younger sister, had thrown a toy against the wall, or perhaps her grandma, who was pretty deaf, had turned the radio up and upset the animal and made her run outside. Hugo loved the dog too, he adored her, and he was really ticked off that Vicky had blamed him and made such a fuss.

'She'll come back,' Adela said, and started up again with her anecdotes about dogs who were faithful to their owners. Gaspar finished writing Vicky's phone number on the poster, then got up and went to knock on her door.

'We're going to make copies and put the posters up. Come with us, give it a rest a while.'

There was a tense silence, and then Vicky opened the door. Her eyes were red, but she'd stopped crying.

'Come on,' Gaspar repeated. 'We've finished the poster.'

The bulb in the hall lamp had blown, and they looked at each other in the gloom. Gaspar thought back to the past summer, which he'd spent with Vicky and her family in Mar del Plata: playing paddleball on the beach, swimming a little (though not much: they got scared when Gaspar went into deep water, and he didn't want to make them nervous), and walking on the damp sand at dusk. He and Vicky had talked a lot, sometimes they didn't fall asleep until very late, the bedside lamp still on. That was the second summer Gaspar had gone on vacation with the Peiranos, who rented an apartment near the semi-deserted beaches around the lighthouse. It was large and comfortable, and Gaspar suspected they didn't pay for it. He was almost sure he knew who did pay, but he never would have insinuated anything. His father hadn't said a word about it, neither of those summers. He had given Gaspar permission to spend a month at the beach. If they're inviting you, go ahead. I trust them. Both summers, envoys bearing money had also appeared on the coast, to be sure he had what he needed. They weren't always the same people, but Gaspar knew them all by then, there were seven or eight of them, including the drivers who took his father to the doctor or wherever else he wanted to go. When he was younger he hadn't noticed, but when he got older it was clear to him that no one else had assistants or caretakers like that. When he'd asked his father about it, his entire reply had consisted of, 'Your mother was rich, and you are too. I'm sure you've seen on TV what can happen to rich people.' Gaspar remembered the stories on the news about kidnappings, and the explanation Vicky's mother had given: It's the former agents of the dictatorship, she said, they have new jobs as extortionists, because they're experts at kidnapping. 'So, am I in danger, will I be kidnapped?' 'No,' said his father, 'because those people watch over you.' And the next time Gaspar had asked, his dad's reply was the same and his irritation extreme. So now he just accepted it.

The first summer with Vicky, Gaspar had had a great time. But the second summer, he didn't really know why, he'd felt afraid for his father one night, and he snuck out of the apartment and went to a public phone. Leaning against the perforated plastic in the round cabin that reminded him of a giant egg, he called his house several times. No one answered. So he tried again the next night. Still no answer. It was January. Gaspar knew that in the summer, his father would usually leave for a few days, he had friends he visited, but he was never away from home long. Ten days max. It was 15 January and he wasn't answering and Gaspar was about to ask Lidia and Hugo Peirano to let him go back home, to please buy him a ticket, though he didn't exactly know what he could do when he arrived at that empty house. Call his uncle in Brazil? Talk to the accountants? Ask to speak to his maternal grandparents, whom he hadn't seen in years, and whom he barely remembered? Sitting on the steps leading up to the door of the building in Mar del Plata while the tourists went in and out – some dressed to dine in restaurants, others carrying groceries to cook in their apartments – Gaspar had started to cry. Vicky had told him: 'I'm sure he'll turn up. Let's not say anything. We'll call again tomorrow.'

And this time when he called, his father said hello in a tired, exasperated voice. Gaspar's knees gave out when he heard it.

'I've been calling you,' he said, angry. 'You never leave for so long.'

'Gaspar, you just go have fun,' his father replied, and hung up.

As he looked at Vicky now in the dim hallway of her house, Gaspar remembered those days of uncertainty, just three months ago. And she nodded. She understood. She pulled her silky dark hair back into a ponytail.

'Sorry, I should have helped you with the poster.'

And then she hugged Gaspar again, and he kissed her head and lingered to smell her hair, a scent of rain and the shampoo the girls liked so much that year, a green one that smelled of apple juice.

The Peirano house was always under construction. It sat on a large plot of land, and the long house stretched out along a walkway that joined the front yard and the garage with the backyard; there was a modest garden with a shed, where the dogs slept in the shadow of a lemon tree and the grill was pressed into service almost every Sunday. In that noisy, messy house, everyone went to bed when they wanted; if they felt like eating together at the table, they did, and if they didn't, they took their plates to their rooms or outside; the grandmother listened to tangos on the radio, and anytime someone mislaid papers they never turned up again.

It didn't seem like the house of a pharmacist and a doctor. Victoria sometimes thought that her parents were unfairly poor, because other kids with doctors for parents lived in a different kind of house. She had overheard her parents talking about what bad luck they'd had, the opportunities they'd missed out on. Her mother worked in a public hospital and took shifts at a clinic twenty blocks from their house; her father didn't want to leave the pharmacy where he had started out at the age of eighteen – he adored the owner, and didn't care that the salary was low. They argued a lot about money, but they were happy. They had fun together. And what money they had, they spent: vacations to Bariloche, Pehuén Có, Mar del Plata, the mountains of Córdoba, Valle de la Luna. Gaspar spent a lot of time with that family. His own house was spacious and elegant, and he knew it was the envy of the neighbourhood; but it was also dark and empty, with a withered garden, scant furniture, imposed silence.

'Why don't you all stay for dinner?' asked Lidia, Vicky's mom. She had gotten home from the hospital close to nine at night with some pizza bases to put in the oven. Only then had she found out about the dog's escape, and after listening to the story she told her husband:

'You're a real dummy, Hugo. Really.'

And she congratulated the kids for having made the posters. They'd left them in all the shops, at kiosks, at the café in the park, at the bike shop, on lampposts. The next day was Sunday;

if it didn't rain, people would be out on the streets much more, and if anyone had seen the dog, they'd just have to call one of the numbers on the poster. They had included Adela's and Pablo's numbers on the signs, along with Vicky's. But not Gaspar's: his father couldn't stand the sound of the phone ringing.

After putting the pizzas on the counter to cool a little, Lidia went to her room to take off her white uniform, and again urged Pablo and Gaspar to stay to eat. Pablo said his mom was waiting for him. Gaspar just said no, thanks.

'How's your dad?' Lidia asked him before getting into the shower.

'I don't know,' Gaspar replied honestly. 'That's also why I want to go home. But he's better than he was a few days ago, thanks for asking.'

'Let me know if you need anything.'

Gaspar waved on his way out. He missed his bike. He'd asked the mechanic to also change the light he used at night, because lately it had been flickering. Adela walked back with him: of his three friends, she was his closest neighbour. He liked to be with her – he felt he could relax with Adela, because sincerity didn't make her uncomfortable.

'You think Diana's going to turn up?' she asked him now.

Diana – her dry fur, her tongue always hanging out, that loving eagerness – Gaspar suddenly remembered it all and felt a rock form in his throat. He loved the dog. Since he wasn't allowed to have pets, he grew attached to other people's. Diana was his favourite.

'No,' he said. 'I don't think she'll turn up.'

'Me neither, but I didn't want to say anything.'

'Maybe we're totally wrong and she'll come back.'

'Here's hoping. How come you don't have a dog?'

'Dad hates animals.'

That wasn't exactly it; his father had told him once, 'I don't want anything alive in this house.' But that was going to sound too strange even for Adela.

'Your dad's so mean.'

They laughed. Adela had said it mischievously, but she could also relate. Betty, her mother, drank a lot when she was sad. She wasn't violent, didn't mistreat Adela, just locked herself in with a bottle and sometimes threw up in the bathroom. Or in the house. Several times, Gaspar had helped Adela empty the glasses full of wine that appeared in the corners, and had sprayed air freshener in the bathroom when Betty didn't clean up her vomit properly. She didn't go on binges very often, but the days when she did were difficult. Gaspar slowed down, partly so he could spend more time with Adela, and partly because her missing arm meant she walked more slowly, as if she lacked an oar to propel herself forward. The rain had stopped, so Adela had left her raincoat at Vicky's house; now she was just in a red sweatshirt, the sleeve rolled up over her stump. She always said she hated to let the empty sleeve hang down; better to let obvious things be obvious. Gaspar also liked Adela's company because she talked a lot and wasn't uncomfortable with his silence. Now, though, she was quiet. And it wasn't because of the dog, who was no friend of hers – she preferred to keep her distance from dogs, a stance she held firmly to back up her story of the Dobermann attack.

Gaspar decided to break the silence:

'Is something up with you?'

'It's this thing that always happens to me, but lately it's been worse.'

'Well, tell me.'

'It's kind of gross.'

'Even better.'

Adela shoved him playfully, and he stumbled.

'Moron.'

She looked down as she spoke, as if paying close attention to her steps.

'My arm itches. This one,' she said, and moved her stump.

'So scratch it.'

'Don't be dumb. It itches on the part I don't have. I already went to the doctor about it. He told me it's called a phantom limb. It's because the brain doesn't register that you don't have it any more, and it still feels things.'

Gaspar glared at her closely under the yellow street lights. Adela's hair had a kind of halo around it: it bristled in the humidity.

'No way.'

She looked at him, the hostility narrowing her dark eyes.

'Why don't you ever believe me?'

'Something that doesn't exist can't itch.'

'It itches a lot and you just don't get it!' Adela yelled, and she went running towards her house, crying, her face turned away so he couldn't see. Gaspar almost went after her, but then let her go. He was tired, he was hungry, and he would have to wait a while for the cutlets to heat up in the oven. He didn't know if there was bread to make a sandwich. He should have accepted Lidia's dinner invitation, but he had wanted to go home, spend some time alone and see his dad.

He went quietly into the cool darkness of the house, and before heading into the kitchen he peeked into the ground-floor room where his father slept.

The lamp was on the floor, an empty glass on the nightstand, and his father bare-chested and sitting up in bed; he never slept lying down any more. Gaspar couldn't tell if he was asleep or not: he could only see that his eyes were closed.

Gaspar turned on the light in the kitchen, the only room in the house besides the bathroom where he was allowed to use the overhead fixture. He found two milanesas in the freezer. He smelled them: parsley and breading and a little lemon, and the metallic scent of raw meat. He poured oil into a pan and lit the oven. He had to hold the knob down for a long time, almost a minute, for the flame to stay lit. If he let go before it was ready and the blue semicircle of light disappeared, he'd have to wait more than ten minutes before trying again. He didn't dare fry the milanesas that night, he didn't want to wake his father with the noise of sizzling oil. Plus, when he went to sleep right after eating fried food, it sometimes brought on one of his most hated nightmares, the one with the man who floated above his head and dripped hot liquid from something he carried in his arms, something small and alive that was dying – that was very clear in the dream. He couldn't tell if it was a person or an animal, he couldn't see it, all he saw was the floating man's feet and a little of his legs, pale like bones, just overhead. So, oven-baked milanesas it was. And a tomato cut in half, with a little oil and oregano.

He liked to cook. He wished he could cook more for his father, who lately ate little and without any appetite. Gaspar knew he was very ill, he'd always known that, but now he felt something worse that he didn't want to think about: he sensed his father was going to die soon. He was always so tired now, so angry, so weak, so incredibly delicate – his father, always so tall and powerful, with such large hands that, in a tender moment, they could hold Gaspar's whole head, and when they hit him, they were like boxing gloves without the protection of fabric and padding, the pure fury of bones in the heavy palm and the brutal backhand.

He took off his sneakers and socks, which were wet, and took some dry socks off the line in the kitchen. He wasn't sleepy, so, after serving himself a milanesa with tomato, he set the political map of Asia that he had to fill in next to his plate. He looked at the lines demarcating the countries, and although the teacher allowed them to use an encyclopaedia for homework, he tried to remember the names without consulting one, as that's how it would be in the test. China, capital Beijing. Almost as a joke he coloured the enormous country yellow. The island above it was Japan. Tokyo. He made it red. He liked geography. He didn't like math, especially geometry, but for that he had Belén, his classmate who wanted to be an engineer and with whom he traded solutions and protractor diagrams for English and languages homework. The exchange was perfect, except for the fact that he really liked Belén. He liked other girls too, but he didn't think any were as pretty as Belén, and none made him so nervous and so happy at the same time. He liked her even more because she wanted to study engineering: she was different from the other girls.

He still hadn't gotten up the nerve to ask her out or to go steady. He knew the other girls teased her about their names: Belén, or Bethlehem, Jesus's birthplace, and Gaspar, one of the three wise men. It was a joke. Put together, his name and that of the girl he liked were a joke. And she was arrogant, so pretty with her wide mouth and her dark eyes and skin so delicate it looked transparent, you could see all the blue veins in her cheeks; Gaspar thought it also looked like a kind of map. And the socks she used, white, pulled up over her shins, and the silver ring on her pinkie.

Now he couldn't remember the capital of Iran. Tehran or Baghdad? Tehran, he decided, and he coloured the country purple. He still had several more countries, the ones he always confused: he remembered the names – Malaysia, Indonesia,

Cambodia – but he couldn't identify their shapes on the map. He didn't feel like going upstairs now to get an encyclopaedia; he could look it up tomorrow.

In his socks, he walked to his room: it looked out on to the street, or rather the front yard, which was narrow and had several dry flower beds. The window was shut with the blinds down, and Gaspar didn't open them. He looked at the books on his nightstand but none of them appealed to him, not even the poetry books, which were his favourites even if he didn't always understand them, because sometimes when he read two words aloud and they brought about a beautiful effect, he almost felt like crying. Nor did he feel like listening to music on the new Walkman his uncle had sent him from Brazil for Christmas. Nor could he watch movies, because he'd lent the VCR to Pablo. He needed to sleep. He took off his pants but left his T-shirt on, and tossed his hoodie on the chair. The scrapes on his knees were dry now; the next day they would itch and he'd pull off the scabs and then they'd take forever to heal; he always did the same thing.

Before getting under the covers, after folding the pillow in half and arranging it just so, he opened the bedside table drawer and took out a booklet that his mother had written, part of a series on indigenous and popular art; her photo was on the back. There were other articles of hers in different books in the house, some of them in English. Gaspar had memorized the titles of all of them. 'The Tupí-Guaraní World on the Eve of Conquest', 'If God were a Jaguar: Cannibalism and Christianity among the Guaraní', 'The Sociocultural Dimension of Epilepsy: An Anthropological Study among Guaraní Communities in Argentina', and many more, and on other subjects, but none of those chapters or monograms had her photo. This booklet did. It was part of a collection with ten instalments, his father had told him, but they only had five in the house. Your mom was proud and also very angry that she was the only woman in the collection, his father had said. Why angry? Gaspar had asked. For a lot of reasons. Because there weren't many female anthropologists, because the few that existed weren't invited to lectures and conferences, because she was tired of working only with men.

The collection was published by the Center for Visual Arts at the Museo del Barro in Paraguay, as it indicated on the first page. The title was *Indigenous and Mestizo Art of Aboriginal Guaraní Groups*. It began with a four-page text without images that was very difficult, at least for Gaspar, explaining the indigenous 'linguistic families' and defining 'popular' or folk art . . . it was boring. But the next ten pages had photos, in colour, which he loved: a wooden carving from the seventeenth century of Christ's bloodied head, another full-length Christ that was called *At the Column*, with Christ all wounded and with his hands tied to a post that came up to his waist; a very strange Virgin – a kind of legless torso with the heart, made of tin, outside the chest and pierced by swords – was titled *Dolorosa*; then there was a painting where the crucified Christ had blood pouring out of the side of his chest that an angel was collecting, holding a golden chalice like a bucket. The second part of the booklet was titled 'Popular Santeria', and it was his favourite. There were four photos of skeletons, all different, called San La Muerte. In one, a very tall skeleton held a scythe in its left hand and a broom in its right; in another, the skeleton was fat and short, with a smiling mouth drawn on, and it held a short scythe that looked more like a knife: that one was funny. The next one was not: a skeleton in a black-painted coffin, serious and half sitting up. And the last one was the strangest: the caption said it was carved in bone (it didn't specify whether animal or human) and was only five centimetres tall, and the skeleton was sitting down with its head in its hands, as if it were waiting on a bench. Then came San Son, a man dressed in red with a sword in his hand, on a jaguar: that one was made of wood. And then Santa Librada, a crucified woman. The final section, of indigenous drawings, was the most boring: birds and armadillos and enormous spiderwebs between trees, fish in the river, crocodiles, people planting large vegetables that looked like squash.

The back cover had his mother's photo and biography. It said: 'Rosario Reyes Bradford was born in Buenos Aires in 1949 and was the first Argentine woman to earn a doctorate in Anthropology at the University of Cambridge, in the United Kingdom. She specializes in symbolic anthropology, anthropology of religion, and Guaraní ethnography. She is a professor and researcher at the University of Buenos Aires. She has published over twenty articles in Argentina, Paraguay, Brazil, Colombia, Mexico, the United States, England, France, and Belgium. She is the author of the book *Tekoporá: Anthropological explorations on Guaraní history, religion, and ontology.*'

Beside the photo was text his mother had written in which she thanked Cristino Escobar, director of the museum, the publisher, the Mbyá communities of Misiones and southern Paraguay, and a number of other people, and then came what interested Gaspar most. It said: 'Thanks to Tali, my sister, my best friend, and my research partner. I am grateful to Juan for his unconditional love and to Gaspar, the love of my life, who put up with his mother's absences bravely and received her with joy and without reproach every time she came back.' Gaspar had asked his father why she referred to Tali, a friend of the family whom he saw on occasion, as her 'sister', and Juan told him it was a figure of speech, because they loved each other a

211

lot. Gaspar was disappointed: he had hoped she was his aunt; he could use a little more family.

He tried to call up all the memories he had of his mother: he remembered her walking down the stairs, putting a cold cloth on his forehead when he had a headache; he remembered her telling him she'd be right back and to stay nice and still (he remembered the 'nice and still' very clearly), then walking down a hallway – but where was that hallway? He also remembered a walkway or pier like the ones in the ocean, but instead of water, there were trees beneath it. Treetops. She was holding his hand and her hair was very dark. He remembered her in bed, teaching him what the cards meant. He remembered her kissing his father on tiptoe while Juan bent down, holding her waist.

The photo beside the acknowledgements showed his mother looking straight into the camera. The booklet was from 1979, but his father had told him that the photo, in black and white, was taken before that. She was wearing a white short-sleeved shirt: her arms were very thin but – and Gaspar was a little ashamed at this thought – she had large breasts. She was very pretty, that's the thing, and he didn't like to think that about his mother, but she *was* very pretty, with her hair loose and a little messy and very full lips. His father had told him once that she had always worn very little make-up, which was unusual for women at that time. Ask any of your friends for photos of their mothers from ten years ago, you'll see. And Gaspar had asked, and it was true: Vicky's mom wore so much dark eye shadow she looked like the raccoon from the cartoons, and her mouth was smeared red and her cheeks stained with pink powder. The eyebrows were the worst. Pablo's mother, for example, simply didn't have eyebrows in her wedding photos; or no, she had really thin eyebrows drawn on to her skin. His mother, in this photo and others, had normal eyebrows. Why did women get rid of their eyebrows? Gaspar had wanted to know, and his father, smiling, had replied that his mother had wondered the same thing. Your mom was crazy about clothes and fashion, he'd said, but she didn't look like anyone else. In the photo she was wearing a thick bracelet: if you looked closely, you could see it was a snake with its mouth half-open and a forked tongue that rested on her wrist.

He closed the booklet and dried his eyes with the bed-sheet. From his hoodie pocket peeked one of the photocopies of Diana's face. He'd left the others on the stove. He thought about the dog. She spent all her time lying around and gnawing on a tennis ball. She had a problem with her hip and that made it hard for her to get up: on walks she'd go slowly at first and then gather speed, as if her hip needed a little practice before it could work again. She was good and a little dumb, and that's why it seemed so strange she would run away.

Gaspar had read somewhere – a magazine? A story? He didn't remember – that if you wished for something hard, if you concentrated and shut your eyes and asked for what you wanted sincerely, it was possible to make it happen. He pictured Diana, her big head and sloped back, the way she sometimes seemed to perk up, especially when Electra, Vicky's younger dog, would pester her and they'd run together, with their tongues hanging out and that kind of smile dogs sometimes have, in the back-yard of the house. It was a small backyard with flower beds all around, flower beds with flowers, hydrangeas and roses and azaleas, explosions of purple and red against the white-painted bricks. He fell asleep thinking about Diana eating the jasmine and Vicky's grandmother yelling at her not to ruin the plants she worked so hard on.

First he woke up feeling cold and realized he'd kicked the blanket off in his sleep. He did that a lot. Vicky had told him, on their last vacation, that he moved a lot and talked in his sleep. What do I say? he had asked, and Vicky, looking very serious, told him she couldn't understand anything. Gaspar didn't believe her. One of these nights he'd have to set up a recorder so he could hear himself.

The second time he woke up he wasn't sure where he was: he'd been dreaming about Diana. A strange dream: he found her floating in the fountain at the park, and he was sure she had drowned. But when he called to her, she lifted up her head and swam to him, panting and happy, struggling to paddle with her front paws. It wasn't the dream that had woken him: it had been, precisely, paws. Dog paws scratching at the shutters and the whining of an animal that wanted to get in.

'Diana!' he said out loud, and he thought he would take her to Vicky right away, now, in the middle of the night. Gaspar got up quickly, opened the window and raised the shutter. There was nothing outside. Nothing but the bars over the window, the closed garden door, and the empty yard, the soft but continuous rain on the pavement that turned it slippery and silver under the street lamps. The sky was cloudy and light: it was a damp and luminous night. He stuck his head out the window and said, 'Diana!' softly, but then he felt a violent yank on his hair that pulled him back into the room and a shove that pushed him into the wall, though not hard. He saw his father, naked except for his black underwear, close the shutter and slam the window shut with a speed that seemed strange, overly urgent. Then his father looked at him. He wasn't angry, not really, he wasn't enraged. He was shocked.

'What are you doing?' Juan asked, though not in a very loud voice – he wasn't shouting. Gaspar relaxed his shoulders, which he had braced reflexively. 'Why were you summoning the dead?'

'It was Vicky's dog.'

'What dog? What are you talking about?'

'Vicky lost her dog and I just heard her scratching at the window!'

Now his father softened, dropping his threatening pose and running a hand through his hair. His left eyebrow was arched, his habitual gesture of incredulity, sometimes showing con-tempt and other times – less often – that he found something funny. He sat on Gaspar's bed and covered his shoulders with the blanket.

'Go and bring me what I was drinking, it's on my night table. And my cigarettes.'

Gaspar didn't like it when his father smoked in his room; it left a terrible smell. He didn't like that he smoked at all, but he had already asked him to quit and there was no point in insist-ing. He brought the glass of whiskey and the cigarettes. His father lit one and then crushed it out right away on the floor.

'Come here.' And he made room beside him under the blanket for Gaspar.

After he took a sip of whiskey and slowly licked his lips, he said:

'The dog is dead. That wasn't Vicky's dog you heard. If it was even a dog at all.'

Gaspar felt his fear dry out his mouth. His father was staring at him. He had dark circles under his eyes and slightly purple lips, like a drowned man.

'Are you sure? She just ran away this morning ...'

'I'm sure.'

His father smelled of alcohol. He was a little drunk, Gaspar thought, but you never really knew. He shifted to get more comfortable and accidentally touched the booklet, which was on the pillow. He moved it to the nightstand.

'Did you ever try with her, with your mother?'

'Try what?'

'What you did tonight when you called your friend's dog.'

'I didn't call her . . .'

'Gaspar, we both know perfectly well what we're talking about.'

What should he say? He was afraid of his father sitting there under the blanket, and of the lamplight, of the rain suddenly coming down harder – with the wind blowing so hard, the drops pounded the shutter – and of the ghost dog's paws scratching in his head.

I have to tell him the truth, he thought.

'Yes, I tried, but nothing ever happened.'

His father took a deep breath, and when he let out the air, it was slow and shaky.

'We must not keep what is dead alive,' he said. 'Don't ever do it again.'

'I didn't know the dog was dead.'

'No, of course not. But don't do it again. It's very dangerous.'

'I never would have called her, why would I call her if she's dead?'

'But you called your mother.'

Gaspar hesitated.

'I didn't know that thinking about her and wanting her back was the same as calling her.'

His father downed his whiskey in one gulp.

'Usually it's not. I don't want you to do it again.'

'I've got it, Dad.'

'Ghosts are real. And the ones who come aren't always the one you've called.'

His father lit another cigarette, and this time he did smoke it in the darkness. Sometimes, when he exhaled, he coughed. He had taken the blanket from his shoulders and now it was only draped over his long, thin legs that were covered in blond fuzz. The cigarette slowly went out in what remained of the whiskey in the glass. Gaspar expected his dad to leave, but instead he stretched out in the bed. Beside him, Gaspar bent his knees against his chest.

'I can't sleep,' his father said, by way of explanation.

They looked at each other in the half-darkness. Outside, the rain lashed the trees and Gaspar thought he heard dog paws again, this time running over the pavement, but he tried to ignore them.

'Can I ask you something?' he said.

'You're not tired either.'

'No, plus I already slept some. Yesterday I was talking to Adela and she told me that sometimes her missing arm itches. I called her a liar because it's obvious she was lying, right? But she went away crying and, I don't know, I know when she's lying, she does it all the time, and I think maybe this time she was telling the truth.'

Juan smiled and sat up straighter. Gaspar realized that it was too hard for him to breathe lying down, especially if they were going to talk.

'She wasn't lying. It's very common with an amputation. I think the brain still has an area for that missing member, and it produces sensations that it considers logical. We don't feel with our skin, son, we feel with our brains. Pain is in the head.'

'Really?'

'Let's try something. Bring me, let's see ... one of those gloves they use in medical exams, do we have any? Didn't the nurse leave some?'

'Yeah, they're in the bathroom.'

'Good. A glove and two toothbrushes, and a knife and a spoon. And I need a piece of wood.'

'Your drawing board?

'Not so big.'

'The other day the cover of the shutter in the living room fell off. It's leaning against the wall.'

'I didn't even notice.'

'I'll fix it later; when the maid comes or the people who bring money, they can hold the chair for me.'

'That cover will work well, it's tall. Bring some dictionaries from the library to hold it. Hurry, I want to show this to you.'

Gaspar ran out of the room, trying to hide his eagerness. If his father realized how happy he was to play with him, to spend some time together, he could very well leave without an explanation. Gaspar had lived with those sudden mood changes for a while now, and he no longer tried to find a reason for them: quite simply, if his dad wanted to have some fun now, he had to make the most of it, that's just how it was.

He gathered the things his father had asked for and placed them on the mattress. Juan knelt down on one side of the bed and positioned Gaspar across from him. Then he told his son to put on his hoodie and inflate the glove like a balloon.

'Let's see if we can tie it off so it stays inflated and looks like a hand.'

Gaspar managed it after a couple of tries. The glove was small, and once inflated it was a hand with a short palm, all fingers.

'Now take your arm out of the sweatshirt sleeve. Your right arm. Let the sleeve hang empty, and lay the empty sleeve on the bed.'

Juan put the inflated glove where Gaspar's hand should be, at the end of the sleeve. Then he placed the wood vertically on the bed, like a divider, propped it up with four stacked dictionaries, and asked Gaspar to put his real arm on the other side.

'They call this the rubber hand illusion,' he said, and he placed Gaspar's real hand, on the other side of the wood, in the same position as the rubber hand, with the fingers up like a spider on its back, and parallel to it.

'Don't look at your real hand. Look at the rubber glove and look at your other hand, the one that's not behind the wood. Put that one on the bed too, as though you had three arms.'

Then Juan picked up the toothbrush and softly ran it over the middle finger of Gaspar's hand behind the wood, and also over the middle finger of the rubber hand.

'If we're lucky,' he went on, 'this is going to make you feel like the rubber hand is yours.'

Juan repeated the movement with both toothbrushes at the same time, and said nothing. Gaspar held his breath. The toothbrushes ran simultaneously over the two middle fingers, then over the index fingers and thumbs.

'Don't take your eyes off the rubber hand,' said Juan. The movement of the toothbrushes continued; outside, the rain had lessened, and now they heard only a slight wind along with the occasional car.

'When I run the brush over the glove, do you feel like I'm touching your hand?'

'Do it again,' said Gaspar. Yes, that was what he felt, even though he saw, very clearly, the yellow glove inside the sleeve of his blue hoodie. 'I feel it, yeah, like it's my hand.'

'Good. Keep looking,' said Juan, and very quickly he picked up the knife. With a precise, well-aimed movement, he stabbed it into the middle of the glove. Gaspar saw the knife coming and thought, No, no, he's going to stab me! and stifled a scream, because even as he recoiled from the knife he had already realized the trick. He'd felt the blade pierce his hand, when really it had only burst the latex glove.

219

'Holy shit,' he said. Juan smiled at him. 'You should do this at birthdays and stuff! It's better than a magician!'

'You do it, now that you've learned how. With a plastic hand, like a mannequin's, for example, it's better. You see? We feel with our brains.'

'It's so cool. Want me to do it to you?'

'No.'

'Where'd you learn it?'

Juan suddenly turned serious.

'In the hospital. Once, when I was sick, a doctor taught me. He was trying to entertain me.'

He wrapped the blanket around himself again and climbed into bed. Gaspar moved the books and the wood to a corner of the room. His father didn't mind if the house was messy or if he left things where they didn't belong.

'So what Adela told me is true.'

'Not only is it true, it's very common. I'm surprised you didn't already know, or that she hasn't mentioned it before.'

'What should I do?'

'You'll have to apologize.'

Gaspar rolled his eyes.

'You were wrong, and it's what you have to do. She'll have the right to make fun of you for a while.'

Gaspar stuck out his tongue. Then he settled into bed beside his father, who gave him part of the blanket.

'Dad, you can find out where Diana is, if you want.'

Juan ran a hand over Gaspar's hair, so fine and very clean, and scratched the back of his neck.

'I don't like to use clairvoyance for such a small thing, and I really shouldn't.'

'But you could.'

'I could. Did you love the dog?'

Gaspar thought for a second.

'Yes. Plus, I love Vicky and I love Electra, the other dog. She's upset. She was crying all afternoon. Diana is like her mother because she's older, even though she's not her real mom. She misses her.'

'She misses her because she already knows she's dead. Animals have a perception that we humans have lost.'

Juan got up from the bed and covered Gaspar fully with the blanket. He picked up the knife and the burst glove and said: 'Go to sleep now.'

If it were possible to see that part of the neighbourhood from above, flying over the blocks as if in a dream or a helicopter, you would see houses with balconies, most of them with back patios, some, very few, with swimming pools. You would see many trees along the sidewalks, a rarity in the city, and a few small factories that are either shuttered or only operate for a few hours a day. An avenue divides the neighbourhood into two equal halves, and though it is a narrow avenue, people usually stay on the side they live on; they shop on their side, have friends on their side. It's not that they distrust those on the other side or believe themselves fundamentally different, it's just that the avenue acts as a river, a kind of natural border.

Victoria, Gaspar, Pablo, and Adela live on the left side of the avenue. Adela's house is on Calle Villarreal, twenty metres from the avenue. To the right of her house is the Turi grocery, to the left is Doña María and Don Ramón's yard, which has fruit trees and a chicken coop that's now boarded up.

Gaspar's house is on the same block as Adela's but on Calle R. Pinedo, perpendicular to Villarreal. It's almost exactly in the middle of the block, and takes up a quarter of it. It's the only luxurious, elegant house in the whole neighbourhood, but it's dirty and gone to seed from neglect. The backyard, with its graceful flagstone paths and the remains of what might have been a fountain, is completely barren, the grass doesn't grow, there's nothing but a rotary clothes line that spins a little when there's a breeze. The veranda is encrusted with glass, thousands of shards from green and clear bottles, as though to ward off any people or animals thinking of climbing or landing on the house.

You have to cross R. Pinedo and return to Villarreal to reach Victoria's house, which is situated between a modest and always warm kiosk and the Italians' house, which is sometimes used as a small foundry. Behind her house is a lumberyard that operates only two days a week but leaves a fresh smell in the air, vegetable and earthy, a smell of newness that lets you forget that the small business, with only two employees, is on the verge of collapse.

Pablo's house is the most striking one on Calle Mariano Moreno. It has two floors and a tile roof, and the front yard has hydrangeas and rose bushes and pansies. Pablo's mother is an English teacher. His father works as an executive at a company selling compressed natural gas for cars that's opening branches and service stations throughout the province. Many people think it's going to fail, that drivers will never make the switch from gasoline, out of habit and a fear that the gas tank in the back will explode. They're wrong. The business is going to make him rich. Pablo's mom wants to have another baby because she's lonely. She and Pablo don't see eye to eye. She doesn't want to repeat what her husband says about his firstborn son. She's realized it, too. If she were a good mother, she would love him all the same, no matter what, but she's not such a good mother and she wants to try again, to see if a new baby will turn out 'better'. The back of the house borders on to the warehouse of a printer's shop. It's silent. Beside the warehouse, whose entrance is a green-painted iron curtain, is the abandoned house at 504

Villarreal, between Moreno and Ortiz de Rosas. A lot of the neighbours unconsciously walk faster when they pass its rusted front gate; without even realizing, they want to leave it behind as soon as possible. They try, as well, not to look at it.

One day, after school, Victoria went with her mother to the grocery store and realized that Lidia not only hurried to pass the bit of sidewalk in front of the abandoned house, but she actually ran over those old, broken yellow paving stones. Victoria asked her why. Her mother laughed.

'I'm silly! Just ignore me. I'm afraid of that house.'

'Why?'

'No reason, just because it's abandoned. I told you, don't pay any attention to me. I get the feeling someone is hiding in there, a thief or something, but it's just my imagination.'

Victoria kept asking questions, but she couldn't get much information. Just that the owners, an elderly couple, had died some fifteen years ago. Did they die together? Vicky wanted to know. No, they died one after the other. That happens to old couples sometimes: when one of them dies the other fades right away. And since then, their children have been fighting over succession. What's succession? Vicky asked. It's the inheritance. They're fighting to see who will keep the house. But it's a pretty crappy house, said Vicky. Maybe so, but it could be the only one they have.

The house isn't so special at first glance, but if during your overhead flight you could descend and hover in front of it, the details would come into view. The door, made of iron, is painted dark brown. The front yard has very short, dry grass. It's burnt, razed, there is no green: in that yard there is drought and winter at the same time. The house at times seems to smile. The bricked-up windows are two closed eyes that give it an anthropomorphic look, and then there are the neighbourhood kids who rattle the lock in useless attempts to open the front door, and sometimes leave the chain hanging in a way that looks like a semi-circular mouth, the smile between the window eyes. One New Year's Eve when a lot of people were out in the street, Victoria approached the house. She had the impression the two of them were looking at each other, that its bricked-up windows were two square eyes that told her, I was tricking you, all these years when you passed by on my sidewalk, I played dumb, I hid, but now I want you to know, I want you to tell people I have something inside. Victoria went running back to her parents, who were trying in vain to light a bottle rocket, and she said nothing. But her eyes met those of Juan Peterson, who, unusually, was out in the street too, a cup of beer in hand. He didn't say anything to her, though he looked very serious. Hugo Peirano finally got the fuse lit, and Victoria covered her ears and closed her eyes. When she opened them again Juan Peterson was not among the crowd, and an empty beer cup had been left on the roof of an abandoned car that was rusting out on the kerb.

Gaspar woke up late. He often did on Sundays, when there was no noise to interrupt his sleep, especially if he had gone to bed late the night before. But once awake he never lounged or lingered in bed, not even on the coldest winter mornings. He felt a certain apprehension about lying down for too long: it reminded him of his father's illness and exhaustion. Plus, sometimes he had the feeling that if he stayed there sleeping, wrapped in the covers and breathing in his own smell, he would just never get up again, surrender to that empty state, so like the feeling of floating when he was tired out from swimming too much.

He made breakfast thinking about what to do that day: keep looking for the dog, maybe after first locking himself in the bathroom with a porn magazine? He didn't want his father to catch him looking at those glossy pages – though he was sure his dad wouldn't get angry, he still felt a little ashamed. Maybe he'd listen to the game at four, and get something to eat, because if he let too many hours go by on an empty stomach, his head would start to hurt. While he heated the milk in a jug and cut bread to spread with dulce de leche, he peered out the kitchen door to see if his father was awake. The door to his room was closed, which didn't necessarily mean he was asleep, but it certainly implied he didn't want to be bothered. Maybe it was best to leave right after breakfast, and have lunch later at the cafe in Castelli Park.

When he sat down at the kitchen table, he saw the note. His father had written it on the back of one of the flyers with Diana's picture on it. In his clear handwriting, it said: 'The dog is in the Llaneza parking lot. Bury her before she rots.' Gaspar understood right away: Llaneza was the supermarket on the other side of the park. He didn't doubt for a second that Diana was there. He picked up the pen his father had left on the table, wrote 'Thanks' under the message, and went out with his mouth full of bread. It wasn't raining, but it was damp and a little cool, so he zipped his hoodie all the way up.

The bike shop opened on Sundays because, in addition to selling and repairing, they rented bikes to people who wanted to ride in the park on weekends. Gaspar picked his up, with its new light, and paid with the money he always kept rolled up in the pocket of his pants or jacket. His newly tuned bike felt lighter now – the mechanic had oiled the chain – as he rode to the Llaneza parking lot. He slammed on the brakes when he saw Diana's paws and tail. She was unquestionably dead. She had the same stillness as the pigeons squashed on the sidewalk, something definitive and distant, repulsive in its foreignness. He didn't look at her face, but raced back towards Vicky's house, without sitting down or pausing his pedalling feet. He knew that at that time of day, Hugo Peirano would be out washing the car in the street, surely listening to one of the matches that were on at noon.

And so it was. Hugo Peirano was smoking and hosing down his yellow Taunus. A ridiculous colour for a car, thought Gaspar. He braked noisily by the kerb, and without getting off his bike greeted his friend's father. He let Hugo speak first, about the championship that was starting in July, about how the wind last night had blown the lid off the grill, how he had to take the car in to the mechanic.

When he finished, Gaspar said: 'I found Diana.'

Hugo stiffened, the hose still in his hand. In that position only a little water came out, but it was enough to get his pants wet. He had realized from Gaspar's expression that having found the dog was not necessarily good news.

'She's in the parking lot of the Llaneza near the park.'

'Are you sure it's her?'

'Yeah, I saw her when I went to get my bike.'

'Goddamn motherfucking shit,' murmured Hugo, and he looked down so Gaspar wouldn't see that he'd understood, and that the dog's death had affected him. Gaspar lowered his head too; he knew that most men didn't like anyone to see them cry, especially not another man, and above all not a kid.

'Well then. What a shame, poor thing. Should we tell Vicky? Or should we pretend she's still lost?'

Was he really asking, or was it rhetorical? Just in case he was being serious, Gaspar answered sincerely: 'Of course we can't hide that Diana died. If she found out, she'd hate us.'

'You're right. Come on then,' said Hugo, and Gaspar brought his bike into the Peiranos' garage, closed the door, and followed

Vicky's dad down the hall. He could hear the rest of the family – the girls, their mother, and their grandmother – playing cards in the backyard, just like they did every Sunday before lunch.

'It's in that house,' Adela said, pointing. 'Right, Mom?'

'I don't know which house it is. Nor do I think any hanged man is going to appear.'

Gaspar looked at Betty, hearing the anxiety in her voice. She was wearing a blue shawl around her neck and the effect was odd: it gave her a bird-like look that was only intensified by her sharp nose. Sometimes Gaspar thought calling her Betty was a little unfair, because a woman so tall and graceful deserved her full name, Beatriz, and not a diminutive.

Adela went on with her story. The bulldozers had come to raze the houses and build the highway – this one that's above us now. Some people didn't want to give up their houses. This one guy, when they came to force him out, hung himself. They found him like that. They took him out and demolished the house. And now some nights you can see his shadow, swinging. I've seen it. Next time I see it, I'll show you.

'Is it true they knocked the houses down like that?' Gaspar asked Betty.

'Yes. How could people defend themselves? You didn't argue with the dictatorship.'

'Didn't people protest? I read there were protests.'

'There must have been some resistance, sure, but there wasn't much that could be done. The dictatorship decided to put a highway here and they forced people out. You couldn't negotiate. They just sent them off to some shoddy apartments and that was that.'

Cars passed over the top of the café: there were businesses built all along the space beneath the highway. In recent years some tennis courts had opened and a few pools were under construction, even some schools and one or two plazas with concrete roofs. Gaspar liked to look at the walls of what had once been two-floor houses or apartment buildings: the wallpaper in the children's rooms, with monkeys and tortoises; the showers and taps set in dark tiles; even a wall that still had the marks of the paintings that once hung there.

'I swear I see him. His legs are wide apart and his hands are really big.'

Betty sighed.

'I believe you, dear,' she said. Gaspar couldn't decipher her expression: whether she really believed, or was just saying she did so that Adela would forget her obsession and eat her ham and cheese sandwich on Vienna bread. Gaspar had ordered a grilled cheese. That day he'd gone to do his homework at the café because his father was restless and pacing around the house, and it was best to avoid him when it was impossible to guess what was bothering him or why.

Suddenly, Betty asked:

'Do you see things too, Gaspar? Like Adela does?'

She was looking for his complicity? That was weird. Parents, in general, preferred their kids not to talk about things like the hanged man's shadow over the highway. Betty still seemed anxious, and she adjusted her shawl. She had very long hair that she always wore loose.

'No,' said Gaspar. 'Those things don't exist.'

'So nothing, not ever?'

'Do you, Betty?'

Adela interrupted them.

'You know what would be awesome? To go to the refrigerator cemetery. That's what they call it. It's close to the school's sports field.'

'I don't know why those refrigerators are there,' said Gaspar.

'The factory threw them out when it shut down,' explained Betty. 'It's one of the many national factories that closed. They couldn't sell them because production stopped. It's a dangerous place because that model of refrigerator has a door that locks, and it's easy to get trapped inside.'

'Exactly,' Adela went on. 'I heard people leave their dogs inside the refrigerators when they don't want them any more.'

'That's dumb,' said Gaspar, after taking a sip of his milky coffee. 'Why would they stick them in there when they could just let them go?'

'Dogs come back, they even stay at the hospital when their owners die, or sleep on top of their graves.'

'Again with the dogs that come back! You're obsessed. If you give them a really bad beating, they won't come back, they're not stupid. There's no need to stick them in a fridge. You're making that up.'

'No I'm not. And people also say that women leave their unwanted babies there. And murder victims. Disappeared people. Come on, take me there, Gaspar.'

Betty poured sugar into her tea and said nothing. She knows I'm not taking her there, thought Gaspar.

'No way. Probably none of that is true, but I'm sure people are living there, because it's close to the slum. It's too far away, and we don't know who could be hiding out there.'

'What if we found something!'

'Adela, that's enough,' said Betty. 'You get obsessed and you don't let up, Gaspar is right. Can't you see he doesn't want to take you? Plus, you shouldn't talk about the disappeared like that, it's disrespectful, I've told you before. No one knows where the victims are. But I'm quite sure they aren't in some refrigerators by the Riachuelo. Enough.'

'Gaspar always says no at first and then he gives in. Don't you, Gaspar?'

Adela smiled and cocked her head; one of her braids was coming undone – they never lasted long – and Betty started to redo it neatly.

'You didn't answer me, Betty,' said Gaspar. 'Have you ever seen anything?'

Betty's eyes looked watery, as if she were sad or they were irritated. Night was falling outside, and the waiters of the nearly empty restaurant were watching a soccer game on TV.

'I'll tell you some other day. With Adela all worked up like this I'd rather keep my mouth shut.'

'Come on!' begged Adela. 'You never tell me anything.'

'That's because you get crazy,' said Betty, kissing her forehead. 'Can you help with her language and literature homework, Gaspar? She doesn't understand a thing. They want her to diagram sentences. I'll come and pick you up in an hour. Sound good?'

Gaspar said yes and Adela handed him her notebook. It was messy, with the edges of the pages all folded and handwriting that looked like a younger kid's, the trembling lines of childish fingers.

Pablo was supposed to go with his parents that day to have dinner with his grandparents, but the outing was called off. His parents had a fight before the car even pulled out of the driveway. His mother shouted that she didn't want to see those old fuckers, and his father replied well, he didn't want them to see her like that, all messy and unhinged. It was true: his mother *was* messy and she smoked all the time and cried in front of the TV. He'd heard her say on the phone that maybe it would help to have another baby, but that she couldn't 'go through the experience' of losing another child. Pablo didn't want his mother to get pregnant, didn't want a sibling if his parents weren't getting along: he didn't think a baby would improve things. He had classmates with younger siblings and they said their parents fought, they couldn't sleep because the baby screamed, and they were always tired and in a bad mood.

When his mother went into her room to cry and his father drove away at a furious speed, Pablo decided to go and find Gaspar. It was always complicated because he couldn't just call him. He *could* knock on the door, but sometimes – Pablo didn't really know why – he was afraid to. Juan Peterson rarely responded if he was home: sometimes he looked out the upstairs window, and if he saw it was Pablo, he might let Gaspar know, but most of the time he just went on with what he was doing and ignored the interruption. He wasn't afraid Gaspar's dad would open the door, because that never happened. He couldn't say exactly what it was that scared him.

It was cold, so Pablo put on a sweater and a down jacket and ran all the way to Gaspar's house to warm up. There was no one in the street, and the closed windows of the houses he passed blocked all but a faint murmur from the TVs, though their flickering lights were clearly on display, more brilliant when they came from a colour set.

When he arrived, he froze in surprise on the sidewalk. Both doors were open, the one leading into the withered front yard and the main front door of the house. What could have happened? Pablo peered in: the house was very dark and seemed empty, but that was normal. Sometimes the only light came from Gaspar's room, which looked out on to the street.

Pablo went inside soundlessly; the wooden door let him enter in perfect silence, without a creak, when he pushed it further open. But as soon as he set foot in the spacious entrance hall ('foyer', Gaspar had called it once, an odd word he had surely copied from his father), Pablo knew something strange was happening. He hadn't been inside that house enough times to know its sounds or its movements, but he could hear something hitting the wooden floor upstairs, and he could feel that the air inside the house was muggy, like at an indoor pool. Even the little noise there was, the knocking from above, reached him as if through water, and he couldn't pinpoint where it came from. Maybe from the connected bedrooms Gaspar's father used upstairs, the ones no one else was allowed to enter, or from the giant room on the first floor that was like an empty ballroom. Pablo walked around the ground floor that was lit only by the street lights; the shutter on one of the living-room windows was open, another oversight. No one was there. The door to Gaspar's room was open and it was empty; so was the kitchen. And the living room, which changed colour every time a car went by on the street, frightened him. The best thing, he thought, would be to go back outside and wait. Gaspar must be at Vicky's, or at another friend's house, or running errands. If he came home he would turn on the light, and Pablo would see it from outside and get his attention the way he always did, by throwing a pebble or a stick at his window. But his heart was pounding, he was dying of curiosity, and the sounds from upstairs didn't sound threatening. Occasionally he could hear voices, distant, filtered through that weird watery buffer. He realized he was sweating: the heat in the house reminded him of the steam in the bathroom after a very hot shower, the kind his mom used to relieve his cough when he got sick. But there was no humidity in the air or on the walls; Pablo touched them and found them perfectly dry.

He went up the stairs with his cheeks burning; he knew they were flushed – how he hated the way he blushed. The climb grew harder with each step, like when he tried to run in dreams and his legs wouldn't move. The stairs were wooden and probably creaked, but now the only sound Pablo could hear was his own breathing, too fast for such little effort. When he reached the first floor, he leaned against the wall to catch his breath. The bedrooms there all led off the central hall; the last three were occupied by Gaspar's father. There was also a shorter staircase that led to a corridor with two bedrooms that served as a library; that corridor had a wooden railing, a kind of balcony or mezzanine from where you could look down at the hall with its wooden floor and, at the far end, enormous glass doors behind dark curtains, like on a stage. On the other side of the doors was a balcony that looked out over the inner yard, which must once have been beautiful but was now as barren as the flower beds at the entrance. Panting, Pablo sat down to rest on the steps of the short staircase leading to the library. He didn't see anyone, and the knocking had stopped. He still felt a little dazed, and he noticed his neck was soaked in sweat. Maybe the house had central heating? Gaspar had never mentioned it. On the contrary: he often complained about the cold.

Pablo was standing up to leave when a movement in the empty hall made him gasp. He crouched back down on the stairs, with his eyes just peeking over the railing. A man was in the room, and he opened the curtains and the glass doors. In the moonlight – the backyard was unlit – Pablo saw he was naked. Then Gaspar's father came out of one of the bedrooms. He was naked too, and Pablo thought he seemed huge under the silvery light, tall and strong. The man who had opened the windows was also tall, though less so; he walked to the other end of the room, where he knelt down and lit a candle. Pablo, of course, hadn't seen the candles before, but as he followed the movement of the naked man – who had grey hair though his face

233

wasn't old, not at all, he seemed like his dad's age or a little older – he counted seven. Seven candles. And then he saw that there was a drawing on the floor of the empty hall: a white circle with something else drawn inside that Pablo couldn't really distinguish. Lines, some circles. Gaspar's dad entered the circle as though passing through a door, and, on his knees, he waited for the other naked man. The two of them sat for a moment face to face, completely still, until Gaspar's dad kissed the other man, without tenderness, nothing like the kisses Pablo had seen in movies or like people gave in public, and suddenly he had trouble breathing again, because he had never seen two men kiss, he'd never imagined they could, he'd thought it was . . . forbidden? Something like that. Gaspar's father sat on the floor, and Pablo watched as the naked man did something incredible, impossible: he sat on Gaspar's father's penis and they started to have sex, like the pictures in the porn magazines, only moving. He'd seen it in the ones Gaspar hid in the garage, sex like that, but not between two men: he'd seen a man putting it in a woman's ass, and he'd thought it was gross. But he didn't think it was gross now. He did feel ashamed for watching, but at the same time he couldn't look away: Gaspar's father made the other man get on all fours on the floor, and, very upright, shining with sweat like a wet statue, he got behind him and they did it like dogs, in complete silence except for the slapping of bodies. Pablo was afraid they would see him hiding there, spying, but it was the best moment to run away, because they were so focused on what they were doing. But how to cross the stretch between the hall and the stairs without them noticing? Now Pablo felt all his sweat dry up and turn icy – the house wasn't hot any more, but something worse was happening: he sensed people in the rooms. He even heard the murmur of low conversations and the rise and fall of door handles. Upstairs and down. Footsteps on the stairs. The shadows from the candles made disproportionate shapes above the men's bodies. His legs were paralysed with dread, and at the same time, when he looked at the men – who were face to face again – he felt dizzy, as though his blood was growing lighter, and he felt like crying even though he wasn't sad or scared; he didn't understand what the men were doing inside that circle but he liked it, liked the strong arms braced against the floor, the backs damp with sweat and saliva, the way they grabbed each other's cheeks and necks when they kissed, and the sweet, metallic smell that reached him there where he hid on the stairs. What could he do? Gaspar's dad had his eyes closed and he was different, beautiful, thought Pablo, beautiful; everyone said he was sick, how was that possible? Weren't sick people always ugly? In the dim light of the candles and the moon Pablo could see Gaspar's dad's chest and the long scar, but it looked like that, just a scar, not a sign of weakness. It didn't make him any less beautiful. The other man had scars on his back, Pablo could see. It looked like the two men had been cut by a single knife stroke, or were separated Siamese twins.

The sounds from downstairs faded or stopped entirely, and again Pablo debated leaving. The men should have been able to hear his breathing – he couldn't control it and it was fast and noisy like after running. Gaspar's father was kneeling with his head twisted to one side, a strange, slack position, as if he were listening to something, music coming in through the window or from the roof. The grey-haired man pulled away from his embrace and stood up; he walked alone towards the room they'd come out of, but then he stopped, and Pablo knew it was because he'd sensed his presence. The grey-haired man turned around and looked him straight in the eyes: his own were sunken and had heavy lids. Pablo could see those details in the light from the moon and the candles, while Gaspar's father sat unmoving in the centre of the circle, distant and tense, his enormous hands fully extended; the shadows made them look longer than normal. The grey-haired man didn't speak out loud, but his lips very clearly mouthed 'Get out.' Pablo nodded, and the grey-haired man kept watching him until he reached the stairs. Pablo ran down them and tried to ignore the voices that had risen up again, a woman talking about a church in ruins, another who said we need smoke and earth, a man repeating a phrase in a language Pablo didn't know, and something that was dragging, he could hear it, it was the sound of shoes walking through dry leaves. Were there people in the other rooms? Was it some kind of club? Pablo was exhausted when he reached the door, as if he'd had to cover several blocks to get there and not just a few yards, and he ran to his house thinking about Gaspar's father's blond hair, about the way he'd wet his fingers with saliva, about the strength of his arms when he'd kissed the grey-haired man. Now, as he ran towards his house, what he had witnessed seemed unreal. The voices and the suffocating heat and the circle drawn on the floor, it all made him think of something dark and deathly, of spiders and abandoned cemeteries, or the cold floor of the bathroom at night and the blood that came from between his mother's legs and smelled like metal and meat, of the chains that the wind banged at night on the empty factory down the street and on the abandoned bricked-up house on Calle Villarreal, of the silence that came after a blackout, of dreams about cold hands that caressed his stomach until he woke up, and of the mildew stain on the ceiling that some nights looked like a fat cat and other nights like a horned beast.

Gaspar woke up before Vicky and Adela, and from the sofa bed he heard Lidia Peirano talking in low tones while she got

Virginia, her younger daughter, ready for school. The girl was snivelling, still half asleep. Despite the cold, Gaspar didn't stay curled up under the blanket; he put on his pants and ran to the bathroom. Then he went into the kitchen and had breakfast with Lidia and Virginia before they left for school. The little girl was still yawning and sniffling; I think she's about to catch a cold, Lidia told him. She's really cranky.

Gaspar folded up the sofa bed where he'd slept, loaded the sheets in the washing machine, and waited to see if either Vicky or Adela would appear, but the door to the room where the girls were sleeping was shut, and he heard only silence. He stayed over at Vicky's pretty often: if it got late, they always invited him to sleep there. Sometimes he forced the invitation if he noticed his father was in an especially bad mood, or if Esteban was visiting, like last night. He preferred to leave them alone. It was less common for Adela to spend the night at Vicky's, but her mom had supposedly gone to a friend's wedding; the party was at a country house far away, and she'd be back late. But Adela didn't believe that. I think she has a boyfriend, she'd said, annoyed. Adela still held out hope her father would come back.

But Adela and Vicky didn't wake up, and Gaspar left without seeing them. It was early and he could walk to school quickly, so he passed by his house first. Esteban's car was gone. Had he left alone? He didn't have time to go in and check. Several times, Gaspar had seen the way his father and Esteban caressed each other distractedly, and once he'd even found them sleeping together, naked. That time he'd gotten scared: it seemed to him, from the things he'd heard, that it must be illegal for a man to have a boyfriend, and they could be arrested. But he looked into it and learned that they couldn't. People are very prejudiced, Vicky's mom had told him, they can't stand people living freely. But it's not illegal. He realized that if people at school or around the neighbourhood found out, they would tease and bully him forever for being the son of a fag. Gaspar was willing to put up with it, though. Sometimes he thought that if Esteban moved in with them and they kept it a secret, things could improve. Esteban seemed capable of dealing with his father – not of controlling him, but at least he was someone Juan listened to. His father had various reactions to Esteban; at times he seemed calmer, and Gaspar could see how even his shoulders relaxed and he slept better; but sometimes, especially after Esteban left, he would lock himself in or have fits of fury or do irrational things, like cover the terrace with sharp shards of glass (last year) or make Gaspar always keep the lights off, except in the kitchen and bathroom (starting last summer, and still in force); or else he'd disappear for several days, leaving money on the table with a short note that gave no information and that terrified Gaspar: what would happen if he didn't come back? What if he never saw his father again?

Gaspar got out of school a little early that day because of a bomb threat. There were threats almost every week and he knew they were made by the kids in seventh grade, but the principal didn't dare ignore them. When the calls first began, she had summoned the sixth- and seventh-graders to an assembly and given them a speech about how democracy had only recently returned to Argentina, and it could easily be lost again. Unfortunately, she said, these matters must be taken seriously, because we have lived through very hard times in this country. Many of the kids exchanged looks during the talk, not understanding what the principal was talking about. Gaspar did.

He walked home despite the cold and a slight headache that, he thought, wasn't going to turn into a migraine. Just in case, he stopped at the pharmacy and bought a blister pack of aspirins.

They didn't have much effect on him any more, but the doctors, including Vicky's mom, said he was still too young to take anything stronger. He took stronger things anyway: his dad gave them to him. There's no reason for you to suffer, he said. Gaspar agreed. Sometimes his headaches kept him from swimming; they didn't go away even after he slept, and not long ago he'd dreamed he was scooping his own eyes out with spoons, as if they were servings of custard. It was always his eyes that hurt first, and it was hard to move them; then came that feeling of wearing a tight helmet. First, sometimes, he'd see black shapes like flowers opening, especially if he looked up: flowers in the sky. An aura, he knew it was called. It was a warning.

He swallowed the aspirins without water, and it felt like the bitter taste stuck to his palate. He went inside intending to go straight to the kitchen for some water to wash away the aftertaste, but he stopped when he found his father in the living room, sitting on his yellow sofa in front of the TV, which was on though he wasn't watching it.

'Come here, son.'

Gaspar approached and saw that his father had a cardboard box beside him, fairly tall, the kind a small appliance would come in.

'Esteban left?'

'This morning. Look what I have, Gaspar, check it out.'

Gaspar looked first at his father's face. He was smiling with one eyebrow arched, and he was drunk. That was a terrible sign. Every time he took a breath, his chest made a noise. Oh, this is bad, thought Gaspar. It's one of *those* times: Esteban took off and left my dad all crazed. He was going to have to obey if he wanted to avoid the beatings, the shouting, or some worse punishment.

'Put your hand in.'

Gaspar did, apprehensively: he knew that box could hold nothing good. He felt a painful throbbing in his temple. Inside the box, his fingers touched what at first he thought were dried bugs: they had a fragile texture and made that pearly sound; hundreds of small things that had once been alive. When he picked up one of the bugs to see what it was – less afraid now, the thing seemed inoffensive, maybe kind of gross – he saw it was much more compact than an insect. They were all the same size, and he put three in the palm of his hand and crouched down to see them better in the light from the TV. Then he realized that what at first touch he'd thought were legs were actually hairs. It couldn't be. He looked more closely at what he had in his hand. They were hairs, yes. Eyelashes. In the palm of his hand, he was holding three dried eyelids with their corresponding eyelashes.

The whole box was filled with eyelids. Gaspar threw the severed lids to the floor and threw up in front of the TV; a little vomit spattered on to his father's legs. He's crazy, he thought. I have to get away. I also have to know. And I also have to take another aspirin before it hurts so much I can't walk.

'Where did you get them? Where did you get the eyes?'

'They're not eyes and they're not mine, they're a gift.'

'Who gave them to you?'

His father sank one of his enormous hands into the box of eyelids and toyed with the almost translucent scraps of skin as if they were coins.

'Did you cut them off? Are they from dead people?'

'Some of them. People can live a lot of ways. Your friend can live without an arm, for example. I live practically without a heart. Some people can live without eyes. Or without eyelids. Some let them be cut off.'

His father stood up with the box in his hands. For a moment

Gaspar thought he was going to dump the eyelids on to him, a rain of dead lashes, and then he would scream and scream until he went crazy too. But no: his father was going upstairs, to his room, probably.

'Clean that up.'

'You clean it up.'

'I'm leaving for a few days.'

Gaspar took in that information with relief, even joy. When his father started up the stairs, he ran to the kitchen and took two aspirins with a lot of water, straight from the tap. He thought he was going to vomit again, but he held it back until his eyes started watering. And once the tears came he let himself go, lay down on the kitchen floor and cried until his headache became unbearable and he felt like his head was burning on the inside, as if someone had hidden a knife within his brain and it was stabbing him.

If you could travel the streets of the neighbourhood at night or in the early morning, you would hear the radios of people who can't sleep without music or voices; you'd hear the sound of spinning fans, plus nightmare cries and the footsteps of insomniacs. In general, though, the neighbourhood is very silent, and the sounds begin mainly in the morning, when those who work far away leave their houses in cars, or else on foot to wait for the bus on the corner.

The wee small hours are the most silent time.

And on some early mornings you might see Juan Peterson emerge from his house, close the door without locking it, and walk two blocks, all alone, to the bricked-up house on Calle Villarreal. The cool night breeze ruffles his hair and reveals a wound on his scalp, a fresh wound that drips blood down his neck to his shoulder. The door of the house has a padlock and the lock is filled with cement, but when Juan steps on to the burnt grass of the abandoned front yard, when he advances along the yellow-tiled path, kneels down, touches his wound and smears his blood on the door, just a little blood, the door vibrates and opens for him. The house is expecting him.

Juan enters without looking behind him; from inside – if someone could see, though no one does, as no one is following him – a tenuous light shines. The door closes behind him, and if anyone were to try to push it open, the attempt would be futile. It's not the padlock or cement that keeps the door sealed.

It's impossible to see inside the house. The windows are bricked up. Even if the bricks could be knocked out, there would be only darkness.

It is possible to hear, just a little, from outside. First, it's a vibration. The house is trembling: it's like an insect trapped inside a room, and the buzzing grows as it gets closer to the listening ear, fades when it pauses in a corner or flies more slowly or lands on the wall. Juan emerges before first light and staggers back to his house; if anyone saw him, they would think he was drunk, but no one sees him, the house protects him, at least until he reaches his own, and usually he collapses as soon as he opens the door. But he doesn't always return destroyed, panting, from the abandoned house. Sometimes he walks home easily, undisturbed, and locks himself in his room.

Once, Gaspar had tried to follow him. He'd heard his father coming in and out at night and was curious to find out where he was going. He was around eight years old then, and the night was cool. He'd gone out to the sidewalk, looked both ways, and was surprised not to see his father, who had just left the house. He thought maybe a car had been waiting for him – sometimes a driver came to pick him up – but when he looked closer, he saw that Juan was simply leaning in the doorway of the house next door, hiding, waiting to catch him. Gaspar didn't hesitate and ran back inside. Before he could start up the stairs, he felt his father grab him by the ankles and in the same movement slam the door so hard that, Gaspar thought, it could have woken the neighbours. Juan knocked him down with a single motion, and when Gaspar tried to get up, he pinned his arms against the floor. It was like being held by metal handcuffs. He still remembered his father's face so close up, his pale lips and furious eyes: the hands that pressed him to the floor were trembling with rage, and Gaspar was mute with terror. He didn't understand why it had been so wrong to follow him, but lying on the ground with his father on top of him like a savage animal, sniffing him – he remembered thinking he was a wolf about to bite his throat – he understood it was worse than he'd imagined, that it might just be unforgivable.

His father spoke to him. What are you thinking, following me like that? And then he wrapped his hands around Gaspar's neck and squeezed. Not hard, but Gaspar was so scared he couldn't breathe. Sometimes even now, years later, he woke up feeling like he was being choked, and he had to get out of bed and take deep breaths while he paced around his room. The strangling hadn't lasted long. His father let go of his neck, picked him up – Gaspar tried to kick him and received a slap that made his nose bleed: he couldn't fight his father – and carried him up the stairs, holding his legs to keep him from struggling. When they got upstairs, Juan opened one of the rooms that were closed off, the walls stained with dampness and the wooden floor burnt in parts. A completely empty room with broken, fallen blinds. You're staying here, he said. Gaspar looked up at him from the wooden floor. He'd hit his head, but he was so scared it didn't even hurt.

Gaspar didn't know how many hours he spent there. He knew he slept on the floor, that he got hungry, that he peed against the wall in the dark and that the smell in the airless room disgusted him, but he got used to it. He knew he had a dream about school: the walls of his classroom were collapsing slowly and he was running, but the crack in the walls seemed to chase him. He knew that in the darkness he cried and begged to be let out and pounded on the door and screamed for the neighbours and his mother until finally he sat with his back against the wall imagining soccer set pieces while he waited, a spectacular goal, the world's best-taken corner, or a cross that he headed into the corner of the net, but the smell of sweat and grass couldn't reach him in that damp room that now stank of piss and tears. When his father opened the door, one or two days or a few hours later, Gaspar ran to the bathroom stumbling because his legs were numb and his eyes had grown used to the dark, he ran to the bathroom because he urgently needed to go and there, standing in front of the toilet, he had the unmistakable feeling that came before a headache, those black flowers that floated in the air and opened, and then the stabbing in his eye. While he looked for pills in the medicine cabinet, he was grateful the pain was only coming now that he could go to his bed, though it wouldn't go away if he didn't eat something first, but his father wasn't about to feed him and, in those days, he hardly knew how to cook anything, and there was surely nothing to cook in the house anyway. Trembling – from fear, from his wobbly legs, because he could hear his father stomping around the house, obviously still angry – he went downstairs and got a dishcloth from the kitchen, opened the freezer and took out some ice cubes, wrapped them up and pressed them above his eye, and finally checked the time: two o'clock. In the afternoon, because it was daytime. The fridge held only a glass bottle of water. With the makeshift ice pack on his eye, he went outside. It wasn't cold, and he walked towards Vicky's house slowly, because if he ran, the pain would become a hammer. And when he got there, he lied. Vicky was still at school but her mother was home: strange, because she worked every day. She'd said something, Gaspar remembered, about taking a furlough. He didn't know what a furlough was, and between waves of pain he lied, he said his dad didn't feel well, that he was in bed and Gaspar didn't want to wake him, that his head hurt and he needed to eat, if he ate it would get a little better, that he could cook but not with that pain, and the supermarket was closed and he couldn't buy anything, he could pay or they could go somewhere else that was open, he didn't know, and Lidia knelt down to look at him. She told him, don't cry or it'll hurt worse. She said, I'll make you a steak, and we have some salad. She said, it's lucky you caught me at home. She said, Later I'll go by and see how your dad is, and Gaspar wanted to say, No, don't go, but he said nothing, he ate and then lay down in the trundle bed, and when he woke up his head was only throbbing softly though his hands were still shaking, the bedroom door was closed so he could rest, Diana the dog was sleeping at his feet, and he never knew whether Vicky's mom had gone to his house or not, if she'd seen his father, he didn't ask and no one told him, but that night he stayed over to sleep, it was one of the first times, and he couldn't remember when he'd gone home or anything else, and the hours in the darkness and the days following had gradually faded. But he had never again dared follow his father when he went out in the early morning.

Gaspar pedalled to the woodshop. Though it was only two blocks away, he'd felt like riding his bike. He hadn't seen his father that morning. He was still mad at him, and scared. It was always the same when he saw, whether by accident or not, some fragment of the secret world his father lived in. Why would he show him those things? Later, Juan would seem remorseful. Or worse: Gaspar felt it was like in those movies about people who were possessed, as though something got inside him and transformed him into someone else; the person who had shown him that box was not his father. He couldn't explain it. The box with eyelids had been one of the most horrible souvenirs his father had let him see, but, like the others, it gradually transformed into a dream, the memory withdrew to a region where it was hard to access, where it lost strength. Gaspar realized that, even while the numb forgetting was comforting, it was also a strange thing. The incident with the box had not been a dream, that was clear, but he felt it like one, and it was more bearable like that. It was the same way he had almost forgotten the red handprints on the walls upstairs. Or the voice that had resounded in his head one night, so powerful he ran upstairs and banged on his father's bedroom door until he opened it, dishevelled and with something like a film of oil over his eyes. Or when he'd found his dad walking like a sleepwalker through the house with something written on his inner arm, two words he couldn't forget: *Solve* and *Coagula*. He'd looked them up in the dictionary, but it turned out they weren't Spanish words: they were Latin. There was a Latin dictionary in his school's library, but it was always checked out. And anyway, sometimes he preferred not to know. His father had disappeared for a week after showing him the box of eyelids. Now he was back, but they hardly saw each other.

Gaspar had to pick up his present for Adela at the woodshop. He'd found the diagram in a book in the library at his house, and he'd torn out the page and given it to the carpenter so he could copy the design. The workshop was open but there was no one at the counter; Gaspar clapped and the sound of his hands echoed in the warehouse. Then he heard a door open, and when Don Sixto saw him, he shouted: Oh, wait just a sec, kiddo. And then he came from the back with the diagram and the box.

'Let's see if it's what you wanted,' he said.

Gaspar looked first at the diagram to be sure it was at least similar.

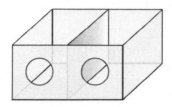

It was. The mirror in the middle, separating the two compartments, a hole in each of them. Gaspar stuck his own arm in the right-side hole: it fit comfortably. The box was pretty big, but Don Sixto had used a light wood and Gaspar could lift it effortlessly. The mirror has to be a little heavy, Sixto said, but pine doesn't weigh a thing. Is it what you wanted?

Yes, replied Gaspar, and he looked at his own arm in the mirror. The box was perfect.

Adela was celebrating her birthday at her house. The Peiranos, of course, had offered theirs, but Adela had said no thanks, and later she'd admitted to Gaspar that she didn't want to use that big yard for her party, which would have so few guests. It'd be more noticeable that no one had come, she said, and Gaspar understood. It was better to do something simple at Adela and Betty's small but pleasant apartment, because one particular absence was always felt: her father's, whom no one knew. Once, while they were washing dishes, Vicky had asked her mom if it was true that Adela's dad had been taken away, and Gaspar, who was drying the silverware, had heard the reply: The truth is, Vicky, Betty was already alone when I met her. I don't know who Adela's father is and I never asked. You don't ask about those things unless the person brings it up first.

Betty had decorated the house well. There were streamers hung all down the passageway to the last door, the one to Adela and Betty's apartment, which was hung with a Sarah Kay poster that said 'Happy Birthday!' beside a picture of a girl smelling a rose. Adela's grandparents were already there when Gaspar arrived, plus Vicky, and Virginia with her water game she never put down, Lucrecia, a classmate who was quite tight with the girls, and that was it. They were only waiting on Pablo, who was always late. He finally showed up with a thousand-piece jigsaw puzzle of a German castle with an unpronounceable name; Adela thanked him with a hug: she liked puzzles, but she liked castles even more. Betty seemed pleased and excited; the grandparents, on the other hand, sipped their sodas in silence. They were taciturn in general, not at all affectionate, not your typical grandparents. They only appeared at birthdays, and when they did speak, it was only to Betty. Adela, though, assured her friends she had a great time with them every summer when she went to their vacation home in San Isidro. The cake was very good: a sponge cake filled with dulce de leche and custard, with chocolate icing decorated with little silver sprinkles. Gaspar ate a piece after clapping during 'Happy Birthday' – he never sang out loud in public – and he felt full; he'd eaten a lot of hot dogs. The grandparents asked Adela to try on the dress they'd given her; it was white, like a First Communion dress, and she mod-elled it with a fake smile – it was obvious she didn't like it, but didn't want to offend them. They left soon after. The kids waved goodbye to them and then, finally alone, they felt relieved. There was something about the grandparents that made them uncomfortable: they seemed to be there out of obligation, like they were following orders. Lucrecia also had to leave early, and then Adela sprawled out theatrically on the sofa. Pablo, who was finishing a piece of cake, offered to cut her another, and she accepted. Then, with her lips smeared with dulce de leche – it wasn't easy for her to hold the napkin and eat neatly with only one hand – she told Gaspar: 'I want my present!'

The bag holding the box was in a corner beside the table. Gaspar picked it up and brought it to Adela, but told her: 'I have to show it to you alone, I can't give it to you in front of anyone.'

'Why not?' she asked, and she wiped her mouth and fixed her dark, short-lashed eyes on him.

'Because I don't know if it works.'

'Such secrecy,' Betty said with a smile, but her eyes were serious. Adela moved fast, grabbing Gaspar's hand and half-dragging him to her room, shutting the door behind them.

'So? Show me.'

Gaspar went to Adela's bed and set the box on the turquoise bedspread.

'Come here,' he said.

Wary, she went closer.

'What is this?'

Gaspar scratched his nose; he was a little nervous.

'It's called a mirror box.'

'Is it magic?'

'No. More or less. It sounds like it, right? Let's hope it is, I guess. Stick your arm in here,' he said, pointing to one of the holes. Adela bent down obediently. 'Now stick your other arm in the other hole.'

Adela looked at him with annoyance, with incipient anger.

'You know what I mean. You told me you can feel your arm, right? So put it in.'

Now she was looking at him with eyes full of tears. Gaspar

felt sorry for Adela as he looked at her there, kneeling on her bedroom floor in a pink dress, her hair in two braids, a girl who never wanted to be different. He felt older than her.

'Ade, I don't know if it's going to work,' he said, and he had to clear his throat. 'I got it from a book. But I swear it's not a joke. I would never pull a prank on you like that. Never. Let's try.'

She hesitated a moment, then said okay, and with her eyes closed, she made a small movement with her stump.

'Done,' she said.

'Great.' Gaspar knelt down beside her. 'Now look at the mirror. See? It's like you had two arms. Tell me where it hurts.'

'It doesn't hurt. It itches.'

'Okay. Where? But don't look at me, don't look at your real arm, just look at the reflection. Tell me.'

The box was open on top, with no lid, so Gaspar was able to put his own hand in and follow Adela's instructions: the side of the elbow. No, down a little. No, up a little.

'Sometimes it takes a while,' said Gaspar, and instead of continuing to look for the place that itched, he caressed Adela's hand, her fingers, her arm, and moved her bracelets, for a long time, in silence, until she said, I can feel my arm! And then Gaspar followed her instructions again and found the place that itched, the phantom itch that had been impossible to forget until that moment, until that twelfth birthday on a turquoise bed.

'There!' Adela said in a low voice, and Gaspar scratched softly with his short nails while she stared disconcertedly at the reflected arm. He kept going until Adela said, That's it, and took her arm out of the box. Sitting on the floor, she covered her face with her hand. She wasn't crying. Gaspar didn't know what was going on. He wanted to ask her if she wasn't happy, and why wasn't she happy, and had it had worked or not, but he knew he had to keep his mouth shut for a while. They could hear Vicky and Pablo's conversation coming from the kitchen, and also the noise of dishes: Betty was cleaning up after the party. Adela broke the silence.

'Why?' Adela asked, and Gaspar realized she was angry. Then he tried to explain that he'd had the idea after a conversation about phantom limbs with his father, who had told him there was a diagram in a book in their library, but she interrupted him.

'No, stop, I'm not asking you. What I mean is: why did the doctor never do this? Or my mom? Why didn't they ever tell me there's a cure for when my arm hurts or itches?'

Gaspar opened his mouth, but he didn't say anything, only shrugged.

'Didn't they know? Are they that dumb? I'm gonna kill them.'

Now she *was* crying, from pure rage, her lower lip trembling. Gaspar knelt down in front of her.

'They might not have known.'

She was still mad, and Gaspar let her be. He let her stand up, didn't insist on asking if she'd liked his gift, let her yank open the door and run to the kitchen, and when he heard the noise of dishes crashing to the floor, Gaspar told his surprised friends we'd better leave, and he pushed Vicky and Pablo through the open door and into the passageway. They heard shouting from Adela and from her mother, but it was impossible to make out what they were saying because one shouted over the other and they were both crying.

'What the hell did you do?' Vicky asked, half running down the passage, while Pablo sighed in relief on finding the gate to the street unlocked. Gaspar didn't know how to answer. He needed to talk to them to figure out what he'd done wrong.

'Let's go to the kiosk,' he said, and he checked his back pocket to be sure he had enough money for a Coke.

*

Gaspar didn't want to go back to Adela's house, as Vicky and Pablo suggested, and after finishing his soda he put on his jacket and said goodbye. She'll get over it, Vicky told him, and Gaspar didn't answer. He went home. When he closed the door, before he could take a step towards his room, he heard his father's voice calling him from upstairs.

His tone held no threat and Gaspar wanted to ignore him, to keep walking and pretend he hadn't heard, but instead he answered. What do you want? he yelled. For you to come upstairs a while, his father said, his voice loud but not a shout, free of any violence or mockery. Gaspar obeyed. The wooden steps creaked a lot; there used to be a rug to muffle footsteps, he remembered, but it was gone now. Maybe his dad had pulled it up – it could have been fuel for one of his periodic bonfires. He didn't know, and in fact only remembered the existence of that rug now, as he hurried up the stairs.

The door to his father's library-study was open, and once Gaspar saw him lying on the sofa with a book beside him, he entered without fear. He didn't sit down, but leaned against the desk, surveying the messy books, an unfinished drawing, the closed notebook with its dark covers.

'How are you?'

Gaspar shrugged and heard his father stand up; he didn't look at him until he sensed him very close.

'You can stay mad at me forever, but I don't know if it makes much sense.'

Juan's eyes shone in the room that was lit only by the small lamp he used for reading. He was wearing a grey long-sleeved shirt that was too small for him and showed how thin he was. Gaspar took a deep breath before speaking.

'Why did you make me touch what was in that box?'

The library was hot and smelled of dust; his father, freshly bathed and with still-wet hair, smelled of soap.

'Sometimes I'm not myself. I apologize.'

Gaspar shivered.

'What does that mean, you're not you?'

'It means exactly what I said: sometimes I'm not me.'

Gaspar rested his elbows on the desk and idly picked up the drawing his father hadn't finished. It looked like a small city, a few houses on a plain and in the sky a black sun or maybe a scribble, but very big and centred.

'Why do you never tell me what it is you do, what all of this is?' Gaspar indicated the books, the closed doors, the dark corners.

'Your friend Vicky – does her father tell her what he does, for example?'

'Yeah. He's a pharmacist.'

'And what else does she know, other than that he's a pharmacist? Does she know how many antibiotics he sells in a week? Does she know how the prices change? Whether insulin is free? Does she know if he'd like to have a specialized section for homeopathy?'

Gaspar clenched his teeth.

'Maybe she does.'

'Of course she doesn't know. What does Pablo's father do?'

'Something with gas.'

'What does he do with gas?'

'I don't know! Puts it in cars.'

'Why is it put into cars? You think Pablo knows more than you?'

Gaspar gave in.

'But it's not the same thing. What you do is weirder.'

'How many times have we had this conversation before? It's boring, Gaspar.'

'I just want to know.'

His father leaned down to his level. His eyes were as puffy as if he'd been punched, but he looked better than on other days, less tired.

'Pick whatever book you want. Read whatever you want.'

'Really?'

'Really.'

Gaspar tiptoed over to the bookshelf. There was so much to choose from! Above all the books, in a wooden box on the shelf nearest the ceiling, were his mother's ashes. Gaspar had once asked his dad to open the box so he could see them. Nothing shocking: it looked more like dirt than ashes. He had cried because his mom was nothing but that, a pile of dust in a box, but he hadn't been scared. He wasn't disturbed by that box in the corner. His dad told him that when the moment came, he was going to throw the ashes into the river. But the years went by and they stayed right where they were.

Now Gaspar looked over the shelves and through the piles of books, turning around the ones whose spines were facing the wall. Some were in English. Dion Fortune, he read, *The Training and Work of an Initiate*. Others were in Spanish: Juan Carlos Onetti, *El pozo*, Thomas Hardy, *Jude el oscuro*, Françoise Sagan, *Buenos días, tristeza*. García Lorca, Keats, Yeats, Blake, Eliot, Neruda: the poetry books Gaspar liked and always borrowed. He moved to another, taller shelf: *Babylonian Magic and Sorcery*, Leonard W. King. *The Magical Revival*, Kenneth Grant. Finally, at the end of one somewhat sagging shelf, he found the spine that seemed to be the chosen one: *The Doctrine and Ritual of High Magic*, by Eliphas Lévi. It was a paperback, grey and very worn. He pulled it out and showed it to his father, who nodded.

'Read anything you want.'

Gaspar opened the book randomly. Page 44 had a drawing of a six-pointed star, a little similar to the Star of David. He read: 'This is why material elements which are analogous to the divine elements are thought of as four, are explained by two, and only exist in the end as three. Revelation is the duality; all verbs are twofold and suppose two.' I don't understand a thing, he thought. He turned to the chapter called 'Black Magic', and was disappointed that it was only a single page. It started by saying that fearful people should close the book, but the warning meant nothing to him. Nor did the chapter. What it said was much less terrifying than what he'd seen himself in lots of movies. He looked curiously at his father, who smiled at him again without mockery, but with a certain sadness.

'Boring, right?'

'Can I try another one?'

'No. They're not much different. Gaspar, that's what I do.'

'What?'

'I study what those books say.'

'Alone? Is there a place where people study that?'

Gaspar saw his father lie down again on the sofa and toss a cushion down on the floor, close by.

'I'm self-taught. I'm too old and sick to go to the university. Sit down.'

'You're not old. How old are you? Did you ever teach, like Mom did?'

'No. I'm thirty-four, but it feels like two hundred.'

Gaspar sat down on the cushion, and his knee almost knocked over a bottle. His father steadied it to keep it from spilling, then picked it up and took a long drink. How had he not smelled the alcohol on his breath? Now Gaspar understood why he was receiving so much information: his dad was drunk. Again.

'Do you study that stuff because you could always predict

things, or is it the other way around? Did you study in order to be able to predict things? Did you always see people?'

'Yes, but they don't bother me. There's a technique to avoid seeing them – you can turn it off at will, and I'm good at it.'

'It never fails?'

'Everything fails, but I'm not afraid of them. They're echoes. Manifestations. They can't touch us. It's just disconcerting.'

'What does disconcerting mean?'

'Something that surprises you, that catches you unawares. What kind of vocabulary do they teach you at that school of yours?'

'They're not bad teachers,' Gaspar insisted, 'I just don't use the dictionary that much.'

'If you say so.'

'Dad, am I going to see those things, those echoes?'

'No. But if you did, you'd know, no question.'

Gaspar sat thinking. Another long drink. The book his father had been reading fell to the floor and Gaspar looked at the title out of the corner of his eye: *Selected Poems*, John Keats. Then he picked it up, opened it, and read: 'Season of mists and mellow fruitfulness . . .' He tried to translate it into Spanish: *Estación de nieblas. Temporada de nieblas.*

'Can I take it?'

'It's hard. Use the dictionary. You'll like Keats. He died very young, you know. At twenty-five. What else are you up to, son? I want to know what normal things you've been doing. Talk to me.'

Gaspar leaned his head against his father's legs and decided that the episode of the box of eyelids wasn't important, it had been part of a nightmare, it was forgiven, forgotten. He felt his father's hand caressing his hair as he told him how Adela hadn't liked his gift of the mirror box.

'Sick people are different,' his father told him.

'She's not sick,' replied Gaspar.

'I know, but still, people who have physical problems are all alike, and we're different from healthy people. If, for example, you gave me a wheelchair, I wouldn't thank you for it.'

'Do you need one?'

'No, not yet. But if someone gave me a wheelchair, I'd burn it. You don't need to understand it, you just need to know.'

'Will she get over being angry?'

'Probably – missing a limb isn't the same as being about to die.'

'Don't say that, Dad.'

'How do you want me to say it? Anyway, what else? Do you have a girlfriend? I heard you talking to a girl on the phone.'

'You heard? You were locked in here, I didn't think you could hear anything. I had one, but she broke up with me. Her name's Belén.'

'She broke up with you?'

'Yeah, she gave me a note saying she didn't want to be my girlfriend any more.'

'And what did you do?'

'Nothing. Pablo told me that if I wrote her back and asked to stay together, she would say yes, because that's what girls do. But I didn't feel like it.'

'You don't like her?'

'Yeah, I like her, but I don't know what to talk to her about, she doesn't talk much.'

Gaspar heard his father laugh softly. 'I can't help you there, son, I don't know a thing about women.'

They were silent for a while. Gaspar closed his eyes. There wasn't a sound in the house. He felt his father stroking his hair, slowly, with an almost feminine gentleness. What he hadn't told him was that Belén's letter, short and written in all upper-case letters, had made him punch the tiles in the bathroom. Not so much because of her – she bored him a little, except when she let him kiss and touch her – but because he was mad at himself for not knowing how to keep her. He shifted on the cushion to stretch out his legs and lean his head against his father's ribs. He remembered how it had felt to sleep beside him when he was little, beside that enormous body and the heart with its violent and irregular beat.

'Gaspar, your friend is at the door.'

'What friend?'

'Adela, I think.'

'How do you know?'

'She was calling you. She threw something, a pebble, at your window. You dozed off.'

'I'd rather stay here with you.'

'And I'd rather you went. She's waiting for you, go on.'

Gaspar stood up grumpily; he had drifted off, it was true, he could taste the sleep in his mouth. He picked up the Keats book and stood looking at his father from the door. He was going to say something (what? That he loved him?), but his dad had already taken another drink from the bottle, and his eyes were closing.

Adela was waiting in the street; at that hour, on weekend nights, there wasn't much traffic. Any approaching cars could be seen and heard from far enough away that there was no danger, and both kids and adults had gotten in the habit of walking on the sidewalks and streets indiscriminately. She was sitting cross-legged on the pavement with her eyes on the ground. She had changed her clothes, Gaspar noticed; she was wearing her light blue Kickers, burgundy school sweatpants, and a shirt printed with tiny flowers that had ruffles at the waist. Gaspar felt overwhelmed by the silence of the street, and he went over to Adela and gestured with his head for her to walk with him on the sidewalk towards the avenue. She didn't speak, just trotted to keep up, nor did she look at him, so Gaspar decided to start. He didn't like to hold things back, he never had, just as he didn't like evasive looks or uncomfortable silences, the way people – especially adults – would exchange glances and bite their tongues, or the way his father would tell him this is all I'm going to say and you will know nothing more. He felt like if he were ever allowed to talk and ask questions he would never stop; he felt curiosity invading him like ants on a jar of jam left open in the kitchen.

'I'm sorry if you didn't like the box,' said Gaspar. 'I thought maybe it would help you.'

Adela grabbed him by the elbow, hard. Sometimes Gaspar forgot how strong her one hand was.

'It's the best gift anyone's given me in my whole life,' she told him. Her cheeks were flushed from crying.

'Then why'd you get mad? Tell me. If one more person just says "I don't know" . . . I'm sick of it.'

She started walking again. They were getting close to the house on Villarreal, and Gaspar instinctively turned them away from it and towards the small arcade, which was open very late on Sundays.

'I got mad at my mom, not you. Why did she never think of it? Why didn't she ask the doctor? She never believed me that my arm hurt or itched. I wasn't mad at you. Still, you guys took off, you left me alone.'

'We felt weird, and I thought you were mad at me.'

'Not at all. You're the best. I already saw the others and I told them they were chickenshit for leaving.'

Gaspar felt his ears burning. He had liked hearing that

'you're the best'. So he pushed the hair back from his forehead
and said:

'Whenever you need it, I'll help you scratch or massage your
arm, whatever you need. But I won't always be there, sometimes
you'll have to ask your mom.'

'My mom can go to hell. I already asked Pablo and Vicky. If
you'll help me too, I'm good.'

Gaspar had managed to guide Adela away from the house on
Villarreal in a detour that had taken them back to the front door
of his own house. Like everyone else in the neighbourhood, he
felt creeped out by the abandoned house, and he'd already heard
Adela suggest that maybe they could sneak inside. An adven-
ture, a visit to the neighbourhood haunted house. Gaspar didn't
think that sounded at all fun. He was hungry, but he couldn't
invite Adela in to eat: he was forbidden from having guests over
unannounced. The bike locked up to the bars outside gave him
an idea.

'Have you eaten?'

Adela said she wasn't very hungry after the cake and hot
dogs. That's how girls are, thought Gaspar, they don't like to eat:
so weird. He was always hungry, and his guy friends were too.

'Well, if you don't want to eat you can still come with me.
Let's go to Curva, okay?'

'Yeah, I could eat a slice of pizza,' said Adela.

'Hop on.'

Gaspar adjusted his belt: he'd grown thinner and his pants
were falling off him.

'Why don't you buy a belt your own size?' Adela laughed, and
Gaspar said he always forgot.

'It's my dad's, that's why it's so long. Do I look like a clown?'

'No,' she replied. 'I don't know why, but it looks really good
on you.'

Adela climbed on to the footrests on either side of the back wheel. That way she could ride standing up, holding on to Gaspar's shoulder. She asked him to go fast, to pedal hard, and since there was no one in the street, Gaspar did, and he took the long way to the pizzeria so she'd have more time to enjoy the speed and the wind in her hair.

There were many stories about the house on Calle Villarreal, though not all of the stories were told. One day Haydee, the wife of Turi the grocer, had told her customers about the owners. She said they'd been an old couple who lived alone without help from anyone, no nurses, no children around, and they went crazy in there. Old-people crazy: senile dementia. The old lady, when someone went by the house, would go to the window and open her mouth as if she were screaming, but didn't scream. Then she'd run away. Sometimes she was naked. The old man was much more placid, but he refused to take the trash out. One day someone had come – a relative or social worker – and hauled away bags of stuff, mostly rotten food, while the old man sat in the front yard – which in those days had a plant or two – and cried, muttering about how they would find him now, now they would.

Turi said he hadn't heard that story, but he did know that when the old woman had died, they found her in bed with two cat skeletons beside her, one on the sheet, the other on the pillow. The owner of the restaurant in the park mostly corroborated that story, except he was sure the cat skeletons were around the refrigerator, which was full of mould and old cold cuts and unopened loaves of sliced bread.

The strange thing was that none of the old people in the neighbourhood, none of the grandmothers or grandfathers, remembered the owners of the house when they were young.

As if they'd always been old. Or as if they were imaginary. Once, Vicky's grandmother had said: When your grandpa and I came to live here, the owners, who were already old . . . and Vicky had interrupted, almost shouting: But you were young when you got married – they were already living here? And they were already old? Impossible, that's crazy. Her grandmother hesitated and said she thought so, they were already old, yes, maybe they were Polish. What does their being Polish have to do with it? Blond people age badly, replied her grandmother. You won't have to worry about that, Vicky, my pretty little creole girl. Vicky pulled away from her hug, and later, when they talked about it at the table – her grandma had already gone to bed – Hugo Peirano wiped his lips with a napkin and said well, she's getting on in years, old people get confused.

That time Vicky kept quiet and cleared the table – green glass plates and brown cups: the forest table, she called it. She hadn't eaten much. Adela was eating less too. They were both feeling the same thing. They were afraid. The fear was diffuse and Vicky couldn't really tell where it came from, but it had started less than a month earlier, in front of the TV. She was in the living room with her family and the eight o'clock news was on. It was boring – stories about how the radicals had won the legislative elections, about the bomb threats in schools and the state of siege, which was making her mother hysterical – when a story came on that caught her attention: a volcano in Colombia had started to erupt. Vicky both liked and was afraid of volcanoes; for a while she'd been obsessed with Pompeii and Herculaneum. That night was only the eruption, but the next day Vicky sat down on the sofa with Gaspar sprawled beside her to see if they were still talking about the volcano, and what she saw left her speechless and trembling, so much so that she reached for Gaspar's hand. The volcano's lava had swept up ice and mud and all that material had flowed into the rivers, swelling them to four times their size and flooding the nearby towns.

'Oh, I'm terrified of floods,' her grandmother said, and Vicky shushed her.

In a village called Armero, lots of people were trapped inside their houses and waiting to be rescued. But all the cameras, in a shaky transmission with strange colours, were focused on a thirteen-year-old girl named Omaira – what a strange name, thought Vicky – who was half submerged in the rubble and mud; she couldn't move, but she could talk, and when they gave her the microphone, far away in Colombia (where's Colombia? Vicky asked Gaspar, and he told her it was a Caribbean country, but it wasn't an island, it was next to Venezuela), the girl said something that made Vicky feel like running away, and she squeezed Gaspar's arm until she got a 'Hey, quit it' out of him, which was a lot, because nothing ever hurt him. The girl, Omaira, said: 'Under my feet, I can feel my aunt's head'. Her aunt who had drowned, of course, thought Vicky, imagining slippery feet on a dead head while she mechanically adjusted her shoelaces.

They kept showing Omaira for three days, not just on the evening news but also in the afternoon. Vicky saw her when she came back from school and later at night, when she got home from her gymnastics class. Omaira knew they couldn't get her out, but Vicky didn't understand why, and her mother, blunt as only a doctor can be, had told her that the only way would be to amputate her leg, and in that mud they didn't have the right 'sanitary conditions'. Omaira said, I want you to help my mom, because she's going to be left all alone. She said she wanted to go to school. She was afraid because she didn't know how to swim, and if the water rose above her head, she would drown. She sang a song. She wanted to study for a math test. She called out to her mother – who was far away, in Bogotá

– and asked her to pray that she could walk again and that these people could help her. She told her mother she loved her, said she hoped she was listening, and she also said she loved her father. Vicky's grandma said, I can't watch this, that child has such dignity, they shouldn't be showing this, and she left and never sat down again to watch Omaira die.

One of those days when Vicky was watching Omaira's televised agony, Lidia Peirano came in with Juan Peterson, who stayed a while for a cup of tea – he never drank coffee – and Vicky observed him attentively because Gaspar's father almost never came to her house. Her mom held him in high esteem, always insisting he was a good and fascinating guy. That's what she said: 'fascinating'. Vicky knew he and Gaspar fought a lot, and she got angry when she saw her friend sad and, too often, bruised. That evening, though, Gaspar was sitting beside his dad and they were talking in low voices, intermittently, as if they were alone. They weren't alike physically but they shared certain mannerisms: their way of pushing their hair back from their face, how they leaned back on the sofa with their torsos always erect.

'You want something to eat, Juan?'

'Thanks, but I'm not at all hungry.'

Lidia persisted, offering him a pasta frola she'd bought at the bakery, but Gaspar's father refused again. Lidia said:

'These kids are obsessed with that Colombian child, it's awfully morbid. Adela, Betty's girl, doesn't talk about anything else either. I let them watch it because if you forbid it, they just go and watch somewhere else.'

Juan said nothing. They all went quiet in any case because, in Colombia, a doctor was announcing that they'd tried to suction out the mud around Omaira, but unfortunately the gangrene in her legs was too advanced. It's over, poor thing, said Lidia.

She's going to die, sweetie, it's done. Don't watch any more, it's too sad.

But Vicky wanted to watch and she saw the doctor crying, he cried and said this isn't fair, not after we fought so hard and she's held on. And Lidia asked Gaspar's dad: Juan, you remember how years ago there was another case like this with an Italian boy? And he nodded very seriously and said nothing and put an arm around Gaspar's shoulders. Gaspar was now hypnotized by the TV too, because the thing was that Omaira was about to die on camera and they were going to broadcast her death, they weren't going to let her spend even that moment alone. Omaira took up the whole full-colour screen and she was clear, no ghosting or static: her eyes were totally black, no irises or whites, her eyelids swollen, and her hands holding on to a piece of wood were disproportionately large and very white, too white, already dead, not like the skin of her face, which was still dark and pretty. Her hands looked like they were covered in wax; it's from being underwater too long, thought Vicky, they get like that, wrinkled and whitish, but they still looked strange. Why are her eyes all black? Vicky asked her mom, who only replied, I'm going to turn it off, okay? It's an abomination they're showing that on TV. But she didn't turn it off, she stood there watching too as the girl agonized in her grave of mud and filth, her legs trapped and her feet resting atop her dead aunt's head.

It was Juan, who hardly ever spoke, who answered the question about the eyes. It's blood, he said suddenly. Her eyes are full of blood. It's not circulating through her body any more and it accumulates there. Vicky looked at her mother for confirmation and Lidia said yes, it's something like that. If it were dilated pupils, she wouldn't be able to hold on any more, she wouldn't have the strength. And then she kept her word: she turned off the TV. Enough. You'll never get that image out of your heads if you keep watching.

Vicky protested and went into her room with Gaspar and the phone, which had a very long cord so it could be moved around. She called Adela, who was also watching Omaira die. Pablo was with her because they hadn't let him watch at home. Why does your mom let you? Vicky wanted to know, and Adela replied from the other end of the line: She's not here, she went out for a while. Maybe she wouldn't let me. You guys want to come over?

'Do you want to?' Vicky asked Gaspar, and, after thinking about it, he said no.

'You go if you want.'

'I'm going, of course. Why don't you want to?'

Gaspar was silent a moment and then said:

'Did you see the part when she said, like, she asked the people to go and rest and then come back and get her out? She was already pretty out of it, hallucinating, I think, but it was like she was asking them to leave her alone, right?'

'But she can't see us, we're far away, we're not bothering her.'

'How do you know we're not bothering her?'

'You're so weird.'

And Vicky went running to Adela's, despite her mother's threats, to watch Omaira's last gasps in high definition and full detail. She, Pablo, and Adela cried together, holding hands in front of the TV. Betty never came home to stop them. Adela said later that the worst part had been the noises at the end, that painful gurgling, like a whining dog. Is that how people die? she asked, and the others didn't know how to answer. Pablo said he was never, ever going to forget those hands, which were grey and looked like a bird's claws; he'd also been afraid of her eyes full of blood. For Vicky it was the feet, her dying feet touching a lifeless head in the mud, losing feeling in her feet but knowing they were still resting on a rotting thing. Never again was she able to sleep with her feet hanging off the bed, never again could she sleep without wearing socks, and the nights when she collapsed exhausted into bed after a lot of studying or stress, she tended to dream of Omaira in the water, clutching a branch, sticking out her tongue at Vicky, a tongue that was as black as her eyes while she died there in the mud.

Hugo Peirano managed to finish the pool he'd promised his daughters just before Christmas. They couldn't use it on Christmas Eve because they had to wait until its paint was dry and it was filled and they were sure the filter worked, but they got to celebrate New Year's Eve in the water: Hugo carried a glass of champagne out to the pool while Vicky and Virginia did cannonballs, ate nuts, and waited for the fireworks. Vicky didn't want to get in the water barefoot: she had bought some plastic sandals because the floor of the pool could be slippery and it reminded her of Omaira standing on her aunt's head and all that deathly mud in Colombia.

At the pool's inauguration on New Year's, after the midnight toast, Gaspar, Pablo, and Adela came over. Gaspar and Pablo swam, Adela only ventured into the shallow end, and Vicky floated on her back. After everyone else went to set off bottle rockets in the street, Gaspar and Pablo remained in the water, dunking each other, holding their breath underwater, and, especially, play-fighting until they set the dogs barking (a new puppy had arrived since Diana's death). Vicky didn't understand why they'd started horsing around all the time, especially in this heat. With Gaspar she could understand it a little more – he was strong and tough and almost always won, and by then she knew boys liked to win at anything. But Pablo, who was as tall and thin as Gaspar, was not as strong, and sometimes she could tell he was suffering when Gaspar sat on his back on the floor or twisted his arm. In sum: she didn't understand why they hit each other if they weren't mad, and they clearly weren't mad; on the contrary, they got along better than ever.

That summer was strange for her. She was afraid, and didn't know why. She had told her mother: sometimes she was so scared that when she took a deep breath, she felt like her lungs wouldn't fill up all the way. It had been a mistake to say that to her mom, who had listened to her chest and then taken her to the hospital so she could breathe into a kind of whistle – they called it a 'spirograph' – and when everything came back normal, there was a long conversation about whether she should go to a psychologist or not, which was resolved, for the moment, with 'wait and see' and 'she's at that age'. Vicky knew her age had nothing to do with it. She couldn't explain what it was that seemed so threatening and that at the same time obsessed her. It was Omaira, a little, but not just Omaira. Vicky was scared of seeing her in the dark, but it went beyond the black-eyed girl. If she had to pee at night she didn't dare get out of bed, but at the same time she could spend hours listening to every sound in the house and waiting for that one different noise, the one that would finally prove there was a presence, a hand that intentionally messed up the books and dishes, something black that floated up by the ceiling and could come down at any minute to show its face.

And then there was the buzzing, so loud on some nights. At first, she'd thought it was flickering streetlights, or maybe the fluorescent tube in the garage or some new electric wires in the neighbourhood, but it grew deeper and more intense with the heat and it seemed to come from the ground. She'd asked her dad if the subway passed nearby, but he said no, that although there was a station six blocks away, the train turned in the opposite direction when it reached the park, it didn't even come close to them, and it would be impossible or very strange for them to feel any vibration. Plus, how dumb of me, thought Vicky, the subway doesn't run at night. One hot evening, to check if the buzzing really did come from the ground, as it seemed to, Vicky went outside to touch the asphalt. Her parents and grandmother were sitting in the garage after dinner; the house was almost cool there, maybe because the ceiling was higher, or maybe because for half the day it didn't get any sun. They were sitting on chairs around a standing fan – the opposite of a bonfire – and chatting apathetically. It wasn't coming from the ground. She had mentioned the matter again to her father after the subway theory was ruled out; he told her it must be the racetrack. You're so sensitive, honey! Victoria was familiar with the hum of the racetrack; it only happened on Sunday mornings, and it was distant and came in waves. The nocturnal buzzing had nothing to do with car races. And anyway, there were no races at night. She didn't talk about it again with her family. When they saw her go out to the sidewalk and crouch down in the middle of the street, they peered at her with lazy curiosity; at some point her grandma called out: Careful of cars!

Adela found her there in the street when she and Betty were on their way home from the pizzeria. Vicky hadn't told her friends about the buzzing, not yet: she was afraid to name it, because that was like admitting it really existed. Now she told Adela, and Adela started looking all around as if the buzzing could be seen, as if it were a shadow in the air. Betty made Adela go home with her so they could eat the pizza, but afterwards she let her meet back up with Vicky. It was summer. In those months, Betty was more permissive.

'I think it comes from the house,' said Adela. 'The house around the block, on Villarreal.'

Vicky saw herself reflected in Adela's pupils, and the fear she already felt, the fear that never left her, intensified as if it were being injected straight into her veins.

'You already knew!' Adela said triumphantly. 'Let's go see if it's coming from there.' And she grabbed Vicky by the arm. Vicky thought: I don't know her. I don't know who this girl is.

'No. I'm afraid of it. Let go!'

She didn't have to fight. Adela let go of her immediately. Vicky saw sweat beading on her forehead. Nothing strange about that, with the heat.

'See?' said Adela. 'That house is scary. You know the things they say, right? If you go in and sleep there, you start to think there are a bunch of pictures around you. Portraits. Weird, you think, but since it's dark and there's no light, you can't see them well. Plus, the house makes you sleepy. Once, my mom took me to a healer, and she also made me sleepy.'

'She took you to a healer? Why?'

'I don't really remember, but I think I couldn't sleep at night, so that lady made me sleep. Anyway, so you sleep in the house and when you wake up, in the daylight, you see that there are no portraits around you.'

'So?'

'So, if they weren't portraits, the faces were people, dummy. People who watch you while you sleep!'

Vicky felt like crying and Adela seemed to realize, but didn't stop. As if she were angry, as if she were punishing Vicky.

'Didn't you ever see, when you walk past, the old woman with her mouth open in the window?'

'No one lives in that house,' said Vicky in a quiet voice. 'And the windows are all bricked up.'

'Maybe the old lady sneaks in, right? And how do you know no one lives there? Sometimes people live in abandoned houses. Bums. There are people living in the refrigerator cemetery, too. Gaspar doesn't want to go with me. You think he'd take me to the house on Villarreal? It's what I want more than anything in the world.'

'I don't know,' replied Vicky, and she told Adela that now she had to go eat dinner. As she ran to her house, she felt like her throat was closing off, and yet also like the idea of that abandoned house was growing in some part of her head, the idea of following that buzzing sound and confirming that it came from there, a colony of insects, an ant hill, flies rubbing their legs together as though planning an attack before assailing a piece of rotten meat.

It was two days after New Year's, most shops in the neighbourhood and on the avenue were closed for the holidays, and Gaspar knew that he wasn't going on vacation with Vicky that summer. The Peiranos would be leaving in ten days, going by van to stay in a cabin on the outskirts of Esquel until early February. The unusual thing was that Betty and Adela were going with them, and weren't spending the summer at Adela's grandparents' country house as they usually did. They had rented the van so they could all ride together. Vicky and Adela had talked to him about Patagonia, the forests, the desert, the lakes, and Gaspar felt a stab of envy, but his father had asked him – hadn't ordered or forced him: it was a request – to stay home with him. Gaspar understood immediately. His father hardly slept and barely ate and had trouble getting to the bathroom: he had to stop several times to catch his breath when he walked there. Then he'd spend a long time in the bathtub, and he let Gaspar talk to him while he lay back in the warm water with the door half-open. During those days of heat and illness, they got along very badly and very well. On one of the doctor's visits Gaspar had overheard her tell his dad he needed to be hospitalized, that it was madness to stay at home, and his father had sensed he was listening because next came the slammed door and later, when the doctor was gone, a slap that made his lips bleed, and the warning to 'never, ever eavesdrop on me'. He slept with oxygen every night and let his beard grow out, and he almost never put down his notebook, where he sketched symbols that Gaspar didn't dare try to get a look at. One morning, he had found his father in the bathroom trying to shave, his hands trembling and a cut on his cheek that was bleeding, and Gaspar felt with blunt certainty that these were his final days. Instead of getting scared and crying – that's what he wanted to do, beg him to get better, wail that he didn't know how to be alone – he went into the bathroom, took the razor from his hand, and cleaned his chin first with a towel, then with alcohol.

'You're half-finished,' he said. 'I don't know how to shave, but I'll try if you want.'

His dad said it didn't matter, but Gaspar insisted: you have half a beard, it's a mess. And he helped him stand up and get to his bed.

Another night, lying back on the pillows, Juan told him:

'Your uncle Luis is coming back sometime in the next few months.'

Gaspar had talked to his uncle over the phone on his birthday and also at New Year's: just recently he'd received his yearly gifts, always two: this time it was a box with four toy cars from the Chevrolet Bel Air 1957 collection and a robot watch; but no gift was ever going to beat the Scalextric from two years ago that was in the garage. The news surprised him.

'He didn't say anything to me.'

'He just decided. He and his wife are separating. He was always planning to come back when the dictatorship ended.'

'He's a little late.'

Juan smiled.

'He wanted to come back with his wife, but he couldn't convince her. Now he's coming alone.'

'Is he going to visit us?'

'He's going to stay here. We have to start the process for him to adopt you when I die.'

'I don't want him to adopt me, you're not going to die.'

'Son, don't talk nonsense. Wise up a little.'

Gaspar crossed his arms, a bit offended, but decided not to respond. I'm going to make something to eat, he said. His father answered by closing his eyes. Gaspar glanced over to be sure he had oxygen and went to the kitchen. Minutes later, when he opened the refrigerator, he felt his father calling him in his whole body. He would never be able to explain how it felt; it was something like the moment you realize you've lost your wallet or that the teacher has found your cheat sheet, an alarm under your skin and in your throat. He went running back upstairs and found his dad sitting on the bed, pale and shining with sweat. He was struggling to take in air and Gaspar could hear the rattle in his lungs, a whistling noise of suffocation. He knew what was happening, it had happened before and he had to act fast, with the full emergency plan that he, his father, and the doctor had designed, a series of steps he had to follow in order and without losing his calm. First, though, he went over to his dad and took his face in his hands.

'Take it easy,' he told him as he brought the oxygen closer. Had he not been able to get up to reach it? That was very worrying. Juan obeyed and put on the mask. Gaspar ran to the bathroom to get a towel and dry his sweat a little, especially on his chest and forehead. Only then did he follow the plan. First, call Dr Biedma. She always answered right away, as if she knew who was calling, and she would arrive, if needed, in minutes. She lived close by, but Gaspar had never seen her around the neighbourhood. Maybe she worked all day. Next, call the lawyers: he had to let them know his father was having a crisis. Then, call Esteban. This call was harder for Gaspar to make, because of what it meant. Once, his dad had told him: 'If I die, he's the only one who knows what to do with you and with me.' Esteban took a little longer to answer than the others.

'Can he talk?' he asked.

Gaspar looked at his father, sitting up with his eyes closed and his breathing making that desperate, wet rattle.

'No,' he said.

'I'll wait for you at the hospital, then.'

And he hung up. Gaspar sat beside his father and took his hand, which was trembling. He couldn't do anything more than stay there and not let him lie down, because if he did it was worse, he couldn't breathe at all. His fingertips were already blue. Gaspar concentrated on listening for the ambulance, which always came fast, the wait never reached five minutes. Everything was well organized. Doctor Biedma said they needed a permanent nurse and Gaspar agreed, but he'd heard his father say, very calmly, If you bring in a nurse you know what I'm capable of.

Gaspar knew what the coming days would be like: fifteen minutes at noon and fifteen more in the evening visiting in intensive care; wait for his dad to be moved into a general room, and then the slow recovery and the bad mood. He would feel like he was living inside a plastic bubble, isolated, able to hear and see everything, but floating, as if he were tiptoeing and his body were lighter and he had to make an effort not to lose his balance. He stroked his father's back. He felt a pain in his throat as though he were trying swallow a nut whole, and then he heard the ambulance's motor: it never arrived with the siren blaring.

'I'll be right back,' he said, and he ran downstairs to open the door for the doctor and the medics. They rushed up the stairs while Gaspar waited outside. He didn't want to hear or see any more. It would be enough to go with his dad in the ambulance, the cables, the machines, the explanations from doctors who treated him like he was stupid, the dash inside, the uncomfortable hospital chairs.

They arrived very fast because it was night time and the hospital was nearby. Gaspar rode up front with the driver; they wouldn't let him ride with his dad, and he didn't argue. He jumped out as soon as they pulled up, but the stretcher was carried in at a run and the doors closed in his face; he had to push them open to get in, and then he found himself alone. He didn't know which corridor his father had gone down or if they'd taken him in the elevator, and he unconsciously brought his hands to his eyes; the fluorescent light hurt, the flowerpots with their plastic flowers bothered him, the laminate floor, the smell of disinfectant, the people with exhausted expressions on that hot early morning. No one came near him until he heard Esteban's soothing voice very close:

'Gaspar, I'm here. We have to wait on the third floor.

They rode the elevator up in silence. Esteban's hair was tousled and his shirt wrinkled. They reached the small waiting room for intensive care and Gaspar watched the green-clad nurses go in and out for hours, until finally Dr Biedma appeared, with her short hair and white uniform. She seemed calm, and before looking at Gaspar, she nodded a 'yes' to Esteban. Gaspar spoke before she did.

'Can I see him now?'

'Not now. Tomorrow. He's sedated, resting. Gaspar, your dad had an acute pulmonary oedema. Do you know what that is or should I explain?'

'I know what it is, he had one before and you explained. I don't forget things.'

And then she turned to Esteban and told him that Juan was in serious condition, that luckily – Gaspar clung to that 'luckily' – it was caused by an arrhythmia, that he had decompensated heart failure, and that they were going to try some new drugs. Then, with a familiarity that surprised Gaspar – they knew each other that well? – she rested a hand on Esteban's shoulder and said: You two don't need to stay here, but go somewhere with a phone. Esteban replied that they would be at Juan's house. Before Dr Biedma went back into the treatment room, she told Gaspar: You did very well, dear. You were calm and, especially, very fast.

'You just said it was serious.'

'Your dad's condition is very serious, Gaspar, but he could be dead.'

Gaspar had crossed his arms and was looking at the doctor with an anger he didn't understand, a rage he could barely contain; he didn't want to keep talking. He followed Esteban to his car, a grey Mercedes. The hospital parking garage was immense and the sound of the keys echoed. Esteban had hardly spoken to him in the waiting room, though they had been there for hours. He never did say much to him. Gaspar settled into the front seat and thought about how little he knew about his father's best friend. He worked at the Spanish consulate; Esteban had once explained that a consulate was like an embassy, only less important. His father and Esteban had met in Europe, when his mother was studying in England. He didn't have family, wasn't married. And that was all Gaspar knew about him.

'Why don't we go to your house?' he asked.

Esteban started the car, lit a cigarette, and said: 'Because your dad doesn't want you to know where I live.'

The sincerity of the answer surprised Gaspar; he sat looking at Esteban, who was smoking and in no hurry to put the car in motion.

'Really?'

'Does that surprise you? Let's go. To your house, then.'

Day had already broken and Gaspar shaded his eyes from the sun: he hadn't eaten in hours, and that could give him a headache. He said as much to Esteban, who quickly parked in front of a diner to have breakfast. He doesn't know what to do with me, thought Gaspar, and he's very worried. Though he was hungry, it was hard to choke down the croissant. I hope he dies, he thought. I hope Dad dies once and for all and puts an end to all this and I can live with my uncle or with Vicky or alone in the house and I don't ever have to think again about locked rooms, voices in my head, dreams of hallways and dead people, ghost families, boxes full of eyelids, blood on the floor, where he goes when he leaves, where he's coming from when he returns, I wish I could stop loving him, forget him, I wish he'd die. The croissant hurt going down. Esteban downed his coffee in one gulp and smoked another cigarette. He paid without calling the waiter over, leaving the money on the table, and he signalled to Gaspar to get in the car and wait for him: he had to make a phone call from the café's public phone. He must be calling work, thought Gaspar, or maybe he was letting someone know about his dad? There was no time to figure it out: Esteban came back to the car quickly, after a conversation of only a couple of minutes. They got home equally fast: there was little traffic, but also Esteban drove with precision and a certain risky brutality that Gaspar loved. They still weren't speaking. But once they were inside, Esteban said:

'Sleep for a while, I'll wake you up if anyone calls.'

'Why don't you talk like an Argentine?' asked Gaspar while he took off his sneakers. He wasn't tired.

'I could never get used to using "vos". Some of the turns of phrase escape me, or mix together, rather. You and I never have talked much.'

'Why not?'

'Because you're a child. I don't get along with kids.'

Gaspar nodded, and then said:

'I don't believe you. Well, maybe you don't like kids, but I'm not a kid. He doesn't want you to talk to me. I know it. I don't understand why, but I can tell.'

Esteban seemed unruffled. Gaspar kicked off his sneakers and ran barefoot across the living room to his bedroom. He sat on his bed. He wasn't going to be able to sleep. He didn't know what to do. Esteban appeared in the doorway of his room: he'd followed him.

'You have a lot of albums,' he said.

'I bought a record player for Christmas. Some of the records are mine, but most are my mom's.'

'You want to listen to some music?'

Gaspar tried to stay offended, but Esteban seemed uncomfortable too, and he was trying to be nice. This isn't his fault, thought Gaspar. It's because of Dad and his craziness.

'I haven't been able to try out the speakers yet because the music bothers Dad, he doesn't like it or something. Was he always like that?'

Esteban sat on the floor, picked up half of the pile of albums, and set them on his crossed legs. He's much younger than he looks, thought Gaspar.

'There was a time when your mother and I used to listen to a lot of music. She was the one who bought records and went to concerts. He always preferred silence, and since she's been gone, well, music reminds him of her, I guess. You know which songs were your mom's favourites?'

'She marked some of them. Dad doesn't tell me anything.'

Esteban looked through the pile of records and put a few chosen ones beside him, on the floor. Gaspar pointed to one: *The Rise and Fall of Ziggy Stardust and the Spiders from Mars.*

'I love that album. She marked it up a lot.'

'This musician was a friend of your mom's. Friends, well, as much as we could be in those years, but they knew each other. Then he got famous and they didn't see each other any more.'

'I don't think he's very well known here.'

Esteban put on a Led Zeppelin album.

'When your mom liked a song a lot, like this one, she'd play it over and over until it drove us crazy.'

Gaspar looked at the marks beside the title. There were about ten exclamation points, in red.

'I don't do that,' said Gaspar. 'I don't know if I like music that much. Is that weird? I like movies better. Or books. You?'

'Music? Not so much.'

'What do you like?'

Esteban thought for a moment.

'Houses,' he said. 'Architecture.'

'Like my uncle.'

'Wow, look at this. I sent this one to your mom from Barcelona when it came out. You must have been less than a year old. I don't know how it made it safe and sound.'

'You sent it through the mail?'

'With some other things.'

'My friend Vicky's mom likes Serrat a lot.'

'And you don't.'

'It's a little boring.'

'*Very* boring. This album has a really pretty song, though, one of your mom's favourites. If you get bored we'll put on another one.'

Esteban lingered over several covers, but he seemed surprised when he got to *Space Oddity*.

'Mom marked everything on that one. See, she made notes beside every song title.'

'Can you read English yet?'

'Yeah, but those words are hard to read.'

Esteban translated the title – 'The Wild Eyed Boy from Freecloud'. 'Let's listen to it.'

Gaspar tried to understand the story, but even with Esteban's help it was hard. A young man was hanged, and he went smiling to the gallows. 'And the day will end for some / As the night begins for one / ... Oh, "It's the madness in his eyes" ...' He saw Esteban shake his head and flip the record to play another song. 'Letter To Hermione'.

'Is that for his girlfriend?'

'That's right, and a real girlfriend, too. A beautiful girl. Do you have a girlfriend yet, Gaspar?'

'I had one, but I didn't fall in love or anything.'

'How's that?'

'When I think about her, I don't get sad like that, like in the song. The song is nice but I don't really like the instruments.'

'It hasn't aged well. There are a lot of musicians who should re-record their entire catalogues. Anyway, it's always sad to fall in love.'

'What about you?'

'I don't have anyone, no.'

'Do you want to?'

'No, it's too complicated.'

'Is it complicated because of the stuff people say and all that? Do they treat you bad? Dad says it's all prejudice and people are stupid.'

'I don't care about what people say, but falling in love is just awful, Gaspar. You're right about that.'

'Aren't you in love with my dad?'

Esteban smiled. He didn't seem surprised. It had been hard for Gaspar to ask the question, so hard he'd had to squeeze his fists and look out the window.

'What do you mean? No.'

'But there's something there. I'd like it if he, I don't know, I don't like that he's alone.'

Esteban looked at him directly, but said nothing.

'Did my mom like this song a lot?'

'She also liked happier things. Let's see what we have here.'

They listened for two hours. The Rolling Stones, the Beatles – which seemed to Gaspar like kids' music, and he said so to Esteban, who nodded and said then let's move on to more serious things – Donovan, Leonard Cohen, Bob Dylan, Pink Floyd, Janis Joplin, Jimi Hendrix, more Led Zeppelin, Caetano Veloso, Maria Bethânia. Gaspar lay down still dressed while Esteban played songs, and at some point he asked him to turn it down because he'd started to yawn. Gaspar closed his eyes listening to a woman singing in Portuguese: *Para além dos braços de Iemanjá/Adeus, adeus . . .*

The days passed as they usually did when his dad was in the hospital; Gaspar felt free and worried, feelings that, he intuited, should not go together. The short visits, Juan half-upright and drowsy, the moans of other patients, washing his hands before entering, and listening to the doctor, before and after, saying the same thing as always: The first twenty-four hours are the most crucial, we're trying a new medication, et cetera. After the first visit, Esteban dropped him off at Vicky's house. What's going to happen when they go on vacation? he asked. They're leaving in ten days, more or less. Adela and Betty are going with them. What happens if Dad hasn't gotten out of the hospital? He will, Esteban said. Gaspar didn't argue. He spent the day with Vicky and her little sister Virginia, who had received a simple Christmas gift, a plastic toy shaped like a magnifying glass but without a lens, which, along with a little bucket of soapy water, was used to make bubbles. Now she spent all her time blowing bubbles in the yard, under the dogs' curious gazes.

Gaspar went to the hospital every day: sometimes Esteban came to pick him up, sometimes Vicky's mom took him, sometimes his dad's driver came. He wanted to go alone, but they wouldn't let him, at least not until his dad was better. Esteban was quite clear: you're my responsibility and I'm not going to let you out in the streets alone. I don't care if you're a bicycle king.

On the fifth day, the doctor moved his dad to the general ward, and Gaspar prepared himself for the coming demands to leave the hospital. Juan hated the beds, too short for his height, hated the discomfort and the schedules and the noises; it all made him so nervous that on several occasions they'd decided to discharge him just because the stress was keeping him from improving. But Dr Biedma was disciplined and turned a deaf ear to whims. You're going to stay, it's not your decision, she told him, and Gaspar pretended to be looking out the window so his dad wouldn't see him smile.

Gaspar respected the visiting hours, the daily schedules, because spending any more time at the hospital was boring. Esteban had taken care of bringing clothes to Juan, as well as the books and notebooks he wanted and needed, so all that remained for Gaspar was to wait.

'You don't need to come every day,' his father told him on one visit. 'Stay at your friend's house, play. They have a pool, right?'

'I already went swimming today. It's really sunny out, it gave me a headache. Can I lie down here a while?'

As always, his father wasn't sharing the room, so there was another bed, made and empty. Esteban slept there some nights. On other nights, a hired nurse stayed so he wouldn't be left alone, or even Dr Biedma herself, who, in crisis situations, was exclusively dedicated to his father. They must pay her a fortune, Gaspar thought.

His father's attitude changed and he motioned Gaspar closer.

'Why didn't you tell me?'

'It's just starting, it's only in my eye, if I sleep it'll pass.'

Juan rang the bell beside him, above the pillow, to call the nurse. The woman, dressed in light blue scrubs, came immediately. My son has a migraine, he said, and asked for a painkiller; she left and came back with a glass of water and a pill. She also handed Gaspar a damp, very cold cloth for his forehead. Gaspar put it over his head like a hood, and the nurse smiled on her way out.

'Go on, use the other bed.'

Instead, Gaspar sat on Juan's bed and carefully touched his father's hand. There were IV tubes stuck into both arms and the skin was mottled with bruises, some of them already turning green. Gaspar adjusted the cold cloth on his head and studied his dad's face, which looked more tired than ever; he saw how the hard plastic oxygen tube was irritating the delicate skin of his nose. He was surprised when the hand he was stroking withdrew, took him by the back of the neck, and gently pulled him down. Gaspar lay against his father's shoulder. He didn't get up when Esteban came in; with the extreme sensitivity that accompanied his migraines, he smelled the faint odour of cigarettes. The painkiller made him doze off a little, and he only woke up when Esteban picked him up and carried him to the other bed, laying him on the hard mattress with his head on the pillow.

He didn't sleep right away: he wanted to enjoy the coolness of the pillow. And, as though in a dream, he heard Esteban and his father talking.

I've gotten what I needed, and I also know what the necessary sacrifice is.

The effort almost killed you.

I got it, it was finally given to me. In the coming days I hope to complete the sign alone.

'What sacrifice?' asked Gaspar, and the two men stared at him open-mouthed, with a surprise that made them look very young and far removed from the exhaustion, the oxygen, the hospital at dusk. Their faces held an almost comical astonishment.

'You heard?' Esteban asked.

'I'm not asleep,' Gaspar laughed.

'Shit,' said Juan.

'Did you know about this?' Esteban asked.

'Are you joking? Of course not. Fix it.'

'Easy for you to say. Fix it. Sure.'

'What are you talking about? What sacrifice?'

Esteban got up and came over to Gaspar. He patted his shirt pocket automatically for a cigarette, then clucked his tongue when he remembered there was no smoking in the room.

'Your idiot father is talking nonsense about how your uncle is going to have to take care of you when he moves on to a better world, the sacrifice he'll have to make. Listen, I've known him for twenty years now and he's been dying that whole time, so the sacrifice will be all ours, because we'll have to keep putting up with him.'

Gaspar laughed. He was a little high from the painkiller.

'We'll have to be more careful for a few days,' said Esteban. 'Fuck.'

Gaspar dived in, and in five strokes he'd reached the other side. The Peiranos' pool was great for cooling off, but no good for swimming. He'd have to wait until they opened the one at the club, in March, before he could swim again for real. All four of them were in the pool: Pablo submerged up to his neck, Vicky on a float with her plastic sandals, Adela walking in the shallow end in a fuchsia one-piece suit.

'She was really scared,' Adela said. 'but I brought her there anyway. The house is different during the day. And I swear the buzzing she hears comes from there.'

'Maybe it's a generator, there are a lot of blackouts,' offered Gaspar.

'What's a generator?'

'It's like a motor that gives electricity, some stores have them so their food doesn't rot when the electricity goes out. Since the house is abandoned, maybe someone put one in the yard.'

Pablo went underwater to wet his hair and get it out of his face. It was long and very curly.

'If you girls want to go in so bad, why don't you just do it already?' he asked.

'We're scared to go alone,' said Vicky.

Gaspar sighed.

'Your heads are full of the stuff people in the neighbourhood say about the house.'

285

'You're not scared?' Adela asked. 'My mom says it's weird that you're not scared of it.'

'I'm a little scared,' he said. 'The stories have gotten to me too.'

'What've you heard about it?' Vicky wanted to know.

'There are lots of stories,' said Pablo. 'My mom says the owners boarded up the house because they didn't want anyone going inside, because horrible things happened to them in there. She wouldn't tell me what the horrible things were.'

'Adela doesn't hear the buzzing,' said Vicky. 'But it's evil. Seriously evil. It's not a generator. It's something alive. Sometimes it's like it's singing. None of you have heard it?'

Pablo and Gaspar replied honestly that they hadn't. Plus, Gaspar thought, even if he had heard something he wouldn't admit it in front of Adela. He didn't want to encourage her any further.

Gaspar got out of the pool and didn't take the towel Pablo offered him. He liked to let the sun dry him off.

'I'll go with you,' he said. 'Once my dad gets out of the hospital.'

Adela started jumping up and down in the water, so fiercely happy, it was as if she'd just won an amazing prize. As if she'd been informed that, thanks to a newly discovered medical advance, she could now get her arm back.

'We're leaving on vacation in a few days,' said Vicky. 'Is your dad going to get out soon?'

'I don't know. We'll do it when you get back if he doesn't.'

'I'll go too,' said Pablo.

'But you're scared.'

'We're all scared,' sighed Pablo. 'I think if we don't go inside that house, the fear will never go away.'

*

Juan had spent ten days in the hospital and had recovered faster than the doctor expected, a nurse had told him. By now he was itching to leave, and he'd told Gaspar that they would be spending a few days at a country house that year. Whose house? Gaspar wanted to know. Technically, your mom's. Actually, technically yours. Your maternal family's. I thought you didn't get along with them, Gaspar said, and his father replied, That's true, we don't get along at all, that's why we never see them, but they're not going to refuse me a place to recover. Esteban would be going with them, and maybe Tali too. It had been a long time since Gaspar had seen Tali; she called on the phone often, but his father always locked himself in to talk to her. Dr Biedma would check on him every day and there would be a full-time nurse. There's a pool, said Juan, and horses, too. The caretaker can teach you to ride. Gaspar liked the idea. His father had moved on from the moment of warmth they'd shared on the day of his headache, and he was treating everyone badly. Gaspar was used to it, but he preferred to keep his distance. How he hated those movies and TV shows with heroic patients who bore their suffering in silence and inspired others. He'd been around hospitals and illness enough to know that most sick people were bossy and mean and tried to make the people around them feel just as bad as they did.

The last thing he remembered was the car. Getting into the car with the driver, Dr Biedma, and Esteban. He had asked about his father: Juan was riding in another car, alone with the nurse, so he'd be more comfortable. Gaspar thought that was strange, but he was used to accepting strange things. He wanted to know how long it would be to Chascomús, and they told him it was less than two hours. And as they left the city, he fell asleep.

Now he was waking up in an unfamiliar bed, a double bed in

a very large room that, when he turned his head to get a good look, started to spin; the dizziness forced him to lie still, face up. This pain was different: it wasn't a migraine, it came from outside, two iron hooks in his temples, and then he realized he was naked under the blanket and sheets. A blanket in the middle of summer? Weren't they going to Chascomús? It wasn't far, the weather shouldn't change. He pulled off the covers and tried to focus: this wasn't a normal kind of dizziness, it was more like the time he and Pablo had gotten drunk on coffee liqueur. That time, he'd thrown up and Pablo had laughed and then started crying and ended up vomiting too. It was better if he didn't turn his head: he'd learned that much. The pain was intense, but in no way worse than what he already knew how to endure.

His arms were covered with bruises. Of all sizes, but, between his shoulders and elbows, bruises without a doubt caused by hands: someone had grabbed him. Someone had held him.

against the floor, no, against a table, a dark table, several hands while he struggled, what were they trying to do to him? – he couldn't remember, but he remembered the hands

One of the hand-shaped bruises looked a lot like the mark, the burn, that his father had on his arm. It was in almost the same place. It's his hand, thought Gaspar, those are his fingers, I know them.

it's not just that I recognize them, I feel them, it's his hand, he tried to hold me down, too, why did he want to stop me, where was I trying to run

He almost screamed when he saw the rest of his body, his chest, his stomach. It was covered in scratches and bruises; he didn't understand what could have hurt him like that. He wasn't bleeding, because someone had cleaned his wounds, and anyway, they weren't very deep. Scrapes. Fingernails? Had he been trapped somewhere, and these injuries came from when he'd been yanked out? What about the blows to his chest and ribs?

I have to run, he thought. I'm naked because they don't want me to run, but I don't care about being embarrassed, I have to get out. Kidnapped, maybe. He didn't recognize anything in the room, and his clothes weren't there. But neither was he tied up. He got out of bed, and no sooner did his foot touch the floor than the door was unlocked – he heard the key turn – and his father entered, Dr Biedma behind him.

And then the certainty came, clear as the knowledge that he had five fingers on each hand or that teeth are used for chewing or that it is cooler in the shade than in the sun. He only had to look at his father to know he was responsible, he was the one who'd attacked him. He hadn't been kidnapped by strangers. He couldn't remember why, couldn't imagine why, but it was the truth: his father had hurt him. Now, he looked satisfied. It had been a long time since Gaspar had seen that expression, his mouth relaxed and smiling.

He tried, first of all, to get back in bed, though he wasn't embarrassed by the doctor seeing him naked. The window was close, but there were bars over it. If he was going to escape, it would have to be through the door, passing between his father and the doctor. He thought he should try to be smart about it, talk to them, deceive them, and only once he got out start to run. But something very primal was screaming that there was danger, and his whole body tensed up in fear and anticipation.

He leapt from the bed, but it was a useless movement and he knew it, they would cut him off. He had to try, though, even if he had to bite his way out. But he couldn't stand: the pain in one of his feet sent him to his knees. Only then did he see his ankle was swollen up like a tennis ball. It was a sprain; he knew because he'd seen soccer teammates who had them, and also, if it were broken, it would have a cast. He heard the doctor say, He's scared; she tried to get him back into bed and Gaspar resisted like a cat, wriggling out from under her and then attacking her face directly. She had to use all her strength, which, Gaspar noticed, was considerable, to sit him down. Be still or I'll have to put you to sleep, she told him. And then she started to explain what had happened – she spoke calmly and with long pauses, trying to get him to meet her eyes – but Gaspar didn't look at her, he looked at his father, whose arms were crossed with a frightening serenity. Why didn't he come closer? Why didn't he intervene? The doctor was still talking and now Gaspar did start to listen, because it was better to know, it was always better to know. She was explaining, patiently, that he was hurt because he'd had an accident. A car accident, two days ago, when they were on the way from the hospital to this estate. We're at the house, she explained. The vacation house you and your dad were coming to: our car crashed on the way. Esteban is hurt too, but not as badly as you are. I wasn't hurt. In any case, you don't have any fractures or significant trauma, although, since you hit your head, we had to leave you under observation at the hospital.

I wasn't at any hospital, said Gaspar. She insisted: Yes, you were. You don't remember the accident or being hospitalized. It's common to have periods of amnesia after a concussion, even a slight one. It's possible the memory will come back to you gradually, or that you'll never remember.

Gaspar stared at the doctor and then at his father, who didn't seem troubled. He felt the humiliation filling his cheeks with blood.

You're telling me I have amnesia like we're in a soap opera. You're treating me like I'm stupid. Then he pointed a finger at his father, who remained impassive. It was you, he shouted. You did this to me.

His father finally spoke. Slowly, like the doctor. The scrapes are from when we pulled you from the car. The bruises are from the crash. I wasn't driving, I didn't hurt you.

You're lying, said Gaspar, and he got out of bed again. Putting weight on his foot was terrible, but he tried. He took three steps; the doctor, following an order from his father – a slight hand movement – let him go. Gaspar hopped to the door; outside, in the hallway, Esteban was waiting. He had a bandage around his neck, and his right arm – he was wearing a dark short-sleeved shirt – was covered in bloody scrapes. When he saw that, Gaspar hesitated: what if it was true about the accident? No. Amnesia, they'd said. He wouldn't let them lie to him like that, it was ridiculous. He acted fast: on one side, the hallway led to more bedrooms, but to his right there was light – a yard? He ran towards it. Now it didn't hurt to take steps. His gym teacher always said you shouldn't run when you're wounded, that you wouldn't feel the pain because of the adrenaline, but he didn't care. No, not a yard: it was a luminous great room, with an enormous window with two types of panes, one clear and the other mustard-coloured, in the form of a chessboard; the floor – he glimpsed it as he ran across – was of ceramic tiles forming shapes like in a kaleidoscope. The door was open and led out to a park. Gaspar sped up as much as he could – he was limping now, and could no longer run – and heard his father shout, Let him go! and he thought the shout was surely directed at Esteban, who must be following him. Outside, he went down a concrete path that led to a table with benches, all made of stone and decorated with tile mosaics, and then to a tree with a swing, and then to the edge of the park, marked off with a wire that, even injured, he had no trouble lifting up and going under. Then, open fields, idle land, and Gaspar ran as best he could, which wasn't very well; his foot made him cry out in pain, but as he ran he remembered, *he was on a table and his father was on another and there were people, not many, it looked like something medical, an operation, his father looked asleep, Gaspar tried to wake up but he couldn't, and he couldn't distinguish the people's faces, or were they too far away? He remembered someone grabbed him by the arms, hard, as if their fingers were metal, fingers that closed around his arms. Maybe that was in the car?*

No, the story about the car was a lie. He still felt dirty under his skin, he couldn't explain it, had they injected him with oil? He looked at his arms. There were needle marks. He ran. His ankle twisted again and he fell, and when he tried to get up he couldn't do it, the pain immobilized him now. There was no point in crawling. He had fallen face first and his lips were bleeding. He turned over and looked at the sky. It was dark grey, a compact, cloudless mass that looked very close, about to crush him. Only once before had he seen the sky like that, in the city, and from that low darkness had come powerful hail, chunks of ice, some as large as golf balls or plums. His entire body hurt, even more so after the fall, and his foot was on fire, but he tried to get up again when his father's face appeared, his transparent eyes taking on the grey of the sky. Gaspar moaned when he tried to stand, and he fell again on to his back. He wanted to believe the story of the crash and the amnesia, but, with a certainty that he recognized and wasn't about to ignore, he knew that his father had hurt him. In a deep and unimaginable way, of which the bruises and cuts and the bump on his head were merely slight, superficial vestiges.

He couldn't get up: the pain in his foot made him lose his balance. And then his father, with an incredible strength – wasn't he dying? Shouldn't he be weak? – held him down on the ground, on the grass, resting his enormous hand on his chest, an elephant's foot, the wheel of a truck.

'Gaspar, I'm not going to argue about what you're feeling. But I didn't hurt you. I'm protecting you the best I can and as far as I know how to do it.'

'Protecting me from what?'

Gaspar felt his father's hand letting up, reducing the pressure on his chest, but he didn't run away. He sat up. He was crying, he realized only then: the tears had soaked his neck. His father looked calm and aloof, as before.

'I don't believe you,' said Gaspar.

'That's okay. I wouldn't believe something I didn't understand either. But I need you to trust me. What do I have to do for you to trust me? When I die, I'm going to leave you protected. It's the last thing I'm going to do, and I know I'll make it in time.'

Gaspar saw Esteban standing next to his father. He was looking up, sniffing the storm, his jaw tense. He had taken the bandage off his neck and the wound – the one from the supposed crash – looked bad, dark, with very red edges. It looked like a bite.

'Prove it. If I was in the hospital and they did X-rays, I want to see them.'

'All right. Let's go now.'

Gaspar watched as his father stood up. Esteban came over and offered him his shoulder to lean on, but Gaspar refused it. The house was about forty metres away; he hadn't run very far. He wanted to get ahead of them so they wouldn't have an advantage. He fell twice on the way back: the electricity from the storm, the humidity, the blow to his head – it was all making him dizzy. Esteban and his father let him have his head start.

Esteban brought him to the bedroom so he could get dressed – his clothes were in a bag, no one had unpacked them and put them into the empty drawers – then helped him into the front seat of the car. Gaspar wasn't so suspicious of Esteban, at least not as much as he was of his dad. The wound on Esteban's neck somehow made him feel that maybe he had defended him. His dad didn't have a scratch on him.

His father's hands had grown: very large hands. He had that image, that memory – where had it come from? His father with very long fingers, like an animal's? With golden claws? He didn't want to look at him. The sky was black now and Dr Biedma stated the obvious, that a storm was coming and they needed to hurry. She and Juan rode in the back seat. Gaspar saw his father rubbing the short beard he'd let grow. How could he be so calm? Gaspar knelt on the seat, hugged the backrest, and peered over: that way he was in line with his father's face.

'What did you do to me? Tell me what you did.'

His father was losing patience, and Gaspar felt the stifling heat in the car and the danger in the air, the electricity of the storm that made the hairs on his arms stand up. For a second he thought about opening the door and jumping out on to the road.

'I didn't do anything to you. You're wrong, and you're stupid.'

'Don't call me stupid.'

'You're behaving like a stupid person.'

'Then help me.'

'I pulled you out of the car. And you remember that.'

'Liar. I don't remember.'

Esteban took Gaspar by the shoulders, firmly, and made him turn around and sit down. That's enough, he said. We're here.

Gaspar was surprised – the hospital couldn't be more than four blocks from the estate. So close, he said in a low voice, and Dr Biedma replied that otherwise they wouldn't have brought him to the house after the accident. And nor would his father have chosen to convalesce in a place that was far away from a health centre. She put it like that: a health centre. Gaspar decided she was believable, and the story of why the hospital was close by also seemed credible. But if that was true, the whole story could be true, and they would be right. And he didn't want to listen or to think anything reasonable, his own body still reeked of danger and he felt that if he cut the skin on his arm he would see a black film, like gelatin. He felt infected, like a black river was pulsing in his veins. He raised his shirt to look at the wounds. The dried blood was still red.

It was Esteban again who came to his aid as he hopped up the stairs to the hospital entrance. His dad didn't get close and Dr Biedma went ahead, but Gaspar could see all her movements and hear her; he had never been so alert. There was a sign that said PEDRO GALÍNDEZ INTENSIVE CARE CENTER, but it didn't include a location that would indicate where they were. At the reception desk, Dr Biedma asked for another doctor, the neurologist, and when she gave her own name the receptionist asked her to wait five minutes. Gaspar was still standing on one leg and leaning against Esteban. Juan had sat down on a long wooden bench and seemed worn out, but Gaspar wasn't concerned, he felt it was all a performance, even his father's vaguely blue lips, even that hospital, so solid and old. A front, it's all a front, he thought.

Suddenly he heard hammering that quickly grew into a fusillade: the storm had finally burst and it was hailing, a summer storm so intense that through the hospital's open front door they could see tree branches fly by, swept up by the wind as though sucked by a giant mouth.

The neurologist, a woman with short grey hair, came rushing up. She listened to what Dr Biedma had to tell her – He's confused, he's scared – then asked them to come up to her consulting office on the first floor. Through its window there was lightning and a black sky; it was night in the middle of the day. Gaspar went in alone with Dr Biedma: Juan and Esteban waited outside. The walls were hung with posters of brains and the doctor's degrees. Once Gaspar sat down – she made him prop his foot up on another chair – she said, Normal, normal, normal. Gaspar hopped over to the X-rays that shone on the wall, lit from behind. He checked that they had his name and the correct date. Gaspar Peterson. 18/1/1986. They were his. Or could they have faked them that fast?

The neurologist explained that blows to the head produced temporary amnesia, that it was the most normal thing in the world. Again with the soap opera, said Gaspar, and the doctor, to his surprise, laughed. They do use that a lot in soaps, don't they? But it's nothing strange. It's possible you won't ever remember the accident.

'I don't remember being here, either.'

'I once treated a soccer player who hit his head at a championship final and forgot the game. That's a little worse than forgetting an accident.'

Gaspar felt himself relaxing a little, but he resisted.

'It's not just that,' he said.

Dr Biedma interjected:

'He thinks we hurt him.'

Gaspar said nothing. He preferred not to reveal the extent of his distrust. The neurologist told him she understood that what he was feeling was real to him. She explained that sometimes the most insignificant blows produced effects that could be very scary. Yesterday you didn't remember anything, not even who the people with you were. That's why I thought that, since the lesion is organically insignificant, it was better for you to go somewhere familiar rather than stay in the hospital.

'That house isn't familiar, it's the first time I've been there,' said Gaspar.

'A homey place,' the doctor went on. 'With a normal bed and a normal room and a park. They told me it has a pool, right? That's lucky, in this heat. Hospitals sometimes confuse people more because they feel too unfamiliar. And I was right, because even though you were upset, you remember who everyone is now, right?'

Gaspar didn't reply.

'Who is she?'

'My dad's doctor.'

'And who is the grey-haired man outside?'

'Esteban, my dad's best friend.'

'And the blond man?'

'My dad.'

'Were you riding with him in the car when it crashed?'

'I don't know, I don't remember.'

'What do you remember?'

'We left the city in two cars. I went with Esteban and her,' he pointed to Dr Biedma, 'and a driver. Then I woke up in that house.'

'Do you know when you left the city?'

'No.'

'Day before yesterday. This is the X-ray from yesterday.'

The doctor took another set of films and placed them on the light boxes. Gaspar, still standing on one foot, saw the date. 19/1.

'You're not going to take one today?'

The doctor explained that the exam hadn't detected anything abnormal. That was why she had discharged him. There was no need for another X-ray. She told him again that he'd been sedated those two days because when the sedation wore off, he got upset.

'Like now. A lot more, really, but it's perfectly normal. Let's go to the orthopaedic specialist.'

Gaspar let himself be led along. He heard ice, immobilize, no cast. He watched as his father told Dr Biedma he was leaving, she protested, and he, as always, ignored her objection and left on his own, possibly walking.

Esteban was waiting in the hallway.

'I want to see the car,' Gaspar told him.

'You're worse than your father,' said Esteban.

'Worse how?'

'You're intractable.'

'What does intractable mean?'

'What you're doing right now is intractable. And enough with the hopping, you're making me nervous. I don't know where the car is. We're going back to the house. Or do you think this is all put on? That's enough nonsense.'

Esteban picked him up. Gaspar realized how strong he was; his arms were very muscular.

'How did that happen to your neck?'

'It was the broken window.'

'How come I know that my dad wanted to do something to me?'

Esteban hunched over. As they walked through the rain, Gaspar saw the hairs on his arms were very long and dark. Only the hair on his head was grey.

'I think you remember it like that because your dad pulled you out of the car, and when he did, he hurt you a little.'

'Why did he hurt me?'

'Because he yanked you out. He was afraid the car would explode. Your mom died in an accident and the mind can play tricks. Let's go to the house, you need to rest that damned foot.'

Gaspar leaned against the car and let the rain stream down his face.

'I don't want to be with him.'

'Then you'll be with me or Tali. Are you afraid of us?'

'No. I don't know why.'

'That's good to know.'

'You wouldn't lie to me. Or would you?'

Esteban smiled at him.

'Gaspar, of course I would lie to you if it were necessary, but there's no reason to lie. What do you think happened?'

Gaspar drenched the seat when he got into the car. The sky was growing dark again and a peal of thunder crashed above them; they drove blind back to the house, very slowly, deafened, too, by the downpour. Esteban carried him inside, and Gaspar felt physically relieved when he didn't hear or see his father anywhere; he was there, Gaspar could sense him, but for now he preferred to stay far away.

Esteban sat Gaspar down on one of the sofas in that living room with coloured glass windows, then said he was going to change clothes. From the hallway emerged a tall woman with long dark hair. She was wearing jeans and a sleeveless top, and for a moment Gaspar forgot his confusion, his fear of his father, and the void of those two days he couldn't remember; he forgot his suspicions. The woman, though older, was beautiful; she wore no make-up – Gaspar didn't like how make-up looked, especially lipstick – and she was barefoot.

Do you remember me? she asked him. And Gaspar talked to her about a party beside a river, a tree, a cat, and her house. Also, you came to visit not long ago, but you were leaving when I was getting home from school, we just said hi. You're Tali. Yep, that's me, she said. Let's see if we can get some ice on that foot.

Tali went to the fridge and took ice cubes from the freezer, put them into a plastic bag, and used a small hammer she found in a drawer to crush them – to make them *curubica*, as she said, and Gaspar smiled because he didn't know that word, but it sounded strange and silly. He felt like he hadn't smiled in ages. He propped up his foot himself: his ankle was swollen and violet. She encircled it very gently with the bag and tied its ends together. Then she turned on the TV and handed him the remote control. There aren't many channels, she said apologetically, but there's soccer.

'I don't want to see my dad,' said Gaspar.

Tali didn't answer right away. She adjusted the ice on his foot and then said: Your dad is in bed now. You'll see each other when you want to, the house is big. She smiled at him and Gaspar felt his head throb along with his foot, and he had to lick his lips. She had very white teeth, and her eyes were as dark as her hair.

They sat side by side, in silence. Gaspar couldn't hear anything that was happening in the house. Its walls were thick. Outside, the rain formed rivulets of mud. Esteban appeared, dry now, and poured a beer. Tali changed the ice when it melted – it melted fast – and then left. She's with Dad, thought Gaspar, and although he was still sick with dread and would have left again if not for his foot and the rain, he felt a little jealous.

The days they spent on the estate were boring and strange. The swelling in his foot went down gradually; incredibly, he could sleep at night, maybe because there was a sedative among the medications Dr Biedma gave him. His father was a shadow who wrote in the park under a tree, and Gaspar hardly ever ran into him in the house because he spent most of his time inside in bed. The strange thing was that the bodyguards were at the estate, and when Gaspar asked why, Esteban told him they thought maybe the accident had been a kidnapping attempt. You have a lot of money. Your father, though he rebels, is the widower of a very rich woman, and her heir. Don't you know that in this country, rich people are kidnapped? Gaspar did know, his father had explained it to him, but were they really that kind of millionaires? The kidnappings he'd heard of were of bankers or businesspeople. 'Well yes,' said Esteban, 'you don't live like a *pijo* because your father has ethical ideas.'

'What's a *pijo*?'

'I guess in Argentina you'd say *cheto*, posh, Richie-rich. But it's more than posh. A rich kid from a rich family. You get it.'

Dr Biedma took him to the hospital one more time: they told him that after the blow to his head he would need check-ups, and his foot would need physiotherapy. He could start either at the local hospital or in Buenos Aires. He decided to start right away, but they really didn't do much. Just wrapped his foot in plastic ice packs and stuck it into a cylinder that gave off ultrasonic waves. After that, the physical therapist moved an apparatus spread with gel over the swelling. To endure those long and boring sessions, Gaspar brought books he'd found in one of the rooms at the house. He suspected they were his father's, because they were mostly poetry and a few novels. But he couldn't read. He just stared up at the ceiling and tried to remember the accident. And what came to him then, as he focused in on a stain on the therapy room ceiling until it turned blurry, or nodded off in restless morning dreams, was something other than a crash. He remembered his father, but his hands were enormous and they had long fingernails. He remembered lying face up, like now, dozing while hands groped him. He remembered more people, further away. If it was true that his father had yanked him roughly from the car, he knew it was possible that in all the confusion from the impact and the accident, he might remember an animal's hands. Face up and dozing: just like being in the hospital. The hands groping him, too: he had never stayed in a hospital, but thanks to his father he knew the procedures by heart, the nurses drawing blood, the bandages, people coming in to take blood pressure and hang and remove IV bags, administer drugs, even bathe him; it was normal for him to remember being handled not only on his skin, but also under it, which was much more revolting. And the distant people could have been doctors in surgical masks, or else the people who always gathered around an accident.

After physical therapy, he ate whatever Tali made. Esteban sometimes cooked, too. He taught Gaspar how to make scrambled eggs, which were much tastier than fried ones, and to fry bacon until it was stiff, like caramel. A black inner tube had appeared in the pool for Gaspar to float on. Some afternoons, Esteban swam for a while. The first time he did, Gaspar saw his back marked by two long, parallel scars. What happened? he wanted to know. I fell from some rocks, Esteban told him. I was jumping, about to dive into the ocean. I used to spend summer afternoons doing that when I was young. The rocks can get very slippery.

'They look like they're from an operation, like my dad's.'

'They're not, but the rocks can cut like scalpels. I spent the rest of that summer lying face down. It was more boring than this summer of yours.'

'How old are you?'

Esteban dried off with a towel before answering. Gaspar would later realize he always did that, he never let the sun dry his skin. As soon as he left the water, he towelled off and then put on a shirt.

'Thirty-nine.'

'That's it? But all your hair is white.'

'Lots of people go prematurely grey.'

'Not anyone I know.'

'Maybe you don't know that many people.'

Gaspar used his hands to paddle over to the edge of the pool. Esteban was lighting a cigarette and Gaspar wanted to smoke. He asked for a drag, and Esteban surprised him by offering him the pack. They both smoked in silence, flicking ash into the pool.

The estate's phone had been out since the storm, and Gaspar tried to call his friends from the ENTel centre in town, but no one answered. They must still be on vacation. Pablo had gone to Mar del Plata with his parents; his mom was now very pregnant. Vicky and Adela must still be in the south. He didn't go out much beyond that, and he hadn't gotten to learn how to ride horses. Since he could barely walk, he spent all his time in front of the TV. There were no kids nearby: when he went to the entrance, he could tell the estate was pretty isolated, or at least the park it sat on was very large. Across the dirt road were open fields where a few cows grazed idly and the horses stood very still; they were pretty ugly ones, white and fat with broad feet. He had studied the terrain a little with an eye to escaping, but every night, his plan to break out faded away. He was scared. He knew his father would find him quickly. The scrapes and bruises he had now were nothing compared with what he might do if Gaspar ever did run away.

Tali slept in his dad's bedroom, and one night, trying not to make any noise, Gaspar sat outside the closed door to listen to what they said. He caught fragments, random words or whole phrases of little importance. Was she his girlfriend now? What did Esteban think? Was he jealous? He learned that Esteban wasn't going to stay much longer. Tali wanted to know who was going to take care of him 'in Buenos Aires' and Gaspar didn't hear the reply. She was walking around the room: those light steps couldn't be his father's. Gaspar closed his eyes and pictured her, with her dark hair pulled back into a very high ponytail, no bra. He felt dizzy when he realized she looked a little like his mother but much, much prettier, at least according to photos. He heard someone, surely Tali, pour water. Now they were talking about the 'next attempt'. 'Six months is a long time,' Tali was saying. 'They already know that the body wasn't hurt.' Now those were his father's steps that came closer and it was his father who opened the door, and Gaspar wanted to run away but there was no point. He squeezed his eyes shut and raised his hands to soften the blow, sitting on the floor to await his punishment, but it never came.

'How many times have I told you not to spy on me?'

Gaspar didn't answer.

'Come in, if you want.'

He obeyed, hopping; the swelling in his foot was completely gone, but it still hurt and, especially, it was stiff: it was going to take time to recover mobility, the physiotherapist had told him. Tali was sitting on the bed wearing denim shorts and a striped shirt, like a sailor's, and her skin was tanned. Her hair was down and her cheeks were flushed. His father kept his distance, as he always did those days. He still hadn't shaved or cut his hair and he looked dirty, unkempt. He went straight back to bed, and Gaspar stayed standing by the door.

'So?' Juan asked.

'What?'

'What did you hear, what do you want to know?'

Gaspar knew that if he didn't answer, the blows would come, and he especially didn't want his dad to hit him with Tali there.

'What's going to happen in six months?'

Gaspar studied his father's reaction. There was none. His eyes were sunken in his head, and they even looked dark.

'Graciela wants me to have another operation. It would be

more complicated this time: I need a transplant. The operation has been done in Argentina, but so far the results haven't been good and she wants me to go to the United States. She had a candidate: that's why we were talking about how my body – or the rest of my organs, let's say – is in good condition. But the candidate turned out to be incompatible. I don't feel like explaining what incompatibility is. Look it up in your dictionary. She thinks trying in six months would be ideal and she wants me to go to the US soon.'

'They're going to give you a transplant?'

'No, because it's not going to work and I don't want to do it. I want to die. It's best for everyone.'

'Juan,' Tali interrupted. 'Don't talk to him like that.'

His father looked furious and weak.

'When I die, I'm going to set you free and maybe you can have a life. Now go. I can't stand to look at you.'

Gaspar opened the door and heard Tali follow him out, but he didn't turn around until she called his name and offered her arm to lean on, so he wouldn't have to limp. They went outside to the park. The night was cool and it seemed like they were alone in the grounds, though the light in Esteban's room was on and soft music came from his window. They sat on the stone benches decorated with mosaics and Gaspar rested his elbows on the table. He was tired.

'Come with us. Both of you,' he said to Tali. 'Don't leave me alone with him.'

'I can't, angel,' she replied.

'Esteban says the same thing. You both say you want to, too. Why do you leave him alone?'

The music coming from Esteban's room stopped and silence fell over the park, barely caressed by the splash of nocturnal insects in the pool and the distant hum of a fan. Tali said simply,

Your dad wants to be with you. He wants you with him and no one else. Gaspar felt defiance hardening his stomach. Let him die alone, he thought. Someone was walking through the park. Esteban. Gaspar turned around to watch him approach: his grey hair shone under the moon.

'I don't want to stay with him,' Gaspar told him. 'Please.'

'Look,' said Esteban. 'The only thing your father has done to you, in all the time I've known you both, is protect you. From your family, even, who are bad people. His methods, son, are ones I question as well, but you're leaving this place with him. There's nothing to be afraid of. Your uncle will come soon. You won't be alone with your dad. And Luis is your family, your real family.'

'Dad always says that my mom's side of the family aren't good people and they don't want to see me. That's true, then?'

'It's the honest truth,' said Esteban. 'They're among the worst people in this country, or anywhere. They're the worst, period. They aren't your family, even if you have their blood.'

'And what are you two?'

Tali and Esteban looked at each other and Gaspar saw them smile, but he didn't understand why. Tali said, We're friends. And Esteban added, as he lit a cigarette: Friends you'll hopefully never need.

The green river at Los Alerces wasn't as green as people said. It was more like a greenish turquoise. But Vicky wasn't disappointed, especially not when Adela was so happy walking along the shore, shouting for photos. Trips with her family were always entertaining, but this one with Adela and Betty was especially fun. They joined in when everyone sang in the RV, which had a cassette player, and they both liked stopping at grills along the highway. Vicky also noticed things about Betty that she hadn't before. She was elegant, she had something to say in every conversation, and her strange face, with its long nose and narrow lips, was pretty, or at least interesting, as her grandmother would say. She always wore long skirts and beautiful rings that looked expensive. And her political opinions were stronger than Vicky's mom's. When they got stopped on the highway, for example, and the policeman asked for the RV's papers, Betty stuck her head out the window and told the policeman that, yes, they could ask for a licence and registration, but definitely not for their personal IDs. The military isn't in power any more, got it? she shouted contemptuously. Vicky saw her father motion her to be quiet, and Betty sat back down. She was furious. Her narrow lips had become two pale lines over her sharp teeth. When she lit a cigarette, her hands were shaking.

Maybe it was true what they said about Adela's dad, that he'd been disappeared by the military.

Now, at the campground, Vicky and Adela were sharing a tent. The adults slept in the RV. Adela was happy not to have gone to her grandparents' country house. I like it there, but it's always the same. They have horses but they're ugly, with fat feet, not at all like Arabian horses. And there's nothing around, all the other houses are far away. The pool is nice, though. The girls talked about all kinds of things before going to sleep. Adela confessed to Vicky that she liked Gaspar. I already knew, said Vicky, I don't know why you didn't tell me sooner. And Adela, who was lighting her face with a flashlight, replied, Because he'll never go for me, he won't want to go out with me because I'm deformed. And he's so cute, Vicky. Isn't he cute?

They were allowed to leave the campground a little and walk under the trees, and they could also dip their feet in the river, though they weren't permitted to swim; the water was too cold, anyway. Betty taught them to bury their used toilet paper

– there were filthy people who left it hanging in the branches and it stank – and how to defend themselves from the horse-flies, which were big and buzzing. At night, Betty and Vicky's parents drank wine and sang songs with the guitar: Vicky liked one really sad one that said '*y en las multitudes el hombre que yo amo.*' She was surprised because Betty knew a lot of songs and could even play the guitar. One night, Betty and Vicky's mom took turns singing Violeta Parra songs. Betty sang very well: in the night breeze, her green silk dress rippled like the river and Vicky pictured her with a rifle in the fields. Someday, she'd get up the nerve to enquire about her life, but for now, Betty intimidated her. Plus, she drank a lot of wine every night. They had bought a bunch of bottles of Chilean wine, which, apparently, was better than the Argentine kind.

At night, Vicky and Adela ventured into the woods to tell stories. They didn't go far: they could still hear the conversations at the campground, and even the showers if someone went late to bathe. They didn't invite other kids: they hadn't managed to make friends with any. They sat across from each other and passed the flashlight back and forth, holding it under their chins so the light would distort their faces, and told stories about axe murderers and cannibal ghosts. Adela talked again about the black dog that had torn off her arm, and also about the shadow of the hanged man that appeared in their neighbourhood in Buenos Aires, and some of her other classic horror tales. Vicky went along with the stories until one night when Adela said, Look what I found. Someone left it in the dining room, with some park guides and books and maps of Patagonia. They're myths and legends from around here. Most of them are pretty boring, but listen to this one. Adela opened the book and read. It was a story about the island of Chiloé, in the south of Chile. There was a sect that lived there called the Brujería. They had two other branches, one in Buenos Aires and another in Santiago. They met in an underground cave, in a forest like the one they were in now. The faithful were called novitiates and they were initiated, that's what it was called. To get into the sect a person had to kill their best friend and skin them: they used the skin to make a vest that shone in the darkness. Imagine, I'd have to skin you! Adela laughed, but that laugh scared Vicky. She put her shoes on over her socks, and when she closed her eyes, she saw Omaira's ashen hands clutching a branch, Omaira in the mud. Anyway, they're really evil. You can distinguish the victims of the sect because the witches leave scars on them. And this is the worst part, said Adela. There's a guard in the cave where the Brujería meets, it's called an imbunche. It's a baby between six months and a year old that the witches kidnap and deform. They break its legs, hands, and feet. When they're done breaking everything, they turn its head around like with a tourniquet until it's looking over its back, like in *The Exorcist*. Finally, they make a deep cut in its back, below the shoulder blade, and they stick its right foot in that hole. When the wound heals and the foot is stuck inside, the imbunche is complete. They feed it with human milk and then, when it's ready, with human flesh, too. It must walk like a half-crushed bug.

They jumped when Betty appeared out of nowhere. What are you two talking about? she asked, angry and drunk. Adela tried to reassure her by showing her the book, but Betty grabbed it furiously and clutched it to her chest. Go to bed now, both of you, and quit talking nonsense. She was shaking. You're really drunk, Adela murmured, and Betty turned around and ran off: the girls watched in surprise as she threw the book of myths and legends into a bonfire.

That night, Vicky and Adela slept in an embrace. Vicky didn't dream about Omaira. She dreamed about a child with his head

309

twisted around and a leg stuck into his chest, not his back. A boy who had a scar just like Gaspar's dad's, except it wasn't dry, it was bleeding. Adela told her later that she had also dreamed about the imbunche. You know where it was? And Vicky could guess the reply. In the house, she said. Adela nodded. In my dream it was the guardian of the house, she said.

Two days later they went back to Esquel. Even though it was summer it was cold at night, and they could light a fire. There was a lot of wood already cut and piled up beside the house, protected from the rain by a roof. One morning they needed to cut more and Betty took care of it: she perspired under her jacket and her hair stuck to her temples. Betty bought a bottle of whiskey in Esquel, for the cold, she said, and Adela got mad, but quietly. She told Vicky later that she was ashamed for other people to see her mother drunk. Betty drank the whiskey without ice, and sometimes sat staring into the fire. They all went together to a ski centre called La Hoya; they couldn't ski because they didn't have money for the equipment or an instructor, but they took photos and drank hot chocolate in a lovely sweet shop. Betty mentioned in passing that she had skied when she was younger, but she'd never liked it because she fell a lot. Where? Vicky asked. In Mendoza, said Betty. At a resort called Las Leñas. That's where the famous people go, said Vicky. Isn't it expensive? My parents could afford it, said Betty. Her parents? Those sad old people who came to Adela's birthdays? They were rich? People really are strange, thought Vicky.

The ride back from the south in the RV had been pretty boring. Everyone slept a lot, and, Vicky thought, Betty must have been drinking on the sly, because she always refused to drive. Vicky wasn't tired when they got back, not like the adults, who went straight to bed. After saying goodbye to Adela and having something to eat, she went to visit Pablo. He had gone to the coast, and his vacation had been awful, he said. His parents fighting, his mother crying because she thought she was going to lose the baby, a lot of rain and cold. The only thing he'd liked was the hotel. His parents had reserved a suite, which meant he had a kind of apartment all to himself. Wow, said Vicky, they have money now? Pablo had to admit they did. His own room had a TV, and he could stay in and watch when it was raining. That, and eating in the port: those were the only good things. I'm sorry, said Vicky, we had a great time. Is Gaspar back yet? I have no idea, Pablo admitted. When I went by it was all closed up, and I didn't want to knock. I haven't gone today.

Let's go now, Vicky said.

She tried throwing a pebble at Gaspar's window: the shutters were closed, but – and this was simply unheard of – there was music playing. Not very loud, but enough that they could hear it from the street. He must be alone, thought Vicky. It was unimaginable that Gaspar's father would allow music that loud, when you could barely talk in that house without bothering him. Convinced that the music was keeping him from hearing the pebbles and that he was alone in the house, Vicky rang the bell. The music's volume didn't go down and Pablo reached up to bang a fist on the shutter. When the door opened, Vicky was prepared to see Gaspar. But no: it was Juan Peterson, and she took a step back. Behind her, Pablo sucked in his breath. He was afraid of Gaspar's dad too.

Juan Peterson didn't yell or get angry. He looked at them with a certain indifference and told them to come in. His hair was very long for a man's and his beard made him look less pale, though he was very thin – his pants were too big for him and his cheekbones stood out. Vicky and Pablo went inside but stayed close to the door, and they watched as Gaspar's father went

deeper into the house. They heard the sound of a door opening and the music grew louder, and they didn't understand well
but they thought they heard a 'your friends are here'. And then
nothing, for a while. The music got quieter and there was no
other sound, no footsteps, no one even coming to close the door.

The music stayed very low, and then Vicky finally heard footsteps, but they were distorted, slow, one foot dragging. Gaspar
appeared looking very serious, wearing only his soccer shorts,
barefoot and shirtless. Then they saw he was limping and had
scrapes healing on his shoulders, his arm, his chest.

Vicky had a sudden and horrible idea that made her keep
her distance from Gaspar, made her not want to hug him as she
would have done any other time. They've switched places, she
thought. He looks like his dad. His eyes are the same.

Pablo did react. He went over and hugged Gaspar and
clapped his back; Gaspar was favouring one of his feet, and he
didn't return the hug.

'What happened to you?' Pablo asked.

'We had an accident and I got a little banged up, I hit my
head, too. My foot is sprained, I twisted it.'

'You hit your head?'

'Yeah. I was in the hospital. Or so they say, I don't remember.'

'What do you mean you don't remember?'

Gaspar lost his patience, got angry. Though he was tanned,
there were circles under his eyes. Plus, he never got annoyed at
them, never yelled at them the way he was yelling now.

'I don't remember! What can I say? What do you want, why
are you here?'

'What's wrong with you?' Vicky said. She wasn't mad, just
worried.

'Nothing's wrong with me,' said Gaspar. 'Nothing! I just
want to be alone.'

And with that he went back to his room, limping but fast; he looked ill, and he was dishevelled, a little dirty. Vicky took Pablo's arm to keep him from following Gaspar, and the two of them left the house, closing the door carefully so as not to make any noise.

That night, Pablo and Vicky met up with Adela. They watched movies at Vicky's on the VCR Gaspar had lent them and had never asked for back. All three agreed that the redhead's dress in *Pretty in Pink* was awful – they'd expected something amazing! The whole movie was built around that dress! They were surprised when Lidia got home from the hospital. Aren't you on duty tonight? asked Vicky, and her mom said she was, but she'd gotten her period and had cramps. She'd switched shifts with another doctor, and she would make up the hours next week. Lidia went to the kitchen to make tea and then sat down with them.

'What's with you guys, so serious?'

The kids looked at each other, and Vicky spoke:

'Nothing, we watched a movie.'

'Something's up, I know you all.'

Then Pablo ventured:

'We went to Gaspar's and he's being weird, he didn't want to hang out with us.'

Lidia sipped her tea, put her feet up on the coffee table, and said:

'You're going to have to give him time. He had an accident and he's not dealing with it well.'

'How do you know?'

'Because I saw Juan, I went over for a drink yesterday. You have to have patience with Gaspar, kiddos. He had a cerebral concussion. A slight one, but he reacted very badly, he was confused for a few days. Don't forget his mom died in an accident, he's reliving some ugly things. And Juan's condition is very, very serious. You're going to have to help your friend, because he's going to lose his father.'

'Really?' Vicky asked.

'It's just so sad. I know you kids don't much like Juan, or you're scared of him, I don't know, but he's a good guy. A little different, maybe. But good.'

Vicky thought, how can you say that, he hits Gaspar and he's crazy, but she didn't want to fight.

'Who's going to take care of Gaspar?'

'His uncle. They already started the paperwork so he can be Gaspar's guardian, and then he'll adopt him.'

'So he's going to die that soon?'

'Sweetie, no one knows exactly when he's going to die.'

'But how can we help him? Gaspar doesn't even want to leave the house,' said Adela.

'You have to give him time,' Lidia said, finishing her tea.

Gaspar found that the easiest way to stay distracted was to watch soccer and read every word of *El Gráfico*. He got a little bored reading about River Plate and having to stomach their unbeatable team, though he had to admit he wanted to play like Francescoli; there was no other player he liked as much, not even on the San Lorenzo team. He hated River Plate because they had Francescoli, plus some brutal defenders who would foul players left and right. But that's a good thing, Hugo Peirano would tell him, they're no sissies. They had watched together when Veléz won the championship against River Plate 3–0. It was like being in a movie. When the movie ended, reality was his dad lying in bed, sometimes at home but more and more often at the hospital. Sometimes he even went out alone, Gaspar didn't know where, and when he came back he was either angry or so tired he couldn't even speak. Gaspar saw the medications piling up on the table and the house filling with papers, sketches, notes that made no sense. Was he not taking his pills? What were those drawings? For all those reasons it was better to be in the soccer movie, or even to study for school while he listened to music, so he didn't have to hear his father's steps upstairs or see him carrying the oxygen tank around. He couldn't read poetry or stories or the things he usually liked: they didn't distract him enough, and some of them had even made him cry. He'd taken a book by an English poet, Elizabeth Barrett Browning, from his father's room, and he'd opened it to a poem that read: 'ENOUGH! we're tired, my heart and I. / We sit beside the headstone thus, / And wish that name were carved for us.' It seemed intentional. To top it off, the Spanish translation was terrible. He couldn't stand reading things that were beautiful or sad. He would rather learn fractions. His foot still kept him from swimming, but he was anxiously awaiting the day he could return to the pool. It was easy to think about something else under the water.

He was finishing a chapter on the solar system in his school textbook when his father appeared in the kitchen – Gaspar studied in the kitchen: there was no desk or table in his room and it was uncomfortable to study in bed. Juan wasn't using the oxygen tank. Gaspar was over the fear he'd had in the days after the accident: he had even gone to the neighbourhood library and the one at school to look in medical books for what could happen after a blow to the head, and he was convinced that, yes, it was possible he'd imagined it all. But with his father, he always had to be on guard. There was no way of knowing when he was going to attack, just like with a wounded animal.

'What are you reading?'

Gaspar showed him the pages with drawings of planets.

Then he realized that his dad's light-blue shirt was stained with blood, and the bloodstains were spreading over his stomach.

'Did you hurt yourself?'

'A little, it's nothing.'

'Did you put hydrogen peroxide on it?'

'I did everything I need to do. Do you like to read about the universe?'

'I have to draw the planets.'

'That's easy.'

Juan poured a glass of water and drank it in two gulps.

'What I don't understand,' said Gaspar, realizing this was a moment when he could talk to his dad, something that had been impossible for months, 'is why the sky is dark at night, when with all those stars there should be more light.'

'There's even a term for that: someone's paradox, I can't remember the guy's name. You're asking a question that still doesn't have an answer, I think. Or maybe they've discovered it and I don't know about it. There's something called dark matter and it pushes on the stars, that's why they get further and further away. Three quarters of the universe is darkness. There's much more darkness than light above us.'

They were silent, and Gaspar saw the blood expanding on his father's shirt.

'Show me. Is it bad? How'd you hurt yourself?'

'Don't worry. I want you to come with me. I've already called the driver. We're going to scatter your mom's ashes.'

Gaspar felt his heart start to pound in his chest and he couldn't speak. His father took his hand on the table.

'I don't need her in the house any more. I was able to set her free. Tonight is a good night, the best one in years. She deserves this night, and for you to say goodbye to her before I die.'

Gaspar let his father caress his hand. What he'd said about

setting her free was weird, but it must be some kind of metaphor. Through the window he saw the headlights of a car coming to pick them up.

It was a short ride. As far as the Costanera Sur, beautiful at night and smelling of rain and mud, the river hidden and silent beyond the stone railing. Why did the city seem so far away from the water? It was strange, a river without beaches that lapped against the ramparts, big like the ocean with no opposite shore, brown during the day but silvered at night. The Costanera Sur with its steps and lights and its roundabouts, totally empty, the sausage carts all closed up, three in the morning in Buenos Aires, walking over the grass and touching the leaves of the trees with his fingertips, not much light except for the moon, three fourths of the universe is darkness, his father had said and Gaspar understood, the universe was night, but not all nights were like this one, cool and beautiful, the driver in the car listening to the radio, a sad tango, all tangos are sad, and walking to the railing, not to the shore, because there was no shore, why couldn't you touch the water? Gaspar remembered rivers in his childhood and the desire to swim at night caressed his skin. In the darkness he couldn't see the blood on his father's shirt; when they reached the river a gentle breeze tousled his hair, and Gaspar accepted the box of his mother's ashes, which was about the size of a notebook, small as if it held a jewel, and this was what she had been for years now, but Gaspar could remember her warm, so far away now, now she was earth, ash, cold like the stone railing. Not here, his dad said suddenly. Let's go out to the reserve. Are you scared? And Gaspar said no. He was never afraid with his father; he could be afraid of him, but not with him. Even though he knew his dad was sick, he seemed invincible and dangerous. Sometimes wounded animals were

317

like that, much stronger than when they were healthy. Can we get into the reserve at night? Gaspar asked. He'd been there several times during the day, with Vicky and her family. They were still building it – or no, not exactly, how can you build something natural? – a swamp of lagoons and grasslands, full of animals and dirt paths that led to the river, because there, you could actually get to the water. They were turning it into a protected place where you could walk, but also where animals could live, and at night it was closed, Gaspar thought, with high bars. Let's see, his father said, and when they reached the fence gate, locked with a padlock, he said, Go in, son, go on in if you can, and Gaspar, confused, handed back the box that held his mother, and when he tried to push the door open he realized he didn't need a key, that if he wanted it open he simply opened it, and how that was possible there was no way to understand, but suddenly the gate was open and he had merely touched it – and he'd thought, yes, he had thought he could open it – and his father followed him without a word, as if it were the most normal thing in the world, and on the other side, on a muddy path through tall grass with pools shining like mirrors under the moon, he took Gaspar's face in his hands, leaned down to look him in the eyes, and caressed his hair, the box on the ground between them, and he said, you have something of mine, I passed on something of me to you, and hopefully it isn't cursed, I don't know if I can leave you something that isn't dirty, that isn't dark, our share of night. I like this, said Gaspar, and his father replied, Of course you do, because now nothing can hurt you. Nothing? Right now, nothing. They walked without dodging the puddles that were impossible to avoid, soaking their feet, muddying their pants, Gaspar stopping from time to time to let his father catch his breath, it was so hard for him to walk now, I'm going to miss him, he thought, I'll be glad when he's gone because without him it'll be easier to stop being sad, but I'm going to miss him. They walked the distance of about two or three blocks: the river wasn't so far, and they parted the reeds to reach the water. There were animal sounds and Gaspar knew there were snakes around there, but not poisonous ones, and he also remembered his father's words, Nothing can hurt you now, how long was now, how long did the present last? Finally at the shore there were sand and rocks and his father told him how in the past, even when he himself was little, people would swim in the water, back then it wasn't so polluted. Gaspar stood and sniffed the night and the water, so huge it seemed unbelievable it wasn't salty, and he took off his shoes, rolled up his pants, and walked into the water. Come with me, Dad, he said, and his father followed him and the two of them stood there, the water around their ankles. His father was holding the box now, and he opened it. He got down on his knees to empty it into the water, and the ashes floated a moment before sinking, and some were still stuck to the bottom of the box, and then Gaspar saw his father take off his shirt and gather ash between his fingers and spread it over the wound, which was already dirty – had he been putting ashes on the cut earlier? Gaspar wasn't afraid: he went closer to see the wound and realized it wasn't very deep and had a shape, it looked like a kind of telescopic sight, or like the sketches his father made and left scattered around the house, and he realized his dad was saying something in a low voice as he rubbed the wound with ash. Gaspar took a little too, but he just sprinkled it on his hand and kissed it. It tasted old, stale, and yet it wasn't unpleasant. I love you, Gaspar said aloud, and he washed his hands in the water and then submerged the whole box. The dead travel fast, he remembered the phrase that had frightened him when he first read it, but it didn't scare him any more, I hope you get where you're going fast, Mom.

Should we leave the box? We'll bury it, his father said, but first he started to stir the water with his enormous hands, his long arms, and when a cloud covered the moon and the darkness was nearly total Gaspar thought those hands grew even bigger, claw-hands in the water, an animal splashing. The moon re-emerged and Gaspar could no longer see the ashes of his mother in the black, silvered water that looked a little like the tar on the neighbourhood streets when the road surface was repaired.

His father went back to the shore and used his hands to dig, more animal than ever. He'd left his shirt floating in the water and Gaspar went to get it. It was soaked. Was he planning to wear it like that? He helped dig; his dad was sweating and his breathing whistled, but he managed a hole deep enough for the box. The two of them covered it with earth, and Juan drew something over the grave of the empty ash coffin, something Gaspar couldn't distinguish, or maybe it was just a final goodbye, the caress of a finger. They sat on either side of the mound of dirt and they both laughed when, simultaneously, they said they could really use a smoke. Finally, said Juan. He seemed happy. Gaspar tried not to think about what his father had done with the ashes, or what he himself had done. They were cannibals under the moon, mud-caked and smelling of river.

The return was like a dream, slower this time but with fewer breaks. When they reached another gate, also locked, his father looked at him: his eyes had turned nearly yellow as they did sometimes, and he hadn't put on the wet shirt, so the dirty cuts looked like a bizarre painting on his chest, a clumsy drawing. Gaspar obeyed the look: when he put his hands on the barred gate to push it, he felt the blood flow through his body at a frightening speed, pounding in his head, in his stomach, his wrists, and once the gate was open he was calm but streaming sweat, as if he'd just crossed the finish line of a race, or like after soccer matches in summer.

In moderation, his father said. Gaspar got up the nerve to ask him, emboldened by the ashes and the moon, if those things had made him sick. That kind of effort. Opening doors like that. No, his father said. No, it's more that my illness held me back. I have to thank it for that. I'm your father because I'm sick. If I'd been healthy, I don't know what would have happened.

When the driver saw them, wet, muddy, and blood-smeared, he said nothing. He wasn't even surprised. He's used to it, thought Gaspar, and when the car pulled away, the gates and the moon and the river and the ashes were left far behind, and there, enclosed in the car with his father half-naked and spattered by blood and ash, he had to fight the trembling of his legs, the feeling that he'd just woken up, that the time they'd just spent in that place was very far away and long ago, and it was beautiful like a secret garden behind a concrete wall, full of purple flowers and plants that eat flies.

Gaspar came out of the pool at a run, and as he was wrapping a towel around himself, the swim coach called out, Not barefoot! If you slip, you're dead. He obeyed and put on his flip-flops. His eyes were burning: too much chlorine in the water. Swimming had relaxed him. The effort of his arms, the sound of the splashing, and the singular stillness under the water distracted him. Thinking about the World Cup also distracted him. It was about to start, and everything reeked of soccer. Hugo Peirano said Argentina didn't have a chance with such a bush league team, but Gaspar believed in them pretty blindly.

Yes, focusing on the World Cup was the best distraction. Because there were other concerns. His uncle. When he was going to come. His dad just wouldn't call him, and if he didn't arrive in time Gaspar would end up in an orphanage or a reform school or something like that. Or could he stay with the Peiranos in the meantime? Thinking was torture. He needed to call his uncle's ex-wife in Brazil, ask her where he was now and if he had a phone in Argentina. He'd said as much to his father, begged him, Please, during a sleepless night, his father doubled up from the pain in his chest and sweating so much they had to flip the mattress. In a brief lull in the pain, his dad had given an unbearable answer: It won't be long, and for now you and I need to be alone. What the hell are you talking about? Gaspar asked, but he kept helping as best he could until Juan fell asleep at dawn, his breathing strange and ragged. Gaspar had been afraid his father would die that morning, but hours later he was awake and even accepted a glass of orange juice. You're really not going to call in a nurse? Gaspar wanted to know. Soon, Juan had replied. Don't even think about calling your uncle, he'd said then, and Gaspar left the house with a slam of the door. At the magazine kiosk he'd bought *El Gráfico* and two newspapers. He saved the sports supplements and studied every article, every interview with Bilardo and the players. It was good to be able to think so intensely about something, sink down into conversations about whether Argentina had played well against Napoli and hear over and over that the team isn't there yet, it's not there, the way Hugo Peirano lamented as he sipped mate in desperation. They move back, it drives me crazy when they play deep like that.

In Gaspar's house they lived according to a different time. His father came and went from the clinic, and when he was hospitalized, Gaspar didn't go to visit. He couldn't, and he didn't want to. The World Cup helped him forget, but at night, as he paged through his magazines and sometimes waited for the car that would bring his father back, he felt his stomach churn.

Who would he stay with if his dad died? Would his grand-parents turn up? Why wasn't he allowed to call his uncle? He was going to do it, even if it cost him a brutal beating or some worse punishment. He could take it, much better than he could take that uncertainty. After the World Cup, he told himself, after it's over, I'll call.

Shouldn't you really have stayed longer in the hospital? Gaspar had asked his father while Dr Biedma was drawing blood. Yes, he'd said. I'll go back soon. I have to finish some-thing here first. Dr Biedma put the blood into a test tube and gave Gaspar a look he couldn't decipher. She obeys him, he thought later, at the pool, while he was under a hot shower. She knows he shouldn't be at home but she lets him. But why? And what did he have to finish? Something to do with the drawings. Gaspar turned off the shower and wrapped himself in the towel he'd brought from home, which was old and scratchy and dried him well.

They were still in the running for the World Cup after a win against England that had made grown men faint and others wrap themselves in flags and sob on the floor. Now the few remaining games were important. Everyone was happy because Argentina was playing Belgium and not Spain in the semi-final. The semi-final wasn't as tense as the match with England and you could sense the final victory, the inevitable, the 2–0 with Maradona enlightened, so elegant, Hugo Peirano would say things like, That son of a bitch is gonna make me cry. It wasn't good news when France lost to West Germany, everyone knew West Germany was a real threat, and the days before the final were a kind of dream. To kill time, Gaspar decided to learn how to make a Spanish tortilla, following the steps in a cookbook. When he finished and managed to turn it over without burning it or mangling it too much, he found that it was so delicious it was a shame to eat alone. That day he hadn't checked where his father was in the house, and he was surprised to find him awake in the downstairs bedroom, his bed littered with books and notebooks full of drawings and annotations.

'You want to eat, Dad?'

'Did you make it all by yourself? I can't get up, son, you're going to have to bring it to me.'

'What do you mean you can't?'

Gaspar went over to his father's bed, and when he was close – he hadn't looked at him closely in days – he saw he'd lost even more weight. And he still hasn't called Luis, he thought. After the World Cup, after it's over, I'll call him myself. They ate together in silence while they watched TV, yet another show with soccer commentary. Gaspar could tell his dad wasn't interested, but that was to be expected. He ate slowly and left half on his plate, but he said, It's just that I don't feel good, the tortilla is delicious. Gaspar asked if he needed oxygen and helped him put on the cable with the new system. He no longer used a mask at home, but rather a tube that went above his mouth like a moustache, with two smaller tubes that went into his nose.

In the fifty-sixth minute in the final match Argentina were up 2–0, and they were all so crazed that Hugo Peirano broke a glass and the girls screamed so loud they had to be shushed just as loudly. You all are like animals, said Lidia. It's like you saw a UFO. The Germans played well and tied with two almost identical goals from the left corner. The silence after the equalizer was absolute. In the eighty-fourth minute, Lothar Matthäus, the West German number 10, momentarily lost Maradona, whom he was marking. It wasn't very obvious, just a second, but it was enough for Diego to make a long, perfect left-footed pass to Burruchaga. What a tough pass to make, thought Gaspar. And then he knew. It's a goal, he said aloud. Shut up, shut up, said Hugo Peirano, who had also realized but didn't want to get his hopes up. Burruchaga moved up, shot diagonally, gently, and scored the goal.

Gaspar didn't see what happened next. He jumped up and hugged Pablo and everyone else, and the remaining five minutes, he knew, would be hard-fought, but useless to West Germany; Argentina were the champions and it felt like flying, as if nothing else existed but that moment, a moment that was forever and joyful and so sad because it couldn't last. They had to go outside, no one could stay in. The streets were full of honking horns and curly-haired dolls wearing number 10 jerseys and flags and confetti. People were chanting, *Mire mire qué locura, mire mire qué emoción*, and what madness, what excitement, some neighbours brought their phones outside so family members living in other countries could hear the shouts, the drunkenness, and could cry from there, from Canada and the US and Brazil and Mexico and Spain and France, exiled by dictatorship, working far away because there was never any work in Argentina, and some had watched the game in bars, others had listened on the radio, they all wanted to come back and be there, even in those provinces where it was raining and people were celebrating drenched, their jerseys stuck to their skin. In the park people brought speakers outside and there was dancing and grilled chorizos and wine, the empanada shop cooked for the people and everyone ended up lying in the grass come nightfall, having cried and eaten their fill and shouted themselves hoarse, dressed in blue-and-white from head to toe.

Gaspar would remember that day, and that night, as the last happy ones in many, too many years.

Pablo saw Gaspar as soon as he came out of school, and hurried over. It was unusual for him to be there waiting. Gaspar offered him a ride on his bike. Pablo said he would rather walk. Then Gaspar invited him to eat at the café in the park. Or were they expecting him at home?

'Is something wrong?' asked Pablo.

'I need a favour. I need to borrow your home phone to call Brazil.'

'That's expensive, man. You've got a phone.'

'The money's not a problem, I'll pay your folks. In advance, before the bill comes.'

'Okay, but you ask them. You want to talk to your uncle? Didn't you say he was coming back to Argentina?'

Gaspar put a hand to his forehead, as he did when he was uncertain, when he was nervous. Pablo noticed his pants hung off him because he'd lost weight. The long belt he used hung down as if he had a snake around his waist.

'He did come back, apparently. But I don't know where he is. And his ex-wife is there, in Brazil, maybe she can give me his new number. Maybe she doesn't have it, but it doesn't hurt to try.'

'And you can't call from your house.'

'My dad doesn't want me to talk to my uncle. He says he'll take care of it when the time comes. But, man, I don't know if he's right in the head.'

Pablo was silent. Gaspar continued.

'I can't call from my house. He'll know. I don't want to make him mad.'

'And what are you going to talk about with your uncle?'

'I don't really know. I'm going to tell him about Dad, I'll tell him he needs to come, he said he was going to be here with us. Otherwise, I'm going to have to get in touch with my grandparents and that really will drive Dad crazy, he hates them. I don't know what to do. He has to be the one to plan it. Or else I'll be sent off to an orphanage.'

'That's not going to happen.'

'Of course it is, that's how it works, Pablo.'

'My mom is home now. We can ask her permission.'

'I have the money.'

'They might not charge you.'

'I want to pay.'

The phone conversation was very strange. The whole situation was, really. Pablo's mom accepted payment for the call immediately, and it seemed pretty rude to Gaspar: he'd expected her to start out saying, 'No, no need', then he would insist, then there'd be a resigned 'Well, okay.' That's how most people behaved. He didn't like that woman. She was quite pregnant, sure, but she wasn't about to burst, and she moved with an exaggerated slowness that Gaspar didn't find believable.

At his uncle's house in Brazil, a woman answered the phone. Gaspar knew Luis didn't live there any more and he was expecting a woman to answer, but until that moment he'd thought it would be a Brazilian woman. He'd even learned how to say hello and a few other words in Portuguese with a dictionary he'd consulted at the library. But the woman spoke Spanish. A strange Spanish, with an accent he didn't know: she used *tú* instead of the Argentine *vos*, and she rolled her double r's. But she was nice to him. She told him his uncle still didn't have a phone at his new place, but she could give him the address. And she did. The woman told him, as well, that his uncle – she called him by his name, Luis – sometimes called her, and she would ask him to get in touch with Gaspar. He said, That'd be good, thank you, and immediately regretted it, but at the same time, he thought, his uncle did call on occasion, it wasn't so strange, there was no reason for him to say he'd received a message from his ex-wife. It occurred to him to ask that Luis not tell his dad he had called, but it seemed too complicated, and the woman clearly wanted to get off the phone. She was friendly enough, but after answering his questions she fell silent. Gaspar thanked her and hung up, and he looked at the address he'd jotted down.

'Do you know where Villa Elisa is?' he asked Pablo, who shook his head but knelt down to find the T-Guide his father used. They paged through it and soon found the place: it was near La Plata, the capital of the province, and the streets were numbered, just as the woman had indicated. Gaspar felt that the knot he'd had in his throat for days was loosening: now at least he had somewhere to go. He could even visit if he wanted: the T-Guide said you could get there on a train from Constitución.

The cold was good for walking Ariadna, Vicky's new dog, who was still a puppy and pulled desperately at the leash. After what had happened with Diana, Vicky wouldn't let her loose in the street for a second. Gaspar liked to go with her on walks around the neighbourhood after school, at dusk; the leash was red, like the elastic band Vicky wore in her hair and Adela's cable-knit sweater with one arm cut off. Her phantom limb no longer bothered her, and she told everyone about it, showing them the box Gaspar had given her. The magic box, she called it. She'd confronted her mother and her physiotherapist about the box and neither of them had given her answers. They all lie, she insisted.

One day, after the World Cup, Adela had asked for a meeting with Vicky and Gaspar. She'd said it like that. I want a meeting. Not with Pablo, because he gets idiotic. And at the meeting, which was held in Vicky's room, she told them how during the trip to the south, her mom had gotten drunk one night.

'She was a different kind of drunk this time,' Adela told them.

'She started to cry about my dad. And I took my chance to get information, because she never talks to me about him. She told me he'd been murdered, that he's one of the disappeared.'

Gaspar and Vicky drew sharp breaths, but exchanged glances: what if this was another story, like the one about her arm and the Dobermann?

Then, Adela went on, her mom hadn't wanted to tell her anything else, and she'd gone into the bathroom.

'I didn't even realize that happened,' said Vicky.

'It was in Esquel, when we were at the cabin. I couldn't bring myself to tell you, I don't know. Plus, she told me something really important: that she dreams about Dad, a lot, and she always dreams he's in the house on Calle Villarreal. I asked her if he'd ever hidden out there and she said yes, but I don't know if it's true, because she was pretty out of it. At a certain point when she's drunk, she gets kind of delirious and she'll say anything, she'll say yes just to get out of something, for example. But maybe he did hide there, right?'

'Did you ask her again?' Vicky asked.

'Now she denies everything, same as she always does, but she was really clear when she talked about the house.'

'Come on, Adela,' huffed Gaspar. 'Don't make stuff up. I know you want to go in, but not like that.'

'What do you know?' Adela had shouted. 'Everyone lies. I do want to go in, yeah, I want to see if I can find anything of my dad's in there.'

Gaspar had left the meeting irate, but the anger had passed quickly. He was too worried about his own father to stay offended about the imaginary disappearance of Adela's.

Vicky ran, pulled along by Ariadna, and they turned on to Villarreal. She instinctively crossed so as not to pass the door of the house, and Gaspar followed her, but Adela didn't. She went over to the iron door and then into the yard. Gaspar and Vicky waited for her on the opposite sidewalk.

'I haven't heard it in a long time,' said Vicky.

'The buzzing?'

'Yeah, that noise like of insects I heard before is gone. Maybe it'll come back in summer.'

'Maybe it was a generator after all.'

'You know it wasn't.'

'I don't know anything.'

'Don't fight with me.'

'I'm not fighting. What's she doing?'

'She wants to see if she can pick the lock. But even if she breaks it, there's a padlock on it.'

'It won't open. I'll take you both when you want to go in.'

'She wants to climb on to the roof.'

'There's nowhere to grab hold. There's not even a tree, it's all dry, it looks like my house.'

And when he said that, when he said 'it looks like my house', Gaspar felt a shiver run through his entire body.

'Adela, come on, the dog's going crazy,' shouted Vicky. And then she told Gaspar: 'Now she thinks her father was a guerrilla fighter and she's reading books and magazines about the dictatorship.'

Gaspar said nothing. Adela came running over.

'When are you going to help me go in?' she asked Gaspar. 'You said after the World Cup.'

'In spring we'll go in.'

Gaspar looked at the house. The two bricked-up windows, the yellow grass, the grey walls. He couldn't explain it, but he felt like the house was challenging him. Let's just see if you can get in, it was saying. Was he crazy? Pablo had told him he'd had to cover Adela's mouth to get her to stop talking about the house, but not just because he was sick of it: he was scared. Ariadna saw a neighbour coming towards them with his dog, and Vicky had to struggle to keep her in check. And so they left the house behind, but Adela shot Gaspar one of her definitive looks: it would be in September, and now no one was going to take that date, that goal, away from her.

It was winter vacation, and Gaspar spent a lot of time at the heated club pool. He also stayed home a lot, waiting for his uncle to call. His enthusiasm for watching soccer had evaporated after the World Cup, and the only thing he wanted now was to hear the phone ring. But when he finally found out Luis had called, the news took him by surprise. His father informed him, calmly, while drinking a cup of tea in the dried-up backyard. He'd been feeling better for a few days now.

'Why did you call your uncle without telling me, son?' he asked, downing the rest of the tea. 'Don't try to lie to me.'

Juan set the mug down in the yard and went inside. Gaspar followed him, angry.

'Because you're never going to call him!' he shouted. 'You're going to leave me with I don't know who, or all alone. Maybe you *want* me to be alone.'

'You don't know anything, son.'

Gaspar saw his father was heading up to the first floor. If he went into the upstairs room, he'd get away. And he didn't want to let him hide. He wanted to tell his father what he was feeling. He grabbed him by the arm on the stairs and felt the rage burning in his eyes. He managed to make his father stop and turn around. He looked so tall there, two steps up, looking down at him with his eyes that were a little yellow and a little green, beside the stairway window that looked out on to the patio.

'Gaspar, your uncle is going to come when I ask him to.'

Gaspar smiled and pressed on his temples.

'I don't want to be with you,' he said. 'Maybe I'll go sooner, you can't stop me. I have my uncle's address. Or else I'll look for my grandparents. Maybe they do want to see me. Maybe you're the problem. I know you're sick but, I don't know, let your friends take care of you. I can't take this any more.'

His father gave him a look that was so different, so deeply disappointed and furious that Gaspar got scared. He'd seen him angry thousands of times, but now he felt he was in danger, the same kind of danger he'd felt at the Chascomús estate. He turned around to go down the stairs, to retreat from the confrontation, but he couldn't move. His father had grabbed him by the waist. Gaspar thought he was going to hit him and he cowered; the punch he was expecting landed on the window, which shattered and left sharp, jagged edges. And then, quickly and unexpectedly, Juan turned Gaspar back towards him. Terrified but also surprised, Gaspar watched as his father yanked his arm to the window and pierced it with the broken glass; he cut the skin with precision, with cruelty and precision, as if he were drawing a design. Gaspar screamed; the pain was cold and unbearable and it blinded him, and when he heard the glass hit bone, he felt dizzy and moaned. There was a hot wetness on his pants: he was pissing himself, and when he looked at his father to plead for mercy, he saw he was completely concentrated on the wound, studying it. The pain made his body go slack and he hung there, and the only thing keeping him from rolling down the stairs was his wounded arm that his father held on to, and he screamed again when Juan brought his lips to the wound and licked it, sucked it, filled his mouth with blood. Without letting go of Gaspar, he cut his own arm with a shard of broken glass. Brutally, he pressed his wound against Gaspar's lips.

'Drink!' he yelled. Gaspar, with the strength he had left, bit. But his father didn't pull away, not even when Gaspar's teeth opened the flesh. Now Gaspar's mouth was also filled with blood, and he swallowed it.

When Juan finally let go of him, Gaspar closed his eyes, but a slap in the face woke him up from his faint. His father, now kneeling, was looking at him with unfocused, transparent eyes. His chin was smeared with blood and his lips were red. He didn't seem to be alone. It seemed like there were people moving in the shadows behind him.

'Go now. Run!'

Gaspar didn't understand, and Juan dragged him down the stairs by his good arm and pushed him towards the door. He opened it and shoved him out and closed and locked the door, all without a word. Please, Dad, Gaspar said in a quiet voice, and then he looked down at his pants, covered in urine and blood, and his mangled forearm. He got up and thought fast. A taxi, ask someone for help, what time was it? Pablo could take him to the emergency room, a hospital.

He raised his arm to stem the bleeding – he'd been taught that once, when he'd cut his finger on a box cutter at school – but it didn't work, and he left a trail of blood behind him. As he walked the block to Pablo's house, he didn't meet anyone. It was incredible, but the neighbourhood was empty.

The sound of the doorbell was constant, as if it had gotten stuck. Coming, shouted Pablo, but the endless buzzing was disconcerting. Who would ring like that, and why? He was alone in the house. His mom had gone to the hospital for her pregnancy check-up – her due date was just weeks away – and his dad worked all day. He looked out the window before opening and recognized Gaspar's sneakers.

He was about to say, Why are you ringing like that, dummy, but he was left speechless by the sight of Gaspar's arm, his wounded arm: in the bloody cut, so red, the skin and muscle hung down like something edible, like the meat under the display-case light at the butcher's; he could see the white of bone. The skin of Gaspar's face was grey and sweaty, and he was leaning against the doorbell because he couldn't stand up. What happened? Come in, said Pablo, and Gaspar shook his head. No. Take me to the hospital right now on the motorcycle.

Come inside, said Pablo, and he pushed Gaspar towards the living room, then ran to the bathroom for some towels and wrapped the wound. When he did, Gaspar screamed. Pablo's mother never used the motorcycle; it was his father's, for weekends. Pablo himself barely knew how to ride it: his dad had taught him a little, but only let him go around the block, or as far as the park on some Sundays, when there wasn't much traffic. But the hospital was only ten blocks away and he could go straight there along a side street.

'I have to throw up,' said Gaspar.

'Hold it, we're going. Lean on me.'

Gaspar stood up and let all the weight of his good side fall on to Pablo's shoulder. The towels weren't soaked through with blood yet. He wasn't bleeding so much. But his pants were soaked, and Pablo had caught a glimpse of a small puddle on the sidewalk where Gaspar had waited for him to come to the door.

Pablo opened the garage door and wheeled out the white Zanella as fast as he could. Gaspar had sat down on the ground to vomit almost silently. Would he to be able to get him up? He got the motorcycle as far as the street and Gaspar stumbled over to climb on to the back seat, but his body drooped to one side, then forward; he couldn't control his dizziness. He's going to faint, thought Pablo, and then he had an idea.

'Let's do this,' he said, and quickly put down the kickstand, lifted up Gaspar's shirt, and pulled the belt from his jeans. He knew Gaspar was wearing one of his father's very long belts. Pablo sat on the driver's seat and asked Gaspar to hug him tight with his good arm and to get as close as possible – Gaspar obeyed mechanically, as if listening to orders in a dream – and then he checked to see if the belt could reach around them both, if it was long enough to act as a tether to hold Gaspar's body against his. It was. Barely. It was very tight, and he struggled, partly because his hands were trembling, to fasten it in the last hole, to close the buckle, to check that his friend was more or less stable on the back seat. Hold on to me and don't faint, he said. Pablo felt Gaspar's head on his shoulder, and his soft hair gave him shivers on the back of his neck. He started off.

The ten blocks to the hospital seemed like forty, and the minute-long red light at the crossroads where Zuviría intersected the avenue was so endless he thought the stop light must be broken. He felt Gaspar's breath on his neck, and every time his friend's arm slackened its hold, he adjusted it again. No buses ran on that street, and he was grateful. He asked Gaspar several times what had happened, mostly just to hear his voice, and Gaspar answered, I tripped on the stairs and fell into the window, you remember the window on the landing. Pablo remembered. He didn't understand how that accident could have happened, but he said nothing.

When they reached the hospital, Pablo parked the motorcycle between two cars and didn't chain it or lock the wheels. Gaspar had recovered a little and needed less help to reach the emergency room; on the way, he pulled off the towels acting as a bandage by himself. He did it with dry eyes and a deep breath, trembling a little. Pablo thought he would never have been able to manage on his own with a wound like that, he

335

would surely be scared and crying for his parents. Gaspar was scared, he could tell, but he also had a self-control that Pablo found incredible.

As soon as they went in, some people who were sitting on the long bench in the waiting area – Pablo glimpsed a woman caressing the head of a girl with braids, an elderly couple, a man his father's age but fatter, whose foot was bare and swollen – stood up to make room for Gaspar, and a tall, fat woman pounded on the door to the attending rooms and shouted, 'It's urgent, it's urgent!' Out came a doctor with grey-streaked hair pulled back in a ponytail and a serious expression that said she was used to anxious patients. But when she saw Gaspar, she held the door open and said, Come in, while she led him along by the shoulder. Pablo followed them, carrying the towels.

'Are you two alone? Where are your parents?'

'We're not brothers,' said Pablo. 'They're all working.'

Of course, Pablo didn't know what Juan Peterson was doing, since he didn't work. Or why he wasn't with his son. Was he in the hospital? He'd been spending a lot of days hospitalized lately. Not here: at a very expensive, exclusive clinic, his mother said, adding, if only I could give birth to your little brother at a classy place like that.

The doctor sat Gaspar on the cot and rested his arm on an aluminium table covered in white sheets. She looked at the wound with her glasses on.

'You're going to need surgery,' she said. 'I can't just give you a few stitches, it's very deep.'

Gaspar nodded.

'How did it happen?'

Pablo intervened and explained the accident just as Gaspar had told it to him. The doctor didn't object and went back to studying the wound. With gloves and tweezers she lifted one of the swollen edges of the wound, revealing the bone. Gaspar stifled a scream and then his eyes did fill with tears, but he brusquely wiped them away with his good arm.

'Now we'll get you to the operating room.'

And she left after injecting him with a painkiller. Right away, before Gaspar and Pablo could speak, another doctor appeared, a man this time, and he repeated the same questions, the observation of the wound, the insistence on the need for surgery. He spoke of the type of suture, asked about parents. I need a responsible adult, he said. Pablo suddenly remembered the obvious. He couldn't explain how he hadn't thought of it sooner.

'Dr Lidia Peirano works here, maybe you know her? Her daughter is our best friend, she's our neighbour. She's friends with Gaspar's father.'

'Ah, Lidia. She's here today, I saw her on the floor.'

The doctor picked up the phone and spoke into it. Then he prepared another syringe, lowered Gaspar's pants a little, and gave him the injection. He also smiled at him, for the first time. You're going to be okay, he said. That's one ugly cut, were you running on the stairs, were you two playing? I was alone, said Gaspar, and yes, I was running down the stairs. You need to be careful, said the doctor, and he smiled again, but Gaspar didn't smile back. It wasn't just the pain, Pablo realized. It wasn't just fear.

He was lying.

Lidia Peirano came in dishevelled and talking loudly. Oh, sweetheart, what happened to you? Again, the story of the fall on the stairs. Were you together? No, said Pablo, he came to get me like that. We rode here on the motorcycle. Lidia looked at them in astonishment. You can tell me all about it later, for now we have to sew you up. I've given him a tetanus shot, an antibiotic, and a painkiller, said the doctor, who was taking

Gaspar's pulse. He wasn't talking to them any more, only to Lidia. He has tachycardia, he lost a lot of blood. Lidia looked at the wound too, and shook her head. Lie back, she told Gaspar, and she placed some pillows under his feet. That way you won't get as dizzy. Then she told the doctor, his father is a cardiac patient; as far as I know Gaspar doesn't have problems, but let them know and monitor him, order an ECG right away. And then: How did you cut yourself so deep? I got stuck on the glass and I pulled on it to get free, said Gaspar. But honey, you could have broken the glass with your other hand. I wasn't thinking, said Gaspar, it really hurt.

The look he exchanged with Pablo had something ferocious about it. Silence, his eyes ordered, their pupils dilated, dark blue eyes in the badly lit emergency room.

We'll talk later, Pablo mouthed in reply, and Gaspar nodded.

The doctor took his blood pressure, and Gaspar closed his eyes. A little low, said the doctor. Let's take him in. Miller's on duty in surgery, the kid's lucky. You're lucky! The doctor smiled at Gaspar, and then he said something to Lidia about nerves and tendons. And about how strange the wound was: there wasn't a scratch on the underside of the arm, which was much more delicate.

'You wait outside.' Lidia went with Pablo as far as the waiting room. 'I'll let you know. What about Juan? We have to tell him.' She gave Pablo two tokens. 'There's a pay phone in the hall, call him. If he doesn't answer, call my house, tell Vicky and have her keep calling.'

Pablo hesitated and started to say something, but Lidia interrupted. 'I know he's a strange person and he's not good with you guys, but he's his father. And that's a very, very ugly wound. Do as I say.'

At Gaspar's house the phone rang and no one answered,

but Pablo imagined Juan Peterson sitting on his yellow sofa, listening to those peals like screams until they stopped.

Pablo listened while the man with the swollen foot told him how when he was young, he'd cut himself on a metal sheet at the factory, and the tetanus shot had hurt worse than the cut. He showed him the scar on his hand. I thought it was going to affect my fingers, but it didn't. Then the factory shut down, but that's another story. Your brother is going to come out just great.

He's not my brother, Pablo repeated. Why did people keep making that mistake? They didn't look anything alike. He called Vicky and told her what had happened, and she kept asking, But is he okay? until Pablo got mad. Finally she said:

'I'm not going to Gaspar's house, especially not alone.'

'Your mom didn't say to go, she said to call.'

'I want to go to the hospital. I'll bring tokens and call from there.'

The call cut off as Vicky was telling him she was going to get Adela's mom: she should be home by now, let her talk to Gaspar's dad, or go and look for him if he wasn't home. And Pablo returned to his seat and the wait. He was still holding the bloody towel. He suddenly remembered the motorcycle and went out to secure it. No one had stolen it, but he had forgotten to bring the chain. He ran back to call Vicky with a token he'd found in his pocket and asked her to bring it, and he also told her he'd left the garage door open. Then he sat on a bench outside the ER under a small tiled roof, facing a flower bed.

They fought and he hurt him, Gaspar's dad had hurt him. Pablo was sure of it even though it was unthinkable and he had no proof beyond the way Gaspar was acting. He remembered that window. It was big, placed right where the stairway

339

turned. He had brushed against it that night when he'd gone into Gaspar's house and seen Juan with his friend, his boyfriend, that night Pablo still dreamed about and then woke up sweating, damp between his legs; sometimes he had to lock himself in the bathroom, get into the tub, close his eyes and remember Juan's back, smooth and pale under the moonlight, and his friend's back, marked by two painted lines, or were they scars? He tried to think calmly, to forget the circle on the floor, the smell, his own fingers clammy under the sheets every time he dreamed of those men or thought about them before going to sleep. It would be easy to fall into the glass if you slipped or tripped: it *was* in a dangerous location. Still, he knew Gaspar well enough to know when he was lying. And what should he do? If Juan was capable of such a thing, he had to get Gaspar out of that house. He had no tokens left, but he found some money and ran over to the kiosk to make another call.

'It's a mess,' said Vicky. 'My dad had to leave because who knows what happened at the pharmacy, they got an order in or something, and I'm stuck here with Virginia. I can't leave her with my grandma because she's feeling bad. Adela's mom went to Gaspar's. She says she'll take care of it.'

Pablo bought a Coke but couldn't get it down, the bubbles felt too big, and then went back inside the hospital. He sat down next to a newly arrived patient who was clutching his arm against his chest and saying he'd fallen like a dumbass in the street. Pablo could smell the alcohol on his breath. Should he call his mother? He looked at the clock: four in the afternoon. Would she be back yet? Sometimes she took a long time at the doctor's. He had to call because she would get scared, there was blood on the front step, on the sidewalk, on the sofa, in the garage, and the towels were missing from the bathroom. The motorcycle was gone, too, though Vicky had taken the time to run over and close the garage door, so that wasn't a problem. But the blood was. She's going to think it's mine and she'll get scared, it's a lot of blood, Gaspar might even need a transfusion. What if they give him the wrong blood type? That can kill you. Though here in the hospital they must know. What's his blood type? I'm a universal donor, they told me, I can give him blood if he needs it.

Just then Lidia startled him from his thoughts. She was wearing her white uniform with the stethoscope hung around her neck – he rarely saw her dressed any other way, not even on weekends, because she always worked either Saturday or Sunday.

'It's all moving along, they're sewing him up. He's going to come out of this perfect. Did you tell Juan?'

'Betty's telling him.'

Pablo lowered his head and squeezed the towels. Where had he left the belt? He felt Gaspar's breath again on the back of his neck when they were on the motorcycle, hot in the cold air of the winter afternoon. Maybe he could sleep with me, we'll use the new bedspread Dad bought me, it's made of down and it's really warm. That's if he doesn't die, he thought.

'I'll be right back,' said Lidia, and Pablo stayed in the waiting room. There was a girl around his age who couldn't catch her breath, and her mother was screaming about her asthma. The suffocating girl was growing more and more agitated until finally a doctor ushered her in and closed the door in her mother's face. Pablo thought about Gaspar, who was alone while they were sewing him up. And Juan? Maybe he was hiding out in one of the rooms of that big dark house, or maybe he was with the grey-haired friend who had moaned as if it hurt, did it hurt a lot? Ever since he'd seen them he'd wondered that, whether it hurt or not.

I hope I'm wrong, he thought, squeezing the towels tighter. I hope Juan is in the hospital and Gaspar is telling the truth.

Lidia came back with several pieces of news: You can go in to see Gaspar, he can leave in a while, but I'd prefer him to stay a few hours until Juan can come. If he doesn't turn up, I'll take him to my house. What bad luck, poor thing. He just hit his head two months ago.

Gaspar wasn't alone. There was a doctor with him, a different one.

'Your friend is a champ!' he said. 'He's no sissy, this one! He's going to be good as new.'

Then he led Lidia to one corner and Pablo couldn't hear much of what he said, something about dressings and antibiotics. When they came back – Gaspar hadn't looked at him once, just stared down at his bandage – they said, If you need anything just knock on the door, we'll come for you.

As soon as the doctors closed the door, Gaspar sat up in the bed and looked Pablo in the eye.

'You didn't say anything, right?'

'About what?'

'If you said anything, I'll kill you.'

'Say anything about what, man?!'

Gaspar lowered his voice and hunched over: he seemed like an animal.

'We had a fight; he was the one who cut me. You realized it. If you tell anyone, I'll kill you.'

Gaspar was threatening him, he was furious, he even looked like he wanted to hit Pablo. But Pablo couldn't get angry. The revelation had left him exhausted, like he couldn't catch his breath. He moved closer to Gaspar though his friend put out his hand in a clear 'leave me alone' gesture; he ignored it and sat beside him on the bed and saw how Gaspar was trying not to look at him, his eyes instead exploring the peeling green paint on the wall, the poster that labelled the human skeleton, a taped-up sheet of paper with X-ray schedules, the many glass bottles and syringes. Pablo touched Gaspar's hand and Gaspar let him, and he also let him put an arm around his shoulders, but he wouldn't accept more consolation. You going to tell me what happened? Pablo asked in a low voice, and Gaspar nodded, looking at his friend with dry eyes when he said: But I can't right now. That's okay, Pablo told him.

'Thank you,' said Gaspar after a while, after taking a several deep breaths. Was he trying not to cry, or to calm himself? Pablo didn't understand, he had no idea how someone would feel after being abused like that by their father. 'Really. I don't know what I would have done if you hadn't been there.'

'You would've taken a taxi.'

'Maybe. The belt was a great idea.'

He said it without smiling. Pablo thought he was never going to see Gaspar smile again.

'Otherwise you would have fallen on your face. Are you still dizzy?'

'A little.'

Lidia came back in, almost slamming the door behind her. Let's see here, she said, and she took Gaspar's pulse. We're going to your house. Betty says your dad got home a while ago. Arm up, like they told you, don't leave it hanging.

Before following Lidia out, Pablo stopped Gaspar with a hand on the shoulder of his good arm.

'Are you sure about going to your house?'

'I'm not scared of him.'

'Why not?'

'It's between me and him. Pablo: if you say anything, I'm not going to kill you, but I'll never speak to you again for the rest of my life.'

And with that he left the room, arm held high, the belt back in place, his pants dry now and stained with blood.

Gaspar felt a little dizzy from the car's movement but didn't say anything to Lidia. Pablo had left on the motorcycle. See you later, Gaspar had promised him, but he wasn't sure there would be a later. He couldn't explain it, but he didn't know if he really was going to see Pablo again, if he was going to be able to leave his house. Now there was no possibility of escape. But he didn't want to escape. He wanted to see his father.

The door was half-open. When the car stopped, Adela's mom Betty came out of the house to meet them. Always so thin and sharp-boned. He was surprised to see her there. Betty had known his mother. What had she and his dad been talking about? She seemed a little nervous. Gaspar felt his knees go slack when he saw his father standing in the hallway, his face full of false concern. He had to lean against the wall. Lidia realized he was dizzy and led him slowly to the living room, where the sofa was. On the ground floor, that sofa and the three kitchen chairs were the only places to sit apart from the floor. Betty left and closed the door behind her. That woman is hiding something, thought Gaspar. Why am I only now realizing something so obvious? Maybe Adela is even right about her father. Parents should not exist, we should all be orphans, grow up alone, let someone teach us how to cook and bathe when we're little and that's that.

Lidia went over to Juan, but Gaspar couldn't make out what she said. He saw his father pretend to listen and then say thank you – Gaspar could read his lips – and nod as he accepted the box of medicine, disinfectant, and gauze. His father's hair was very clean and a little long, and he was trying to push a fine blond lock behind his ear. Lidia put a hand on his shoulder – she had to extend her arm almost completely – and Gaspar heard, Whatever you need, you know very well we're here for you, and his father, such a liar, saying he had found the window broken and seen the blood and hadn't understood until Beatriz arrived.

'I was in the clinic. It's like a bad joke, this whole thing. When I was leaving for the hospital to find you, you all were already on your way here.'

'Whatever you need, Juan, really.'

'There won't be a problem. The nurse will help us.'

They went on talking like that for a while. The dizziness had passed, but Gaspar was no longer interested in what they said. He felt the throbbing pain in his arm; it wasn't very intense, they'd given him a lot of painkillers, but it smarted. It was going to get worse.

When he closed the door, Juan only grunted. Instead of going to Gaspar, he went towards his room: on the way, he tossed the box of gauze and medicine and disinfectant on the floor.

Gaspar wasn't about to let him lock himself away. He wasn't going to let his father abandon him in the living room, alone and in pain.

'Come here!' he yelled, and he felt that he no longer had pain or painkillers in his body, only a rage that made him tremble. He could kill his father now. He wanted him to realize it. 'Say something, you son of a bitch!'

Gaspar stood up in the living room and waited for his father, who walked slowly back. He felt the urge to rush him and smash his head against the wall. But when he looked at him, the rage dissolved and he felt like lying on the floor and ceasing to breathe.

'Where are you, Dad? You're not my father. My father loved me. Who are you?'

The silence was so complete that Gaspar thought this man who couldn't be his father must have left.

'I'm empty.'

'No. No. I want you to tell me where my father is.'

'He's here. He's still here.'

Gaspar heard the footsteps approaching and he put out his good arm. Don't hurt me any more, please, he said. Juan sat down on the floor beside him. Gaspar smelled his scent, recognized it.

'You are what I love most in life, Gaspar.'

'So, what's wrong with you? Kill me, Dad, please, I'm not scared.'

Gaspar looked into his father's eyes and saw a horrible craving there, a desire completely new to him, like an unknown colour.

'Don't ask that.'

'It's what you want.'

'No. It's not what I want.'

Gaspar felt rage well up again. Liar, he thought. He was acting. He hadn't even asked if his arm was okay.

'I didn't ask you because I know it's okay.'

'Get out of my head,' growled Gaspar.

'I'm always in your head, even if you don't realize it. Don't close yourself off. If you do, it's going to hurt. Enough pain, Gaspar.'

And then Gaspar felt something that he would remember for years to come, but didn't know how to name: a blood transfusion, hot water in his veins, images he didn't see with his eyes. He saw himself sleeping with his father in a bed with white sheets, beside a fan. And before, when he was very little, a baby, lying on his father's chest while he read a book at an impossible angle so as not to wake him. The back seat of a car. The sound of the waterfalls. Swimming. His parents dancing beside a record player. A black light in the night, a woman with no lips, his mother in an orange shirt playing with him in a garden, his father talking in a dark room, the geometrical sketches in the notebooks and the memory of a damp house with people all around, stains on the ceiling and his father beside him shaking his head no. The smell of gasoline and laughter in the water. And above all, along with the images, that heat in his whole body that made him lunge at his father, beat him with his fists. His father made no move to stop him and Gaspar tried to punch his eyes, scratch his cheeks, until he got tired. And when he got tired, he dropped on to the floor and looked up at the ceiling, at the lamp that was swaying as if moved by a current of air from an open window. I wish it could have been different, he heard.

'People who love each other don't hurt each other,' said Gaspar.

'That's not true,' replied Juan. 'I hurt you to save you.'

'Are you crazy?'

'It's possible that to you I'm crazy, but it's too late for you to understand and I don't want you to understand, son. I'm prepared for you to hate me. I would like to die and leave you with a good memory of me, but that's not possible, and, I think, it's for the best.'

'I don't hate you,' sighed Gaspar. 'But I'm afraid of you. Why did you cut me? Tell me the truth. You made me drink your blood, Dad.'

'It was necessary. Every step was necessary in order for you to be protected.'

'From who, Dad? You're the only one I need protection from!

What if I tell someone? You could go to jail for hurting me like that, this isn't the same as smacking me around.'

'I'm also prepared for you to turn me in.'

'You just lied to Lidia.'

'I could tell them the truth. I don't care.'

Gaspar sat up. How long had he been there, on the floor, beside his father? Hours? His arm was hurting terribly.

'We always took care of each other. I took care of you all this time. You shouldn't have done this.'

'I'm going to keep taking care of you. Wait,' said Juan, and he gently touched the hand of Gaspar's wounded arm. 'Don't be afraid of me, there's no need to be afraid of me any more.'

Juan rested his hand on the bandage and Gaspar gave a start, but then, immediately, the pain disappeared. It didn't fade away: it disappeared as if it had never existed. His father looked at him. His eyes were bloodshot. He looked dead. He *is* dead, thought Gaspar.

'The wound is still there. Take care of it as if it hurt, but it won't hurt any more. Don't take the painkillers, you don't need them. Do take the antibiotics.'

'Where did the pain go?'

'I think you can guess the answer to that, son.'

Gaspar lay back on the floor. He wanted to sleep without dreaming, he wanted to sleep for years.

He was sitting on the front stoop when his uncle arrived. He recognized him immediately: the family resemblance was unmistakable, though Luis wasn't as big as Juan and he had some grey hair. He was older, Gaspar knew, he must be around forty years old. His uncle waved at him and came running over. He was wearing a down jacket over a flannel shirt, and a bag was slung over his shoulder. When he got closer Gaspar noticed he was tanned, and it was a strange contrast to his blond hair, lighter because of the grey; he also had a lot of wrinkles. They looked at each other for a second until his uncle smiled and hugged him, tousled his hair, and said, You're so big, it's been over three years since I've gotten a photo of you. Gaspar's voice came out shaky when he said:

'There's coffee from this morning. Do you drink coffee?'

Luis said yes, but before going in he paused to look at the house. Wonderful, he said, pointing out the wooden door, the iron shutters painted dark green, and finally the names inscribed beside the front door: O'Farrell and Del Pozo.

'They're two famous architects,' he explained. 'You live in a fantastic house.'

Gaspar felt a little ashamed when his uncle entered, because inside was not fantastic. It looked uninhabited. Luis said nothing, though he did look surprised as he glanced around. Not a picture on the walls, no furniture to store things, just that yellow sofa. Gaspar was grateful for his silence. The kitchen was more welcoming, and Gaspar started heating the coffee.

'Where's your dad?'

'I think he's asleep.'

'I'm going to stay for a while, kiddo, you two can't be on your own.'

Gaspar took a deep breath before asking:

'Why didn't you come sooner?'

His uncle smiled.

'I heard you talked to Mónica in Brazil. Your dad asked me not to come until he called me. You know your dad isn't an easy person. Nor is it easy to get divorced.'

'I bet,' said Gaspar. His uncle's voice was soothing. It was the same one he'd heard so many times on the phone, on his birthday, at Christmas, sometimes for Three Kings Day, every year for as long as he could remember. Luis didn't feel like a stranger, though he'd only ever seen him in photos. He hadn't called for the World Cup, and that was odd. He asked his uncle about it.

'I did call!' Luis said, and he laughed the laugh that Gaspar also recognized, a short and pretty loud peal of laughter, a little like a shout. 'But there was never anyone here during the games.'

'Dad was here, I think, but he wasn't about to answer. I watched at a friend's house for good luck.'

'Too bad, I would have liked to talk to you.'

Gaspar spilled a little milk when he poured it into his coffee. He thought it was strange that his uncle drank coffee without sugar, but he said nothing.

'Did you break your arm?'

Gaspar was expecting the question because his arm was still partly immobilized. He'd be getting the stitches out soon. He didn't want to talk to his uncle about his injury. From repeating the lie so much, someday he might just end up believing it.

'I cut myself bad falling on the stairs. I'll show you later, the staircase has a window and I slipped and put my arm through the glass. They operated and everything.'

'Really? Your dad didn't tell me anything.'

Of course not, thought Gaspar. The wound itched, pulled; he scratched carefully over the bandage. His uncle sipped his coffee: he wasn't suspicious, he'd believed the story of the accident. And why would he suspect anything? Just in case, Gaspar kept talking. He told Luis how he'd be going back to school next Monday and he still wasn't allowed to play soccer, though he didn't understand why, when there were players who did it after injecting themselves with worse things.

He wasn't able to finish his tale or receive a reply because he was interrupted by his father's footsteps in the living room. Gaspar was surprised to see him enter the kitchen: it was unusual for him to get out of bed. And it was with even more surprise that he took in their hug, the emotion in his uncle's eyes, his father's tall body that seemed so fragile as it made that affectionate gesture. The two of them left the kitchen; Luis gestured to indicate he'd be back in a while, and his father didn't even glance at him. Gaspar started to wash the mugs one-handed, because he couldn't get his wounded arm wet.

Vicky was surprised to come home from school and find Gaspar's uncle Luis drinking mate with her mother in the messy living room of her house; Lidia was off from the hospital that day and the next. Her mom introduced her as 'one of Gaspar's best friends', and Luis said he'd heard about her. Vicky thought he was like an older and nicer version of Gaspar's dad. The important conversation was over, Vicky realized, because now they were talking about Luis's life in Brazil. A neighbourhood called Gamboa, near Santa Teresa. How lovely, her mother was saying, and Luis replied: More or less. Maybe I didn't think it was so beautiful any more because I missed home. They talked about exile, and Luis said he'd missed the smells, the food, that Rio was a wonderful city, but also very melancholic. And this return is also sad, he said, and here they both looked at Vicky, but she reached for a pastry filled with dulce de leche and stayed put.

'He'd be much more comfortable in a hospital,' said Lidia suddenly.

'So they tell me, but he wants to be at home as long as possible. They're going to hospitalize him soon.'

Gaspar's house was already like a hospital. Vicky had only been by once lately, but she'd noticed the change. It was warm, with the heaters turned on. She'd gotten a look into Juan's room: they'd bought a new bed that would make it easier to tend to him, tall, with railings and a lever to raise the head, and she'd seen all the medicines neatly organized on a bedside table. The nurse slept there, and the doctor almost always did too. Vicky's mom also helped out on her days off. That was all fine, Vicky thought, but she realized that in the meantime, no one was paying much attention to Gaspar, who rode his bike around the streets or went swimming or to the movies, where he watched one film after another. He looked so sad, so skinny, and he didn't even seem happy when he was watching soccer any more. Plus, he was skipping school.

'Gaspar is doing really bad,' said Vicky.

Luis looked at her, the mate straw between his lips, his turquoise eyes very attentive. He set the gourd on the table, poured hot water in, and handed it to Vicky.

'He's really messed up, it's true, because of his dad. And on top of that he had two accidents in a few months, poor thing's had some bad luck.'

'Still, they don't really get along.'

'My brother was never an easy guy, and I think Gaspar is having a hard time accepting that he's going to have to say goodbye to his dad.'

Vicky was taken aback by this man who spoke to her so seriously, like she was an adult, who looked at her so frankly, and who made great mate.

'Are you going to adopt him?'

'I already started the process. I'm now Gaspar's guardian.'

'What's that?'

'It means I'm the adult in charge of taking care of him.'

'Then maybe you should pay a little more attention, because you sure aren't taking very good care of him.'

Luis folded his hands on his lap and thought for a bit before answering.

'Look, Vicky. What you're saying is true. I would like for Gaspar to listen to me more, spend more time at home. He's still very young. Everyone deals with the death of their father or mother as best they can. My mom died when I was just a little older than Gaspar. It was a very ugly illness and I rebelled a little, too. I'm sure that you all, as his friends, can help him better than I can, because you know him better.'

Vicky was wearing her gym sweatpants, and she crossed her legs on the sofa.

'I don't know how,' she said.

'See what I mean?' said Luis. 'No one knows.'

It was late when Gaspar got home. His father was in the hospital now and things were calmer at the house, no bustling nurses, no need to be silent. He didn't know if his uncle was there; he divided his time between the clinic and trying to be there for Gaspar. There was pizza in the oven, and though it was cold and several slices were missing, he ate it standing at the kitchen counter. It was a stroke of luck: the café in the park had closed without warning, and he was really hungry after spending the afternoon at the movies. The bedroom door was cracked open and for a moment he thought he saw his dad's shape in the bed, but it was just a movement of the shadows.

He heard keys in the door. The steps that followed were his uncle's: decisive, fast, sneakered. They headed straight for the kitchen, and when Gaspar saw his face, tired and frowning, an expression between worried and sad, he thought: There's a talk coming. *The* talk.

His uncle sat down on one of the kitchen chairs and asked for a glass of something cool. Gaspar poured some apple juice over ice. Maybe he wanted wine? No, he would have said so.

'You want to come to the clinic with me? You haven't visited your dad since he's been there.'

'What for? Did something change?'

'Why so angry, son?' Luis shook the ice in his glass like it was whiskey on the rocks, then said: 'Something's changed, yes. Your dad is no longer conscious. He had an embolism this morning. You know what that is?'

'No.'

'They explained it more or less, I don't understand it much either. In the end, what it means is that they don't know if he's going to wake up.'

Gaspar felt his knees start shaking, and at the same time he felt such an immense relief that he didn't know how to react.

'It's time for you to say goodbye, I think. They don't know if he can hear or not. They say your old man is unpredictable.'

'Why should I say goodbye if he's not even going to know? You're lying,' said Gaspar, and he didn't want to hear any more. He went to his room and locked the door so his uncle wouldn't bother him. In case he came knocking on the door, Gaspar lay face up on the bed and put on his headphones and an album by the Cure – the one that was on his stereo, on repeat – and he cried in the dark, trying not to make any noise, until he fell asleep with the music in his head. He dreamed his father was talking to him while he held a giant knife, like a hunter's, in his hands. He sat there on his deathbed and talked to Gaspar, and he had cut off his eyelids, with the knife, maybe, though Gaspar didn't see any blood in the dream, only his father's yellow eyes wide open, and on the sheets blond eyelashes stuck to bits of dried skin.

He couldn't understand what his father was saying, and that was what disturbed him the most in the dream, because it seemed important.

*

That Saturday was the day. They had agreed to meet there, in the barren front yard of the house on Villarreal, after dinner. Gaspar said he would rather go in when it was light out, and by 6 p.m. it would be dark, but his friends ignored him and he didn't insist. His father hadn't woken up now for two days. In the end he had gone to the clinic; his uncle stopped insisting but he decided on his own. Juan had a special room in intensive care all to himself. Gaspar sat on the bed. His dad's eyes were closed. Gaspar opened them. The pupil on the right was fixed and black, like a beetle. The other one was normal. Touching his body was like touching clay. He couldn't believe his father had been extinguished like that. He wasn't dead but neither was he fully alive, and although Gaspar was still angry, he would have liked to talk to him some, maybe for the last time, tell him that he didn't forgive him but that he loved him. Was his father going to die without ever speaking to him again? Had it really ended so suddenly? When his dad moved slightly Gaspar leaned closer, relieved – he wasn't dead yet. But it had only seemed he was moving because of the strange way he was breathing: he would go nearly a minute without breathing at all and then gasp suddenly, as if just remembering he needed to, quickly, frantically, and then stop breathing again. He didn't open his eyes, but could he hear? Gaspar leaned down close to his ear and said: Wake up, Dad. He took his father's hand, but there was no reply. When he left the room his uncle was waiting for him, and Gaspar asked if he'd noticed how he was breathing. Luis said yes and put an arm around his shoulders, but Gaspar pushed him away. He didn't want to be touched. And where were Esteban and Tali, if they were such good friends? Why had they left him alone? On Friday morning, before going to school, Gaspar stopped by the bedroom and thought he saw his father lying dead in his bed, so motionless, the sun filtering in through the metal shutter, and he stood in the doorway until the image vanished. Yes, he was going to move in with his uncle, whom he liked, who was so different, so similar to his friends' parents, but he felt expelled from his real house – a house he didn't fully know and where he'd only been allowed to enter some rooms, yes, but a secret house that was completely his. He felt like a door had been slammed in his face, like he'd been sent to a different world to be raised by a stranger, like in *Star Wars*.

He had arrived early at the house on Villarreal. On the way there he'd seen some boys playing soccer in the street and a group of girls jumping rope. It was Saturday evening, the weather was already starting to turn a little warm, and the sky seemed painted, not a cloud in it, darkening towards the blue that came before the black of night. Gaspar had a large crowbar in his backpack to use as a lever; he'd borrowed it from the tyre repair shop. Pablo was in charge of bringing the flashlight, Adela would be bringing keys to try in the lock, and Vicky wasn't bringing anything because all of a sudden she was against going into the house. She'd told him very clearly: I'm scared, there's something in the house and I don't know if it has to do with Adela's dad or not, but I don't care. Don't come in if you don't want to, Gaspar had told her. I'm not going to leave you guys, she'd replied, but I sure hope the door doesn't open.

The door would open, Gaspar was sure of it.

He sat down on the sidewalk to wait for the others and lit a cigarette. From his position he couldn't see either the house or the door, but he could picture them clearly.

He remembered how, when they were scattering his mother's ashes at the Costanera, his dad had told him to open the iron gate leading down to the beach. What had he done then? Just obeyed. He thought he could do it again on his own. His father was going to be cremated, too. No one ever got cremated. Why did his parents? He had asked his uncle, who, clearly uncomfortable, had said he thought it seemed like a healthy habit, though he preferred the earth, a grave. Cremation was expensive, too, though that wasn't a problem. Gaspar asked if they would get the ashes, and his uncle replied that it would be up to them. He added that Juan had told him: If you scatter them, do it in the river. But as long as they're in the same house as Gaspar, let him decide when. Again, the box of ashes on a shelf. That's what it meant to be an orphan: to have boxes of ashes and not know what to do with them.

Adela arrived first, as he figured she would. She had the keys. She sat down beside Gaspar on the sidewalk: she was wearing a pair of jeans a little too big for her and an old pink sweatshirt with wide sleeves. Pablo arrived next, with Vicky. Gaspar could tell she was scared, more scared than the rest of them. Of course, she was the only one who'd heard that buzzing from the house; Gaspar had tried to hear it too, but for him the house was silent.

'Let's not go in. Please,' said Vicky.

'Don't come if you don't want.' Adela was getting mad, and she went up to the front door with a padlock key in her hand. Gaspar let her try to open it, let her fumble with the key in the lock for a while, though he knew that even if it was possible to open it, she wouldn't be able to with only one hand. He let it go on until he started to feel sorry for her. He thought about his father, pictured him as he lay dying alone in the hospital bed, breathing intermittently, and he said to himself, Come on then, let's get into this house, what can really happen to us? If Adela thinks there's some clue in here, let's see if she's right; let's find out what the buzzing is, why people are so afraid of this shitty little house, what's hiding in here. I can open it. I can enter what is hidden, he thought, and he repeated it to himself: I can enter hidden places, I always could, but I don't know if I want to live like that. Did my dad live like that?

He gently pushed Adela aside and positioned himself to block his hands and the lock from the others' view, so they wouldn't realize he wasn't even manipulating it. He merely took it between his fingers, and under that minimal pressure, the padlock opened.

'You were right,' he told Adela, trying to hide the droplets of sweat forming on his forehead and dripping down his back. His body hadn't made any effort, but it behaved as if it were exhausted after a run: his heart was beating fast and hard. 'That key opens everything. Now let's see what we can do about the lock on the door. Hand me my backpack.'

Adela handed it to him: Gaspar tried not to meet her eyes. She was looking at him with an infatuated expression, the same look as when he'd given her the box to fix her phantom limb. Why did he do things for Adela? He cared about her, she was his friend, it wasn't because he felt sorry for her. It was as if he owed her a favour. He wedged the crowbar in the door, which was made of iron and didn't seem like the original – they must have removed the wooden one to secure the house with this one.

'You want some help?' Pablo asked him. 'Doesn't your arm hurt?'

'A little, but I'm okay,' lied Gaspar. His arm was cured. He'd lost some feeling in a couple of his fingers, but he was going to recover it. He could move them, he just felt them less than the others. They were phantom fingers. Phantom fingers on his right arm, the one Adela was missing.

Gaspar pretended to exert himself, to clench his teeth from effort, to pry the door with the crowbar. Really, he was doing nothing more than resting the tool in the door frame. It was already open. He kicked it hard so it would seem like all one movement, that the kick accompanied the effort of his arms and the lever. When it opened, his friends stepped back. Gaspar had to lean over to catch his breath and calm down: once again, he hadn't exerted himself physically, but afterwards his body reacted as if it had moved something very heavy. During those moments of recovery, he didn't see what it was that had made the others retreat.

There was a light inside the house.

Adela went in, determined. Gaspar went after her and sensed the other two following behind him. Vicky grabbed his hand and he squeezed it. What they saw was impossible, because the light seemed electric, but there were no lamps hanging from the ceiling: there were holes from which old cables peeked out like dry branches. The place also smelled like disinfectant; a little like a hospital, thought Gaspar, but he didn't say anything. Just inside the door there was an old black telephone. It was unplugged, they could see the cord, but Vicky said into Gaspar's ear: Oh, please don't let it ring. Pablo, who had gone a little further in, was turning in circles and looking around.

'It's too big,' he said, without looking at them. 'This house. It's bigger inside than out.'

He was right. The living room, or foyer, or whatever that first room was, seemed empty and had three windows, though from outside only two were visible. There were only two. Gaspar felt Vicky's nails digging into his arm, his good one – she was careful, as he'd never told her the injured one didn't hurt, or Pablo either, even though Pablo knew what had happened. Then she said out loud:

359

'Let's go. It's buzzing.'

Now Gaspar heard it too, thought it was very faint, at a low frequency, like when the stereo was left on and it vibrated almost imperceptibly. It was as if colonies of bugs lived behind the walls, hidden under the paint. Tiny bugs, maybe winged. Night butterflies. Black beetles. He thought that any second now the paint, a very light canary yellow, would start to peel and let the bugs fly out. He imagined swarms of moths, those creatures that turned to ash when you caught them.

Being an orphan meant bearing ashes.

Adela went ahead, excited and unafraid. She went further into the house that was lit by its own private sun, the house that was a different house inside. Pablo called to her to wait, wait, but she didn't listen. The vibration drew her onward. The light, which was not electric or at least didn't come from any ceiling lamps, made her look golden.

They followed her to the next room, which had furniture. Dirty sofas, mustard-coloured, greyed by the dust. There were glass shelves stacked against the wall. They were spotlessly clean and held a lot of tiny ornaments. Adela went closer to see what they were: the shelves reached almost up to the ceiling. The lowest one held yellowish-white objects, semi-circular. Some were round, others sharper like claws. Gaspar went to touch one but immediately snatched his hand away, disgusted.

'They're fingernails,' he said.

Vicky started to cry. Pablo and Adela kept looking. Gaspar watched them. They were acting strange. Entranced, but as if they'd just woken up, still half-asleep. Not like him and Vicky, who were alert. The feeling that something horrible was going to happen was very clear, at least for him, but he acquiesced, he went along. The house had sought them out and now it had them, in its hands, in its claws. The second shelf was decorated with teeth. Molars filled in with black lead; then the canines, which, he'd been taught in school, were called cuspids. Front incisors. Tiny baby teeth. Gaspar guessed what was on the third shelf before he saw it; it was obvious. Eyelids. Arranged like butterflies and just as delicate. With short eyelashes or long, dark ones, others with no eyelashes at all.

'We have to collect them!' said Adela, excited. 'Maybe there's something of my dad!'

Gaspar stopped her. He grabbed her hand before she could touch the delicate human remains on the shelves. And then a door closed inside the house. Gaspar was going to remember that sound for years, very clearly. A firm slam, not from the wind, no creaking. A dry, definitive sound. Where in the house did it come from? It was impossible to tell. Vicky turned, frantic, and started to run, but she didn't know where she was going. Pablo grabbed her by the waist without a word. Gaspar looked at him admiringly and took charge of Adela. He looked her in the eyes – dark, bewildered eyes – and he said, very clearly:

'We're going to try to leave now. There's someone here.'

'Don't talk out loud,' whispered Vicky, and Gaspar thought, Things need to be clear now because we have to try to save ourselves. He felt cold and determined. He gripped the crowbar in his hand and knew he would be capable of using it.

'Vicky, they already know we're in the house.'

'We never should have come in,' said Pablo, and just then Adela took off running to the next room. Gaspar tried to grab her, but she slipped away. They followed her. It was a little hard to run in the house, as if it were poorly ventilated or lacked oxygen. No one shouted at her to stop, but they didn't let her go alone. The next room was a kind of kitchen: at the back they saw the remains of a rusted-out stove. There was no table. And what *was* there didn't make any sense. A medical book with satiny pages, open on the floor. A mirror hung near the ceiling – who could see their reflection way up there? A stack of white laundry, apparently clean, neatly folded. Sheets. Adela started to pick one up and Gaspar stopped her firmly, ready to slap her. We can't touch anything, he thought. It's like it's all radioactive. Like Chernobyl. If we touch the house, it will never let us leave, it'll stick to us. He said it aloud; though he was afraid the presence in the house would hear his voice, he had no choice. It was impossible to hide.

'Don't touch anything. Seriously, I'm telling you.'

I just have to get her out of here, he thought. I'll drag her out if I have to. He felt the attraction, too, not as strongly as Adela did, but he felt it: they had to leave but they didn't want to, or something was holding them there.

'But why?' she asked. 'There could be things of my dad's!'

'You don't know your dad.'

'Maybe those teeth were his. Maybe they had a lot of people in here. A lot of people. We've both read about how the army used regular houses to torture people. Maybe they used this one and no one knew. There are parts of a lot of people here.'

Adela spoke in a tone that terrified Gaspar. He thought of Omaira in the mud, her eyes like cockroaches; he remembered his father's fixed pupils, and he thought of a world of black and shining crystals. There are parts of a lot of people here. It wasn't Adela who had said that, though someone had used her voice. Who was speaking through her?

'We have to get out,' said Gaspar.

Adela shimmered under that artificial light. Gaspar felt like they were in a theatre: he knew he was being watched. And when she darted towards a hall that was just past the rusty stove in that house that on the inside seemed to never end, he stopped her. He threw her down and heard her chin hit the floor. She wriggled under his weight and with an inexplicable strength managed to extricate her only arm and stick two fingers in his eyes. In a second she was free. Gaspar couldn't believe it. He must be at least fifteen kilos heavier than Adela and he was strong, he swam, he knew how to fight. Still, he was no match for her.

Because he wasn't fighting with her, he thought; he was fighting with the house. Or with the owner of that voice.

Vicky tried to catch her too, and couldn't. Pablo merely ran after her, panting. And then the three of them followed her down a wide hallway that had several doors to either side, an impossibly long hallway, metres and metres long, impossible for it to exist in that little house, its wooden floor a bit dirty, but not abandoned, and the walls papered with a fleur-de-lis pattern. It looks like a hotel hallway, Gaspar thought. All three of them watched as Adela opened a door that must lead to a bedroom. Before entering, she turned around and waved at them with her only hand. No one stopped her, because they planned to follow. They couldn't have imagined that after waving, she would close the door behind her. Or that *someone* would close the door.

And then, when he saw her yellow hair disappear into the darkness – there was no light in the room she had entered – Gaspar knew that this was one door he wasn't going to be able to open. It was out of his reach. He felt it in his body and his mind with a luminous clarity. First Vicky tried to open it: the doorknob turned, but that was all. None of them had heard the sound of a key turning. Then Gaspar tried, though he already knew it was useless. All three of them tried, not giving a thought to the presence, the someone else who could be in the house. They used the crowbar, they kicked, they ran at the door and tried to break it like they'd seen people do in movies. There was no opening it.

'We have to get help,' said Pablo, and in that precise second, as if he'd given an order, the light went out.

Vicky screamed and then started to cry very hard and loud and Gaspar realized her sobs were coming from below; she had sat down or fallen, it was hard to know which in that utter darkness.

'Hand me the flashlight,' he said, and Pablo fumbled with it behind Gaspar's back until he found his hand. Gaspar took it and switched on the beam. The light was feeble, but it would have to be enough. Pablo was crying too: Gaspar recognized that contained, quiet sobbing. He didn't feel like crying himself. He had to get them out of there, because they wouldn't be able to do it on their own.

'Vicky,' he said. 'Get up and grab my waist. Pablo, you grab her, that way we won't get lost.'

'Why would we get lost?' cried Vicky, and her voice sounded childish, so paralysed with terror that Gaspar squeezed her arm and held on to it with his free hand while his other tried to hold the flashlight steady. He'd put the crowbar in his pocket; he knew it must be sticking out, but he couldn't see it in the darkness. He didn't answer Vicky. It was obvious why they could get lost: the walls of the hallway were no longer there. This wasn't a hallway any more. He was scared by the thought of crossing the room with the shelves again (what was on the highest shelves? Hearts, lungs, brains, maybe heads?), but he knew they couldn't go any further into the house. Whatever was further in was very far from the street, from their homes, from the neighbourhood, from their parents. If Pablo realized they were no longer in the hallway, he didn't say anything. Gaspar heard him sniff in the darkness. He could hear his own heart beating too fast, skipping some beats. He raised the flashlight to neck height and shone it on what was no longer a hallway. Vicky's breath was on his ear and he heard her say:

'Turn on the flashlight, please, please.'

He was surprised. Were her eyes closed?

'It's on,' he said.

'Don't lie, asshole! I can't see anything.'

Think fast, think fast, Gaspar told himself. If she finds out the flashlight is on and she still can't see, she's going to think she's gone blind. If I pretend it doesn't have batteries or doesn't work, she'll get mad at Pablo. If Pablo can see, maybe he'll understand enough to keep quiet. That was better. Vicky furious was better than Vicky terrified.

'I can't see anything either,' said Pablo. He wasn't crying any more. Gaspar felt he could trust him, didn't have to take care of him. He didn't understand why his friends couldn't see. The flashlight illuminated only a little space, but very well. He could tell the batteries were new. It was a detail Pablo never would have missed.

'It went out. Vicky, take it easy, I can see a little.'

Vicky never acted like a baby. That's why it was so easy to be friends with her. But now she was hysterical. And she started to say aloud, right by Gaspar's ear:

'I can't stand this buzzing any more, and now they're talking! Can't you guys hear someone talking?'

That's why she's acting like this, thought Gaspar. Vicky didn't lose control so easily: she was hearing things, something different was happening to her than to him or to Pablo. She was locked inside her head as well as inside the house. Gaspar didn't hear anything at all. Not the buzzing – which he'd heard when they entered but had now faded – and of course not any voices. He cried out in the darkness:

'Pablo, are you okay?'

'Yeah,' said Pablo, doubtfully. 'I don't hear anything either.'

'Okay. Hold on to Vicky, and walk. I'll guide you; you guys just walk. Don't let go.'

And I'm not going to listen to you two any more, thought Gaspar. Because he had shone the light to either side and seen the walls covered in vines and moss. And, when he lit them better, he saw little white things in among the plants. Bones. Some very small. Animal bones, he told himself. Chickens. At least now it looked more like an abandoned house. He moved the flashlight and saw a black piano, and, nearby, what looked like mannequins hanging from the ceiling. The floor was covered in burnt-down candles, and he said aloud:

'Careful, it's slippery.'

Vicky and Pablo didn't ask why; maybe they imagined something horrible, but Gaspar couldn't reassure them that it was only wax because just then the flashlight revealed a window, and what he saw through it was impossible. Gaspar didn't want to stop and look, but he did: on the other side of the dirty glass he saw the moon above trees, many trees, a still forest, as if the house were high atop a hill that allowed for a panoramic view. It wasn't a pretty forest. It could also be a very detailed painting, he thought. A painting of a window that looked out on a forest. That's what it was. Still, there was something off about the painting; it looked like a trap. The whole house was a trap.

He didn't shine the light on the walls any more. Or on the floor. He kept it pointed straight ahead, painfully aware that if someone really was in the house, they could snatch the flashlight from his hand at any moment, hit him, hit all of them, and drag them into one of those dark rooms, like the one Adela had chosen. Why had she waved to them like that? It had been such a small gesture, a goodbye.

What if the person who'd slammed a door somewhere in the house was Adela's father? What if he was still alive? Not disappeared, but a serial killer? Pablo gave a feeble scream in the darkness, and Gaspar asked, What's wrong, what's wrong?

'Something touched me. On my back,' said Pablo.

'Enough,' said Gaspar. 'We're getting out of here. Don't turn around.'

Vicky said nothing. Had she heard Pablo? She must have.

The flashlight illuminated a wooden staircase with a beautiful handrail: it led to another floor upstairs. The problem, of course, was that the house on Villarreal didn't have a first floor.

'Do you see the door?' Vicky asked. Her breath was very hot and smelled of pennies. But now she sounded less scared. Her hands squeezed Gaspar so tight that it hurt a little.

'We're almost there,' he said, and he thought: Adela is locked in this house, Pablo is about to have a little brother, and Vicky is loved. Enough, he thought. Dad, show me the door. We have to get out.

'Vicky, do you hear anything?'

'The buzzing, but less.'

Gaspar repeated without moving his lips: Dad, show me the door, and he felt the sweat drenching the back of his neck, his back, and he kept walking.

The flashlight beam fell upon the door, which was wide open. Had they left it like that? It didn't matter. He sped up without a word, just in case, and he felt Vicky's relief when she, too, saw the streetlights, the night outside, and let go of his waist and went running out to the sidewalk, safe. Pablo did the same, instinctively. Gaspar turned off the flashlight and looked at the house. From outside, it looked the same as always. Small, ugly, grey, its windows bricked up. Dark. He handed the flashlight to Pablo. He couldn't speak. Vicky was different now: her long, tousled hair gave her an adult air. She hugged him fast but tight, and said, you're soaked in sweat, and then, thank you, thank you. Outside, she was back to being decisive.

'Let's go to my house. My parents can call the police, we have to get Adela out of there.'

And with that Vicky took off running straight to her house; Pablo and Gaspar followed her. Are you sure someone touched you? Gaspar wanted to know, and Pablo, running but looking him in the eye, said, Yes and no. He could have imagined it. Are you going to tell the truth? Pablo asked, and Gaspar said yes. And he *was* going to tell the truth about what he'd seen, but only up until Adela went into the room. He wasn't going to talk about the flashlight beam the others couldn't see, or the magnificent staircase, or the piano, or say that he had opened the door himself without any effort, as if the door had obeyed him. As if it had been waiting for him.

He had brought Adela there. He was sure of it. He had delivered her to the house. He hadn't been able to stop her when she ran – a girl as light as a toy, a girl who was missing an arm! And he, big as he was, hadn't been able to stop her because she'd stuck her fingers in his eyes! Now the guilt twisted his chest from inside, now he knew the only person who could tell him where Adela was and who had taken her was his father, and his father wasn't going to talk to him ever again.

Everything that happened after that happened for Gaspar through a kind of fog. As if he had rubbed his eyes until he was half-blind. And as if that partial blindness, that grey mist, had spread throughout his whole body. A distance between him and everyone else, between him and what others said and did, as if he were watching a movie on mute through smoke.

His uncle, angry because they'd gone into the house. And because he had to go with him to talk to the police, to the juvenile court judge, to other people Gaspar could no longer distinguish. Betty had fainted at the news of Adela's disappearance:

she'd wanted to go into the house, she'd pounded against the walls and the door, she'd clawed at the bricks in the windows. Someone told Gaspar that the door was locked again. Also that Betty had blamed him, that she'd shouted, it's Juan's son's fault, he brought her, he handed her over. Gaspar wasn't surprised: Betty was right. But he could no longer respond. He did talk, just a little, to the police and the people in court, which came much later.

He went to visit his father between one thing and another. Juan was still motionless. How many days had passed? Dr Biedma said he was in a coma, that it was definitive, that he wasn't going to wake up. Gaspar didn't know how to reply. He *had* to talk to his father. They let him in to see him. He was utterly inert except for his breathing, which was still strange, very intermittent. Gaspar whispered into his ear: If you can hear me, tell me where she is. Why couldn't I open that door when I can open others? Who took her? How do we get her out? Why did I take her there? And he sincerely expected those words to wake his father, but he waited in vain. Juan's lips were cracked and bloody and nearly purple. His fingers, too, were bluish. His arms were covered in bruises and so was his chest, big bruises, and patches of his skin were burnt. They had tried to resuscitate him.

I don't want to go to school, Gaspar told his uncle, who told him that was fine. He could still feel Adela's body beneath him, the way she had struggled, like she was made of rubber, and then her fingers in his eyes, but he knew, he knew, that if he'd made a little more effort she wouldn't have gotten away. She had gotten away from *him*. When he wasn't being called in to talk to some detective or yet another woman in an office (the judge? A psychologist?), Gaspar was in a bed beside his father's. They let him stay. The sound of the cardiac monitor kept him from sleeping, but he didn't want to budge. His uncle had to press him to bathe and eat. On one of those breaks from the clinic he found out that Betty was gone, no one knew where she was, and how was it possible that she left right when her daughter had disappeared? Gaspar closed his eyes. Maybe Betty had gone looking for Adela. He had to return to his father's side because, if he woke up even for a second, two seconds, he would tell Gaspar where Adela was or how he could find her. He had looked at his father's eyes again. Now they were both completely black, as if they reflected the night sky. Like Omaira's, the girl Vicky still saw in dreams.

His uncle had sat beside him while he devoured some empanadas at the hospital restaurant, which was so nice and had such good food it was like a regular restaurant. He clearly didn't know what to say, but first he apologized for having gotten angry. He said he 'understood', and they were just getting up to 'mischief', that it was normal for him to try to 'escape' what was happening. Uncle Luis, said Gaspar, Adela got away from me. I tried to grab her in the house and she got loose. I let her go. She wanted to go inside and I took her and that was wrong, but on top of that I let her go. It's not your fault, don't do that to yourself, his uncle told him. Someone took her. Because of me, said Gaspar. Who else could be to blame?

He went back to his father. If he hasn't died yet it's because he wants to talk to me, he thought. Leaning over, he insisted: You know where she is. You know how I can find her. You helped me find the dog. This is the last thing I'm asking. You owe me. Open your eyes. I could open the door, the first one, but not the second. Why can I open some but not others? You have to talk to me.

Pablo came to see him. For Pablo, he left his father's room and sat down in the restaurant. They ordered coffee with milk.

Pablo told him the police had gone into about twenty houses. Including his. Raids. Then he said the police hadn't seen doors in the house, or pretty much anything else. And no one believed them. They say what we saw in there was an optical illusion. From the shock. They don't believe us about the teeth. Apparently, they found clothes in the house, new clothes, and they think they might belong to the guy who took Adela. They say maybe the guy put light in the house to attract us. They say someone kidnapped Adela. Was it the guy who was in the house?

'We don't know if there was someone in the house,' said Gaspar. 'That house is a trick. It told us a big lie. I'm going back to my dad.'

'Not yet,' said Pablo, and he went on talking: 'A TV channel came round and interviewed the neighbours, including Hugo. They interviewed Vicky after she gave her statement in court. They're talking about Adela on TV,' he said. 'Haven't you seen?'

'I'm not watching TV.'

'They want to interview you because I told them you got us out.'

'I'm not going to talk to anyone.'

Gaspar stood up, though he hadn't touched his croissants. He looked at Pablo, who bowed his head, and suddenly he felt very alone. Without thinking, he pushed the table aside to get closer to his friend, who, astonished, stood up. Gaspar hugged Pablo tight, without tears. I have to get back to my dad, he said. I miss you guys. Vicky too, but I have to be with him.

Someone was in the room, sitting on the bed and talking to his uncle: The kid is in shock, he's stressed, he's depressed. Gaspar had gotten under the bed, and, from the floor, he watched what went on in the room. He didn't even come out when a nurse came to 'sanitize' his father, as they called it. They summoned him to court again and his uncle told them Gaspar couldn't go, that he was sick, and they excused him. He found out later that a family lawyer intervened with a writ so they couldn't summon him any more. A psychologist evaluated him and determined that he was in no condition to give any more statements.

Gaspar felt sick and tired because sleeping meant dreaming of Adela, Adela who slipped from his hands like a little fish; they'd been in a fish tank where giant eyes had seen everything. Whose eyes, only his father knew, and he was so far away, his own eyes black and impenetrable. Gaspar talked to him every day while his uncle watched them and cried a little.

Juan died in the early morning and Gaspar sensed it. First there was the silence: no more breathing. Then no more heartbeats were registered, just a single, continuous sound, an alarm. And then he felt the pain, so intense it forced him into a foetal position, though that was no relief. Still, after a while he stood up to look at his father. He wasn't alone in the room: his uncle was there, and Dr Biedma. On other occasions, especially in the hospital, Gaspar had seen her direct teams trying to revive his father. He had even seen her on top of him, pounding on his chest. She had done that just days earlier. Now she did nothing, because there was no point. Gaspar approached the head of the bed still hunched over: the pain he felt was as if invisible hands with nails like knives were tearing at his body. He saw his father's eyes were black and open. He didn't understand. Had he opened them to die? When he was about to ask, Dr Biedma came over as well and closed his fixed eyes, two shining stones, and then Gaspar began to cry, and he cried standing beside his father's bed – he didn't dare touch him, couldn't touch him – and then sitting on the bed where he had slept those final nights, and his uncle had to pick him up and carry him out of the room because he didn't want to leave. Gaspar closed his eyes, and it was like turning out a light. He only had dreams. Dreams where he opened the door and found Adela. Dreams where she didn't get away from him and he threw her over his shoulder like a sack of potatoes and carried her out of the house. Dreams where his father explained how to do it. Or where his father woke up and directed him in the search. Dreams where Gaspar got up from the mattress, his father already dead, already ashes on the bed, and went to the kitchen and slit his own throat with a knife, blood pouring out, drenching the walls, his pants, his face, his hands, until everything he saw was red and he could let himself die once and for all. He, too, could have black eyes.

IV

Chalk Circles

1960–1976

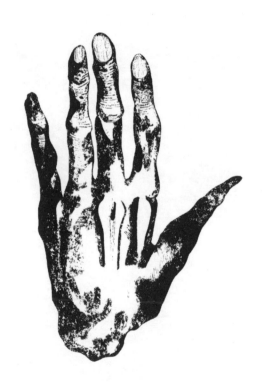

Gods always behave like the people who make them.
Zora Neale Hurston, *Tell My Horse*

1

MY MOTHER'S HAIR IS FINE AND GREY AND HER SCALP shows through it. She's nearly bald above her forehead, and for a long time now she hasn't taken the trouble to comb her hair over the bare spot there. My mother's family loses their hair very early, and they also go grey very young, as if they suffered from premature old age. It hasn't happened to me, and my father assures me his creole blood saved me; he raises his fist to the sky when he says it, but never his eyes.

I was born in Buenos Aires, in the family residence on Avenida Libertador. The three of us – I'm an only child – got the fourth floor. My maternal aunt inherited the fifth, and my uncle, the third. The bottom two floors were used for parties and dinners and other rare social occasions, so they were almost always empty, though impeccable, with polished floors and shining dishes. I never liked that solemn building with its dark and heavy furniture, the floors of such expensive wood that we could never wear shoes, and my father's art collection that didn't leave a single blank space on the walls.

I liked our country house in Chascomús a little more. We never went to the other estates, which were more comfortable – some of them magnificent – because my mother preferred this modest *quinta*, the first house her family had occupied when they came to Argentina from England two hundred years ago. Near the house is the cemetery that in town they call 'English', even though it's mostly Scottish people buried there. It's small and very well cared for. My grandmother is buried there: she died really young and I used to like to visit her in my black dress and patent leather shoes. The cemetery is ours, in a way, because it's my family that pays the expenses of the church, which is always empty, and for the cleaning, keeping the place up for the very few tourists who are interested in this pampa curiosity, with its Celtic crosses and its dark green moss that will stick to your clothes.

When I was little, Florence Mathers used to stay on Libertador only long enough to recover from her trip, and then she'd accept our invitation to stay at the house in Chascomús. I don't know how many properties she has in the pampa, but it must be a lot: she raises horses and livestock. She likes the Argentine countryside, its emptiness and its sad sunsets, the perpetual smell of burning leaves in autumn and the smoke from the grill night and day.

Our families are joined by history and by a friendship that has lasted hundreds of years, but hers is the one that leads the Order. I've asked my grandfather many times why that privilege is hers. According to him, in Europe they were much more consistent with the Cult of the Shadow than we were. Plus, Argentina is very far. Far from what? I asked. It's the ass-end of the world, he'd reply. We can't participate in the organization the same way they can. Still, at crucial moments, there has always been a Bradford present. We are important, though secondary at times. Money is a country where some cities are more prosperous than others, but they are all rich, he told me.

What I learned over the years is that the nation of affluence is monotonous. The properties, the land, the companies that others manage for us, the old, dark houses and the new, luminous ones, the leathery skin of women who spend summers in the south of France or Spain or Italy, the silver, the Gobelins tapestries, the paintings, the art collections, the gardens, the people who work for us about whom we know nothing. Doesn't matter if it's Buenos Aires or London. It doesn't matter either that our families are founders of the Order. Being rich makes us like all rich people. Being founders of the Order differentiates us from the whole world.

It was my grandfather who told me the story of the Order. The descendants of the original families are called blood children, and we all learned our history thanks to the stories of the elders. My grandfather, Santiago Bradford, sat us down – me and my cousin Betty, his two granddaughters – in the yard at Puerto Reyes. Of all our properties that's my favourite, my beloved house in Misiones, uncomfortable and hot and absolutely beautiful. It's the house my mother hates, because she hates everything beautiful and wants to destroy it; that is her true faith and her nature.

He told us the first story near the orchid garden, lit by a lamp that lent his dark eyes a yellowish gleam. My grandfather Santiago was born in Argentina and inherited all the fields and yerba plantations and sawmills and ships from the family, which had gotten rich in the nineteenth century. How did they get rich? The usual: looting, partnerships with other influential people, understanding what side to take during the civil wars, and allying with powerful politicians. The first Bradfords came to Buenos Aires in 1830 or 1835, versions differ, but that date isn't the important one. Our year zero is 1752. My great-grandfather, William Bradford, was a bookseller and owner of a printing press back in England, and his best friend, Thomas Mathers, was a landowner. The social difference between the two was important – I think that origin continues to mark the positions of our families – but they became friends because they shared a passion for folklore and occultism. In their free time they travelled the country together, buying books and collecting the stories that interested them. They were educated men, researchers and collectors of stories and testimonials of people with magical abilities, people who were gifted or cursed.

They found the Darkness, and the first medium, in Scotland. They didn't just come across it; they weren't searching blindly. They had read oblique references to a spirit that manifested as a black light, and that had capacities of prophecy and divination. Those references, very brief, said that certain people could contact it and make it speak. In its words there was knowledge, and in the contact, the possibility of obtaining its favour. It is clear, said my grandfather, that they were not searching for the Darkness specifically, but for some reason it did catch their attention, maybe because of the mention of how those capable of contact would undergo a physical metamorphosis in some part of the body, especially the tongue or the hands.

The medium was the son of a peasant: he predicted the future using the scapula of a sheep, a detail that always made me laugh because of the precision in the choice of bone. The boy alerted his community about useful matters like how they should care for the livestock, how much money they would earn or lose in the next harvest, when a storm was coming, if they were in danger in a time of political violence. I liked the name of the method and the way my grandfather pronounced it: *silinnenath*.

Where in Scotland? Beatriz always asked. Near Inverness, said my grandfather. Far to the north. The town was called Tarradale, but if you look for it on a map, it will be called Muir of Ord, because they changed the name. The town was isolated by two rivers: it was hard to get there, but they managed it, fortunately, because they wanted to meet the seer.

The two friends frightened the youth, who was weak, thin, and had eyes that Thomas described in his journals as 'like codfish eyes'. They convinced him to go with them to London. It was a period of rebellion in Scotland and they insisted he would die in the conflict if he stayed, because, with his build and sickly constitution, he wasn't a fighter. They offered to take care of him. It wasn't hard to take him from the village: his parents trusted the elegant English gentlemen. And the locals, though they appreciated his prophetic ability, also feared him. The most religious among them believed his gift had come from the Devil.

They brought him to Thomas Mathers' house, and they didn't have to wait long for the first manifestation. He showed them the black light in a nearby field. In those days the ritual was done diffcrently. The boy had to be lying down on the ground when he summoned the light, which, they say, didn't wound back then. It was less savage, or it was asleep. 'We touch it, and it's cold and wet to the touch, like rain,' wrote Thomas Mathers in his diary. 'The boy is Dee's black mirror. He's a medium, like Kelly.'

It's because of those words that we refer to those who bring the Darkness as mediums, though technically they should be called something else, maybe priests or shamans. That young man, like Juan, experienced a metamorphosis in his hands. Thomas Mathers described claws like a cat's. The boy spoke in the trance, pronouncing the words of the Darkness. That's different now too: the Darkness speaks, but not in the medium's voice.

Once, when Grandfather was telling us the story – he repeated it regularly, so we wouldn't forget: he would even question us about the details – I asked him what the boy's name was. I must have been eight years old. Grandfather had to admit they hadn't recorded his name. The diaries just called him 'the

Scottish youth'. That is also what it is to be rich: that contempt for beauty and the refusal to offer even the dignity of a name.

The Scottish youth's trances occurred almost daily and always in the same field. He floated in a dark halo and spoke with his eyes closed. After two months he suffered, according to the doctor who attended him (and in the terminology of the period), an apoplexy. That is: a brain haemorrhage. He survived, but he had another attack days later from which he didn't wake up, and he died without ever recovering consciousness. They had forced him to summon almost every day, sometimes twice a day. After one of the trances, the youth had threatened to kill them, and one night he managed to get out of the room and bite Thomas Mathers on the neck. The wound wasn't serious, though in those years before antibiotics, dental germs from a bite could be deadly. They tied him up. The restraints probably caused the clot that killed him. He hadn't gone crazy, as the diary claimed: they had driven him mad. His words held instructions, very complex ones, on how to summon the Darkness without a medium. There were also other methods, brutal and dangerous ones, to ask for favours.

William Bradford's sons emigrated to the Americas in search of better business opportunities. The one who settled in the United States had a press, like his father, and died young. The one who came to Argentina participated in the Conquest of the Desert and received government land in payment for his military action. The most fertile land in the world. That man, in addition to being a very efficient murderer of natives, was also a researcher of the occult, and he never tired of searching for the Darkness in the pampa. He didn't find it, never learned to summon it, though he was capable of trying out the cruellest methods without remorse. He died screaming his failure at the Chascomús house, the same one where today we go to rest and ride horses.

I became an anthropologist because of these stories. My notebook, all my notes, my recordings, everything, it all goes back to my childhood. I started to collect stories and myths before I even knew I could study them. I know how to listen, how to ask questions, how to follow the fingers pointed towards the healer's house or the grave that grants favours; I recognize the fear in the eyes of those who make the sign of the cross, and I like to wait for night to see will-o'-the-wisps over the graves. I'm grateful to have been born into this family, but I don't idealize it, or at least I try not to. All fortunes are built on the suffering of others, and ours, though it has unique and astonishing characteristics, is no exception.

I have my father's dark hair and brown eyes, but I lack his elegance, his slender body, and his beauty. When I was very little, he told me that if I wanted to be a pretty woman I would have to make an effort. He made me cry, but I was grateful to him. Riches can replace beauty, but not entirely. And I am not like my mother, who finds authority in her repulsive appearance. I learned, effortlessly, which colours make my skin glow, which stockings look good on my legs, and why I should always wear accessories: the long necklace to make my neck look slender; emerald earrings to contrast with my brown hair; rings on several fingers, to let others know that I have character. My cousin Beatriz isn't pretty either. She inherited the feline features of our English family, the narrow nose, the thin lips. She always had a hard face with a cruel expression. A little bit leopard and a little bit bird. I remember her in the stairway of our building, the one that was only used by maids, drivers, and the rest of the service personnel. Our parents and Uncle Jorge only used the elevator. Buenos Aires had a lot of blackouts, but they never affected us: we had a generator. The first legend I wrote in my notebook is from the urban folklore of our neighbourhood. The family at one of the nearby properties went to Europe on vacation, and the electricity went out just as the last of them got into the car. They didn't realize that the maid, who was going to stay and take care of the house, was in the elevator. No one heard her screaming and she died in there, from hunger; it was a cage-style elevator, so she had oxygen, which only prolonged her agony.

For a while, Beatriz and I didn't use the elevator and we met up on the stairs instead, our secret place. One night before dinner we were in the stairwell, and she asked me if I really believed in our grandfather's stories and the Order. I remember her, with her small teeth and big nose, in possession of a truth she was about to throw in my face. It's all rubbish. My dad told me so, and he doesn't want me to listen to those stories any more. The tears burned my eyes and I wanted to hit her, but instead I asked, why they would lie to us? The Englishwoman has them under her control, she replied. I don't remember what she said after that, but it had to do with the business the two families shared. That was the night Beatriz announced they were moving to her father's house in San Isidro. We don't want to participate in this farce any more, she insisted, a sentence she had taken word for word from her father, because she didn't talk like that. Are they going to let you go? I asked. Why wouldn't they? she replied, defiant. That was when I learned that it's customary in the Order to let members leave without trying to retain them. My mother says they must be allowed to go because they always come back, they come crying back, all beaten down, because the Darkness is a god with claws that sniffs you out, the Darkness catches up with you, the Darkness will let you play, the way a cat lets go of its prey just to see how far it can get.

I still saw Beatriz, but only at school, which she lived close to now. Living in downtown Buenos Aires, I had to be driven there and back by the chauffeur. The same year Beatriz moved away from the building with her family, Uncle Jorge brought Juan to live with him. They didn't have to tell me anything, but I was so curious and asked so many questions about the boy that they told me part of the truth. He's your uncle's patient, Jorge operated on him. He has a very serious cardiac deform-ation and his parents, who are very poor, can't care for him. He's going to live with Jorge. I was little, but I already knew that my family, especially my uncle, were incapable of such generos-ity. My grandfather added: It's a case that could change Jorge's career, because no one in the whole world has successfully carried out the surgeries that this child needs.

I wonder sometimes whether Jorge might have wanted to have a child, after all. I never knew him to have a woman, but he wasn't homosexual, either; it's clear he couldn't reproduce. Families in the Order don't have many children: it's a punish-ment, I think, or a mark. What to do with the Order's young people is a difficult question to answer precisely because of their scarcity. Training the young should be a priority, but since it's also dangerous, why risk the future?

I asked if I could see the boy, and after a few days they let me. They gave him one of the main bedrooms, which surprised me, because I figured he would be put in the service room. I went in on tiptoe, I remember. They had told me I should be careful, because if he was startled it could kill him. But as soon as I saw him, I knew this boy wasn't going to die easily. He had a hardness in his gaze that reminded me a little of the kids who worked the fields, but there was also a certain haughtiness.

I said hi to him, I remember, and he didn't answer. He speaks when he wants, Jorge told me, nothing is easy with him. His lips were dark, bluish, as were the fingertips resting atop the white sheets. The circles under his eyes were like stains on his pale skin, and his hair was cut too short, so blond it looked white. You're like a ghost, I told him, and his gaze pierced me and I giggled a little. That same night I went to visit him again; the nurse had orders not to let anyone in, but she wasn't about to stop the daughter of Mercedes Bradford. My mother inspired an unparalleled terror.

'Don't laugh at me,' Juan said as soon as he saw me come in. 'I'm not a ghost. Ghosts exist. I see them if I want, and if I don't want to, I don't see them.'

Thus began our habit of talking every night. Juan not only filled the void left by Betty's departure, he became my brother and my confidant. There were things he didn't understand, like when I came back fuming over something at school or upset by some insult from Mercedes or a classmate, but even when he was so little, he wanted to help me. Sometimes I stayed and slept with him: the bed was big and he had to sleep in a seated position, propped up by pillows, because he couldn't breathe when he lay down. I adored him from the start. I always wanted to take care of him, but I also respected him, and in some way I feared him, and also honoured the distance he imposed. He didn't go to school, and I loved to supplement the lessons from his private tutors by reading him poetry, which he liked from a young age, or myths, and even taught him to listen to music, something he never really learned. We weren't allowed to run or play any rough games, but he showed me his scars, in bed at night, lit by the moon. You're like Frankenstein's monster, I told him, and I remember how he didn't understand and I promised to read him the novel. And we read it, for months.

Except for my visits and those of his older brother Luis, Juan lived practically alone in Uncle Jorge's gloomy apartment. His mother came to see him at first, but she soon died. I remember her well: she came dressed in her factory uniform, and sometimes her fingernails were dirty. She had even offered to work in the house as a maid so she could be near her son. She looked so sad. Her hair was cut short and neat. Her size was impressive, and so was Juan's father's, whom I only saw once. They were Swedish immigrants from Misiones, workers on the yerba plantations who had left their town because it didn't have the medical resources to treat someone as sick as Juan. The father acceded to my uncle's deal and handed Juan over in exchange for a lot of money, but the mother didn't give up, and on every visit she would ask, please, when were they going to let her live with her son again. I heard her crying and I felt bad for her, but I didn't want her to take Juan away. I asked my uncle not to return him and he told me: Don't worry.

In any case, I never imagined what Mercedes, my mother, was going to do. I've had enough of this woman, she said one day, and soon after that we learned Juan's mother was sick: she died in a matter of weeks from a sudden and terminal cancer. Juan's brother Luis informed us of his mother's illness and death. The father had already disavowed Juan by then. That man wanted to get rid of his sick son because he was expensive. Luis, on the other hand, came to visit every weekend, and whenever he could he took Juan out for walks or to swim, listening closely to my uncle's instructions about what he could and couldn't do. My mother used to make him wait on the landing, and sometimes, if it was raining, she would tell the doorman not to let him inside. One time Luis shot my mother a murderous look, heavy with the hatred of generations, and then I loved him eternally. I'm going to help you, I promised him when he brought

Juan back that day, I won't let her separate you. I was just saying it, because I never had and never will have any power over my mother. If she didn't kill Luis, it was because she didn't want to or because she was bored or because she didn't think he was a danger.

Juan changed a little when his mother died. He would sit on the wooden floor near the window, and sometimes I'd have the feeling that we were meeting in a desolate place. From the balcony, we could look out on to the avenue's jacaranda trees. He was sad and very distant: I spent all day thinking about how to entertain him, what kind of stories would satisfy the young rajah. When I realized my family had gotten Juan's parents out of the picture so they could keep him, I wanted to know more. This wasn't just about Uncle Jorge's career. I confronted my grandfather: I have a right to know, I said. And he told me without much beating around the bush. We believe the boy could be the medium the Order is looking for. Your uncle had a revelation when he operated on him, which has not been repeated. That's why sometimes, when we take him to the hospital, we visit the operating room. We want to see if he manifests again. It hasn't happened yet, but I think we have to give it time. He's too young.

It's a good thing he told me. Otherwise, when Juan did manifest, I would have been in danger. That day, my grandfather saved me from the Darkness.

That was the year Tali, my half-sister, came to Buenos Aires to study. It was a violent, difficult time. Tali couldn't stand the city and she cried, pleaded for her mother, pulled out her hair. Mercedes beat her; if I intervened, I was in for it too. We tried to run away once, with Juan. Our plan was discovered, and we had to go without dinner for a month.

Mercedes hated Tali because she hated her mother, Leandra. She never cared that my father had lovers; plus, in the Order that kind of possessive jealousy was and still is considered shameful. But Tali's mother was competition for something other than my father's erotic attention. She was a healer, and she had her own temple to San La Muerte in Corrientes. And she was a beauty; I don't know if I ever again saw a woman so naturally magnificent and alluring. My father spent a lot of time in the north with Leandra, and whenever he could, he took me with him. Tali and I would run along the dirt roads and shake the lemon trees to make white flowers rain down on us. Leandra received the faithful in her temple; Tali and I would clean the effigies of San La Muerte while we listened to the sobs of the pilgrims. The heat was suffocating: Tali always wore her hair down, and when she perspired a lot she would jump into the river. I never learned to swim like her. The Paraná has whirlpools: it's said they're made by the dead who live under the water and long for company, so they produce those swirls of water to drown swimmers. Leandra taught us how to avoid them, and she kissed my father on the beach. I understood why Tali didn't want to stay in Buenos Aires: I wouldn't have stayed either. The city, especially our apartment, was an opiate. The only bad thing was that my uncle wouldn't let Juan come with us to the north, saying he was in no condition to go so far away. Juan, however, listened enthusiastically to our adventures.

When the news came that Leandra had cancer, my mother clapped and celebrated with those little steps she always does when she's euphoric, one hand over her belly and the other in the air, like in a tango. Then she dropped on to a sofa and told us, me and my father: You two are some real cowards, you never dare to get rid of what bothers you. Just look at that kid Jorge's got his mind set on – I've already gotten rid of his mother.

And just how does Leandra bother you? Dad asked her.

That squaw doesn't bother me in the slightest, replied my mother. My father told me to go to my room, but Mercedes said: Let Rosario stay, let her listen, she has to learn – you all just teach her little stories and nonsense. Your Indian lover, Adolfo, is irrelevant to me. But you care about her. I'll let you sleep with all the whores in this country, but I cannot allow you to care about any of them. You want to know, Rosario, how I made Leandra sick? You want to know how I made your dying little friend's mother sick? Come visit me tonight and I'll tell you. It's time you learned who you really are. This bunch of sissies coddle you too much.

I never went to her room to learn how she had made Leandra and Juan's mother sick. When she tired of waiting for me, Mercedes went out: she put on lipstick and high heels and went across to the hotel sweet shop she liked, and she celebrated with champagne. She wouldn't let me go visit Tali in Corrientes, and Tali never came back to Buenos Aires. My father gave up on his plans to educate her in the capital, and he responded to my pleas with a convincing argument: If your mother starts gunning for Tali, you've seen what will happen.

My mother sent me to the Chascomús house that summer, alone. I knew it was a punishment, but at first I didn't really understand how it could be. I had always liked the countryside, the horses, running with the dogs, nights around the bonfire, all the stories I could write down in my notebook, the smell of smoke at dusk. I begged to have someone come with me, Juan or Tali or some friend from school, even Betty, but Mercedes refused and slapped me with her ring-covered hand until she drew blood from my cheeks. Make friends with the little Indians who work there, she told me. You always get along with those people, you little brat.

She drove me herself to Chascomús. And she gave me her instructions. I was to feed the caged ones every day. My mother is not the only member of the Order who searches for a medium or tries to summon the Darkness on her own, but as far as I know, she's the only one who uses this method. She brought me to the shack where the cages were, and then she left. The smell made me vomit and I ruined my red Mary Janes, my favourites. I ran out. But the next day I went back: one of the employees left the food at the door of my room, and he had orders to force me to fulfil the task. Otherwise, my mother would come back. That possibility was worse than the shack. It was kept locked with a padlock, and inside, the darkness was absolute. I left the trays inside the cages. The smell of shit and piss and blood made me throw up every time. All that summer I brought plates of food, very often spoiled, to the caged ones. I walked with my hands extended, and if I noticed they were very still, I prodded them to see which ones were alive and which dead. If there was a dead one, I also had to take care of the body. I buried two under the pear trees, following instructions my mother gave me over the phone. They didn't look human, and the smaller one had no eyes. One day, I heard a howl so intense coming from one corner that I disobeyed the orders I'd received and went to get a flashlight. The light made all the others shriek and for a moment I thought I was surrounded by winged demons, but I took a deep breath and steeled myself. I could always be tough when I needed to. I recognized the face that was wailing: they were looking for him in town, there were posters of a rough identikit drawing up every-where, in the shop, on light poles, in the police station. Someone wanted him back, someone loved him. The rag over his eyes was so dirty it had maggots. I bore the filth, his suffering, for several days, until I couldn't take it any more and removed the bandage. I cleaned him up as best I could, but I'm sure he'd already lost his eyes by the time Mercedes decided he was no good to her and threw him out like all the others. His name was Francisco, and he was four years old. The identikit said he had dark hair, but in my mother's prison he'd gone completely bald.

My mother had gone to that shack to perform the rituals that enabled her to get rid of Juan's mother and Leandra. There are other ways of getting rid of enemies that don't involve the Darkness. More classical, less exhausting methods that everyone in the Order knows. But she prefers this. The caged ones, some of them, in the trance of their suffering, manage to make the god appear, and that's when the request must be made. The apparition is brief, but pleading with it works. Of course, it's not just about keeping the prisoners locked up, it's also necessary to practise invocations I had refused to learn; hence this punishment. I know them now, but I don't perform them. My grandfather and some older members believe it's not exactly the Darkness that comes, but a figment that resembles it, a shadow, though sometimes it turns an entire room black. It's not the same indomitable Darkness that the medium summons, the one that speaks and cuts and takes. It's a copy, the other side of the mirror: it's false. But it's very effective in destroying, inexorable and pitiless. In Misiones, my father's yerbatera company had competition, another very rich family who cultivated tea as well as yerba. There wasn't room for two. My mother asked the Darkness to get rid of them. The other yerbatera family had a beautiful house, with white neoclassical columns, beside a lake: we went to see it once the destruction was complete. The sky was pink and the palm trees cast long shadows on the water. We didn't keep the house: when something is touched by that kind of affliction, it's better to abandon it. The eldest son, who would inherit everything, drowned himself in the lake in front of his jungle palace.

I watched Juan arrive from my bedroom window in Chascomús. My uncle and grandfather had brought him. It was close to Buenos Aires, so they were letting him make the trip. I was eleven that summer, and he was eight. He got out of the car and climbed the stairs slowly; he did everything slowly when he was little. He later changed completely in that respect. I sat on the bed and waited for him. From the doorway he said: I'm not going to leave you alone. I started to cry and reached out my hands, asked him to come in. He rested his head on my bare knees so I would caress his hair. We cried together. He knew about the caged ones. My mother told him, though there was no need to, of course, she just wanted to scare him. After that we did the job together. My uncle stayed to take care of Juan, and Juan went with me every day to the shack. It was easier with him because he could find his way in the dark, and he led me by the hand to each cage. None of them died while he was there.

Despite the tragedy of the caged ones, now that we were together we could have fun: we were young. In the afternoon we played with the coloured panes of the window in the entrance hall. A blue hand, a green eye, a yellow foot. We moved so the light would paint us. Many years later I remembered those games when I moved my hands and the LSD made a rainbow between my fingers.

In Buenos Aires, when I got back, my mother screamed: if that fucking kid doesn't make himself useful soon, I'm kicking him on to the street. I told her she'd have to throw us both out and she hit me on the back with her cane. I had trouble breathing for days. It was possible she cracked a rib, but she forbade my uncle from taking X-rays. That same night I went down the stairs, and from then on, I lived in the apartment with Juan and Jorge. And although later we spent some years apart, really, we never left each other's side again.

I would like to say that I fell in love with Juan before any other man, that I loved him from childhood, but the truth is that my first love was George Mathers, the man who found the medium Olanna. I even had his photograph, and I kept it in my little-girl's purse: I'd asked Florence for it once, and she sent me a copy from London by mail. George Mathers had the face of a romantic hero, with high cheekbones and round, guileless eyes; his hard, square jaw made him look strong and virile. He was perfect.

Florence was the Order's current leader, and George Mathers had been her great-uncle. He found Olanna when the National African Company, where he worked, established itself in Ibadan, a British protectorate that would eventually become Nigeria. His whole story is told in detail in his diaries: I saw the originals when I went to London, with their beautiful pencil drawings preserved by the Order's conservation experts, but when I was little, I read the facsimile edition that all Initiates receive. It was my favourite book. George loved the region, the beauty of the tall, thin natives, the white clothes, the forest, and even the food, which the other British people hated. He was the one who communicated the most and the best with the natives, and soon he was chosen to negotiate with the chiefs. In a few months he was receiving invitations to banquets and witnessing local dances. He was interested in the native rites and religion; he saw something profound in their sophisticated simplicity, something that from England and its salons, where the Order's members wore tunics and used swords and flasks, was unimaginable.

In one of the ceremonies he attended, the natives let him see Olanna, a distant niece of the Priest-King of Nri. The royal family, it was believed, had descended from a celestial being. The kingdom no longer existed: not long before, in 1911, the British Empire's troops had forced the king to renounce his ritual and political power. With the help of some priests, Olanna had escaped to Ibadan. She was fifteen years old, fragile, her forehead marked by scars, a maze of inflamed skin forever above her eyes. George Mathers fell in love with her, but at first he could not speak to her, they couldn't communicate. And Olanna, a priestess from a noble family, would never have touched a white man. The portrait George drew of Olanna, very delicate and retouched several times – you can see the erratic lines, later retraced neatly – shows a teenager with a tired gaze.

They called her She Who Brings the Night. Also, the Serpent of the Moon. With the scant English that his guides and friendly chiefs spoke, plus the little he had learned of the native language and a few more phrases in dialect, George Mathers understood that Olanna was not just a priestess possessed by spirits. She was the one who communicated with the occult gods, the ones who slept underground, in the riverbeds, and up among the stars. What his family, who belonged to the Order, referred to as a medium. In the first ritual they let him witness, in a clearing in the woods at night, drunk on palm wine, he watched as Olanna's body moved with impossible fluidity under the priest's hand, and how she bled. The women participating bled too; unlike Olanna, they were clothed. The meaty, metallic smell filled the woods and left him dizzy and excited. After the rituals, Olanna was taken away by the local healers and carried to her spacious hut: she was burning with fever and sometimes refused to drink, which only worsened her condition. When she recovered, she allowed George to take her hand and she talked to him in her language about other gods, many others, as well as a secret forest. George Mathers learned, took notes, sometimes even refused the woman assigned to him as a night-time companion so he could write alone in his bed, protected by the white mosquito net. The priests told him about Sopona, the deformed god of illness who appeared in the form of mosquitoes and flies; they didn't understand how he remained untouched by the deity. All his companions had suffered some form of illness, and many had died from malaria. George had only gotten a bit thinner and darker since he'd left London. He paid little attention to the business of the National African Company, but no one demanded he tend to the enterprise. He still went to the offices every day, even when he was very tired. He listened to his colleagues talk about the Niger River, the rebel tribes, the country's riches, and relatives and friends who had been killed in Europe during the Great War.

It was 1919. One September night, in the forest, George finally saw how Olanna brought the Darkness. The silvery light, a reflection of the moon on her sweaty skin, was slowly overcome by a darkness that emanated from her, flowing from her pores. The women and priests cried out: the drums flooded the night and George Mathers watched as a forked tongue emerged from Olanna's mouth, and as every nocturnal butterfly that got near her fell dead as soon as the black light touched it.

After that particularly intense ritual, in the doorway of his house, George Mathers found a very small clay statue of a naked man sitting with his hands on his knees, with a long, erect phallus. The great god Pan? he thought, in Ibadan, in the African forests? He was afraid, and he decided to return to England. But he didn't want to go alone: he wanted to take Olanna with him and give the Order a medium. She had come to him, for him: he was sure.

Taking her was very simple for a man in his position. For us, it is always easy to get what we want.

The trip over land and sea was exhausting for the girl, who was also on the receiving end of stares and pointing fingers. George Mathers realized then that her weakness was not just the result of the ritual; Olanna was also ill. She often lost consciousness. The rolling of the ship made her so sick she couldn't get out of bed. But as she lay in the bunk in darkness – necessary to relieve her constant headaches – she learned English with frightening speed. He told her about London, about his wife Lily who was waiting for him though he had been gone for over a year. He told her about the cold sea and the snow. Olanna listened seriously: George noticed how she learned, but at the same time did not consider anything he said to be wondrous. It was simply different from what she knew. She spoke too, and when she couldn't make herself understood, she drew in the air with her hands. She told George about a forest where thousands of demons lived, but there was one that reigned; it would hang from the trees and its feet were on backwards, so its footprints never gave away where it was going. She told him about the wood carvings her uncle made and about her father's riches and honour. She missed her jewels. She told him about forests of bones, about skulls that rolled between the trees. One night, while the ship swayed gently, she told him that certain beings were content with wine and flowers, but real gods demanded blood.

By the time they reached London – her, skinny and hollow-eyed; him, hale and hardy as if the trip hadn't lasted for months – Olanna of Nri spoke English and George Mathers loved her, but forbade himself from touching her. The members of the Order were waiting for them in London, and they seemed disappointed when they saw Olanna disembark from the *Vauxhall*. They had imagined, George would say later, a tall, thin woman, more like the ones in photographs from East Africa, with their long necks; they didn't expect this slight girl with her round head and a face marked by scars. But they treated her with reverence. She seemed astonished at the city, but in no way overwhelmed. I want to see the train that goes under the ground, she told George. And he went with her to ride the Underground, to walk through Hyde Park, to admire Kensington. Olanna was very tired when she reached the Palace, and she was cold; he covered her with his jacket and had the urge to carry her to his father's house in St John's Wood.

Christopher Mathers – George's father and the leader of the Order at the time – and the cult's senior members were all waiting in the main hall of the house, on the red sofas under the chandelier. Olanna blinked as she looked at the decorations, and George studied his mother's rigid demeanour, the envy in all the women's eyes and in his younger brother's. He realized he was not going to be able to save Olanna, and he understood: the Order comes first. They had endured years of frustration, and although their practices had made them rich and powerful, they needed something more. My father always believed that the Order and its rituals aid in maintaining riches, but that one must help them along with inheritance or good business. He's right. I've read Ramon Llull, and he says exactly the same thing about alchemy: to make gold, you must first have gold. You can't make something from nothing. Riches, in those years, were no longer enough for them. They wanted to evade death, and they thought the Darkness was going to grant them that gift. It's the same thing we believe now, of course. Christopher Mathers knew that in order to build a faith, an incalculable promise was required.

George's mother decided to hold the Ceremonial. She was a bitter woman, he wrote, who spent hours in front of the fireplace crying with rage because she had lost her favourite son, her eldest, in that Great War she considered stupid and unnecessary. Her beautiful son who had died in a trench from typhus, and who had gone to that massacre voluntarily, in defiance of her and of the Order. He was the only one in the family, as well, who had the gift. Not a considerable one, but more than the nullity possessed by George and Charles – young, ambitious Charles, who studied eight hours a day and could spend ages explaining the meaning of the Sefirot, but was incapable of the smallest glimmer of natural magic. More than the incapacity of George, who preferred to travel and take notes, but always ended up as the captivated recipient of the magic of others.

The Ceremonial was set for 31 October 1919. It would be held in the hall specially prepared for it at the house in St John's Wood. It's the same hall used today, the one where I myself drew chalk circles, and where I was taught the most exquisite calligraphy to improve my seals. George Mathers promised to be there and went home to his wife Lily, who decorated her hair with gold ribbons and spent hours tending the garden. Lily, who wrote violent and romantic love poems. He embraced her against the iron door and regretted that he couldn't give her a child, a smiling little one who would keep her company during his absences. Other people, his parents, even the doctors, all believed that Lily was sterile. But he knew the truth, because he had been with many women, not so much because he wanted to, but as a test, and none of them had gotten pregnant. The Mathers were dying out and their only hope was Charles, so young.

He opened the suitcase that held his gifts for Lily: carved masks, the extraordinary cloths from West Africa, the perfumes he'd bought in Paris – she liked bottles of unexpected colours – lithographs by Alphonse Mucha, an illustrator who was already considered somewhat antiquated but whom Lily loved. The suitcase also held the little clay statue someone had left at the door of his house in Ibadan, possibly as a warning. When Lily picked it up, George snatched it from her. The great god Pan also lives so far away, she said. Lily was a disorganized adherent, incapable of naming the constellations or of drawing a seal, but she believed. And she wanted to know if the medium really was powerful. You'll see her soon, said George, and he showed her a necklace, his last gift, that made her smile. The wind blew one of the windows open and Lily closed it, but couldn't keep a flurry of dried leaves from entering.

Today, the statue is protected behind several panes of glass in the Order's library in London. Except for the phallus, it reminds me of San La Muerte. There's something about its seated position, a pose identical to a particular representation of the skeleton saint that we call the Lord of Patience, because he seems to be waiting. I study in order to find these correspondences and connections, but they always make me a little dizzy. The statue seems to follow you with its eyes, and it is repulsive in a way that's hard to explain.

The Initiates arrived at the appointed time. Many of them chose to wear masks, mostly Venetian, some of animals: they wanted to be known only by the leaders of the Order.

Olanna was waiting on the altar, naked and face down. The only light came from candles. Everything happened very fast. The chants began and then the women, some with a scream, others with a strangled gasp, felt the blood start to flow from between their legs. Olanna moved like a snake on the table, and the smell of semen and blood made her nostrils flare. Soon she threw herself to the floor. The Serpent was out of their control. They couldn't touch her when the black light shone, and they didn't.

Do you hear her? shouted Christopher Mathers, the leader. Do you hear? Many people nodded, and Mathers broke all the rules and protocol and left the protective circle. He went to get paper and pens and gave them to those who could hear. The Serpent was speaking, and they transcribed those words that were murmured in the spaces between the stars, between life and death. Each used their favourite writing system, and each wrote in the language they heard. That's how it's still done today, though the Ceremonial is very different, because no one bleeds – not menstrual blood, at least – and because it's no longer sexual, and it continues until early morning, when the medium withdraws. The transcriptions, like now, turned out very different from each other, and some were impossible to comprehend. No matter, said Christopher Mathers, euphoric: the Black Serpent speaks to us and says more than we can understand, but the little we are capable of learning will suffice.

Christopher Mathers called this stage 'the oracle phase'. When it ended, Olanna was unconscious in a pool of her own blood, her forked tongue hanging from between her half-open lips. Women and men embraced and cried, naked; some couldn't look at her, others dropped their masks. Only George sprang into action, and when the black aura left Olanna, he approached her and picked her up. They hadn't prepared a room for her, though George had explained the procedure. He lay her on the first bed he found, and the sheets were soaked through right away. She was racked by fever. He knew she was going to die. Not that night, but soon. Nobody could endure the intensity of the Darkness's visit. And his father was going to use her often. Every day, if he could. George had seen the man's ambition. Everyone would support him: Olanna was the medium but she was also a savage; none of the Initiates believed her fully human.

Lily burst into the room and covered Olanna and sent for

ice, fresh water, jasmine flowers. In the other room they could hear Christopher Mathers explaining to the male Initiates that they must contain their semen, and he beat those who had ejaculated. He also enquired about the ecstatic visions they'd had. Olanna burned with fever for two nights. Christopher Mathers didn't want to call a doctor, saying that the chemicals could ruin the energy fluid, and he spoke of Apanga and Bindu and the purity of secretions. He was worried, though. On the third day, Olanna emerged from her semi-unconscious state and accepted some soup Lily had ordered the chef to prepare. That same night they held another Ceremonial.

Olanna survived two months. The night of the final ritual was almost no different, except that the Darkness surrounding Olanna lunged – there was no other way to describe it, George said in his diary – and when it touched one of the Initiates, a young woman with her face covered, it opened a deep cut in her left arm. She was rapt in ecstasy and didn't feel the pain, but later she almost lost her arm, which required several operations. After the Darkness leapt, Olanna was motionless as always, silvery and red, but now frighteningly thin, her teeth protruding, her skull perfect under her skin, her eyes sunken. She no longer stuck out her tongue. When George picked her up, he was surprised: she was cold. No fever. He didn't think it was a good sign. In her final delirium, Olanna wept. Lily dried her tears: her father-in-law had ordered her to collect them in small vials, but she had only done it once before telling her husband that she would not obey that cruel man. Couldn't he see the ribs that seemed to want to rip through Olanna's skin, or how her beautiful colour was turning grey, how the scars on her face looked white? Olanna, you don't have to do this, Lily had told her, naked except for her flapper's headband that crossed her forehead and kept her short hair in place. In less than an hour, the Princess of Nri and medium of the Darkness stopped breathing. Lily cried with her hands submerged in a bowl of ice.

Lily and George took care of Olanna's burial in Highgate, the most beautiful cemetery in London, though it was in decline in those days. Lily had a stone sphinx carved and ordered it placed beneath an oak tree. The grave had neither name nor dates: the burial of an African teenager in a state of malnutrition caught the authorities' attention, but the Mathers' money could silence any scandal. Christopher would have preferred to keep her body or use her ashes for rituals, but George put his foot down. Don't take all her dignity, he pleaded. She gave us so much. His father permitted the grave.

Years later, however, it would be desecrated. Few people know this, but Olanna's skull, embellished with jewels, is used by the women of the Order in secret meetings, in dances and invocations. I attended at least two, in London. I say at least two because Florence let me use psychedelic drugs in certain rituals, and sometimes, in my dreams, I remember the skull with its forehead shining red – it's set with rubies – and I remember a woman lifting her skirt and displaying, between her legs, what looked like a long tail.

It was Lily who decided to go with her husband to Africa: George had to return and oversee the family's business, this time at trading posts on the Niger River. On the long, happy voyage there, Lily got pregnant. But they didn't turn back home: the child would be born in hot lands and, with any luck, he would be a great master, powerful and compassionate. A child who would come to change the Order and its practice of exploiting mediums.

George Mathers, who had never before gotten sick in Africa, not even with a stomach ache, came down with malaria during his first week on the Niger. He died without ever recovering consciousness. Lily lost her baby, and she also had fevers – what illness it was exactly, the western doctors didn't know – it seemed like malaria, but it could have been anything – and she survived it, but only for a few months.

The news reached London quickly. Christopher Mathers handed over control of the Order to his youngest son, Charles. He had lost two sons already, and he felt worn out and old.

It would be Charles Mathers' daughter, Florence, who would confirm the arrival of the most powerful medium the Order had found, in Argentina, one winter night in 1962: the fragile blond boy who brought the Darkness, this time in the house of another blood family, the Bradfords. Again, in the jungle and the heat. Florence confirmed his arrival, but I found him. The medium manifested in front of me and for me.

What the Darkness dictates to the Order are instructions about how to achieve the survival of consciousness. To call them 'instructions' is imprecise, but it's the simplest term to help explain what happens. Every time it speaks and communicates through the medium, it dictates the steps necessary for that transition. Those steps are what the Darkness dictated when it came to Olanna, and also during the trances of the Scottish youth, though in those first sessions they couldn't decipher the meaning of the words. The method is transmitted in a very slow, spaced-out, and enigmatic way. Everything is written down in a sacred book. What we believe, and what the Darkness – and therefore the Order – offers, is the possibility of maintaining existence on this plane forever. But the Darkness is fickle. Sometimes it speaks and there's no way to find meaning in what it says. Sometimes it utters only isolated words. Sometimes it dictates methods for other ends, generally hurtful ones, because such a god can only be cruel. Often it tells brief stories about its solitary existence in an empty wasteland: it invites us to visit but it doesn't say how, because its nature is fickle.

Only the mediums can summon this Darkness that speaks and that will help us live forever, help us walk like the gods. Mortals are the past, Florence once said to me. It took a long time for the method of survival to be revealed, and it is, of course, repugnant. I should also add that, so far, it's not only repugnant but also a resounding failure. There is no arguing with faith, though. And it's impossible to disbelieve when the Darkness comes. So, we trust, and we go on. At least, many of us do. Others are sick with doubt.

Before 1962, I spent two years living in my uncle's apartment, with Juan. I spent half the day at school, where I'd see Betty, as if our families had not decided on a separation that at the time seemed definitive or at least unusually long. I never again set foot in the Chascomús house, although I missed it: the underbrush of spiny hackberry, the acacias, the Jerusalem thorns, and especially the dogs. I understand and have always understood that the Order must go to extremes to obtain knowledge, and that in many cases this entails forgoing affection or embracing madness; it entails cruelties that are hard to comprehend, even for Initiates. But when I had to feed the caged ones, I found out what my limit was, or one of my limits.

My grandfather taught me to draw chalk circles; he said they were magnificent. I wasn't allowed to invoke yet: at that time, the youngest in the Order were preserved until adolescence. (Florence broke that rule with her youngest son, but no one knew until the damage became impossible to hide.) My grandfather, however, allowed me to learn things that he considered minor. Tarot. The circles. Some local rites that both delighted and disgusted Tali and me, like crucifying frogs in a circle of salt

407

to ward off storms. He also let me help Juan, who, when he felt very bad, lost the defences that kept presences and discarnates at bay. So, I'd leave a sign beside his door or a talisman under his pillow. He always needed those small assistances at certain moments in his life, though most of the time he could deflect any intrusion on his own. He once explained to me that after he had mastered the method my uncle taught him, it felt absolutely natural, like not wetting the bed.

Those two were the most pleasant of my formative years, away from my mother, whom I never again called Mother, only Mercedes. Away from her and close to the men of my family, failures and alcoholics, hunters and collectors, who reminded me of the Order's founders and of George Mathers, my first love.

In Puerto Reyes I started making lists. I always liked writing everything down: recipes and instructions, catalogues and advice, dictionaries and indices. When Juan revealed himself as a medium, I was working on a basic dictionary of all the beings who were said to live in the area around Puerto Reyes. I talked to people, collected testimonies, kept notebooks. My grandfather told me I could study religion and culture if I wanted to; I could major in anthropology at Oxford or Cambridge or whatever university I chose. The Order always kept up its profile in research and study: the Darkness had to be interpreted, not merely worshipped blindly. It was a difficult balance to strike, but it was done by incorporating other esoteric traditions and magical systems; so there were specialists in the Kabbalah and the mystical doctrine of Judaism, and in Sufism, spiritualism, necromancy, alchemy. The Order gathered together the most distinguished students of the Graeco-Roman mysteries, and they even brought in doctors, especially neurologists, because epilepsy, schizophrenia, neuronal hypersynchronization or hyperia, mystical ecstasy, it was all thought about and investigated. I wanted to be part of that tradition, which, of course, also involved practice. 'Study, know, then dare; dare to will, dare to act and be silent!' This is the definition given by Eliphas Lévi. A charlatan, as my grandfather said, but a charlatan who wrote very well.

I remember the day and night of the revelation perfectly, partly because, over the years, I've had to tell the story to various Initiates. I was tired from swimming and from the sun, and also a little sick from the boat. Tali had gotten sunstroke a few days before and she was with Marcelina, the woman who took care of us and of the house. That was the only reason she wasn't there that night. I hid the revelation from her until my father decided it was time to initiate her. Tali isn't of blood, and the timeline was different for her. She never reproached me for it.

That winter, my uncle had agreed to let Juan travel north for the first time. He brought him by plane himself. Juan and I had spent the day together, and I went with him to his room that night: he wasn't all that tired after a full day of boating, or maybe he was so excited by the novelty of it all that he wasn't sleepy. I told him, Quit fooling around and shut your eyes, if they catch us awake and talking, they'll kill us.

I went up to my room, turned on the fan, and lay down with my blue notebook. I remember I was wearing the silk nightgown my grandfather had brought me from Paris, lovely, cool, with delicate details on the straps. I remember I wrote with a Parker pen that had a gold-plated lid, another gift from my grandfather, which I've since lost. My father also gave me beautiful gifts: every year, for example, a piece of jewellery with a different stone. That year he'd given me a Lalique ring. The girls in my class were all pining after Vendôme rings, but I preferred the ones my father gave me, much stranger and more expensive – museum pieces.

I opened the notebook and added two new beings. Guachu Ja Eté. I wrote: They call him 'the ruler of the deer', and he whistles. He also changes people who steal into deer. That's what Marcelina told me, but she didn't say what shape this particular whistler has. There are many whistlers and scream- ers. The scariest screamer is the Mbogua, which is identical to the Irish banshee. It screams to announce a tragedy, but only the person the tragedy will befall can hear the scream. I traced the correspondence with an arrow: banshee, and 'keening', the name of its howl. Marcelina was teaching me a little Guar- aní. I dreamed of writing books about the local mythology, like the ones I read in English about the beings from the British Isles.

Since I wasn't tired, I put the notebook away and left the room to get a glass of water. The house was silent. My grand- father and my father had withdrawn early and were already asleep. My uncle was asleep, too. I had to go past the door of Juan's room on the ground floor to get to the bathroom, and I remember how I tiptoed so I wouldn't wake him. At night, Reyes is a beautiful house. Mercedes never went there, and for that reason, too, it was a sanctuary for me. At Reyes I was far away from her rage. She still hit me often, though I no longer lived with her. She would ask me to come up for dinner, and afterwards she would let fly if I said something inappropriate – and I always said something she didn't like. The beatings from Mercedes never made me cry, and if at some point my eyes watered, more from fury than from pain, I didn't let anyone see. Only Juan.

Descending the steps without making any noise was easy because they were carpeted, but the hallways had wooden floors and they creaked. My father would say they should have been made from marble or tile, that it was crazy to use wood in that heat, but they were definitely prettier. I tugged at the hem of my nightgown, which wasn't short, but I didn't want to meet anyone at night, any man, who might look at my legs. They weren't very long but they were nice, at least back then they were – my body changed a lot with the pregnancy. When they dried in the sun, on the shore of the river, they took on a very soft colour, like varnish.

When I tiptoed up to Juan's door, I found it open. That wasn't strange: my uncle wouldn't let him close it. I had a premonition, though, and I peeked in. He wasn't in his bed. I figured he had gone to the bathroom and I waited. Ten minutes, fifteen minutes, until I got worried. What if he was feeling bad? I went to the bathroom to look for him. It was empty. Then I went out to the garden and called his name. The only response was from some nocturnal birds, which fell silent, and from the house dogs, who came running up to me. It was a lot of silence, which alarmed me, because the jungle roils with sound. When it is quiet, that means it's on the alert. I petted Osman, the youngest dog, a black puppy who was very sweet and who had to be constantly told to heel or he went on the defensive.

I remember I didn't want Juan's disappearance to be my responsibility. I went back into the house, still barefoot, and knocked on the door of my uncle's room. He got up very quickly, his shirt unbuttoned but already on over some loose pants.

Juan left, I announced. I wasn't sure he had left, of course, but that's what I blurted out, stammering. The knocking at the door woke my father. Son of a monkey! What the hell's going on here? he asked, and I explained the situation. My uncle was wringing his hands, and I felt a wave of disgust.

Soon, the three men had laid out a plan for the search party. They ordered me to stay put, but I didn't listen, I couldn't care less about their drunken instructions. The three of them went out half-dressed, my grandfather carrying a kerosene lantern, the other two with flashlights. The dogs went with them, barking. They yelled Juan's name. I went out behind them in my nightgown and boots.

I don't know why we were so sure Juan wasn't hiding in the house, but no one questioned the intuition. Osman left the men and came back to be with me. I patted him and raised the flashlight to the height of my head. I imagined Juan drowned in the river. I imagined Juan fallen into some pit, out of reach. I imagined Juan attacked by an animal. Then I saw the clothes on the ground, or rather I stepped on them. I shone my light down and realized it was what he'd been wearing to sleep in, a long sleeveless nightshirt with blue and white stripes. Was he naked in the jungle? I screamed his name, I shouted, It's me, Rosario, where are you? and I ran through the trees, the tall grasses scratching at my legs. Then I copied something I'd seen in a movie: I had Osman smell Juan's clothes. The dog didn't understand, and whined.

I ran deeper into the jungle and stopped in a clearing among the trees. The flashlight wavered a little, but I shook it and the beam steadied. I could no longer make out the house from where I was standing, and I thought I couldn't go any further without getting lost in the brush. I shone my light on the trees, and that was when I saw Juan. Beside me, Osman whimpered as if he were being tortured. I didn't shush him because I was speechless from shock. Juan was totally naked and walking through the trees like a sleepwalker; he didn't notice us or the light from the flashlight, and he was stumbling. His eyes were covered with a yellow film, like an animal's second eyelid, and he was exhausted: he tripped over a stump in his path, and though he didn't fall, he stopped, panting and sweating. I shone the flashlight on his hands. They were no longer a little boy's hands. They were very big and had long, golden nails, like a bronze animal's. I hesitated; I thought, That boy is not Juan, but I could see the scar from the surgery on his chest. He started going in circles again, now on all fours, his giant hands scratching the earth, the trees, his own skin. He was searching for something, desperately, and he didn't respond when I called his name. I realized what was happening. I waited for the black light. I remember how the pride made my legs tremble, but I was afraid, too. My god, I said, and for the first time in my life I said it not as an exclamation, but as a recognition.

He stood up. Juan's body, thin and tall, was surrounded by what looked like insects, lots of beetles or black butterflies, buzzing, darker than the darkness of the jungle. He did something very simple when the blackness started to surround him: he reached out his arms and brought his hands together, palm against palm at the height of his chest, as if he were about to dive into water. The silence was absolute: Osman was still, and there wasn't an insect, not a leaf or the wind or the distant river, nothing, just the silence and that dark blur that silhouetted Juan, a line of shadow around him, and it all let me know that something was changing and the change was terrible and wonderful.

His body was alone and floating in the blackness, and then I stepped backward, because I knew the Darkness could leap, cut, wound.

Just then the men arrived with the heat of their breath and the flare of their lights. My grandfather raised his kerosene lamp and we saw that the Darkness covered the trees like a heavy, impenetrable curtain. He fell to his knees and backed up, like a Christian pilgrim. The silence was broken by the noise of the Darkness, which was marine and voracious, the sound of water. It didn't have an odour. I never did smell it. Some people smell decomposition; others, freshness. It's different for every-one. My father's mouth hung open like an idiot's, but my uncle was crying and he rushed towards Juan, he lunged at him with his arms extended, he cried out, I don't remember what he said or I didn't understand it; my grandfather moved to stop him and he did, but not before Jorge's left hand touched the open Darkness. Then he fell to the ground, his hand bloody: several fingers were gone. He was screaming, but we ignored him. We were looking at Juan, whose head was hanging down, his hair over his face, and he looked dead. He hung suspended for a few more seconds until the Darkness seemed to re-enter his body. (I still believe that's what happens: he takes out the Darkness and then recovers it.) When he raised his head, I didn't recog-nize his eyes. They still weren't his. He walked upright and sure out of the clearing in the trees, and the shadow followed him, surrounding him like smoke, and he knelt down beside my uncle, who stopped howling when he saw him. Juan touched the wound with his enormous hands and it was cauterized. But first, blood spattered his naked body.

Then my grandfather's kerosene lantern went out and the men went to tend to my uncle. They stopped paying attention to Juan, who crawled away from them on all fours. I don't know why they didn't see him or follow him; maybe the Darkness wanted the two of us to be alone. Juan couldn't get far, he didn't have the strength, he was pouring sweat and clutching his chest, which hurt, with one hand. He looked like an overgrown new-born, wet and drowned. I sat on the grass and called to him like a dog, because he wasn't going to understand anything else. He dragged himself over to me and I embraced him, I took him in my arms, and he was so wet he was slippery but he looked up at me, and I told him it was okay, he was with me. Then I kissed him. A very childish kiss, with my mouth closed, but long and inappropriate. Why did I do that? I still wonder. I was crazed. He put his arms around my neck and I started to cry, and the only thing I felt was his body getting my nightgown wet, his hot hands, his breathing that burned my cheeks, the irregular beating of his heart.

The men came to get him and I resisted, I didn't want to hand him over, but of course I couldn't fight with them. I started to menstruate at that moment; the blood stained my nightgown, and I felt the grass beneath me grow wet. They carried him at a run back to the house, to tend to him. As I followed them, my legs bloody, I was thinking the whole time that I found him, he's mine, they're not going to take him away from me.

I think I was crazy during those minutes, touched by the Darkness. If Dad hadn't given me the well-aimed slap that he did when I got to the house, I wouldn't have come out of the hysteria. My father always says that everyone in the Order goes crazy in the end; that day, I understood what he meant. Once, the day after a Ceremonial, Dad came in with his whiskey to see me and I asked him: how can we go on after this, how do you all do it, the world is stupid, the people who know nothing are contemptible. And he gave an answer that was so true I some-times repeat it out loud. The thing is, nothing happens after this, dear. The next day, we get hungry and we eat, we want to feel the sun and we go swimming, we have to shave, we need to meet with the accountants and visit the fields because we want to keep having money. What happens is real, but so is life.

They wanted to keep him from me during the first days, which were full of running feet and cars that sped out of the driveway, throwing up a cloud of red dust. Mercedes came. I tried to get into Juan's room in a moment of distraction, but she yanked me out by the hair and I ended up on the floor. She smelled of rose perfume, a cheap, disgusting fragrance; she could buy any bottle she liked but she chose that one, because she wanted to stink. They had sent Tali back to Corrientes, where her aunt was taking care of her.

I couldn't sleep or think or write, and all the doors were shut in my face, but I could listen. My uncle talked about his lost fingers. He said he had felt Juan's hands to be cold. He was crying as he said it. He mourned the fact that he would never operate again. He was destroyed and happy at the same time, and so was my grandfather. The only one who kept it together was Mercedes. She walked around the house and the gardens in a white shirt and beige high-waisted pants. If she had been a different woman, with her hair down to her shoulders, a little hat to cover the bald spots, and the dark glasses she wore even in the house, I would have said she looked pretty, or at least that she maintained a certain elegance amid the chaos and all the running. But all I could see was smugness and arrogance. She walked with superiority, she mocked the men, she mocked me. She shouted: None of you have enough character to deal with this, you bunch of capons! Capons: that's what they called the castrated bulls on the estate.

I endured two days without seeing Juan, and then I went looking for my grandfather. I found him sitting in one of the iron chairs, smoking, the skin on his arms irritated from the sun. When he saw me, he motioned for me to come sit with him. Below, in the river, a man and a woman in a rusty boat were tossing white flowers into the water. I asked for permission to see Juan. I found him, I said. I have a right, and plus, he needs me.

My grandfather shook his head no, and added: Florence Mathers is coming tomorrow. She will tell us what to do. And she's going to explain to you, too, because you're going to have to take charge of him, you're the custodian. Like George was for Olanna. You have the primary responsibility.

Is she going to take him away? I asked, and my grandfather's reaction was surprising. He grabbed me by the shoulders and I saw that his eyes were different, jumpy, as if he thought someone was after him. No, he told me. They're not going to take him. He came to us. He sought us out. He could have died as a baby but he held on. We waited for him and he came through. Then he started to mumble without much coherence, saying what an honour, the doorway was here, it's here, where could they take him? I didn't want to be there with him any more and I ran to the catwalk. I wasn't so sure. If they take him, I'm going too, I thought. They're never going to separate us, Grandfather just said so. The men wouldn't have found him. Without me, I thought, the medium wouldn't have appeared.

2

I vomited during the whole flight. The stewardesses thought I was nervous or sick: they kept bringing me bags, napkins, even a towel. They gave me a new seat away from the annoyed, disgusted passenger next to me: I was flying first class and there were several empty spots. The plane shook and the turbulence was constant, but that didn't matter to me one bit; I wasn't afraid like the other passengers. Going to study and live in England, leaving Juan for several years – it was the most decisive thing I'd done in my life, and although I was sure about it, I couldn't stop going back over the goodbye, which had been long and desperate and furious. Juan did everything he could to keep me from going. He swore that he would kill himself if I left him. That he wouldn't summon in another Ceremonial. That he would never speak to me again. Every time, I stood listening with my arms crossed in the living room of my uncle's apartment, and every night I let him kiss me soaked in tears, and I always repeated the same thing: I needed to be far away from him, I needed to be someone without him. I had thought it out very well. He had someone who would be with him in the Ceremonial: Stephen, Florence's eldest son. He could replace me in my ritual duties for a time. I didn't want to throw myself into an existence dedicated to Juan without first learning what life was like without that obsessive and devotional bond. I was exhausted in every possible way, and scared, because I realized that he and I were going to be together, we were going to be a couple, the Order's heirs, and I wanted to flee from that certainty. I felt as though if I didn't make the most of the time, my whole life was going to consist of being his companion. That made him furious: what was wrong with that? He needed my company, he had revealed himself to me because I had to be his companion, and we were in love, something he repeated without knowing what he was saying, because he was only fifteen years old and he had never known another girl, he'd never even liked anyone else, and I didn't want that for him or for me. I didn't know if my departure was going to fix things, but my presence certainly wasn't helping. You can visit me, I told him, which was cruel, because he wasn't allowed to fly, at least for the moment: his heart was decompensated and would soon have to undergo another operation. In our arguments he also blamed me for his relapse, and I suppose he was right. Between the Ceremonials, which were fairly frequent, four per year at that time, and the anxiety, the symptoms of his heart failure had worsened. Despite his weakness and deterioration, I thought he would be capable of hitting me in one of those arguments. He was so tall and crushing in size and I was so small and clumsy; he desired me with all the rage of a teenager and all the arrogance of a demigod. Only once did he not want to let go of me after our kisses, and I had to shove him brutally, get him off me and accuse him of being a violent, macho idiot. You can abuse your power with everyone else, I shouted at him, but not with me. He spent the night on the other side of my bedroom door, begging forgiveness. That's what any violent man does, I told him – beg forgiveness. That was the only thing, in our whole awful goodbye, that did any good.

Juan wasn't the first man I had sex with. Before I left, when he found out, he got one of my grandfather's shotguns and shot at Mercedes' crystal glasses and French ceramics. The police came because the neighbours reported the gunshots. It was a few days before Christmas, and we lied and said the fireworks we were storing for the festivities had exploded in the heat. They partially believed it. My first lover was a long-distance runner I'd met at the Regatta Club. He attracted me because he seemed to understand my feeling of haste, of time running out. He had told me that as an athlete, he had a different notion of time. The runner wasn't very good-looking and I never saw him again, but I think of him often because he talked to me of the importance of seconds, how nothing was more complicated than fighting against them, two or three made all the difference, and at the same time it was so stupid, so futile, to fight every day against thousandths of a second, against something the clocks barely registered, something almost no one else even noticed.

My grandfather said, Damn, Juancito knows how to shoot, who knew? And that was it. He was already very depressed in those days, and he killed himself a few years later. I miss my grandfather every day, even though it's a predictable fate for members of the Order and we're taught to accept it. The house smelled like gunpowder for weeks – weeks that Juan spent locked in his room. When he came out, I told him he could find someone else too, and he shouted, Who's going to want me? I told him, Oh, anyone will, you can take your pick, but he dismissed my words with a gesture of defeat. He never has realized what disquiet and fascination he provokes in other people. I was telling him the truth. At fifteen, Juan didn't look like a teenager, and though he was delicate and pale, he had all the look of a man, with his broad back, prominent veins in his arms, that sad and haughty look in his eyes.

I departed at night and left him crying: the driver was waiting for me, the suitcases already in the car. The drive to Ezeiza was long but hypnotic, and I didn't feel sick until I boarded the plane. I didn't know how much I was going to miss Juan or how unbearable his absence would be, but I felt free and distant and alone. It was what I wanted. Vomiting during the entire trip was a cleansing.

Stephen was waiting for me at the airport. The wind had tousled his hair and his streak of white hair covered his eyes. The white had appeared the day after his first Ceremonial: that was when Juan marked Stephen's back with his golden claws. It was an unforgettable moment, because Stephen was very young, because he was Florence's son, and because the wounds were deep and long, running from beneath his shoulder blades to his waist. All the participants screamed: they thought Juan had killed him. The healing was as definitive, immediate, and perfect as when he cauterized my uncle's mutilated hand. The two elegant lines, Stephen would say now, proved he was a fallen angel, and were very attractive to his lovers. But even so, when he received them, the trauma left him speechless and gave him those sudden white hairs. The mark also indicated that the medium could have him as his companion, if he wished. I never felt jealous: on the contrary, it was a relief to have someone to share the task.

We embraced like lovers: he picked me up and spun me around amid the travellers and tourists, the porters, the voice announcing the next flights. I adored Stephen; he had all the joy and defiance I was lacking, at least in those days. He carried the suitcases to the car that would take us to the Order's headquarters, his mother's house in St John's Wood. Though my family had houses in London and could also rent one for me, Florence preferred, at first, for me to be her guest. She wants to understand why you're leaving Juan, Stephen had told me. But I wasn't leaving him. Was it so hard to explain? My life had been dedicated to him for the past six years. I wanted to miss him and go back to him with real desire. I wanted him to become a man. I understand perfectly, my friend, Stephen said. If only Juan could understand too, I replied. He will, and if not, I'll beat it into him. I laughed and kissed Stephen on the cheek. He was in love with Juan too, but he never interfered with us and I always wanted him nearby, like the other spouse, the peacekeeper.

The house in St John's Wood was surrounded by a brick wall that blocked its view from the street. I had been there before, some years earlier on a brief trip. It had a garden that was lovely but sad, with a stone fountain, red and yellow roses, and gravel paths. The intense green of the grass made you squint your eyes. The house held the Order's main library. A group of experts cared for more than three thousand books; there were also two rooms dedicated to contemporary editions. And in the most closely guarded place, the Book that was written in the words of the Darkness, the Order's sacred Book, to which Juan had contributed the best and most extensive pages. Because of that crucial contribution, he was granted a normal life, with less frequent Ceremonials and a new method that wasn't based on using him to exhaustion, like all of his predecessors had been. Florence was proud of having made that decision, because the results were clear: never had the Darkness given so much information, though it was at times erratic and confused. Our task is to interpret it, she said, and we must learn patience.

She greeted us with a hug: she was alone except for the servants and Eddie, her younger son, who lived with her because there was no institution that could contain him. The first thing she did was ask me if I wanted to take a bath before eating, because I must be exhausted after the overnight flight. I *was* exhausted, and famished: the nausea and disgust had passed. Florence took me upstairs to the guest room, and one of the servants left my suitcase on the straps of the luggage stand. The wallpaper was of thorny roses, like the ones in the garden. From the window I could see the damp street and people walking quickly, freezing in the February cold. The bathtub, to my surprise, was already full. Florence took care of those details that, in my house, my mother had never learned how to organize. When I started to feel cold, I got out of the water and put on a simple black dress, long and loose, and a pair of moccasin boots. The house was warm and I didn't need anything else.

We had a somewhat uncomfortable lunch, the three of us. Florence listened to my plans to study at the Warburg Institute and Cambridge; she said only that it was all arranged, I could start classes in two weeks, and, when the time came, begin the regular school year. We didn't talk about Juan, but we did talk about Eddie. While we were downstairs eating, he was upstairs tied to his bed, because he would try to bite himself, and he'd already managed to destroy his wrists with his teeth. Florence kept the secret of exactly what she had done with her younger son, but she told the basic story because, she thought, Juan's arrival had been a wake-up call about her arrogance, a way of showing her that neither she nor anyone else could influence the Darkness's decisions. By training her son to be a medium, she had laid waste to his psyche. Eddie was crazy and he was dangerous, to himself and to others. She regretted it and her pain was sincere, because she loved Eddie desperately.

Stephen didn't let me rest after we ate. When they cleared the plates and Florence ordered the tea, he told me, We're going right out, you have to see the city, it's wonderful. The rest of the country is worthless, but London is the centre of the world.

Florence didn't stop us. She didn't like the company of young people like us. We reminded her of what she had lost as a teenager, when she had to take over the Order. In her mind, we had no responsibilities. Stephen kissed me in the doorway of the house, under the umbrella, and with the tip of his tongue put a tab of acid on my palate. It's only a fourth, he told me, to see if you have a bad trip. It's good to fly low your first time. And we climbed into his moss-coloured Lotus Elan – a convertible, even though, he would say, you can only put the top down three days a year on this damn island. He was exaggerating, of course, but not much.

Before Florence, the Order was led by Charles Mathers, the grandfather Stephen never met. Charles was determined to find a medium for his generation, as his older brother George had when he'd found Olanna. But he was frustrated at every turn, though his search was frenetic. He spread the Order throughout the globe with the promise the Darkness had made: members would be given the chance to perpetuate their consciousness on this plane; that is, to experience a form of immortality on earth.

He found, in fact, many mediums in various parts of the world, but he couldn't keep any of them alive very long or achieve significant advances. It's all in the Book. A young woman who died during her first Ceremonial. A teenager who killed himself after barely a month as the Order's medium. A young man in the United States who tried to strangle several Initiates before dying from a stroke. Charles realized how difficult it was to keep these sinister children alive and lucid, but he couldn't figure out how to do it. Florence was the first one to understand.

The news of Encarnación, the teenager found in Figueres, Cataluña, reached him after the bombings in the winter of 1939. Charles wasn't afraid of travelling to a country at war, nor of entering a region that was so troubled during that time. He went through France. He found the girl still traumatized, mad from grief and terror: she had lost her whole family in the Francoist attack. He brought the girl to France with the help of the Margaralls, an aristocratic family that belonged to the Order. The chosen city was Perpignan.

The child was raped many times, and I call it rape even though the Order speaks of sexual magic. No kind of sexual magic is required in the Ceremonial or with the medium, and Charles knew it. He let himself get carried away by ambition, he ceded to the perversions of members of the Order who were challenging his power, and he gave in to the demented vortex of war. After months of imprisonment, Encarnación escaped through one of the ground-floor windows, and then she returned to the house, where most members of the Order were sleeping, with a shotgun stolen from a nearby farm. She killed them all. Charles was there with his sons, Florence's brothers – her father had instructed Florence to stay in London, which saved her life. The Margaralls were there, and all the most important families in the Order, at least the ones who had dared to cross Europe.

In addition to killing them, Encarnación used a knife to destroy the genitals of all the Order's men. She was fourteen years old and pregnant. Stephen showed me a photo of her: a thin child with a headband holding her dark hair back from her face.

Stephen says that the cycle must be halted, the wheel stopped. And he insists that every medium corresponds to their time. A peasant during the Industrial Revolution, a black woman from the British colonies before decolonization, a poor teenager in the war whose butchery went unnoticed amid the general butchery of the time. That's what we are, he says, and it's possible that the Darkness feeds off that pain and exploitation. I don't want that to be true, I told him once, and he replied that I would have the chance to try to make changes if I became leader. But I know he doesn't think it's possible.

After killing and mutilating everyone, Encarnación jumped out of the highest window of the house. She died instantly.

Stephen's father, Pedro Margarall, found her body. He had left the house for a trivial reason: it was cold and they needed supplies: alcohol to start the fire; light bulbs, because they burned out regularly; plus candles for the blackouts, some of which were related to the electricity system that failed in the war, others to the forces unleashed by the Ceremonials. He found the medium dead on the gravel, the dogs gone mad, and the Order murdered. Pedro Margarall was twenty years old, a student of philosophy and religion, and the son of a marquis: he didn't know how to resolve anything. So he packed his suitcase, took some pictures so he would be believed, and crossed the border before he could be arrested. He reached London with the notes taken by the scribes, because he was a meticulous Initiate even before the disaster. Florence and her mother asked him to stay with them.

Pedro and Florence rebuilt the Order during and after the

war. She called a meeting attended by fewer than ten Initiates and announced that she was the new leader. Many disdained her, but others recognized her bravery. A purge had been necessary, she told them. My father was not obeying the Darkness but rather his own ambition, and he dragged us into unnecessary perversions. Florence did everything, really; Pedro's help was consistent but minimal. She even personally took over the businesses in England, Argentina, South Africa, and Australia. Stephen says that his father, who is a scholar and a soft, delicate person, totally different from Florence, fell in love with her willpower. And she chose him not just because he was the only living witness of the massacre, but because he was, and still is, the person with the best intellectual training in the Order. Pedro Margarall is alive. I should call him by his title: the Marquis of Margarall. He is locked away at his house in Cadaqués, and refuses to see anyone except Stephen and Florence. He made a mistake with Eddie for which he cannot forgive himself. That willpower he fell in love with ended up destroying him.

My year zero: 1967. Bengalis on the street selling shawls with magical symbols, buskers dressed in Elizabethan costumes, plastic bracelets from Biba, Indian saris that never fit me right and that I ended up mailing to Tali, who was with Juan now but I didn't care, or I was a little jealous but I understood: he and I needed separate lives so we could find each other again. The boutiques on Walton Street, the thigh-high boots with miniskirts, which were hard for me to wear because you have to have very thin legs for them to look good. A designer on Carnaby Street explained the best options for my body type and style: long skirts or wide-legged pants with high heels, boas, bronze earrings, hair teased when it went limp in the humidity. I bought earrings shaped like pentagrams, big and black, from a girl on the street. I learned to draw the sigils of the *Key of Solomon* to perfection. I'd started doing them when I was very young, but in London, the Order perfected my technique. I didn't use the traditional materials; instead, I used chalk. Sometimes blood. Time seemed infinite. I drove my Mustang to Cambridge, went to classes, which I juggled along with the ones at the Warburg, and there were still hours left over for magic and clothes and exploring. Time, suddenly, had stretched out. I knew that's how it would be: it was what I'd come looking for. The pasta at Alvaro's place when we were very hungry. Baghdad House, the restaurant where they played *maqam* music and people smoked hash out in the open. Going with Stephen to King's Road, where my favourite dress shop was. The 7½ Club, where I saw Jimi Hendrix play in a basement so stifling and smoke-filled that the acid closed off my throat and made me cry. The incredible shows at the Marquee. We planned our acid trips to predictable places: the Uffington White Horse, which we stared at from a distance for hours, its stylized chalk shape that was so incredibly minimalistic; the neolithic stones at Avebury, Glastonbury, and Stonehenge, where we always encountered hippies and travellers and the hundreds of neopagans and mystics who populated the country: once, we ran into a 'Druid' ceremony and my girlfriend Laura, who was tripping and drunk, laughed so hard they kicked us out. You don't know anything! she shouted at them. If you only knew! And Stephen covered her mouth because if Florence found out we were going around insinuating our secret, the punishment could be serious. I liked going to Stonehenge: a lot of musicians visited the circle, and there was nothing I liked more than music. Some of them brought guitars and it was beautiful to sing with them wrapped in a jacket of Afghan leather, smoking hashish. Our outings almost always included Edward James's house in West Sussex, that surrealist mansion with its forest and its hunting preserve. Years later, Tali would often ask me how we managed to drive while high. How did I manage to study in those conditions? The truth is that you can function under the influence of drugs a lot better than people think, plus, I was so young I could wander around on acid all day, and the next attend several classes and study as many hours as I needed to. We had enviable stamina.

When I say 'we', I'm referring to Stephen and our friends, most of them children of members of the Order: Sandy, who was studying Middle Eastern history at Cambridge; Tara, Stephen's most stable lover, heiress to a shipping company; Robert, who brought us to the best concerts in the city and helped to organize some of the free festivals; Lucie, who wanted to be a photographer but worked as a model and was horribly jealous of Penelope Tree. But, above all, when I say 'we', I mean the trio that was me, Stephen, and Laura. It wasn't a requirement, but the Order encouraged us to live under the premise of the magical androgyne; that is, we could choose lovers of the same sex for rituals and for life, so that that energy would embrace us and aid us in our mystical work. Stephen was nineteen years old, I was eighteen, Laura twenty-two. We were young and bold: we never hesitated to follow the suggestion because almost everyone our age and in our circle lived like that. Acid is a very sexual drug, and under its effect, the idea that sexes should relate only to their opposites is revealed as absurd.

The world seems like the Order, Stephen would say, and of course he wasn't referring to the world as a whole but to ours, the world of young bohemian heirs, libertine and powerful, who had invented the London scene in the sixties. Radical political positions, hedonism, sexual promiscuity, weird clothes, kids with too much money: that stuff was *similar* to the Order. But the spirit of the age, the hippie canon, now *that* was identical.

It has never been easier to blend in, said Florence, and that was partly why she allowed the young Initiates to participate in the ambient esotericism. People talked about thought police, William Blake, and Hölderlin at parties, they read Castaneda and Blavatsky, they looked at Escher pictures to stimulate their trips, they discussed UFOs and countryside fairies. It was common to smoke hash, and, while the pipe went around, page through *Le mystère des cathédrales* or argue over whether the best Tarot was Crowley's or Rider–Waite's (or, as Laura and I insisted on calling them, Frieda Harris's or Pamela Colman Smith's). The I Ching was consulted, the Ouija board used, trips taken to Primrose Hill where the ley lines started, demarcating a map with megaliths aligned across the magical territory of the islands; we sought the spiritual sun Blake had glimpsed. One morning, Sandy thought she saw a black light, the god Brân and his crows, on Tower Hill. We went on the alert, but nothing happened. Tara, with her enormous fortune, brought us objects, rugs, and clothes from Morocco, her favourite place in the world, which I never got to see.

Our epicentre was Stephen's house in Cheyne Walk, right by the river in Chelsea. Stephen had chosen it because it had a staircase designed in the thirties by Sir Edwin Lutyens, with a marvellous iron handrail, and, underneath – because it snaked in a curve – a small table was placed atop some slightly arcane art deco mosaics. I moved in with him two months after I arrived in London. It was far away from St John's Wood and from Florence, but that helped me get to know the city a little. My bed was always littered with books and albums, like the beds of almost everyone I knew: it was a meeting place, a normal thing among the people who went from Mandrax to hashish, all that languor and lethargy we lived in. Sometimes when Robert spoke we couldn't understand him, and he had to write down the dates and times of the concerts because his tongue got tied. Incense, Tiger Balm, and sleep.

Laura was the only one who didn't lead that kind of life. She would lie down beside me, smoking tobacco, and take off the straight masculine pants she wore; I would admire her firm, thin legs while she asked me questions about Juan. She had never attended a Ceremonial, so she'd never met him. Laura was the adopted daughter of Anne Clarke, Florence's aunt. She was missing her left eye and wore clothes that made it impossible to get an idea of the shape of her body: men's clothes, and several sizes too big. Her hair was long, though, and always greasy, and she drank atrociously, so much that she tended to get lost, and Stephen would have to go out and search the city for her. He'd find her sleeping in a park or a cemetery, her favourite places, because Laura was, out of all of us, the one who had best studied communication with the dead, or, as they are called in the Order, the discarnate. Her hands would often smell of earth, and sometimes of blood; if she didn't bathe, she could stink of decomposition. I took care of cleaning her, sometimes: I'd scrub her skin with the sponge and trace the scars she'd given herself when she got too drunk. We read *The White Goddess* aloud until the water got cold and then, when we dried off, we'd tickle each other and she would bite my ass. She still had her eyelid but refused to wear a glass prosthesis: she preferred a leather patch. I thought she was beautiful.

I met Laura at a ritual at Florence's house and her ferocity shocked me: the way she used a knife to cut her arm, and shushed the woman who squealed when she had to cut her, too; the way she pronounced the words with authority and without wavering; how she stimulated me until the sexual energy became a palpable thing over my chalk circle; how she addressed the entity we summoned with surprising familiarity.

430

Laura was infallible and demanded respect: she didn't attend all the rituals, or agree to perform lesser spells. We used to walk around Highgate Cemetery and caress each other atop the graves. I confessed that George Mathers had been my first love; she regretted that the Order hadn't recovered his body, which was buried in Nigeria.

In bed at Cheyne Walk, Laura wanted to hear about Juan. You know what he thinks about the words the Darkness dictates? I said to her once. Juan believed that the utterances were all in the mind of the scribes. Or, in any case, that what the Darkness said could not be interpreted on this plane. Laura turned over in bed, and her unbuttoned shirt revealed a tattooed breast; she tattooed herself, if she could, or else she asked a friend of hers whom I hardly knew, a fox breeder who read viscera as a system of divination, and who hated me because she wanted to be Laura's only lover.

He's right, she told me, and the smoke from her cigarette took on the smell of danger, because what we were saying meant shaking the very foundations of the Order: we were questioning the Book. She went on holding forth, fuelled by the alcohol, while I put on an album so we couldn't be heard from outside. The Book contains fragments that are worthless, she was saying. There are passages of text that were supposedly dictated by the Darkness, but that are identical to fragments of grimoires in the Order's library. Or that even copy modern texts more or less faithfully, texts from occultists in this century. There are excerpts from *The Lesser Key of Solomon*! 'Ars Paulina' is there in its entirety. It's clumsy. But doesn't Florence know? I asked. And Laura would repeat: Florence is one of the scribes, at least when she wants to be. She's a great woman, but it's not the first time she's been wrong, and if she admits any of it is fake, she has to also admit that the method to preserve consciousness dictated by the Darkness could be false too. And she can't admit that, because she would lose her power.

When Laura said those things, I felt anguish. My throat closed off, my chest hurt. All a lie. The possibility of living forever, or at least a very long life, a lie. She kissed me on the lips, and as her teeth collided with mine, she'd say, I could be wrong, baby.

A cult that doesn't offer everlasting benefits, or ones that last an unusually long time, does not construct a faith. And belief is non-negotiable. Florence believed. She had to, not just to preserve her own power, but because she had destroyed her son in the process. Hermes is the god of writing, but he is also the god of falsehoods, I thought, but I didn't say that to Laura: instead, I started untangling her hair, which was about to turn into the kind of dreadlocks Brixton's West Indians wore.

Apart from my room, apart from my books, my albums, and my companion, Stephen's apartment was glorious. Tara wandered naked among the clothes, the newspapers and magazines, the cushions and rugs. We always sat on the floor, even to eat. Sandy wore white lipstick because she wanted to look like Juliette Gréco, and she listened to chansons while reading Camus. Lucie took our pictures without warning. Cheyne Walk was a strange mixture of velvet, William Morris, and some Victorian extravagance, like the obscene paintings Stephen collected, along with the classic hippie decoration of pashminas over lamps to dim the light, Moroccan hand drums, African masks, photos of Rimbaud, and architecture books. Stephen used to say that the tailoring of the time was the most exquisite since the Restoration, and I had to agree, especially when we were visited by David, a musician friend of Lucie's who I thought was extraordinary, with his long blond hair and feminine blouses designed by Michael Fish. He was like a doll with strange teeth, so attractive that sex with him made me a little afraid – I didn't want any infatuation with that boy. Once, I wrote his own name on his back, with ash, down his spine; there was something reptilian about David, even about his English teeth, what a national disgrace. That time, he started talking about mirrors, his fear of mirrors. I told him Borges' story about the war of the mirror, how one day the silver was going to rebel and stop reflecting us, it would disobey and stop replicating our movements while we looked on, astonished and scared to death. And how the first thing that would appear, in the depths of the mirror, would be an unknown colour, then the rumble of weapons and conquest. David sat in front of the mirror and looked for the colour and I think he found it: he was on acid, as always and like all of us. He was afraid. Study, know, then dare; dare to will, dare to act and be silent! I said, to soothe him. And he was soothed, and he fell asleep on one of Tara's golden blankets, a blanket that was for Juan. We're gathering his court, Stephen would say, the court of the golden god. When he comes to London, I thought, I'm going to wrap him in this blanket that smells of peaches. I missed him a lot but I never said so out loud. Secretly, I called him my Persephone. How can I get you out of hell? I can't, I am one of the mistresses of hell, but hell has its corners, and we can rule there, rule and disobey. My grandfather used to read us Milton in the orchid garden, but Juan preferred Blake, and when he gets to London, I'm going to take him to see the Blakes at the Tate Gallery, and all the houses of the poets he likes.

During that time, in the spring of 1967, while we kept an eye on the papers and TV to follow the trial of Mick Jagger, Keith Richards, and their friends, who had been caught with drugs at a country house in Sussex, I talked to Juan again, over the phone. And we started calling each other every day. At any hour. He was usually at the apartment on Libertador; when he went to Reyes, he let me know. Sometimes I heard his agitated breath even over the static on the line; every time I talked to him, I imagined cables under the water, along the ocean floor, bitten by blind fish with enormous teeth. Jorge had told him that his surgery would be performed in London. He was afraid of dying. Tali helped him with his night terrors, but no one could help him like I did. He was devastated because Florence had told him that when they died, mediums were claimed by the Darkness, they spent eternity there, like in the Christian myths. One night he cried until he fell asleep and he didn't hang up until the early morning, or someone hung up for him, maybe my uncle. He didn't talk about those things with Tali, which gave me a vague feeling of pride.

They're all such shits, I said to Stephen. Why do they scare him like that, talking about an eternity with the gods? Because they want to keep him from leaving any way they can, Stephen replied. A professor at the Warburg had explained to me that alchemy was never a technique meant to multiply riches. It was and is a mystical exercise. The search for gold is the attempt to find the substance of immortality. Juan opened the path towards that substance. They would never leave him alone, never say, Enough, his body can't give any more.

I still dream about the wallpaper in my room, the way it morphed into spiders and dancers; I still remember how my hand, when I reached it out towards the sun, would be wrapped up in the colours of the rainbow. Also the rituals where we danced until our bodies disintegrated into particles of light, and how Laura opened the belly of a hare over my chalk circle in Florence's house. Juan, over the phone, talked alternately about Tali and my grandfather, whom it was sometimes necessary to go searching for in the jungle where he hid out, naked and drunk and terrified. In the jungle, under a tree, he finally shot himself. I was still in London, and I didn't go to his funeral. One night, Juan talked to me about doors he could open and houses that looked one way from the outside, but inside were completely different. What are you doing? I whispered. Nothing, he replied, it just happened. I passed by the door of a house that seemed strange, and when I opened it, I found that it wasn't a house at all. Don't tell anyone, and don't go in, I warned him. I told Laura about those doors: I was thinking about liminal spaces, and she suggested we not mention the doors over the phone any more, in case someone was listening, and they almost certainly were. If there was a new path opening up, I had to protect Juan. That was a horrible morning in London, when the sky looked like wet sugar and the people, who in general were used to it, ran down the street under umbrellas to escape the freezing rain. We need to protect him, Laura told me. I have a bad feeling, she said, and I'm never wrong.

We used to go to a club in Soho called Hive. It was beside some ruins that still hadn't been rebuilt after the Blitz. It was a place for gay and queer people that closed in early 1969. David played there once, as did several others of our musician friends. To get in you had to knock on a small green-framed door on a short street, and an eye on the other side of the peephole would ask if we were members, though there was no membership, Hive wasn't White's, and that was just a strategy to avoid the police. A dirty mirror on the wall, feather boas, cheap high heels, tall men teetering atop platform shoes, and the best music in the city. For a time, I gave Tarot readings at a little table near the bar. One night, when I was drunk, a blue-eyed boy asked for a reading. He was so thin he looked sick with TB, and so beautiful he looked like a girl from Carnaby Street. In fact, it took me a minute to decide whether he was male or female. Unable to hold back, I told him all about the theory of androgynous magic: *solve et coagula* and why Baphomet has the torso of a man and the breasts of a woman. I explained about the number 11, the number of homoerotic magic, which represents the double phallus. I taught him that all magical instruments must be doubles, two swords, two wands, two cups, two pentacles, and why occultists should all be homosexual. He thought it was funny. He wasn't interested in what I was saying. He listened to me as if to a madwoman. The boy spoke Polari with astonishing ease and I told Stephen to please take him home, please let me see them together, but Stephen likes masculine men and I had to content myself with staring at him until he left. Quit recruiting, Stephen told me, annoyed.

At Hive, Stephen made crude, vulgar jokes and knew almost everyone, because he'd slept with half of them and gone to school with the other half. Once, I led Laura by the hand to the bathroom and we ended up screaming, me holding on to the sink and Laura on her knees, and we made such a scene that some queens getting high in a corner applauded and asked for an encore. We used to lose Stephen, and Tara too, when they went to Regent's Park with their occasional lovers, or took them back to Cheyne Walk. But Laura and I would walk until dawn, taking different routes each time. We'd end up at Hawksmoor's church in Spitalfields, the area where Jack the Ripper committed his crimes. When she met Juan, Laura spent hours explaining Hawksmoor's churches to him, and he took photos for his brother Luis and mailed them with a long letter. Laura designed alternative cartographies. Lines on maps that were an underground text capable of divination and prophecy. You had to traverse those alternative paths without thinking, draw the seals standing up, and finally the way would be revealed.

Like in alchemy, I told her: they seem like regular walks, but they're a process. The meaning lies in the time spent on that process, not in the result: the discipline of repetition. That's it, she replied, enlightened boredom. One night I told her about how Mercedes had made me feed the children she kept locked in cages, how Juan had lightened the task, how Mercedes beat me every day to let me know that I may have found Juan, but she was still the boss; also how Juan let me sleep beside him after the beatings and promised to kill my mother, but hadn't done it yet. To defend me, though, he told Mercedes that if she laid another finger on me, he was going to take an overdose of his medication. It's easy for me to die, he shouted at her, and you'll lose everything. Mercedes didn't hit me after that.

He's faithful, Laura said. I really love him, I replied, and I miss him. We sat down on the grass and I heard squirrels skittering along branches. Laura handed me a bottle of wine she'd bought at Hive. Who took your eye? I whispered into her ear. I liked the oily smell of her hair, and also the colour it shone with when it was so dirty. Your mother, she said. She did it at Florence's house. Without anaesthesia, but I didn't faint from the pain. You're strong, I told her. No, I was just surprised.

Someday, we're going to get rid of her, I assured her. If Juan doesn't do it, someone else will.

Juan came to London in the summer of 1969. His health had deteriorated after the Ceremonial earlier that year. The surgery that they had been planning – because the one when he was little had only been palliative, or at least had become obsolete as he grew up – was set for the month of July. It would be at the Heart Hospital, where my uncle had studied and was regularly invited to give classes, though he rarely accepted because he couldn't bear to be away from Juan. He wasn't going to perform the operation himself, of course, because the Darkness had taken his fingers. He was even more legendary after the mutilation – attributed publicly to a hunting accident – or maybe thanks to it. It was going to be a long and risky operation.

It was hard to keep calm when the arrivals door opened. Juan looked weak and exhausted; he wasn't carrying a single bag and he needed to lean on Graciela Biedma, the doctor who would be with him from then on. My uncle was already in London preparing the team of surgeons. Brown Oxfords, white shirt, and blond hair almost down to his shoulders; Juan was already six foot five, and he wasn't at all awkward like other tall boys. He was elegant and slow, regal, as the British would say, and he had the air of a giant cat. He let go of the doctor to hug me: he could cup my whole face in his hand, his fingers tangled in my hair, his palm on my cheek, wrist at my chin. He'd lost any remaining trace of adolescence, and he was all aggressive cheekbones, a chin so cleft it looked wounded, darkened eyes. Not even his smile of recognition was the same: Juan used to smile with a touch of shyness, and now it was a dry, sideways expression, which only I could perceive as happy or relieved, because I knew him so well. I buried my face in his chest, smelled his sweaty shirt. I don't know if he had a fever, I suppose he did, because I could feel him breathing with difficulty, his heart beating fast and irregular, always the same, so many nights spent sleeping at his side, next to that body. He bent down to kiss me, and I put my arms around his neck and received his breath that was heavy with the hours of confinement and the ordeal of flying, his soft lips and the ferocity of the beard that was already growing in like a man's. He was about to turn eighteen years old; he looked twenty-five, at least. I caressed his forehead with my thumbs so he would stop frowning: his head hurt. He caressed my back under my shirt. I closed my eyes;

Juan's hand on my back reminded me of a claw. I forced myself to pull away from the embrace because if I didn't, someone else would break it up for us, possibly my uncle or Florence, who were waiting anxiously.

We went by car to the house in St John's Wood. Juan would wait there for the operation, and there he would recover once he was discharged. The doctors checked him over in the bedroom, while I waited outside. My uncle came out wringing his hands, clearly displeased.

'The surgeon who is supposed to operate has a cold, and we have to postpone until he's better. This is very bad news.'

'How long?'

'I don't know. Juan will have to go to the institute every morning this week, for tests. I'm not going to hospitalize him; I don't want him to be stressed. He had a difficult flight and he needs to sleep, but he wants to see you. Go on, before the tranquillizer kicks in. Then we need to talk about your behaviour in the airport. You went there to mark your territory, like a cat. Like a whore.'

I felt my eyes fill up with tears at the insult and the contempt behind it, but I said nothing. There was a simmering feud between us. Outside, the rain had started to pour, so hard it didn't seem like just past noon, with the grey sky so dark and a tree lashing the window. There was a green blanket covering Juan's legs. The room was heated, and now he was wearing only a white cotton T-shirt. Despite his paleness and his heavy eyelids, he looked powerful against the pillows. He was only fragile because he was sick. Fragile like relics, ancient ruins, sacred bones that had to be cared for and protected because they were incalculably valuable, because their destruction would be irreparable.

*

His recovery from the surgery was very slow. I was allowed to visit him in the hospital, but my presence did him no good. He was unconscious, on a ventilator, unrecognizable. He was losing weight, and no more tubes could fit in his arms. Once he could leave the hospital he would finish recuperating at Florence's house, with me. Stephen had fought with his mother because he thought it was wrong for Juan to have to spend his convalescence under the same roof as Eddie, Stephen's brother. Eddie hated Juan because he thought he had usurped him, Stephen told her, and he was capable of anything. And he has a gift for escaping. Don't you remember when he was little and he could get into any house, at night, and he'd move things around, smear dirt in the beds, wake up sleeping people by biting their legs? Anne found him slithering around like an eel not long ago. He can get into Juan's room if he wants.

Florence did not agree. Eddie doesn't know Juan, he doesn't even know he exists, she said. Eddie doesn't talk, Mother, but he's not an idiot: he listens, he understands, and he perceives so much more than any of us. And you know full well what he wants: to die, after killing the one who took his place. Florence shook her head and insisted that Juan was perfectly safe: Eddie lived in the west wing of the house, where he was guarded by a small army. Stephen gave up on the argument and turned to me. She's blind, he explained. You know how my brother escaped from the psychiatric clinic? He talked to the nurses and convinced them to inject themselves with an overdose of tranquillizers. She's the one who trained him, and she knows what he's capable of, it's ridiculous that she thinks she's in control. She owns dozens of houses in London, and Juan could go to any one of them. The arrogance, fuck. She wants to have them both in the same house, who knows why.

I hadn't seen Eddie in months. The last time, I'd noticed

he was missing a little finger. He had chewed it off himself. Eddie was progressively mutilating himself. The pain relieved him, according to Stephen. He had red hair, like his mother, and very light grey eyes; he was colour-blind. Sometimes, when he walked in the garden, he saw me in the window and waved, smiling. His teeth scared me. They had been sharpened, and they were pointed and yellow.

I've always needed to be well dressed to have serious conversations. With the right clothes, all my insecurity vanishes. I called Sandy and Lucie for a shopping trip. Juan was going to be discharged in a matter of days, barring any complications. My back was hurting from sleeping in a hospital bed beside him. He could walk on his own now, his legs didn't tremble, and he wasn't in pain. Managing the pain had been the hardest part, because he could only tolerate light painkillers. It was going to be good for me, as well, to leave the hospital; I'd spent days inside those greenish walls, listening to moans and cries.

Sandy had been crazy about Ossie Clark's chiffon pants for years, but that was never my style, so I let her try on clothes while I waited. Everything looked good on her. I had to be more careful. I loved the fabrics of Ken Scott, a designer I'd met on a quick trip to Rome with Stephen: Lucie took photos of me in a dress of his printed with owl faces, so psychedelic my friends would often ask me to put it on and dance when they were on strong acid. I'd seen a marvellous dress near our house, at the Fulham Road Clothes Shop; black, long, and ample, made of silk and wool, with a V-neck hung with a fringe that had red, yellow, and green beads. It was a little like a tunic, a little ceremonial, a little African. It would be perfect with some high Biba boots made of green suede. I didn't need anything else. Going to Biba, in Kensington, always gave me a euphoric joy: it was a dark place with a tenuous, golden luminescence, and there were mirrors and peacock feathers in every corner. Their models would swan around the rooms: Biba's owner said they had suffered from malnutrition in the post-war period, and that's why they were beautiful and thin now. I had been raised as a millionaire in South America, all protein and milk products, and I didn't look like those kids who wandered around the store and sometimes chatted up the actors and other celebrities. The gossip in those days was that Anita Pallenberg, Keith Richards' partner – at the time: she'd been Brian Jones's girlfriend before, and she was so beautiful I didn't like to look at her – had a Hand of Glory. I don't know what the girls who chattered about that really understood: all they knew was that it had something to do with black magic. I was dying to have one myself, and I'd asked Laura for one many times; the Order kept theirs in the library, near George Mathers' statuette of the African god. They were used regularly, though they were precious relics: the left hand of a hanged man that was cut from the cadaver while it was still strung up. The hand was then treated with wax to turn it into a candle. How could Anita have one? She had no ties to the Order, though she did flirt with the occult, like all the rich kids in London. A Hand of Glory, used correctly, could achieve many things: I was most interested in its ability to open doors. Juan and I had already spoken several times about his discovery, about that door he'd found that he could open. I didn't go in, he said, because the air in the passageway seemed foul and I didn't feel good. When I get better, he told me, we have to find those passages. I kissed him: his lips were no longer cracked, though his nose still bled sometimes because the plastic tubes had injured the delicate mucous membranes. He'd had a birthday in the hospital, while he was semi-conscious and in pain. All my energy, at that time, was directed towards getting him to be able to stay with me, with us, to share our life. I was sure it was possible.

I had to convince Florence. I always forget, because I didn't believe it then and I don't believe it now, that she was convinced other members of the Order were conspiring to take Juan away from her – or should I say from us? – as, she also believed, were other secret cults that referred to themselves as 'cults of the shadow' or 'cults of the left-handed path'. As she understood it, the constant bodyguards were necessary in order to prevent that kidnapping, and as a guarantee that the medium wouldn't hurt himself or try to flee, all of which I thought was highly unlikely.

It wasn't raining, so I dropped Sandy off at the Warburg and left Lucie at Biba and walked to Florence's house. The city becomes both greyer and greener as you enter the more elegant neighbourhoods. Still, I missed the purple flowers of the jacarandas that the wisteria couldn't replace, though it's also lovely: there was a particularly lush one growing beside our house in Cheyne Walk. I had to tell Florence the whole truth and propose a simple plan. Juan and I were together, and in love. She knew that, and disapproved. To her, love was impure. I, on the other hand, have had so little love that it seems to me like a delicate jewel, and I'm terrified of losing it. My fear is not just that I'll misplace it, like an earring on a night of sex or sweaty dancing, it's that it will evaporate and vanish like alcohol.

I waited for her reclining on the chaise longue in front of the fireplace. I was served tea. I heard footsteps the whole time, though I was alone. Sounds were treacherous in that house, and there were currents of cold air in every corner. I sat up very straight and smoothed my hair when Florence arrived. She listened attentively. My request sounded reasonable. Juan was going to spend his first days out of the hospital in this house, But after that, please, Flo, don't send him back to Argentina,

443

I want him to see the city. And it would also be good, especially for him, if we could spend some time alone.

She was displeased, but not enough to refuse. We'll have to talk about it with your uncle first, and I also want to hear what Juan has to say. Doesn't he trust me?

Of course he does, but he's very tired. We want to be together, Florence. We accept the surveillance, we'll accept it if you set up a hospital next door, if necessary. But it's easier for him to communicate through me, for now. I'm not manipulating him; I would never dare. There's never been a medium like him before, and that's partly because he's been pressured less. I'm asking you for a period of peace.

Florence gave me a look I will never forget, and for the first time I was afraid of her. Her power was being diluted. I was calm and very assured, and my tone held a veiled threat, although, of course, I was also in danger. I couldn't become an obstacle, or they would eliminate me.

We'll continue this conversation when he is out of the hospital.

Just then, that was all I needed to hear.

Stephen sat down on the bed looking happier than I'd ever seen him, and he embraced Juan with that particular tenderness they shared. I fought back an unexpected wave of jealousy that made my mouth taste sour. Even so, it excited me a lot to see them kiss unabashedly, with that discomfort of men's kisses that at first makes them seem like a fight, and then spills over into an emotion I didn't understand, a lost and recovered fraternity.

You're freezing, Juan told him. This city is cold as a crypt, replied Stephen, and I know what he was referring to: the damp cold that sticks to your skin and never leaves. The saying 'chilled to the bone' gets it so wrong, it's more like there's a second skin that forms, like that of an animal made for cold waters. Stephen stood up to get the albums he'd brought us: the North American ones I'd asked for, the Byrds and Leonard Cohen and the Velvet Underground. Neither Stephen nor Juan understood music. Juan did a little more, because he liked poetry. Stephen preferred structures, buildings, the night.

Stephen added a lot of sugar to his tea so that, as he always said, he could forget it was tea. Why don't they make coffee in this country? I will die with that question on my lips, he said. You should play these albums at night, to drown out my brother's screams. Don't listen to him. You should really have something more than a few records to protect yourselves from him.

When he screams, your brother talks about hands, Juan said suddenly. Stephen and I looked at each other in surprise. Juan had only spent one night in St John's Wood. You didn't sleep? He nodded with his head a little cocked, as if he were hearing something right then. The screams woke me up. There are hands that touch him. Can't you all help him? I can, I've felt the same thing many times. I know how to get them to leave.

My brother talks about hands and about rapes, said Stephen, and he lowered his head. You can't help him, no one can, not even you. Don't think about Eddie, fuck.

Juan insisted. He asked if Eddie had also been kept in a cage, and Stephen said he didn't know the details about what had been done to his brother. My father admitted to certain practices, but not to everything. What he has done is his dirty secret, and he's ashamed. They were trying to get Eddie to achieve a state of hyperia, which means an excessive number of neurons in his nervous system are turned on.

Juan looked at us. 'I was told they raped him with human remains.'

445

'Who told you that?' I asked in horror.

'Mercedes,' replied Juan, and Stephen swallowed hard.

'I don't know,' he said, 'but if Mercedes said it, it's possible. Why would she tell you that while you're recovering?'

'Because she's a piece of shit,' I said.

'Well, in short, they achieved that state of hyperia in my brother, and that's why he's crazy. The state of clairvoyance, when it's permanent, is madness.'

Juan didn't ask any more about Eddie that day. From an enormous bag, Stephen took a very long Afghan coat made of suede and goat leather: it was big enough for Juan. This will keep you warm, he said. That afternoon we went to Kew Gardens, and on the following days, which were rainy, we went to the museums. The Tate holds Juan's favourites, Turner and Waterhouse. I told him I would like to pose for a photo as the woman in *The Magic Circle*: go to the countryside and reproduce it, photograph myself like that, with the crows, the cauldron, the witch in a sensational dress as she drew the circle without looking, as if leaning on the wand. Lucie could help me. Juan spent half an hour in front of his favourite Blake, the yellow monster, *The Ghost of a Flea*. Some art-school girls stared at him brazenly, giggling and nervous. If only they'd known the truth, they would have died of fright.

When we were back at St John's Wood, Stephen decided to go to Hive; Laura, he told us, had been drunk for three days. She's afraid to meet me, Juan said. She'll come when she can, said Stephen nonchalantly. In our room, Juan opened the window because a perfect breeze was blowing, and I embraced him from behind. He asked if I wanted to know the truth about Eddie, and I told him I was very curious. I can find out, he said, if we get close to him. The whole floor is guarded, I told him; they don't want you getting near him and I'm going to obey the rules, because they're right. Florence's son can't control me, he whispered. But the guards can, I said. He pulled away from my embrace and huffed in annoyance. Bring me something of his, then. Anything. Hair, for example. Or do they not let you in, either? Why do they keep him prisoner? You're more curious than me, I said, and he replied: I want to know what they're capable of.

I couldn't go to the part of the house where Eddie lived either that night or the following days, but I spent the time studying the movements of the guards. I finally managed to get into his room when his custodians took him out to walk in the garden. There were always two who went with him, and Eddie raised his face up to the sun. When he went downstairs, the guards in the left wing relaxed; they were only there to keep him from escaping, so I was able to get into his room. I stood for a minute taking it in. They kept the place neat, but it was impossible not to see the dried bloodstains on the sheets, the bars over the window, and Eddie's drawings on the walls. Markers and paints were scattered over the floor. Above the headboard of the bed, like a mural on the wall, he had painted an enormous black tombstone with no name. And in other places he'd drawn Tarot arcana – especially, overwhelmingly, the Hanged Man. It seemed like the bedroom not of a madman, but of a mystic. A monk at war with Satan. I went over to the pillow and collected several bristly hairs, nearly a handful: his hair was falling out, I'd noticed it months ago, the last time I saw him close up. Or maybe he pulled it out. I took it back to Juan without encountering anyone on my way, but constantly startled by the creaking and groaning of that house.

I put the hair in Juan's hands and he stood up. The room seemed to grow bigger and I got dizzy. Juan held me up, gripping me hard by the arms, and then he spilled out: I don't know how to explain it well, though he would do it several more times in the future. Maybe spilled isn't the word: maybe transfused is better. An intravenous invasion of images: I saw amputated limbs, coagulated blood on golden claws, a black lake with a hand rising from it like a buoy in the Paraná, cliffs on the horizon, naked men hanging from a lamp with a gigantic fringe, a withered, beautiful dead body caressed by a thin woman with a dark cloth covering her face, a pond surrounded by reeds, a lagoon, a swamp from which hands emerged, desperate to catch hold of something, clutching at the air, and a man hanging from a branch, very still. And then I felt a violent lurch that laid me out on the ground, and I heard a voice, extremely clear:

another son, she said, and the branch burned in the desert. The rest was coldness and the darkness in the sky. The fire hid the stars from view. Right now, let the demons of dust come. A son who can open the doors for us. The smell of hash and smoke, and Pedro removed Florence's clothes on the sand while she intoned the necessary words and someone in the shadows traced the protection circle with a burning branch. It wasn't enough protection. She cried out that it didn't matter, let her be rid of the blood of the moon, it didn't matter, nothing mattered except the desert son who would have hair like fire and colourless eyes.

If the chalk circle was closed around the house, they couldn't leave until the ritual was complete. They would be locked in as long as the ritual lasted, and some lasted for months. The book clearly said that a child could not be used, nor could his writings or words be trusted. But Florence believed that this child was special, she had seen him outside, his eyes closed and his hands extended, playing, laughing. The boy learned and repeated the indicated words as if they were his own. They're of his language, Florence said. He was conceived at the necessary time in the necessary way. Pedro closed up the house. They had provisions for months. The boy was bathed a quarter hour before dawn, dressed in a very loose white nightshirt. His freck-led face looked towards the window where the sun would rise. They would give him little to eat in the coming days, and every dawn he would be in this room. They would give him drops of the experi-mental hallucinogen that would take him further than they could go. It was reckless to use it on a child, but they had to be reckless, the left-handed path was of recklessness. The women drew the symbol on the floor, in chalk. Eddie repeated the words along with Pedro in front of the altar. Six moons. The father covered the child's hair in ash. Six moons.

If a word was pronounced incorrectly, the spirits would turn against the speaker. Or if the person said the words mockingly or with evil intentions. Eddie had pronounced them well, and yet they had all seen how the shadows pulled him by the hand and out of the room. Slammed doors and running feet. A locked door and behind it Eddie's voice calling for his mother, and then his feet run-ning upstairs, the footsteps of his little feet so clear. Florence behind a locked door, her knees wounded from crawling under the furni-ture because she saw Eddie's eyes there, the son lost in the house, taken by the Darkness, and it did no good for his great-aunt to shout that they had to return to the chapel, protect the lamp, that the boy would return if they went on with the ritual. Pedro returned to the chapel. So did Anne. The two of them continued. Florence was loath to abandon her son to the shadows. She loves him too much, Anne said as she lit the lamp, and love is impure.

Florence returned and asked to be washed. Anne took off her clothes and used cold water. The boy didn't return until dawn. He said he was blind, and he was crying. His eyes were white.

The boy chose the form the spirits would take at the invocation. He chose mouths. He prayed looking to the East and he invoked look-ing to the West, without needing to be told.

Days of hunger and cold were necessary before they were able to banish the spirits. Eddie wouldn't let them leave. The battle of wills made Pedro ill, and he was in bed for months, his body consumed by a rash that kept him from sleeping. Sucked at by hundreds of tiny mouths. His whole body burning, gnawed at.

The boy couldn't retain the symbols, he couldn't remember them and thus could not place them under pillows and beds, in thresholds and doorways, in the necessary places. Let him feel only night, Florence heard. Then he will think only of the symbols. She put Eddie in the small basement. First, she traced the symbols in the air and ordered him to remember them. She left him a basin of water. She let him scream day and night, not from fear, but from hunger and rage. The boy wasn't afraid, he hadn't been afraid when he'd walked blind with his hands tied, hadn't been afraid when he'd been offered to men and to the dead for them to take pleasure in. He had cried later, but because he'd been hurt in the Offering, he had cried from the pain. Nor was he afraid when he was brought close to death. Florence, however, did feel fear. Love is impure, said her aunt, but Florence believed that love was inevitable and could also be set aside. That was the sign of true strength. To put love aside. When he came out of the darkness, dirty and hungry, the boy would remember the symbols and she could ignore how, when he was alone, he clawed at his arms with his own nails and woke up with his lips bloodied from clenching his teeth and chewing his cheeks. She started to speak to him, to explain that he would be the doorway, he would be the blood that brought the night, he would be the medium and people would bow before him, and that it hurt now but when he was touched it would all be worth it, and no one would ever replace him, she had chosen him, he would be the only one, he couldn't doubt that. He would be like a god. The final Offering.

I tried to move. I didn't want to see any more. Juan let go of my hands and I opened my eyes, though they were already open. I re-opened them, I opened them to this reality.

I can't take any more, I told him. I had to process what I had seen and heard.

Juan bundled up Eddie's hair and put it in his jacket pocket. Then he reached out a hand to help me. I sat down on the floor. What did you do? I asked him. You couldn't do that before. Juan shrugged. I've learned a lot of things since you've been gone. I wanted to tell you about some of them over the phone, but you asked me not to talk about it, so I didn't. Other things I kept for myself. No one taught me to display like that. I practised on Tali. She hates it. It made me tired at first, but not so much now. But I don't know if it's good for you. For other people. I'm going to keep this – he pointed to his pocket – for when you want to know more about Eddie.

I crossed my legs and a shadow of worry flitted across Juan's forehead. Do I scare you? Never, I told him. I'm surprised. And I'm cold.

That tends to happen, he said.

Florence invited us for a goodbye lunch. I had class that day, but I skipped it because I thought the meeting was important. Juan had been in London for three weeks, and he was past the critical stage of his recovery. In fact, he spent all his time walking around the city with Laura while I studied. They'd become friends once she managed to overcome her reluctance to meet him, the sacred respect she felt for him, and sometimes they stayed out late, which annoyed Florence.

We drank beer while we ate and Florence talked about the Book, about the progress made, and she gave me two volumes as gifts: *Tell My Horse*, by an anthropologist I admire, and *The Palm-Wine Drinkard*. She was very friendly in spite of her anxiousness – because more than anything, what she wanted was for Juan to return to Misiones and for the Ceremonials to continue. But she agreed to give us a kind of vacation. It's just that the Revelation is very near, she said, and I feel that pressure, but I've realized that a break can also be beneficial.

Since I was a little drunk, I asked her why she thought the Darkness would give us that revelation, and what it would be in exchange for. What were the terms of the trade? We feed it in the Ceremonials, I said. All gods, in every culture, ask for and receive offerings of food. But is that worth immortality? I feel like we're giving very little.

She got uncomfortable and said it wasn't the right time for that conversation. I knew she was going to dodge my questions and avoid explanations. Talking about all of that in front of Juan, in any case, was delicate, because it always meant talking about him, because the Order depends on his sick body for the Revelation. He can't run away. If he did, they might return to the traditional method, the one Mercedes supports: use him more often, treat him as a mere messenger or slave, and let him live as long as his body endures, which would not be long.

I need you to be happy, Juan, she told him suddenly, and he was caught off guard, but only for a second. He has the inexpressiveness of a statue, when he wants. Florence took him by the hands. All of this is yours. Nothing would be possible without your help. Sometimes we have disagreements, sometimes you'll feel like a prisoner. That's to be expected. Your situation is unique. The world will be everlasting, and it will be ours, Juan. I often say that mortals are the past, and I believe it. I can never thank you enough. Or the others, the ones who came before, and who suffered so. I want you to have a different life. I won't let a medium suffer like that ever again. I myself fell into that trap, the trap of suffering, and with my own son. Do you like your life, Juan? It's the one I can give you.

Juan didn't let go of her hands or lower his head. Then he

spoke more than I ever heard him talk to Florence in my life. I'm going to tell you what I want, he told her. I want to live with Rosario, near the sea. Here or somewhere else, it's best if it's warm, so I can swim. I want to wait for Rosario to come back from school or work, I want to learn how to cook. I want to reach old age. If Rosario agrees, I want to have a child. I don't think you understand what it is to have nothing: a child would be mine, the only thing of mine. And I want to be able to open the Darkness when I feel like it, no dates, no obligations, no fear of dying every time. I don't want bodyguards, I don't want surveillance. You can't give me that and I understand, but don't ask me if I like my life or if I'm happy. I'm poor and I'm sick. I have no education, no family, no money. I don't think I'm capable of working. I need the help you all offer me. I am a servant.

Only then did he pull away from her hands.

I didn't know what to say at first. Juan stood up and apologized, then left. I apologized to Florence too, and I followed him.

Stephen and Laura were waiting for us in our room. In the hallway we passed Genesis and Crimson, the couple who used genderless names and had begun sex-change operations in order to take the idea of magical androgynes as far as possible. Crimson has breasts now, Stephen told me. They've just shown me, you two missed it. They turned out really nice.

The surgeries are done in the same hospital where Juan was operated on. If the British citizens ever knew that the Heart Hospital and so many other NHS clinics are infiltrated by the Order, it would be a real scandal.

What did my mother talk to you about? asked Stephen, and he put on an album. *Beggars Banquet*. Did she give you the old saw about how we're the future and mortals are the past?

Frankenstein's monster could say the same thing, of course, if the monster were capable of thought.

Something like that, said Juan, and he pushed Stephen over to make room on the bed. She'll let me live at your house for a while.

I have a story about a woman who lived forever, said Laura, excited. She stood on the bed and opened her arms wide, to declaim like in a play. There once was a woman who ate and drank happily, and she had everything the heart could long for and she wished to live forever. For the first hundred years all went well, but then she started to hunch over and shrivel up, until she couldn't walk or stand or eat or drink. But neither could she die. At first, they fed her like she was a child, but then she got so tiny that they stuck her into a glass bottle and hung her up in a church. She's still there. She's the size of a rat and she moves once a year.

From the way he laughed at that story, which was much more macabre than funny, I realized Stephen had taken acid. She moves once a year, he repeated, and then lit his marijuana pipe. While they talked and laughed, I thought that if immortality was really possible, I wanted to share it with them. Not with the old people. If only Juan could control the Darkness to get rid of the others.

The first weeks were beautiful. Stephen left the house to give us time alone, and Juan and I didn't separate even for breakfast. We were together in bed and in the bath and in the beautiful winter garden, talking in low voices. Buying fruit and chocolates, the surprise of discovering he could sleep through the night without waking up coughing. The surgery had helped him a lot, especially with the dyspnoea; he wasn't cyanotic any more, his fingers weren't blue, and he looked at them in astonishment, and also studied his lips in the mirror every morning, as if he expected the colour of death to return. I watched him sleep with his legs tangled in the sheets in our room, which stank of sex and salt. We spent whole days in bed and I caressed him in silence, the golden hair on his legs, his broad, abused chest, his sunken belly, the scars, the veins of his arms dark grey under his pale skin, his long hair that gave him the look not of a Viking or a rock and roller or a hippie, but rather of something that was only visiting in the present, something savage and desolate.

Graciela, Juan's doctor, along with two bodyguards and some assistants, had moved into the house next door: the neighbours, who were renting, handed it over immediately thanks to an exorbitant cash offering. Still, we could ignore their presence. My uncle visited us too. My friends weren't going to come until they were invited. Nothing interrupted our days of exploring and reading, of dancing naked in the kitchen in the light of the open refrigerator, or of telling secrets without fear of being overheard. I thought I had gotten pregnant during those weeks, and I cried when I found blood on the sheets. The mattress was bloodstained too, and Juan flipped it over.

After the first two weeks, the subtle changes began. Stephen still wasn't back, I think he'd gone to Athens, one of his favourite destinations: he chased heat like a lapdog. The first sign happened at night, when Juan got up and didn't come back to bed. I wasn't asleep yet, I was reading with the bedside lamp on, and I waited for him, sure he'd gone to the bathroom. When he didn't come back, I had a déjà vu of the night of his Manifestation in Puerto Reyes. At first, I had the hope, though faint, that he was only feeling bad. He'd had prolonged arrhythmia despite his medication, but we hadn't informed the doctors: he asked me not to, and I went along with it because I understood that he also needed a break from the constant examination and groping of his body. I found him in the first-floor hallway, looking all around and towards the stairs, that iron staircase that had so beguiled Stephen. Did you hear something? I asked. He and I both knew that the possibility of an intruder was remote, since one of the bodyguards stayed awake all night and the house didn't have many doors, just the front door and an emergency entrance. He nodded: his eyes were shining. Can you open that door? He pointed. It was one of the smallest bedrooms. My hands trembled as I took hold of the doorknob, but behind the door there was only a narrow bed lit by the moon, a small armchair, and two paintings by Forrest Bess that Stephen had bought from a New York gallerist.

He went back to bed without a word. Did you think it was one of those doors you could open in Argentina? He embraced me and nodded, but that night he didn't get up again. In the morning, he hardly spoke at breakfast. There's something there, he told me, after toying with the toast that he couldn't eat. It's not a presence or a discarnate, it's much more powerful. I can't explore it alone. There are two of us, I said. Not enough, he replied. Why did Stephen choose this house? No one ever realized? Not even Laura?

Juan was always very suspicious, much more than me.

Let's go in, I said.

No. We need Laura and Stephen. You won't be enough.

I went for a walk alone, frustrated. I wanted to be his companion in this as well, to follow him into the unknown; I was never afraid. But I can only help him in minor things, with my stupid protections. He hates when I call them stupid because he loves and respects me, but they are. All the little spells in this world are dust, they're nothing, they're specks of dirt in the blood of someone like him.

When I got back from my walk I called Laura, who arrived in under half an hour. Judging from her expression when I opened the door, she thought we'd invited her to a dinner party, one of our fun-filled nights at Cheyne Walk. She realized her mistake when she saw Juan. They sat down on the rugs and he told her what he'd felt. She denied having perceived a door before – I believed her, I still believe her – and, to my surprise, she refused to go with him. The reason she gave made me gasp in shock.

The Book doesn't say anything about opening doors, she murmured. What does that matter? asked Juan. He got up from the floor calmly, his hands folded, and went over to Laura, who looked so small sitting there, her head at the level of his knees. Why are you talking about the Book? Laura was trembling a little: I put my arms around her shoulders. The transcriptions don't say anything about any door or any house, she repeated. Juan got angry and told her: I have no doubt that there is something important and repulsive behind that door, and I don't believe in the transcriptions, and neither do you. Why are you so afraid? He looked at her, and his eyes were dark green.

'Because to follow you is to disobey,' she said.

With his index finger, Juan touched Laura's patch, just barely.

Who took it? Rosario didn't tell me anything. She keeps those kinds of cruel secrets to herself. In the Order they say it was your father who pulled it out, and that was why Anne adopted you. That's the lie they tell. A brutal father who emptied out your eye socket because he didn't want a daughter with second sight. Your father was a gypsy? A traveller? That part is true? I'm sure it was Mercedes who did it with her own two hands. Though Florence would also be capable. They believe in pain more than anything else, they lie when they say those methods are in the past. If, as Rosario says, gods resemble their believers, then this cruel god is the one who wants and allows

457

them to mutilate you. I'm not going to spell out what they did to me, or to Eddie, or to all the others. Did your father sell you, too, like mine did? We are servants to those people, we are the flesh that they torture. We're the rickshaw drivers transporting rich little girls in India. I'm the lumberjack who fucks the plantation owner's daughter. You're going to have to disobey them if you want to follow me. There is something behind that door and I need you. Don't be a coward.

Laura slipped between us and ran out. She left the house, but stayed sitting on the front steps. She was crying.

Juan went upstairs. I followed him, angry. I told him there was no reason to treat her like that. But he wasn't furious: he was devastated. I asked if he felt bad and he shook his head, but I took his pulse and it was so fast I made him lie down. He put my hand on his chest so we could monitor his tachycardia together. I don't like to talk to her like that, he said, but I need her. If she follows me, she's going to have to keep the secret and turn against them. You're going to follow me and you don't mind betraying them. But Laura is different.

He put a pillow under his head and undid his pants. That summer he was wearing very dark corduroys that only made him look taller. Come here, he said, and I got on top of him. Why does Laura smell like that? he asked. She never washes well after she does her spells, I explained. She stinks like a butcher, he smiled, and I added that sometimes she also stank of death. When he entered me, I felt vertigo, a sensitivity in my uterus that scared me. I stayed still, looking down at his glorious face against the pillow; he is glorious, his body, his feigned coldness, his sweat that smells of chemicals. Don't destroy Laura, I said, and he told me he was trying to do just the opposite. I closed my eyes and imagined the three of us on chalk circles; he could split Laura in two, she's so little. I always pay lip service to my preference for gentle, soft men. Just two weeks ago I was arguing in class about the authoritarianism and hypermasculinity of Christianity, saying how sick I was of phallocentrism and Eurocentrism, but when Juan dominates and orders me around, I start panting like a submissive dog. He sat up and toyed with my earrings, the giant lightweight pentagrams that I always replace when they break.

Juan told me that he wished he could buy this house. I guided his hand to caress me the way I like. I thought about taking a tab of acid – Stephen had brought me a lot of boxes that I kept in my drawer. I told him the house was going to be his, everything would be his, because we were going to get married. I'd been thinking about our recent conversation with Florence. It's not possible for you to have nothing. The Order owes everything to you. I asked him to bite my belly and I circled his neck with my hands to feel his irregular pulse in my fingertips. I always liked to see in his eyes that he was unafraid of dying. Or, at least, that he didn't mind as long as he died with me.

When Juan fell asleep, I went out to find Laura. I found her sitting looking at the river. It was hot, and she had unbuttoned her shirt. Her tattoos looked like insects on her skin.

If it were night time, I told her, we'd have to get naked and look at the stars here. We can do that whenever you want, she replied. She had taken off her patch, and her eyelid, sunken and loose, trembled. It's better in winter. The wind off the river hurts. Every time she spoke, the air filled with the smell of alcohol. If he's right about there being something in the house, if it's like he describes, it's a passage, she said. He wants me to help him cross the threshold and not report anything to the Order. He's asking a lot. I don't know why he was so mean to you, I said. I do, she replied. He wants to know how broken I am. I'm going to do it, but I'm scared, because if they find out, they will be merciless. Also, he scares me. I told her there was nothing to fear from Juan and she laughed, she split her sides laughing until I thought she was going to fall into the river: the lights came on in some nearby houses, in protest.

In a low voice, I asked her what was going to be required of us in exchange for moving our consciousnesses into another body. She thought about it, her legs crossed, and asked for a cigarette. The sun, shining down on us just before the blue hour, didn't bother us. I don't know, she finally told me, but it will be something obscene. I've decided I don't want it. Her reply surprised me. Who doesn't want to keep their consciousness alive? Who would refuse being practically immortal? I asked her if she knew that before the Chinese figured out what gunpowder was for, they'd thought it could be used in an immortality elixir. How did they find out they were wrong? she asked me. The most logical way possible: it blew up in their faces, and ever since then they've used it in fireworks. And the truth is that when I see particularly beautiful fireworks, I really do feel immortal. You and I are different, she replied.

She put out her cigarette and we went back together.

We told Stephen before going through the door. He thought no one else should know, not Tara, not Sandy, not any of our other friends. At least not for now. Juan asked Stephen, as he'd done with me, to open the door. He did, and we saw a normal room, with its bed, its turquoise curtains, its paintings. A sink by the window and then a small bathroom. The English are so absurd, said Stephen. What kind of riffraff puts carpet in a bathroom – it's clearly not meant to be used, am I right? Juan almost smiled. We left, and Juan closed the door behind us. When he was the one who opened it, there was no longer a bedroom on the other side. No bed or paintings or sink. There was a dark tunnel, like an underpass, the kind you see in train stations. Something lit it, but it didn't look like electric light. I immediately thought about Arnold van Gennep and Turner and liminal spaces, thresholds, internal or external. Crossroads, bridges, shores. I said nothing. Laura squatted down on her heels.

Through the door, the air ran out quickly. I stopped Juan when I started to feel suffocated. I was afraid for him, and I put my hand on his chest: his heart was beating fast and too hard, but it was regular. Laura was panting, breathless. This feels just like altitude sickness, she said. I nodded. It reminded me of La Paz. When Dad and I went there, I hadn't been able to walk and I got scared. I'd thought: this is how Juan feels all the time, and I cried in a corner that reeked of urine while Dad yelled at me because we were late to a meeting with the ambassador.

The duct or underground passageway led to a very narrow mountain path. There was running water nearby. A river, but not rapids. It was night time through the door, though it wasn't dark. We didn't need the flashlight we'd brought with us. Laura and I were exhausted after three hundred metres, but not Juan. He approached what looked like the end of the path. We followed and saw it was not a precipice, but that the path continued down through trees. It wasn't so steep and you could descend fairly easily. Below, we saw the silvery flashes of a river.

The silence was powerful and horrible. A place like that, a forest with a river, cannot be so still. Where were the animals, the birds, the rustling leaves? Maybe our ears were clogged by the height. Nor was it cold or hot. The place was still in every sense. Laura said it reminded her of the mountains in Wales, but it was like an imprecise copy. A sketch. It's cold in the mountains, there's fog, she said, and the colours here are wrong.

461

It's all wrong, said Juan. It's a stage set. He kept walking. After the curve, the path straightened out again and opened on to a footbridge flanked by trees. Laura pointed to the branches, and Juan went closer. There were bones in the trees, bones littering the ground. Fleshless, most of them, very clean and old. The ones in the branches formed strange decorations, adornments of interlaced phalanges and femurs, fastened with slender twigs into delicate shapes, carnivorous geometries. Juan touched some of them, like he was trying to memorize them. They look like writing, Laura said. On the ground, the bones were scattered with no clear goal. Would someone come, later on, and assemble them into pendants? When Juan touched another of the decorations, it came off and dropped into his open hand like a ripe fruit. We studied it. It was a sign, a seal. Juan kept his hand open and three more fell. He gave thanks and put them into his pocket.

The path was covered with bones as far as we could see. They were from all parts of the body and of all sizes. Were they the remains of centuries of banquets? Were people brought here to die? Or had the bones been carried here in order to make this mortuary path? There was no smell. They were old bones, or they'd been savoured until there was nothing left on them, no trace of flesh.

Getting down to the river was easier than I expected. The air was still dry despite the nearby water. I reached down to touch it but Juan stopped me, roughly, as if waking me from a hypnotized state. He's right – we all know what happens if you steal something from faery. True, this is no fairyland, but there's no reason the rules would be different. The rules almost never are. The forms can vary, but not the rules.

Someone sleeps in the Other Place. That's what Juan calls it. That's why there is silence. So that presence can sleep. And the bones are a temple. He took a deep breath. There is absolutely nothing here, he said. The river has no fish. There are no insects. How much further are we going to have to go before we find something?

Laura asked him to be patient. It's our first time.

He looked at his hands and spoke. We listened, and from his tone we knew he was confiding a secret. When I summon the Darkness, or when the Darkness takes me – you choose the term – I can't see what's happening. I'm blind in my trance. I know that the Darkness cuts and takes the Initiates because I'm told. Once, Florence showed me a recording of the Ceremonial, which she burned later. I don't know what has happened until I return and cauterize the wounds and mark those who must be marked with scars. But I'm not unconscious in the trance. I go to a place, or rather, I see scenes. I thought they were hallucinations, like the ones people see in a coma or during a heart attack.

They're like this place? asked Laura.

Yes and no. I see a hallway I don't dare walk down. There are people, or beings, hanging from lamps. I saw a piano. And there's a window, and through it there's a forest. That forest does look like this one.

All forests are similar, I interrupted him.

I know, but these are identical. I've seen that window many times, at every Ceremonial. Sometimes it's closer than at others. And it's this place, I could distinguish it from among thousands of similar images.

Laura gave him her hand and he took it, interlaced his fingers with hers. Let's keep going, he said.

On the other side of the river there was more forest and a gentle hill that we could barely see in the darkness. We went back to the path of bones and to the ornaments: the femurs arranged in intricate shapes, the skulls hanging as though on door knockers, very still, the little bones of hands and feet mounted like delicate jewels, and on the ground, trampled bones. How many metres of them? How long until the bones turned to dirt? Some of them edged the path like sentinels, complete ribcages upright, and there were delicate tracks of vertebrae, some of them whole, with the little tail of aquatic animals.

Then something strange happened to me. I felt nauseous. A bitter taste filled my mouth and I started to retch. We are profaning this place, I told Juan, and he placed his hands on my belly and managed to soothe me so I wouldn't vomit there, on to the bones. The retching took all the air I had left, and we headed for the exit.

On the other side, Laura and I dropped to the floor to recover. Stephen was waiting for us, and turned all his attention to Juan, who was pressing on his eyes and blind from his headache, a monstrous migraine. Stephen led him to bed. I followed them, and Stephen asked me to get ice and water. He didn't want to hear anything about the expedition, not just then. We have to take care of him, he told me, and I went down the stairs squeezing my fists. I left water and ice on the night table and went back to Laura, inexplicably irked. She and I weren't about to rest or sleep, we were too excited. We had to put oil on our lips they were so dry, the Place turns your skin rough, the air scrapes your nose, and if we stayed any longer it could draw blood. We discussed whether it would be better to open the door again soon or if we should wait before returning. I talked to her about San La Muerte and the bones of the Guaraní, and how it was so obvious something was looking for Juan, that it had come here to seek him out. Laura drew the path on the floor: she remembered it in incredible detail, while I'd been more distracted than I thought. I hadn't looked at the sky, for example, hadn't ever raised my head. Laura had, and she'd seen a black sky with no moon or stars. I feel like I'm giving away a secret, drawing the map of a forbidden land, she told me. We have to document everything, I replied. And she copied the map from the floor on to a piece of paper she had with her, because she's always drawing her maps and alternative plans. The good thing is that no one who sees this map will think anything of it. It could be a map of Middle-earth, I laughed.

I felt enormous that first time, because that place was ours. We can use this to take control, I thought. I went back to our room to check on Juan, and I found he was fine, calm in Stephen's arms.

We went on a second expedition when Juan decided he was going to make an offering to the Other Place and ask for something in return. What will you ask for? I enquired. To be able to have my secrets, he replied. I thought it was so strange. Why not ask to be cured? It needs me sick, he said, pointing to the door. It's only capable of finding me because I'm close to death.

This time, there were even more bones on the path. The number of ornaments hanging from the branches had also grown. Juan took off his shirt, knelt down on the bones, and plunged his arms into the remains. His bare back grew broad, and we heard the sound of his knees breaking ancient skeletons. The river sounded like it was running faster. It grows because it eats. Juan is its mouth, and the gods are always hungry.

Being on the other side of the door for too long is like spending hours looking through a telescope. From so much gazing at the stars you feel lost, outside the world. In space, human life

465

has no meaning. Not in this place, either. Juan crumbled the bones with his fingers. He was bleeding, and he left his blood as an offering. Laura shaved part of Juan's scalp, above his left ear. I tried not to look, because I thought bringing a razor into the Other Place was a mistake; I said as much, but they didn't listen. Juan used the sharp edge of a bone to draw a design on his scalp. He barely bit his lip from the pain. I don't know how he could do it without a mirror, but the sign came out perfectly.

That communion was dangerous but necessary. We needed Laura to decipher the drawings on the ornaments. We needed to keep those incursions, that place, a secret. And in order to do that, a gift from Juan was necessary. When he finished drawing the design on his skull and set the bone down atop the others, an ornament, a small one, dropped from a long tree branch in front of him. He looked around, and I think his eyes held gratitude.

There was a new path now, besides the path of bones; it was the grey colour of night and the very dark green of a strange vegetation, mosses and lichens on the trees. The floor was like that of a pine forest. I sensed that the silence was going to be broken long before I heard a distant sound. I can't call it music; it was like a wind instrument, but disjointed and clumsy, sporadic, as if the flautist was out of breath. It lasted less than a minute. Someone was there, but very far away from us.

I don't know if it's an instrument, said Juan. Maybe it's an animal. Something or someone's mouth. A chant. I leaned against his shoulder and he ran his bloody thumb over my lips. His blood is delicious. What would happen if we had sex here, under the moonless sky? What kind of child could we conceive?

We kept walking. There was more oxygen now, too. The trunks of the trees grew thinner. Laura noticed what was on the trunks before we did: it wasn't easy to distinguish at first glance. There were hands gripping them. Many: one on top of another. Amputated hands, severed, clutching the trunks, the whole palm bent and the fingers arched. Human hands, rigid in the position of claws. The whole forest was like that along that stretch. Trunks and trunks with dead hands. Someone had mounted them when rigor mortis set in. The first trunk we saw had twelve hands. Some had more. Others just one. I thought of the Hand of Glory I longed for.

It's a collector, I said. An artist. Or several. To the right of the Forest of Hands, as we baptized it, was what Juan would later mark on the map as the Valley of Torsos. They looked like headstones: a cemetery of soldiers, so symmetrical. But they were human torsos. No arms, no heads, no legs. Torsos with the spotted skin of elderly men, torsos with young girls' lovely breasts, torsos of children, of fat men, of thin men, torsos with dark skin and torsos with very pale skin, flat bellies, huge obese stomachs, torsos of women who had breastfed. I recognized claw marks on one back, like the ones Juan gives in the Ceremonial, like the ones Stephen has on his back.

Never leave us alone in this place, said Laura. We couldn't survive away from you. This is a mouth. Maybe it's asleep, maybe it's eating somewhere else, but it only respects us because we're here with you.

At that point, Juan told us he'd had enough, and we should go back. His head was hurting again. His eyes were irritated and he looked like he was about to cry.

Laura deciphered the meaning of the ornaments the next day. Surprised, she told us she had been distracted by other possibilities instead of considering the one that was the most obvious, because it was the closest to her. I was looking for different symbols, seals, and I couldn't find any meaning. But they're letters. I looked at the details, the imperfections in the bone ornaments. They're notched, and they're trying to communicate precisely and exactly. It's just one word, she said, and a number.

She put her drawings on the table, the progression of how she had deciphered them, her mistakes in search of a more complicated meaning.

HUNGRY, the ornaments said.

Juan leaned against the doorway of the kitchen and motioned for me to give him a cigarette.

It's hungry? What's the number?

It's a 4, said Laura. I don't understand, unless it refers to the house next door, where the bodyguards and your doctor live.

I looked at Juan, who had closed his eyes.

I know how to recognize a Place of Power. Mine is back in Misiones.

It doesn't have to be like that, insisted Laura. The dogma doesn't say that the Place of Power is always obvious to the medium. Sometimes he has to look for it. Women carry it with them and can invoke it. Men must find it.

And I wouldn't have noticed it already?

Not necessarily. Have you ever been to the house next door?

Never, admitted Juan. The doctor, or her assistant, always comes here.

We could pay it a visit.

The house at number four was extraordinary, more spacious than ours and more outmoded: Graciela hadn't changed the furniture; plus, she was no hippie, and her only interest was in being Jorge Bradford's best possible disciple. Juan didn't want to hurt Graciela, so he decided to explore while she was out taking classes or working a shift at the hospital – I never really knew what her activities in London were, she didn't talk to me. So the only people at 4 Cheyne Walk were the bodyguards and Graciela's assistant, a very young medical student who always greeted us with a sincere smile. He offered us something to drink and apologized because Graciela wasn't there. Juan asked his permission to tour the house, then: I've never seen it, he explained. The assistant, whose name I don't remember, said it was a very pretty house. Juan nodded and went in, determined. The bodyguards stayed outside.

The discovery happened so incredibly fast that even today I can't explain it, I just can't understand how he didn't find it sooner, how it could go unnoticed for so many days. When Juan reached the middle of the living room, we heard him take a deep breath and start to speak in a very low, fast voice, words of recognition and relief. His back was to us. When he turned around, he was almost unrecognizable. He reached out his arms in a clear gesture: we should not come any closer. I saw the transformation before the others did, in his hands. I screamed, I couldn't help it, and my scream was so shrill and hysterical that one of the bodyguards opened the door. Stephen acted fast. He asked the guard to come in, and to bring his partner with him. I understood. Juan was going to open the Darkness, and the Darkness would come and eat. Graciela's assistant was asking what was going on, but everyone ignored him.

Juan took off his clothes. He always had to be naked before the Darkness. It was necessary, it was part of the ritual. Rituals must not be questioned because rituals protect. The bodyguards surely thought, in those seconds before the Darkness invaded the house, that we were in the middle of an orgy and that they had been invited to take part. I don't think they had time to imagine much more. Juan moved to stand in the requisite place and touched the floor with his animal hands. Something responded, and we could all feel it. When he stood up, there was a dark line all around his body and it was widening, as if it emanated from him. The Darkness is different when it's unleashed inside, in a closed space. Enclosed, it bellows. It's a continuous thunder of low vibrations. I backed up as far as I could, but it would take more than that to escape.

In the Darkness, Juan's body rose just a few inches: there wasn't enough room, but he hung suspended in a black stain that grew. Laura took a few steps forward and Stephen ran to stop her, throwing her to the floor. I heard the thud as she fell.

The Darkness became so large and pulsating that we could no longer see the walls or the stairs, nothing. It was hungry, I could feel it in my body. Stephen was the one who guided the bodyguards. Dumbfounded, they stopped very close to Juan, and Stephen told them, C'mon, go, and they did, of course, because they no longer belonged to this world and they never thought to escape. They accepted the blow. The Darkness stretched out like a whip to take what it wanted. They didn't even have time to scream. In an instant they were no more, swallowed in one bite. The assistant walked on his own towards the embrace of the blackness, attracted by a force he would have been unable to explain. Juan's face showed no change. I prayed that the assistant would be the last, because if the Darkness wanted more, nothing would be able to stop it and we couldn't escape. We couldn't see the front door any more. But the Darkness was content with the bait. It wavered for a few seconds, then slowly returned to form an outline around Juan and set him back on the floor, standing up but still surrounded by the black halo. Stephen approached him before I did and laid him on the floor, gently and assuredly. There was a reason Juan had given him his mark of trust all those years ago. With his own shirt he gently dried the sweat from Juan's chest and neck. Then he sat beside him. If he didn't wake up soon, we'd have to go and find Graciela. I took his pulse and was surprised: it was very fast, but regular; his breathing was anxious, but not desperate. By the time Laura finally dared approach, Juan was almost quiet, though still unconscious. He didn't have a fever, either. It wasn't necessary to take him to the hospital or summon the doctor. Between the three of us, we got him outside and back into our own house.

Later, Laura told us she had heard the voice of the Darkness. She opened a bottle of whiskey and drank straight from it before adding that she hadn't understood anything, not in any language, that it had seemed like a completely unknown language. No one understands it, my friend, said Juan, who was resting with his eyes closed but was completely lucid. The question is not whether it's impossible to understand it. The question is whether it's talking to us or just speaking inside its abyss, whether what speaks is merely hunger in the void. Whether it has anything more than the intelligence of the storm or the earth when it shakes. Whether it's anything more than another blindness, and it only seems illuminated because we don't know it.

That same day we got a call from Florence to tell us that Eddie had escaped. She wanted to know if he was with us. Eddie's disappearance and the appearance of the Place of Power were related, no doubt about it, but we didn't dare speculate as to how.

I woke up alone in bed and found Juan sitting on a sofa, looking out the window. Outside, the sky was very blue and there were birds in the trees across the street. I went and sat on his lap: he'd been crying, and that unnerved me, because Juan almost never cried. I took off his shirt and leaned naked against him: I needed him to feel my body.

'I'm so sorry,' I told him. 'I wanted this place to be different for you. You have no idea all the things I pictured us doing. Taking the train, going to Brighton, you wouldn't believe how good the fried fish is there, though the seagulls are really bold and they'll snatch it right out of your hands. People eat fish at the beach here the way we eat churros. I thought about asking Dad to buy us a house by the ocean. I also thought we could throw parties in this house, invite all the kids, no one complains about the loud music. I imagined filling this room with books and records, taking care of you, putting off the return; I imagined them letting us. And then this happened, first the door and the Other Place. At first I liked it. We're like explorers, I thought, and you know how I get a kick out of expeditions, how jealous I am of the women who opened the Pyramids. But every time we've come back from the Other Place, I've thought how unfair it is. It won't leave you in peace. I wanted a different life for us, a break. A respite. And now this. A Place of Power right next door. I brought you into a trap.'

'The traps find me. That's why you went away from me, right?' he asked, kissing me gently on the cheek. His lips were cracked. 'Because deep down, you knew that kind of life was impossible with me, and you wanted to try it alone. Because you knew that with me, the gods will always come first.'

'Can you forgive me?'

'There's never been anything to forgive. I'm glad you did it.'

I curled up against him. I took his hands and placed them on my neck, my stomach. I wanted him to feel the movement of my belly as I breathed. His eyes looked too dead.

'Go on, my love. Leave me. I can't go, but you can, you can escape me, and them. There is nothing, Rosario, it's just fields

of death and madness, there's nothing, and I am the doorway
to that nothing and I'm not going to be able to close it. There's
nothing to find, nothing to understand.'

'I'm never going to leave you. Ask me for something else.'

'If you won't leave me, don't leave me alone. Not even if you
die. Follow me as a ghost, haunt me.'

'Of course,' I answered. 'I'd do anything for you.'

Florence asked that the Ceremonial be held quickly and Juan
agreed: he understood that she needed to see in order to believe.
She had almost fainted when we told her there was a Place of
Power on Cheyne Walk. It's not possible, she kept repeating.
In Chelsea? You would have sensed it. He looked for it and he
found it, I told her. We never told her exactly how or why Juan
had found it. We'd forbidden ourselves from talking about the
Other Place. It was ours. What for, we still didn't know, but
it belonged to us.

The Initiates lit the candles. It looked so much like a
Christian vigil: it had the same tenuous and sinister beauty
as those streets lit with amber light, the village churches and
the murmuring faithful. It was dangerous to do it in London,
Florence said, and so she had asked everyone to come dressed
for a party. They arrived wearing masks and silk dresses, exquisite cravats and vertiginous high heels. Some people kept their
clothes on. Others, like Stephen, waited in the nude. I envied
the scars on his back. I wanted them too, but it wouldn't be
possible that night. Juan had asked me not to participate. The
scribes settled in to one side, as always. There wasn't enough
room for many Initiates. Graciela was relocated to another
house nearby. Because she was the medium's doctor, she wasn't
allowed to attend the Ceremonial. My uncle never missed one.
It was unwise, but he was of blood.

Juan lifted up his arms in the room we'd chosen for his preparations. He would descend the stairs and preside over the Ceremonial. My mind strayed to Laura and I thought: if only she could be the one to receive Juan's scars tonight, his medals; she deserves them. I dressed him, covered him with a beautiful tunic of black lace that obscured his face and draped over his chest. My mother was present among the Initiates, her nearly bald scalp visible through her sparse grey hair, her horrible, withered body with its meagre fat distributed in all the wrong places. I took Juan by the neck without any delicacy – it wasn't needed – and I could feel his pulse in the palm of my hands. Do not die today, I ordered him, and I looked into his eyes that were a little green and a little yellow. Don't die, and if you can, take my mother.

Ready now, he took my hand and placed it on the scar on his arm, the burnt imprint of another hand, the left hand of the Darkness. Do not die tonight, I repeated, though he wasn't listening any more. I watched him go, down the hallway, the stairs, and I caressed the caburé feather that Juan had handed me before going, the payé I gave him long ago and that he never brings to the Ceremonials, where the small spells of this world are worth nothing. Alone, listening to the screams of the Initiates as they were mutilated and eaten, locked in with the implacable Darkness, I was coming to understand the power of a secret. You walk among others but are not one of them. Some – I suppose Florence, for example – must feel that they walk above the rest, but not me. I feel I walk along passages of colours no one else knows; I feel like the others are lit by a weak little bulb, while I am lit by a blinding light. It's strange I would think of light, because it was always explained to me that we are for the darkness.

*

After the Ceremonial, which by Florence's standards had been a success, Juan decided we would go a few months without entering the Other Place, and I would dedicate that autumn to starting my thesis. It already had a title: 'Bone Worship among the Mbyá People: Origin and Urban-Migratory Redefinition: The Figure of San La Muerte in the Creole Culture of the Littoral'. I was missing much of the fieldwork and interviews, of course. I was planning a trip to Misiones exclusively to gather testimonies: Tali had promised to help me, and had already put me in touch with a Paraguayan anthropologist who knew more than anyone about Guaraní religions. Juan wanted to study with Laura, and she was entranced. The house filled up with circles and the two of them were like kids, locked in the bedroom or strolling the cemeteries of London, as if dealing with spirits were a game. Stephen and Juan were perfect as magical androgynes: the double current, as the ritual sexual encounter is called, worked to perfection between them. They took my breath away: they were capable of convoking several entities in a single day, and they did it with such carelessness and abandon that my scrupulous nature made me resist. I was the girl of books and lists: though I would take risks, I also liked order. One day I refused to draw the circle and seal because, I told them, this is all just fun and games to you, and I'm sick of it. Juan picked me up, laughing, and promised that as soon as he learned of a suicide, he would get me that Hand of Glory I was so obsessed with. And he told me to quit being so serious. *He* told *me* that.

Plus, during those days, Laura and Stephen and Juan had managed to communicate in secret. Laura called it *pishogue*. They couldn't use it often, and never without Juan, because it emanated from him: it was the result of the seal he had drawn on his scalp in the Other Place, when he'd requested the capacity

475

to have secrets. It had to do with altering other people's perception so they would see and hear whatever he wanted them to. A blinking of reality. They spoke, and other people heard something else. They did it right in front of me, with no consideration at all, and it was infuriating. Juan had taught me the method in detail, but it just didn't work for me, though we tried many times, for hours, until I got fed up and locked myself in the bathroom to cry. I couldn't do it, nor could I get pregnant and guarantee the continuation of the blood. Stephen couldn't have children, and Eddie was still missing, and I couldn't or didn't know how to acquire any ability aside from the same old chalk circles. I didn't feel like studying. All I wanted to do was go to the Other Place and take one of the dead hands clutching the tree trunks in the forest. But Juan refused to go with me. I was frustrated and furious. I even said to him, what if it's you who's impotent? But he wasn't offended in the slightest. It's possible, he said. We'll have to ask Jorge to examine us.

The thing is, my dear friend, it's not like riding a bike, Stephen told me. It's like playing the piano. Take Juan out of the conversation, because he's different from us. If you don't learn certain things when you're little, you'll never reach the level you need for this. Laura and I received instruction as children. You did too, but of another kind. You should thank your father, because it's not right to use kids like that. Mercedes always accused me of being useless and sterile, and she was right, I said. Your mother is never right. You *will* be a mother, Rosario. And Juan loves you. I have my scars, sure, but they're all I have.

In an attempt to soothe me, Stephen suggested a trip. We could get Tara and the others and all go to Spain, Italy, Greece. We'd have to travel with the bodyguards, Graciela, and the whole crew, but we wouldn't be all that different from other young millionaires. Didn't the Getty heirs and the Rolling Stones travel the same way? And we could get away from the Darkness, from this island and the obsession with finding Eddie, which was making Florence crazy. There were private detectives all over Great Britain looking for clues about her younger son, and, of course, the police were looking for him too. I pictured the sun on the ocean and the white houses of Cadaqués and I said yes immediately, and I was so happy I almost started packing right then. I had to buy a bikini, nicer sunglasses, sandals for walking around Rome. I would take my books, too. I was going to be the first Argentine woman with a doctorate from Cambridge, and it made me ridiculously proud. Someone had to be happy about it, because aside from Juan, no one else cared. I needed to review *Purity and Danger* by Mary Douglas, and *Les structures* by Lévi-Strauss. That could take me a month. Laura agreed to come too: she had hardly ever left England. It took some work to convince Juan, but not too much. He was worried about Eddie. He thought Eddie was a loose end, and he was convinced that as long as he was missing, we wouldn't be safe.

Eddie's escape had been extremely violent. He'd done it in the morning, and no one heard the attack on his guards, though there's no doubt that they screamed, because Eddie ate their eyes with his sharpened teeth, the teeth that had been filed into a saw when he was a child. Afterwards, he'd managed to paralyse them or put them to sleep, no one really knew; the men didn't remember what had happened, they woke up from their trance blind and mad with pain. Eddie had taken clothes and money, clear signs that he wasn't as crazy as people thought. I was sorry I had never spoken to him. Florence would have let me. Stephen said that a relationship with Eddie always ended the same way, and he listed all the animals he had abused, the classmates he'd driven to suicide, the various caretakers who'd ended up dead or mutilated. Juan listened. They have to find him, he said over and over. Why did they let him live?

They let you live, too, Stephen answered once.

And maybe that's a mistake, Juan said in a low voice.

The night before our planned trip, Tara and Sandy came to visit. They brought other friends, all of them members of the Order, children of high Initiates. Navid, who was Sandy's lover; Lucian, one of Anne's sons and Laura's adoptive brother – her other son was a true old Etonian, with his suits and shiny shoes: he wanted to be the youngest Member of Parliament. Susie, who lived in Scotland and always invited us to her house near the sea, in Portobello. Lucie, with her camera. The twins Crimson and Genesis. With all of us there, we could almost reproduce life at Cheyne Walk before Juan arrived. We put on *Blonde on Blonde* and Otis Redding and the Velvet Underground, we took acid and danced until our bodies disintegrated into shining particles and we couldn't see them any more. Laura shouted that no one should leave the house, that we couldn't disconnect the trip, the group must stay united. It's true that it's strange when someone abandons a trip: something is disturbed. Juan didn't dance, but Sandy sat on his knees and kissed him. I let her do it. I remember she was wearing a bright red feather boa, and it looked like a stream of fake blood. Suddenly I had a horrible sense of foreboding, and to get rid of my fear I put on David's new album and lay down beside the speaker. The first song made me cry and laugh because it talked about being far above the moon, and only then did I realize we had missed the moon landing, months before. Even worse, we'd forgotten! We hadn't seen it, we'd never even turned on the TV. Where had we been that evening? Gazing at torsos? At hands? Walking over bones?

I think I slept for a while, and when I woke up, everyone was in a circle. I thought they were looking at the pictures of the Other Place and I almost screamed to high heaven, those idiots, Laura and Stephen, getting high and showing the secret to our friends – we couldn't trust them with something like that. When I saw Juan was listening very attentively, I realized he would never allow that, and it had to be something else.

Tara was reading a letter. Sandy told me it had been slid under the door, but they didn't know when. Time, on acid, was impossible to measure. They'd seen it when I'd separated from them, but they didn't know how long it had been there waiting for someone to open it.

It was a letter from Eddie.

'Are you sure?' I cried, and Stephen said yes, he recognized his brother's handwriting.

I remembered the headstone Eddie had drawn over his bed, the images of hanged men on his walls, and I looked at Stephen and Laura: they were pale from fear. I listened closely to Tara's voice. *Never locked up again, there are hands in the darkness and they won't leave me alone. You don't care if it hurts me, Mother, and neither does the old lady, she's the one who sharpened my teeth, she wants me to bite her. No one helps.*

The old lady. Mercedes, I said. The children in cages all had sharpened teeth. I had to make sure they didn't bite me, because she had warned me they could give me rabies and I would die convulsing and they'd have to shoot me in the head like the country dogs. Did he leave a letter for Florence, too? I don't know, said Stephen. My mother isn't in England. She left yesterday to go and visit my father.

No one helps. I want to go to the mountains, I can fall and the rocks will pound my whole body, and then I'll have bruises I can touch and feel the pain. I'm in darkness and pain. Is the usurper, too? He is not the medium. The pregnant one told me. You all think I don't know him, but I do. He looks like a lion. I'm like a fox and I move better than him.

The paranoid lucidity of the acid, which was no longer a tranquillity of colours but rather a state of alertness in my whole body, my hair standing on end as if it were wired, forced me to break the circle and take Stephen by the shoulders. Your brother is looking for him. We have to leave right now.

The one-eyed girl is also a usurper, like the lion. They deserve nothing, they are not of blood. Mother, you pulled out her eye with your teeth. Or else it was the old lady. Was she in the Darkness, too? It's never clear who is real and who isn't, everyone is real, there's no point in trying to distinguish. I don't know if the hands are real. They won't let me sleep. Mother, you wouldn't let me sleep, either. We have to keep him awake, you'd say, and I heard you, I was standing up. You all always think I can't hear because I don't speak. You all are smart, because it is smart to hurt with simplicity. I am smart, too.

Stephen asked Juan if Eddie had ever seen him. I don't know, said Juan. I recovered at your mother's house, and he lived there. I spent the nights with Rosario, but she went out during the day and I was alone. I don't remember having sensed someone's presence in the room, but that pain medication is pretty strong and I spent a lot of hours asleep.

You understand why I ask. Ever since he was little, my brother has played this very simple game. He sneaks into houses, into bedrooms, at night, and moves things around. Or he does other nonsense, leaves some kind of mark on a wall, a drawing. If there's a garden, he tramples a flower bed. In the morning, the owner of the house sees the changes and the little acts of vandalism, but can't understand why someone would do them. Eddie calls them 'creepy crawlers'. Before my mother locked him up, he would do it with some friends he'd managed to make in Mayfair, some really demented people. They've all gone to California now. I think he's seen you. He knows you, somehow.

I looked at Juan. We had stolen Eddie's hair so we could learn his story. Maybe he had realized. Juan looked back at me and I understood the instruction in his eyes: not a word. I tried to compose myself, but I couldn't stop thinking about how the doors of the house weren't locked.

What can he do, exactly? Tara finally asked. Eddie can't have power over anything or anyone, he can't control his actions. That's not true, said Juan.

You're not going to find me. There are always methods to change how a person feels, I only have to find the words. I can write them on my skin. Does the lion have scars? All your children have scars. I never wanted to die, because there's not so much difference between death and life, Mother, you taught me that in this house and I learned it from the holes I dug, something living died and it wasn't so different. The pregnant one knows, that's why she visits me. She was taught wrong. You all teach wrong. You should stop teaching us like that, with the hands, with the night and the pain.

The pregnant one is Encarnación, said Laura, but not everyone listened. A lot of Initiates don't know the medium was pregnant when she killed herself, they only know about the massacre and the suicide. Sandy stood up: my distress had spread to her. We have to search the house, she said. We all understood. We had to find Eddie if he was hiding there. Juan took me by the waist and whispered into my ear: Don't worry if they open the door. All they'll see is a bedroom. The key to the Other Place is mine.

This house isn't safe any more, said Stephen. Let's get out as fast as we can. We have the cars, we have our passports. We have the bodyguards. The needle lifted off the record and we were left in silence. We divided into groups to scour the house. The kitchen, every one of the drawers, and the cupboards. I heard someone lifting the loose floorboards on the stairs: it was Laura, the only one who knew about that defect. I don't know how much time we spent like that, drugged, jumping in fright, uselessly checking every corner, sometimes rolling with laughter, sometimes shrieking in fear because at the back of a drawer we felt the squeeze of a ghostly hand. We performed a ritual to find him, but we couldn't concentrate and Laura annulled it. I don't remember it clearly, either. I drew the circle, as always.

We slept with the house locked up using all the keys we found. We were sure there was no one else inside, but we were scared anyway. I don't know why we didn't leave. We were too high to hold on to a decision. We all shared beds: I remember five of our friends settled into one. Stephen managed to get hold of Florence in the early morning. She was already in Cadaqués. He read her the letter and she ordered us to get out immediately. Eddie couldn't leave England, he didn't have a passport and there was an all-points bulletin out for him at the borders. We didn't listen to Florence.

I go back over it, but I can never reconstruct exactly why we didn't leave the next day. The acid is the only excuse I can come up with, but it's not enough. Sandy felt bad, I'm sure about that: it hit her hard when she mixed acid and alcohol, and she'd been doing it all night. But Sandy didn't matter: the ones who had to get out of the country were Juan, Stephen, Laura, and me. Our frantic search of the house had lasted a lot longer than we thought: even Juan woke up after noon. We hadn't packed. The bodyguards reassured us: there was no one on the property, there was no danger. This was one of the poshest streets in London, we lived surrounded by rich and famous neighbours who had security of their own. An intruder would have been detected. We were hungry, so Susie and Tara threw together some spaghetti, and somehow the mood changed. We were young. We started to remember the previous night as a bad trip, the ghost of the Order's lost son, the one we, somehow, had avoided becoming. Though as Eddie said in his letter: all the Order's children have their scars.

We spent the afternoon sprawled on cushions and rugs, as always, drinking wine to calm our nerves because weed might turn us paranoid again. We did nothing but lounge around the house, listen to the storm, jump at claps of thunder. We packed our suitcases with abnormal slowness, or at least that's how I remember it. I spent hours deciding whether to bring one or two saris, for example, and I never wear saris. Genesis made tea and we ate a gooseberry pie that the cook had left for us. The storm was intense and we convinced ourselves it was impossible to go out in weather like that; we were sure, too, that the ferry wouldn't be able to leave the dock. None of our friends left, either. As if something was keeping them from going.

Genesis and Crimson embraced under a blanket and were the first to go to sleep. The others withdrew one by one: they yawned, stretched, said the stress of the night before had left them exhausted. Stephen said we could go anyway, the four of us, and leave them there, but he didn't seem very enthusiastic. I was the one who gave the last word: It'll be better if we leave when it stops raining. Tomorrow morning. Early, he said. Very early, I replied. I'll set the alarm for six.

I let Juan take me in his arms. There was a smell of wine and earth on his hands and his breath. I kissed him, but we didn't have sex that night. We fell asleep under a white Afghan blanket that I can't forget, and still dream about.

*

The shot split the night: a thunderclap that awakens, a rock shattering a window, a frozen lake cracking. Juan sat up in bed, and I jumped to my feet. It wasn't the storm, it wasn't a fallen piece of furniture, it wasn't a magical or supernatural phenomenon: it was a gunshot. I knew that dry sound because my father and grandfather had taught me to shoot. It was a large weapon, for hunting, and I knew that too, because my father hunted his whole life, and when he was drunk he would fire it inside Puerto Reyes.

The second shot came accompanied by a man's indecipherable screams. Juan got out of bed too, barefoot. A sudden modesty made him quickly throw on pants. When I started to peer out into the hallway he grabbed me hard by the arm, but I pulled away to go and look out the window. We could normally see the bodyguards from our room. They weren't at their posts. I heard Genesis's unmistakable voice, the Scottish accent, begging, Please. Saying Eddie's name. There were running feet. Bodies hitting the floor. More screams. Some minutes later, the door opened. I screamed, I couldn't help it. It was Stephen. He was half-naked, pale, and furious as always when he was afraid. It's my brother, he said. He's coming for you.

Another scream, a woman's, along with another gunshot. Laura. More screams and crashing furniture. Three more shots. The progression was slow. Eddie had to reload the shotgun, but he was killing everyone. After each gunshot, a howl.

He was here, then, said Juan.

But we checked everywhere! I yelled at him.

He was in the Other Place, Rosario, Juan murmured.

I understood, but it was too late. Juan had also understood late. I'm a fox, I thought, and I know how to move better than him.

No running, whispered Stephen. I had covered myself with the white blanket, because I was naked. The goal was to reach the service stairs at the end of the hall, which led to the kitchen. We heard more gunshots, and slamming doors. The running footsteps didn't get very far. Neither did we. Another shot, and Eddie came out of the corner bedroom, turned around, and saw us. His face and clothes were spattered with blood. The hallway light was off but we could see him clearly. On his young, freckled face, with its light eyes and halo of hair as red as his mother's, an expression of relief appeared. He had found the one he was looking for. And he took aim. Incredibly, he missed Juan. Only by a little. He's missing a finger, I thought. He can't handle the gun well. The shot grazed my arm, which bled and stained the blanket. It was a superficial wound, but it was enough to enrage Juan: when Eddie tried to reload the gun, fumbling with the shotgun's two cartridges, Juan lunged at him, and in a single movement he wrenched away the gun and threw it over the railing. It fell to the floor downstairs. I don't know how he dared do it: the manoeuvre required the reflexes of an animal. I wasn't afraid for him, I remember. I always intuited he was going to win that fight. I wanted to help him, I remember that, too, but I didn't know how. It wasn't my story, I think now. They had to resolve it between the two of them. Juan grabbed Eddie by the neck and dragged him downstairs to the door that led to the Other Place. He opened it. I followed them. My arm burned like it was in flames. Juan kicked Eddie into the Other Place and dragged him to the end of the passageway. I followed them, running silently. Juan knew what he was doing. He walked with the assurance of a predator.

It was Stephen who closed the door behind us, I learned later. He didn't want to witness his brother's fate.

Eddie tried to get up, but Juan placed a foot on his chest.

They must have been the same age, but Eddie looked like a teenager, or even a child. He tried to fight back but he was very scrawny, and Juan had an impossible advantage: the Other Place was on his side.

When did you get in here? Juan yelled at him. Eddie bit his leg and received a kick in the face that broke his nose and choked him with blood. The temperature of the Other Place had risen. It was a heat like breath. I finally understood why Laura said it was a mouth. Juan let go of Eddie, who tried to get up again but couldn't: he collapsed, face up and gasping. Juan approached him calmly and sat on his bony hips. Florence's son: the one they had trained to be a medium, as if that were possible, as if all the experiments over many years had not amply proven that the Darkness found the medium, and not the other way around. Why do you want to kill me? Juan asked, and he brought his mouth close to Eddie's. It was a love scene. I couldn't see them well through my tears. They were beautiful as they fought under the starless sky, with the heavy breath of the Other Place around them.

'She said you were in the first one, but it wasn't true. Stupid girl, stupid.'

He meant the first bedroom, on the ground floor, where he'd started shooting.

'Who told you that?'

'The pregnant girl. She can't see well! They burned out her eyes.'

'You knew this place?'

'Not this door, but I've been here before. In a different place. It's endless. It shouldn't be opened. She showed me the door. The pregnant girl. It shouldn't be opened.'

I don't know what language they were speaking, but I heard the conversation clearly. Eddie was making an effort to get up, and he opened his mouth: his fox-child's teeth were all he had against Juan. 'It has to end,' I heard at one point, and it was Eddie's voice, calm and convincing.

'You're right,' Juan replied. 'It shouldn't be opened. It has to end. But I can't do it, because this is my land.'

Eddie kept fighting and gnashing his teeth at the air. I think he wasn't afraid because he knew where he was. The Other Place accompanied Eddie's bites with fetid panting: now everything stank like a hungry mouth. Juan kicked him, and in the silence of the valley I heard the crunch of his cheekbone as it broke. Eddie didn't know how to fight; he was just tenacious and felt no pain.

'Why?' Juan yelled. With a single yank he dislocated Eddie's shoulder. The Other Place seemed to applaud, to concur with the crack of the joint.

Eddie finally answered. Because you're an impostor. Because all of this should have been mine, it was promised to me. It couldn't be anyone else's. The pregnant girl had told him he had to end the lineage, there could be no more children, the doors had to close.

Eddie no longer resisted. He was moaning. It's not the pain, he told Juan, I don't care about the pain. The pain is to lose and lose and lose.

'Help me,' Juan said to me, without looking at me.

I went closer, and once I was beside him, he stood up and smashed Eddie's sternum with a kick. Eddie screamed and fainted. Why was he so weak? He had fought and it was hard to breathe in the Other Place, but I felt like he hadn't put up enough resistance. Outside, he had killed. Inside, he surrendered. Eddie started to cough blood, and he was bleeding from the nose. I handed the white Afghan blanket to Juan. Being naked in the Other Place made me feel vulnerable in a new, obscene way. I expected at any moment to feel a hand hit me or touch me between my legs, or to be carried off to the Valley of Torsos, where my body would be used as decoration. But I was with Juan and he was the guardian; he would protect me.

Juan placed Eddie on the blanket and motioned for me to pick up the end with his feet. He did the same with the other end. We carried him like a wounded soldier being removed from the battlefield on an improvised stretcher. My feet were wounded as I walked over the bones, and I felt the breath of the Other Place directly on my skin. Eddie weighed very little, but I couldn't take in enough air. Juan only looked at me once, to check that I could do it, and I nodded.

I didn't know where we were going, but the path of bones we were following had broadened. It was a road now. We came to a narrow passage leading away from the Valley of Torsos. We picked our way down it until we reached a clearing that was like the others except the trees were further apart, some of them only trunks, others with treetops. I asked Juan for a break and he nodded. Eddie was moaning. When I could focus on the clearing and its trees, I saw the shapes hanging from the branches. They were people. Juan took Eddie out of the blanket and pushed his body so it would roll down the hill. Then we went down on our own, more easily. Juan carried the blanket and gave me his hand: it was freezing, unlike mine, which was burning. It's because you're alive, he said, and I didn't answer. He was going to hang Eddie with the others. It was a mechanical act, an old, repeated task. There were several empty trees, and he chose one with a relatively low treetop, its branches within reach.

He wasn't going to hang him alive, though. Under the tree, he circled Eddie's neck with his hands and squeezed. I watched, enthralled. Juan killed seriously and surely, as if he had done it many times before. It was the sacrifice the Other Place wanted. I could almost hear it savouring Eddie's death. There was a clicking sound through the whole valley and it wasn't the branches, it was the satisfaction of an enormous tongue. I felt bad for Eddie, but I was fascinated watching him die. There is no greater disappointment than to believe oneself the chosen one and to not be chosen. To this day, I think he accepted his end. Maybe he even sought it out. Eddie's eyes were red, his mouth blue, he had blood on his lips, his neck, his sunken sternum. He was ruined. He had cut his tongue on his teeth. Juan stood up. The air of the Other Place reeked. I had often wondered why a place decorated with human remains had no smell at all, and now I realized it was a matter of perception, of recognizing the territory. The Place gave little by little: as if it were turning on the lights in dark places and revealing new scenes, hidden doors, horizons that thus far seemed like paintings.

There were ropes beside each tree: everything had been prepared. Juan didn't know how to tie knots, but I did. My father had taught me on the boat. I showed him. Juan had to be the one to hang Eddie, but I could offer my advice. First, I went closer to the ones who were hung around us, to understand the procedure. It was very simple. They were all upside down. Juan had to tie Eddie's right foot to a branch and drop him.

When Juan took Eddie in his arms, he struggled to lift him: he was tired. The price he would pay for this effort was incalculable. He supported Eddie with the strength of his own body to keep him from falling, but he still slid to the ground several times. I moved to help him, but he stopped me with a gesture of his hand. I must not profane the sacrifice. Eddie's eyes were open, and as he lay face up on the ground, he seemed to be staring at the starless sky. Juan managed to hang him on the third try. Then he bent Eddie's left leg so it was behind the one he hung by; he used some of the rope to tie Eddie's waist to the tree, and the rest he used to tie his hands behind the trunk. Some versions of the Tarot left the hands loose, but there in the Other Place it seemed appropriate to respect the traditional version.

When it was ready, I observed his work. The Twelfth Arcana. Eddie had painted it in his bedroom. This story was old. We walked away from Eddie to visit the nearest hanged people. Some knots were professional, others looked like bows: it wasn't really the rope that held them up. There were men and women, and their bodies were conserved; none showed any signs of putrefaction or of any clear violence, though of course they had all been murdered in one way or another. There was nothing more for us to do, but something was keeping us there, and Juan realized what it was. He could take something, as always when he offered a sacrifice: the Place wanted to repay him. I looked at his hands. They were surrounded by black light. Thank you, Juan said out loud. With an unerring touch, because now he was blade and weapon, he cut off Eddie's left hand. For my companion, he said. The Hand of Glory that she so desires. He offered it to me and I cried, in grief and in thanks.

We went back to the house. Stephen was waiting for us. He wasn't going to call the police: the Order would take care of cleaning up the massacre. The gun his brother had used was still on the ground floor, all the proof we would need to avoid being accused, now that Eddie would never be found in this world.

The dead were dead, and it was the fault of this life that one chose or received as condemnation, depending on how you looked at it. Eddie's sacrifice had been necessary, and so had the purge. The only survivors were Stephen, Juan, and me. I was irritated that Juan couldn't understand and believed it was all his fault, believed it with a desperation that was black and (I thought) exaggerated. The monster always lurks inside the Labyrinth, and he who enters knows that if it's not around the first bend, it will be around the next. Some know how to let out a rope and escape. He who makes it too far does so knowing the price. Juan thought Eddie's shot could have killed me, and he blamed himself. But I didn't want him to take care of me. I had told him so many times. Who could he protect, destined as he was to live in the abyss?

We travelled as planned to Cadaqués, several days later. In the beautiful Margarall house we followed the news of the massacre at Cheyne Walk, which mixed with the other terrible bloodbaths of 1969. Eddie Mathers, the Manson Family, Hells Angels, the bomb in Piazza Fontana, the news of Mỹ Lai. Eddie was presumed guilty: the gun had his prints on it, and he'd also left them all over the house. We told the police he had escaped; I was wounded and couldn't go after him; Juan had to abandon chase because of his health; Stephen had gotten further, but lost him. We also told this story to Florence and Pedro, and they believed it: why wouldn't they, when they themselves had met thanks to a similar purge? Florence was surprised Eddie hadn't killed himself; she had her own vague doubts. They looked for his body in the river, with no luck. The other living witness was Graciela, the doctor: when she'd heard the shots, she'd tried to call the police, but the phone was dead. Eddie had cut the line.

On the terrace, looking out at the blue sea, the puny boats, the white houses, I had time to think. Encarnación, dead by her own hand after being raped by the men of the Order. Eddie, the destroyed son. Both of them wanted to extinguish the lineage, and both had almost put an end to the Order in different ways: Encarnación slaughtered the old people; Eddie, the children.

Not everyone, of course. They were right, Juan said, but I wanted a child now more than ever. My son would not be handed over or abused. And he would be the first child of a medium. I would have a family with Juan, and when the time came to lead the Order, or when the correct interpretation of how to keep consciousness alive was found, it wouldn't be Florence, Mercedes, and Anne who gave the orders. Or at least they would have to negotiate with me.

Dealing with Juan's depression was the hardest part. During the days we spent in Cadaqués, he never left his room. He couldn't stand to be in Eddie's parents' house, and he was constantly on the verge of confessing the crime. He didn't commit suicide only because he was always being watched. He ignored me, didn't want to see Stephen. I understood I had to wait and, moreover, I was sure that a child would restore him. He needed to take care of someone defenceless, someone of his own. To forget about himself.

Juan's depression wasn't only about the deaths he thought he was responsible for. Or about Eddie's sacrifice. After the massacre we spent a day making statements, and the day after that we were at Florence's house. We had no reason to return to Cheyne Walk: if we needed clothes or documents, an assistant could get them. But Juan wanted to go back because he was convinced about something, and Stephen went with him. The passage to the Other Place had closed. Now, when Juan opened the door, he only saw the bed, the paintings, the window. He tried several times. He leaned against the wooden doorway, begging please. The Other Place had disappeared after receiving its sacrifice. *Pájaro que comió, voló*, as they say in Argentina. It had got what it wanted. Eddie was lost in that dead world. Of course, the Place of Power had also dried up. Florence received that news with a scream. She didn't know how to interpret it.

She related it to the purge Eddie had inflicted, of course, but she was missing the necessary details to fully understand what had happened. Just one Ceremonial in London, she said. What a waste.

Juan felt free and at the same time desperate when he found that his centres of power had vanished. I thought about leaving, he said later. Walking to the nearest train station, getting off in a town, drinking a beer in the pub, squatting on one of the abandoned farms, letting myself die in the ruins of some castle or at the side of a highway.

Why didn't you? I asked. They always say they can find you, but what if you're the exception, the one who can escape? We were in the darkness of his room in Cadaqués, and I could feel his heart beating, arrhythmic and frantic, against my own chest.

I don't want to choke to death in a village hotel with my lungs full of fluid and my body half-paralysed. I don't know how to work. I can't find my way with a map. It's easy to talk about getting away, leaving, dying, changing, when leaving it all behind means nothing. But to feel the power in my whole body, to claw and mark people, to have a role as the companion of the god of night – it means something. It's mine.

I'm yours too, I told him in a low voice.

You're mine too, he replied.

For Juan, returning to Argentina meant failure. For me, it meant recovering my language, my hands freed, my blood cleaned of drugs; it meant finishing my studies at home, trying for my son in the place I knew I would find him. Puerto Reyes, the summer storms, having a drink on my father's boat, going with Tali to the jungle and the reservations, travelling to Paraguay and laughing with her the whole way there. It meant having a bourgeois marriage, my fragile and beautiful husband waiting on the terrace reading poetry. It was the life of young million-aires waiting for their inheritance. Though we were no longer young, not after the massacre. Before returning to Argentina, I was able, finally, to visit Laura's grave. I also wanted to leave so I could forget her. Everything in the city reminded me of her. Every street had a meaning on her alternative maps. We had walked through every park and every cemetery. They had placed her near the medium Olanna, at Highgate. Strawberry plants grew over the graves. Stephen had told me that on his first visit, he'd seen a fox. I lay down on Laura's grave, remembered her dirty, tattooed body, and I said goodbye and promised to think of her. But when I got up and felt a pull in my shoulder, the muffled pain of the inoffensive wound that, nevertheless, some-times hurt, I thought how this was my moment and Juan's, and I knew that this death and the others had to be left behind, as, in her time, Florence had left others behind.

The Other Place had also changed me. Walking naked with its breath on my skin left me with a kind of shell. And, though it wasn't easy, Juan and I were able to recover our intimacy. Now we shared a secret. Now, we were both marked. We had sex with sweetness and frenzy, and more frequently than ever before. I lost my pregnancies and didn't tell him. I would sit looking at the thick, untimely blood floating in the water of the toilet or bathtub. The moment would come. My child would be conceived at Puerto Reyes. There, as well, Juan's black depres-sion would lift, and a permanent anger would replace it: I could never rid him of it. He feared for our child. He was afraid of being unable to take care of him or of not knowing how, or of dying before he met him; of loving him too much or being indifferent to him. I don't know what I should feel, he told me once.

You will feel what you need to feel, I told him.

3

'I think Marcelina buried my knife. I can't stand that mania of hers any more.'

Tali ran a hand through her long hair. It was hot, but there was a wind that augured rain and moved the trees, cooling the back patio of Puerto Reyes, just in front of the garden, and beyond that the park, the guest house, and the rest of the property that blended with the jungle. After settling in on the cushions, she poured a mate and handed it to me. We didn't drink it cold, even in summer. Juan was still recovering from the Ceremonial in the infirmary-bedroom, and we were near him but outside: it was unbearable in that room, with the doctors, the noisy machines, the waiting. Most of the Initiates had gone back to where they came from, and only family remained at Puerto Reyes. My father, sleeping off the booze on the beach. The three women, locked in with the scribes for days now. Stephen, who did stay with Juan; he was the most faithful, much more faithful even since Eddie's death. Gaspar was at my feet, crawling around and trying to eat leaves, flowers, bugs.

'Did you take the baby in to him? It does him good.'

'Him, yes, but not Gaspar. Today he realized Juan was suffering and it took me hours to calm him down.'

'*Angá*, you didn't tell me that.'

'It was just this morning.'

Tali took a jacaranda flower from Gaspar's mouth. He was crazy about them and ate them like candy.

'I really liked that little knife.'

'Ask her where it is and she'll give it to you. The Guaraní love to bury things, she got that habit from her grandmother.'

'When Juan gets better, we have to go back to Asunción. We can take the baby. All four of us could go.'

We were collaborating on a folk art exhibit at the Regional Museum of Asunción, and we had gotten the director to let us use a whole room for the collection of San La Muerte statues. My father had protested, but he didn't have any authority any more: most of the time he was so drunk he couldn't even remember what it was he wanted. Of course, we weren't donating the statues: the collection was simply on loan for an indeterminate period. And the most important statues would remain in Tali's temple, in Corrientes. She would never part with the powerful ones.

I'd finished my dissertation at Puerto Reyes and gone by myself to defend it at Cambridge. I was only in England for a week, and I went to visit Laura's grave every day. Later, I published chapters of my dissertation in anthropology journals in several countries. Soon, I would start teaching classes at the University of Buenos Aires, and I needed a home in the capital that was not in my family's building, which I didn't want to go back to. Juan, meanwhile, took care of Gaspar, studied and read, and, with Stephen, looked for a door, a passage to the Other Place. They hadn't found anything yet: Juan thought that Puerto Reyes could hold a portal, but it wasn't in his reach, he only sensed it. But if not there, where else to look? Stephen had an idea: near the hospital where Jorge had operated on him and where the Darkness had first come to Juan. They travelled often to Buenos Aires, with any excuse, though they were no longer required to give so many explanations now. In the new phase of the Order, after the massacre and Eddie's disappearance, many things had changed.

Others hadn't changed at all. After some explosive arguments, Florence agreed to monitor Gaspar in an accepted ritual, simple and effective, that I proposed. Twice a year he had to be brought to Juan's Place of Power, and the women would draw a blood circle around him. Arterial blood, which is the kind that seeks and finds, as Laura taught me – blood offered by the Initiates themselves. They also used Olanna's ruby-encrusted skull. At two years old, Gaspar had already been in the circle several times, and each time he had crawled around and looked at the expectant members of the Order with a mixture of curiosity and worry, never with fear. He didn't give a single sign of understanding what was happening or of being in contact with any energy that arose from the Place of Power. Juan and I were always present. Gaspar was a normal baby, perhaps more clingy with his father than was usual for his age. He slept a lot, cried little, and sometimes sat looking at some insect, or the TV, with too much concentration.

We fought a lot about Gaspar, Juan and I. A lot, and every day.

'If he manifests, I know how to avert it,' he'd tell me. 'There are a lot of ways to nullify his power, and you know them.'

I didn't like that.

'Gaspar has the right to be part of the Order, if he wants. I have power, too. They're not going to do just anything with him.'

'I trust you, but I don't trust them. I can keep him from being part of the Order, if I want.'

I didn't like arguing, but other than him I didn't have anyone to talk to about my son and what awaited him. Before he was born, I wanted the unlikely to happen: for him to inherit his father's abilities. I really believed it could happen, and that Gaspar would be a different kind of medium. I had conceived him on the correct date and under the correct signs. Juan hadn't opposed it, at least not actively. My pregnancy was incredibly easy. I only had nausea and discomfort during the first month. After that, it was as if I'd been injected with light. I worked every day, I was so full of energy. Ideas, writing, interviews in the jungle, even fights with my father over the yerba fields. Along with Tali and Betty, who was totally dedicated to politics and sometimes visited us – her partner Eduardo was a leftist militant who felt enormous contempt for our family – we had practically forced the yerbatal to formalize its workers. They earned a pittance now, but at least they earned something. And that's how it was every day, from then on: I didn't even feel tired, just ferociously hungry. I was fat and I cried about being fat, which made Juan laugh. But I was never unhappy: my excitement wouldn't allow it.

Juan smoked now. It made my uncle desperate, but no one could convince him to change any of his habits. He smoked more when we had our shouting matches. The Darkness had dictated the way to preserve consciousness: we had to transfer it from one body to another. Transmigrate, they would call it in other traditions. I called it occupation, because that's what it was: stealing a body. It was a repulsive method, because it meant hijacking another life and another identity. What they didn't know yet were the details of the method: who would be the receivers of consciousness? Could they be chosen or did they have to be marked, or discovered? The Darkness still had to dictate the steps that must be followed, and, as usual, it was hermetic and capricious. According to Juan, there was nothing true in the dictates: the Order would never achieve the transfer of consciousness because it was interpreting the words badly, or making them up, imagining things. The arguments started because I didn't agree with him on that. I didn't distrust the dictates like he did, or like Laura had. I believed. Didn't the Darkness emerge from Juan, didn't it cut and wound? Didn't his hands turn into claws – and wasn't that impossible, too? The difference of opinion, though, didn't come between us. We spent nights awake, talking, and none of our fights were wholly bitter, even if they ended in slamming doors and shouting. Certainty was impossible and disbelief was impossible, because there was physical proof. It was impossible to trust, because everything was blurry. And there we were, in a place that seemed like the end of the world, full of secrets and doubts.

'Why do you want that little knife, sis?'

'For some plants. I know there's a gardener, you don't have to tell me, but these are my plants. I like to work on them myself.'

The impending storm was suffocating: even Gaspar had lain down on the blanket and was staring up at the sky. Was that normal, I wondered. He pays such close attention to things. I distracted him, and Gaspar, who rarely got angry, seemed on the verge of tears. Nearby, the old dog Osman was panting. It was cruel to make him spend his final days in that Misiones heat.

I saw Stephen emerge from the house. He was so pale as he entered the little garden that I got scared. Juan is fine, he's awake and alert, he said, and my shoulders relaxed. It's my mother. She needs to see you, alone.

'This can't be good, judging from your face.'

Gaspar put his arms around Stephen's leg, and Stephen picked him up.

'Come on, let's go see your dad.' And he added: 'He doesn't need oxygen any more; Gaspar won't get scared.'

They were waiting for me in the first-floor room where they always met. The wooden staircase creaked and the carpet was very damp. I didn't want to go in nervous, so I dawdled a little, looking at my father's paintings. The one by Cándido López, so beautiful, was starting to crack. I'd have to take it with me one day, steal it and give it to a museum. He wouldn't notice.

I went a little warily into the room where Florence, Anne, and my mother were waiting. The three of them all together was always a reason to be wary. What was that poem Juan had read me a few days ago? 'One is a harlot, and one a child / That never looked upon man with desire, / And one it may be a queen.'

Florence greeted me with a kiss and smoothed my hair. Her hands smelled like Tiger Balm and the bracelets on her wrists tinkled. Mercedes looked me up and down: possessiveness mixed with mockery. The same way she had always looked at me.

'My dear, this is a wonderful day,' Florence said as she opened a bottle of wine. A Leroy. The smell of Burgundy filled the room. Florence's unchecked joy tended to augur bad news. I was especially annoyed that she was celebrating whatever this was while Juan, in the room downstairs, was suffering the Ceremonial's ravages on his body. She rattled on, peppering her Spanish with English.

'I couldn't wait, dear. Juan should be here, I know, but it wouldn't be right to give him the news in his condition, *it might upset him*. I'll wait until he's stronger. We owe him so much; we owe him everything. My darling, we now know how to keep consciousness alive. *The words were so clear. I heard them too.* The gods have dictated the Rite for the medium and his recipient. The medium will transfer his consciousness into the body of his son. The continuity of life will be given to them, first, and then our turn will come. What we mean to say – *I'm so excited*, it's hard to find the words – is that the Rite is complete. The details of its execution have been given to us. First for the two of them, then for others. You can consult them yourself.'

I went over to the pages open on the table beside the window. I was too dizzy to read, but I pretended. Of course, this was not the actual Book, which was kept in London. There were copies, whose location no one else in the Order knew, not even me. I read sigils drawn in Anne's elegant hand.

When I had finished turning pages and faced them again, the three of them toasted. I had left my glass on the table, and I forced myself to drink. I felt blood rush to my head and my body turn cold, and the dizziness made me stumble. This was it? This was how it happened? There would be no thunderclaps, no sign in the heavens? No great speeches for the Initiates from a pulpit in the jungle? They weren't going to gather for a festival that would last for days in London, or on the estate in the pampa, or on Mediterranean shores? Just this celebration of old ladies in a stifling room? I would have to spend eternal life with them?

Did I want that?

'Oh, she's in shock,' said Florence. And she lit a cigar like a man celebrating his firstborn child.

They were euphoric, their vulgar faces reddened by wine. My mother, her grey hair ever more sparse, spoke.

'If Gaspar is not a medium capable of continuing his father's work, it doesn't matter any more. If he didn't inherit the gift, he is of no interest to us. But in a way, he *is* the gift! The Darkness said that consciousness is preserved by moving it into another body. We knew that. Now it has told us that the medium can continue indefinitely. That is what the Darkness desires, of course. And your son will be his Recipient.'

'I got it, Mercedes.' I tried to make the annoyance clear in my voice, but I didn't want to insult her. Certainly, I detested her way of always repeating Florence's explanations, as if her clarifications were necessary. The Recipient. That's what they called him. Like a bucket. Gaspar's body would receive Juan's consciousness. They knew how to do it. I tried not to cry, not in front of them. I spoke, and my voice didn't shake.

'And when will that transfer be possible? When will Juan have to leave his body and move into our son's?'

Florence frowned. She hadn't liked that I said 'Juan' and 'our son'. It made her doubt. Can she possibly expect me not to resist? I wondered. To let my baby go so easily, and to lose my man as well? Because, of course, I would not be the partner of someone occupying my son's body! Even if that someone was Juan. But these three would not brook a conversation in those terms. In these formal talks, distance and precise terminology were required. I knew I should have said 'the medium' and 'the Recipient', but I didn't care if they could intuit my unease. Love is impure, that's what Anne's eyes were saying. And it was true. It contaminates you and makes you possessive, savage, destructive. Florence had once told me: We love our children and our partners until we must let them go. The sacrifice for something greater demands that we remain detached.

'Not immediately, *we'll have to wait.* The boy must be twelve years old. That is the age indicated by the Darkness.'

'Are you going to try with others, first?'

'The attempt has not been forbidden us.'

'You won't lack candidates,' I said.

'Your son is the continuation,' they repeated. 'You can go on living the normal life we promised until the moment comes. The Rite will be held in ten years. The medium and the Recipient must be preserved with life for ten years.'

'I want you to demand less of the medium, then. If you want him to live for another ten years, you'll have to space out the Ceremonials even more. You had to resuscitate him yesterday. Jorge is planning more surgeries. He can't keep that up for so long. We have already talked about this too many times.'

'My agreement with the medium can be renegotiated. The Ceremonials are already held *when he wants to do them.* I'm not going to go to war when there is good news. We're all a little worked up. The important thing is that *we can go on*. Be happy, dear. Your family will be the one to bring the future.'

I finished the wine in several sips and asked permission to go outside to think. Of course, Florence said. We understand. It's so much responsibility! Today, no one in the world is more important than you. Of course you need to be alone.

When the door closed, I walked as slowly as I could until I was sure they couldn't hear me. Then I ran towards the river. I went down the steps so fast that I was out of breath when I got to the beach. I sat down, dried my sweat with my skirt, and dug my big toe into the sand. I had come the long way around the house to get to the beach. I couldn't go back to Gaspar and Juan yet, or to Tali and Stephen. I had to compose myself. I needed to find out what I thought beyond my first reaction.

I had birthed a replacement for Juan's body. Maybe I had known it all along.

I looked at the brown water swirled with oil from the boats. The circularity of the process seduced me. It was closure. I had seen the medium summon the Darkness for the first time, in the jungle: I had found him. We had fallen in love. That was inevitable. I had given him a son in the same place he revealed himself to me. Finally, I would offer him that body as a means to remain alive. The Darkness had guided me by the hand every step of the way. I was the real priestess. Not those three crones.

But Juan would never agree. He was capable of killing himself first, and of killing me. And he was right. I accepted his arguments. Never give them a child for the Darkness, he repeated. Don't let the slavery continue. But I rebelled against that idea now, sitting by the river. It didn't have to be like that. Gaspar was of blood. Gaspar was not a slave. I thought about my son. I hadn't loved him instantaneously, hadn't felt that overflowing love women always talked about. I had protected him and fed him on my own, without any help but Juan's. I never wanted nannies. And I had watched him sleep every night, trying to fall in love with him. All I felt was a wave of tenderness that I didn't recognize as love. Until one early morning, when I stayed with him because he had a little cold, and I thought I saw him stop breathing: an effect of the dim light from the hallway made him look completely still. He inherited his father's illness instead, I thought then. His weak heart had stopped beating before my eyes.

I ran over to the cradle, and in that short run to pick Gaspar up, I wet myself. I soaked my bare legs and left a puddle on the wooden floor, such was my fear when I was confronted with the certainty of my child's death. I understood. That was love. After the death of one's child, there was only more death. A blackness with no future.

I was toying with the sand, and down in the wet layer I saw a wooden handle and dug it up. A knife. It could only be Tali's. I put it in my skirt pocket, and thus armed I went up the stairs: from the beach to the house was less than two hundred metres, but I felt I was traversing kilometres, because I was heading into an endless fight and I was my own main enemy. I had fantasized with pride, with arrogance and joy, about giving a child to cruel gods, because Gaspar was of blood, and Gaspar deserved the possibility of a princedom. And I had thought I deserved all the dominion that a powerful son could give me. I, who had never had abilities, who envied Olanna, Laura, even Tali, had imagined myself crowned in shadows.

And I would imagine it again. I was always capable of betrayal. But whenever I doubted, I clung to the memory of that night when I'd believed my son dead. And the unmitigated joy when I heard him cry.

It was our worst fight, the one that seemed definitive, and I was afraid of it even in advance. It was the first time Juan mistrusted me. I had seen that look and its dark depths of disappointment before, but never directed at me.

'How long have you all known? How long have you been hiding it from me? Why put on that whole farce of having a child if you were just raising him to die?'

I had asked Tali to take Gaspar away from Puerto Reyes: he was in Corrientes with her. I believed that in his fury, Juan would be capable of killing us. What's more, in Puerto Reyes, near the Place of Power, it would be very easy for him. Finish it all off where it had started. That would be his form of closure.

'They can blackmail me however they want, they can, I don't know, torture you and kill you, and Tali and Stephen. I will not occupy Gaspar's body.'

I tried to reason with him, but it was useless. It was never just that he found it unthinkable to take his son's body. Juan identified with Eddie and with Encarnación, with the Scottish youth, with Olanna: that was his lineage, the line of mediums used against their will. His lineage was not the Order and its exploiters. At the same time, his position in the cult had changed: now, with Gaspar, he was part of the family. I managed to convince him I hadn't known about the Rite. It was the truth, and Juan was never stupid. What he questioned was whether I would actually refuse to carry it out – and he wasn't wrong to wonder. The doubt made me scream, the ambivalence kept me awake at night. We were both desperate, and he decided to leave. He was gone for several days, with Stephen. They were capable of escaping together. My mother cursed me, beat me like she had when I was little. You can't hold on to anything, it's the only thing you have to do, keep the medium with you, that's all. She sent for Gaspar, and warned me that if I let someone take him again without her authorization, there would be consequences. He is the medium's body, she told me. He is valuable. Much more valuable than you.

Florence was more merciful. We can find them easily, they're not going to escape. We have employees who can find them, and we also have the police. Still, she looked at me with scorn. I was disposable. I had given birth to the heir, and they saw me as disposable. They knew Juan's temperament and they suspected he would be opposed to the Rite, but they were sure that in the end, they would break his will. They didn't need me. I was alone. Some nights I let Osman sleep in the room with me: the dog was practically breathing his last, but he still kept me company. He died early one morning before Juan returned, and I cried with all the anguish of our separation, of my son's uncertain future, of my own doubts.

Juan came back without Stephen, stinking of sex and cigarettes. Ever since then, every time he's left and come back, the first thing I've done is open his shirt, unbutton it, lift it up: I need to touch his skin. The days without him are physically painful for me. Getting him back after that absence made me feel insecure for the first time. He didn't need me either, and he was capable of leaving me. I had never before imagined that possibility. Such was my arrogance. When he came back, Juan said things like, I miss you, I need you, I forgive you, I'd kill you, I can't be away from you or from Gaspar. I felt his love had hardened, and his need.

That night, the night of his return, we slept together with Gaspar between us. Or more like Gaspar slept, and Juan and I put a record on loud enough that no one could hear us talk. In that giant room, we had danced with Tali and Stephen while Gaspar clapped: I bought records in Brazil, and Stephen always brought some from Europe. The three of them could talk in secret, but they didn't do it in front of me any more. I could never learn. And how could he do it with Tali, who had never been trained? I felt, and was, ever more alone.

Juan gently took Gaspar's arm and used his index finger to draw a phantom image on his wrist. A large design that almost reached his elbow, on the outside of his arm. Then he touched the scar under his hair.

'I need a specific seal to keep Gaspar far away from the Order when he turns twelve. A sign that will keep them from finding him. I have to ask the Darkness for it: what we know won't be enough.'

'What are you thinking?'

'I'm not going to live ten more years, and I don't want Gaspar to belong to the Order. If I can mark him with a seal that will prevent them from finding him, I'm going to do it. There are a lot of things that would have to happen first. I have to find the Other Place and get it to offer me the sign. It will surely require another sacrifice. I'll give it one, of course. A sign on his arm, visible, that will disorient them. If they try to find him, they'll get lost. They won't be able to find out where he is, and if they do, they won't be able to reach him. A sign, a mark, to hide him.'

'What about me? I don't want to be apart from my son. Are you going to hide him from me?'

He kept drawing the phantom seal on Gaspar's arm. The mark could only be made with violence: it would have to be a deep, painful, unforgettable wound, he told me. He would have to hurt Gaspar.

'And yes, he would also be hidden from you, even if you left the Order. But I want the seal to work only in one direction. It will keep the Order away from Gaspar. That's what it would do, and only that. Gaspar could approach the Order, if he wanted.

If he wants to see you again, he'll be able to. He deserves that horrible freedom, and you do too, I suppose. I hope I won't be alive for it if he wants to go back. The mark is going to drive him away from you and from me. I'm willing to make that sacrifice, and you should be too, in order to save his life. He will live with my brother. Luis is the only one who isn't contaminated. It's already decided, Rosario, and you're not going to be able to stop it. If you aren't with me, you'll have your own decision to make.'

'You're going to drive our son away from us, and you call that love.'

'Of course. Or is it love to steal his body?'

The most incredible thing was that we weren't arguing. Even our voices were low, so the music would cover our conversation.

'And the Rite, Juan? Are you going to mark him before it takes place? Gaspar is the Recipient for your consciousness . . .'

'Gaspar is not the Recipient for anything. I'm going to mark him whenever the seal is given to me. I can also make the Rite fail, or pretend I can't do it. You have to find out the rules. You or Stephen. That way I can make my plan, figure out how to stage a failure.'

Gaspar turned over in his sleep and rested his hand on Juan's chest. He would often make that movement when he was asleep. I cried from jealousy. I was also crying because I didn't want to decide, but I had to. The ceiling fan made the light from the bedside lamp seem to flicker; I looked into Juan's yellowish eyes. He, too, was going to leave me behind. I didn't answer him immediately.

'How can you even think of giving them our son?' he asked me.

'They trained me to obey,' I said.

508

'That convenience is over. Do I have to save Gaspar alone? Maybe I shouldn't tell you my plans. Can't I make you change?'

'Yes,' I replied. 'I can change. Yes.'

The beach was still clean though the brown water was starting to wash up branches, dead flowers, wayward hyacinths, even animals. It was always the same after a flood: the river robs, drowns, sullies, and scatters. I looked at Gaspar, who was playing on the shore. Physically, he was very different from his father. Dark hair, blue eyes, overwhelming energy. He already had a personality, and he wasn't even three yet. He rarely threw tantrums. I only saw anxiety in his eyes when I went to spend a day in Asunción with Tali, or to teach class in Buenos Aires. But when I came back, I always found he'd been good during my absence, with Juan taking care of him, the two of them alone in that silent world they shared.

Since we'd learned the information about the Rite, Juan, Stephen, Tali, and I were united. We were all in agreement that we had to save Gaspar, to stop the cycle. The discussion was settled. I didn't have any more doubts that it was the right decision, but sometimes, still, the possibility of continuing Juan's life, of keeping him alive inside Gaspar, seemed like a horrible miracle that was worth trying.

Juan was in Buenos Aires because he had found a door. Stephen was with him. This trip was to make sure the door was still open, that it was in effect a passage to the Other Place, and that it would open again for him. Finally, after so many years, the Other Place had appeared.

Something else had appeared, too, unexpectedly. Something the Order didn't know how to deal with and that I had to take care of, because, in part, it was my fault.

Betty was the new problem, my cousin, distanced from the

Order for so many years now. Why had I felt compassion for her? Some days earlier, we had listened together as the radio announced the coup d'état. She had cried; luckily, my parents were in another room, because they surely would have celebrated. My father had told me, though, that I needed to be careful with those who had taken power. He said the same about Stroessner's soldiers every time I went to Paraguay. My dad was in agreement with them ideologically, but he insisted that they were animals. But I knew how to take care of myself. If I couldn't ward off a few idiot soldiers after so many years learning from the Order, then it had all been for naught. And that's without taking into account that I possessed a Hand of Glory. I'd never had any incidents. They didn't even look at me. At the border, they waved me through respectfully.

Betty came down to the beach with her daughter, whom she sat beside Gaspar. They liked to play together. Gaspar didn't seem to notice that Adela was missing an arm. Of course, Gaspar didn't know that Juan had cut it off, certainly against the baby's will and her mother's. Not Juan, of course. The Darkness. The girl had been chosen. Betty had ignored my order not to leave the house during the days of the Ceremonial, and the Darkness had seen baby Adela, so tiny, younger and slighter than Gaspar. The mutilation on such a little body was shocking.

When Betty had arrived, I hadn't been able to turn her away. She was my cousin, my childhood friend; plus, the Order wanted her back. She had shown up with her daughter in the middle of the night, covered in insect bites and scratches, panicked and dehydrated. She had run through the jungle with the baby, trying to escape. I'd known she had settled in the jungle nearby with the organization she belonged to, and I had always intuited how badly that plan would turn out, but Betty believed in herself. She and her comrades were trained, they had an arsenal. When she announced herself to the guards at the entrance to Puerto Reyes, alone and defeated, I took her in. I talked to Florence, to my mother, my father. Of course she's welcome, they said. She's part of the family, she's a Bradford. The Ceremonial was in a few days. She would have to stay locked away until it was over, because Betty was not an Initiate. Later they would decide what to do with her and her return, which they had long hoped for.

Betty, however, had left her isolation, despite my orders and my pleas. She wasn't rebellious, she was disobedient. She could be brave, I won't argue with that, but she didn't understand where the limits were. Why did she leave her room? Why didn't I lock her in? It was my fault. And her moment of curiosity had created another weight for Juan to carry, because now he also had to suffer for Betty and her daughter. How hard it had been to calm her down after she had unwittingly stumbled on the Ceremonial. She had no idea what she had seen, she didn't understand it. She was in shock for weeks, raving about a black light that had taken her daughter – though that wasn't what happened, it only cut off her arm – and then the man, she screamed, the man had healed the wound with his hands! With his hands! she repeated. The black light and the hands. She screamed all night. She went crazy. I half-heartedly took care of her daughter. It was lucky that Marcelina and Tali were there, because I didn't have any patience with Adela, who was nervous and whiny. I didn't really like kids, just my own son, and not even him all the time. I had told Betty that the man with the hands was Juan, but she never did believe it. How annoying.

And how pleased Mercedes, Florence, and Anne had been with what they considered a gift, a black miracle. That's what they called it: the youngest child ever touched by the Darkness – and she was in the family! Adela was a gift to the Order.

Toss them both in the river, Stephen had told me. I would have happily done it, too, but there would have been consequences and I was still in danger, because I was disposable. I saw it in Mercedes' eyes. You never deserved the honour of giving birth to that boy, she would tell me. By that point, my love affair with Puerto Reyes was over. The project at the museum was coming to an end and I wanted to live in a city, go back to Buenos Aires. I had offers not just from the university, but from foreign institutions that had satellites in the capital.

'Where's Juan?' Betty asked. I looked at her in profile: she had the Bradfords' long nose, and widely spaced eyes.

'He'll be back tomorrow,' I said.

I couldn't be specific. Betty was not authorized to know of Juan's activities. Maybe someday. One way or another, she could eventually become a good Initiate. She had witnessed the Ceremonial in the most brutal way possible, with no guidance or warning or explanation. And she hadn't gone crazy in the end. Belonging was in her genes. Her mother, Aunt Marta, was a Bradford, and had timidly returned to the Order in recent years, terrified because her daughter was a militant revolutionary. Was that worse than the Order? To her it was. The Order wasn't wrong in its conviction that the disobedient will return: there was Betty, with the most spectacular return ever recorded. She'd made every effort to get far away from her family of bourgeois bloodsuckers, and yet chance and violence, night and terror had all brought her straight back into the heart of the Order.

Adela, the black miracle. Right now, Gaspar was sticking a dirt-covered finger into her mouth, as if he wanted to feed her, and Betty was smiling. If anyone had been watching us from the Paraná, they would have seen a tender picture. Two young mothers with their babies. It was about to rain, as always.

'We're going to stay here for a while, right?'

'It's safer for everyone,' I replied.

Betty pushed her hair behind her ears.

'All of my comrades around here were killed. You tell me it's safe, but I don't know whether to believe it.'

'We're going to take care of you. They're all captivated by Adela. You'll live close to us in Buenos Aires, once we find a house.'

'Are they going to let us lead a normal life?'

'That's one of Juan's conditions. They want Adela to be near him. We'll be watched, as always, but that will be good for you.'

Betty laughed, a bitter and ironic laugh that annoyed me.

'If you don't want our protection, you can leave, Betty,' I told her.

'I don't know what I want,' she replied. 'I want to go back in time, I want to be with Eduardo, I want to forget everything.'

She picked up her daughter, and Gaspar complained the way he did when something bothered him, a whimper that vanished right away. A gentle breeze carried the scent of jasmine to the beach, and I saw Marcelina coming out with tereré, ice, and oranges.

'There are prisons worse than this one,' I told Betty.

She didn't answer me but ran to help Marcelina, who was balancing the glasses, the pitcher, and the bag of fruit. Behind Marcelina, I saw Juan. He was back early from Buenos Aires. He wasn't alone, but it wasn't Stephen who was with him: it was another blond man, shorter than Juan but still imposing. I hadn't seen him since I was a teenager, but I recognized him, and was surprised by the audacity of the visit. It was Luis, Juan's older brother. He looked exhausted, his turquoise eyes sunken in his face. They had travelled together from Buenos Aires.

'Please, Marcelina,' said Juan, 'could you bring the drinks inside? By the picture window, if you don't mind. We've had a long trip.'

I went over to Juan and received, along with his kiss, the smell of gasoline and sweat. I caressed his damp back. Betty followed Marcelina inside: she didn't like strangers to see her, not her or her daughter. She shielded Adela from the eyes of others, always focused so coarsely on her stump, and she also wanted to protect herself. She couldn't be too careful, and she didn't know this man with Juan.

The three of us went up to the house, Juan carrying Gaspar. Before going in, Luis paused for a second.

'It's wonderful,' he said. From the catwalk, you could see almost the whole house. I remembered Luis was an architect.

'Von Plessen designed it. It's very hot, it doesn't work for this climate. The gardens are the nicest part.'

'They must be by Blanchard.'

Juan ignored us and went inside, while I stayed with Luis. Large hands with broad fingers; wrinkles at the sides of his striking eyes that seemed not to blink, their colour compact, artificial, similar to Gaspar's; jeans with slight bell bottoms. Juan was twenty-four years old, so his brother must have been thirty, but he looked older. He was polite, but clearly on edge.

Juan sat down on the sofa facing the picture window looking on to the orchid garden. Marcelina served the *tereré*, left the oranges in the middle of the table, and left. Juan took off his shirt and sat Gaspar on one of his legs.

'Luis is here because he needs to get to Brazil. He can't do it alone, and we need you to help.'

'Well, aren't you blunt,' said Luis.

'What kind of runaround do you want me to give her?'

'Not a runaround,' said Luis. 'But I'm asking for a favour. Let me do the talking.'

Juan raised his hands in a gesture of surrender.

'Take it easy,' I told him. Then I turned to Luis: 'Your brother gets like this when he's exhausted. You must know already that his health has deteriorated.'

Luis looked at his hands. He was wearing a broad gold ring, but it wasn't a wedding band.

'You travelled all the way from Buenos Aires and didn't say a word to each other,' I guessed.

'We took turns sleeping,' said Luis, and he looked at Juan with a hint of reproach.

'Well. His heart is quite decompensated, so I suppose that if he went to Buenos Aires to get you, it must be for something important.'

'I didn't go to get him,' said Juan. 'I went for what I had to do, and we met up. He told me he needs to get out of the country, so I offered him help.'

Gaspar leaned against his father's bare chest and yawned. The circles under Juan's eyes looked like he'd been punched. The ride back in the car had destroyed him. I was a little annoyed by his bad mood, but I knew him well enough to recognize his way of showing affection – behaving like the world was a por-cupine and he couldn't find anywhere to sit.

Luis took a sip of water and explained. He was precise: I was grateful that he didn't underestimate me.

'I work as an architect, and until last year I also had a position at a ceramics factory. My role in the factory was, or is, political. I also did community work. Over the past year everything got more complicated: the union secretary, a close friend of mine, was assassinated. They made it look like a car accident. I went on with my architecture studio, but two weeks ago a guy came and cornered me in the doorway and told me, "The only reason I'm not killing you is that you have a sick son." He was wrong: my partner in the studio is the one whose kid has problems. It won't be long before they figure that out. My girlfriend has already landed in Rio. I want to meet up with her, and I can feel them breathing down my neck. Since the 24th, I haven't been safe here any more.'

'Your girlfriend, she couldn't get you out?'

'She thinks I'm chickenshit because I don't agree with armed struggle. She left on her own. If I meet up with her, we'll see what happens. I don't know if she'll take me back, but I hope so.'

'And? Are you a coward?'

'Now that they're killing us, it doesn't matter. From her point of view, I'm a coward, but I still believe she's wrong.'

'You don't have kids, Luis?'

'My girlfriend has two daughters and I've raised them as my own. I don't have my own kids, not yet.'

'Can we talk about how to do this?' said Juan. I ignored him.

'Do you want to freshen up, Luis? The hot water in this house is a pain in the neck, but if you don't mind lukewarm water, you can take a shower or a bath, whatever you prefer. Then we'll work out the details. I go to Paraguay once a week, for work, sometimes with my sister. And we also go to Brazil a lot because there's a really nice restaurant on the border. We could do it today, even. Or tomorrow morning. The soldiers know me.'

'Things have changed,' said Luis.

'I'm sure they haven't changed that much. They'll let us cross without problems. Have you been to the border here? It's pretty lax, and there are surnames that carry weight in these parts. Like mine.'

Luis got up to thank me, and his hug was sincere.

'Thank you,' he said into my ear. 'We barely even know each other. You once promised to help me, and I haven't forgotten.'

'I haven't either,' I said. And it was true. Juan loved that man, and so did I. He had always been unwavering, even when they'd hidden Juan from him behind threats and lies. Without Luis, Juan wouldn't have been capable of loyalty and affection. I remembered him from years before, insistent, stubborn, waiting for Juan in the plaza if Mercedes' cruelty kept him from entering the apartment. He had never abandoned his brother. And Juan hadn't ever forgotten him. From England, he had mailed Luis a beautiful book on the architect who had designed Big Ben; I couldn't remember his name, but I did remember that he'd gone mad and died at the age of forty. His life had seemed so brutal, and so had those monuments, those churches imagined by the feverish insistence of a young man who wanted to be close to God and found only dementia. And wasn't that always the way?

Luis apologized for his sweaty hug, and said he would accept the shower. He only had the clothes he was wearing because you couldn't flee with a suitcase, it had to seem like a short trip. I called Marcelina and asked her to give him a clean shirt. When Luis left the room, I closed the door and went over to Juan. He needed a bath, too. I took Gaspar from his arms and put him on the floor, where he had a toy car he would soon throw against the glass window.

'How did you get away from the bodyguards to make the drive?'

Juan touched the side of his head to remind me of the mark.

'That's a long time to keep up the secret. That's why you're exhausted.'

I wet my fingers in water and refreshed his forehead. As always, my husband had gone too far, got what he wanted, and as a result would go even further the next time.

'Tell me.'

'The door is still open, it obeys me, I can go in and out. It's the Other Place, no doubt about it. Stephen is working on getting a house for us nearby. We shouldn't talk about the Other Place, I can't keep up the secret with you and for now we can't go somewhere we won't be heard, because frankly I can't get up from this chair. Are you going to take my brother? It was impossible to let you know we were both coming.'

I moved back to get a better look at his face. He was telling the truth about the doorway. When he felt better, we'd have to go to our private place near the beach, where we held our secret conversations. I had a moment of euphoria. The Other Place had returned. It was ours. We could ask for things, ask for Juan's health, ask for wisdom about how to manoeuvre politically in the Order, finally ask for Mercedes' death and my entrance into the power of the Three. And, of course, we would also ask for the seal to mark our son and save him from his destiny.

'Yes, I can take him,' I said, drying my tears. 'The soldiers know us. I'm going to tell him, though, that he can't talk about this with his comrades. We can't be an exit door or put this place in danger. Betty is already putting us at risk, in my opinion. She can't find out about this, either. She would beg us to get her and Adela out, and that's impossible. There are plans for the girl. Does Stephen know?'

'He's looking for a house for them, too.'

Juan massaged his temples and I recognized the signs of a migraine, his red eyes, the right side of his face a little stiff. I took his pulse: weak and dangerously fast. It was a severe arrhythmia.

'I can go with you,' he said. 'When it's all ready, we have to give our address to Luis. We can't lose contact with him. Your parents aren't going to understand why we want to live in that neighbourhood, and I don't want them to suspect anything. It's far from Libertador and near the hospital, just like we thought.'

'They're going to think we want to antagonize them, that's all. You know why they want Beatriz and Adela to live near us, right? They got it into their heads that the girl will grow more powerful if she's near you and Gaspar. It's not the best time to move to Buenos Aires, but I no longer expect anything to be easy, and I can't stand this house any more. I need to work.'

I pulled Gaspar out from under the table so he wouldn't hit his head, and picked him up. He was sleepy.

'You don't need to come with me. The soldiers will confuse your brother for you. They don't know you well enough to tell the difference. They just know my husband is a tall blond man, and that's enough. You need to rest.'

'I know,' he replied.

Down below, the gardener was getting ready to water the plants. It was better to go the next day. The bodyguards didn't follow me to the border when I didn't have Gaspar with me. We had time. We would drive to Asunción like we did every week. And I'd take a quick detour into Foz. They would let me pass. The yerbatero's daughter. The daughter of the powerful family. The guards at the border had arrangements with my father. In Foz, Luis could take any bus or rent a car. As soon as he was in Brazil, he'd be safe. He could be in Rio in two days.

We were all going to survive. I could sense it. My son, Juan, Luis, Betty, Adela. For a while, at least. The Darkness was open and the night was clear.

V

The Zañartú Pit

Olga Gallardo, 1993

'HERE, WE KNEW,' SAYS THE WOMAN, HER EYES RACKED by cataracts and her skin too taut for someone nearing one hundred years old. 'They put the bodies there.'

She indicates the exact direction of the mass grave, as if she weren't blind.

'But us, what could we say, miss? My sister used to hear them cry out at night.'

'Hear who?'

'The dear little souls. *Angá*. Hundreds of them!'

The woman, Margarita Gómez, is Guaraní. She lives in a house made of logs and mud that's collapsing, five of her ten children are dead, and her grandchildren are all 'potbellied'. Still, though, she braids her long grey hair, and still puts a flower behind her ear when she finishes; the red petals illuminate the grey. She remembers the war. That's what she calls it. She remembers the kids mown down in the light of day. She remembers them with sorrow but without horror, because Margarita Gómez has seen a lot. She's seen her own children die, she's seen her surviving children weep from hunger. She's seen her neighbours beaten, their backs scarred by the whips of plantation overseers. She feels sorrow for those kids, but it's not the first or only misfortune her people have seen. So she prefers to water her plants and serve tereré before continuing the conversation with me.

I'm tired, though the trip wasn't all that taxing: no more than two hours from Posadas to the village. The heat, the lush vegetation, the humidity that'll make you grow gills, it all permeates you with a sense of languor. After I speak with Margarita – my first interviewee in the village of Zañartú, 15 km from Puerto Iguazú in Misiones – sleep knocks me into bed at the modest inn where a handful of us journalists are staying. We have all come for the same reason: the Justice Department, finally, ordered excavations in the fields around the Casita de Zañartú, the sub-prefecture unit that was used as a clandestine prison for the area. It was, in addition, the centre that launched Operation Itatí, perhaps the least famous of all the genocide practice sessions carried out before the coup in March of 1976. And the excavations uncovered an enormous mass grave: a pit twenty-five metres deep. They have only excavated ten so far, yet some thirty bodies have already been recovered. Identification of the bodies is complicated, and forensic anthropologists in Misiones don't have the necessary technology. The remains will be sent to Corrientes, where the work will be done at the central hospital's morgue with assistance from the university. In this first phase, a group of journalists was invited in to observe the proceedings. There are remarkably few of us considering the magnitude of the discovery. At the inn, while I resign myself to the fact that my sleep will be intermittently disturbed by insects of a terrifying size, I take stock of the media outlets that accepted the invitation from the Misiones government, and I'm astonished. Most of us are independent. For now, the Zañartú pit is not a story that sells newspapers.

The thing is that, unlike other operations in preparation for genocide – most notably, Operation Independence in Tucumán – the conflict here between the Liberation Army and the Argentine military had almost no reverberations outside the immediate locality, for many reasons – above all, because of how short-lived the actions of both groups were. The Liberation Army settled into Zañartú and its surroundings and tried to do too much: on the one hand, they tried to raise the consciousness of the historically exploited and abused yerba mate workers, and on the other, they tried to improve the living conditions of the Mbyá-Guaraní aborigine population. They did make some inroads with the province's *tareferos*, or artisanal yerba harvesters. (At the time of writing, 70% of *tareferos* make their living from off-the-books labour that in many cases could be considered slavery. They tend to inhabit precarious houses, have no access to basic services, and have high rates of child labour.) Most are employed by the Isondú company, property of the powerful Reyes Bradford family, and to a lesser extent by Obereña, owned by the Larraquy family. The army had a strong presence near the border and acted in cahoots with the companies; they had long-standing relationships with the families and even acted as their security. The extreme consolidation of property here meant that the army attacked the guerrillas quickly, though not efficiently. The young fighters were trained, which surprised the soldiers, and they resisted in the jungle for almost a week. In the end nearly all of them were wiped out, and except for the survivors, Agustín Pérez Rossi (twenty-two, from Béccar, Buenos Aires) and Mónica Lynch (twenty-three, from Martínez, Buenos Aires; almost none of the revolutionaries were native to the northern provinces), they all remain disappeared. Pérez Rossi and Lynch, who spoke with me from exile – they live in Paris and are still friends – are convinced that their comrades are buried in this mass grave that has just become public. Neither of them wants to return to Argentina; they say they will, though only to visit, once the bodies begin to be identified.

When we speak, what neither Lynch nor Pérez Rossi mentions, and I don't either – sometimes it is hard to name the horror – is that the Liberation Army had twenty-two members in the jungle. And since thirty cadavers have already been recovered from the pit, that means the army used it as a cemetery for all of its clandestine operations on the border. That is: there are many more dead here than those who fell in Operation Itatí.

Bones in the Jungle

Our Lady of Itatí is the most important church in the Mesopotamian Littoral. It's in the province of Corrientes, but veneration of the Virgin of Itatí is consistent throughout the zone, and it blends with other popular beliefs. Just outside the marked-off perimeter of the ongoing work in the pit, someone has placed an image of the Virgin under a lapacho tree. In the larger of the town's bars – there are only two for around 700 inhabitants – people drink firewater with leaves of a male rue plant and debate where to get the most effective *payés* (amulets). They're afraid of the bones. Not all of them, of course. Señor Segundo, the bar's owner, says that in his house they've always worshipped San La Muerte, and he is not shocked by the bones.

'The shocking thing,' he says, 'was seeing those kids from Buenos Aires setting up around here, easy targets. How could they think they'd be able to get the people on their side? Folks around here put their heads down and keep 'em there.' I start to defend them, the revolutionaries, but then I realize Señor

Segundo isn't attacking them. He simply remembers what happened here almost twenty years ago with a certain astonishment. And he insists that they were well trained militarily, in spite of their naivety. 'They rented some little houses. They came here to live, with furniture and everything. One couple even had a baby.' He's not the first person to mention the child. She was the daughter of Liliana Falco, both of them disappeared, possibly killed in the operation. Will mother and baby be in the mass grave? The remains haven't been identified yet, but so far all the bones are of adults.

Pérez Rossi and Lynch told me about the little girl months ago. Neither of them know if she was murdered or stolen from her mother to be handed over for an illegal adoption. 'The girl was blonde,' Mónica Lynch told me. 'Someone was bound to want her or buy her.' Pérez Rossi remembered the mother, Liliana Falco. 'She was your typical uptown girl from the Zona Norte, like all of us. I always thought it was strange I'd never met her before, but she moved in other circles, and she'd left home. She came with Eduardo, her partner, who was from the Zona Sur. They were already living together, and she was pregnant. Taking a pregnant woman to Misiones may sound crazy now, but at the time we thought that as revolutionaries we had a duty not to conform to the norms of the bourgeois family. Plus, there was no leaving her behind. Liliana wanted to go to Zañartú, and we didn't think it was a security problem. We wanted revolutionary children.' What we do know is that the baby was born in a hospital in Puerto Iguazú, and she was over a year old when Operation Itatí pulled the revolutionaries from their houses by dint of boots and bullets. Pérez Rossi and Lynch don't think the mother survived. They're sure about the father's death, because they saw him gunned down from behind on the second morning of resistance in the jungle.

The survivors don't know why their lives were spared. Arresting them was very easy: they'd both run out of ammunition, and then had simply fled until they couldn't run any more. Pérez Rossi spent six years as a prisoner in Unit II in Oberá; during his first years there, he saw other inmates be tortured and taken away, and their whereabouts are still unknown. Mónica Lynch was transferred to the women's prison Nuestra Señora del Rosario in Corrientes, and her well-to-do family finagled a pardon after a year. They both say they could never move past their guilt, the question of *why*. Why was everyone else murdered and disappeared, while they had the privilege of surviving? 'It's a refined form of torture,' says Pérez Rossi, and then he thinks better of what he's just said. 'Really, I don't want to compare. We didn't suffer at all.'

The work of recovering remains is not necessarily slow, but it is painstaking. They let the press in on the second day. The pit is covered by a roof of netting, a kind of tent to protect the people who descend into the brutal heat – it's stifling outside, but inside the pit, say the anthropologists, it's hell. Wearing white jumpsuits, they go ten metres down on a platform elevator. If it breaks, there are ladders against the walls. They pull out the bones with their hands. The bodies, they say, are all mixed together. As if they'd been dumped in from a garbage truck. And maybe that's really what happened. People in the village don't know what kind of vehicle was used: the area was cut off by a military checkpoint. They do remember, though, that the Casita's lights were on all night long, and that trucks would arrive from the highway, coming from both directions.

Señor Segundo tells how on the night of the attack, his obsession (that's what he says: obsession) was to find the baby. 'They lived right here in town, Liliana and Eduardo. Liliana was sophisticated, but she was homely, bless her heart. I thought what they wanted to do was admirable, educate the people and all that. Folks around here are illiterate. When I found out they were armed, now that vexed me. Still, I wanted to save the baby, I ran straight to their house. They were already shooting. I couldn't get to her.'

Most of the bones are grouped by type. Femurs with femurs, hips with hips, vertebrae with vertebrae. Only in some cases can bones belonging to the same body be grouped together: the position gives it away. With others, it's impossible to tell. I ask one of the anthropologists why they're like that, fleshless, when some had only been buried for around ten years. He explains that it's because of the humidity. He is not authorized to tell us much more. They'll answer technical questions, which are the least important, though they can inspire morbid fascination. There is a pit full of bones just metres away from a clandestine detention centre. There are no arrests and there never will be any, because this country's laws command amnesty for the armed forces. The victims will be identified, but they will never have justice.

The prosecutor on the case, Dr Germán Ríos, holds a press conference just metres away from the mass grave. It's a disturbing location, another white tent, more appropriate for a cocktail party than for a meeting to report on the discovery and identification of human remains. Ríos confirms thirty-two bodies, all adults. The anthropological team is working on identification, but, unlike with the databases in Buenos Aires, in the north of the country people have not come in to give genetic information for DNA studies and they aren't even clear on the process, which, moreover, is not publicized. Human rights organizations have launched their own campaign, and they hope to get results. In general, their campaigns are successful.

'But many of the militants buried here come from Buenos Aires,' I interrupt.

'That's true,' replies the prosecutor. 'We suspect that this pit was also used to bury disappeared people from Corrientes, Misiones, and Formosa. Even tobacco and yerba workers who participated in labour claims. Up to now we've had reports, but no information about their bodies, though we knew the dates and locations of their arrests. There were three confirmed clandestine detention centres within a sixty-kilometre radius. We believe all three were using this mass grave to bury remains.'

There is silence in the jungle. I'm discovering, during my time here, that the jungle is much more silent than I thought. I'd imagined a pandemonium of birds and other animals, that even the plants would make a sound as they grew; in fact, they do seem to grow several inches every day, with an abnormal, stimulated vitality. There is life everywhere, but the stillness is remarkable. The electricity at the inn will often go out at night, and some of my colleagues get nervous. Nervous from the heat and the humidity that seeps through the walls and makes the mattresses stink, and nervous from knowing that we are in a land of massacres and secrets. The jungle is silent and so are the residents of Zañartú. After the first few days when they talked at the bar about what they remembered, they went back to their work and no one mentioned the lights of the trucks at night or the dead yerba workers, many of them known in town, some even regulars.

Spending another day at the pit seems excessive. I dream about bones. I don't understand what else I can do. Maybe go to Corrientes, where the remains are being identified. I've already witnessed the process in Buenos Aires: it's sad and meticulous. I want to find out about the lives of the detained and disappeared workers. I want to know what the locals remember about the incursion of Liberation Army revolutionaries, but I have trouble getting testimonies. Doña Margarita Gómez's son tells me she is tired and can't talk, but then his mother comes out of the hut, offers me a slightly stale *chipá* and an orange, and sits with me a while in the yard. A girl, maybe a granddaughter, is sweeping the ground with a broom made of palm branches. Doña Margarita tells me how her people have always been nice and quiet, quiet, and maybe that's how it has to be, because only God shouts. It's possible that one of her sons, a yerba worker, is in the pit. She doesn't say it this way.

'He was a proud man, and pride was bad for him. Drink was, too. But I loved my son, I love all my children.'

'He was one of the leaders. Did he talk to you about that?'

'They were treated bad, and he complained a fair bit. How he didn't have food to eat or clothes for the little ones. That's how it's always been.'

How it's always been. Margarita is right. The pit, its atrocity, ruptures the quotidian resignation of this place. An atrocity so far removed from this village stopped in time, with its noisy refrigerators and soda brands imported from Paraguay. The anthropologists clean the bones carefully. They have to remove the dirt, but without breaking the bones or altering them in case they still have any evidence. A bullet wound, for example. In spite of my reluctance, I go to the pit anyway for the second visiting period, in the afternoon. One of the anthropologists shows us a skull without a jaw, a hole in the left parietal. We ask if it's a gunshot and he, professional that he is, replies he can't be sure, but it does look like a lesion compatible with a firearm.

That night, we eat in silence. We're leaving the next day. The pervading feeling is one of defeat. There's a grave, there are crimes, and there will be no investigation into the perpetrators. In all this oppressiveness, I've decided to take a short detour before going back to Buenos Aires. There's a town nearby where local tourists go, along the shores of a lake called Totora. A lot

of people prefer the calm of lake fishing, the sunsets over scrubland, to the river, which is more unpredictable. Motorboats are
forbidden on the lake and there are no palometas, the local, less
fearsome version of piranhas. I'm not going in search of calm,
though perhaps I'll be able to write a little: its hotels are better
than the inn – really, the inn isn't made to house people longer
than a night or maybe a few hours. It's said that the family
members of the disappeared and murdered who could be in the
pit are gathering in that town. As if they needed to be close, to
keep vigil. Why don't they come to the village? I wonder. And
I realize it's a question I should ask them directly, if it's true
they have occupied the town on the lake with their suspended
mourning.

The Dark Twilight

The town at Lake Totora is called San Cosme del Palmar. It
gets its name from a saint who is very revered in the area and
from a nearby palm grove that can be seen from the shore, in the
distance. The place surprises me, subverts my prejudices. One
of the hotels is simple but truly comfortable and pretty, with
airy rooms, wicker furniture, the smell of wood and oranges.
The concierge is also the owner, a woman maybe sixty years
old who bought the place in the eighties. The house, she says,
was pretty well abandoned; it had been one of the weekend
properties of a moneyed local family that fell into poverty after
various misfortunes. She doesn't name the misfortunes, as if
relating them could contaminate the diaphanous atmosphere
of her adorable hotel. She lets me know the breakfast schedule,

gives me directions to the beach, recommendations for where to buy sunscreen if I didn't bring it, and the few – but, she assures me, good – restaurants ('you have to try the pacú, they pan-fry it in yerba mate, it doesn't sound good but it's delicious, you won't regret it'), then takes me to my room, the only one available. In the doorway, after she explains that the key is a little tricky ('but the room locks up tight, and around here it's totally safe'), I ask her if there are family members of the dead from the Zañartú pit staying here. I ask like that, no beating around the bush, because for days now the silence has had me depressed and paralysed. The woman stands straighter and says, sincerely, that she doesn't ask her guests why they come, and it's not her place to tell me. That hotel owners, like bartenders, are similar to psychologists; they hear confessions and the secrecy is implicit. 'You can ask them, though,' she says as she turns on the light. The room doesn't need it: it's very bright and looks out on to an inner yard with lemon trees and freshly cut grass.

The pacú coated in yerba mate is indeed delicious. And I'm surprised to see that there are almost no empty tables in the restaurant. The small pier I walked along to get here was overflowing with boats. At this hour, just past noon, no one is fishing; they go out at twilight. Near the hotel is a small board-walk with jacaranda trees: you can see the ruins of the weekend house that used to dominate that part of the lake. I wonder which of the region's rich families was its owner. The town has a regional museum where I could find out about its history – the hotel concierge's discretion is exaggerated – but it's closed, and it's possible that, as often happens in small towns, it has no employees, or maybe just one person who occasionally checks in at the office to organize old papers.

After eating, many people head off to take siestas. I can't get used to the custom – I didn't even take them in Zañartú, where the weight of the humidity and the anaesthetized village can make you want to spend hours in a dreamless sleep. Instead, I get water for mate at the hotel and settle in on the boardwalk, under the trees, in one of the wicker chairs that turn out to be more comfortable than they look. I take notes in a note-book. I read for a while. There are others out, sitting on the little beach or the boardwalk. From where I am I can see a couple, a man and a woman of about sixty years of age, and a young woman, very thin with pale arms, who is wearing a long dress. I approach the couple and dive right in, asking what I want to know. They open up immediately. They want to talk, or at least the woman does. That isn't unusual, but I'm still surprised. People always want to talk, they want to tell their stories to a stranger, even knowing that that stranger is going to publish and surely distort what they've said, because that is the nature of the job.

They are the mother and father of a young man from Corri-entes, a student leader at the National University of the Littoral. He was taken in April of 1976, just after the coup. He had lived with them in one of those large provincial houses where they build for all the family members on one piece of land: the business looks out on the sidewalk; the main building is for the parents; the back one, past the yard full of azaleas, is for the children. The parents had been tied up and gagged and couldn't defend their son. They only took him; he had a girlfriend, but she wasn't at home.

'He never believed they would come for him. He said those things happened in the capital, you know? We didn't think so either. He had friends who'd gone to Brazil, and others who were in hiding, clandestine, all that. Honestly, we thought they were coming to... My son was just a student activist. I can assure you of that because he told us, and he said we shouldn't be afraid. I'm not justifying what they did with the kids who chose armed struggle, but that just wasn't the case with Gustavo.'

The woman participates in the small collective Mothers of the Corrientes Disappeared. I would have guessed as much from her way of expressing herself. The man says nothing. The victims' fathers tend to be silent companions. Many have died during these years spent in the background, accompanying their wives. They're killed by impotence and love; they're unprepared. Women know how to manage these emotions better.

They offer to introduce me to other parents, even a few wives. It's not a large group, they say, maybe eight or so, though there are some who don't talk or are more reserved. I want to know why they're at Lake Totora, and that night, when we all meet to have dinner at the restaurant that serves pacú à la yerba mate – I'm the only one who orders it – they all give me a different but similar explanation. They won't let us near the pit, and there's not enough room for everyone in Zañartú. The people in the village recommended this place as nearby and comfortable. They're not staying long. They've been coming for two months, since the pit was discovered. All of them go to Zañartú every day, to try their luck, see if they can get in, if someone will talk to them. They've already realized there isn't much they can do.

'You might want to go to Corrientes, where the identifications are being done,' I tell them.

'It's the most logical thing,' agrees one mother from Castelar, in the province of Buenos Aires. Her son, Guillermo Blanco, alias Piru, was one of the militants. She's the only mother of a Liberation Army member here. I tell her about the survivors I interviewed, but the information makes her eyes fill with tears and her face harden. She never learned their names, her son never told her his comrades' names. She doesn't want to hear about the living: she can't avoid the rage.

'We'll find out about the identification anyway: I already gave a DNA sample, and when they identify him, they'll call me at home. My husband is there waiting. He couldn't come with me. His health is bad. He was estranged from Guille when he came up here. I myself didn't even know he was in the north. My other son, his brother, only told me after it was all over.'

'Being here is the closest we can get to a funeral,' says Sonia, the mother of the student leader from Corrientes, Gustavo. 'We want to be close, keep vigil over the remains. We're several miles away, but I know he can feel me. We put flowers out, here at the lake and near the pit, in the trees. Did you see the Virgin of Itatí? They won't let us get very close. They should, don't you think? It's disrespectful.'

'This country disrespects its victims,' says María Eugenia, some fifty years old, the wife of a yerba overseer who supported a strike attempt. When they killed him (that's what she says; though there is no body, she knows they killed him), she had been in disagreement with him.

'"How can you go on strike, the *patrón* will fire you, how will we feed the kids?" That's what I yelled at him, morning, noon, and night. He would tell me that people were suffering. I understand him now, and you just can't imagine how sorry I am.'

'Who did he work for?'

'For the Reyes family. More than half the people around here work for them. I met the owner once, Adolfo Reyes. I even thought he was a good guy. But he wouldn't see me after my husband disappeared.'

María Eugenia is crying and the waiter brings her a Cachamai tea. Outside, the moon kisses the lagoon and insects hit against the restaurant's light bulbs. Beetles. I think how I'm afraid of beetles, but I know that if one of them falls on me, I'll take it out of my hair like it was just a hair clip. Fear changes, accommodates. I don't want to get used to that. That night I don't dream of bones, but I do dream of a huge darkness over the lake, a fat storm heavy with hail.

The Skinny Woman

At breakfast, I say goodbye to some of the relatives. The ones going to Zañartú to leave their flowers and see if they'll have any luck, and others who are headed home. Some to Corrientes. Others to Posadas. María Eugenia and the mother from Castelar are staying a few more days. Last night I saw them together at the edge of the lake, lighting candles. It's a secret ritual that belongs to these families, a delicate, intimate one, shrouded in water and heat. I also greet the new guests. Some are coming from Zañartú, they say as they're checking in: they couldn't find housing there and were sent to San Cosme, the same story. Others already knew they should stay here, María Eugenia tells me. Mostly those who are from the area.

There's one person, I call her the skinny woman, who didn't come to dinner last night and who eats breakfast alone, smoking, at a table on the patio. She has an extraordinary face that, moreover, seems familiar. Maybe it's just the peculiarity of her features: it's such an angular face that from the front it's pretty, but in profile and in a certain light she looks like one of Picasso's *Young Ladies of Avignon*. I know she's here for the bones, too. I want to respect the distance she imposes, but I find her fascinating, with her long, barely greying hair, and her dresses, always different, that go down to her feet.

I get the chance to talk to her after breakfast. She's the one who approaches me: she asks me for a light on the Costanera. I give her one. She smokes constantly, like me. Now that I see her in the merciless light of day, I recognize her, but I can't believe what I'm seeing, I refuse to believe it. About seven years ago, on the boundary between the neighbourhoods of Caballito and Parque Chacabuco, in Buenos Aires, a twelve-year-old girl was kidnapped. A girl who caught the press's attention because she was missing an arm. It was never known whether it was a congenital defect or the result of an accident. The disappearance was the outcome of a game that turned macabre: the girl and her friends went into an abandoned house in the neighbour-hood. A prank. Something happened in the house that the kids couldn't see very well, and the girl never came out. Remark-ably, the disappearance, which was labelled a kidnapping, didn't spend long in the news even though there were a lot of inter-views with the mother, who didn't avoid the TV cameras. The hypothesis was that she was kidnapped by a mysterious man, who was never caught: the police found an adult's clothing covered with blood inside the house, though no relationship could be established with any individual, and the girl never turned up. I wanted to interview the mother at the time, but my editor wasn't interested. I turned to the editor-in-chief. He told me people didn't want to hear about such a morbid story, and we should run good news. I never believed him. He said it mechanically. In other circumstances, he would have killed for a story like that. It's true that those were some horrible months, with the Carapintada uprisings and the desecration of Perón's body: no one could believe someone would cut off the hands of the most surveilled cadaver in the country. There was some-thing bleak about the story of the disappeared girl, it's true, and maybe that's why they didn't follow it up. Those things happen in journalism. The public's imagination falls in love with certain horrors and is indifferent to others. When I tried to interview the mother anyway, maybe for a different outlet, she had already left her house and the neighbourhood. Her whereabouts were a mystery.

'I came for my partner,' said the skinny woman, and when she spoke, I had no doubt. Voices tend to kick-start memory. If it wasn't the kidnapped girl's mother, it was her twin. Or else the resemblance was supernatural. It was noon and the heat could kill a bird mid-flight, but I remember I felt a shiver. I was scared. The coincidence seemed like a sinister piece of fiction.

She recognized my fear, and paused before speaking.

'My husband and I were militants in the Maoist Leninist Liberation Army. That was its complete name, although even the history books and articles just call it the LA. I survived.'

I was shocked. I asked her name. She told me. Beatriz Bradford. I stared at her. I had fully reconstructed Operation Itatí and I had no record of any militant with that name. That wasn't the disappeared girl's last name either. She was Adela Álvarez. I remembered it now, even after years of not thinking of her.

'It's right for you to question it,' she said. Her voice was thick, and I noticed she had marks on her neck and arms. Little scars from fine, superficial cuts. As if she had scratched herself too much with long fingernails. 'My nom de guerre was Liliana Falco. Only my husband knew my true identity, and our leader, because part of our plan, which failed, was to kidnap a member of my family to finance our operation. My family, you must know, is immensely rich. They're also some terrible sons of bitches, complicit in the dictatorship. They used their means and their influence to help bodies disappear. That's why I don't mix with the people who come here. My family was complicit in the murders of many of their loved ones. Eduardo wanted to save me from them, but he never knew what he was up against. I didn't fully know, either.'

I felt dizzy. If she had used the name Liliana Falco as a fighter, then she really was the mother of the baby who was possibly murdered or stolen to give to another family. And if she really was a member of the Bradford family, I was looking at a monumental story. And a believable one, because the family's legendary house was only ten kilometres upriver. How could she also be the mother of the girl with the missing arm who disappeared in Caballito?

I tried to formulate my question just right. I was afraid she would run away. There was something elusive about her. Already in that first conversation I realized she was unbalanced, that her family and her history had wreaked havoc on her psyche.

'Comrades of yours told me you had a daughter in Zañartú. They were wondering about the girl's fate.'

'Adela isn't in the pit. Maybe Eduardo is there. I don't know why they take so long with the identifications. Eduardo's mother already donated blood. She has no love for me, but she told me she did it. I tell Eduardo every night, I tell him how I tried to save the child. The ones who come here don't know how to get close to the pit because they don't study the terrain. You have to study the terrain.'

I had turned on the recorder without asking her, and it was vibrating in my hand under the book I was reading. She said:

'Don't hide it. You can record me if you want. I have nothing to lose. Plus, if they don't want this conversation to be published, it won't be. They play by other rules. They're not so skittish any more. You know that my aunt's house is near here. Mercedes Bradford. She's my aunt, make sure you get that, I don't want anyone thinking I'm that monster's daughter. My mother and father are different from her, in spite of everything.'

'Are you in touch?'

'With my aunt, or my parents?'

'Any of them.'

'I'm not going to talk about my aunt. I can't. With my parents, I do what I can, and so do they.'

Starting here I'll transcribe the conversation. It would be very hard for me to paraphrase it. Our exchange that day was short. So was the one later that night, but both of them felt very long to me, and I remember checking the recorder several times to be sure the cassette didn't get stuck.

'Do you remember the operation?'

'We were woken up by gunshots and we knew it was them, so we ran. Or rather I ran, with my daughter. I knew what path to take through the jungle to reach safety. We had planned it, I had to get to the house of a woman who helped us, the wife of a *tarefero*. The only one who helped us in that shitty village. I never would have said they were shitty people back then, but these days I can't talk about class consciousness or about con-tradictions, I don't have the patience. I don't care about them. I couldn't find the house, I was disoriented. So I made my way to my aunt's house. I needed to save my daughter, and I thought I would leave her there and go back to find Eduardo. I was tired and terrified. My family has private guards. I decided to stay with Adela in the house. We should have died that night. Sometimes, cheating death is the worst thing that can happen.'

Beatriz's thick smoker's voice never once broke. She spoke with the hardness of one who isn't afraid of dying, or who wants to die but has a few things to resolve first.

'I stayed in the house with them. With my cousin Rosario and the others. I'm not going to tell you about my life. I want to tell you that what you've guessed is true: my daughter is Adela Álvarez, the disappeared girl. I never hid my first name: I told the cameras my name was Beatriz Álvarez. I never married Eduardo, but I took his last name. Adela was registered with her real name and she didn't die in the jungle. They didn't kill her in the operation. I tried to save her. I tell Eduardo. I tried, but there were other plans for our daughter.'

'You're the mother of the girl who disappeared in Buenos Aires?'

'That's what I just said. The girl who went into the house on Calle Villarreal with her friends, near Castelli Park.'

'I recognized you from TV. Your family is very rich. As I recall, your house in Caballito was fairly modest. I mean, the house where you lived with your daughter.'

'The house was fine. It was what I wanted. I didn't live with them or live like them, if that's what you mean.'

'Did your daughter lose her arm in the repression?'

'My daughter came out of the jungle in one piece. She lost her arm at my aunt and uncle's house.'

'She had an accident?'

'Do you know what is in this jungle? I don't either. I never fully understood. It's big and it's terrible. Voracious. My family has venerated it for hundreds of years. What lives in this jungle, asleep for now, it took my daughter's arm and marked her as its own. She was no longer mine. I always wanted to escape from the Bradfords, and when I fell in love with Eduardo, I believed in what he did, because it was a way of getting away from them, and a noble way at that. But they brought me back, and they kept my daughter.'

'I don't understand.'

'Better for you.'

I thought, then, that she was unstable. But when she left

and I was alone in the silence broken only by the splashing of animals in the lake, I felt an irrational dread of the jungle and all that beautiful and hostile landscape, capable of harbouring so much suffering and so much death. What did she mean that her family 'venerated' something terrible in that wilderness? Was it a metaphor? Was it literal? I was disturbed by that first part of our conversation, by the coincidence and her instability, which was clear from her dark, jumpy eyes, from her hair that, close up, I saw was fine and brittle, from her ragged, neglected nails. She was an elegant woman destroyed. I was also disturbed by the insinuation of that voracious monster she'd mentioned, the one she related to her daughter's disappearance. She went to walk under the sun, without a hat. I didn't follow her, but instead went back to the hotel to transcribe the recording. I wanted to ask more questions. The list of Operation Itatí's victims includes Eduardo Álvarez (alias Mono Álvez), disappeared, husband of (alias) Liliana Falco. She wasn't lying. The metaphors she used to understand the tragedy of her life moved me, but also shook me, especially those almost mystical ravings about the powers of the jungle. Though I understood why she could go crazy in that regard. If you travel by car along a road through the jungle in Misiones, the bush is like a prison, with walls on either side, and the red earth is a river of lava. There, near the lake, the jungle seemed more distant. Maybe that was the real reason the family members chose that village – because of its openness. I imagined the bodies in trucks driving down muddy roads to be tossed in a pit, the nocturnal birds hushed by the sound of the motors. Earlier, I had seen an altar to San La Muerte. And the first day, when we arrived by car from Posadas, I'd seen one to San Güesito, a dead, venerated boy – an *animita*, as they're called in Chile. I thought of bones left dry by the heat, heat that eats the flesh until nothing is left.

I encountered Beatriz Bradford again that night, in the hotel hallway. Her room was at the end that led to the breakfast area. She was drunk. So drunk that I felt pity or solidarity and I brought her into my room. I locked the door and she collapsed on to the bed, face up. I was afraid she would choke on her own vomit. I hadn't seen her eat, and I don't think she ever ate much. She was drunk, yes, but still fairly lucid. She wanted to talk. I recorded her again.

'No one remembers my daughter. You do.'

She used the formal *usted* with me. I told her to call me by my name, Olga.

'Olga. What an ugly name, like Beatriz. Rosario, on the other hand, now she had a lovely name. Poor Rosario. She was a mean one, but she wanted to save us, and herself. She was mean, but she had love, you know, Olga? She had love.'

'Who is Rosario?'

'My cousin, Mercedes' daughter. She let me in that night and she said to me, Betty, don't come out, not tonight, people are coming, they're holding the ceremony, you know you can't participate in the ceremony, you're not authorized. Stay in here, Betty. But I went out. What an idiot.'

She started to scratch her arms, to run her nails over her neck – that was how she got the scars. Her despair was awful to see. I took her hands from her body and offered her water, but she wanted a cigarette. I made her smoke it sitting up, so she didn't burn the sheets.

'I went out even though she told me: No, Betty. And then that *thing* cut off my daughter's arm. Don't ask me to explain what it is, it doesn't have a name. It used Juan to do it, but he wasn't Juan any more, and the black light touched my daughter. Why did I take my daughter when I left the room, Olga? Why didn't I listen to Rosario? She was always sensible. Juan was dark, but she loved him, and without Rosario's love I don't know what would have happened to him. What am I saying! I do know. He gave up my daughter. He tricked me. He told me he was going to save her, he was going to save his son and my daughter, that was the pact and he didn't fulfil it. I should have realized – he didn't even talk to me! Now I can't get near his son. Gaspar, his name is Gaspar. He's like Juan, but he doesn't know it, someone should tell him. You want to tell him, Olga? My aunt wants him to know. I haven't seen my aunt in a long time. You can run away from them for a while, they'll wait, they know you'll come back. Oh, I don't know if you'll be able to get close to Gaspar. Juan marked him, and the mark keeps him away from us forever. They can't find him, and neither can I. Because of the mark. The mark keeps us away. He's protected. They hate him, you know, Olga, they hate Juan because he beat them, sort of. It's the only thing I'm glad about. I'm alive because they hate him and because I want to bury Eduardo and tell his bones that I took care of our daughter but I couldn't get her away from my family. You are not your last name, he told me. You are not doomed to be an exploiter. Maybe not to be that, but I was certainly doomed. He didn't know. He had love, too.'

She took a long drag on the cigarette. It's on the recording. It sounds like she smoked the whole thing. Then she sat up straighter on the bed.

'Juan betrayed me and exchanged my daughter for his son. He handed her over. He saved his own child. In exchange for mine. Though sometimes I think he also saved her, in a way. When she disappeared into that house, he saved her. My family won't have her any more, they can't use her. They hate him for that, too. There were plans for Adela. But where is she? And his son gets to live a peaceful life. It's not fair, Olga. Can I call you Olga? It's not fair.'

'Was your daughter kidnapped?'

'Olga, you don't want to know. You don't want to know! You're already in danger because of me. I ruin everything I touch. I didn't know how to take care of her. But Eduardo has to know that I wanted to save her and I couldn't, I couldn't, but it's their fault and the fault of the black god who guides them. The black god, Olga. They call him the golden god, but he is dark. Juan was afraid of the god. He was decent, in the end. I would have handed over his kid in exchange for mine too. That's why he kept his plans quiet, because he knew how I am. He played dumb. Pretty handy, huh, playing dumb. He knew he was no one. The god lives in the shadows. Be careful, it sleeps, but it lives.'

She went running out of my room and into hers, locking the door. I heard her scream and cry, beg forgiveness, and, I think, hit herself. There was a dry pounding like a head hitting the wall. Then, silence. The concierge decided to go in and check on her and she found Beatriz asleep. Passed out drunk.

'It's not the first time,' she told me, and clucked her tongue. 'Poor thing can't hold her liquor. She's not the only one, it happens to some of the others who come here. Plus, she eats like a bird.'

'Has she stayed here before?'

'Twice. I think she lives nearby, although I haven't asked. Once, they brought her to me because she got too close to the pit. I don't know how she got past the guards. The police brought her here. She left and I didn't think she'd come back, but she did.'

I wanted to tell the concierge who that woman was, what had happened to her, but I kept my mouth shut. Beatriz had never asked me for discretion or secrecy, but I didn't want to spread her story. I considered I had her permission to write it, though, as I'm doing now.

Although I didn't think I'd be able to fall asleep, I slept soundly that night, with no nightmares that I remembered, though I woke up sweating. The electricity had gone out and the ceiling fan had turned off. I took a long shower. The hot water ran out soon, but the cold, after the first shock, lifted my mood.

I was late to breakfast. Beatriz Bradford was not in the dining room. The concierge told me she'd left in the early morning, in her car.

'I don't think she'll be back for a few months,' she told me. 'Sometimes when she drinks a lot and makes a scene, she leaves early. She's ashamed. She's a refined woman.'

I stayed a bit longer with the concierge. I don't know why I thought Beatriz might have left something for me. Her address, her phone number. But she hadn't. I spent that day meeting the newly arrived family members, and at night I reserved a flight from Posadas to Buenos Aires. I didn't go back to Zañartú or the pit.

The Forgotten Girl

Back in Buenos Aires, I wrote up my article about the Zañartú pit, the last in a series on Operation Itatí and the repression in the yerba plantations in the Littoral near the border. This essay, however, is different: it's a personal text, less concerned with information and history. My encounter with Beatriz Bradford hit me hard, and after I finished my assignment, I turned to confirming her identity, and to finding out if she really was Adela Álvarez's mother.

She hadn't lied to me. There aren't all that many news articles about the case of Adela Álvarez, but I can direct readers to the piece by Guillermo Triuso published in *Panorama* two months after she vanished (*Panorama Magazine*, 'The Disappearance of Adela', 27 November 1986, n.139). It's a unique document, because it cites the investigation reports; these, stored in a basement of the courthouse – odd, because it was an active case – were lost soon after, in the flood of July 1987. Just two folders, nothing extravagant. Very little attention was paid to that girl and her circumstances, or to the statements given by the other minors, Pablo Fonzi, Victoria Peirano, and Gaspar Peterson, which were not contradictory but were very fanciful. While the judicial file containing Gaspar Peterson's statement no longer exists, his testimony to the police remains in the fifth precinct of San José de Flores, and it attests to his complete name and parentage. Beatriz Bradford hadn't lied: the boy's parents were Juan Peterson and Rosario Reyes Bradford. Both deceased. Gaspar had been legally adopted by his uncle, Luis Peterson. The statement includes a description of what happened the night of the disappearance. As the kids told it, they were inside the house for about an hour and a half. Maybe forty minutes after they entered, Adela went into one of the bedrooms; the rest of the time was spent trying to open the door the girl had disappeared through, which had been hermetically sealed. They gave up after almost an hour. Then they left and told Victoria Peirano's parents, who reported it to the police.

To summarize, all three kids said that the house had light inside, that it was enormous, that it had shelves with human remains arranged like decorations: teeth, bones, and fingernails. Adela went into a room, closed the door behind her, and they couldn't get it open again. Victoria was convinced, the official record said, that someone in the house had locked that door. It was over five hours before the police went into the house, already the next morning. And starting then, it's one misstep after another. In the following days, Judge Carmen Molina ordered a series of raids on the neighbouring houses, including Adela Álvarez's. It's conspicuous that she did not order an inspection of Gaspar Peterson's house. To this day, there are no suspects or clues about who took Adela Álvarez, if in fact someone did take her. Between the time the incident was reported and the arrival of the police on the scene, the kidnapper or kidnappers had time to erase all signs. The children's statements are bizarre and they're included, cited directly, in my colleague's investigation for *Panorama*: I recommend my readers look at his work. Unfortunately, Guillermo Triuso left Argentina in early 1988 because of the economic situation, and currently works as a journalist in Mexico. I called to consult him about certain details and he was polite, but the matter is closed for him. What he did mention, when we spoke on the phone, was how perplexed he'd been at the kids' statements regarding the size of the house. That house at 525 Villarreal is about 40 square metres, 44 to be exact, plus 10 extra metres distributed between the small front yard and a backyard that includes a small shed, according to the original blueprints, which are accessible in the city hall archives. Its layout, moreover, is very simple: a multipurpose room at the entrance, a kitchen with space for an everyday dining area, a single bedroom, and a bathroom. But the kids described very spacious rooms, hallways, and several bedrooms. There is no doubt that they entered this house and no other. That is: they testified that the house was much larger inside than out, a physical impossibility. Plus, when the police went in, they found that the wall separating the dining area and the bedroom had been knocked down, as well as the walls of the bathroom, which was open to view. There was still rubble piled inside, and only some of it had been moved to the small backyard. It had no electricity, though the kids were sure there was light, and it didn't have any doors: the bathroom and bedroom doors had been removed. The house was for sale, though it didn't have a sign in front: it belonged to a family named Ordóñez, and a realtor was offering it privately. It was being sold as land: the house was in ruins. The owners' son also gave a statement, but what he said is irrelevant: he hadn't even been to Buenos Aires in years. He and his sister had moved to Córdoba for business. They'd put the house up for sale after their mother died. There was no reason to suspect them; their alibi was airtight.

The judge confronted the kids with this information, according to Triuso's article in *Panorama*, and although they were surprised, they didn't change their statements.

The Marked Boy

A cold case, say the criminal lawyers, and too old a subject for journalists. I wasn't able to look for Beatriz Bradford again for a while. Work and personal matters kept me in Buenos Aires. I managed to speak with Eduardo Álvarez's mother, who asked for my discretion. She had donated a DNA sample to help identify her son, but she wasn't active in any human rights organizations. She was angry with her daughter-in-law and with her son, and she thought the disappearance of her granddaughter, whom she had seen only on occasion ('Beatriz's fault – she's a bad person') could be linked to her son's activism. I couldn't get anything else out of her except the promise of an interview that never came to pass.

I couldn't get access to Beatriz's family. After a call to their offices, I immediately received a reply from a lawyer: if I continued, I would be accused of harassment. The lawyer's tone was menacing. Was it possible Beatriz lived with her mother? Some of my sources who'd heard rumours about the Bradford family assured me it was her mother who took care of her. I persisted through other routes, but reaching the Bradfords turned out to be extremely difficult: at every attempt, I received a reply from their lawyers. The phones were always answered by icy secretaries. The properties were guarded. That family is a country within the country.

Meanwhile, I wanted to talk to one of the kids who had gone into the house with Adela. They weren't kids any more, though. It wasn't so easy. Victoria Peirano's parents wouldn't see me, and over the phone the mother told me her daughter had worked too hard to recover from what had happened only for me to come around years later and remind her of it just for the sake of my own vanity. I wanted to argue that my vanity had nothing to do with it, but she hung up on me. I got a similar reply from the Fonzi family, although, surprisingly, they gave me an address for Gaspar Peterson, the third kid, who lived with his uncle. They gave it to me with what seemed like indifference, as if it were a trivial thing. They didn't give me a phone number, nor could I find one in the phone book. I decided to visit him. He lived in Villa Elisa, a middle-class suburb near La Plata.

Villa Elisa is a small place where it's hard to get lost. The streets are numbered: from north to south they go from 31st to 1st, and from east to west, 32nd to 60th. Curiously, the larger avenues and streets are numbered from 403 to 426, but this apparent complication is very clear on the map. Moreover, the municipality is efficient and the streets are numbered on every corner. Luis Peterson's house was at 6th and 43rd, near the train station. I drove there and quickly oriented myself in the right direction.

And here begins the part I don't understand and that, in the end, made me abandon the investigation. The part that made me renounce this case and my journalistic instinct, and made me suspect I was at the beginning of a story I didn't want to know. Because what happened that day, and the next, is impossible.

I couldn't find the house. I don't mean that I got lost. I reached the intersection of 6th and 43rd, turned on 6th and looked for the house number, 147. The address was 147 6th Street. There was no question. I talked to some neighbours. They all knew Luis Peterson. An architect, they informed me. They knew Gaspar, too, and described him as a lovely young man. They all gave me the same directions, easy. But when I drove down 6th Street, the numbers didn't coincide. I saw 451, 453, 455 . . . and then, when I turned around, I realized I had turned on to a different street. On to 7th, most of the time. Also on to 8th, 43rd, 44th. I tried with a taxi driver, but as soon as he turned the corner, he got sick and vomited all over the steering wheel. I thought he was drunk and I argued with him, but the man told me he never drank while working and that he'd felt a sudden headache that had frightened him, 'like a stroke'.

I abandoned my attempts that day. There was something strange in the air or in my head: the swampy feeling of those nightmares where you can't scream or walk, the dreams where you're sure something else is lurking inside the house you can't get out of.

I went back the next day, facing my fears.

On this second attempt, I tried asking a neighbour for help. I told him the truth, that I couldn't find the house. The man offered to help and we went together. We got lost. Twice. The man got a little mad, frustrated: he felt, I think, that same dreamlike unreality. 'Find it yourself, ma'am, I don't have all day.' I tried a few more times, but I remembered what Beatriz Bradford had said. You won't be able to find him. Juan marked him. You won't be able to. I realized with all the lucidity of the irrational that I was being kept from reaching the house at 6th and 43rd. I don't know why. I spent a few hours on the corner: I thought that if I stayed long enough, I would see one of them. I never did, plus, I didn't know what they looked like: the people I asked told me to just go to the house on 6th and 43rd. One of them gave me the phone number. I called from a public phone by the road. It was busy at first. Then I got an answering machine. When I went back to the corner, I felt afraid and impotent and I decided to go home. Next time, I told myself, I'd come back with a photographer to document that strange defeat, or to find, at last, the elusive house.

I couldn't get there on the third try. I took the train to Villa Elisa. The Roca line's bad reputation is well deserved: windows without panes, many of the seats destroyed, constant theft at the stations of impoverished neighbourhoods, and an unusual number of street pedlars and buskers. At Hudson, generally one of the less frequented stations, I saw a bum traversing the cars. There were always so many bums that there was no reason for him to catch my attention, but I couldn't help staring at him. The man was missing an arm. The coincidence with Adela's missing arm was disconcerting. I tried to reassure myself. There were a lot of homeless people with missing limbs. A lot. None had ever scared me or given me any reason for alarm. People with mutilations, if they're poor, don't adapt well in society.

The man was selling pens. He hawked them as the best on the market at an incredible price. People bought them: there was something friendly about him, warm and charming. My aversion grew. And when he approached my seat – which I wasn't sharing: the person beside me had gotten off at Pereyra – the man stopped. He stashed the pens he was selling in a small shoulder bag. I realized he was well dressed: a high-quality short-sleeved shirt, pants with leather or faux leather hems to protect them from the grime on the ground and ensure their long life, a new digital watch, and clean, neatly combed hair. From up close, he didn't look like a street vendor. With a prosthesis, he could have passed for an office worker.

'We all want to see him. But you won't be able to,' he said.

'What?' I asked, and the adrenaline made me grab him by the shoulder. I didn't want him to leave. He didn't.

'There's no point.'

His eyes, large and brown, stared directly into mine. His grey hair was smoothly styled.

'See who?' I asked.

'You know who. You won't get to him. You can't interfere. Leave it.'

He stared at me, but his face showed nothing. He was inscrutable. He jumped off the train while the wheels were still slowly turning, and I saw him walk quickly away down the platform. I got off too, intending to follow him. I didn't notice that the shoelace of one of my sneakers was untied. And I fell slowly between the platform and the car, in that terrible space so close to the tracks and the wheels of the train. The smell of hot metal filled my mouth: I screamed, and my scream could be heard over the squealing train. It's not true that when death is near you see your life pass before your eyes. The only thing you feel is horrible fear and sorrow, sorrow for what was left to do, for your children, for your own stupidity, for the waste. But, above all, you feel fear.

The train stopped just before it hurt me. The wheels were less than a centimetre away. The station chief called an ambulance and they pulled me out. I was convinced the train would start up again, but I didn't want to move in case the slightest touch would roll the metal wheel into my belly. When they managed to get me out – and I say 'managed' because for some reason I resisted – I sat on the platform and cried while the doctors checked me over. Unharmed but very scared, I swore I would abandon this investigation I had begun beside a pit of bones.

I don't know who the man on the train was. I thought about reporting him, but what would I say? I could have been hallucinating. I wonder if my inability to find the house and my encounter with that man aren't all one big hallucination. Or if, on the other hand, it's all part of a plan with rules I don't know. I can barely leave my house without looking over my shoulder. I'm even afraid the armless man will take my daughter, who is the same age Adela was when she disappeared. As I put a final stop to this article, I have my doubts about publishing it.

VI

Black Flowers that Grow in the Sky

1987–1997

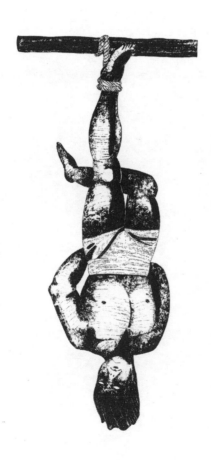

One need not be a Chamber – to be Haunted

Emily Dickinson

LUIS PETERSON MOVED INTO A NEGLECTED HOUSE HE had bought cheap with money he'd saved up in Brazil. A house in Villa Elisa, near La Plata, and it was falling down but it was beautiful, and Luis wanted to fix it up. And so he started working obsessively on restoring the house and on restoring Gaspar.

The boy was angry, and when he wasn't angry, he was depressed, an adult depression that collapsed him into bed. He couldn't go to school. He barely ate a few mouthfuls at mealtimes, slowly nibbling a prosciutto sandwich (that was all he wanted to eat: prosciutto and cheese on French bread), and he'd cry heavy tears that left little puddles on the wooden table, like the first fat drops of a summer rain.

The treatment with the first psychologist had been a disaster. She told Luis she thought Gaspar was schizophrenic, and recommended a psychiatrist. The psychiatrist accepted the diagnosis outright and prescribed pills. Gaspar took them sometimes; sometimes he threw them back up. His headaches made him writhe in bed. He fought with the psychiatrist and shouted to Luis that he never wanted to see him again, that he knew they were going to lock him up, that it was obvious they wanted to get rid of him. Why do they say I can't tell what's real? he screamed one night in the kitchen, with ice wrapped in a cloth held to his temple to alleviate the migraine. But as long as he kept saying the inside of the house on Villarreal had been different from the outside, there weren't many possibilities for a second opinion. That wasn't true for the other kids, and Luis could guess why: Gaspar was the one who came from a strange family, the widower's son, the boy who raised himself. The weird kid. The others, the judge had told him, were only following his lead.

The day Luis found a knife under Gaspar's mattress he almost agreed with the doctors, and he was afraid. But he called the kid in, put the knife on the table between them, and asked why he'd hidden it. Gaspar sighed, but didn't cry. To kill myself, he said. I was wondering if it's better to stick it into my neck, and he pointed to his jugular, or here in my chest. But I think that would be harder because of the bone. Luis didn't know him very well yet, but he was sure Gaspar wasn't lying, that he wasn't planning to use the knife to attack him or anyone else. That same afternoon, after hiding the knife, he decided to talk to Julieta, the woman he'd met just after moving back from Brazil, a young and unexpected lover who was surrounded by psychologist friends. He hadn't seen her in months, not since he'd had to move into Juan's house. She would understand, he thought. He left Gaspar with Negro Sánchez, a comrade from his activist days in the seventies, an ex-delegate like him who'd been one of his best friends before he went into exile and who now lived nearby; he'd helped Luis find the cheap house. Luis trusted Negro Sánchez more than anyone else in the world.

At a bar in La Plata, he told Julieta everything. How the judge had made him Gaspar's guardian, and the boy was technically his son now. He told her about the knife under the mattress and how Gaspar had said he wanted to die, that he didn't want to live if he was crazy. That they'd diagnosed him with schizophrenia. He insists he isn't crazy. They told me

562

it's normal for him to deny it, that he can't distinguish reality from his own hallucinations. But, I don't know why, Julieta, I believe Gaspar. I know it's absurd, he's a kid, how can he know more than the doctors? But he's very rational. He talks like an old man.

He told her what he knew about his brother's final years. He told her about Rosario's death, about the psychiatrist and how Gaspar couldn't go to school because the pills gave him a headache and terrible exhaustion and there he was, at thirteen years old, doing nothing all day but thinking about himself, banging his head against the wall when he couldn't stand the guilt about his friend Adela any more. It's obscene, Luis told Julieta, it's obscene to see this in a boy of his age.

What do you want me to do? she asked.

I want you to meet him and help me find a good professional, not this son of a bitch who just wants to put him on drugs, lock him up, or whatever the hell else.

Let's go now, she said, take me to see him. Let's all have dinner together. Do something normal. I don't understand how you could leave him with Negro. Negro is the most loyal person in the world, said Luis. Sure, but he doesn't know how to take care of a kid with problems. No one does, replied Luis.

On the way there they talked about the political situation, to relax; they had met through politics, and Luis had avoided talking about his family situation in their first meetings. He was still bitter that Menem had won the primary. Alfonsín is going to hold the elections early, Julieta said, and Menem will be president. You're going to have to accept it. She had supported the Riojan governor in the primary. What we're all going to have to accept is what a disaster the next few months will be. Luckily, I have dollars, and Gaspar gets an allowance, in dollars too.

The house in Villa Elisa, with its red tiled roof and white

walls, looked pretty ruined, and it was. The restoration was going to take a long time if the economy didn't improve, but Luis had managed to fix up the kitchen a bit. Gaspar's room was in good shape, though the parquet floor needed replacing or months of waxing and polishing. The most difficult problem was the seeping damp, but for now he couldn't afford repairs and he'd have to live with it. After a very good contract that had allowed him to buy the house, he hadn't found any more work. He still had some savings and had finally managed to finish the cumbersome process of separating his money from his ex-wife's in Brazil. Hoping for a job in March of 1987 seemed crazy. Hoping to find a good psychologist did too. Everyone was scared, impoverished, worried about only themselves.

Gaspar and Negro Sánchez were in the kitchen, kneading pizza dough. Luis was visibly relieved – his shoulders slackened, he relaxed the fingers of his left hand that he always unconsciously squeezed into a fist – when he saw Gaspar look up from sprinkling flour. It was just a flash of normalcy, he well knew; but it was those flashes, so clear and fresh, that made him hopeful he would eventually see Gaspar healthy, or at least suffering less.

Negro Sánchez greeted Julieta and looked at the two of them curiously; Luis made a movement with his head that could either mean be patient or shut up. He took Julieta out to the garden to show her the progress he'd made. He was a dedicated gardener, and a good one.

You're all good-looking in this family, she said. That kid's straight out of a fairy tale.

She grabbed Luis's face between her hands and kissed him, but said nothing more. He knew then, though, that she wasn't angry, that now she understood why he couldn't see her for all that time, and that his predicament had overwhelmed him.

They ate the pizza in the kitchen: it was still March, but already a little cold. Gaspar managed to choke down a slice and a half – Luis kept track obsessively – and asked a lot of questions in that direct, slightly brutal manner he sometimes adopted, and that alternated with periods of muteness.

'Are you my uncle's girlfriend?'

'We haven't seen each other in a while.'

'What happened? Was it my fault?'

'Nothing is your fault, Gaspar, please,' said Luis.

'It makes sense she wouldn't want to be with you now that you're taking care of me.'

'I didn't really know what the story was with you,' explained Julieta, smiling. 'Your uncle left me before he explained. Take it easy. Men just don't know how to handle two crises at the same time.'

'What do you do? Do you work?'

'I'm a lawyer. But I'm not an asshole.'

'Most lawyers are assholes, right?'

'Unfortunately.'

Then Gaspar turned on the TV and stopped paying attention to them. Julieta tried to start another conversation, but now his replies were curt.

'What are you watching?'

'Nothing.'

'Do you like TV?'

'I don't like anything.'

'Everyone likes something.'

'Not me.'

'Come on, you have to like something. Tell me or I won't leave you alone.'

Gaspar looked at her, and Julieta thought that in a few years, if his growth spurt and adolescence didn't deform him too much, that look was going to drive women crazy. Or men, if the kid preferred men. Whoever.

'I like to swim. And to run, play soccer.'

'Does your uncle know that?'

'I don't know if I told him. I don't think so.'

'So why don't you swim, if you like it? There are several clubs with pools in this neighbourhood.'

'Because I'm tired all day.'

And with that he put an end to the conversation and turned up the volume on the TV. Julieta went to help in the kitchen. That night she stayed over to sleep with Luis, who got up several times during the night to smoke on the patio. On the way back to his room, he always paused a few seconds in front of Gaspar's door.

It wasn't easy to convince Gaspar to go to another psychiatrist. Julieta had recommended one who specialized in children with serious problems – with psychosis, but that word wasn't mentioned. She was the sister of a famous paediatrician in La Plata, a leftist but very anti-Perón, and very sweet. Luis went to meet her himself before making an appointment for his nephew: he liked everything he saw, the house with its wooden stairs, the simple decorations on the tables – handicrafts, family photos – and the cats who barely opened their eyes when they sensed movement. And he especially liked the doctor herself, short and a little stooped, a woman over sixty years old who hugged him as if they were friends and seemed to understand him immediately: he didn't need to tell her about the weeks of withdrawal after the first, failed treatment, with Gaspar screaming that he saw Adela in the corners of the house or his father beside him in bed. That's how the boy woke up: he opened his eyes and saw his father lying down, his head on the same pillow. Sometimes he saw Juan dead, other times alive, but the day always started with those screams, sometimes followed by hours that Gaspar spent motionless in bed with his eyes open and his pupils dilated. Luis talked to him and the boy didn't respond, didn't seem to hear him, just blinked and furrowed his brow; he was somewhere else.

'Another psychiatrist told me hallucinations can be common after a trauma.'

'That's what we're going to evaluate. Go on, tell me about it. It must have been atrocious for him, being there when his friend disappeared. Does Gaspar talk about death?'

'He says that if he's crazy there's no point in living.'

'You just told me you found a knife under his mattress and that he talked about suicide.'

'He's thirteen years old – I don't know whether to take it seriously.'

'Teenagers often commit suicide.'

They also talked about how to initiate treatment and break with the other psychiatrist. Let me talk to him, I know him, we all know each other in this profession. It's best for Gaspar if his doctor is near his home and he doesn't have to go into Buenos Aires several times a week. A bad relationship with his doctor could bring on unnecessary crises. I'll take care of it. There won't be legal problems, I know the system, too. I used to work in institutions.

'What about the medication? Gaspar says it doesn't help, just makes him feels worse.'

The psychiatrist hesitated.

'We're going to lower the dosage,' she said. 'I can't make a diagnosis in the first meeting, but I can try a different approach. Also, I don't want you to force him to come to the sessions. He needs to come, but you should act as though you weren't forcing him. Keep talking about it. Let him feel you're worried. Talk about it every day.'

Luis talked about it so much he was left exhausted: by Gaspar's sobbing, by the violence of his screams. But that wasn't the worst part, and neither was Gaspar's horrible thinness, which, Luis thought, would surely have merited the urgent intervention of a social worker, if not for the fact that the country was a hellscape of power outages, protests, hyperinflation, and early elections, and that no one from the juvenile court ever visited them (maybe they were on strike?). The worst had been one day when they'd had a strange, nearly silent argument, and afterwards Gaspar had started to go back to his room – as he did every day; he spent too much time lying down, in bed or on the living-room sofa – but then stopped in the doorway, motionless. From the hallway, Luis saw that the boy's knees were giving out, and he ran to catch him before he collapsed to the floor. He didn't faint but he was drenched in sweat, even though the autumn afternoon was pretty cold. Luis, as he embraced him, felt his body shaking.

'Dad is in my room, don't go in,' Gaspar told him.

Luis picked him up. He weighs less than a chair, he thought, and he carried Gaspar out to the yard because he couldn't think what else to do. Still, he couldn't help but steal a quick glance through the open door into the bedroom, and he swore he saw the intimidating, unmistakable figure of his younger brother, a flash of blond hair and his broad shoulders, long fingers, arms hanging down by his side. Unnerved, he sat on the garden bench and cradled the boy. You're going to be okay, he said, you're going to be okay, until the boy interrupted him unexpectedly:

'Quit lying.'

'You *are* going to be okay, Gaspar, I'm going to help you.'

'It was him. It's better when he comes. Adela comes at night. She waves at me. They ate her face.'

'There's no one else in the house, it's just the two of us.'

The silence affirmed his words. In the distance, there was the sound of a neighbour mowing grass. The murmur of a TV, a few birds. The sun was still out. It was a beautiful day. The yellow roses swayed gently in the breeze: Luis had managed to revive the rose garden. The fact that Gaspar couldn't enjoy the day seemed unfair to Luis, and he said so. He told Gaspar about the school he planned to send him to, about how he imagined them fixing up the house and the garden together, about his wish to start working, and about a nearby club where Gaspar could go back to playing sports, if he wanted. He didn't know if Gaspar could hear him, nor did he notice when he fell asleep, but eventually he carried him inside to the living-room sofa and sat down to wait, in silence, until he fell asleep too and dreamed of hallways and iron bars and the sea. When he woke up, Gaspar was looking at him in the half-darkness; the garden lights were on, and the house was full of shadows.

'Aren't you uncomfortable there?'

'I'll be sore everywhere tomorrow.'

Gaspar sat up, the blanket draped over his shoulders.

'Can that doctor see me tomorrow?' he asked.

Luis realized how much he loved his nephew as he watched him go into the office to see Isabel, the psychiatrist. The boy looked back before the door closed, and Luis gave him a dumb wave that Gaspar didn't return. He had never felt so helpless and adrift, not even when he'd had to go into exile, or when, at his house in Brazil, he'd gotten news of comrades and friends who had disappeared or been murdered. It had all been monstrous, but that one look from Gaspar was worse. There'd been several nights when he imagined finding Gaspar dead in the bathtub, and he'd had dreams where the boy was covered in blood, others where he simply died in his sleep.

Gaspar emerged with the psychiatrist's arm around his shoulders. They had been in there for a long time, almost two hours.

'See you on Friday? Gaspar and I decided we need to meet twice a week. We might add a third visit, if it's necessary.'

Luis expected the psychiatrist to invite him in, but she said goodbye to both of them with a kiss on the cheek, saying, you can pay me next time.

And that was it.

In the car, Gaspar only said: I think this one is better.

Her mother had finally allowed her to call the house where Gaspar lived now with his uncle. Why had they taken him away like that, without warning? Gaspar has problems, dear. So what? We all have problems. Adela disappeared or she was killed, whatever, in the damned haunted house, and then they took Gaspar away too.

And Victoria cried and couldn't sleep, and her mom called Gaspar's uncle and told him about the situation and he told her about his own, and they went on talking.

'Gaspar's uncle promised we'll stay in touch. I'll call him once a week. Everything's fine. Gaspar is in treatment.'

'Treatment for what?'

'Vicky, you go to the psychologist too, it's the same.'

'It's not the same if I can't see him.'

'Gaspar is in worse shape than you.'

'He's not crazy.'

'You will get to see him, but he has to get better first.'

'Why do you all think I'm going to be bad for him?'

And her mom hugged her, but didn't explain any more. And Vicky saw Adela at least once a week, but out of the corner of her eye, like a shadow just behind her, and when she turned around no one was there. She told Pablo about it, and after he listened to her in the cool living room of his house that seemed so quiet to Victoria, he went to the bookshelf, took out a thin book with a green cover, and read: 'There is the Hide-behind, which is always hiding behind something. No matter how many times or whichever way a man turns, it is always behind him, and that's why nobody has been able to describe it, even though it is credited with having killed and devoured many a lumberjack.'

'Why the hell would you read me that?'

'You just reminded me of it. It's Borges.'

He showed her the book's cover.

'Is it a story?'

'No, not a story, it's a legend. A legend from the United States, it says here.'

'Pablo, you mongoloid. I'm telling you what's happening to me and you come out with Borges and some bullshit of his.'

She left in a huff, ignoring Pablo's apologies and thinking that he was also pretty crazy. Thinking that Gaspar would understand. How could I be bad for him, explain that to me, she asked her mother later. I'm his best friend. Give me his phone number, don't be an asshole.

'You curse at me again and I'll smack you.'

'You always say the same thing, the same old shit. Like you'd ever smack me. Give me the number!'

'We do not curse in this house!' said Victoria's father, who had come in from the kitchen holding a cup of coffee, the paper tucked under his arm.

'Hugo, stay out of this.'

He slammed the kitchen door.

'I'll give you the number, but Luis won't let you talk to Gaspar. You can talk to Luis.'

She snatched the paper with the number from her mother's hand and called: her fingers were trembling, and she had trouble dialling the new phone. Luis was very friendly and explained that Gaspar was sick, that he needed time.

'Time for what?'

'To recover.'

'I've never even seen you with Gaspar. When your brother was all crazy and sick, he was always alone. Pablo and I were with him. Where were you? Who do you think you are? I don't know what you were even doing. We're his friends. I miss him, he must be missing me.'

Silence from the other end. Fucking old man, thought Vicky.

'You're right.'

Well now, Vicky thought.

'But he's my responsibility now. I'm taking care of him and his psychologist says that for the time being, in order to take care of him, the best thing is for him to get away. Not from you, but from everything that reminds him of what happened.'

'You're a dick.'

'Child, give it time. He's going to get better.'

Victoria hung up and went into her room. She had to go back to school the next day, but how she was going to do it, she didn't know. It was high school, it would be different, and luckily it wasn't a Catholic one any more. She'd be going to a normal school where she didn't know anyone, although some of the kids must know she was the girl from Adela's house, and if one of them knew, they all would, eventually. She called Pablo. 'I forgive you, get over here, but don't give me any bullshit that's gonna scare me, I'm already plenty scared. Aren't you scared? What's with you?'

'I'll come over and tell you,' said Pablo.

What Pablo had to tell her was so simple and so horrible that Victoria wanted to call in her mother and ask her to fix it; she was an adult, she had to be able to change things and make them better. Pablo told her something that had only happened to him twice, but now he didn't move from his room until the sun came out. If he had to pee, he held it; he'd brought in a bucket just in case. Never again would he leave his room at night. He'd gone to take a piss, as normal. In the hallway before he reached the bathroom, someone had grabbed him by the hand. And not a friendly touch. It had been a sharp yank, so hard he'd almost lost his balance, and the hand was hot and dry, fevered. He screamed, thinking someone was really there – the house was totally dark, and a thief could have broken in. His father got up, sent Pablo to his room, and searched the house, while his mother shouted at him: Don't act all macho, think of the baby, stuff like that. She even wanted to call the police, but in the end his father said no. He said he didn't want to make a scene. He said Pablo was just afraid of the dark, and then he sent everyone back to bed.

It had happened again a few nights later. He'd wanted to hold it until morning, but the moment came when he just couldn't and he had to get up. He decided to turn on the light. The hand had grabbed him while he was fumbling in the darkness, walking with his arms outstretched to keep from running into something. This second time, the hand had grabbed him by the shoulder: it was behind him, in the darkness of the living room. And it had thrown him to the floor. He couldn't see a thing. There was nothing there, or the hand had escaped quickly. Pablo ran, too, back to his room, and from then on, he never left it at night. He had the bucket if he needed it. He wanted to move.

'I'll kill you if you leave,' Victoria told him. 'You didn't tell your dad?'

'No. It's the same hand as when we lost Adela. When we were in the house, it touched me from behind.'

'Yeah, you told me.'

'It's the same, it feels exactly the same. I'm not gonna say anything to my dad. Every time I tell him I'm scared he calls me a fag. He's right, anyway. Not about being scared.'

Victoria was quiet. It was the first time Pablo had said it out loud.

'Have you told anyone else?'

'Are you crazy? Gaspar knows, he realized on his own. Anyway, he doesn't care.'

'It seems natural to him,' said Victoria.

'I miss him so much, I'm afraid something bad's happening to him.'

'Do you like him?'

'Obviously, Vicky.'

Vicky sighed and said: 'Listen to me. We have to make a plan so they won't call you a fag at school, because they're going to make fun of you and you don't know how to fight. We'll come up with it later.'

That night they slept together in Victoria's single bed, their arms around each other, and before going to sleep they pricked their fingers with needles and mixed their blood together and promised they would never separate. Then, so that their sleep would be dreamless, they took the pills that Victoria stole every week from her dad's pharmacy.

Gaspar went punctually to his appointments and almost never seemed angry with Isabel. She was Isabel now, not 'the doctor' or 'the shrink', just Isabel. She had gradually cut out the anti-psychotic medication and left him only on anti-anxiety and antidepressant drugs that helped him eat. But he still had those blackouts when he lay paralysed, sprawled in bed with his pupils dilated, unresponsive to touch.

Luis had had a meeting with Isabel, and she'd told him she thought Gaspar had been misdiagnosed. Luis felt his forehead relax in relief. Those blackouts Gaspar suffers, she told him, are flashbacks, he experiences the trauma all over again, with all the same sensations and emotions. It's post-traumatic stress disorder, the flashbacks and anxiety attacks are clear symptoms. I want him to see a neurologist again to see whether it's also a case of epilepsy.

'He doesn't have fits. Not that I've seen.'

'Epilepsy doesn't always have generalized tonic-clonic seizures – that is, convulsions. Sometimes it manifests as black-outs: you've described them, but Gaspar doesn't remember. Sometimes the episodes are similar to night terrors. Epilepsy can also be accompanied by complex visual hallucinations. In general, hallucinations tend to be very simple, but we could be looking at an exception.'

'Is it curable?' Luis wanted to know.

'It's treatable,' she said. 'Gaspar told me about an accident and a blow to the head. He had amnesia, he says. They did some examinations and I've sent for them. I have a good friend who's a neurologist, with whom I often work. I was surprised those exams hadn't been sent for before, but Gaspar didn't mention the accident or his memory loss to the other doctors, and I assume not to you either. I understand, there's no reason you would know. Sometimes epilepsy is the result of a lesion. It's true that there don't seem to be any signs of that in the tests they've done so far. But, again, some cases

575

of epilepsy are difficult to diagnose, and each one is different.'

'I don't know what was going on with my brother. Gaspar told me very little. He did mention a car accident, but he didn't seem to give it much importance.'

'He'll tell you what you need to know. In general, everything he tells me, what goes on between the two of us, is confidential. I don't think there is anything, yet, that you need to hear from me. When a person remembers the past, their autobiographical memories are verbally accessible, which means they can relate them in words. In trauma, memories are isolated and the person cannot access them voluntarily; that's why Gaspar relives them in nightmares and flashbacks. It's not just his friend's disappearance. His father's death took away his structure: they were very close. My job is to try to get some of those memories to become biographical, to get him to integrate them so he can tell them as stories.'

'And that's possible?'

'Not always. I've seen patients after years of abuse who barely suffer a slight depression. Others collapse. Gaspar was very vulnerable. But we're going to try.'

And she gave him instructions regarding three things: establish a routine – four meals a day, schedules, outings, movies – monitor Gaspar's medication, and have him exercise. Luis wanted to know if Gaspar could see his friends again: the kids had called to ask. Not yet, said Isabel. We can't risk them being a trigger. When he asks to see them, we'll consider it.

'He likes to read.'

'That too, then. Get him a library card. That way he'll leave the house, and he'll have a commitment to return the books. I need him to establish ties, to have simple responsibilities.'

The whole previous week they had watched on TV as the Carapintadas took over the Campo de Mayo military base. An attempted coup d'état, but this time the people had taken to the streets to defend the democratic government. Luis wanted to go to the demonstration, but he decided to stay with Gaspar instead. Negro Sánchez and Julieta did go into Buenos Aires, and they stayed in the plaza until Alfonsín came out onto the balcony and said, 'Happy Easter', the greeting that put an end to the attack on the base. Gaspar had said to him: 'With me being crazy and all, we didn't even notice the country was going to hell.' Instead of worrying him, the joke had given Luis hope. When Carlos Menem won the election in the midst of a disaster that barely registered in the house in Villa Elisa, there were fireworks at a Peronist meeting house a block away, and Luis took Gaspar. He ran into an acquaintance who started raving about the new president; Gaspar sipped a Coca-Cola and wandered out of Luis's view. When he came back, he was eating a sausage.

'You're hungry! It's a Peronist miracle!'

'It's delicious,' Gaspar said with his mouth full. That night he ate a sausage and a half, more than he'd eaten all week. Two months after that, Luis noticed that the flashbacks, those terrifying blackouts, were no longer as relentlessly frequent. By the end of the year, they were happening so sporadically that even Gaspar dared to say out loud, over breakfast: Now I'm scared I'll have an episode, because I'm having them a lot less, right? That's what he called them, 'episodes', surely a term taken from therapy. Luis started to invite people over, friends of his, friends of Julieta's. They stayed up late talking about politics, drinking beer, and smoking. Gaspar was suspicious at first – Who are these people you're inviting? he'd ask. Eventually, he accepted it. And once he gained confidence, he stayed up with them, eating pizza and asking curious questions. By the end of the year Gaspar was eating almost normally, so much so that he even requested different pizza toppings and wanted to make sure Julieta would be there to keep the sauces from burning, and enough with the zucchini torte, it's gross. He also agreed to go to the neurologist. When Luis watched the news or political programmes and shouted at the TV, Gaspar would tell him, 'Uncle Luis, don't act crazy, they can't hear you,' and the two of them would laugh. He wanted to sign up at the club to swim and run; only then did Gaspar tell Luis that he was bad at soccer. Luis wouldn't believe it until they played a pick-up game and ended up rolling with laughter on the ground, clutching their bellies, because they were both equally clumsy.

'So what team do you root for? And show some respect, jackass, don't laugh at me like that.'

'Don't call me a jackass, I'm mentally unstable and you have to watch out for me. I support San Lorenzo.'

'How about that. Me too.'

'Dad said all the men in the family support San Lorenzo.'

'It's true, your grandfather did too.'

There was a silence.

'You know, Dad wasn't always mean to me, Uncle Luis. There were times when he read to me every night. Sometimes I'd read to him.'

'What did he read you?'

'Poetry. But don't say anything because then people will call me a fag.'

'It's not gay to read poetry.'

'I know, but I don't need those problems. I know there's nothing wrong with poetry or with being gay, he taught me all that. That's what I mean, he wasn't always bad, sometimes he was really good to me.'

'Your dad suffered a lot, and there are people who turn bitter when they have such a bad time of it.'

Gaspar leaned one elbow on the grass and his head on his hand to look directly at his uncle, who was sitting with his legs crossed and the ball on one of his knees.

'That's true. But it's not just that. I tell this to Isabel. I can remember a ton of things, but it's like I've forgotten something important. I remember hardly anything about when we went alone to Misiones, for example, to my grandparents' house. Mom had just died. And something happened there.'

'How did you get there?'

'By car.'

'And he drove? What a crazy son of a bitch. You both could have died. You don't remember your grandparents?'

'Barely. But Dad didn't want me to be with them, and he said Mom didn't either. And they never tried to see me.'

'That's true. But goddamn, you were alone. I'm sorry I abandoned you, son.'

'You didn't abandon me.'

Luis tried to hug him, but Gaspar put out an arm to stop him: he wanted to talk.

'When we go back to my house, we have to go into the room where he kept his things, and you'll see all his books. I want to keep some, I like to read. Sometimes he'd lock himself in for days at a time, and I wasn't allowed to bother him.'

'And who fed you?'

'I know how to cook. And there was a lady who cooked for us. Otherwise, I'd go to Pablo's or Vicky's or the café in the park. Dad would also leave. Sometimes he'd be gone a whole week. I don't know where he went, he never told me. I miss him a lot.'

Now Gaspar was sitting up and his eyes were filled with tears. Luis was afraid something would happen to him, a panic attack, an episode. But Gaspar only said:

'I'd like to see them again, Pablo and Vicky. But I don't know if I can.'

'How about we wait until after New Year's.'

'Sure. Have they ever called?'

'Kiddo, they call all the time. Your friend Victoria cussed me out once, she's a real handful.'

Now Gaspar was smiling, and his face had changed so much that Luis didn't recognize him.

'Tell them to wait for me, because I think I'm getting better.'

'See? What'd I tell you.'

On New Year's Eve, Luis let Gaspar have a glass of champagne. That summer of 1988 they went with Julieta to a house in Mar del Tuyú. Gaspar went fishing with Luis and ate the *cornalitos* they caught; he swam with Julieta, and when he raced the other kids on the beach, he left them panting on their knees or half-dead. There were no crises, and they didn't have to call Isabel even once. Gaspar asked Julieta for a book of poetry. She was surprised, and Gaspar told her simply that his dad had a lot of books and the two of them had read a lot; he said he wanted to go back to their old house to get some books. His uncle had only gotten his albums, and he liked music a lot, sure, but he liked reading more. One afternoon, when Luis and Negro were taking a nap and the two of them were drinking mate on the beach, Gaspar told Julieta that he wanted to 'know things', that being sick had 'made him dumb'. That when he was with his friends, they'd listened to music, watched movies. And that he missed them.

'You just say the word and we'll work it out for you to see them. You want some toast?'

'I want it with dulce de leche, but this damned sand sticks to everything.'

'I brought churros. Are you sick of being around old folks, Gaspar?'

'Sick of it, no. But I think I should go to school.'

Gaspar started classes at an evening high school in La Plata; it was less demanding, and the teachers, who were used to working with adults and problem students, were less strict and more understanding. After the first day, when he went to pick him up in the car, Luis promised that now he was going to look for work. That's going to be even harder than dealing with my insanity, I think, Gaspar told him. We've got to be optimistic, laughed Luis.

The school was across from a plaza, and many of Gaspar's classmates – mostly older than him – arrived early and would sit on the grass before class and smoke pot and listen to music. On his first days everyone ignored him, but one Friday, when they were told classes would start late because the history teacher couldn't make it, they offered him a beer. Gaspar accepted, but he only took a couple of sips and he refused the joint. Don't even think about drinking or doing drugs, his uncle had told him recently while the two of them were trying to fix the bathroom door, which didn't close right. You know it's not a question of morals, I couldn't give a damn and I'm certainly no saint, but you're taking pills. And last year was really rough. For now, Gaspar had decided to listen to him. The other kids didn't say anything, didn't make fun of him. They wanted to know why he'd come to night school. Gaspar half-lied, saying he'd been recovering from an accident almost the whole previous year. The scar on his arm, which was large and hard to miss, backed up his excuse.

He and Isabel had talked a lot about what he should do if he was recognized. If someone realized he was one of the kids from Adela's House. She had told him that if they asked, he didn't have to answer. He could just say: I don't talk about that. It wasn't so easy for him to flatly refuse to talk, but he had an advantage: people hadn't seen his face. When the cameras came to the neighbourhood, they hadn't filmed him: he had spent almost all that time at the hospital with his father. People did know what Vicky, Pablo, and Betty looked like. Adela too, thanks to the photos that were shown during the futile search. People knew he existed, they knew his name, but they hadn't seen him, and names don't resonate the same way.

Plus, there were other things happening. Supermarkets looted; people in the slums so poor they ate cats; a truck full of cows had turned over and some local people, with no shame at all, had butchered the animals for the barbecues they'd been missing. Adela's House was old news. Not for Gaspar, though – every time he dreamed of her, he woke up to vomit and then kept throwing up all night, entire nights spent in the bathroom, where his uncle brought him a pillow and sat down beside the bathtub to wait for it to pass. At least he didn't see her when he was awake any more.

He couldn't talk about that with his classmates.

Nor did he need to. The kids in the plaza were nice to him and always invited him to play soccer. Gaspar told them that he was awful and no one would want him on their team, but that he'd play if they wanted. It's just a little field close by here, and we've got a few klutzes, said the owner of the cassette player. He went, and as usual, he played very badly but had a great time, laughing hard at the other kids' jokes. The field was close to the school and to a rugby club that had a pool and a track. Gaspar joined so he could get back to running and swimming. He got along well with the people who went to the club. He ran or swam every day if he could, if it didn't rain; often he went after class and before eating dinner, alone, accompanied only by the light of the club's buffet and the owner of the restaurant, who listened to music behind the bar. At the club, late, he'd smoke a few cigarettes sitting on the grass; when he ran, he'd leave the pack beside the track along with his keys, his water bottle, and the hoodie he put on once he was sweaty. His uncle and Julieta didn't know he smoked. Isabel did: she let him smoke during their sessions, but never more than two cigarettes.

As night fell he would smoke in silence, and he'd often watch the fireflies as they blinked among the eucalyptus trees and above the dirt path that led to the pools and the tennis courts and rugby fields. They were especially pretty when there was still a little light: at sunset they seemed like sparks given off by the sun. But after it was fully night, Gaspar wasn't sure if he liked them or not: they reminded him of eyes that blinked and were suddenly gone, or else were too close to see. And yet they were beautiful, flickering like that among the tall grass and tree trunks.

The house in Villa Elisa was so different from the house Gaspar had shared with his father that it felt deeply foreign to him, even while he enjoyed it and loved it as if its walls were a careful person who always thought before speaking. And it was never silent: his uncle tended to keep the radio on, and other times, when Julieta would stay over for several days – she was ever closer to moving in – she listened to music on a boombox she'd brought over or turned up the volume on the TV, saying it kept her company. They both got up early, even when they stayed up late – and they often stayed up late, the empty wine bottles like green glass decorations on the patio and kitchen tables – and opened the blinds to let the sun in. At first the light bothered Gaspar, but once he got used to it, he ate breakfast outside at the patio table unless it was very cold.

Plus, there was nothing in the house. Nothing dangerous, nothing evil. The house was clean. The things he saw, the apparitions of his father or Adela, belonged to him, not the house. He would bring them wherever he went. Ever since his father had hurt him, the scar on his arm had acted as a kind of alarm: it throbbed and burned when he went near certain houses, some that seemed threatening, others that looked perfectly innocent. Gaspar understood that it was indicating places he shouldn't go into, other houses like the one that had swallowed Adela. He couldn't share that with anyone, either. Vicky and Pablo were the only ones he could tell, but he still couldn't bring himself to see them.

That feeling and the inexplicable horror certain places provoked in him could have been caused by whatever it was the doctors and psychiatrists were struggling to name: the aftermath of trauma, epilepsy derived from the accident, some kind of mental illness. Gaspar played dumb, but he heard them talking. And he thought maybe one of them was right. Adela was nearly gone, but she still appeared in the corner of his room sometimes and stared at him in accusation. I loved you, she told him, her lips not moving, and you betrayed me. Still, he could live with those feelings, and the guilt. As long as the house in Villa Elisa existed, his uncle arguing with the radio in the morning, Negro Sánchez trying out different pizza toppings, and Julieta bringing him poetry books, he could trust that someday he would see his friends again. And if some impossible memory left him mute and paralysed, he now knew it was also possible to re-emerge from that immobility and sit in the sun with the chocolate his uncle always kept for him in the refrigerator.

The backyard of the house in Villa Elisa had been the first thing to improve, and Luis had started there just because it was the only thing Gaspar had mentioned. Without too much enthusiasm, and it wasn't a request – he didn't ask for anything in those first days – he'd said it would be nice to have a garden. Surprised, Luis remembered the postcards his brother had sent him when he went to have an operation in London, where the treatment options were better. Juan had always talked about the gardens and flowers and the English green; he sent photos of old, secret gardens, of public parks, and also of buildings and castles and churches. He'd thought they were very odd postcards coming from a boy who, though he did have physical limitations, was living it up in one of the world's capitals. He decided not to show the postcards to Gaspar, not yet, but instead set to work: he broke up the cement and tiles, bought dirt and grass, dusted off some ideas from a landscaping class he'd taken in Rio, and spent afternoons at the nursery choosing plants that were already grown. He thought about adding a pool, but didn't have enough money. A canvas one would have to do. Plus, he would rather Gaspar go to the club to swim: it was better for him to get out of the house, and that was also what Isabel recommended. He and Gaspar had fun fixing up the garden. The kid was very good at following instructions, and he liked repetitive tasks. Luis thought they helped give him structure, and he understood, because he felt the same way.

With Gaspar's improvement came some adjustments. Luis tried to make him understand that if he wanted money he had to ask for it, but Gaspar took that instruction as a mere suggestion. When his weekly allowance ran out, he would go into Luis's room and take what he wanted from the drawer, and sometimes he took too much. He didn't ask for help with anything: if he wanted to get something that was out of his reach, he climbed; if one of his buttons fell off, he sewed it back on, and he sewed Luis's while he was at it. That was good, endearing, even. But if he went into La Plata and it got late or he felt tired, he would take a taxi back: it was several kilometres, the taxi was really expensive, and they couldn't afford it. Even worse: sometimes he didn't come back until very late, in the early hours of the morning, and when he arrived and found Luis awake and anxious, he'd ask what was wrong, as if it were the most normal thing in the world for a mentally ill fourteen-year-old to stay out all night. If Luis scolded him, he shrugged his shoulders, not exactly with rebellion or indifference, but with a genuine lack of understanding. He couldn't comprehend why he shouldn't come home late, or why it worried others when he did. He cooked – always simple dishes, but he did it well: pasta with sauce, ham and cheese empanadas, and sometimes he ventured painstakingly into a potato pie, a Spanish omelette, a sponge cake, oven-baked hake with cheese. But he didn't clean the kitchen or change the sheets or clear the table, nor did it occur to him to pitch in on weekends with a mop and bucket. He's a rich kid, Julieta told Luis whenever he got angry.

For some months now, Julieta had been having meetings with lawyers representing Gaspar's mother's family. They had communicated to her that Gaspar's grandparents would not demand custody or visitation. Really, they couldn't intervene in the matter of custody, because Juan had done the paperwork while he was still alive. But Julieta had the feeling, peculiar but distinct, that Juan had bypassed them by giving his son to Luis before he died and that it bothered them immensely, which was why they had mentioned custody for no reason. Bypassed? What do you mean? asked Luis, and she didn't know how to answer. It was an instinct. The lawyers seemed to concede from the start that the boy would not go with his grandparents, like it was a fight they'd already lost. The meetings were held at one of the properties of Gaspar's maternal family – not the main offices, but a smaller branch. The meeting room was bizarre, Julieta thought. In addition to the fireplace, which was already out of fashion with its false firewood covering the gas screen, there was a wood stove and a samovar that looked authentic. It was never cold enough in Buenos Aires to justify such a display of heaters. The walls were covered with what she supposed were hunting trophies, but that were only the horns of different animals. Stags, bucks, she'd been told. Without their heads. The table was oak and very large, and they always had her sit at one end. The lawyers, a man and a woman, were polite and meticulous, but they took a long time, many months, to approve Gaspar's inheritance, the list of property that would belong to him. Whenever she was leaving one of those meetings, Julieta had the feeling she would never see them again. But Gaspar's monthly allowance, which was a lot, continued to appear punctually in the bank. Luis didn't want to touch the money: he wanted to save it for Gaspar's future. Julieta disagreed. She had told him so while the two of them were smoking in bed, talking in low voices so Gaspar wouldn't hear them, though he tended to fall asleep wearing his headphones or with the radio on.

'He's mature, we always say so. He'd be happy to share his money.'

'Maybe later. I don't want their cash. It's a nasty story, but I never knew how to unravel it, or never had the courage to. What am I talking about? That guy, the doctor, kidnapped my brother for his own professional benefit, and who knows what else.'

There was a silence, and Luis finished his cigarette in three drags.

'Do you suspect something?'

'I suspect, but Juan never told me anything. Bradford was a prominent figure, the most respected doctor in the country. Hell, the other day I went to La Plata and I found out they named the new medical school building after him. The guy was weird, and when he lost his hand, he got worse, he was like Narciso Ibáñez Menta, but more British. Like the guy in the Saturday movies.'

'Christopher Lee.'

'The other one.'

'Vincent Price. Luis, he didn't look at all like Vincent Price, he was a totally different physical type. Plus, Vincent Price was American.'

'I'm talking about the vibe he had. Kind of degenerate. He saved my brother's life, and he even went on treating him after he lost his fingers. The way he died was really strange. A guy like that, driving without a chauffeur? And then everything burned because they didn't get there in time to put out the fire, I don't know.'

'I'm surprised your folks didn't fight to keep him. Juan, I mean.'

'Mom tried. My dad didn't want that problem, he said Juan would be better off with that filthy rich family. Dad wasn't exactly a great guy. When I found out they'd bought Juan, I had a fight with my old man and I never spoke to him again. I don't even know if he's alive.'

'They paid him off, then.'

'Those sons of bitches bought my brother. And on top of that, my dad supported me with that money when I was in college. I owe them, too. You have no idea how mad it makes me. That's why I don't want their money. I know Gaspar would share, that's not it. He's got a big heart, like his mother, who was a brave, extraordinary woman. It was a shock when I met her because I didn't think anything good could come from that family. Gaspar's mom was first-rate, and I don't think she knew how my brother came into her family.'

'Does Gaspar know she got you out of the country?'

'I don't know how to talk to him about that. I'm afraid it'll upset him.'

'Why would it? It's his mother, he has a right to know. Well, that's between you and him. Another thing: when they finally give me the full list of his inheritance, it's gonna knock you on your ass. I did an informal investigation. You have no idea. Plus, they don't have any debt, apparently. Gaspar is rich.'

'Just my luck.'

'It's not like it's going to be bad for you.'

Luis growled in the darkness.

'My brother made it very clear he didn't want Gaspar to have any contact with his grandparents. They still haven't asked to see him?'

'Even if they did, you're his father, they have no legal claim.'

'Still, they have all the power.'

'They'll never let go of that.'

That summer they didn't go on vacation, but Luis's ex-wife came to visit from Brazil with her two daughters, one older than Gaspar and one younger. The girls ignored Gaspar, or maybe it was just that they were shy and spoke more Portuguese than Spanish. Luis had raised them as his own, he missed them and wanted to see them, and his ex had agreed to a visit. Luis spent a week taking the girls on all kinds of outings, and Gaspar was grateful he didn't insist he go with them.

By then he was used to the parade of people in the house, and he almost never felt overwhelmed. He was interested in the conversations, the men's way of speaking. Especially Negro and his soccer expressions. This guy made an argument but it hit the post. Hell is when your clean sheet gets ruined with two minutes to go. And his judgements of teams: the rival's rigid defence versus our solid example of the beautiful game. And his accusations: You'll be playing billiards soon, buddy. It reminded him a little of Hugo Peirano; he missed Vicky and Pablo more and more. He hadn't made any new friends, or not friends like them, at least. One of those nights, Negro was playing the guitar and he dedicated a song to Luis's ex, Mónica, a song that said beautiful and terrible things, like how traitors would pay (*Y pagarán su culpa los traidores*), and he sang with a trembling voice and everyone cried and shouted a name and then 'present, now and forever'. He thought that was beautiful. It was beautiful that his uncle hugged the girls and his ex-wife and that Julieta was moved: they seemed like perfect people, Gaspar thought. The moment always came when they put on music and started dancing, and Negro would shout a *sapucay*. And it turned into a party, glasses would break, men would sweat, women would lose shoes and earrings and their make-up would run – the ones who wore make-up, not many – and they'd hug, proclaim their love for each other, just like that, I love you, fucking Negro, and Gaspar felt he couldn't ascend to that level with them. He'd said as much to Isabel. It's like we're all going up a flight of stairs together and at a certain point I say 'this is as far as I go'. And on that step, higher up, they're all happy and I watch them from below. Had he always been like that? It wasn't shyness or reserve or adolescence, as other people thought. He wasn't going to get over it. He could dance when he was alone, he could get emotional in his room with a book, but when the party started he disconnected, the others turned into a movie that he could watch but not participate in. So he acted like he was invisible, which wasn't hard when everyone was drunk. And he withdrew into his room, where he felt the purest kind of relief.

Once, as he was retreating, he'd bumped into Negro.

'You feeling bad, champ?' he asked.

Gaspar said no. Later he heard Negro say to his uncle, 'He's a sad kid.' And he waited for his uncle's agreement, his yes, his disappointment. But Luis surprised him. No, he told Negro. He's not sad. It's his temperament. And even if he was sad, so what? He is the way he is. Getting plastered and shouting to high heaven isn't for everyone. We make noise to fill the hole we have inside.

That night, Gaspar flopped on his bed with his headphones on and thought how he needed to go back to his house, the one where he'd lived with his father. He wanted to go through everything that was left. Had someone taken their things away? His uncle had told him it was all untouched. Why didn't Stephen call? Gaspar preferred him out of his life, but was curious about what had happened to him. And Tali. Was Tali uninterested in him, too?

That night, for the first time since he'd come to Villa Elisa, he had thought without fear – or at least keeping his fear in check – about Adela and the house. He pictured her. Pictured the street. Remembered the walk in the darkness. He closed his eyes and saw her again in the doorway where she had disappeared, waving. The shadows behind her. The darkness behind her. The memory of Adela had made him start to tremble. But not so much. And without nausea.

Tomorrow, he decided, when his uncle woke up, he was going to ask for Vicky's number. He didn't want to do it now, in the middle of the night, when it might scare her family. And he wanted his uncle to be there, in case things went bad.

But they weren't going to go bad, he was sure of it.

*

Not much was left in his house, simply because there hadn't been much in it to begin with. His uncle had cleaned the rooms so that when Gaspar had his re-encounter with the books, objects, clothes, he wouldn't find neglect as well. Going inside made him nervous, but not afraid. Crossing through the doorway of his father's room had been the hardest part, but once he was inside, the musty smell obscured his memories.

What he did avoid was going down Calle Villarreal and seeing the house where Adela had disappeared. He was not ready for that, and he thought he never would be.

In his house, he had a superstitious impulse. He took the clothes out to the patio and burned them, just as he'd seen his father burn his mother's clothes years before. Vicky and Pablo loaded books into boxes while he tended the flames with a shovel and remembered those pants, that shirt with the rolled-up sleeves, the white T-shirt now moth-eaten after years in storage. His father had been cremated. He didn't know where his ashes were: he hadn't wanted to ask. It seemed like enough to burn his clothes.

Vicky and Pablo were now reincorporated into his life. For some time, the contact with Vicky had been only by telephone, but the conversations were always torrential and direct, no evasions, no careful euphemisms. Vicky had been the first: she interrogated him, and told him how at night she still slept in socks because she felt Omaira's head; how she didn't avoid passing by the house on Villarreal, but she had to sneak off to see it, because she wasn't allowed to go; how she'd switched schools, and if her classmates knew who she was, they'd never said so. I want to see you, it's not going to be bad for you, there's a reason we can't make new friends, or have you? Gaspar admitted he hadn't. She came to the house in Villa Elisa happy and anxious; Gaspar thought, as well, that she looked very different, tall, her familiar, heavy hair now very long and cared-for, and her skin so fine you could see tiny vessels in her cheeks. Pablo's return had been more careful. The phone calls were uncomfortable and nervous, but his first visit was an immense relief, one cold afternoon under a blanket on the sofa, like reaching shore and being able to tie up and forget the storm. It was always Vicky and Pablo who came to the house in Villa Elisa, never the other way around. And Pablo's visits would soon become more frequent: his dad, who had gotten rich off the natural gas company, had signed a contract with the province's Ministry of Production, and he would soon be moving the family to La Plata. He was already renting an apartment downtown, which he was using as an office, but soon they'd need a house for the whole family. Gaspar told Pablo he felt like someone was bringing them together. Pablo listened to him, thought about the hand that sometimes touched him in the darkness, and said nothing. Vicky wanted to move there too, once she finished high school, to study medicine at the National University of La Plata. Luis had his reservations about the reunion: he thought if the kids re-formed their group it would only bring back all the drama. He would have preferred them to maintain a friendship of phone calls, birthday parties, an occasional concert. The way they understood each other disturbed him. He talked about it with Isabel, and she surprised him when she said it didn't seem like the best thing to her, either. But they were teenagers: forcing them to separate was no longer an option. Suggesting distance after years of keeping them apart could also be counterproductive.

Gaspar had asked Vicky to go through his father's drawers – he didn't dare. There wasn't much. A few photos of his mother, which Gaspar put in his backpack. Several decks of cards: he kept those, too. She threw away all the expired medication. She found drawers with candles and chalk and little aluminium pots stained with something brown that could be rust or coffee. Gaspar also kept some postcards from Europe and some notebooks. The books went into a suitcase.

While Pablo was washing his hands in the bathroom – Luis still paid for the water and electricity – he admitted to Gaspar that he'd tried to get into the house a few times. He didn't have a key, but raising the shutters didn't seem so hard, nor did climbing over the flat garage roof. But he never could. It was as if the house didn't want me, wouldn't let me in. It ended up scaring me. Plus, the last time I tried to get in, it was later that night I felt the hand, it grabbed my shoulder in the bathroom at my house. And that was the end of that.

Gaspar handed him the towel and leaned against the bathroom wall with his arms crossed.

'I'm sure the house kept you out.'

He felt his scar burn and he rubbed it: he wasn't worried about hiding it in front of Pablo.

'It's been months since I felt the hand grab me. Almost a year.'

'It's not gone. Or do you think it is?'

Pablo shook his head. 'I think it's waiting. I was afraid of seeing you again, too, I told you that. I thought if I saw you, the hand would immediately come and find me again, and it wouldn't let go. But it was the opposite.'

'Let's go,' said Gaspar. He had started to feel a slight twinge in his eye, the sign of a migraine; he had to take something before it got worse, and his pills were in his backpack. Pablo followed him down the bare corridor. They passed the empty room that had once served as a place of punishment; they looked at the hall, which seemed to be waiting for a party, guests, laughing people, everything that had never happened in that house. When they went down the stairs, Gaspar saw that the glass in the window that had wounded him had been repaired; he hadn't noticed before. Who had replaced it? Pablo put his arm around his waist just when he started to shake. Let's go down together, he said into his ear, it's okay.

The care, the constant care; Gaspar was sick of all the protection, which seemed excessive, and now he understood his father and his refusal, the confrontations with his doctors and sometimes with him or Esteban. Still, he could let himself be cared for by Pablo. They understood each other, he trusted Pablo, though he had changed a lot. All three of them had changed, but Pablo's change was more significant because he was homosexual (Pablo preferred to call himself gay, and they were all getting used to that much nicer word), he didn't hide it now, and he had his group of girlfriends from school who went out with him, called him, acted as his companions and his shield against cruel boys. Plus, he wanted to study art, and he painted graffiti. He had slept with several classmates, he said. Watch out, warned Vicky, be careful, you can't imagine how many patients my mom sees at the hospital. Oh, don't be dumb, I'm careful, he replied, plus, it's older people who get infected.

Gaspar went back to his father's room. He paged through the notebooks he was going to take with him. He had the feeling one was missing: he remembered a notebook with drawings, a lot of symbols that his dad went over and corrected very attentively. They weren't doodles; he didn't know what meaning those geometrical signs held, and his father had always lied and said he drew them for fun. You always thought I believed your lies, Gaspar said in a low voice as he opened the backpack. But I was also inside your head. Not so much, I could never break through the barrier, but I knew there was a barrier, Dad, I felt it. Why did you have to put it up? That's what I wonder.

He looked for the notebook in every drawer, even in the kitchen. He couldn't find it. He asked his uncle, who said, I didn't touch anything. I don't know if your dad's friend had a key, I don't know if he took anything. Esteban: Gaspar could imagine him taking the special things, the ones they shared, the secrets they surely kept. The notebooks he did take, though, had some unnerving notes. One said: '"When we call upon the devil with the required ceremonies, the devil comes and we see him. In order not to die, struck down by this vision, in order not to become cataleptic or insane, one must already be crazy." Levi.' So that's what you did. You invoked the Devil. Or maybe his dad was only interested in the subject out of pure boredom. From spending all his time alone in bed with no one to talk to. But no, there was something more, it wasn't boredom. The cuts, the ones he'd given Gaspar and the ones he'd given himself. The night they'd scattered his mother's ashes in the river. The way he could divine things. His father could find what was lost. His father knew when someone was going to die. His father had talked to him about the dead who rode in on the wind. *The dead travel fast.*

His last year of high school, Gaspar discovered the Princesa Cultural Center, just two hundred metres down from his school. The façade was painted red and the paint was recent, because that colour was impossible to miss – it looked like blood had been spilled over the house. Also, the name of the place was in both graffiti and neon, so it could be seen at night. That first time, at seven in the evening with the neon already lit and the music drifting out through the open door, the place attracted Gaspar enough that he ran across the street, ignoring the car horns. It was raining a little, and his black sneakers got wet.

Outside, under the terrace balcony that acted as a roof, a girl was smoking with her leg bent, her foot resting against the wall. She was dark-skinned and wore cut-off jean shorts, a white sleeveless T-shirt, combat boots, and a lot of bracelets on both wrists; some of them shone, glittery like a little girl's, and others were black plastic. Her hair was short and black. Gaspar thought she was beautiful like no other girl he had ever seen. He approached her unabashedly, attracted as if he were suffering from terrible heat and she were melting ice; he had to be fast, decisive.

'Is it open?' he asked, after saying hi.

From inside came a song that talked about skin flying all around. What weird lyrics, thought Gaspar. The lazy guitar seemed very fitting for that evening of humidity and rain.

'For now you can only drink beer at the bar, but there's a poetry reading tonight. And a band is on after that.'

The girl looked at him curiously.

'I never noticed this place before,' said Gaspar.

'It's been here about a year, but we just painted it red so it would stand out. Are you in school?'

'The Normal two blocks from here. I'm behind. I'm a senior, but I'm eighteen already.'

'You repeated a grade.'

'No,' said Gaspar, and didn't explain further.

She was older, he realized. Not much, a couple of years. She must be in college. He hadn't been with many girls, a fact he was ashamed of and tried to hide. There was Belén, an old class-mate. They'd gone to the park and he'd kissed her belly; it had tickled her, and when she moved and the smell from between her legs had reached him, he'd gotten a sudden and somewhat painful erection. He'd tried to lie on top of her and he kissed her behind the ear, but Belén got scared and he stopped immediately. I like you a lot, said Belén, but I don't want to. He felt like his head was pounding, but since she was on the verge of tears, he told her no problem, and said, Sorry, it's just that you're really pretty. Let's go, I'll walk you to the bus stop, okay? And she said yes and soon they were talking about something else, though Gaspar didn't remember what because his erection was hurting and while they were waiting for the bus, he told her he was going to pee and he jacked off quickly and furiously behind a tree, before the curious gaze of a grimy white cat that blinked at him. When he returned, calmer now, Belén told him about her vacation at the Valley of the Moon and how the landscape had looked like *Star Wars*, and then the bus came. He hadn't seen her again. He had slept with other girls after that, but every time it was both memorable and profoundly unsatisfactory; he was sure he should do something else, that it had to be more than just that desperate feeling of haste and joy and then the unease of not knowing if the girl had liked it, if what he did was okay, if he'd put the condom on right, if it was bad to fall sleep afterwards, if he had to stop or if he was allowed to ask to go again, when to ask and when not to. He'd talked to Vicky about it and she just said, 'It's so obvious, Gaspar.' How could it be so obvious if it was so difficult for him?

'Do you have a smoke?' the girl asked.

Gaspar pulled a pack from his hoodie pocket and offered it to her. She looked at it suspiciously.

'Le Mans?'

'I ran out of money. They're my uncle's girlfriend's. She doesn't notice when I steal them. He does.'

'Does he smoke something better?'

'No. Jockey.'

The girl let him light her cigarette. Gaspar looked at her legs. She had visible muscles. The lighter had illuminated her very dark eyes, lined in blue like a punk Cleopatra. She said her name was Marita, and when he told her his, she said she thought Gaspar was a great name. One of the Magi.

'That's what my dad used to say, that's why my mom chose it. Because of the wise men.'

Marita peered at him through the smoke and Gaspar hastened to explain, because he didn't like uncomfortable questions.

'I don't have parents. They died a while ago. I live with my uncle.'

Her face showed no pity or sorrow, she only nodded and murmured, That sucks. She held the cigarette between her lips when she knelt down to tie her boots. And just like that, feigning nonchalance, as if it were as casual as adjusting her long shoelaces, she told him she had seen him go by some nights, running to the bus stop. Do you live far? No, Gaspar replied, in Villa Elisa. I stay around here until late, sometimes.

'Come dancing whenever you want,' said Marita. 'We have parties on Saturdays. I don't imagine you like poetry.'

'I don't know how to dance but I love poetry,' replied Gaspar.

'That's weird,' she said. 'The poetry part. Because no guys know how to dance. Except for gay guys, of course.'

Marita handed him the cigarette for him to finish. The filter was sticky with her lip gloss, but Gaspar didn't mind. He liked the world of girls and women, though he didn't fully understand it. He liked how girls giggled behind their hands, how they wrote on their clothes and shoes and preferred things to be shiny and silver, how they worried about combining colours and decorated folders with stickers of their favourite groups, or with photos of actors protected by strips of Scotch tape. He liked that they cried and worried about smells, the good ones and the bad, and the intensity of aromas, if this girl wore too much perfume, if the imported scent they'd bought at duty-free was incredible or a waste of money, if boys' skin had a smell and whether damp underpants smelled like peaches or fish. He liked that Julieta cursed more than his uncle and that she spent hours at the beauty parlour, and although he didn't understand why a bad haircut made her cry, he felt sorry when he saw her sad, it didn't irritate him (as it obviously irritated his uncle, who would grumble, I really don't get that shit). He liked that Julieta noticed when his jacket zipper broke and that she knew how to fix it; he knew it was better not to argue with her when she'd had a bad day in court. He liked that Vicky would call him up and tell him: I know how to avoid being teased at school. You have to be either good-looking or weird. That's why no one makes fun of you: you're good-looking *and* weird.

Gaspar didn't stay at the Princesa that night, but he decided it would be his spot: he liked it even before he got to know its walls painted red to hide the stains of dampness, the creaky stage, the beer that was never really cold, the big table on iron legs where they sold fanzines, used records, art books with some of the pages loose.

Vicky rested her head on the steering wheel and sighed. I'm so tired I can't even get mad, she said.

Gaspar lit a cigarette for her.

'We'll sit here until the car starts; I've got nowhere to be.'

The move to La Plata was becoming torturous. The apartment Vicky had rented was dark, had no balcony, and the tiny kitchen couldn't fit two people. She wondered what size refrigerator she'd have to buy: the one her father had offered her, an old model that still worked, was too big. She signed the lease anyway: the rent was low, befitting its miserable appearance. At the realtor's office, the owner consoled her by saying the place was well located and convenient for the university.

Vicky had only asked her if the electricity went out in the building or the neighbourhood. If there were blackouts. Gaspar had gone with her to sign the lease, since he was on vacation – and he was alone: Luis and Julieta had gone to Brazil, and he'd decided to stay in Villa Elisa to spend the summer with Marita – and he arched an eyebrow when he heard that question, sensing the anxiety in Vicky's trembling voice. It never went out when I lived there, the owner assured her, except during Alfonsín's programmed blackouts.

Now, as they sat in the car and smoked, Gaspar wanted to know why she had asked about the electricity.

'So it's not true, then,' he said.

'What's not true?'

'That you're over what happened with Adela.'

'I *am* over it. I just have these residual effects. I'm scared of the dark. I can't stand blackouts. When a lamp flickers, I panic. I can't control it.'

Gaspar flicked ash out the window and scratched the scar on his arm. It was hot.

'Can you sleep without socks?'

'What about you? Do you still see Adela in corners?'

'Less often. I told Marita everything.'

'And?'

'She feels sorry for me, I think. I don't care. At least she's not afraid of me.'

Vicky leaned against Gaspar's shoulder.

'I'm happy for you and Marita. She really cares about you, I can tell.'

'Let's go to the Princesa tonight. You have a place now, or

else you can stay with us. Pablo's got his drawings up and Marita told me Andrés Sigal came to see them.'

'Who's that?'

'Don't be ignorant, he's famous. He's a photographer. He directs the photography gallery at the Fine Arts School and he has his own gallery. He's big time.'

'I'm in med school, my friend. Different ball game. Anyway, sure, I'll go tonight.'

The engine finally turned over, and Gaspar thought he should never leave Vicky alone in the dark. He had to make sure she got a phone line soon so she could call him or Pablo if there was a blackout. In summer, the city often had outages: the apartment's owner had been lying. Plus, Gaspar had noticed some disturbing details about the woman. Her socks, for example. They were visible under her pleated and seemingly elegant skirt, and they were men's socks, one of them army green and the other navy blue. The army green one seemed to cover a wound, and he imagined a slash that hadn't come from a cat or the corner of a table, the kind of accidents he could imagine for a woman of her age. Something more like a claw mark. He thought of the hand that touched Pablo. It wasn't cold the way one imagines ghostly hands. It was fevered, a knife heated in fire. A tool to mark with. The woman's make-up was exaggerated, as if to cover up bloodless skin, especially under her eyes, where cheeks start to sag at a certain age. And when she looked at him, Gaspar saw a horrible desire, a kind of envy: that woman would be capable of biting him. Isabel had often told him those sensations he experienced could be auras, manifestations of epilepsy, very personal hallucinations. Though he trusted in Isabel, above all in her good intentions, for some time now, whenever she explained his symptoms, he nodded without believing. He was no longer sure. That woman intuited something, she was hiding something, or else he had provoked something in her that had been asleep, lurking.

And that's why Vicky should never be alone in the dark. If she was alone, she could be caught. Taken, the way Adela had been taken. He couldn't explain this intuition or any other, just as he couldn't explain his aversion to certain houses, certain corners, abandoned lots. In his father's notebook he'd found a fragment of a Neruda poem that had left an impression on him. Julieta liked Neruda – she read poems about love and politics, typical of her. He was a shitty old man, she said, he was awful to women, but what a poet. Gaspar had shown her the poem fragment copied out in his father's nervous but clear handwriting, and she had told him what book he could find it in. Now he had it in his room, atop the towering pile on his nightstand. 'And it pushes me into certain corners, into certain moist houses, / into hospitals where the bones stick out of the windows, / into certain shoestores with a smell of vinegar, / into streets as frightening as chasms. / There are brimstone-colored birds and horrible intestines / hanging over the doors of the houses that I hate.'

Houses that I hate. He hadn't felt hatred in the ugly apartment Vicky had rented. He didn't think it was dangerous, despite the deadened skin its owner was trying to hide. Still, he was going to visit a lot to be sure it was a safe place. He couldn't lose anyone else.

The Moreno Theatre may have had an illustrious name, but it was the only porno cinema in La Plata, and anyone who more or less knew anything about the street and the night understood it wasn't a place for pencil pushers or kids looking to jack off, nor was it for dipping your toes in the water. It had been once, but by 1992, people who wanted to see porn had video stores. And now the theatre was the epicentre of cruising, the place where the city's gay men sought each other out to have sex at any hour, any day – except Monday, when a discreet cleaning was done, testified to by the persistent smell of cheap disinfectant.

'That's where I caught the bug,' said Max, the Princesa's DJ and general sound engineer, while he wiped his grease-covered fingers; he also took care of the precarious maintenance. 'I won't set foot in there again. It's a hospital full of the infected.'

'Well, I want to see what's up, but I'll be careful,' said Pablo. 'You know I double bag.'

'Look, Paulie, if you've got a death wish that's your problem. I'm not taking you and I won't come running if they raid the place. I'm not in the psychophysical condition to be bailing out fags from police stations, I've done that enough. Especially underage kids.'

Gaspar declined the mate Max offered him.

'I'm curious, that's all. And I'm not underage, I turned eighteen months ago. You're getting senile.'

'Well, isn't she sassy? Do what you want, no one can stop a damsel in heat. Don't go alone, take a little boyfriend with you. But you,' he said, pointing at Gaspar, 'don't even think about going with him to experiment. With how pretty you are you'll be gang-raped.'

'Not a chance I'd go in there.'

'This kid is such a hunk, and with that tragic face, it drives me crazy.'

Max had just finished rehanging the bathroom door, which had fallen off several nights before. He wanted to make the place presentable because Andrés Sigal had come in for the second time now, and he was hoping, at least, for a donation. 'Surely the big-name fag could take up a collection for us, the poor cutting-edge queers,' he'd say. Pablo's drawings were now sharing space with photos of transvestite girls who all lived together in a squatter hotel near the station. Andrés, who was a collector, had bought one: the girls were celebrating a birthday around a cake covered with meringue, and they looked happy. It was the only happy photo of the series. Andrés was rich because he took photos of Argentina's tourist spots, and his books were sold in hotels and airports and souvenir shops. In addition to those commercial photos, Andrés had traversed the country several times to document the lives of gay people and transvestites from the time of the dictatorship through the early eighties. On his last visit, he'd talked about wanting to do a mixed retrospective with a little of everything, the photos of Argentina, of gay men, of all the people he had met in almost fifteen years of coming and going.

The Princesa Cultural Center had become a lightning rod of agitation in La Plata. Max and Marita, who were good friends and knew each other from high school, ran the place but were very flexible. The poetry readings overflowed with people. There were local poets who read their own work and others who interpreted poems by famous authors; the Pizarnik and Plath nights were great successes. The space had also given rise to the city's one and only – so far – gay pride march, sparsely attended but intense. Marita, as well, had started to record conversations with Max's HIV-positive friends. She was interested in finding out about how they were treated by their neighbours, their families, their doctors; about their difficulties getting medication; whether they were discriminated against, whether they felt represented by the activists in Buenos Aires, whether they knew about ACT UP. Sometimes Pablo stayed to listen to these conversations, occasionally interrupting with questions of his own. Marita was delighted to have him. She wanted, one day, when the right medication or vaccine was discovered – and she was sure this would happen – to write a book using those testimonials, or to simply publish them as they were. She was studying journalism, and had thousands of plans. One night, after making out on the sofa at the empty house in Villa Elisa, Marita had asked Gaspar why he didn't feel uncomfortable around so many gay guys. Gaspar, toying with her skull earrings, had told her without thinking: I think my dad was gay. Or bisexual, because I know he loved my mom and he had women as lovers, or one, at least. Tali. Catalina.

'Really? And he was open about it?'

'Nothing was open with my dad. But he had a boyfriend, yes, a lover, though they didn't see each other much.'

'You haven't seen the boyfriend again?'

'He disappeared, and I think it's so shitty of him that I don't ever want to see him again. My problem is with him, though, not because he was my dad's boyfriend. It was the opposite: I wanted them to live together.'

'So that's why you're so comfortable.'

'I don't know why I wouldn't be.'

And he wasn't lying: he felt as at ease in the company of gay people as he did with his five-a-side soccer teammates. Sometimes Gaspar thought maybe it was because he couldn't really get close to anyone, and so he found it easier to accept everyone. At the Princesa, too, when the parties made the walls sweat and everyone danced and shouted and clutched their cups of beer, he had to go outside. It's fear of losing control, said Isabel. For many years, because of the chaos you lived with, you needed to be in control, on the alert. Excess could destabilize you, that's what you believe. I'd like to change, he'd told Isabel, but she, as always when he expressed a desire, smiled and stayed silent.

'Gaspar, my love, do me a favour,' said Max, wiping the grease off his right hand. 'Did you bring the cards, like I asked?'

Marita, who was in charge of the kettle – mate water was her obsession, she thought no one else was capable of getting the temperature right – said:

'Don't bug him about that, he doesn't love doing readings.'

'You're so overprotective.'

'Well, maybe I am: My boyfriend's half-schizo and my best friend has AIDS. So fine, I'm overprotective. Don't give me shit.'

'So you're hot for crazies and you're a fag hag. You can't go all Florence Nightingale now. Please. I don't know how you put up with her, Gaspar. Sure, she's pretty, but swarthy chicks like her are a dime a dozen.'

Gaspar told them to quit bickering and took out his cards. Max had to shuffle them and hand them back. The deck hadn't been used much, except for one card, the Hanged Man, which had been handled so much it seemed to come from a different deck. Why had his father touched that one card so much, the strangest card of all, and the one Gaspar found the most frightening?

Pablo wiped off the table so the cards wouldn't get wet. Gaspar took the deck from Max's hands and looked at him before laying them out. Max was serious. His dark eyes were shining, maybe from fever. Marita leaned back on some cushions and Gaspar felt her hand, rings on all her fingers, caressing his back.

'Do you tell me, or do I ask?'

'Ask.'

'I've got some heavy questions.'

Gaspar raised his left eyebrow. It was an expression he'd inherited from his father, and he couldn't help it, though he tried.

'They always are. Heavy, I mean. I don't know anyone who asks dumb questions when the cards are down. That doesn't happen.'

And to himself he thought: Tarot is an old language. He'd read in one of his father's books – skimming through, but he hadn't forgotten this – that the cards hold the secret to something that perhaps has been forgotten. The cards are that secret.

'Ask if I'm going to die of AIDS.'

'Oh, Max,' said Marita, and she stopped rubbing Gaspar's back, as if she didn't want to distract him.

Gaspar was expecting the question, so he didn't react. Whenever he read, which wasn't often, it was always the same: he had the calm of an expert. He chose a simple spread, the one his mother had taught him when he was very little. So little he hardly remembered that lesson. He laid the cards on the table and didn't make any mysterious pauses, because he never put on an act, the same way he couldn't fake the abandon of parties.

'You're going to be okay, Maxima, so I'm going to have less patience with you. Look, down here, it's the only one that matters because it's . . . the future, let's say? The conclusion. And it's the Sun, which is the best card. Of course, you may die of something else.'

Max couldn't hide a tremor in his throat, so it was a few seconds before he spoke. Gaspar's eyes seemed to blink infrequently, like the eyes of certain reptiles, and that fixity gave them a special coldness; it also provoked a certain distrust, as though he belonged to a hybrid species.

'If you're lying, I'll kill you.'

'You won't be able to kill me from your deathbed.'

Max rubbed his eyes with his fingertips and then said:

'Now I want to ask about the breefcake at the grocer's.'

'I can answer that without the cards: put the moves on him and he'll punch your lights out.'

'You've sure got a lot of faith that straight is straight, dollface.'

Gaspar stacked the cards, put them back in the deck, and looked around.

'You don't want me to read for you?' he asked Pablo.

'Not today. Tomorrow, if I see you.'

Of course they would see each other. They saw each other every day. Pablo was studying art and he was already so good in his first year that they'd offered him a position as an unpaid teaching assistant. Gaspar had seen some of his projects and drawings. He was bold and brilliant. If Andrés Sigal gave him a hand, he would be a star.

Pablo thought seven in the evening was too early to go to the theatre, but Julián told him that's how it worked, you went early to avoid the police. The owners paid them off, but sometimes they missed a payment and then the pigs could raid the place, and they were vicious with fags, mocking and violent. Julián was a boy Pablo had met at the Princesa, and with whom he often went dancing at other clubs – less artsy, more fun ones; someone he could be silly and drunk with and kiss random people. He thought Julián was cute and nothing more, but he was the ideal companion for this foray into the theatre, to help him learn how older queers met and found each other, and what it was like to fuck someone faceless in the dark.

There was no one at the door and that seemed strange, but once inside they were greeted by a man half-hidden behind the glass in the ticket window: he was the one you paid. Then you went downstairs, to the theatres. Along the floor where it met the wall there was a tube of neon light: the only light by which to guide yourself from one theatre to another. Julián laughed, a silly and excited giggle, and Pablo felt a fit of anger, the desire to slap him and hightail it out of there. Suddenly he was scared and felt a vague claustrophobia; it was the artificial light, so similar to the light in Adela's house.

There were three theatres, and Julián told him they had to go first into the Wilde and then into what they called the Tunnel. He had never been, but it was the best, people said, you don't know whose dick you're sucking, you don't know anything. Pablo followed him. The Wilde theatre's only light came from the movie being shown, plus two small bulbs to mark the entrance. Some men were fucking on the seats, others were walking along the middle and side aisle, stopping to touch each other, ask for a light, or even chat. It was almost a club thanks to the music from the movie, a hetero porno with girls with plastic breasts, blonde hair, and semen in their eyes, and brutal men with hairy chests, tanning-bed skin, and disproportionate cocks. He lost Julián in the theatre. A man with his jeans unbuttoned came over and told Pablo into his ear to suck it, and Pablo knelt down and obeyed, excited, too, at obeying that thick voice, and while he sucked and the man – much older than him – grabbed his curly hair, he also unbuttoned his pants and masturbated. Much later he would think about whether he had any cuts in his mouth, or why he hadn't looked to see if the man's penis had sores. He got scared whenever he was careless, but once the anxiety passed, he felt desire again. Desire to meet a man on a corner and take him to the plaza and laugh when a passer-by got close, wondering if they'd be reported. Desire to get into a car that stank of semen and shit. Desire to feel a strong chest on top of him, and to spend the whole night drinking wine from the bottle and snorting coke off a plate or a back, the ashtray filled to overflowing.

He found Julián again up near the screen: he was breathing heavily as if he'd been running, and when they kissed, Pablo tasted the cocaine. He asked in a low voice why he didn't share, but Julián didn't hear and started telling him about some bear or silver fox, congratulating himself for getting him to wear a condom. He sounded proud, and Pablo thought it was the worst moment to have to worry about that, and he wondered what it had been like for older people who hadn't given a thought to being careful or dying or getting sick, but it was also true that people used to have to hide in the closet and get married. Had it ever been good to be gay? He turned around, and at the entrance he thought he saw Andrés Sigal, with his fine grey hair, his shirt unbuttoned, and a cigarette in his hand. He should have gone straight for him, but Julián insisted on not changing course, and Pablo thought there would be time to meet Andrés. Everyone said he was crazy about much younger men.

They headed for the Tunnel. Pablo didn't love the name, but he thought if he started to feel claustrophobic again, he could just leave. It was a basement, and it felt subterranean even in the way the sound grew more muffled at each step down. There weren't that many men at first. They had to go down another short flight of steps. But by the time they were halfway down, Pablo could no longer see the stairs. Julián had to help him descend, struggling with the railing, with the bodies. There was no light down there. Nothing. No screen or movie. A furtive lighter revealed bodies that seemed too pale, and it was so dark you couldn't see the walls, as if the basement were infinite.

Pablo stepped backward and someone yanked on his arm, and then he felt the unmistakable adrenaline surge of panic. Later, talking to other friends, he would say that place was really dangerous, people could die in there, the music would drown out their screams, that it was easy to imagine someone with a knife because they didn't search you – a gay serial killer, a fag-murderer, a madman. It would be the easiest thing in the world

611

to kill down there. And he did think that: the place was a trap. But only Gaspar and Vicky knew the truth, because only they could understand. He knew what he'd felt was the ghost hand, that same hand that had lain in wait for him so long in the dark hallway of his old house, the fevered hand that wanted to take him, and that, he thought, could leave a permanent mark if it held on too long. These days he was safe, living in the family's La Plata apartment that his mother proudly described as having 'Rationalist' architecture and 'Slovenian oak floors'. He hated it, though, and wanted to move, but couldn't afford to yet. He hated his little brother, such a spoiled brat, and the smell of frustration in the air. But he had to admit, at least the hand didn't wait for him in its hallways.

In the Tunnel, in the movie theatre's black basement, the hand – which could have been Julián's, though he was never able to convince himself of that rational possibility – was the same one he'd thought had left him alone. And now, instead of hair and hide and asses, he saw a man on the floor with his head between another's legs, but the other man was a desiccated cadaver: a man had his head between death's legs. He saw a broken bottle in the hands of an eyeless woman. He saw a man with a rope around his neck: he was missing an arm. He didn't want to see any more. The tunnel was a festival of the dead, it was one more room in the house that had taken Adela. He couldn't remember if he had screamed, surely he had and the music had drowned out that humiliation, but he ran up the stairs, he fell, he felt someone dragging him back down, and he kicked a stranger in the darkness, and he also ran down the aisle to the exit, and if anyone looked at him strangely he didn't notice, nor if anyone sounded a warning, insulted him, or expressed concern. There was nothing but the exit and Calle 2 with its linden trees and tired people heading to or from the station. He ran across the street oblivious to the traffic, and on instinct he called Gaspar from the public phone on the corner with the only token he had left. He prayed his friend would be there while he dried his tears and crouched down in the booth, trying to control the tremor in his legs and the pounding of his heart, which wouldn't let him speak.

'Take a taxi,' Gaspar told him. 'I'll pay for it. We'll call your folks and you can stay here. Take a taxi now.'

Pablo never went back to the Moreno Theatre. Six months later Julián was infected and there was a string of hospital visits. In the hallways, Pablo would remember that basement, the armless man, the mummy with an erection. Julián died quickly, within months: he spent his final days talking in a little boy's tiny voice about the toys of his childhood. They held the wake at the only funeral home in the city that accepted people with HIV. Max, the DJ at the Princesa and Marita's friend, died three weeks later. She cried under the blankets in Gaspar's bed, and she was angry, furious, and a little scared: she almost never wanted to have sex, or she asked for exaggerated safety measures.

'You lied to him,' she said to Gaspar one afternoon when they brought flowers to Max's grave. 'You told him he wasn't going to die of AIDS.'

'What else was I going to say?'

'He thought he was going to survive. He talked about the Sun, said it was the best card. Was that a lie, too?'

'It is the best card, but it was inverted for him. When they're dealt upside down, they mean the opposite.'

Marita sat on a gravestone and dried her tears.

'I don't want you to lie to me, don't ever lie to me.'

Gaspar said okay and kissed her mascara-streaked cheeks, but he thought: sometimes you have to lie to take care of someone. I already lie to you. I hide things. And I'm going to keep lying to you.

Pablo had asked Gaspar for a reading after Max's wake. It said the same thing as his tests: he wasn't in danger. It was true that he was careful, that after the theatre scare he'd decided not to go for any more dangerous encounters, but he was amazed to be the only healthy person in the hurricane of illness. That winter had seen the deaths of two more friends who frequented the cultural centre. One was older, around twenty-six. The other had just started college. At the march that Marita organized with Max before he died, some people had been so weak they attended in wheelchairs. They still sang and took the microphone on the stage in front of the Ministry of Health; they always finished by cursing, and then it was back to the singing and the sequins in the air.

That winter, too, Gaspar's childhood home had finally been rented out. A young family with kids. The rent was high. It's a pricey house, Luis would say, because it's an exceptional house. Your dad didn't make much effort in its upkeep, but still, it doesn't have any major problems, not even dampness.

Those months had been so sad and intense that Gaspar had paid almost no attention to Julieta's pregnancy, which was an event from the start because the news had led him to fight with his uncle. Gaspar had asked him: Aren't you a little old to have a baby? And the question had unleashed an argument full of reproaches (You want a normal kid, huh, the crazy son's not enough for you?), and taunting (You going to take him to soccer with a cane?). The fight had escalated, and in one of the fits of rage that sometimes consumed him, Gaspar had thrown a pitcher of pomegranate juice: the red liquid had spattered the floor and tablecloth. Luis had demanded he clean it up, and Gaspar had refused with a slam of the door.

Julieta wanted to be a mother: she was young, but not so young, and if she was going to have kids the time was now. That information had not been shared with Gaspar, but after all, he could have and should have assumed it. His anger passed the next day, and he apologized so much that Luis told him to hush. At least congratulate me, goddammit, you sure can get jealous, if you only knew how much I love you. Gaspar wasn't jealous, he didn't think. He hated change: that was it. If only things could always be the same, if only this house, so like a port in a storm, could be standing forever, and always for us, no additions, no time, no future. That the baby was actually twins was a strange bit of news: two babies would be expensive and labour-intense, and meant Julieta would have to stop working for much longer than she'd planned.

The babies were born by Caesarean and baptized Salvador and Juan. Gaspar got dizzy when he realized he felt nothing but a vague tenderness for them, and a whole lot of boredom. I'm never going to have kids, he thought, when he held them and wanted only to hand them back, to get away from the smell of milk and the excited smiles, from the money worries and the price of disposable diapers, from the tears. What was he going to do if Marita wanted a baby? They had never talked about it, and lately they weren't having much sex, either, because she was paranoid. Or something more. He didn't know. He understood she was in mourning for her friends and it was difficult; he didn't pester her. If she got the idea to get pregnant, he thought, better for her to tell him, because he would have to leave her. No matter how much he loved her. When the twins came home they turned out to be fussy and annoying, and, in Gaspar's opinion, they took up too much room even though they were so small. Despite the silent request in his uncle's and Julieta's eyes, he decided not to take care of the babies for one second, which meant spending less and less time at home. He had plenty of places to stay, even to sleep. His uncle wanted him to go to college, but Gaspar didn't know what to study or why he should even study anything, and he spent all his time at the Princesa. Pablo had practically moved in there. We've both been exiled by babies, he said to Gaspar one day. My brother is evil incarnate, and my mom doesn't want me near him because she's afraid I'll infect him. The Princesa was a squat, and the owners had never turned up to reclaim the place. Marita had investigated, because a house so close to downtown was very valuable and she didn't want to be kicked out. Nor, she said, did she have the energy to dig in and defend the place. There were owners, she had their names, but as long as they didn't complain, the house was there for them to use.

Gaspar had been unsettled by that information about the owners. Just like the house on Villarreal: no one claimed it. He had never sensed anything disturbing in the Princesa and he trusted his instinct, but he didn't much care for ghost owners, he didn't like houses no one wanted that beckoned to visitors with their windows like half-closed eyes, houses like whores showing their legs on the corners, their mouths red and their lights neon, the sickly light that was the same as the lights at the hospital where their friends died and where Vicky did her internships and where he'd said goodbye to his father, whose eyes, at the end, had been black like beetles, and like Omaira's, who still came back to touch Vicky's feet at night, black and shining like insects, like the bugs that hit against the patio lights at the Villa Elisa house on summer nights. He had to think less, sometimes, deactivate the connections. Marita always wanted him to smoke pot – it'll relax you, she'd tell him.

Pablo was finishing his latest project: drawings and photos of lovers with the faces of poets. Gaspar helped him make the masks and was also teaching him to read poetry. I want them all to be thirty and under because the project's going to be called '30 under 30', and there'll be thirty guys, some in photos, others in drawings. Now that I think about it, I could really include some women.

Gaspar had started researching. He knew of several poets who had died before the age of thirty, but he had to hit the library to find more. His father's books also helped a lot. His list for Pablo grew every day. Sylvia Plath, she was thirty, she just makes it. She killed herself by sticking her head in the oven, her kids were in the next room and she closed the door off with tape, towels, and rope so the gas wouldn't reach them, and she left them milk. Why'd she kill herself? asked Vicky, who didn't come to the cultural centre much because medicine was a demanding programme. Sylvia had just gotten separated, and apparently that made her really depressed. Emily Brontë also just squeaks through, thirty, she died of tuberculosis. Keats. He was my dad's favourite, and I love him too. He died of tuberculosis when he was twenty-five. I had a hard time reading him when I was younger, but now he's one my favourites. Chatterton, I think he was seventeen, he killed himself with arsenic. Shelley drowned at thirty, he was the husband of Mary Shelley, the one who wrote *Frankenstein*. Novalis, tuberculosis, twenty-eight. There's one who's older, thirty-five, he fell down when he was drunk, in London, but hold on, he was closeted and a cousin of Bosie, Lord Alfred Douglas, Oscar Wilde's boyfriend. Lionel Johnson was this drunk's name, he was really crazy. I like him a lot. A book of my dad's had a selection of his poems chosen by Yeats. You don't know Yeats? He won the Nobel. Doesn't matter. Use Lionel Johnson, he's old, but he fits. Asunción Silva shot himself in the heart, he made his doctor mark the place he had to shoot. What an ass the doctor was, if he didn't realize, said Vicky. Georg Trakl, twenty-seven, died of a cocaine overdose, can you believe it, in those days? Teresa Wilms Montt, a high-class Chilean girl. She killed herself in Paris at twenty-eight. I found her in the library and I photocopied everything. You see one photo and you fall in love. There's one from around here, too, from La Plata, this is really crazy, apparently they found his body mummified at the Tolosa Cemetery. His name was Matías Behety. He died crazy and drunk, but they put the mummy in the chapel for a while and he had believers, apparently he could cure illnesses and they set up a kind of altar to him. He was also over thirty, but just tell me the story isn't fantastic. I looked up his poems, but the poor guy was really bad. Why don't you quote the poems, the good ones, I mean? Trakl has some tremendous ones, really dark. You could put the photos or drawings and a quote. Yeah, said Pablo, only I don't want it to be too systematic. Quotes if they fit and from the ones that make sense. You choose the quotes for me; you have a clearer idea. Then I'll veto them or not. And don't bring me older ones, even if they have really good stories. Especially not that one about the mummy, I don't want to hear anything about mummies.

'I don't know if you're going to have enough poets, but there are painters, too,' said Gaspar.

'I know about those,' said Pablo. 'And I already thought about it. I don't want them. Only poets. And I especially don't want musicians, that's too obvious and really tacky.'

I'll keep looking, said Gaspar, and he spent nights with Marita asleep beside him, underlining dead poets, most of them suicide victims. Sometimes he read to her in bed and she asked him to repeat some parts. Aren't you going to use Rimbaud? she'd asked. He was punk. And he was beautiful, like you. Gaspar snorted. He wants them to be younger, all thirty or under, plus, there's a famous photographer who already did a similar project using Rimbaud's face.

'Oh, so he's copying,' said Marita.

'He calls it "citing". They're kids in New York with Rimbaud's face,' Gaspar told her. 'Some of the photos are taken in an abandoned building near a river. They're wearing Rimbaud masks and they're really skinny. Some are shooting up heroin in their arms, others are reading a newspaper, others are walking around the city at night. Pablo has the photos. They're really good.'

'What's the photographer's name?' asked Marita, and she pulled the blanket over her bare legs.

'I don't remember, but he died of AIDS a few years ago.'

'Ugh, no, enough with all the dying,' she said, and asked him to turn off the light. When Gaspar tried to caress her belly, she turned over with a low complaint, as if she were sleepy. He knew it wasn't tiredness or a bad mood, it was rejection. And how was he going to manage that rejection, he wondered. It would pass, it was a phase, she didn't love him any more, everything he wanted to ask her was left hanging in the darkness of the room, in the flickering bedside light, in the unease of two bodies together that wanted to be apart.

Marita had yelled at him during a fight, telling him she had a right to be in their meetings, after she had put up with so much from him. Gaspar only half-understood the meaning of the reproach, but he knew it wasn't jealousy. Marita was, as his uncle said, extracting her pound of flesh. But he couldn't let her come to his meetups with Vicky and Pablo. They were theirs. Those who weren't with us are against us, he again cited his uncle, who had apt phrases for everything: he was the most old-fashioned and the most modern guy in the world, thought Gaspar. And

Luis had never extracted any flesh, not after years of taking care of him, years of dealing with a crazy nephew and neurologists, psychiatrists, diagnoses, schizophrenia, epilepsy, hallucinations, and now this limbo – stabilized, it was called. He was stable, so balanced that Luis had dared to start his own family.

After the first few months, Luis had stopped asking Gaspar to help with the twins. The meaning behind that wasn't so good – Luis trusted Gaspar except in one respect: every once in a long while, but with real ferocity, Gaspar got angry. And when he got angry, he broke things and hurt himself and was unstoppable, strong – there was something of the terrified animal about him. He had kicked in the wardrobe, which still had the holes. Another night it was all the dishes, after a fight that wasn't even about anything important. He had thrown his own clothes out into the street, and one time he'd intentionally hurt himself in front of his uncle: sitting at the table during an argument, nervously tapping his fork, he had suddenly stabbed the utensil into his own hand. Isabel, the psychiatrist, talked about anger management, but hadn't recommended anything as being urgent. 'My daughter screams that she hates me, quit your bitching, he's a great kid,' Gaspar had overheard one night during a barbecue; Negro talked too loud when he was drunk. So far Gaspar hadn't gotten violent with anyone except himself. But sometimes, when he was coming back from swimming or from Marita's house or from the soccer field, it occurred to him that he could insult someone in the street just because, start a fist fight to get the release. The desire to break something or someone was sometimes like the desire to run, or like thirst: urgent. Soothing.

The house was big enough to have privacy, in any case. In the spacious backyard, Luis and some construction worker friends had built a small enclosed porch, nothing fancy, but well made.

Since the parties at the house had grown less frequent after the babies were born, Gaspar had taken it over, and no one objected. It was his studio apartment, warm in winter and cool in summer: the porch had a heater and a fan. He brought out his mattress, his stereo, he took one of the small TVs, his books. It became a much more convenient place to be with Marita, who had left some of her things there. Underwear, a pair of pants, pads in the nightstand, all with her little touches: the pants with black hearts drawn on with marker, the underpants white and cotton, the pads inside a black faux velvet pouch so no one could guess what it held.

There, on that double mattress in the studio, the heater on and the window cracked, Vicky, Gaspar, and Pablo would gather whenever they could, which was often. Marita was not invited to those meetings. They sat and remembered and talked about things that were still going on now. When they were together, it wasn't bad for them to remember. Sometimes, when the memories got very intense, Gaspar had to take a deep breath and announce that he was stopping, because otherwise he would feel the horrible caress of a fear that paralysed him, that drove him into bed, that even fixed his pupils. A neurologist had explained how some epilepsies had symptoms that were only mental, like the sensation of fear – sometimes of euphoria – and of déjà vu, and sometimes the fear was paralysing. They had never found definitive signs of epilepsy or a brain injury in Gaspar. The tests were always questionable, indeterminate. He took medication erratically – mostly, he pretended to take it. Vicky got mad – Doctor Vicky, the rational one. For a long time migraines used to be diagnosed as epilepsy, she told him, and you have them really often, too often. True, but his father had suffered from migraines, his uncle did too, and neither of them was epileptic.

Still, they didn't talk about that. They talked about Adela and about the house. It had recently been demolished with authorization from the owners, who had never managed to sell it and clearly never would. Vicky had gone to the site several times; her parents still lived a few blocks away. There was some graffiti on the only wall that was still standing, but not much. The ruin scared everyone. It had the look of a place where something bad has happened: an expectant air. Evil places wait for evil things to reoccur, or else they seek it out.

'It's like a magnet,' said Pablo, who had walked by it on a visit to Vicky's parents. 'It always was.'

And Gaspar said he would rather avoid visits to his old neighbourhood. He felt bad about Hugo and Lidia Peirano, because he missed them. I don't want them to think I'm ungrateful, he told Vicky, and she reassured him. Call them every once in a while. That's enough for them. Gaspar sometimes felt about the Peiranos the same way he did about Esteban or Tali: he didn't understand why he'd stopped seeing them. Or why they'd left, like Betty, Adela's mother. As if his father had ordered everyone not to bother him.

Gaspar had taken a sheet of the very large sketch paper his uncle used for his designs. And there, little by little for the past year, they'd been reconstructing the house they had seen when Adela disappeared. Pablo sketched it out. It had taken them some time to remember where the shelves were. The doors. The staircase. The piano. The old clothes. The medical books. What could those books be, and why were they there? One was green, said Vicky. Pablo remembered it as sky blue. In the drawing they didn't colour it. They wrote beside the sketch: 'uncertain colour'.

'Write that it wasn't red,' Vicky said once. 'We can at least narrow it down.'

She had recently started to talk about the buzzing and the voices she had heard. It was hard to remember what they'd said, but she remembered certain tones. An authoritative voice, a frightened voice, a monotonous voice.

Pablo talked about the hand that had touched him in the house. On his back, especially. And his arm. Always his arm. Maybe the hand that grabbed him in hallways wasn't a ghost hand, but a memory that materialized, thought Vicky.

'I saw, you heard, Pablo felt,' said Gaspar. 'We're going to get somewhere with this.'

Vicky, leaning against the wall, put on an album she liked and said:

'We're not going to find Adela, Gaspar.'

He touched the drawing, the blueprint, and clicked his tongue in displeasure because it seemed incomplete. He didn't answer Vicky. They all thought it was possible to find her. Otherwise they wouldn't have been there, recalling the steps in the darkness with the buzzing in their ears.

'Oh,' he told Pablo, changing the subject. 'I found two more poets. Rupert Brooke, who died of an infection in the war when he was twenty-six. World War One. They called him the handsomest man in England, look up his photos. Did you read *This Side of Paradise*? Well, the title is from a poem of his. You guys don't read enough. He was gay or bisexual. And Wilfred Owen, he was younger, twenty-five, and he died a week before the war ended, seriously. He's great.'

'Where'd you find them?'

'In a book of my mom's about art and World War One. It has some incredible paintings. It's a really sad book.'

He hadn't been surprised when he found out, because Marita had been looking for an excuse for months. Gaspar hadn't known what to do, so he decided to go running. He'd had the same circuit for a long time now, out where the paved streets of Villa Elisa ended and the dirt roads began, first with weekend houses on both sides, and then empty fields, and then small farms until it was open countryside. Now he was slowly drinking water before heading back, sitting in the grass. He'd seen it coming. She never wanted to go out with him any more, or, if she finally did agree, suddenly she got a headache or she was cold and wanted to stay home. She had also yelled at him over the phone after a silly argument over some albums he had forgotten to return. Fucking kid, she had called him, trying to hurt him. She wanted to make him mad. And now Gaspar knew why. He hadn't been surprised to find out she was cheating on him. What did surprise him was his own rage. He barely knew the boy in question. His name was Guille. Gaspar knew he was with Marita because he followed them. He'd seen them drinking beer at the Meridiano bar. Guille was the son of someone important, Gaspar wasn't sure who, a politician, a legislator. Tall and dark, he wore military coats and combat boots and Gaspar thought he looked more Nazi than punk. He knew him the way everyone knew each other in La Plata: from going to pick up tickets to get into clubs on Calle 8, from shows, from protests, even from the Princesa. He didn't like or dislike him, he'd never given a thought to the guy. Until now, when imagining him with Marita made him crazy with jealousy. He'd seen them kiss at the bar. Guille put his fingers under Marita's shirt, a black-and-white-striped one that Gaspar knew well. She'd spray it with her favourite perfume, Calvin Klein Obsession, which was expensive, so sometimes she'd get her dad's friends to buy it for her at duty-free when they travelled to Uruguay. Still, sometimes the shirt stank of grilled meat, because Marita's house had poor ventilation and the smell of food would often impregnate her clothes if she left her bedroom door open. Guille's other hand rested on her jeans, some very tight ones Gaspar hated because they were hard to take off. He didn't touch her hair, the dumbass. Marita's hair smelled like the rain on dry earth.

He hadn't been able to sleep after seeing them, and that's why he was running now, wide awake and exhausted, his knees a little shaky and his chest closed off like an asthmatic's. He'd wanted to run until he passed out, but his body didn't work like that. It wasn't weak. He went back home thinking about whether he should fight Guille or call Marita, but when he got in the shower and the hot water hit the back of his neck, he felt a ferocious urge to hurt himself. He hadn't been able to keep Marita with him. She knew it didn't make sense to stay with a crazy, sick man, a ruined person. What could he give her? They didn't even get drunk together, he and his pills kept her from having fun; he often had to go to sleep early because he was dead tired. He talked to her about poets and his childhood in an empty house. He'd gone with her to bury her friends because he knew all about that, about death and friends who were never coming back. He hit his forehead against the bathroom tiles and the pain gladdened him, filled his body with euphoria, so he kept going until he saw blood mixing with the water. He got out of the shower and looked at himself in the mirror, his forehead wounded, his pupils dilated, his longish hair dripping on to his shoulders. He gave the medicine cabinet a punch, and another, until it shattered, and then he pulled out the glass to cut himself. He'd read that it had to be a vertical cut in the inner arm, it wouldn't work on the wrists, you didn't hit any arteries there.

He had started sawing at his skin when Luis came into the bathroom.

'Gaspar, what are you doing?' he cried, and grabbed the shard of glass from Gaspar's hand. Gaspar flew into a rage and tried to hit him, but Luis was fast and grabbed him from behind, squeezing his belly until he couldn't breathe, immobilizing him, and then dragged him out of the bathroom. With a single movement he picked up Gaspar's pants and shirt. He didn't mention the cut on his arm or what he had seen. He didn't say suicide, didn't talk of attempts, nothing. He only said: Gaspar, dry off and get dressed. Then meet me in the kitchen.

Gaspar obeyed, but he was furious. When he came into the kitchen, he grabbed the wine bottle that was on the table and hurled it at the floor. The glass flew everywhere. Julieta came out of the bedroom carrying one of the babies.

'What the fuck is going on?' she shouted.

'Nothing, we're working it out,' said Luis in a calm voice.

'Control that brat, you hear me?' Julieta slammed the door and Luis sighed deeply.

'What?' said Gaspar. 'You afraid to argue with her? You're chickenshit. That's why you ran away from this country, isn't it?'

Luis pushed Gaspar into a chair and then sat down facing him across the table.

'You're not going to piss me off, Gaspar. You're not even going to get a rise out of me. You don't know what I went through and what I didn't, and your opinion about my decisions doesn't matter to me. Not in the slightest. If you're trying to get me to lay a hand on you, know this: I will never, ever hit you. You can call me a coward for hours if it floats your boat.'

Gaspar brought both hands to his head and suddenly, before Luis could stand up and move to stop him, pounded the table with his wounded hand, over and over, hard, and Luis stopped him when he was about to start hitting his head again. He embraced him from behind and asked him into his ear to calm down, the way he'd done when Gaspar was younger. But it was harder to restrain him now that he was a man, the two of them the same height and Gaspar in extraordinary physical shape, with all the strength of a trained athlete.

'What do you want, son?'

'I want someone to beat the shit out of me,' said Gaspar, and although his voice came from a hardened throat, though his voice was thick, he wasn't crying and he wasn't going to cry. 'To be beaten to death, that's what I want. I killed a girl, I deserve it all. Marita left me, she's with another guy, I'm a piece of shit.'

'You didn't kill anyone. This again?'

Luis grunted and let go of Gaspar, who rested his hands on the table and stayed quiet.

'You brought her to the house. But to go from there to thinking you killed her – how many times with the same thing, Gaspar? Well, in this house you will not be punished for what you didn't do. You can go get your ass kicked over some girl if that's what you want. You're not going to lack for girls. Are you really that mad? You really love her?'

Gaspar got up to get a bottle of water from the fridge and held it against his head. Then he poured two glasses. He was shaking. Luis asked him for wine. They drank in silence for a while.

'We all screw up, son. I cheated on Mónica, and you can't imagine how much I loved her. You might just end up forgiving Marita.'

'If she didn't want to be with me, she could have broken up with me a long time ago. Two-timing me is an asshole move.'

'Don't be so hard on her. Life is different in practice.'

It was getting dark outside and Luis said he was going to cook something, if Gaspar wanted to eat. Gaspar decided to wait for the food in a lounge chair, looking up at the night sky.

His head had started to hurt and, as always before a migraine, he was having minor hallucinations. Right now, for example, the tenuous light of the stars was producing a strange reflection, a kind of furrow that shook and opened, the first flower. The black flowers that grow in the sky. Suddenly, his father's presence was so overwhelming that Gaspar could sense him standing there behind him, but he wasn't afraid. He raised his good hand to see if he could feel his father touch it.

Gaspar fell asleep on the lounge chair and didn't wake up even when his uncle put a blanket over him before eating his dinner, alone, at the kitchen table. Julieta hadn't wanted to come out of her room. She was really angry.

When he woke up and went inside to the sofa, the house smelled of grass, milk, and Julieta's perfume. His headache was aggressively making itself known behind his right eye; his face was numb and he could barely extend his fingers, but still, he felt a kind of euphoria.

He heard his uncle's unmistakable steps headed to the bathroom; he had to cross the living room to get there.

'What are you doing there? You startled me.'

Instead of going back to bed, when he came out of the bathroom his uncle brought a glass of wine from the kitchen. He couldn't sleep either. He didn't turn on the lamp: the moon illuminated the living room, and the patio light was on and the curtain was open.

Gaspar reached his arm out towards Luis. It was the arm with the mark, the dark scar of a deep wound.

'This wasn't an accident, Uncle Luis. Dad did this to me.'

The wine glass froze halfway to Luis's mouth.

'He did what to you?'

'He cut my arm with glass. He bit me, too. Pablo is the only one who knows.'

'You fell in your house, you smashed into the window, Gaspar.'

'No. That's the lie I told. I covered for him. He didn't ask me to, though, he didn't give a damn. Well, I don't know: maybe he did care. Sometimes I think he needed to do this to me.'

'Needed to, dear God. What are you saying?'

'It has a shape, see? I remember how he gave it a shape. He moved my arm like he was drawing the cut. He didn't stop even when the glass hit the bone. He was like that, and maybe I'm like that too.'

Luis got up from the sofa and sat beside Gaspar to hug him, but he found that the scarred arm, extended as it was, kept him from getting close. That, and Gaspar's eyes, which wanted no comfort. After a while, Luis spoke. He wanted details. He wanted to know how much of this Gaspar had told Isabel. He didn't doubt his nephew. For Gaspar, the confession brought no relief. Quite the contrary. Now his scar was burning, and he could well imagine his father's contemptuous expression as he called him lazy, and a traitor. Especially a traitor. He felt he had denounced his father.

Vicky liked that summer at the hospital, the first of her internships. She even preferred being at the hospital to going to school, despite the tension and the many sleepless hours and that fevered state of forced insomnia. Some of her colleagues took stimulants – amphetamines, most of them; coffee, everyone; cocaine, some – but she had learned that after a while the lack of sleep became a kind of burning pilot light: she was alert, she smouldered and conserved energy. There was no need to stoke the fire.

The hospital was short on gauze and gloves, its mattresses were old and many stank from the dampness of years, and some of its rooms had cracks and leaks. The staff worked well nonetheless, though on early Saturday mornings they often had to make room for the drunks and knife-fight victims in the hallways, and they sometimes had to argue with patients' friends and family whom no one controlled or stopped from barging in from the ER waiting room, sometimes violently. The head doctor was a young man, very arrogant and very attractive. Some months back, Vicky had caught his attention after a strange afternoon. A young woman had come in with a drooping eyelid, difficulty swallowing, and a numb face. One of her colleagues said it could be facial paralysis. The head doctor was leaning towards a cerebrovascular accident, when the girl added that she was hypertensive and her head sometimes hurt. Then Victoria had a certainty that was so clear she even raised her voice to argue in its favour. It's myasthenia, she said. The others didn't overrule her, but they did rule out starting the exploration there, because, said the head doctor, it was statistically the least likely possibility. It's what she has, insisted Victoria, and she was emphatic. When she saw she was about to lose the argument, she asked the patient if she saw double. The girl said yes. That she'd thought she needed glasses, or maybe she was just tired. Vicky had a very simple idea. Let's do a radiograph of her chest, she said. Myasthenia can be caused by a thymoma. If she has a thymoma, we'll know I'm right. And it's just a radiograph, two minutes, it's routine.

There was something about her insistence and the specificity of her questions (whether the girl had trouble speaking, pronouncing certain sounds, for example; whether sometimes she got very tired at night, to the point where she couldn't move her arms) that pierced through the head doctor's barrier of scepticism, and he ordered the radiograph. In effect, it showed an enlarged thymus. Victoria received congratulations that made her feel euphoric, and only later did she think about how her correct diagnosis was a catastrophe for the patient, and she hadn't even explained to the girl what the discovery meant. Later, when she told Pablo the story, he replied that when it came to that part of medicine, empathy, Vicky wasn't so advanced. She gave him a shove, offended but also really hurt, because there was some truth in what he said. She had trouble seeing the people behind the pathologies. Her mother had told her maybe she should specialize in a scientific branch of medicine – like your sister, who's going to do pharmacology. Vicky couldn't and didn't want to force warmth. She didn't believe it was her job. She had to be efficient and accurate in order to heal. Let someone else take care of drying the tears and calming the panic: she was too busy.

The correct diagnoses kept happening. Not like clockwork, but often enough to make her colleagues alternate between admiration and envy, to make her boss veer between aggression and familiarity, and to make news of her 'ability' spread through the hospital, gaining her the nicknames 'little witch' and 'Dr Crystal Ball'.

Victoria liked it, but she was also disturbed. She felt like her ability came from an irrational place, and had nothing to do with applying deductive methods. Every time she got a diagnosis right – and the conditions she diagnosed weren't always bad: it was just as common for her to find inoffensive cases that only appeared serious as to realize that a child who seemed to be having an asthma attack actually had heart failure – she felt like her head went dark. A momentary blackout, the reverse of an illumination, and then she just knew, without a doubt. Many nights after that kind of diagnosis she had trouble sleeping, or if she did sleep, she dreamed of the house or Adela. Her dreams about Adela were not horrible, strictly speaking. Her friend would appear in the ER, for example, complaining of phantom pain in her arm. In the dreams she was a woman and looked different, she'd grown up along with Vicky. It couldn't be a coincidence. She knew the house had taken things from her – her friend, first and foremost, but other things too. She felt like that distance she maintained with her patients was another consequence of the house, a certain empathy she had lost that night in order to fend off a mental collapse like the one Gaspar had suffered, and was still suffering. Maybe the house had given her this ability. Sometimes she thought it was as thanks for having given it Adela. After she made a diagnosis, she had to sleep not just in her usual socks, but also beneath a sheet: without a doubt, that night she would feel Omaira's dying head under her feet. It wasn't the only unpleasant memory, but she could manage them all.

It wasn't just Adela who appeared to her in dreams. She also dreamed about Betty. Sometimes she turned up in the ER like her daughter. Vicky wasn't afraid of her. Awake, she even wished Betty would reappear in real life. Nothing more had ever been heard from her. The police hadn't looked for her, they thought she had left voluntarily, but where had she gone? It's so easy to disappear, thought Vicky. They often received patients in the ER who had no friends, no family, no past. They were found in the street unconscious, sometimes from hunger, sometimes from alcohol, sometimes from some illness. She remembered one woman with a terminal case of cancer that had never been treated. She wasn't exactly a vagrant. She had left her house, she told Vicky, when she'd been diagnosed with the untreatable disease. That had been at least a year before. The woman wasn't very clear on time. She was disoriented, with cerebral metastasis. She had simply packed a bag, taken out some money, and left. She didn't want to say what place she had left or give the name of anyone who could be with her in her final days. She spoke with distance but affection of her children and husband. She said she had been in the newspaper and on TV and that looking at her photograph had made her laugh, because she was another person now: since this bug got in me (she called the cancer a 'bug'), I've been a different person. People saw the photo on TV, then looked right at me and didn't recognize me. That happened, she said, at service stations.

Disappearing was easy. The woman hadn't given any names. She didn't have ID. No one thought it necessary to conduct tests that would determine her identity. She was lucid enough. She didn't want to be found, and that was her right. Her folks would process their pain as best they could. Vicky hoped that some-day Betty would appear too, and she wondered if she would rec-ognize her. Once, when they were chatting on the patio of her childhood home, the dogs playing on the concrete, her mother had admitted that she was also waiting for Betty. And that Hugo, Vicky's dad, had thought he saw her once as he was clos-ing up the pharmacy. He called out to her, but that woman who looked like Betty had run away. Hugo had been unsettled by a small but ghostly detail: the woman who ran away was barefoot.

Gaspar went to visit Vicky often. He was keeping strange schedules now too. He'd started to work filming quinceañera parties and weddings, and sometimes he came by in the early morning, tired but awake, and they had coffee at the hospital café. Once, she had asked him if he wasn't disturbed by being in a hospital. Because of your dad. And your own past. I was nervous when so many gay guys started getting sick and you went to visit them, I thought you were going to have an episode. I'm not that obvious, Gaspar had told her. Plus, he added as he spread butter on toast, the times when my dad was in the hos-pital were nowhere near the worst ones with him.

One of those mornings over breakfast, Vicky had gotten a strange feeling and thought it was the moment to try to diagnose Gaspar and his elusive epilepsy. She didn't have to do anything special, touch him or hold his hand – she didn't even need to say anything to the patient if she didn't want to. She let the blackout come while Gaspar poured milk into his coffee and thanked the waitress with a smile. The certainty never came and, even worse, the blackout didn't light up again, as had always happened before. Vicky felt herself losing consciousness, and bright points like fireflies appeared in the darkness: she was about to faint. Gaspar realized it too, because he took her hand on the table and she held on tight like she had in the house, and then the black curtain lifted and she withdrew as though from the edge of a black pit, as if she had peered into a deep lair. Are you okay? Gaspar asked her. I just got a little dizzy, I'm tired, these shifts are murder. Can you order me a grilled cheese? At the hospital's café you had to order at the counter, and Vicky needed Gaspar to go away for a moment so she could breathe and let her sweat dry, and, especially, so she wouldn't have to answer any uncomfortable questions. Gaspar had never asked her to use her diagnostic ability on him. It was strange that he hadn't, but now Vicky understood why. Gaspar always knew a little more, that's why he'd been able to get them out of the house. You had to respect his silences and evasions. There was always a reason for them. She would only try again if he asked her to.

Those mornings, Gaspar often talked to her about his hallucinations. His neurologist was very prestigious and trustworthy, but Gaspar insisted that certain apparitions were just too vivid and strange; nether the neurologist nor Isabel could convince him they were rare but possible symptoms, normal within his pathology. Vicky recommended a book that she thought might interest him: *Epilepsy*, by William Gowers, a British neurologist from the end of the nineteenth century. These days it's only read as a curiosity, she told him, but some of the descriptions are so out there that maybe it will help more than what I or your doctors can say. Vicky was right. Gowers wrote about a woman who could smell forget-me-nots, although, of course, the flower has no smell. A certain Mrs B. told Gowers that she always heard a voice to her right saying her name, and it wasn't like a voice in a dream, she said. Nor was it the voice of a man or a woman. After the voice, she suffered convulsions.

Could it be that his father had suffered from the same thing, and that's why he had collected all those books on the occult and magic? Did he believe he was getting messages from other worlds, when really they were epileptic fits? According to Vicky, it was very possible that in one of his first cardiac surgeries, performed back in the fifties, his father had suffered a cerebral lesion from lack of oxygen. That could be the cause of his hallucinations, if he had them, and he could have thought they were something mystical, a parallel reality. They didn't call it the sacred disease for nothing.

Maybe both things are true, thought Gaspar. There was no reason they should be incompatible. It wasn't a cerebral lesion that haunted his father. And Adela's disappearance was no delusion. It was soothing to think of illness as an answer and disorder as an explanation. But the truth had a way of rising to the surface, of scratching at the skin, of kicking you in the back of the neck.

Gowers' book included many stories of depersonalization. That happened to Gaspar, too. He knew he was in his room with his uncle or his friends, but he felt like he was somewhere else, and everything was familiar and unknown at the same time. It only lasted seconds. But during those seconds, if one of those stranger-friends were to touch him, he could go on the defensive. At one wedding reception he had filmed, he'd felt dissociated after drinking a glass of champagne: sometimes alcohol unleashed his symptoms. For him, alcohol loosened something that was tightly fastened, a chain whose lock he'd been trying for years to find. The bride's godfather had approached to ask him to film a few words he wanted to dedicate to the groom, and Gaspar heard him, understood him, but could not answer. In his private reality, he was in a hotel room, someone was sleeping in the other bed, and the reclining figure was enormous but unthreatening. What he *was* afraid of was a pregnant woman, naked and bald, who was in one corner of the hotel room. And the godfather, whom Gaspar recognized but who at the same time seemed a stranger, was clearly saying to him, let's go outside, I want it to be a surprise. The man was a little drunk, and he took Gaspar by the arm. Gaspar shook him off violently with a disproportionate shove, and the man stumbled into a table and yanked off the tablecloth; though he was able to catch his balance before he hit the floor, the dishes and glasses all shattered, and the floral arrangements were spoiled. The crash dispelled Gaspar's vision of the hotel room, the figure in the bed, and the naked woman. The godfather recovered, and Gaspar stammered out an apology: a group of men had formed a circle around them and seemed ready to beat him up. Amazingly, the bride's godfather had believed his lie: It was clumsy, I was about to drop the camera and I tried to shake you off so I could grab it with both hands, but I didn't calculate my strength well. I don't know my own strength either, said the godfather, I've got a heavy hand. He was smiling. Maybe he didn't want to ruin the party. It's okay, he told the other men, and Gaspar followed him to the reception hall's patio and filmed his words for the groom. Things hadn't gotten out of hand. A shove. The man wouldn't remember it as anything more than an accident and a misunderstanding, if he remembered it at all.

Gaspar had had a very clear déjà vu, only it was real. The memory of something true. He knew the figure in the bed was his father.

Pablo stretched out in bed with his arms behind his head, and he let Andrés use some of the goodies (that's what he called the massage oils, 'goodies') that he'd brought back from Thailand. He closed his eyes and tried to think about someone other than Gaspar, but he couldn't, and the frustration reached his erection, which disappeared despite the seductive scent of coconut. It didn't matter. They'd spent the previous night with an employee of his father's gas station. The guy had talked to them about a taxi driver from Quilmes, married with two daughters, who went crazy for a ménage à trois. Next time, they'd told him. Andrés was much more enthusiastic than Pablo, who was more careful. He knew straight guys like that could get violent. That's why you should never pay. Andrés got turned on by paying. He was forty-three years old and was practically the only survivor among his group of friends. And he was rich. He'd always been rich – his family owned a chain of car dealerships. His boyfriend had died two years before and there were photos of him all over the apartment. Sometimes, when he was really high, Andrés cried because his boyfriend hadn't gotten the pills in time, another year and he would have had the cocktail, you understand, you know. Pablo said yes but he didn't understand: two years was a really long time. In that period, Pablo could think of at least five friends and acquaintances who had died. He couldn't believe he wasn't infected himself. Vicky had foretold it in one of her monstrous intuitions: you're never going to catch it. Some people are like that. I think they should be

637

studied, maybe they already are. Cases of immunity. Still, you should always be careful. Over and over he'd heard it, and Pablo, naturally obedient as he was, had been careful. And now he was healthy and alone. He and Andrés were alone: one missed his dead boyfriend, the other was in love with his heterosexual friend. Together they were a playbook for dissatisfaction, and maybe that's why they got along so well.

Pablo was planning a show at Andrés's gallery. Sure, it was in La Plata, but it was every bit as prestigious as a Buenos Aires gallery, partly because it was Andrés's, partly because the periphery held a kind of suburban glamour, like some kind of discovery. Andrés knew it and that's why, though he had a lot of money, he didn't open a second site in Buenos Aires. That would have been the obvious thing, but then he'd lose all that snobby charm, which in the art world is worth more than anything. Andrés had a lot of ideas for the title of the show, but Pablo didn't like any of them. Andrés is kind of tacky, you know I can't call the show *The Survivor*, that's straight out of the seventies, he'd said to Gaspar. Can you think of anything? And Gaspar had suggested *The Plague Years*. No way. You're so tragic. For the moment, Pablo had a tentative title: *This one died, that one got pills, the other one left.* Or something like that. He hadn't told Andrés his idea, but he would surely accept it. He wasn't a picky person. They hadn't been lovers for long. There was a twenty-year age difference between them and they would never have said they were boyfriends. Nor did Andrés know Pablo was in love with Gaspar. He would often tell him, Bring me that spectacular friend of yours. I mean please, it's diabolical, no one should be that beautiful. Are you sure we can't convince him? He certainly is comfortable around fags. Makes me suspicious.

I'm sure, Pablo always said. And he thought: Plus, I wouldn't let you have him even if you tortured me.

The only unpleasant thing about his time with Andrés was the return of the ghost hand that grabbed his arm. He felt it, clearly and with each of its fingers, one night when he was going to the bathroom in Andrés's apartment. The same situation as when he was a kid. Bathroom, night, hallway. But he was different now. He closed his eyes and didn't shake it off, didn't run, didn't lock himself scared in the bathroom. He let the hand touch him. He felt it squeeze him, felt its heat, its contained violence. And then the hand let go. Later, trembling, he looked down at his arm: there were no marks from the ghost hand. He no longer believed it was all in his head. He had realized the hand was also lost in the darkness, like the forgotten remnant of an incomplete memory that was on a mission to touch, to surround with its fingers, to squeeze, to weakly push, and after that it didn't know what to do. The hand was a residue left by the house, another of its side effects, like the socks Vicky used when she slept or her terror of the dark; right now, for example, she was about to buy a used generator. He himself still felt repulsion and at times terror of dark places where bodies touched – he avoided having sex in pitch blackness – and he didn't like hands that were too hot, because they reminded him of that fevered squeeze. Maybe the hand had been a warning. Maybe Vicky was wrong when she said he was immune, or at least she was wrong from a scientific point of view. In the years before the cocktail, he had seen so many people get sick and die, his friends, his lovers, that he'd often thought his survival was anti-natural, as if something wanted to prolong his life so that, in the future, it could give him some kind of task. Or because, in the future, someone was going to need him.

Gaspar gave his leftover meat to Pocho, Luis and Julieta's dog. He hadn't been able to eat much: it was too hot, and everyone near the grill was roasting except the twins, who were splashing in a newly bought canvas pool. Julieta was mad at Gaspar, but he wasn't about to change his mind, not for anything in the world. He was going to live on his own. And Julieta thought it was selfish, given the context, for him not to use that rent money on his family instead. We have to get through this together, she said. You're not being very supportive, she repeated, calmly but firmly. You should stay until the economic situation improves. And Gaspar had flatly refused. The economic situation never improves in this country. If you need money I'll lend it to you, every month, it's no problem. I want to go.

Julieta had been offended by the suggestion of a loan, but Gaspar didn't understand why. After all, what did it matter? He didn't help with the twins. He was hardly ever there. Why did she want to keep him around? There was something strange about the demand, something that was at odds with Julieta's personality, always so generous. After he'd turned eighteen, Gaspar had gained access to the bank accounts and statements of his inheritance and properties. It was an astonishing amount of money that changed his life, and could potentially change the lives of Luis, Julieta, and the twins. Luis didn't want to hear a word about the money – it's all yours, son, he said, it's the money your mother left you; Julieta thought differently. In a very unpleasant fight, Gaspar had told her it's as if you wanted me to pay you for the trouble of taking care of me. And I *will* pay you, if that's what you want! Let's agree on a monthly amount. She had started crying. You don't understand, she'd yelled, and Gaspar replied that no, he genuinely did not understand. They weren't fighting now, but the situation was tense. Julieta didn't ever let him forget who his mother's family was. The Bradfords, the Reyeses. Proprietors. Yerbateros. Landlords. Exploiters. And she sought signs of that origin in him, as if class were a matter of genetics. Now she thought this display of 'individualism' – as she called it – was a whim.

That was another reason he preferred to live alone. Because with Julieta, embraces were mixed with prejudice, trust with control, concern with exasperation. She had changed a lot since she'd had children. Gaspar could understand that. He knew it didn't help that he couldn't hide his indifference towards the twins, but still, he didn't understand her imperious need to keep him in the house. She had put it like that once: You just can't leave the house. Why not? he had asked her, and she'd been silent, as if she hadn't known the answer because no one had told her.

After lunch, Luis, Negro, and Gaspar rode in the same car to downtown La Plata. The three of them were going to take part in a march that would be multitudinous and possibly dangerous, which was why Julieta had decided to stay home with the twins. The whispers of repression had risen to a scream. The new education law was about to be passed, and its obvious goal was to cut the budget in order to pay down the debt, the eternal Argentine merry-go-round, as his uncle said. The cuts in all sectors were suffocating. No one had money and no salaries were raised and every day people were fired and factories shut down and there was such a feeling of looming disaster that the heat of a never-ending summer in the middle of March was asphyxiating.

Negro and Luis had taken teaching jobs at starvation wages because they couldn't find anything else. Negro, to Gaspar's surprise, had once been a camera assistant on several legendary films that had been banned by the dictatorship. Hence his exile. Negro had seen some of the things Gaspar filmed: poetry readings, marches, a short film about Pablo in his studio. He'd told Gaspar he had a good eye, and he'd gotten him the gig filming quinceañeras and university events. Look what the kid does, Negro said when he saw the fifteen-year-olds waltzing, their pink dresses like flowers, their exaggerated make-up too mature for a young girl's features, the sweaty fathers whose expressions were a mixture of pride and fear. Look what he does: he takes this shitty party and that ugly kid and he makes them beautiful, gives them dignity.

It was so hot that the drum played alone at times, such was the players' exhaustion. Gaspar joined in the chanting. 'Let's go, comrades, gotta have more balls than that ...', 'Fight, fight, education is our right! ...', and the loudest one, 'Education for the workers, and if you don't like it, get fucked, get fucked!' Over in the journalism school's column, he saw Marita. She had recently started saying hi to him again, and they even chatted sometimes. His anger had passed. Maybe they could be friends. He had forgiven her for what happened with Guille; she'd never known how much it hurt him. Now Marita worked at the university press and she was a serious activist; her new boyfriend, who went by the name 'El Hueso', was one of the most well-known student leaders. He was a far cry from Gaspar and his banal quinceañera shoots, which, anyway, he did just to have something to do, so he didn't get bored, to make some extra money that he really didn't need. As she was now, distant and with a different life, he liked Marita even more. He'd seen her sitting on the pavement making signs, her face spattered with white paint, laughing. She always wore some very worn-out combat boots that she'd surely bought used; her fingers were ink-stained and her nails painted black. She went to the Princesa often, though she'd handed over the responsibility of running it to Pablo, which he did with a great deal of intelligence and a joy in giving orders that Gaspar found tremendously entertaining.

The assembly in Plaza San Martín was at the boring phase where they read out names of supporting organizations, but right away Gaspar noticed how many cops were there, and an even greater anomaly: there were mounted police. Horses. He waded into the crowd to find his uncle, who was equally disturbed. Let's wait, he told Gaspar, but if they give the order, run. Don't hesitate, just run. Then Luis looked into his eyes and said: Or just go right now, son.

Maybe nothing will happen, said Gaspar. Just when someone from the journalism school was about to take the mic, the sound system squealed with feedback and there was an explosion. And, further away, stampedes. Stampedes in a plaza are seen in the treetops, which shake as people try to escape by climbing up. When it's hot, you can also tell from the waves of heavy air left by the empty spaces. And then come the screams and the sound of running feet. With any luck, there are no gunshots.

That afternoon there were gunshots. The police, both mounted and on foot, broke up the gathering and chased people down streets and avenues. Later, Gaspar would learn they arrested over two hundred people. There would be a full day of waiting and of terrified parents and families, the police silent, the governor spouting nonsense on TV. For now, they had to run.

It would have been better not to flee down Calle 7, so broad and open, but it was the only option. Gaspar's idea was simple: get to the School of Economics. It was nearby, and, more importantly, the police couldn't enter university buildings because they were autonomous. Running in the stampede, he found himself beside Marita and El Hueso, who were panting from the effort. Though it was very hot, he still felt like everyone was running too slowly. He heard shots. Rubber bullets. He could tell the difference by now: this wasn't his first stampede at a protest. The unmistakable smell of tear gas reached him. The best way to combat its effects was by burying your nose in a handkerchief soaked in urine. He hoped it wouldn't come to that. Some people brought lemons to marches, but his uncle said that didn't do shit. Better to pee on your clothes.

He heard the horses' hooves, a groan from Marita, and he saw the cop's baton. He shouted to Hueso to run faster and he guided them at his own speed down the sidewalk, dodging people in their path. Marita yelled, I can't keep up! But he ignored her. He wasn't about to spend the night in jail, or let them, if he could help it.

The economics building had been designed using the blueprints of a prison, his uncle had once explained. It's a panopticon, see it? The open galleries all around, and in the middle, a surveillance tower. The tower in question was for the elevator, not a guard, but the idea was the same. These guys have some evil minds. Gaspar hardly knew the building, he'd gone there once or twice for a party or to meet up with a girl, but that was all. Still, he didn't need a map of the place: they just had to get inside and they'd be safe. The police couldn't go in.

Except, that day, they went in.

Gaspar watched incredulously as a horse struggled up the entrance steps. From the upper windows, people peered out and jeered 'motherfuckers, motherfuckers', and the cops, wearing helmets, made them retreat back into the classrooms by firing gas canisters into the air. Gaspar decided to go inside anyway, and Marita and Hueso followed him. The building was full of people, and a lot of police had entered. They were dragging students out. One girl's belly was bared, her shirt lifted as she was pulled across the floor, one of her sandals left behind in front of a classroom door. Kids had been handcuffed for resisting, one of them bleeding from his temple. Hueso shouted that the cops couldn't enter the building, that it's the law, that this is a bloodbath, and Marita told him to be quiet. They were in a corner, and they watched as the cops went rushing up the stairs, some already entering the classrooms. They were arresting people randomly. Gaspar decided to turn down a narrow hallway he thought he recognized that led to the service personnel bathroom, which was less frequented. When he turned around, he saw they were being followed at a trot by two fat cops who looked pretty fatigued. We're not getting out of here, said Hueso, but Gaspar opened a door with a sign saying PRIVATE that led to a janitor's closet, then closed it behind them. The three of them were left in darkness, waiting for the cops to open the door. They heard the doorknob rattling, voices cursing. Did you have a key? Marita asked. And Gaspar, in a low voice, said no. More turning of the doorknob, so hard it seemed about to break, a kick to the door and then a shout, and furious footsteps running away. Not yet, said Hueso, though neither of them had tried to leave.

They listened. The sounds weren't clear. Some shouts, sirens in the street. No more gunshots, at least not nearby. Marita sat on the floor and took out her lighter in order to see. When Gaspar heard it clicking – it didn't light on the first try – he asked her not to use it, taking her gently by the arm. It was the most restrained gesture he could make in that narrow place, trying to keep his calm. There was nothing evil in the little room. He wasn't going to turn around and see shelves holding teeth, no piano or blonde Adela waving in the darkness. But if Marita used that lighter, he *was* going to scream, and it was possible that after screaming he would end up hugging his knees on the floor, his eyes dry and staring. Marita complied: maybe she thought it was a strategy for hiding from the police. While they waited, the sounds in the building quieted. Raids, by definition, didn't last long. Gaspar felt Marita's arm lightly touching his, and that dispelled his fear. He wanted to get her attention, to defend her; he wanted her to leave that room thinking Hueso was a coward and a good-for-nothing and Gaspar was a hero, who, what's more, was a much better fuck.

'Let's go,' said Hueso.

Gaspar opened the door. For a second, he thought that his father was right beside him, standing there and saying very good, you can lock as well as open, very good. It was an instant, then the feeling vanished. Marita was talking about what incredible luck they had that the doorknob should get stuck right then, and so firmly, it was crazy. I can't believe you could open it so easily now. It must have gotten stuck from outside, said Gaspar, a ludicrous explanation, but one that, amid the panic and adrenaline, she accepted. When they left the janitor's closet and were walking carefully towards the main hallway, Marita let go of her boyfriend's hand, slowed down, and asked Gaspar: Were you scared in there, since it was so dark? Are you okay?

He was okay. A little anxious: his chest hurt when he took a deep breath. But that was all. Marita touched his cheeks with her black-tipped fingers and thanked him.

Then she and Hueso disappeared, mixed in with classmates they knew who were already organizing to find out where the detainees had been taken, already calling lawyers from the hallway phones. Gaspar went running towards Plaza Italia, crossed it, and reached the bar where he and his uncle had agreed to meet if there was violence. It was open, unlike all the others on Calle 7. And right away he recognized his uncle's back, the plaid short-sleeved shirt, the sweat stains under the arms, the hair somewhere between blond and orange that was growing ever lighter from the grey.

*

Gaspar put on his sunglasses so the bright light wouldn't give him a headache. They were going to be a little late because he'd asked Pablo to come and pick him up. He'd forgotten about the opening of Andrés Sigal's show, and he had promised he would be there. He'd spent the night before with one of Vicky's fellow residents, and it had been really fun: who would have thought a doctor would drink and smoke so much? He'd ended up pretty drunk. So Pablo came to pick him up on his motorcycle, and he made Gaspar get on without a helmet.

'I'm not going to throw you.'

'I'm not scared,' said Gaspar.

Pocho, the dog, got so excited by the bike that he chased them for two hundred metres, until they turned on to the highway.

'So, Vicky's friend?' Pablo asked.

'All good.'

'That's it?'

'She's pretty, she's crazy, who knows.'

'Oh, I know. You only love Marita.'

'You just keep your eyes on the road, or your boyfriend's gonna have to pay for our funerals.'

'He's not my boyfriend.'

'Man, quit fucking around.'

Andrés Sigal's opening was an event: photos of Argentina during his youthful travels around the country during the final years of dictatorship. Pablo had to go because he was Andrés's lover and because Andrés still hadn't confirmed the date of Pablo's own opening; also, there would be journalists and collectors, because it was an important show. He couldn't miss it. And Andrés had asked him to bring Gaspar. It's not so much to ask. Come on, please. Pablo had told Gaspar: He's head over heels for you, you drive him crazy. If I bring you as a little gift, he'll green-light my show within the week. Do it as a favour for your favourite artiste, and later you can ask me for whatever you want. Gaspar had laughed a little, but he agreed. He wanted to see the photos, after all, and he liked Andrés.

Andrés's gallery had once been a garage, and now, renovated, it had three exhibition halls. Its façade was completely white, so that when it was closed it was hard to distinguish the edges of the heavy iron door, also painted white. Now it was open, and people had spilled outside to smoke on the sidewalk. Against the wall near the entrance was a table covered with a black cloth where there were glasses of red wine, champagne, water, and Coca-Cola. Waiters dressed casually in jeans and T-shirts were offering empanadas, a common-man touch Gaspar was grateful for, because he didn't much care for the snacks that were usually served at this kind of event. He'd filmed several for his work, especially at the Fine Arts Photo Gallery, because most of his jobs were for the university. The faces of the guests, who had been drinking but were not drunk, held mockery and a trivial kind of cruelty; they were the faces of people who were thinking up their next ingenious phrase, the next biting criticism, the most efficient way to offend someone with impunity, because no one could afford the luxury of causing an affront in that place, with a glass of champagne in hand and a request on the tip of the tongue. Pablo rushed off to mingle with artists he knew: he introduced himself, was introduced, and their laughter rang out in the gallery's strange acoustics. No one had seen Pablo's newest work yet, the pieces from the past year: dolls made from IV tubes on foam mattresses, miniatures assembled from the pills his dead friends and acquaintances had never gotten to take, sheets that looked like shrouds with stencilled figures of bodies in different positions, in many cases real sheets stained with real sweat and shit. That's what he planned to show.

Andrés was at the other end of the hall, surrounded by friends and a few journalists.

Pablo broke away from his aquaintances with a few cheek kisses, downed his glass of wine in one gulp, and returned to Gaspar, who had stayed by the drinks table. 'They all want to meet you. They think you're my boyfriend.'

'You set them straight?'

'Let them envy me a little, they're all snakes, and on top of that they're hacks. Let's look at the photos, come on.'

'And what time do you plan to serve me up on a platter to the lord photographer?'

'When the lord photographer sees you, he'll drop everything, but for now he must attend his court.'

'Good thing you two are lovers, otherwise you'd skin him with your teeth.'

Pablo shrugged.

'He's a good guy, but he just loves for people to tell him how great he is.'

Still, Gaspar thought, the photos *were* pretty great. None of them screamed dictatorship, repression, or death, but the selection was unsettling. A soldier with his bride in front of a rickety house under a cruel sun. They were both smiling. The photo was from 1979. Had that soldier with dark skin and white teeth participated in an operation? Beside that one, a shot of the road muddied by rain. A highway temple to San Güesito. Gaspar was about to tell Pablo the story of the murdered child saint, but then he stopped himself, because he didn't remember exactly how or why he knew it (had his father told it to him when he was little?), and he also thought he recognized the place in the photo. The next image was of a child holding his fingers in the shape of a gun, pretending to shoot. It was a beautiful picture. Also beautiful was the photo of the young man dressed in a suit in a wooden shack, posing beside a boom box, surely just purchased.

'They're really good,' said Gaspar.

Pablo had to admit it was true. A waiter carrying empanadas passed by, and they both ate one. They left their glasses on another tray, and Pablo saw Andrés wave to him from afar, still surrounded by people. Gaspar had already gone back to the photos.

They saw it at the same time. It was a bit larger than all the others. Pablo took a little longer to realize than Gaspar, because of the surprise, the shocking coincidence. Gaspar had raised a hand to his mouth but said nothing. It was him in the photo, as a child, five or six years old. He had the same round eyes and dark hair, and he was thin, he'd already lost his baby fat. He was serious, with dark circles under his eyes – he looked tired. There wasn't much that was childlike in his expression. He was leaning against his father's leg with calm nonchalance. The two of them against a white wall. Pablo recognized Juan Peterson. In the photo he looked healthy and majestic in a black half-open shirt, his hands in his pockets, his fine blond hair grown out long, and that face, that unforgettable face, which in the photo was full of tenderness and exhaustion but had eyes that were heavy with violence, a powerful fury that was transmitted even over the distance of death and years, as was his demonic allure. Juan Peterson was not handsome like a movie star, nor was he beautiful like a model. There was something inhuman about his appearance, and many who gazed at the photo wrinkled their brows, because the father and son didn't seem sweet, but vaguely dangerous. Pablo felt the start of an erection, the memory of that day: Juan Peterson and the grey-haired man who was perhaps his secret boyfriend, fucking like animals in an empty room. My first time, thought Pablo.

Gaspar started towards Andrés and Pablo tried to stop him, because from the way Gaspar was walking, he could intuit a certain rage, and he knew that when his friend had those attacks of ire, things could end badly. But he didn't need to intervene: Gaspar changed his mind and headed towards the bathroom instead. Pablo followed him. Gaspar blocked the door with a chair that was beside the sink. He was mad, but also shocked. That's why he had gone into the bathroom: he needed to calm down.

'Had you seen it? Why didn't you tell me?' asked Gaspar. His voice shook.

'How could I see it and not tell you? I've never seen it.'

Gaspar leaned against the marble sink so hard his fingers turned white.

'Sorry,' he murmured between his teeth. And he rubbed his eyes as if they burned, fighting back tears. Pablo embraced him, and when he heard someone banging on the door he shouted 'occupied'. He could stay in that bathroom forever, holding Gaspar's waist, his taut belly. I love him so much, he thought. I don't care about the others, Andrés, this gallery. If only you'd stay with me. I'd set up house for you. I'd cook for you, I'm not afraid of anything. Just talk into my ear on the motorcycle. The sun and the wind in our faces, and then we'll fuck all night long. Forever or as long as it lasts.

Pablo kissed Gaspar's forehead, and Gaspar stiffened a little and gently pulled away from the hug. He took some paper towels and used them to dry his face. He saw a ghost, thought Pablo, and he must have been afraid he'd have one of those fits that Pablo had never seen himself, but had heard described so many times.

'Sorry,' Gaspar repeated. 'Open up, they're going to kill us.'

They went out and stood under the stairs beside the bathroom, in the shadows. Upstairs, on the second floor, were the gallery's offices. Gaspar said: I don't remember that photo. It must be from when we went to the waterfall, I've told you about that trip many times. I got upset because of the surprise, but also because, though I don't remember much, something really specific came to me, I don't know where or when it was, but I remember that my head hurt and my dad laid me in a bed. It was hot. He left me alone, but it was okay.

'You want to talk to Andrés?'

Gaspar wiped his face again and said yes. Andrés saw them coming and opened his arms wide to welcome them. He was standing next to the central photo of the show, an image of some soldiers kneeling in a church, praying, in the foreground; in the background and a little out of focus, children were taking Communion. In command of the room, he shook off a thin woman holding a long cigarette between two fingers and her elegant friend with perfect, salon-styled grey hair. He hugged Pablo long enough that those who didn't yet know would realize that this attractive young man was his lover. Then he gave Gaspar a kiss on the cheek, but there was something in the boy's expression and the paleness of his face that made him stop his flirting and turn serious.

'What's wrong?'

Gaspar pointed to the wall behind him, the photo, the people gazing at it.

'That's my dad. His name was Juan. And that's me when I was little. I wanted to know where you took the picture. I don't remember it. I mean, I don't remember where you shot us. I can't believe it's a coincidence to find it here, I can't believe we know each other and didn't realize, I can't believe you chose that photo today.'

'Holy Mother of God,' said Andrés. 'Forget this bullshit. Let's go upstairs to my office.'

*

Gaspar opened the diagrams of the two houses: the original house on Calle Villarreal and the one that had taken Adela, superimposed. He had started another sketch based on the Chapel of the Devil and the Karlen Grocery, the places Andrés Sigal had told him about. The chapel was real; he had called the tourism office in Corrientes to confirm its existence. It was an architectural rarity. The photos Andrés had taken of it hadn't turned out well, so he had never shown them. As he told it, he'd been able to enter through a window, expecting something sinister, but inside there was just an eccentrically carved altar, an unsubtle imitation of Bosch in bas-relief, with clumsy, grotesque lines. Then Andrés had taken a fruitless detour to Posadas. His intuition was that maybe Juan and Gaspar were trying to cross the border. It was 1980, the worst years of the dictatorship were past, and he thought they were going into exile. He thought, even, that the scars Juan claimed were from an operation could really be from an armed confrontation. Gaspar confirmed they were not. And Andrés opened an unexpected door for him when Gaspar told him it was true what his father had said: they were going to his grandparents' house. He barely remembered it. A wooden walkway over trees. The river. A park that had an orchid garden. Not much more. A nearby zoo – he remembered some colourful birds and a strange game of hide-and-seek with his grandfather and other adults. Andrés fell silent a moment and then asked his mother's last name. Holy Mother, that house is Puerto Reyes! he said excitedly. Legendary. They have private police so no one can get in to take pictures of it. The family, your family, hasn't let anyone near it in decades. You can catch a glimpse of it from the zoo, which also belongs to the family but is open to the public. Still, you can't see much. It's high up so the river won't reach it if it rises, so from a certain point on the nearest road you can just see the rooftops. There are photos from the forties in the local history museum in Puerto Iguazú. It's a marvel. It's going to be yours? Why didn't you ever go back? Will you invite me to the house once it's yours? I would love to photograph it.

Gaspar gave a general summary of his father's wishes as he tried not to scratch the scar on his arm, which was burning as if someone were dripping hot wax on to it. Don't worry, Dad, he thought, I'm not going to give away any inconvenient details. So you don't have any contact with them, then? They sure are a strange family. No one knows anything about them, they're rich but discreet. Not like my family. Still, there's no comparing the two fortunes. They're the owners of this country, seriously. *You* are! I'm not anything, said Gaspar. I tried to photograph it years ago, Andrés went on; the house, I mean. There's a town nearby, but people there don't see much movement in or out. I didn't even make it a hundred metres down the private road, which is long. To me, the mystery is why they keep using that isolated house, which can't be all that comfortable. Rich people who are *that* rich go for other kinds of summer homes. They go to Punta del Este or places like that. People wonder what they do in there. They have other houses, said Gaspar, I guess they must spend a while at each one. They must have a lot, I'm sure, Andrés replied. Puerto Reyes is near Iguazú. Your dad sent me to Posadas. He didn't want me to follow him, clearly.

Gaspar wondered what had happened between Andrés and his father, because the photographer's story held a certain nostalgia. Plus, he remembered the details too well. But Gaspar wasn't going to ask. Let Pablo ask for him.

Using a map, he located the Chapel of the Devil and, further north, Puerto Reyes. Ever since he'd seen the photograph in the gallery, or maybe after he'd locked the door in the economics building, his epileptic hallucinations had become so vivid he'd started taking notes on what he saw. Near Plaza Rocha, the white-painted iron door of an abandoned house had opened on to a nocturnal swamp. He'd thought it was a garden with its tall reeds, but beyond the door it was night, though he could see clearly thanks to a light that didn't come from the moon – there was no moon. He was able to walk up to the edge of the swamp – more like a lagoon, a recognizable landscape – before it went back to being a door and the headache pounded his eyes. At the edge of the swamp, he saw a man's body hanging from a branch, stiff and old and dry, brown from mummification, naked. It wasn't swaying. He never thought it could be a mannequin.

That night he had dreamed of bodies and trees; of bodies hanging from trees. When he ate with his family, he felt dirty sharing the table with the twins, smiling at them, rinsing their pacifiers when they threw them on the floor. He felt the mummified body on his skin, so still, that otherworldly night. Julieta seemed to notice his discomfort: she'd made a pointed joke about his family. She'd asked him again to keep living with them. It was a dance, Gaspar thought now. A way of pushing him away by insinuating the desire to keep him, a very smart way of going in circles. Julieta loved him. Julieta had saved him just as much as his uncle had. But now she wanted to get away from him.

When he told Vicky about his avalanche of symptoms, she asked for a meeting to speak with the epilepsy specialists at the hospital. They came in rarely, and were very strange. Mad scientists, she called them. And they'd told her things that sounded impossible. Patients who, during seizures, would see fields laid to waste, bombings. They're called oneiric landscapes. If you talked to them and told them about your episodes, you'd have no doubt this is epilepsy.

'My neurologist already tells me, Vicky. He's a pretty mad scientist too.'

'Take the medication. This is no joke.'

'I'm actually taking it now. And it turns out, it's worse. I hadn't seen Adela in a long time. The other day I rode in an elevator with her. She cursed at me, and she didn't have teeth. Plus, how can you explain what happens to you guys? You say you hear voices when there's no light. Pablo is grabbed by a hand, he feels it. Epilepsy isn't contagious.'

'Our stuff could be just in our heads. Trauma. Plus, our symptoms don't keep us from functioning. Yours can be incapacitating.'

Pablo, who was stretched out on the sofa at Vicky's apartment, said: I don't feel like it's in my head. I know the hand now. I don't seek it out, but I'm not afraid of it. If I let it hold on to me for a while, it lets go. As if it didn't know what to do. Poor thing.

'That could be your imagination,' Vicky insisted, and Pablo snorted.

'That attitude is going to kill us, my friend. I know you want to have a life. We all do. Lately, I even want a boyfriend. God, how ridiculous.'

'It's my fault,' said Gaspar. 'Tell me the truth: have you gotten worse? The things you feel happening to you, are they worse now?'

'It's more frequent,' said Pablo. 'Not worse, because I'm not scared of it any more.'

'It's worse,' said Vicky. 'But the good stuff happens more, too. I've made better diagnoses than ever recently.'

Pablo sat up on the sofa and said:

'Hey, why don't you try to diagnose Gaspar?'

Vicky crossed her legs, uncomfortable.

'It's not like that. I can't decide, it's something that just happens.'

'It's so weird it's never happened to you with him, right? Try it. I'm sure that if you make an effort, you can.'

Vicky opened her mouth to explain again, but Gaspar interrupted.

'No,' he said. 'Don't try to get inside my head or anything like that. My dad used to do that. It's repugnant.'

She looked at her hands, her eyes full of tears.

'You already tried.'

'You didn't even realize.'

'What was there?'

'A pit,' said Vicky, and she looked up. 'A black pit. I wouldn't do it again.'

'Why didn't you tell me? You can't lie to me!'

'Don't fight,' said Pablo. 'It's worse if we fight, because there's no one else who cares about this. We've already been over it a thousand times. Vicky, don't you realize, for example, that hardly any articles were published in the papers after Adela disappeared? Gaspar has all of them. There are six. That's it. Any kind of bullshit will get quadruple that coverage. A girl gets lost in a house and they never find her again. A girl who's missing an arm. And then her mother disappears. They were just alone, like two air plants hanging there. And now, I start fucking this guy just to kill time, because he's old so he fucks well, or better. There aren't many like him, I'll tell you. Or out of convenience, because he's powerful, because he's got a gallery and he belongs to the scene I'm interested in. Whatever. And it turns out the guy takes me under his wing, and when he does a photo show, there's a portrait of Gaspar and his dad. A giant, impressive photo, impossible to miss. Vicky, ten years have passed and we're in the same shitty place. Don't argue over whether you could diagnose him or not. It's the least of our worries.'

'You can't hide something like that from me, Vicky. They're getting closer,' said Gaspar. 'They want to get my attention.'

'Who?' asked Vicky, resigned. 'You're sounding paranoid. What do you want to do, Pablo? Let's hear it, what do you want to do? What *can* we do?'

'I don't decide what to do. You've got the captain right here. He's always been in charge.'

Gaspar, who was sitting with his arms crossed, shook his head. Then he said: 'I don't know what to do or what all this means. Not yet. But for now, we wait. And we tell each other everything. In detail. I think we can hold out a little longer.'

Marita had accepted Gaspar's invitation to have a beer after they'd run into each other at the Princesa. She'd seen him there like so many other times, sitting on one of the sofas and smoking, with his thin legs, black sneakers, his high, delicate cheekbones and hands with their long fingers always flecked with scrapes. He was thinner now. For the first time since she'd met Gaspar, she felt intimidated, and not because he acted any different. The girl who was reciting had a dramatic, declamatory style, and her poem was about the lack of work, the shipyards, the country's roadblocked highways. It was political poetry, better than the Morrison emulators but extraordinarily bad, and Marita had been hit by a fit of laughter. It was terribly bad form to laugh at someone talking about those subjects, so she went outside. Gaspar followed her; when they met on the sidewalk, he bent over with his hands on his knees, and the shared, stifled laughter was a relief for Marita. Gaspar imitated the girl's affected style and then, sitting beside Marita now, he told her that this girl may have been a debacle, but lately there'd been some incredible poetry readings at the Princesa.

'You've gotta come more often.'

'I have a lot of work at school. I've started practice teaching, working as a TA.'

'Meaning they don't pay you anything.'

'It could help me later on.'

'The other day this guy no one knew came in. First there was a really pathetically bad poet who acts all suicidal and reads something à la Pizarnik, a disaster. Then there was a more conventional girl, boring, Orozco with no heart. And then this guy got up, this stranger. He recited 'I Explain a Few Things' by Pablo Neruda in full, without reading. Most people looked at him like he was a crazy old man, you know how they are, condescending. It made me cry, though.'

'Yeah right, you cried.'

Marita knew Gaspar hardly ever cried in public.

Then Gaspar recited some parts of the poem, the ones he remembered, and he ended with, 'And through the streets the blood of the children / ran simply, like children's blood,' and shook his head.

'It was incredible, Mari. And to see those people who didn't understand a thing, I just hated them.'

And they looked at each other while, inside, the music started up. Something from the eighties. Bronski Beat. Marita thought they were going to kiss, but Gaspar took a sip from his beer bottle.

'I miss how you used to read to me in bed,' she said.

'Me too,' Gaspar replied, and got to his feet. He reached out his hand to help her up, too. They went inside and she spent the rest of night talking to other people, never losing sight of Gaspar. She was attracted to him, that was never the problem. The day she'd seen him for the first time outside the Princesa, shy, just out of high school, beautiful, with his dark hair combed back, she'd thought he had a tragic face that reminded her of all those dangerous and delicate boys she fell for, James Dean looking at the stars, Motorcycle Boy playing pool. That first sensation had diluted over time, and in their last months together, all that had remained was his melancholy, and also his anger: if he got mad, he could destroy something valuable (she remembered how he'd once thrown a camera against the wall just because it was the closest thing in reach), or even hurt himself if he was too furious. That tension was still telling her it was better not to get back together with him. At the same time, though, it was as impossible to ignore Gaspar as it was a house fire.

Days after they saw each other at the Princesa, Marita had gone to Gaspar's house. He still lived in Villa Elisa but, he'd told her, he was looking for an apartment in La Plata. Marita was going to interview Luis: the university press where she worked was putting together a book on the resistance of Peronist trade unions. They'd had a simple gathering of friends, homemade pizzas, pot smoking. The house seemed warm in comparison to hers, to her boyfriend's, or her friends', who always heated their places with stoves and left the windows cracked so the rooms didn't fill up with smoke, who always had light blankets full of holes, worn out on trips through Patagonia or Jujuy, and houses that smelled of starving dogs, where everyone drank mate and ate plain bread. She understood that, in part, she was fed up. Activism was surprisingly homogeneous, the discussions were circular, the offences identical, the dues to be paid insurmountable. A year ago, the way El Hueso monopolized the party meetings at the university inspired a sort of pride in her. Now she felt like yelling at him to let someone else talk. She saw the frustration on her comrades' faces when they lost votes, and the rhetoric seemed ever more useless, precisely now when everywhere in the country the strikes were layoffs and the layoffs were picket lines. The student branch of the party only answered with articles in its newspaper to express solidarity, denounce the union lockout and neoliberalism, and call for mobilization of workers and students. But the workers remained outside the factory, cutting off the highway or trying to form a co-op to get their jobs back. Marita thought they should participate fully in those actions or join in the strikes – enough with the talking and talking and the theorizing and mate-drinking. She had discussed all that with Luis during their interview.

'There's no solution,' said Negro, who had come by for a few glasses of wine. 'They're Trotskyists, they don't know how politics work and they're disgusted by the people's happiness.'

From the kitchen, Julieta yelled that she deserved a little happiness, too, and could someone please deign to help her clean the kitchen. They ate like pigs, made messes like pigs, she said. Negro huffed a little, but got up to help. He came back from the kitchen with Gaspar, who had made dessert, and sprawled in the lounge chair. After a long time of searching, Luis finally had a job at a construction site downtown. He did a little of everything: foreman, some engineering work. But they couldn't pay very many people well. Gaspar wanted to know how the job was going.

'It's going well, the boys work like beasts, plus, they're much better than I am technically.'

'That's not saying much,' said Negro.

'Go to hell. What can I do, brother? They won't hire an engineer. Still, Sixto, the kids' leader, is a natural at engineering, it's really impressive. It just kills me that I can't hire more people.'

Gaspar sat down beside Marita and served everyone strawberries with cream. She realized, as he leaned over her, that she missed his smell and his supple skin, the chlorine in his hair when he came back from swimming, the sex on the damp grass, at night, in that very yard where they were now eating dessert.

'You do hire some people,' said Gaspar, as he poured everyone a spritz he'd recently learned how to make. 'I don't know if it's better with Cynar or Campari. You all can tell me.'

'This kid's turned out all James Bond,' said Negro. 'Must be his drop of English blood.'

'My, how unrefined,' said Gaspar. 'This drink is Italian.'

'There's nothing better than giving work,' Luis went on, 'and it drives me nuts to have to turn people away every day. Every day, some kid comes by asking for a job, wearing a helmet left over from another site. We need people, but I can't take anyone on. Some of them leave cursing, which is fine, but a lot of them go away resigned. Just two years ago, we used to grill out at lunch. Now we've got pork shoulder sandwiches.'

That day, Marita wanted to be a part of that family again. She stayed at the house even after Gaspar left, without saying where he was going. She suspected he was going to meet a girl, and she enjoyed the stab of jealousy she felt. A few days later she ran into Luis at the university cafeteria, and he told her that Gaspar had gone by the site to bring the workers barbecued meat and some sausages. He seemed moved, and Marita smiled, because Gaspar still had that way of listening, thinking, and acting without announcing anything. Still, Luis told her, I'm worried. He's not doing well, he's depressed. I don't know if he's taking his medication. He won't listen to me at all now, he's all grown up. Talk to him if you can, Marita, you'd be doing me a favour.

She hadn't been able to talk to him, not yet. She would try the next time.

*

Take four hours and make it one. It was always easy to cut, but in this case, this particular party, a ten-minute video would have been ideal. An hour was too long. The editing bay at the journalism school was a windowless room, and Gaspar hated it; he liked to smoke when he edited, and in that confined space even the most insistent smoker would feel suffocated. He didn't have much time: he rented the suite on Saturdays, when there were no classes. Marita was with him that day; she had asked him to show her his videos before they went for a beer. She was curious. Gaspar hoped she didn't laugh. He detested it when people laughed at these parties where people were just trying to be happy.

Now he had her sitting there beside him, Marita and her worn-out jeans, sleeveless white shirt, dark skin, and her hair a little longer, but still short. I can't let it grow out, she'd say, because it gets too frizzy. It's the genes from my Uruguayan grandfather, who was black. He gave me great skin and complicated hair. Gaspar didn't want to think about the fact that Marita wasn't wearing a bra and he didn't want to look at the way her jeans emphasized her hips, so he handed her a notebook and asked her to mark times. She had taken an audiovisual class and knew how.

The fifteen-year-old girl. Valentina. He had filmed her with tears in her eyes too many times. Her hair mussed. Totally, overwhelmingly aware that her party was falling apart. The adults drunk. Her own father trying to touch her classmates' asses. Her mother yelling at the waiters because they brought the food out cold and always late. A DJ so bad he couldn't get anyone to dance.

'I've never seen anything more depressing,' said Marita, while Gaspar decided to cut a full hour of small catastrophes, including a shot of the cake ruined by the clumsy hand of a well-intentioned grandma who, when she tried to adjust the pink-dressed figure that crowned the layers of sponge cake and meringue, had pushed it and almost demolished it. The only option left was a backup shot: he'd filmed the cake in the kitchen of the event hall, before they brought it out to the guests. The Carioca carnival was a fiasco of sweaty men, women dodging their horny advances, and an exodus of teenage girls: some of the kids had made fun of the quinceañera. Valentina. A lovely name.

'Hopelessly sad, right?' said Gaspar, pressing pause. 'That's how it was all that night. I shot some girls who were talking and drinking champagne, they'd brought a bottle outside to the park. It's a really nice hall, have you been there? La Casona, in City Bell. Anyway, so they offered me some champagne, but I try not to drink when I'm working, not because I get drunk, I don't, but it looks bad. The parents see you drinking with the girls and it makes a bad impression, they're fifteen years old. The thing is that whenever the girls talk to me, they tell me stuff or they flirt, the way girls always get with older guys. These girls started telling me how they were all being treated at the Melchor Romero outpatient clinic, which has a centre for eating disorders. I looked at them and they were really skinny, dark circles under their eyes, really sick. That's how it was all night long. One of them told me, "hunger hurts but starving works," in English. They were from a really good bilingual school, really posh.'

'Were they pretty?'

'I don't like girls that skinny. I don't know.'

'People always tell you things. You've got something about you. That look that says, "I have the power of a dark experience, come to me."'

'Don't be mean.'

'I don't mean it in a bad way. You have it, Vicky has it, Pablo too. Your uncle, from being in exile. Negro. I don't have anything. Sometimes I feel like I'm so boring. You have no idea.'

Since Marita didn't say anything else, Gaspar went back to work. They finished a version of the video that was an hour and three minutes long. Gaspar would come back alone during the week to do the final edit. They'd had several beers. Gaspar wasn't drunk, Marita was a little, though she'd eaten two bags of potato chips. They talked about other things, mostly about anorexic girls, about Marita's classmates who wore oversized clothes and looked at themselves in the bathroom mirror, sucked in their stomachs, made their ribs stick out, cut themselves and let the blood trickle down over their pubis. I've never been like that, she told him as they were crossing Plaza Moreno.

'Why do you keep saying that?'

Marita ran her hand over her short hair and tugged on it a little.

'Because I want to say something else and it won't come out.'

'I can't keep walking with you if you're going to give me the runaround. This is new, you never used to torture me, really, and I don't like it.'

Marita said, Sorry, sorry, and hugged Gaspar before taking his face in her hands.

'Is that why you were with me? Because I don't have any issues, I'm just a normal person with no drama?'

'What's so bad about that?'

'Not that it's bad, it's just really boring.'

'I'm the boring one,' said Gaspar. 'Not you. You care about people, you want to change things, you don't lose hope over stupid stuff. Everyone loves you. Same as my uncle. I can't think of anything better than that, truly. Nothing.'

Marita kissed him. Gaspar took off his backpack and took a deep breath.

'I left Hueso,' she said. 'I want to be with you. Do you want to get back together with me?'

Setting up a house could bring some relief. It had worked the first time: ride out the constant headache by trying to get a table into the kitchen. Ignore the dreams and hallucinations by painting a wall with a roller, up and down, right to left, tape on the door mouldings so they wouldn't get spattered, the penetrating smell in his hair and on his skin washed away in the afternoon shower. Choosing light fixtures and fearing electrocution while he stood on the penultimate step of a lopsided ladder. Now that he was having what the neurologist called déjà vu – and what he preferred to call memories – at least once a day, he was setting up house with Marita. Rented, for now, at his uncle's recommendation. You have a lot of cash and a lot of houses: take your time, you need to choose well when you buy. So now there he was, painting the walls purple, a purple house like Paisley Park, that was Marita's dream, and, after painting, two cups of wine while they sat on the floor like in a TV commercial, installing programs on the computer. When she fell into a deep and dreamless sleep, he disentangled himself from her legs and stared at the ceiling and felt the exhaustion of sex and the sorrow like a weight around his neck. That Marita was there only brought him moments of relief, pleasant pangs. He didn't want to describe for her the visions that made him so afraid. He wasn't going to tell her, he didn't tell her, that he couldn't go back to the actual house where Adela had disappeared because they'd demolished it, but he went back almost every night in dreams and searched for her desperately behind hundreds of doors. The dreams were terribly long, like full-length movies; Gaspar didn't know if normal people had such long dreams. The neurologist had said he was experiencing visual and emotional flashbacks from a dream or a series of dreams. That was his latest conclusion. He had a déjà vu of dreams. Gaspar had asked, How can that be, and the doctor had told him it was rare, but entirely consistent with epileptic symptoms, that it was unusual but not unheard of, and on and on. Vicky agreed. Marita said it seemed like a science fiction plot, straight out of Philip K. Dick. How can you have déjà vu of forgotten dreams? Sounds like you should get a second opinion.

After they set up the house, they started going out into the city. Sometimes they talked lying in the grass around the cathedral, Marita smoking pot while the light faded and the lamps in Plaza Moreno blinked on. Sometimes they drank beer and ate peanuts in the bars of Diagonal 74 while they complained about the music. Sometimes they spent the afternoon at the artificial lake in the park that people called the Forest, and Marita always pointed out the rats swimming in the stagnant water and wondered how it didn't smell, how people could keep using the boats as if it were a romantic outing and not what it was, muck and sludge, and how they could eat at the food stands that no doubt also received visits from rodents.

She wanted to hear about the years they'd spent apart. And he told her how, little by little, things had stopped interesting him. As a kid, he said, he'd been an obsessive soccer fan. And he'd never gotten that back. That's for the best, she said, those people are raving lunatics. I get it, though. There's a joy there. When Estudiantes wins the championship, my dad is truly happy, nothing else makes him that glad. Not even when he comes into some cash or things go well for me or my brother. It's a different kind of happiness, it must be awful to have lost it.

'And I can't get interested in anything. You're going to start working at the newspaper, you're planning a book, a radio show. Pablo works like a beast, always planning, he's got seven note-books of sketches. He's going to be famous. Vicky's a genius. And I film bullshit. I started filming because I loved movies when I was little. Now, I like them, they distract me, but they don't interest me much. I used to cry in movies, I acted out scenes. That gradually went away too.'

'You're depressed, sweetheart.'

'Yeah, of course I'm depressed. Sometimes I think I film the quinceañeras because there's something there, I don't know how to express it, some kind of elemental trust in life, and it's a relief. Is that crazy?'

'No. I'm just thinking. I mean, you still like to read, you're still into that.'

'That's the only thing, yeah. Reading. And girls. I never stopped being into girls.'

'Go to hell.'

'Hey now. Still, there was something kind of bitter about girls, you know, I had this really stubborn refusal to commit, I made thousands of excuses, refused to feel. Or it wasn't even a refusal: I didn't feel anything. You're the only one, and that worries me.'

'Why?'

'Because you shouldn't be with me.'

'Gaspar, I hate that kind of self-pity, it's rotten and it really pisses me off. That's excuse number one for guys, "I'm no good for you", "It's not you it's me", always the same shit.'

'I don't mean it like that.'

'That's why I'm not leaving right now, because I know you're depressed. What does Isabel say?'

'Isabel is old and she knows me too well. I need to get a new therapist. I can't keep going to my childhood doctor, it's

shockingly immature, I think. Some of the epilepsy medications are antidepressants. So there: I'm already medicated.'

'You should go to school. You could major in literature. I can
see you as a professor.'

'I don't understand why I have to study.'

'That's what we middle-class kids do, right? Although I
guess you're rich.'

'Don't you start in on that, too.'

Before going to sleep, Gaspar read to Marita from the
poets he'd discovered. This one died at twenty-two, it's crazy. I
found him when Pablo did that photo show with all the poets,
remember? He was Slovenian. I don't know how to pronounce
his first name, but his last name is Kosovel. He wrote about a
thousand poems, and supposedly they're all good, at least for a
kid. I like this one: 'In my temples it throbs, throbs. The shadow.
The cold muzzle of the gun. Ten tons. In my heart a half-tone
in minor key.' And my dad would write names down randomly
in his notebook. You can tell they were writers he wanted to
read. Here he wrote "Sara Teasdale". I've been translating her.
She's great.'

'You could teach English, for example. I don't like you reading about suicides.'

'I'm not going to kill myself. And I don't need money. That's
the only good thing I have.'

'Enough with the poor me. That account where they deposit
your money, is it here? Because it should be in Colonia. Let's go
one day and deposit cash in Colonia.'

'It's already in Colonia, been there for years.'

'Let's go anyway. I went when I was little, it's lovely. Read
me some Sara Teasdale.'

'"There will be stars over the place forever; / Though the
house we loved and the street we loved are lost . . ."'

'I used to want to study astronomy. But I don't know how to divide by two digits, that's why I majored in journalism.'

'You never told me that.'

'I don't regret it, though. Whenever you want, I can teach you the names of the constellations, I'm sure you don't know them. No one does, it's weird how people aren't interested in space. They must be easier to see from Colonia, right?'

That's what she wanted: to travel. To go to Patagonia and write about the Welsh colonies there. She wanted to go to Valparaíso, though she was afraid of earthquakes. And to Minneapolis, to see Prince's house. She deserved a better partner. It didn't matter that she was sincere about wanting to be with him. He had to go, to leave her, and it was so hard. I want us to travel together, she said, and Gaspar replied of course, and he kissed her neck and left his lips there on her throbbing pulse and thought that he would never take her anywhere, because he could only go towards those who were seeking him. There was a black heart that needed him and someday he would fulfil its wishes, because when you can't fight, the only way to be at peace is to surrender.

Though the tension between him and Julieta remained unspoken but clear, Gaspar attended Negro's birthday party in Villa Elisa: they were celebrating at Luis's house. The guests included the workers from his uncle's building site, some of Negro's neighbours and students, and his daughter. Gaspar didn't feel like helping with the salads or the table this time. He was tired. Julieta's lips were thin with disapproval and he knew why: in a recent argument with Luis, Gaspar had punched the door so hard it still had the hole his fist had left. A week later, he was still pulling splinters from his knuckles. His uncle had reacted as he always did to those fits of rage: fearlessly, his outstretched arms reaching for Gaspar's neck like a dominant animal, sub-duing him in an affectionate hug until Gaspar had no choice but to take deep breaths and open his hands. When he was lit-tle, his father used to pry his fingers from the palm of his hand to correct that anxious gesture. Luis had done the same for a long time. Even today, he would occasionally touch Gaspar's arm under the table to make him realize he needed to relax his fingers.

Julieta had been frightened by the punch to the door. It's all under control, Luis had said, and, unable to hold back, she had almost screamed at him, her voice thick with reproach:

'It's all under control until one day he gets mad at your chil-dren and beats the shit out of them. Where the hell are your priorities?'

And when Luis went to reassure her, Gaspar had wiped his tears and his runny nose with a hand that he rubbed on his jeans and left that house, planning not to come back for a long time. The next day he'd gone by his uncle's work to apologize and listen to the same lecture as always: you have to control yourself, son, you have to learn to manage that rage or work on it more in therapy. And: Julieta changed a lot after the babies were born, I don't know if it's the hormones or if this is what being a mother is or what, but she's gotten more fearful. Gaspar had thought about skipping Negro's birthday and just calling, but he didn't want to offend him. He decided to take a seat at the table and wait and applaud the grillmaster. The babies weren't there, which was good: their grandparents were watch-ing them so their parents could have an adult party, with wine, fights, and maybe some tears at dawn.

'Guess who I ran into? Josecito Viola. He was visiting Bue-nos Aires. He lives in France. You remember that fight we had?'

'In Plaza Francia, coincidentally.'

'I was giving him some shit about how rock music was the culture of big business – my god! What a jackass I was. Well, he lives there now and apparently he's teaching sociology. He looks good.'

Marita wanted to know more, and the two men spent half an hour enthusiastically regaling her with tales of the seventies. Gaspar had already heard almost all the stories, but he was vaguely entertained at seeing them so excited to get attention from a young girl who 'was no dummy' (that's what they always told him: 'Your girl's no dummy': that's how sexist they were, though they swore otherwise), and who also had a marked and sustained interest in politics, which was rare ('they're just not engaged' was their most common complaint about their students). She participated in their arguments and wasn't condescending, and nor was she in their thrall: she used them as information sources, thought Gaspar. And they enjoyed it.

The after-dinner conversation drew out and Negro even sang a little, but he couldn't coax the others into what he called 'the chorus situation'. When he got too wasted and started to pick fights – he was an ornery drunk – the others moved away and let him grumble to himself and, finally, start to nod off. That was the moment to invite him to sleep over, and he always said yes. Gaspar led him to the room under the pretext of helping, but really he just wanted to be alone for a while, have a little silence before re-entering the fray. Julieta was being nice to him, for the moment. Negro's daughter had left early because she didn't like to fight with her dad when he was drunk. Things weren't so bad. When Gaspar came back from the bathroom, people were starting to say goodbye. Negro's students, the workers from Luis's building. Gaspar rummaged around the grill and made himself a belated sandwich with a little skirt steak. Julieta announced she was going to sleep. And in the early morning only Luis, Gaspar, and Marita were left, plus all the dirty dishes on the table and three full ashtrays.

Gaspar was waiting for Marita's signal to leave. A little bored, he started to play with the dog, who was still excited by the meat, the smells, and the people. With all the rolling around and pretend biting, Gaspar missed the beginning of a conversation. But then he distracted the frisky dog with a bone from the barbecue. He'd heard something that piqued his interest.

'So, you left through Paraguay?'

'Through Brazil. Two months after the coup, more or less. Gaspar's parents got me out. His mom, really. She drove me in her car.'

Gaspar sat upright and lit a cigarette.

'My mom got you out? She was the one who got you out of the country? You've never told me that before. Why not?'

Luis looked a little ashamed. He had said too much. He was drunk, and excited as he always was when he talked about his past with someone who was interested in listening.

'I don't know, son. Those were hard things.'

'Why is that hard? She helped you, I don't see the trauma. I can't stand secrets. You *know* they drive me nuts.'

'Don't get carried away, now, you're blowing this out of proportion. We're not going to fight about this.'

'We'll just see whether we fight or not. Why did you never tell me?'

The silence in the yard was heavy and pensive, weighted with drunkenness and exhaustion. Gaspar had come closer to the table with his arms crossed, and Marita rested a hand on his shoulder.

'My mom got you out of the country and it never occurred to you to tell me. In fifteen years. Nothing, not a word.'

'I'm telling you now. Some things aren't so easy.'

'You're not telling me, you're showing off for Marita. I'm sick and tired of you all and your harrowing lives. For real.'

'Stop it, you two,' said Marita. 'Gaspar, if he couldn't tell you, he couldn't, okay? You keep quiet about things, too. We all do.'

Luis decided to cut the tension by telling the truth.

'Your parents were living in Misiones, in your mom's family's house. I met up with your dad here. Well, not here, but in Buenos Aires. It wasn't a coincidence, he called me and we set up a meeting. He'd come to do something else, I think he went to the doctor, but maybe that was a lie. He didn't tell me much of anything. You know how he was. Well, straightaway he told me to pack a bag and that he was getting me out of the country. I don't know how he knew I needed to go. Those weren't things you said over the phone, and I hadn't told him anything. We took turns driving all the way to Misiones. It was a demented trip, and his health was bad.'

'I took that trip with dad, too.'

'I know. Maybe that's why I didn't tell you.'

'What does that have to do with it? So you've been to the house.'

'I was there a few hours. Long enough to take a shower and eat something. We crossed during the day. Your mom knew the soldiers at the border because she was working in Asunción, and also because your family on her side, well, they had a good relationship.'

'My mom drove you out. My mom. You never told me about her or about the house. You knew I dream about that house, or I hallucinate it, or whatever the fuck happens to me with that house, and you never thought to mention that you'd been there. You know I want to know about my mom, that I hardly remember her, that I miss her. And you met her. You're such a traitor.

You'd better tell Julieta my mom got you out, maybe then she'll get over her bitch fits and quit judging me and my family.'

'I will not allow that, Gaspar.'

'You won't allow it. Why didn't you tell me? Tell me the truth.'

Luis lowered his head and sighed.

'Juan asked me to never tell you, and I respected his wish. He didn't want you to have any references of your mother's family, nothing.'

Gaspar picked up an empty glass and Marita grabbed him hard by the elbow to keep him from throwing it, to keep that night from ending in violence. The glass fell on to the table, but didn't break.

'I'm leaving,' Gaspar said.

Marita got up to follow him, but Gaspar walked out fast and alone without waiting for her, forcing her to run down the street after him. It was late to go back to La Plata, but Gaspar headed towards the highway and the bus stop. Marita followed him as fast as she could: it wasn't easy to catch up. Luis's shouts also followed them: Quit fucking around, stay and sleep over, I've already made up the bed, tomorrow we can talk more calmly. Gaspar couldn't go any further than the highway: at that hour there were no radio taxis, yellow cabs didn't come to Villa Elisa, and the train wasn't running. The only options were to wait for a bus that passed once an hour, hitchhike, or stay at Marita's parents' house. When she caught up with him, she felt like slapping him. Leaving her like that, making her run through the night like a dumbass, begging him to stop like they were on some soap opera. But she held back.

'Don't talk to me right now,' he said. 'Please.'

'Your dad asked him not to tell you. It wasn't his fault.'

'I said don't talk to me.'

Marita stopped in the middle of the road, incredulous, as she saw the white and red of the approaching bus that would take them back to La Plata.

'We need to buy a car,' she said.

On the bus, she let Gaspar sit alone in the last seat. When they reached La Plata, she went back to the apartment, but he stayed out alone, walking.

Marita ran to Professor Herrera's office. She was late for her appointment with the university press's director, all because Gaspar had been too furious to let her get a good night's sleep. And she had to work. Gaspar was selfish sometimes: his drama came before everything else. She knew, though, that when she got home that evening, he would probably have calmed down and would apologize. She was aware that they had to break that cycle somehow, and she trusted that they would, with the correct therapy. Gaspar was right when he said he couldn't go on seeing his childhood psychiatrist.

The college's hallway was papered with signs on both walls, and paper banners with slogans were also hanging from the ceiling and doors. Elections were coming up, and it was the first time since she'd started school that Marita wasn't involved in the process. That year, her job at the press had absorbed her entirely. Currently, she was helping on the series of great forgotten essays from the seventies onward. Texts that had been published to no great acclaim in alternative magazines or media outlets, by authors who over time became famous. Also articles by disappeared journalists, the occasional overlooked gem. The criteria were eclectic because the choice was up to Herrera, the teacher whose class she assisted in. He was also the most admired and feared professor at the college, though she knew his gruff character was just a show for his classes: outside the classroom he was very nice. Marita still needed to read the essays in the last book, the one that would go to press that afternoon, because she had taken a week off. And now, instead of returning on time and enthusiastic, she was turning up bleary-eyed and half asleep. Herrera demanded meticulousness and Marita loved that job; she wanted to keep it for the coming years. They weren't paying her yet, but it was possible they would hire her soon. Plus, she wanted to show Herrera the testimonies she had gathered about the AIDS crisis in the city, and the photos of the first pride parades. It was a modest project, but with some work and more material it could be published. That wasn't going to happen if she came in late and didn't demonstrate seriousness.

'Finally,' said Herrera without a greeting. 'We need to get to work.'

Marita set her backpack on the floor and licked her lips in case there were breadcrumbs or drops of coffee left over from breakfast. She wanted to seem professional.

'We need to send Volume 12 to press. You didn't correct it, we had a temp last week, so I'm not holding you responsible, but the proofreading is a disaster. We can't send it like this. I need you to sit down and do it now.'

'Professor, there's not enough time to proof a whole book, and I'm not a proofreader, either.'

'No, my dear, I'm not asking for the whole book, I'm not crazy. It's the last article, by Olga Gallardo. I don't know what happened: it seems like the temp didn't even glance at it. Take a look. It's missing accents, it jumps around, it's a mess. Clearly it won't be the same as if the proofreader had done it, but she can't come in today. You and I have to do what we can.'

'No problem.'

'Have you read that text?'

'Not yet.'

'I went back and forth on whether to include it up until the last minute, because Olga was a very particular person in her final years. Mental illness is terrible, Marita, it can devastate a person. I met her when she was young and she was an excellent professional, bold, a little too bohemian, like everyone. And at the end, she was just a shadow of herself. She got obsessed with this case you're going to read, but not just that. It's never just that.'

Marita had heard of Olga Gallardo before, the great female chronicler in a male-dominated world, and also a suicidal alcoholic. She thought the whole legend was an exaggeration, and also unfair, because although everyone insisted Gallardo had been great, they never assigned her in classes. Herrera himself had said once that in her work, it was hard to know where the facts ended and the fiction began. And how that was the mortal sin for journalists, who, though they should by all means employ the narrative tools of literature, must never employ the imagination: public responsibility and commitment to truth-telling were inalienable. Marita made a cup of instant coffee and then printed the article from her computer. It was called 'The Zañartú Pit', and it wasn't very old: Gallardo had killed herself soon after it was published. It was a suicide note. Marita felt a little apprehensive as she sat down to read the text, pen in hand. It meant reading the words of a woman who was possibly crazy, the words she had left as a testimony before killing herself. And it had been a horrible death, from rat poison – that was also part of the legend, her painful last gasps in a hotel, because she had left her house to die. Herrera had his back to her as he talked into the phone, twisting the cord. Marita settled into her chair and entered the jungle, a pit of bones, the heat.

*

The phone rang, so did the doorbell. The brand-new cell phone's battery was dead, and he didn't plan on charging it. He wasn't about to respond to anyone. He had thrown Marita out. He'd done it because she was in danger, and, of course, she hadn't been able to understand. She'd been scared. She wanted to know if it was true what the article said about the house where Adela had disappeared, the human remains, if it was true about the difference in size and area between the inside and out. He hadn't wanted to answer: he couldn't, but he didn't deny it, either. While Marita yelled at him, he was watching Adela, naked in a corner of the apartment, lit by the dusky light shining in from the balcony. Her body was covered in trickles of blood or maybe strands of red yarn, and she was dancing a childish and elastic dance, her blonde hair falling over her black eyes, black as Omaira's eyes and his father's before he died. He tried to look at Marita, but he couldn't stop seeing that little-girl body, white and obscene, skipping near the curtain. Marita insisted. Gallardo made things up, she told him, everyone knew that. Everyone, everyone, who is everyone? That woman had killed herself because of him. His second death. There would be more, he was very sure of that. The fact that this article had found its way into Marita's hands was the final message. He couldn't explain it to her because it would be years of explanations and of silences, and so he'd thrown her out. Pack your bags, I can't take care of you, Marita, I seriously cannot take care of you, you have no idea what this is. I don't either, but I sense, I know, I always knew, that the end is coming and they sought you out. But I can't let them, not you: if anything happens to you I won't be able to forgive myself. And something's going to happen. Get out.

You're crazy, Marita sobbed, we have to call your shrink, and while she cried, Gaspar started to empty out her drawers and pull her clothes from the closet, and to fill the suitcases they had so recently unpacked when they'd moved into that apartment that still smelled of paint. At the back of the closet, once it was empty, he saw a head. Or rather, the back of a neck. Someone had chewed it, there were teeth marks. He slammed the doors shut before the head turned around and showed him its face. He was afraid he would recognize it.

He had to give Marita credit – she'd brought the article to him immediately and told him everything. Not like his uncle. She didn't hide things from him. She was brave. She was scared and crying, and although she had howled when he put her clothes into the suitcase, in a way it was what she'd expected. There could be no other outcome. Gaspar could understand fear and rage, but not secrecy. The price of revealing that secret, of course, was this. When Marita left, Adela stopped dancing: she was dressed now, wearing the old pink sweatsuit she used to wear when she was still his friend and not this ghost dancer. Gaspar could feel only relief when Marita left, saying she was never coming back. That was exactly what he wanted.

The phone rang again. Maybe it was his uncle. It could be Vicky, or Pablo. Had Luis met Betty out at Puerto Reyes? If he'd met his mother – no, worse, if his mother had taken him over the border and out of the country – anything was possible. It didn't matter. The article mentioned his grandparents' house. They were getting too close. They're surrounding me. He read the article until he knew it by heart. He had to be practical. He had to realize that in all the years since Adela disappeared, he had never been this close to finding his way to her and understanding what had happened, what his story was, and his parents', his family's. Adela, according to Gallardo, was his cousin. Betty had never told him, never even hinted. How cruel. He expected that cruelty from his father, but Betty? They were hiding something monstrous. He pictured Betty at that provincial hotel, drunk and raving about a monster that lived in the jungle.

She was telling the truth. That house, Puerto Reyes. He had to go. The Devil's Throat, he thought. He had asked his father if he was going to throw him in and his father had sworn he wasn't. Maybe he had lied.

During the next two days, Gaspar didn't leave the apartment much: just to buy food and cigarettes, and a map of Misiones from the Auto Club. The one he found wasn't very big, but it was good enough. Zañartú was marked on it. So were San Cosme and Puerto Libertad. It was easy to get to Puerto Reyes from Libertad, Andrés Sigal had told him. Puerto Reyes, the Moby Dick of the aristocracy's mansions. His grandmother had a limp, he had a faint memory of it now. She climbed the stairs with a cane. Grandma Ahab. He had to plan out the trip's itinerary. Betty could still be in Cosme. The excavations at the pit had ended. He remembered how they'd talked about that at one of his uncle's cookouts. He had to find the list of identified bodies. Had they found Adela's father? What had Betty done with him? The Corrientes morgue. He'd have to go there, too. It was a lot. Was Betty at Puerto Reyes? If anyone else was at the house, they would open the door to him. Olga Gallardo wasn't the only one after him. And they weren't looking for him so they could welcome him lovingly as the prodigal son. He knew that much, if nothing else. He had to go there, or else the circle closing in on him was going to start to squeeze. If they couldn't reach him, they'd get to someone else. If they got to Marita, he couldn't imagine how he would go on with his life, with life.

He unplugged the phone.

*

The ER had been unbearable from the start. She'd hardly clocked in and she got the worst kind of case: a pregnancy with complications. Vicky hated complicated births because the families never understood. They got angry, they blamed the doctors for the woman bleeding out, for the breached baby, or, in the best cases, for the emergency C-section. They didn't understand the simple explanation that these things happened, that it was nature, that women had died in childbirth for centuries. They couldn't understand that a birth wasn't some sacred experience, all that hocus pocus. These doctors ruining their bliss. She detested the relatives.

And, after the pregnant woman, a boy convulsing from fever who had that kind of hysterical mother who won't let you work and thinks she knows more than the doctors. It was pretty true what her own mother always told her: she had no empathy. All she wanted was for them to let her fix things. Why did she have to be nice on top of it?

Now a patient was arriving by ambulance, and the report said it was an accident. They were never told clearly what was coming into the ER. Communication between the hospital, the ambulances, and the police was a disaster. So it could be anything, a contusion, a hit-and-run, a massacre.

Vicky waited with her co-workers on the driveway, smoking the requisite cigarette before going back in for another fifteen minutes of stress. The ambulance workers lifted the victim down on a stretcher, and when asked, they said the same as always, we don't know what happened; he turned up like this on Rambla 32. Vicky went closer. Rambla 32 was near the projects, where there were often stabbings, shootouts, and fights over drugs. The sight of the man on the stretcher left her openmouthed. It was so unthinkable that on first glance she thought she was seeing the impossible: Juan, Gaspar's father, with his surgery scar on his chest, his pale skin, his sunken eyes. She blinked, stepped back, and realized the truth with a lurch of her own body: the man on the stretcher was Luis Peterson. He was naked and had a wound on his chest, right above the sternum, a vertical wound brutally sewn up. She couldn't tell in the driveway's light if it was superficial or not. Temperature 39.5, pressure nine six, reported the ambulance doctor, and Vicky gave herself a mental slap. She touched the wound. It didn't seem superficial. At first glance, it looked like his sternum had been broken, like in a thoracic surgery. Luis was unconscious. He had tiny cuts all over his body, now somewhat scabbed over. Fine but continuous cuts. Except for his face, his entire body had been delicately lacerated.

She tried to kick-start her ability to diagnose, made an effort to intuit as fast as possible, and her instinct told her the most urgent thing was an X-ray. To find out, right away, what that wound was. Blood analysis, oxygen, IV, check vital signs. The tachycardia was obvious and was another bad sign, as was the unconsciousness. He was in shock. And the wound wasn't recent: it had the sickly red of infection.

The X-ray left everyone aghast. One of the students had to leave the imaging room and Vicky heard the sound of him vomiting from far away, like in a dream. She and the head doctor looked at the films and looked at each other and turned back to the X-rays. The sternum was split, and not by a surgeon's saw. The cuts, splintered and irregular, looked like they were from a giant pair of scissors. They could have been made with something similar. Hedge clippers, for example. And the bone was open, no one had made any attempt to close it: only the skin was sewn up. In the space between the bones of the split sternum, pressuring the lungs, there was an arm. A very small arm, not an adult's. A child's arm. Don't let it be one of the twins' arms, thought Vicky, please, please. The arm could be clearly seen. It had been cut off under the elbow. It had all five fingers and their bones.

God, let it be a mannequin's, said the head doctor, and he went running out. It's not a mannequin's, thought Vicky, and he knows it but doesn't want to admit it, he can't say it out loud. The head doctor gave orders for an operating room, for cultures, for antibiotics. Luis is in septic shock, Vicky thought. While she waited in the ER to hear the results from the surgery – and attended a man who'd cut off a finger with a grill knife trying to pry meat from the freezer – she could think rationally. She realized, with utter clarity, that Luis was going to die. It was a human arm. It had bones. It was in the space between his heart and lungs. All of his organs could already be damaged from the infection. The arm was surely in a state of decomposition. That had caused the sepsis.

And that was only the start of the problem. Vicky apologized to her lead doctor and told him the truth: she knew the man who'd gone into shock. He was the father of a friend of hers. She needed to stop working. The doctor told her of course, that was fine, and Vicky sat in the surgery hallway. They left an arm like the one Adela was missing, she thought. They left it in his chest. Like the imbunche. Where had that memory come from? Chiloé, the sect of witches. Adela in the forest. The river, Betty, furious and drunk, that summer in the south. He's identical to his brother and that's not a coincidence. This is an attack. An attack and a message. For Gaspar, first of all, but also for all of us. Vicky felt like someone was blowing on the back of her neck, like voices were whispering into her ear and always saying the same thing. You'll be next. Or Pablo. Gaspar has to make a move.

The surgeon came out and Vicky approached him, told him

the truth, too. The surgeon looked at her with all the frustration of a doctor who has failed, or encountered an impossible case. Then his look turned to sorrow, then to a slight distrust. He, too, was aware how macabre the situation was. This is black magic, thought Vicky, it's macumba, it's demonic.

'It's a human arm, Doctor, and the sepsis is very advanced. If you know the family, you'd better call them. The wounds on the body are superficial. We're going to report it: this man was tortured.'

Vicky ran out. She hadn't been able to reach Gaspar for a couple of days. He'd fought with Marita and thrown her out. That's what Marita had said through her tears, but she hadn't said any more than that. Sometimes Marita could be complicated, too, though she had the reputation of an easy-going girl. Vicky didn't want to call Julieta: what was she going to say, and how? The only thing she could do was call Pablo, but when he answered, her phone was shaking so much she had to hold on to it with both hands to tell him:

'Bring Gaspar to the hospital. Kick his door down, because he won't answer. Luis is here and he's dying.'

She hung up, then slowly walked to the nurses' station. She needed to lie down, rest her head that was spinning dizzily, and cry in peace around women, without having to explain something she couldn't even think about, just telling them, Girls, you can't imagine what a mess, what a disaster, what a nightmare.

The hatred spilled from her eyes along with the tears and Gaspar heard her scream, It's your fault, even if you didn't do it, you did it. She didn't think he had opened his uncle's chest like a crazed hunter to insert a child's arm inside, a girl's arm, because its little fingernails were painted, that's what one of the nurses

685

had said, such gossips the nurses, those little nails painted coral pink, specific as well as gossipy, those nurses. She didn't say he had committed the crime, in just a few words she said the crime was his fault and she was right about that, he couldn't argue with her there, so he let himself be hit, let her scratch his face, and he liked the salty taste of his own blood in his mouth. He could only think how it wasn't one of the twins' arms and that seemed like a victory, an insolent show of mock compassion. I don't want to go in and see him, Vicky, I can't see him. I'm not going in, period. And he wasn't going to see him, it was a meeting with a ghost, Luis would be just like his father, they didn't look so much alike, they'd never looked all that much alike, but the family resemblance, and like that, in the hospital, with all the tubes, the smell of death, his chest split, he was just like his father and Gaspar didn't want that image and he wasn't going to have it. You have to go in, Vicky was saying, because his whole body is covered in cuts and I looked at them, they're inscriptions, letters. You decipher them. Copy them out, write down what they say. Take photos of him. Julieta screamed after hearing the doctor announce the inevitable and soon the police would come to ask the first questions and in a few hours they'd tie things together, one two three knots. The little girl's arm. Vicky and Pablo and him, especially him, of course, the ones who'd gone into the house with Adela. Armless Adela. A little girl's arm. Adela, my cousin, Adela, my blood. Who had poisoned that blood? A dead father, a dead uncle, both with the scar in the middle of their chests. And he had spent his days locked inside while this was happening. This was happening. Julieta was telling a policeman that Luis had left three days ago. She thought he'd stayed in La Plata for work or with his older son. Yes, that's his older son. Adopted. His nephew. Sometimes he stayed over at his house but he always let me know, he always let me know, we have very young children, he always let me know. So I called Gaspar but he didn't answer, Gaspar is the son, the nephew, the one over there. I couldn't get him, the line was busy and I thought, that happens, the phone wasn't working, they'd let me know the next day. I went to work and it was a tough day, when I finished I called home and nothing, I went to the site and nothing, but they told me the crew had the days off because it was raining and they couldn't work in the rain, so I thought he went somewhere else on his days off, I thought about another woman, I don't know what I'm saying, I'm sorry, I thought about whatever, I even got mad. Why didn't I go to his son's house? Because I got this idea in my head about another woman, I don't know, I was in denial? Because I couldn't understand why he didn't come back? This was happening, thought Gaspar. Someone had taken his uncle when he was on his way to La Plata because the car had turned up, intact, in Gonnet. Near the city. A beautiful place, Gonnet, prettier than Villa Elisa, with modern houses, though it's true the dive bars along the road were horrible, just awful, some of them even dangerous, Gaspar had gone and the girls who danced on the speakers were always high and beautiful and ferocious. The little painted nails, what colour were they? Salmon? Coral? Now there were a lot of colours with aquatic names in addition to good old navy blue, *azul marino*, which wasn't *marino* for marine, but for the *Marina*, the Navy. It had taken him a ridiculously long time to figure that out. Like the ridiculous amount of time he had wasted in his house making maps and plans and reserving plane tickets while this was happening. So, Gonnet. A house in Gonnet, one of those pretty houses. A house into which they had dragged his uncle after pulling him from the car. Surely he had thought that after all this time he was actually being kidnapped, and he was right, but it wasn't the government doing it. Had they knocked him out to cut his sternum? Surely they had, because otherwise he would have fought back and he was strong, he was strong, all those times he'd picked Gaspar up, the way he held him against the wall when he needed to calm him down, the way he sawed wood faster than the others and perspired less than anyone. So they had put him to sleep and then they'd used the hedge trimmers and maybe a saw, they'd find that out from the autopsy, because there would be an autopsy, this was a murder. So, the house in Gonnet. How many people? Two or three? Who? They would tell him. In Misiones. Because they weren't in the city any more. They'd tossed a body at him the way bodies are tossed in Argentina. In Argentina, they toss bodies at you. *Te tiran muertos.* Now he understood what that phrase meant. The arm was from a random child, a little girl who was maybe already dead, the cops would do well to check for dug-up graves or even at hospitals. Maybe a girl had been reported missing. They worked at night, they worked in darkness. Why did they want him so badly? They wanted him, and they hurt him. They wanted him hurt. Hurt, he was easier to manipulate. That's why he refused to see the body. The police would be interrogating him soon. He didn't have an alibi. He'd kicked Marita out. Had he ordered delivery? He couldn't remember. He'd gone out to buy things, that's true. Food, and the map. Surely the guy at the Auto Club would remember, because he'd asked for a bigger map, bigger, as if he were half-blind. He didn't have an alibi, but he didn't care. What Julieta said was true. It was his fault. It was a message for him, they'd tossed a body at him. He didn't want to see. One time, Luis had put bananas in the freezer and taken them out cold and drizzled hot chocolate syrup over them. His idea for a cheap, delicious dessert. He always let Gaspar have the TV remote. He never lost his temper on the soccer field. He said that someday he wanted to go and live in the mountains, but he also really liked the beach, what he most missed about Rio was being able to go for a walk along the ocean, with the wind, the smell of salt in his hair. He had been at the birth of his two children and he hadn't gotten drunk afterwards and he hated it when people congratulated him, I didn't do anything, it's just a joy. A joy, Luis was a joy, and he would have had a peaceful, sweet future. The house in Gonnet, then, they stuck the arm in there and left him unconscious, or maybe not, maybe they woke him up and let him scream and agonize, there was nourishment in that, he had felt it, the suffering that can be eaten. And then, racked with fever and infection from the little arm, they left him lying on Rambla 32, there where the city began or ended depending on your perspective. There were ballads to calm suffering, lullabies, but he couldn't go in and sing any because it was his fault, because he had given that permission to kill and mutilate. Julieta knew it, that's why she was crying like that, with so much rage, because she knew. Vicky came out of the ICU and led him over to a corner. She grabbed his face to make him look at her. Vicky's dark eyes. She was so beautiful. More than Marita. More than anyone. 'The only thing written on his body is "let him come". That's what the cuts say.' 'What do you mean, "let him come"?' 'That's it, Gaspar: "let him come".' 'Okay,' said Gaspar. 'Is he going to die? Tell me the truth.' 'It's a matter of hours,' said Vicky. 'Okay. I'm leaving tonight.' 'You have to talk to the police,' Vicky protested. 'After I talk to them, I'm leaving. They're not going to arrest me tonight. Listen to me, Vicky, and explain to Pablo.' 'Pablo is right downstairs.' 'I don't have time to talk to him. They've crossed the line. I can't live among you all any more. If I stay with you, you'll be next. There can't be any more. They want me, I'm their blood. Take my house key.' Vicky was listening closely now. 'In the apartment, on the bed, I left something, I want you to read it. It's an article by Olga Gallardo called 'The Zañartú Pit'. I can't explain now. I want you to go and read it. Let Pablo read it. It'll be there because they can't go into my house and Marita won't come back. You know how Luis said he was afraid of my dad sometimes? He told me something really strange once. He told me that when he was taking care of my dad, when my dad was little, maybe six years old, he'd just had an operation and my uncle was taking care of him. My grandparents, I don't know, working. Doesn't matter, right? Doesn't matter. So Luis was taking care of him and he told me how my dad's lips were covered in blood, like he'd eaten raw meat. Luis put water on his lips because they were dry and a nurse had brought cocoa butter, and later he used it and they stopped bleeding. But that time, when they were bleeding and my dad was scream-ing in pain, they must've had bad painkillers back then, how could they just let a kid scream in pain like that?' 'Maybe they couldn't give him any, it's possible they'd make his pressure hit the floor,' said Vicky. 'What pressure?' 'His blood pressure, Gaspar. If the painkiller lowered his blood pressure, he'd die.' 'Oh, maybe. Anyway, those nights in the hospital were horrible, Luis said, he was just a kid, too, after all. So, Dad screamed, all of a sudden, he screamed: "No one hears the bones sing." That phrase, like a reproach. It really scared Luis. My grandparents were afraid of my dad. My dad saw ghosts. Luis didn't, because Luis wasn't marked. I don't want to see him. He's going to scream the same thing. Now they've marked him too, but they can't make it last. The truth is I should have stayed in the house with Adela. It would have ended there. All this, all this time, it doesn't matter, Vicky. It's not time. Marita knows it should have been in a different life, don't tell her this isn't life and it isn't time.'

*

How many times had he thought, 'I want to be just like him'? The way he'd told Gaspar while they rode in the car, you have to always be respectful with girls, even if you're not interested in them. The way, after he got mad about something and raised his voice and shouted, he always gave in to a joke and laughed and shook his head. The twins were going to forget him, they would miss out: the permission to do their homework on the patio, the races down the dirt road, the grilled fish at the beach, the, What you wrote is really good, that teacher must be kind of dumb, she doesn't have to understand everything but it's a shame she didn't understand this, because it's so well written, and long! And the words you use! They were going to miss out on having him always accept them even when they messed up, even if they had ridiculous mental emotional psychiatric problems, they'd miss out on knowing there was someone who would never abandon them, would never back down, they could beat their heads against the wall until they broke their heads and the wall, and he would be right behind them, arms crossed, saying, Well then, shall we start by fixing your skull, your anger, or the bricks? You choose.

Gaspar paid a minuscule amount of money to the taxi driver who dropped him off at Ezeiza Airport, and he waited for the flight in silence, his backpack between his feet. He wasn't bringing much, and if he needed anything he could buy it where he was going. It was his first time on a plane alone. He didn't want to think about the previous times, which were few and always with Luis. The flight was short but they still served food, though he didn't touch it because he couldn't eat; he didn't know if he would ever eat again. He remembered Pablo's face when he saw him come out of the hospital: he'd almost asked him to come. Pablo would have done it. Vicky had to stay with Luis. They would follow him, he thought. Both of them. They knew where he was going.

In Posadas he spent an hour looking for a place to rent a car. The heat was going to give him a headache, though he was wearing dark glasses and he'd wet his hair several times. He started to down pills: they would work better on his empty stomach. He found a relatively cheap Clio, rented it for a week, and, after concentrating for a kilometre to be sure it handled easily, he opened the map from the Auto Club. Puerto Libertad, the town closest to the house, was near Iguazú, just metres from the Paraná River: across the river was Paraguay. Three hundred kilometres. How was he going to manage not to think for three hundred kilometres? He turned the map and lit a cigarette, trying not to burn the map or himself. The car had air conditioning, but when he turned it on it stank of gasoline, so he kept it off. He was no expert in cars. In theory, his epilepsy meant he shouldn't drive, but Luis had taught him anyway, because he believed a person needed to know how to drive, otherwise they weren't fully free. Luis wasn't an expert either. All the cars he'd bought turned out to be clunkers. Gaspar remembered him standing in front of every ruined car and saying, What bad luck, his hands on his hips as he stared at a raised hood billowing smoke. It's not the car that's the problem, Negro had shouted at him once, you forgot to put water in, what kind of asshole doesn't put water in a car, I ask you? They'd been on their way to Punta Lara. For a picnic or to go fishing? It was before the babies, before the pregnancy. Why did he never name the twins? Salvador and Juan. Gaspar had thought Juan was named after his father, but Luis, a little sheepish, admitted the name was for Perón. He hadn't been able to negotiate the full name, Juan Domingo, with Julieta. He turned on the radio. Brazilian stations came in clearly, but he didn't want to hear that language, obviously. Would someone tell Mónica and the girls? They hadn't been to visit in a long time, but New Year's cards still came, and phone calls at birthdays and sometimes presents. Luis had gone to visit them twice, alone, just a week each time. Gaspar had stayed with Julieta both times. Luis came back with Garotos and records and some books, saying that book design was much better in Brazil than Argentina. He had promised to take Gaspar to see Rio, a promise that was delayed by the babies. Gaspar didn't much care for the beach, but Rio was more than just Copacabana, it was also dark streets and staircases and twilight at bars in inner neighbourhoods. They were going to miss out on that, too – him, the twins, everyone.

'They're not going to let you in.'

The restaurant at the service station had a name, Los Lapachos.

'They have their own police, just imagine. A lot of people come to take photos. A lot! People are obsessed with taking pictures of it. I give them directions to the place, but it's not going to happen. If you do get in, let me know, I have a lot of interested folks.'

'I'm going to try, we'll see,' said Gaspar, and he took a sip of cold Coca-Cola with two headache pills. It wasn't as intense as he'd thought it would be. With the sun in his face the whole trip, he'd expected to see black flowers start growing in the blue sky, taking over everything. Instead, it was a slight, annoying pain. He could allay it with some food.

'Do you ever see them?'

'No, and they don't shop here in town, either, they have servants who buy further up. My grandpa says that years ago they used to have parties and he'd see the cars, but no one stayed here. The *patrón* used to come around, before. He'd have some drinks, or buy fishing supplies. That was a long time ago. The *patrón* likes his drink.'

The *patrón*, thought Gaspar. My grandfather, the boss.

He had to go to the end of the main street and turn down the unpaved road. He decided to walk a bit first. Red sidewalks, kerbs painted an even deeper red, shops selling ice, girls using umbrellas as parasols, the sky perpetually threatening a storm, white houses. Had his mother walked through that town? Had she bought something in its markets? Would anyone remember her if he asked? Once, Marita had told him, after sex – she said the most intense things after sex – that if he wanted to live he had to give up his dead, let them go. A lot of motorcycles, red earth. The soles of his sneakers were already totally red. The municipal farmers' and artisans' market was closed, like almost all the businesses. The hallowed siesta. There wasn't much to see. He went back to the car and opened a fresh bottle of water before driving down the main avenue and reaching the dirt road to the house. On either side, dense jungle, full of green depths. No animals. He had to go to the house because they had summoned him. He had been repeating that to himself ever since he left, and he kept on repeating it to fight off sleep, hunger, emptiness.

They sought me out, here I am. I don't know how to let go of the dead.

He'd expected abandonment, madmen and women sequestered in the jungle, mouldy tapestries, overgrown plants, underbrush he'd have to hack through to reach the house. He passed a security cabin that was empty, but not abandoned – there was a steaming mate on the reception table and the radio was on – and then he stopped the car and took in the view of the house. He got out and walked in: the giant iron gates were open.

694

A wide expanse of freshly cut grass lay before a house whose mustard-coloured façade was covered with climbing vines – not a sign of neglect, but well-tended decoration. Roofs that were red like the Misiones earth, palms and other trees surrounding its hexagonal shape, which at the front and back gave way to separate buildings; he could glimpse, along a side path, at least two more houses, one small and the other, in the distance, also enormous. The grass was uninterrupted: if there were fountains, they were at the back. And he could hear the river. That's where the catwalks are, thought Gaspar, near the river, and he looked up because suddenly the landscape had darkened. A threatening storm cloud, low and swollen and heavy with hail, hung over the afternoon. When he looked at it, his headache exploded along with the black flowers that opened with carnivorous ferocity. He had the horrible certainty – déjà vu again, but very powerful this time – that his parents were going to come out of the house. The ghost house with palm trees and ghost parents; he even expected to see his uncle emerge, ash-coloured, ashes in his hair, the rotting arm in his hand, the rotting arm he would use as a club to attack Gaspar, to beat him on the head and body. He leaned against the car and saw someone come out of the house, a man. He approached Gaspar and straightened him up by taking hold of his shoulders, making him meet his eyes. The elegant grey hair, the sunken dark blue eyes, a forehead that Pablo would have called 'Teutonic' when he was doing his taxonomy of men: Teutons, fairies, breeders, bears, otters, daddies. The memory of Pablo almost made him smile. He knew this man. Esteban. He hadn't expected to find him here.

On the front steps of the house, a group of people had gathered. Gaspar could see them clearly, the pink light of dusk forming a golden aura around them, a diminished glow. Two old women, one of them elegant in a gauzy Indian dress. The other wore a mask that hid her mouth and jaw, her grey hair cut very short, pants, and a high-necked shirt. Behind were some five or six other people whom he couldn't distinguish as easily from where he was standing.

Gaspar summoned his strength and shoved Esteban away. He regretted not having thought to bring weapons, but what would be the point when he didn't know how to use them? He had never fired a gun. Never used a blade. All he could do was fight: he felt weak, but still capable of going up against Esteban. So as Esteban tried to regain his balance, Gaspar rushed him, pinned his arms behind his back, and threw him to the ground. Esteban knew how to fight too, and he managed to get to his feet and remove Gaspar's arms from his neck with a quick and almost professional movement. Panting, sizing each other up, they faced each other from a metre apart.

The elegant woman left the doorway, came down the steps, and opened her arms in a sign of welcome. She had white hair with orangish streaks. Freckles all over her face. She'd been a redhead. The masked woman followed her, limping. That's my grandmother, thought Gaspar. She took off her mask before speaking to him. For a person with such a horrible mutilation, what she said could be understood quite clearly.

'I was the one who ordered your uncle's death. Be still, you're as savage as your father.'

Gaspar recognized his grandmother's voice in spite of her slavering diction. Again, he didn't hesitate and lunged at her, not caring if she was old or a woman or his family. She had just confessed without even being asked. He managed to throw her to the ground, managed to sit on her bird-like hips – it couldn't be that hard to kill her. Before many hands – how many, he didn't know – pulled him away from her, he managed to hit her in the face, to feel her nose give way under his knuckles, to hear her curse him. Then, a single expert blow from a bodyguard, a man who really knew how and where to punch, knocked him out, and the last thing he saw was the sun through the trees and a flash of river.

Going up in the lookout tower was one way to go. It might be in good condition, and if the stairs gave way, that was good too. Although falling down a collapsed staircase wasn't a certain death – they could still rescue him, and he didn't want to be rescued. They followed him constantly, but he could do it if he was fast. They couldn't watch him all the time. He could also stop eating. That was another way to die that they couldn't control. Escaping was impossible. He had tried all the obvious ways, the river, the night, the jungle, and they'd caught him every time. The beatings weren't so much brutal as they were efficient. They knew how to torture, inflict pain, wound without damaging. He never got far. He couldn't flee. What they wanted from him was demented, but demented things were possible in that house and with those people. But he couldn't give it to them.

The women, especially, believed he could. He should stop calling them the women. Florence and Mercedes. His grandmother, Mercedes. The one without lips. Her false teeth chattered all the time, as if she were shivering. She didn't always use the mask, and never in front of him. She wanted him to see her.

Your father did that, Florence said, pointing to Mercedes' mutilation, her horrible face. Your father also killed my son and never told me where he hid his body. He thought he had arranged your salvation, and his revenge. He also took away the girl, who was of blood. He always had contempt for us, always wanted to destroy us, oh, you could see it in his eyes, *those yellow eyes, like a reptile's*. I trust that he is watching, from wherever he is, and he can see that we have done it. We have the medium he wanted to take away from us, we have you in spite of that potent sign he marked you with. He always was more talented than intelligent. I feel sorry for him. A medium has too much responsibility. They are all dangerous, they all go mad.

'I don't know what you're talking about,' repeated Gaspar.

His grandmother came closer, and the words hissed from between her teeth:

'He didn't want you to know anything, he hid your inheritance from you. Better that way, better. I think mediums should merely be instruments. Still, I'm going to tell you something, wise you up a little. I can't stand those puppy-dog eyes of yours.'

Gaspar observed her skull. She was nearly bald. Very short shocks of hair spiked up from a barren desert. And the missing lips. She didn't look fully human, and maybe because of that he didn't find her horribly ugly, but rather interesting, like a fantastical animal.

'He never told you this, of course, but what the Order wants, and what you can give us – what you *will* give us, because we will force you – is immortality. I see you, Florence, shaking your head. Everything has to be exact with this woman. Really, we refer to it as maintaining consciousness on this plane. Keeping consciousness alive. That is achieved, as the Darkness has dictated, by transferring it from one body to another.'

Esteban came into the room as Gaspar stifled a guffaw.

'What's the Darkness?'

'It's what took Adela,' Esteban answered, and Gaspar stopped laughing, covered his eyes with his hands, murmured, You're all crazy.

'There you go, you heard it straight from your dad's buddy. Though your father also lied to you your whole life. We know you can open the Darkness like Juan did, and you're going to do it for us. The Darkness tells us how to make that transfer and remain alive forever. Your father tried it with you, don't you remember? It's like the kid is retarded, don't you think, Flo? What a shame, my only grandson is an idiot, and on top of that he lost little Adela, who did have promise. Now that was a girl with character. Well then.'

Mercedes sat on the leather sofa near the window and turned up the room's air conditioner with a remote control.

'What a stupid day that was, for us at least. Your father tricked us. Did he erase your memory, is that why you remember nothing? Or does that mark on your arm also give you amnesia? It's a very good mark, I'm surprised. You know that's why he cut you, I suppose. To keep you away from us. Well: we carried out the transfer of your father into your body at the Chascomús house. That place is very special to me because it belongs to my mother's family, not like this jungle monstrosity my father liked, and my husband when he still had some brains left, and everyone else. There is nothing like the emptiness of the pampa. I'm getting distracted. I'm old, I need a new body, now. It's my right and you're going to give it to me. We brought you both out there to Chascomús. There is something you need to know about the Rite. We have achieved the transfer of consciousness many times; what we cannot yet do is keep it in the new body. That's why we believed your father.'

Gaspar listened to her closely. She was talking about the accident at Chascomús, the time he had woken up wounded, in an unfamiliar bed, with the horrible certainty that his father had hurt him. He remembered his twisted ankle, the blow to the head that had supposedly caused his epilepsy, that lazy summer beside the pool with Tali and Esteban.

'The Rite requires preparations I don't need to go into here, and in any case your father didn't need to perform them because he was an extraordinary medium. We put the two of you on altars. And he was able to transfer his consciousness into your body. Oh, it was marvellous! Remember, Flo? We stood in a circle around you, it was sacred. Your body's eyes opened and it was Juan who looked out. But then came the resistance. The receiving body always resists. Never, however, have I seen resistance like that. I don't know about the rest of you.'

Florence said she had attended all the Rites and, truthfully, she couldn't remember any other resistance being as violent. They described it: when he opened his eyes and everyone saw Juan's gaze, he had tried to run away. The Recipient cannot be tied down during the Rite. We think that is foolish, but unlike Juan, we follow the rules of the Darkness as they are dictated, because whenever we haven't, oh, what disasters, right, Esteban? You were there for some of them. They're like abortions. That's what Florence always says.

'*Like losing a child*,' Florence said, in English.

'And we have both lost children, it feels exactly like that. Though when it came to your mother, she was better lost than found. Well then! You struggled so much to get your father out of you that we all had to pitch in to stop you. You bit poor Esteban here in the neck. Florence's son, the younger one, used to bite too. At one point when we were trying to stop you, to get you to quit hurting yourself – because that's one of the unfortunate collateral effects of the Rite, the recipients get desperate and will damage themselves in order to get the Occupant out – we threw you to the floor and you hit your head.'

'*Oh, that was dreadful*,' said Florence, again in English.

'We thought we had ruined your body. But no. They say you're epileptic? What nonsense.'

Gaspar closed his eyes, trying to process the information. So the accident hadn't happened. His injuries were the result of this madness, this forced transmigration that he found absolutely incredible and stupid, but that they believed in, no doubt about it. Maybe not Esteban, who was silent.

'You want me to give you my body? Take it, I don't care.'

'No,' interrupted Florence, and she went on, alternating between English and Spanish. 'We need a medium, *and you are one.* You will tell us how to continue. *We cannot complete the Rite* and we are old. We cannot die, we must not die. *The messages stopped* because of your father, who unilaterally decided to cut off contact. We will continue with you.'

'I don't know how to do it.'

'You'll learn. You're young.'

Gaspar tried to stand up, but a dizzy spell stopped him short. He was eating little to nothing, wasn't taking his medication, and his knees shook weakly. But that wasn't it, he realized, or at least that wasn't the only reason. The dizziness knocked him off balance and he toppled from the chair. He heard his grandmother say: 'He's having convulsions, looks like, maybe it really is just epilepsy,' but no one touched him. He tried to tell her he had never had fits before, and then the memory flooded him, and he recalled that Rite they were talking about in full detail. He had sat up and opened his eyes and seen all those people around him, most of them naked, some wearing sheets or tunics, it was dark, and he had to expel something, a parasite inside him, and then he got up and ran because he'd seen the door, and they grabbed him by the legs and arms, Why do they want to keep me who are they what's wrong with them I have to get out of here, help me! I can't help you now, but fight them, said his father's voice, tired and thick, that voice he missed so badly. He started to cry as he lay on the floor but the memory kept going, implacable. There are a lot of them, where are we? Fight. There's an awful old lady, what are they?

Get up. Run. The others were trying to keep him where he was, but they couldn't, and in the struggle, in the attempt to get him back and lay him down, they dug in their nails, squeezed his ribs, and when he screamed, the shared body had a voice that was both of theirs, his and his father's. They got him back on the board, the altar, his grandmother had called it, and when they did, they hit his head violently, a dull sound, and then a moment of silence. Gaspar thought the memory would end there, that his body, now, in the freezing room in Misiones, was going to stop shaking, but it kept going. It's a monster grabbing my feet, kick its face, make another effort and kick its face, I'll help you, and Mercedes received the precise kick in the neck, she had to retreat, choking, but she came right back and twisted his ankle until the ligament nearly snapped, she was smiling, winning, You brought me here, why? The blood from Esteban's neck when he tried to escape again, I'd better get out, and then the sudden ending when his father withdrew. My father could have stayed inside me, he left because he wanted to, he told me to fight, Dad, you should have told me everything, it all would have been different, maybe I never would have come here, maybe your brother would still be alive. Gaspar felt Esteban's hands as he gently helped him sit up and offered him a glass of water, but the memory granted him one more image: other hands that rocked him, his father's hands, but enormous, with golden nails like misshapen claws. He looked at Esteban, who didn't insist with the glass of water.

'He tried to protect me?'

'He would never have taken your body. Never.'

Gaspar couldn't reply.

'This one's not going to die, is he? Let's see if we can make him eat, he's emaciated. One fuck-up after another.'

*

They visited him every afternoon in the room they'd reserved for him. He had a view of the garden and not much more. It was the ground floor, so he couldn't jump out the window. In any case, the window had bars. There were the two women and a man the same age as them, who spoke to him in English. The women would leave him alone with the man. He explained techniques. *Death posture. Inhale the sigil.* He laid Gaspar on the bed and taught him to breathe. If he resisted, the guards were there to persuade him with some form of pain. The man sometimes frowned or scowled: maybe he didn't agree with the methods, but the women dominated him, and so did something else, something that, like Betty said in the article, lived in the jungle. My family has worshipped it for centuries. His family. The man believed that Gaspar could establish contact with the thing that lived in the jungle, just like his father had. Gaspar didn't want to talk to them and he didn't know if he was even allowed to, or if it would mean more beatings, more prodding, more fingernails yanked out, more submerging of his head in water. But he did tell the man in English: *I can't give you what you want. I am not my father.*

The man insisted as if his life depended on it. Maybe it did. *Shut the lid of your unconscious. You know how to do this, I'm sure your father taught you.*

The same thing every day. Gaspar even started to enjoy the old man's visits. He was teaching him a kind of meditation that allowed him to think less. And after the old man left, he went back to his usual method, the same one he used to try to sleep. The letter A. The last name of a poet. The first line, or whatever he remembered, of a poem by a poet named A. If it was in English, translate it. Example: A. Ashbery. 'Alone with our madness and favorite flower.' How appropriate. *Solos con nuestra locura y nuestra flor favorita.* B. Blake. His father's favourite. Or one of them, at least. The other: Keats. 'He whose face gives no light, shall never become a star.' *Aquel cuyo rostro no de luz nunca se convertirá en una estrella.* C. Cendrars. 'It is my star / It is in the shape of a hand.' D. A difficult letter. There weren't many Ds, or he didn't know many. D'Annunzio. He couldn't remember any lines. Darío. Obviously. '*La princesa está triste . . . qué tendrá la princesa?*' E. Eliot. More than one line. 'Fiddle with pentagrams / Or barbituric acids, or dissect / The recurrent image into pre-conscious terrors—/ To explore the womb, or tomb, or dreams.' Tombs and dreams. Messages, pentagrams. His father's copy of Eliot was almost illegible from so much underlining.

Sometimes his grandfather visited him. He was in a wheel-chair, though Gaspar had noticed he could move his legs. He had a cup with a straw, and he drank something that looked like iced tea, but was whiskey. His skin had the yellow hue of terminal alcoholics. His grandmother came often, and sometimes he had trouble understanding what she said. Her tongue was white with tartar. The girl had been touched, she said. Your father took her away from us too, through you. Your father must pay. We sacrificed our own children because of him. We saved his life. The ungrateful wretch.

Every night, they took him to a clearing behind the house, far enough away that the trees hid it from view. They went through a garden that he remembered, far from the catwalks they still hadn't allowed him to see – they didn't have high railings – into full-fledged jungle. A clearing, that's what it was, like in books: 'In the clearing in the woods.' They took off his clothes at a certain spot and the English-speaking man urged him to repeat the exercises he'd taught him, and to concentrate. He gave Gaspar instructions about what to say and what movements to repeat. Gaspar obeyed. It was ridiculous. He saw the expectation in their faces, then the frustration. There was another red-headed woman, smaller and very old. Esteban hid his face in the shadows of the trees. There was a fluctuating number of younger men and women who didn't live in the main house; at night they withdrew to the guest house at the back: they were in charge of maintenance of the gardens and of the cleaning and upkeep of the house. He wasn't ashamed of nudity, though he was losing a lot of weight: they tried to force him to eat, but he fought back, and starving himself was bringing results. At night he felt feverish and couldn't sleep. In any case, he knew he would live for many days on a hunger strike, though his thirst defeated that plan more than his fear, the beatings, or the desperation. Plus, if he didn't drink liquid, he'd been assured they would connect an IV.

The guards took eight-hour shifts. They didn't let him read or watch TV or listen to the radio. He could explore the house if he wanted. And he did, every day. He was looking for Esteban. He hadn't seen him again except at the night-time ceremonies, and not at all of them.

The lookout tower was a good idea. They would follow him there if he wanted to go up. He didn't have any restrictions on the property, but he had permanent company. The tower was reached by a path lined by hydrangeas and forget-me-nots. He could see it from the window of his ground-floor room. The ones on the first floor had also been barred. This was his house, though. His. The lookout tower: in the night-time storm, it looked like a lighthouse without a light. It didn't have bars, as far as he could see. Maybe the guards would be fast enough to stop him, but he had to try to be even faster. One movement, a jump, and the end.

*

He didn't have to talk to them, he simply led them to the tower. The men followed, and when he reached the stairs one of them went ahead, so that Gaspar trailed him through the structure's interior, illuminated by a lot of small windows. Fast, fast. Get there and run straight to the railing and jump without thinking, he had no one, he had nothing, life before the room in Puerto Reyes didn't matter. Plus, the nights in the clearing in the woods were furious now, with his lipless grandmother screeching like an animal, Florence giving him orders and slaps, the young people spitting. Nothing from before, no one had come to find him, and if they had come, they were surely dead, these people can kill, I ordered your uncle's death, I ordered your mother's, that traitorous slut, that's what Mercedes had said, and he had asked, Why my uncle? And she said, We used to believe in treating those like you well, but now we know they are instruments, mere instruments.

Florence listened to her and smiled. This time we won't make mistakes. I know who you are. We all know who you are. We have ways of getting what we want.

But the truth is they don't have ways of getting what they want, thought Gaspar as he climbed the stairs. They don't. Otherwise, they could have already gotten anything from him, because all he wanted was to die. He didn't even have the consolation of the epileptic images any more. They were gone. The house had cured him. He didn't feel anything in that house, not in any of its corners. It was dead, it was a ruin, it was the place he was going to die: it was his tomb.

They reached the top of the lookout tower, the terrace. The man in front of him looked away for a second and Gaspar ran, put a foot on the railing, and suddenly his other foot was in the air, above the trees, he could smell the river, a bird cawed, and the sun, implacable, and he closed his eyes.

*

Idiots, Gaspar heard from the floor, while he tried to understand what was happening. Two arms had stopped his jump, but not the arms of the guards, whom he had dodged with precision and elegance. There was someone else on the lookout tower, someone who, focused as he was on escaping, he hadn't seen.

It was Esteban. His back was to the guards, and Gaspar saw him mouthing the words, 'Please, Gaspar.' And then:

'Go and get the doctor right away, he hit his head. Later you'll have to explain yourselves to my mother.'

One of the guards went running downstairs, and Gaspar leaned against the wall and thought about the freedom of that instant in the air, the stormy sky, the beauty of the fall. He didn't dare try again right now.

'Your father had a trick,' said Esteban, and Gaspar perceived a change in his voice that forced him to pay attention. *I'm trying to do it now. You and I can speak and that idiot over there will hear a different conversation. I don't know if it'll work, he promised to leave it to me before he died, look, he gave me this mark on my head, but you can't try with just anyone and it's been a long time since I've had someone to practise with, Tali won't let me any more.*

What are you saying?

You don't want to die. Or maybe you do, but you can also get away from here.

Gaspar looked at the guard and then at Esteban, who was sweating as if he were lifting something heavy. His father used to do this, the thing Esteban was trying to do now. He used to get into his head. Gaspar had always thought it was an exclusive communication between the two of them, and its oddness hadn't been apparent to him until many years later.

He can't hear us, who knows what he hears. But come on, I don't have much time. It's painful for me to keep this up. Ask, go on.

Why are you with them?

I'm not on their side, if that's what you're asking. They're my family. They're yours, too. There are plans for them, and you have to carry them out.

I don't believe you.

Well, you don't have many options left, Gaspar, you should really trust me.

Why did they kill my uncle? Why did they take Adela?

Luis's death was out of my control. I didn't even know about it. Adela was going to go no matter what, and plus, you took her there, much as it pains you. I can't summarize decades of history in the ten minutes until the doctor comes and my strength runs out. Your father decided Adela would disappear: he gave her up to save you from your family, and he used you as an instrument. I think that when he did it, he released unknown forces.

Gaspar smiled almost involuntarily.

I don't think the salvation is really working.

You're mocking me. At least that's a change from how resigned you've been since you got here. I remembered you as a brilliant child, one with character. Our family is brutal, Gaspar. You can't allow yourself to be weak. You never used to be weak.

That was a long time ago. I remembered you as a friend.

Enough with the sentimentality. Wake up, Gaspar. You can't do anything out there in the jungle where they take you, but you can do other things. You haven't sensed any doors?

Gaspar looked at this sweating man, his damp grey hair, and he observed the guard, who seemed nervous but wasn't paying them any attention, his eyes glued to the path. It was clear that Esteban was right: either he didn't hear the conversation or he didn't understand it.

I don't sense anything in this house.

You haven't seen all of it. There are two other buildings. You can ask them to take you.

Gaspar felt a shaking in his legs and then in his hands, and suddenly he was shaking on the floor. Four feet were climbing the lookout tower's steps.

It's normal for you to shake, it's the adrenaline, don't worry. Look, I'm going to stop talking to you in secret, okay? Whatever I do from here on doesn't mean anything. I'm going back to the role of my mother's son.

Your mother?

Florence. She's my mother.

When Esteban disconnected, Gaspar felt it. It was as if a hot wind stopped blowing in his face, or as if, after being inside with a heater, he had gone out into fresh air. The two guards carried him down, an unnecessary show: his head didn't hurt, Esteban had used his own arm to soften the blow. He let himself be carried. He heard running steps and phrases in English. *You were friends and lovers. You cannot be trusted. I just saved him, but of course that's not enough for you,* and he looked at the sky, where the flowers were growing along with his migraine, which had been caused not by hitting his head, but by the double adrenaline burst from the failed jump and what Esteban had done, that secret conversation spoken aloud that seemed as impossible as it did familiar. They checked him over, and he obeyed every order: it all reminded him step by step of the false accident months before his father's death, a farce that, he now knew, they'd put on in order to hide the repugnant Rite by which they'd tried to steal his body. The sensation was so vivid, so obvious, that he had no more doubts. It was a matter of remembering. That's what he had to focus on. Remembering, even things he hadn't witnessed. Maybe start eating again. You don't want to die, Esteban had told him, and you can escape.

He had to find the door.

It was hard to get moments alone with Gaspar. They tolerated his nearness because he was of blood and they had already lost too many blood members, but Stephen didn't want to make any suspicious moves. The encounter at the lookout tower had been an intuition. Stephen lived in the guest house. He could see the park from his window, and he'd caught sight of Gaspar and his guardians heading towards the most obvious place on the grounds from which to jump. The fact that the kid wanted to kill himself was so clear that only people who had gone mad from lack of human contact could fail to recognize it. Gaspar was so different from the child he remembered. It had been a real blow to see him in ruins: at twenty-five years old his beauty was simply extraordinary, healthy but so heavy with death. Hearing his thick voice at the lookout tower, so like Juan's, had been a shock, such unexpected virility coming from that faun-like face with its cheekbones protruding from the hunger strike; his rough hands were powerful too, with their long, broad fingers.

Stephen was getting ready to meet with Tali the next day when he saw Gaspar enter the guest house. The members of the Order believed Adolfo's daughter had committed suicide by drowning in the river after Juan's death. Her own father had identified the body. It belonged to a different woman, but in his drunkenness he couldn't have distinguished a woman from a deer. Tali had managed the confusion in part thanks to the Hand of Glory she inherited from Rosario. Eddie's hand, my brother's, thought Stephen. Well, if it lets Tali live 'clandestinely', as she calls it, then it's a good thing. It had been hard for her to leave the house and temple behind, but she had trusted people who took care of them, and she'd taken all the valuable relics with her. She lived nearby, but in a more conventional place. Mercedes, who doubted that death because distrust was her nature, would never look for Tali. About time that Indian fucked off, she'd say.

Stephen went ahead with his plan. He crossed the park and entered Mercedes' office, where she had prepared the accounts and the errands he would have to take care of. Sometimes some other member of the Order went with him, or even Adolfo Reyes himself, who got terribly bored and wanted to spend some time in Buenos Aires on occasion. Mercedes was wearing her mask and sunglasses: she looked like a murderous insect. She was also pretty easy to fool, because she was lazy. Stephen had started the transfer of property to Gaspar years ago. He didn't need Mercedes' signature, Adolfo's would suffice. And Adolfo, who was always drunk, would sign anything. The house was no longer hers alone. All her money was in Uruguayan and British banks, safe from Argentina's financial disaster, but that wasn't under his purview. There were accountants and lawyers everywhere. But he'd made it so that changing the ownership of the companies, the yerbatal, and the real estate would be much easier when the time came. They didn't even need to die first. They had bequeathed everything in life – they were elderly, so it was logical to pass things on to the young grandson. No one had seen them for a long time, and when Stephen went to meetings, he was clear about Adolfo Reyes' alcoholism and Mercedes' insanity. Gaspar's absence was a relief for the lawyers and accountants and managers, who imagined a young playboy capable of ruining everything. The decision to entrust Stephen with managing part of the fortune stemmed from Mercedes' enormous distrust of the living members of her family, who weren't many. She preferred to put someone from the Order in charge. Florence didn't share that paranoia, but neither did she meddle in other people's affairs. She didn't care about Mercedes' empire. Florence thought they were indestructible in earthly matters, that the families' power and influence were impossible to take down for reasons that had nothing to do with putting on a suit and spending hours in banks and offices. In short, she thought Stephen's work was useless and she didn't interfere.

'My grandson is a disaster, a failure,' said Mercedes. 'He doesn't even try to escape any more.'

In Mercedes' language, that meant they were missing out on a magnificent dog chase through the jungle in which she would get to employ a little sadism. Stephen still hadn't said anything to Gaspar about exactly what Mercedes kept in the tunnel.

'No matter. He will eventually manage the invocation. But I don't like to wait. I've always been impatient!'

'I'll leave tonight. If you need anything else, let me know. I'll be around.'

Mercedes waved him away and ran a hand over her sparse hair. Stephen remembered her from forty years before, in this very house. Back then, when he was still almost a child, he had found her repulsive. Juan had always said: Mercedes is a priestess of repulsive gods, and we always take after the gods we worship.

He wanted to see Gaspar before leaving. The kid's visit to the guest house was the result of their talk at the lookout tower, and Stephen was sure he would find the door. Even he could sense it, and he had never dared set foot in the Other Place.

He found Gaspar on the beach and the guards on high alert: the nearby river made them nervous. They were new guards: Florence had decided to change them after the suicide attempt. She had even toyed with the idea of making Gaspar be handcuffed to one of them every time he left his room. The idea was dismissed when Gaspar started accepting food again and exploring the grounds with renewed curiosity. She wasn't stupid. She knew she had to let him find his Place of Power. It wasn't impossible that he would be able to summon exactly where his father had, but it was unlikely. And if it didn't work, Florence was capable of sending the kid to travel the world, even at the risk of losing him. She needed a medium in order to maintain a power that was unravelling, as always happens after so great a disappointment. And with Juan the disappointment had been double: he had died, and when he wasn't able to occupy his son's body, it was clear that either the medium had disobeyed, or not even the Order's most powerful member was capable of carrying out the technique ordered by the gods. She insisted: The technique has not yet been given to us in full. We need a medium to complete it. She treasured those all-too-short moments they had kept consciousness alive inside a Recipient body. She had seen different durations. Mere minutes in the overwhelming majority of instances. Hours on one occasion that had reduced her to tears. Power was slipping from her hands, slowly, just as life was slipping away from her.

Stephen approached, and Gaspar stayed standing beside him. The guards were annoyed and told Stephen: Señora Florence prefers no contact between you two. I know, he told them.

We can talk now, he said to Gaspar then.

You should really work on your technique, then they wouldn't even hear you.

You want to fight. I'm glad, it reminds me of the boy I knew.

You never knew me and I don't trust you. It's the second door in the upstairs hallway. Where they store paintings.

You have to take them there.

Will it be easy to convince them?

They know you found the door that opened for Adela. They don't know anything about the extent of what's on the other side.

I don't know either.

You'll explore it together. We'll explore it. And then you'll be able to do what you have to do.

You have to make sure they all follow me. Were you ever behind the door, in that other place?

You sound like your father.

You're getting nostalgic. I haven't forgotten you didn't stop them when they decided to split my uncle like a chicken. You think my father would have forgiven you for that?

Your father killed my brother and I forgave him.

I don't believe you. Deep down you're a son of a bitch, but you're all I've got. I don't care about your brother, especially if he's dead. Did you ever go to the other side of the door? I know how to come back. I don't know if I'm going to let you come back, you're going to have to risk it. Can you keep this up longer?

No. And it's not safe.

Is it possible to summon all the members of the Order who exist?

No. There are a lot, I don't know how many.

First I'm going to give a small demonstration for the ones who are here. Disconnect now.

Stephen left the beach, walking slowly. He was destined to be a servant, he thought. His family's servant and Juan's and now Gaspar's. A servant and a traitor. But now he was about to light the fire, days away from seeing flames on the horizon.

It was a procession, and Gaspar was its leader.

He heard the others panting and dragging their feet. He pretended to be exhausted and enjoyed the sight of them so desperate as they traversed the marsh, which was crossed by a path through scrubland. It was hard going because, from among the scrub, hands reached out. Hands like the ones that touched Pablo, he'd thought the first time he saw them. The hand that had marked his father's arm. They didn't touch him.

The hands had dragged some Initiates off through the grasses and into the still water. 'Initiates' was the word they used. Gaspar was learning the jargon only from what he over-heard. He was a servant. Esteban had told him that he was a servant, too. But no, Gaspar had told him. It's one thing to be the black sheep. You're the black sheep, the prodigal son, the family's shame. You could conform. All I can do is rebel. My dad could only rebel. Non-conformity is only possible for those who are not slaves. Everyone else has to fight.

The people the hands grabbed and pulled underwater wore smiles of ecstasy as they were dragged away. They didn't scream. They disappeared in seconds. Your father said they are only food, but they don't know that. And if they do know, they don't care, they want to feed their god. Gaspar ignored Esteban. The hands couldn't touch him. With him they were stupid and slow. Esteban had learned to stand near Gaspar to avoid them.

Once the swamp was behind them, Gaspar turned around to look at the landscape. It was beautiful though muted, with no clear source of light. It ended in an open field, small and empty, the solitude of a wasteland in a hollow world. There in the waste-land, things were left for them, the visitors. Small things placed right in the centre of the field, very visible. Gifts. They had to go and get them. The Initiates who volunteered to collect the gifts looked small and frightened. The objects were all different. They looked like jewellery – earrings, sometimes, or bracelets. After the first excursion they'd realized the objects were made of bone. Gaspar didn't know what happened once they were back from the excursions, because everyone withdrew to rest, and so did he. He pretended to be exhausted, though he wasn't tired.

My mother says the bones form letters. She thinks she's getting messages again, Esteban explained. And what do they say? I'm not allowed in those meetings, Esteban answered. It was easier for them to see each other now: the members of the Order were so worn out after the expeditions that no one monitored them except the guards, and they were annoyed at not being invited behind the door, so were less inclined to worry about that contact Florence preferred to avoid.

They still hadn't seen, and Gaspar hadn't pointed it out, that on the other side of the small valley where the forest began, a man hung from a tree. He was motionless. There was no wind behind the door. Gaspar began to dream about the man. In his dreams, the hanged man took the rope from around his neck and plucked bone fruits from the trees.

One night, Gaspar woke up and found his grandfather in the room: he had rolled his wheelchair in and was very drunk. The old man didn't say anything, just tossed one of the objects on to the sheets – small bones tied together with a kind of vegetable twine. Gaspar inspected it in the moonlight. Its shape was identical to the scar on his arm. The guards didn't do anything. They were unsure what to do when the person who entered was Adolfo Reyes. And they didn't know what it was he had thrown on to the bed.

'They shouldn't take those out,' said the old man. 'You don't take things from places like that.'

The guards, realizing the extent of his drunkenness, wheeled him away. And Adolfo Reyes went out yelling that the kid was his grandson and he could talk to his grandson whenever he damn well pleased. Gaspar listened to his shouts until the heavy silence fell again over Puerto Reyes, and he took the object in his hands. By then, they had brought back many gifts. How many expeditions? Six? Seven. They had infested that land by now. He brought the mounted bones close to his mouth and whispered, Dad, it's you, you were here, you know these places.

We must go into the forest, he told them during the next expedition. When he was on the Other Side he talked to them, he went in front of them, he guided them. Florence and Mercedes followed. He didn't let them intimidate him, nor did he feign obedience. On the Other Side he also dominated because he had a secret: everyone got tired except for him. The old people were left exhausted. Crossing the swamp to the field was no more than five hundred metres, but they reached it nearly unconscious. He especially liked to see his grandmother keeling over. Seeing her breathe with her mouth open was extraordinary, a spectacle from hell. How had his father hurt her like that? And why? He would have the answers. It wouldn't be long now.

We have to get to the forest, he said, and he made them follow him. The guards were outside the door, they were never allowed in. That meant he had to leave with Esteban, who knew how to fight. Gaspar needed him. He didn't want to need him, didn't want another father figure ever again. If it weren't for the guards, he would leave Esteban on the Other Side, except that he was also the only witness to his father's life. Him and Tali. He needed Stephen alive. He had a lot to tell.

The forest wasn't dense, the trees were spaced far apart. The members of the Order caught sight of the hanged man. A mummy. Dried-out skin. The body was still. Gaspar backed up and let the others go forward without him. They all saw something that fascinated them. Mercedes: a tree of hands; that is, a trunk with stiffened hands wrapped around it, some of them mummified, others rotting. Grandfather Reyes: a torso skewered on a thin trunk. There were several. The heads on some of them had been replaced with animal heads. Someone was having fun behind the door. Gaspar had known it ever since Adela's house. There'd been something of the collector about those shelves with their fingernails, their teeth. He remembered his father's box of eyelids. He couldn't get distracted. He had to finish, and the arm, his own arm, told him where to go. His scar was burning. Follow the arm. A little further. Past the forest. He didn't know what he was looking for, but he knew what direction to take.

Florence's scream revealed the purpose of the march through the forest. Esteban, behind him, grabbed his arm.

There were many trees with people hanging from them. The first man, the mummy, hung by his neck. And very high up. He was missing a hand. But the position of all these men and women was the same. Gaspar recognized it: they had been hung in the position of the Tarot's Hanged Man, head down.

'That's my brother's body,' said Stephen.

Florence had stopped screaming. Now she was on the ground, her face against that of a cadaver, a young man with very white skin. She was confirming that it was, in fact, her son, and she was talking to that dead head. It didn't seem decomposed, but the eyes were fixed and the neck was bent, broken. There was dried blood on its face and its long hair was red and straw-like. Gaspar felt some pity, in spite of everything. Florence was no longer panting, she seemed rejuvenated as she kissed her son on the mouth. Why hadn't he rotted? How old was he? A teenager, Gaspar realized. His arms were very thin and his neck black, as if time had not been able to hide the bruises of hanging. His father had done that. Esteban would tell him how.

Florence spoke in English to the dead teenager, cooing to him. My magic boy, she repeated, how much you must have learned in this place, in the realm of the gods.

She asked the others to help her get him down, but there

was no response. No one moved. Mercedes indicated the other hanged people: they went as far as the horizon, like in a cemetery of soldiers, a valley of the fallen.

Florence insisted, with all the sternness she could muster in her exhaustion and desperation. No one was paying attention to what was happening around them, nor did they notice Gaspar start slowly backing up, and Esteban with him.

Mercedes was the only alert one. Her beast-like face sniffed at the air. She had noticed the change that the others were unable to perceive, bewildered as they were by that field of hanged bodies, and above all by the reappearance of Eddie, the vanished heir. The place behind the door had never had a smell on the previous expeditions Gaspar had led. Now, however, there was a swelter in the air, a stench of old meat and sun-warmed crypt, of rotten milk, of menstrual blood and hungry breath, of dirty teeth. The breathing of a filthy mouth.

We need to leave, Mercedes said, but they didn't hear her. They ignored her. But she had realized. The place was a mouth.

Gaspar met his grandmother's eyes and nodded. She was right. They had to leave. So he shoved several members of the Order who, not understanding, didn't try to catch him, and he ran. Esteban was behind him, lagging. Some people tried to follow them, but a head start of a few metres in that place without enough oxygen was insurmountable. They couldn't run, no one had any air except for Gaspar, who had time to turn around to watch the useless efforts, to raise his head towards the moonless night and wonder, if there was no moon, no stars, what was the source of that lowering light, so like a cloudy sunrise? When he reached the scrublands, the swamp was giving off a repugnant stench and he felt a wave of nausea. Behind him, he heard Esteban's choking, disgusted cough. He didn't want to help him, but if he managed to get out, he would need him to fight the guards. He retraced his steps and dragged Esteban by the arm, pushed him. They had time to escape from the Order's members, who were falling to their knees on the grass, gasping, but he didn't know how long they had in relation to the resurrection of the world around them. Everything was waking up and crawling, flowing, sticking out tongues, drooling. The hanged man was starting to sway, though the wind was imperceptible. There were noises in the water. There were no hands along the path through the swamp, though. They were allowed to pass. Gaspar touched the wall of stone, like a mountain, and found the passageway, a short, high tunnel. At the end, the doorknob that opened the door. And then, the hallway of the Puerto Reyes guest house.

The guards were on the other side, as always. Gaspar yanked Esteban out – he fell to the floor, his face such a dark red it was nearly purple – and then closed the door behind them. The guards looked at them questioningly. They said nothing. Disconcerted, they turned to Esteban, who couldn't get a word out, couldn't breathe.

Gaspar understood what he had to do. It was so simple.

'We came to get you,' he said. 'Señora Florence says you two should come and see what we found.'

And he opened the door to let them through. For a moment he considered going with them. Maybe just as far as the swamp. Push them into the stagnant water. Skewer them on the trees that were waiting for their torsos. But that massacre was not his. And following them would be dangerous. He shut the door as soon as they were through.

Esteban had gotten up and was looking out the window, trying to catch his breath. Aside from his panting, the house was completely silent.

'What comes next?' asked Gaspar.

'Tomorrow we brick up this door.'

Gaspar felt the trembling in his hands, slight at first and then a violent shudder. The nausea was so intense he soaked his pants with vomit, spattered the wooden floor. His long hair stuck to his face. He closed his eyes, and when he opened them, he was alone. He crept out of the guest house, hesitant: outside, the sun was shining, ignorant and idiotic, and he didn't see Esteban anywhere.

They were waiting for him, they wanted to see him. He had said no. Over the phone, Vicky had threatened to show up at the house without warning. You already tried to push us away and this is how it turned out, this is how it ended. You can come back. No one is looking for you. They know you had nothing to do with what happened to Luis. Don't ever talk to me about Luis, Gaspar had shouted. Never. Who gave you this number? Tali, Vicky replied, but just then Gaspar didn't think about her. He thought: I have to call right now to change the number, or just cut off the phone. Pablo argued with less conviction. They wouldn't come to him if he didn't want to see them, if he didn't ask them to. The conversations were tense. Gaspar had cut off the last one and hadn't answered again. Stephen – that's what he called him now, as Stephen had asked him to – wandered around the house without saying much, but he listened to what Gaspar needed to tell him. Pablo and Vicky had received compensation from the Other Place – without realizing, he'd been calling it by almost the same name his father had given it. They both had good lives. He didn't want to ruin them.

'You don't need them any more,' Stephen told him. 'All this is yours. You decide.'

We went to visit your aunt, Vicky had told him. The man who lives with you told us where she was and we visited her. She wouldn't let us near your house, and we complied. Gaspar felt another wave of rage. Tali. He remembered her well. His father had never told him she was his mother's sister, and she had never said so either. Another liar. And why was Stephen going around sharing out information? Anyway, for now, he couldn't face her. He couldn't look at Tali or listen to her explanation. She could be his ally, but not yet.

Stephen didn't abandon him. Gaspar had killed his family and he stayed on in the house, unsteady, meandering, but with no intention of leaving. If he puts a bullet in me one night, thought Gaspar, it's fair. Still, he felt safe. He wasn't sure what to do with Stephen, and it seemed to him Stephen didn't know either whether he should leave Gaspar. For the moment, they had only been capable of resolving practical matters. Going into town to eat. Buying food. Talking, in the bar in Puerto Libertad, a little drunk. Stephen talked about Gaspar's father evasively and in detail at the same time. They would need to hire workers for the house. Unemployment was so high in the country and in the area that it wouldn't be hard, but Gaspar remembered a woman who had sung him to sleep, her patchwork apron. He didn't remember her name, but Stephen did: Marcelina. We could find her. You can do whatever you want. There's no one to answer to any more.

'Are you sure they aren't alive, in the Other Place? They can't come back?'

'You're sure, too. There's nothing left of them. That place was starving.'

At night, when he went out to the beach to smoke, Gaspar thought about the procession he had led. It had been another sacrifice, like Adela's, but this time he'd known what he was doing. He didn't regret it. He wasn't afraid of retaliation. He slept with a peace he had never known before. Stephen, on the other hand, though he had guided Gaspar in the massacre, and had planned it for so long with Juan, was as disconsolate as the last speaker of a dying language. One night, Gaspar had seen him disappear along the path leading to his father's Place of Power. Hours later he'd heard an explosion. He ran. An underground explosion. The tunnel with the iron door. He asked Stephen why he'd blown up the tunnel and he said because it brought him memories. It was empty, he added. Gaspar didn't believe him, but once it seemed safe, he would visit the ruins. After the explosion, Stephen left for several days. To meet up with Tali, he said. Maybe he also had a lover. A week of absence. No more than that. In the house he ate little and drank a lot. Maybe Gaspar would find his body on the beach one morning, washed up by the river. Or maybe they were going to be two solitary men sharing a secret in that still house, year after year, who would run into each other in the early-morning hours, unable to sleep, incapable of forgetting how the hanged man swaying in the wind had no shadow.

After smoking every night, Gaspar went back along the catwalk, past the orchid garden, and along the path that led from the lookout tower to the guest house. He climbed the stairs to the first floor. They still hadn't bricked over the door, despite Stephen's insistence. The carved wood was still there, the bronze doorknob, the silent hallway.

He hadn't opened it again, not yet. He knocked, timidly, as he did every day.

'Adela,' he said.

There was no answer. He closed his eyes. He saw a blonde, naked girl walking under a starless sky. Lost, but not scared. He saw her dancing on a red dirt path, strands of yarn hanging from her arm and her legs, unfettered, frenzied. He saw a black planet above the river. He saw his grandmother without lips or nose. He saw candles in the forest and a young woman on all fours crawling over bones. He saw men and women running, all of them mutilated, some without legs, who dragged themselves or spun in circles. He saw a starving white dog, its spine like metal balls encrusted into its back. He saw a girl in a red dress sitting beside the swamp; something that came from the water was eating her legs, but she didn't protest. He saw a pale torso in a field of yellow flowers.

He could come and go and search in that land. He was welcome in that land. If she was still there, he could find her. Would she still be a child? What had she been given to eat? Had the place been a mouth for her? He had to be sure. In the Other Place, time was a different thing. He could look for her.

He stepped back from the door.

'Adela.'

He heard no knocks. Nor did he hear Adela's voice, though he didn't remember it. When someone is gone, their voice is the first thing you forget.

'I'm going to come back,' he told her. 'I need time. I was never brave. I'm learning.'

And he left the door, the hallway, the guest house. He ignored the phone that rang every day. It was Vicky or it was Pablo. He still hadn't disconnected it. He wanted to see how quickly they gave up. He expected the calls would grow more sporadic, no longer sirens in the jungle, and then fade away. If it was raining, he didn't cross the park at a run. He liked the short, violent rains of Misiones, the rivers of red earth, the prelude to the hot, black night with its stars throbbing in the sky. A flash, silence, another flash, like an exhausted heart.

Acknowledgements

Thanks to Paul Harper and to Emily.

I would like to thank, for all their help, enthusiasm, suggestions, discussions, and work (as applicable!), Ariel Álvarez, Mauricio Bach, Salvador Biedma, Ariadna Castellarnau, Rodrigo Fresán, María Lynch, Sandra Pareja, Carolina Marcucci, Vanina Osci, and Silvia Sesé.

Text credits

Every effort has been made to trace and contact copyright holders where usage is not governed by fair-use principles prior to publication. Please contact the publisher if you are aware of any errors or omissions.

Lines from *'La casa de la niebla'* ['The House of Fog'] © Elena Anníbali, 2015, translated from the Spanish by Jessica Sequeira, *Washington Square Review*, Issue 42, Fall 2018. Reprinted by kind permission.

Lines from *The Invention of Morel* (*La invención de Morel*) © Adolfo Bioy Casares, 1940 and the heirs of Adolfo Bioy Casares. Translated by Ruth L.C. Simms.

Lines from 'The Dry Salvages' from *Four Quartets* by T.S. Eliot © The Estate of T.S. Eliot, from *Collected Poems and Plays* (Faber and Faber Ltd, 2004) reprinted by permission of the publisher.

Line from 'The Waste Land' by T.S. Eliot © The Estate of T.S. Eliot, from *The Waste Land and Other Poems* (Faber and Faber Ltd, 2002) reprinted by permission of the publisher.

Lines from 'Wild Eyed Boy From Freecloud' by David Robert Jones © 1969 Onward Music Ltd/Tro Musica España, SL.

Lines from 'Walking Around' © 1933 and 1935, Pablo Neruda and Fundación Pablo Neruda, translated by Donald D. Walsh in *Residence on Earth*, copyright © 1973 by Pablo Neruda and Donald D. Walsh. Reprinted by permission of New Directions Publishing Corp.

Lines from 'I Explain a Few Things' (*'Explico algunas cosas'*) © 1947, Pablo Neruda and Fundación Pablo Neruda, translated by Donald D. Walsh, in *Residence on Earth*, copyright © 1973 by Pablo Neruda and Donald D. Walsh. Reprinted by permission of New Directions Publishing Corp.